The Chronicles of Michel du Jabot

Eckhard Gerdes

Journal of Experimental Fiction 22

Aurora, Illinois

The Chronicles of Michel du Jabot

The cover art is in the public domain and is from embroidered front and back covers of a 1791 edition of *Robinson Crusoe*, from the Newberry Library. More informatiion can be found at *The Public Domain Review* website at publicdomainreview.org.

ISBN 1-884097-22-7
ISBN-13 978-1-884097-22-5

ISSN 1084-547X

JEF Books/Depth Charge Publishing
"The Foremost in Innovative Publishing"
experimentalfiction.com

JEF Books are distributed to the book trade by SPD: Small Press Distribution and to the academic journal market by EBSCO

Table of Contents

The Chronicles of Eckhard Gerdes

by Yuriy Tarnawsky

Have you seen whales frolicking in the sea—giant masses of shiny wet flesh gracefully rising up into the air and then just as gracefully plunging back into the water? They do it not to catch flies as trout do, food always on their tiny minds, but to delight at their ability to do it, delight at being whales. I rise and plunge, says the whale, therefore I am! And so it is with Eckhard Gerdes in his massive, whale tale kind of a book, *The Chronicles of Michel du Jabot*—he is not after seducing a reader or two with a suspenseful story into purchasing his book but to exercise the writer in himself, delight at his ability to use language. Gerdes is because he writes. At one point in the book he says, "I swear allegiance to this language and to all languages, spoken and unspoken. What is at stake is playful communication. Do we really want a world in which we could only speak hyperformally? Or not at all?" And a few pages down, "[Milton Roff] said that there are two kinds of artists: the kind who are busy being artists, and the kind who are busy doing their art. I am proud to be one of the latter. I work. I love to write. […] Somewhere is a sentence I can write that is so perfect that no Œðer sentence needs to be written." As the size of this book suggests, we will have plenty chances to read many more of Gerdes's new books. Given the high standard he has set for himself, it is unlikely he will ever write that perfect sentence and therefore will continue striving for it as long as he lives.

The Chronicles is composed on two levels—language play and storytelling. In Editor's Foreword, Gerdes ("the editor") explains to the reader that the book is written in an English different from ours since, as happens with languages separated geographically for an extended period of time such as "Latin and Romansch," it had developed independently of the English we know. In the case of Michel du Jabot's English and ours, the period of time separation was some 200 years and the geographic distance not insignificant, to put it mildly—it developed on Mars. Gerdes calls it *Theirn*, contrasting it with ours, which he calls *Ourn.* This gives him an opportunity to display his knowledge of historical linguistics as well as use it throughout the book in many clever, frequently hilariously ways. The *Ourn* "self" and "other" are respectively "¢elgh" and "Œðer" in *Theirn,* which are used in a quirky way; "rest" has become "rust," leading Gerdes to remark that the fact is "disturbing in the grander scheme of things"; and "ask" is "hax," which makes one think of "ax" used for "ask" in some American English dialects. Double "s" has turned into the German "ß," there are a number of different quotation marks, including unique ones for "violent quotes," "popping," and "sung words," and so on and so forth. But the bulk of language play are puns and other word games, a skill at which Gerdes has excelled from the very beginning, as for instance, in one of his earliest novels, unpublished until only recently, *Hugh Moore*. We have seen this in essentially all of his subsequent books, but here are some vivid ones from *The Chronicles*:

I got us ushered out of the establishment abruptly when I followed one sign to the letter: ⧖Wet Floor⧖. I did. The store personnel seemed upset. [⧖ is the quote mark for a sign.]
<<Remember the tortoise and the hare,>> I said.
<<Tortoises don't have hair,>> he replied, sounding annoyed. [<< and >> stand for regular quotes.]

My mine eyes saw the cave-in not as bad as it could be. [The action takes place in a cave.]

America. Inter-rusting. I hadn't thought of America in quite a while. I guess one would have to start with soil analysis.
How soiled is your America? Mine's pretty soiled. But I'm keeping the faith that it's going to get better someday. [This is an example of the use of the "rust/rest" relationship.]

The Chronicles is divided into eight books: "Aasvogel," "Parkour on Mars," "Never Made Up," "Fitting for My Death Mask," "Michel du Jabot's Journey to the Center of the Earth," "The Eight Immortals of the Wine Cup," "Snail Shells for Slugs, the Diving Duck, and Œðer Dovecote Tales," and finally "The Rest." So what we have on our hands is an octalogy—a rare species in the world of literature, although, I was surprised to find out, not unheard of.

The action in the book takes place interchangeably on Mars and Earth, and there appear to be frequent, easily executed, comings and goings between the two sister planets, which with time blurs the distinction between the locations, something Gerdes has done, no doubt, intentionally, to give himself room for his imagination to roam freer in deforming reality. And for deforming of reality there is a need, since Gerdes devotes much of his energy to poking fun at our society, pointing out its decrepitude and brutality. Note the "rust' quote above and also see the following two passages, the first one from Book Two, and the second one from Book Four:

*On my way to the office I stopped at the Stationary Bus. A long time ago a city bus had broken down in that intersection. It was left there and had become a landmark to *pop* into and grab a newspaper, a cup of coffee, and a seat. I grabbed the ►Condenser◄, Mars Condatis' abbreviated morning paper,* *nicknamed the ►Condescender◄. It wasn't particularly well written, but it was tabloid-sized, so I wouldn't **hit** my neighbors in the face when I folded and unfolded pages.* (The strange symbols are some of the special quotes I mentioned earlier. Mars here and throughout the book looks strikingly similar to Earth, in particular to Chicago and its environs, which is where Gerdes has resided for much of his life.)

America is like Jonathan Edward's spider dangling over the gates of hell, being pulled by its threads in two directions: capitalism for the ¢elghish, democracy for the Œðers. The two are mutually exclusive. All for one or *one for all. The one who'd prefer the former is the capitalist. Survival of the meanest badaßes of all, at least until society finds them and puts them away. Or puts them down like rabid dogs.*

In places, especially in Book One, which deals with Michel's du Jabot's expedition to rescue the Martian potentate Aasvogel, the story of *The Chronicles* reads like an adventure story of the Lost World genre, in particular as exemplified in the work of H. Rider Haggard (he of the *King Solomon's Mines* fame), in whose work one occasionally comes across "aasvogel," a largely obsolete word referring to African vulture. But don't be fooled by it. It is only a carrier frequency for the modulations of language play that Gerdes has set out to engage in. Like a radio or TV wave, it is merely necessary to bring what Gerdes wants to tell the reader. Moreover, delving deeper into the book, one realizes its real topic is Gerdes himself, he the writer. The editor in the introductory piece is obviously a literacy device, "*jabot*" means "craw" in French, and Avery Craw, a character in Gerdes's first published novel *Truly Fine Citizen* and his alter ego, is mentioned a couple of times as the ancestor of Michel. But this becomes especially apparent in the central piece of the octalogy, book four, "Fitting for My Death Mask." Here Gerdes turns uncharacteristically serious and brings in the tragic figure of the great nineteenth century Ukrainian poet Taras Shevchenko, using his famous death mask as a model for his own. Like Virgil leading Dante through Divine Comedy, Shevchenko leads Gerdes through this part of the book causing him to say at one point: "I am finding humor difficult. I tried to lighten stuff up with humor, but I am emotionally exhausted." In the end, though, he concludes (the text is presented inside the cross section of a gently curving snail shell):

Okay. At long last I think I have found a way to stay in my inner home, the one in my gut that says that somehow someday everything will be all right. We will achieve that at some point in between now and eternity. Or is it infinity? I forget which comes first. Perhaps they come simultaneously. My mask is in place. I can return home now. I feel her hand. ("She" is most likely his beloved wife Persis, who died many years ago.)

There is one more topic I haven't mentioned in connection with the book—music, in particular jazz, of which Gerdes has been a long-time student and practitioner. It permeates it as much as do language play and storytelling. Going through the text, we come time and time again across various musicians' names, and its prose is liberally laced with poems which are frequently called "blues" ("dark slow blues," "hard blue paisley," "morning glory blues," and so on; many that are not called blues, clearly are that, being very much like the named ones). In fact, structurally, the whole book may be viewed as a jazz composition, a jamming Gerdes has done with various parts of himself as well as with such writers as Rabelais, Sterne, Joyce, Beckett, Arno Schmidt, whom he mentions in Editor's Foreword, in addition to others, including Kenneth Patchen, whose *The Journal of Albion Moonlight* may have served as a model for the first book—"Aasvogel"—both of which include lengthy treks through a hostile terrain.

All of this, plus much, much more awaits the reader in *The Chronicles,* but to avail oneself of it, one must make the journey through the book oneself. My advice for anyone who plans do it is to read beforehand Gerdes's delightful book-length essay *How to Read*, in which he sketches out various ways of tackling a text. The reader might find in it a way of going through the big tome, which will make the trip through it easier and more profitable.

Editor's foreword

The Chronicles of Michel du Jabot, when first presented to me, had me exclaiming in exasperation with François Rabelais, *Beuveurs très illustres!* "Mighty boozers! What the heck is this thing? I have read Sterne, Joyce, Beckett, Arno Schmidt, and many of the Other great weirdos of literature, but I don't think I've ever seen something like this!"

But what quickly came to my attention was that this was written in an English that had developed independently of the English I had come to know and use on a regular basis. When a language is divided geographically, the halves continue to evolve independently, as with Latin and Romansch. And these *Chronicles* were written in an English that is close enough in time, being separated from us by only a couple of hundred years, to be understood, but we can see that it evolved in ways different from our own. For the ease of discussion here, I will refer to our English as *Ourn*, and the English of Michel's milieu as *Theirn*.

I think the author seems to associate *Theirn* with the colony at *Mars Condatis*, but *Theirn* seems to have been in use elsewhere as well, as during Michel's journey underground. Indeed, Michel seems to have adopted *Theirn* quite naturally, as if it was his native version of the language, which, perhaps it was. Or perhaps he was raised bi-dialectically, as German speakers from mixed High- and Low-German-speaking ancestry frequently have been.

I have, however, noted in particular some of the unusual usage in *Theirn* as being peculiar to Mars because, of course, these are in no way what we do in *Ourn*.

Quickly apparent is the fact that the metaphorical "twin oars of being"—"self" and "other"—are referred to on Mars as *¢elgh* and *Œðer*, as if they are themselves entities who live in some sort of symbiosis with their hosts and the hosts' environment. Curious is the use of the cent sign in *¢elgh*, which suggests perhaps some sort of economically oligarchical origin for the term. This interpretation is also supported by the loss of the word "rest." "Rest," of course, indicates economic fallowness, so its removal would suit the oligarchs well, and on Mars the word "rest" seems to have been removed from the language completely. Apparently that entire concept is lost. “Rust” has replaced it, which is perhaps quite disturbing in the grander scheme of things.

Also note the reintroduction of the Old English and Middle English *eth* “th,” ð, into the language, as well as the Œ digraph, taken from Middle English, but which is here curiously only used with capital letters. Additionally, the double “s” has been replaced by the eszett, ß ,which was common in German orthography and perhaps points back to the shared common ancestry of Old High German and Old English. Note also the use of *hax* as “ask,” an apparent reversion to the Old English *acsian*. These harkenings back to earlier forms of English are perhaps due to some oligarchical application of the Golden Age Fallacy, which suggests that we were all better off back during some mythical “good old days.” Reversion would mean the restoration of some past glory.

In addition to these restorations in *Theirn*, we also can note many symbols that arose neologistically, perhaps in response to situations that were new to the *Theirn* speakers. That *Theirn* has freed itself from gender bias when *Ourn* has not, is, of course, to their credit. *Theirn* uses *ze* as the subjective third-person gender-free pronoun, and it uses *hir* as the objective and possessive. In this regard, we can learn much from *Theirn*.

Some symbols are abstract and seem to function much the way quotation marks and italics do in *Ourn*:

► ◄ is used for individual quoted words, song titles, poem titles, titles of shows, and so forth;

►► ◄◄ for individual quoted words inside a quoted title or expression;

<< >> for quotes;

< > for quotes inside of quotes; for foreign words with odd pronunciation (see the spellings used in Lake Gusev at start of the first book); for parts of words; for sighs.

Additionally—and these symbols in particular delight me—I can imagine visually onomatopoetic, almost concretist origins for the following:

♪ ♫ for sung words;

Ͼ Ͽ for questions of self and for thoughts (don’t these look

like ears?);
✸ ✸ for violent quotes and for hitting (little explosions?) ;
✸ ✸ for onomotopoiea for popping, i.e. ✸pop✸,
✸popping✸, etc. (charged explosions?);
☼Aßhole☼ (self-explanatory);
⅄ is used for signage (sign post?);
↓ ↓ for putting someone down (as in "↓colleague↓");
●stumping around the office● (the sound of a pegleg).

If you are like me, after just a short period of adjustment, these quirks will come to seem natural, and the reading process will no longer be hampered by the strangeness of *Theirn.*

At this point, I am not sure if a person named *Michel du Jabot* ever existed. Many of the persons mentioned were historical figures, especially the musicians who populate the book. Michel's obsession with music is made much of by some of the other characters in the work, and indeed, from our own perspective, his obsession is quite unhealthy. Here I suggest, however, that the reader remember that not too long ago in our own history, music was a dominant art form. What is entirely possible is that it continued to be important among the *Theirn*, and that perhaps our having jettisoned it so readily is our own weakness and not theirs.

Make of this work what you will in regard to its authenticity. I have not been able to verify many of its details. But I offer it to you nevertheless as an interesting examination of a world similar to our own, but also profoundly different, just as Michel himself, albeit in one sense a typical literary *Everyman* is also, in another, suspiciously *No Man.*

To paraphrase Rabelais again, "Enjoy this, my friends. Read it happily—it's good for the body (and the kidneys, too!)"

— Brandish Yar

The Chronicles of Michel du Jabot

Book One: Aasvogel

Part One: The Push Thither

➡*The Twin Oars of Mars*⬅

Two, they in the 22nd Cemetery like the rust[1] of us who bŒðer to hax, will cut the water with the oars ¢elgh and Œðer[2] and bring us there, to Mars Condatis, near Lake Gusev, to plead our case.

We will need to portage to the Ma'Adim River en route, and our boat is large. We have brought many porters and have also brought publican openers to begin negotiations with the mason jarheads who hold the base at Condatis.

The Sestina envoy sent last month has not returned, so we expect to encounter guards who are well versed in the ways of espionage. We'll need to be very careful.

➡*Aasvogel*⬅

The guards are sitting at the entrance *en maße*[3], debating whose shift's beginning and whose is ending.

<<You're coming on,>> says one contingent to an Œðer.

<<No, we're going off>> is the reply.

---

[1] Apparently, on Mars, the word "rest" no longer exists in the English language. Apparently the concept is lost.

[2] The metaphorical twin oars are Martian metaphors for "self" and "other."

[3] The double "s" has long since been replaced by the eszett.

<<Put it in writing next time,>> one side says after conceding.

<<We don't have anything to write with>> comes the lame reply. I say leave 'em alone and they'll come home, dragging their foundry behind them.

Some wanted to hurry back to their horrors. Œðers wanted to escape their horrors. A horror is more whore than a whore. Beyond the horror are the Horus'd. They turned around, but we kept going. I had to honor my ¢elgh, for whom I worked. Even though he was an *aasvogel.*

He wanted Condatis's base. By hook or by crook, I was to get it. He'd swoop in and pick it clean as soon as I'd subdued it. That was our agreement, though it was beginning to make me uncomfortable. But as long as I kept my face to the rising sun, I could also see what was ahead of me. I would then take siesta in the afternoon and rise again in the evening. I never wanted the sun behind me. I couldn't trust it.

➧*The Lake Gusev Market*⬅

The Lake Gusev Market was bristling like brislings in a feeding frenzy. The locals here spoke a strange but colorful homophonic dialect that took some getting used to. George Bernard Shaw had noted it once in his writings when he discußed the ▶ghoti◀, which is pronounced *fish*, <gh> as *f* in ▶laugh◀, <o> as *i* in ▶women◀, and <ti> as *sh* in ▶fiction◀.

Shaw reportedly visited here twice during his long life, though how he ventured here has long been the subject of debate. Nevertheleß, he is a local hero. One sees his influence everywhere, except in the pub district, of course, where he is as reviled as Carrie Nation. Place names like Mrs. Warren Street (hosting the brothel district, of course), Higgins Lane, the Doolittle Theatre, the John Tanner Building (the tallest building in the market), and even St. Joan Cathedral had Shaw as their nominal starting points.

In front of a store with a giant sign proclaiming ⅩTiolocts[4]Ⅹ[5], a local was haggling with the storekeep over the price of a silkscreen. We interject a request for allowance, and the local looks at us wild-eyed and takes off at top speed. We don't bŒðer pursuing him. He's not our guy. Don't know why he took off. After warding off a t-shirt with the frowning countenance of <Stonehaugh[6]> holding a fan made of feathers, I haxed the storekeep if he'd seen any suspicious <gmoughvlmepnpts[7]>. He said he'd seen

---

[4] Pronounced "shirt," as in fic*ti*on+co*lo*nel+indi*ct*.

[5] This was a symbol denoting text from a sign, advertising, brand names, words that are owned by companies.

[6] Pronounced "Shaw," as in "Featherstone-Hugh," which is pronounced "fan-shaw."

[7] Pronounced "movements," as in phleg*m*+thr*ough*+v+pa*lm*+e+*pn*eumatic+*pt*armigan+s

<ghougholo[8]>. Then he haxed us to leave so we wouldn't blow his cover. He worked for us, see. And he said he'd be in touch in a couple of hours over at the hotel. I bought the Stonehaugh tioloct to make the conversation look realistic, and then I slapped down two bills disgustedly, as if he'd gotten the better of me in the haggle.

We were hungry, so we next haggled for some fried haggis-on-a-stick from some vendor who, having seen we'd <<been had>> at the tiolect vendor's, tried to charge us trebletruffle prices for them. But when we threatened to beat him, he quickly changed his <phthoughpn[9]> and let us have the food for the posted price. He'd have besmirched his ¢elgh if we'd have shown him our scepters. Which reminds me of the flavor of the so-called ▶haggis◀ [10]. I swear it was made of ratchet horsefood and rancid carrots sewn into a ratgut. The stick was the best part, especially when I poked it into the vendor's belly and told him to start selling some real food. That vendor was so fat, then when he pulled the stick out of his belly, he didn't even bleed. The fat closed up the wound instantly. And then he put the stick back on the pile of sticks customers had left behind. Apparently he recycled the sticks.

We walked toward the hotel. Hopefully our contact had found us safe paßage acroß the Ma'Adim River. The river near the lake was unnavigable. We'd have to portage 30 miles to where we could safely enter the water again.

¢elgh and Œðer were laid to rust early in the evening. The openers, the Major and I stayed up playing cards and drinking black-and-tans.

➡*My Western!*⬅*!!*

Beginning 23 May 2007 and going back who knows where and how and when? But I'm thinking Western this time. I used to love them. Let's all gang up on Avoidance City! Oh, that was just that one western writer, what's his name? *The Consciousneß of Purple Place* is his anti-Avoidance novel. I know the Avoiders are all tied up in the history of the West, but this isn't about the Avoiders.

Freeze!

Pardon old motormouth back there. He always seems to get to the microphone a step before we do. Now, Sheriff, let me hax you. You gotta believe me. I had nothing to do with it.

Rustate that as a question.

---

[8] Pronounced "four," as in enou*gh*+d*ough*+*colo*nel

[9] Pronounced "tune," as in *phth*istic+thr*ough*+*pn*eumatic

[10] This sort of punctuation mark is common in Martian prose. These sorts of marks are probably self-explanatory. The publisher only paid me for ten footnotes, so for the rest, you're on your own.

With it to do nothing had I?

Okay, you may enter.

The sheriff follows you to the hatcheck room next to an empty concierge booth with a sign on it reading, <<if you want help, hax at the hatcheck room.>> Consequently, the hatcheck room's line was doubly long.

<<I'm sorry, but we'll have to wait. There's no way I'm letting you in there with your guns.>>

So we waited. I thought I saw that outlaw Featherslinger in the line, but he was too far away. They must have had a temp for a hatchecker. But finally we got to the front and got the sheriff's guns secured into *my* name.

➡*Every town*⬅

Every town seemed to have its own feel. Don't you believe in consciousneß of place? I can tell you, I've entered places where I've felt a shudder down my spine and knew I had to get out of there fast. Avoidance City. I can't tell you why, but I got the heebie-jeebies there. And in Purple Place, a year before the Settler's Compound disaster. We'd stopped in for a cup of coffee, and I overheard the local constabulary talked at the table behind me. I don't remember exactly what they said, but they scared the shit out me, and when she came out of the bathroom, I said, <<Let's get that to go. We can't stay.>> And at Fort Hellhole, I think that's what it was called. When we pulled in there, on our way to Cheechako, the freakin' tent zipper broke, rain started pouring, and all of 10,000 hummingbird-sized mosquitoes decided to seek shelter inside the open tent. I was so distraught that I wept. You know what she did, though? She sat out in the rain over a fire she'd gotten started miraculously and was boiling water for artichokes! The absurdity of that gesture was perhaps the most endearing moment of our time together. It was beautiful, and I laughed at fate for the rust of the evening. Then we slept in the car with the radio and the a/c, splurging on gasoline so we'd feel better. I'd wake up every couple of hours to make sure we had enough gas, and I'd turn the car off for an hour or so, but then it'd get so clammy, I'd have to turn it on again. Still, I didn't mind that. The artichokes had been perfect.

The entrance to the city is ahead. I think we paßed through the towns in the correct order. Œðerwise, the gate won't open.

Well, on the way, we might have time for a story.

<<Great. Go ahead.>>

No. I mean for you. Tell us one.

<<Oh, man, don't put me on the spot like that.>>

Okay, never mind for now. But I'm coming back to it.

<<Okay. I'll try to be ready.>>

So tell us one.

<<Not right away. Give me a while. Fifteen minutes, at least.>>

And you'll be a tinker just like Einstein. Okay, I gueß I'm supposed to stall for time. <<Shake it to the left, shake it to the right, do the hip hip milk shake with all your height. Shimmy, shimmy. Do the swim. Jump up. Jump back. Do the Sharona. The Rock Lobster. Going down, down, down.>>

<<Okay. There was once—>>

Where was? ▶There◀ is a pronoun referring to place. You have not established a place. Each pronoun needs an antecedent. If you are constructing a delayed-subject construction, sometimes referred to as an ▶expletive construction◀, then you are making a mistake in logic. Pronouns do not take postcedents. State the subject before the verb. If you are not constructing a DSC, as I call them, then where is ▶there◀?

<<Twentieth-century Lilliput.>>

That, of course, means Liverpool, back on Earth. Beyond the Merseybeat and the Premier League, what the heck do you know about Liverpool?

<<No, not Liverpool. Lilliput. But I gueß you are saying that Liverpool is what Swift had in mind when he wrote about Lilliput.>>

But of course.

<<Okay, I'll start over. A young man lived in a run-down apartment in the Edgewater section of Chicago in the 1980s. He had just finished spraying his shower with mild-and-moldew spray when he—>>

You mean ▶mold-and-mildew◀, right?

<<Look, are you telling this or am I?>>

Go ahead, go ahead. I won't interrupt. Oh, what kind of feeling does Chicago have?

<<What?>>

This is about consciousneß of place, right? What kind of feeling does Chicago have?

<<Chicago is too big to have a single feeling. It's a complex city—fast, quick to anger, yet forgiving of almost everything but lazineß. The biggest problem it has, I think, is that it considers artists to be lazy, and thus it tends to revile them unleß they have enormous incomes. Income level is equated with how hard one works.>>

Everywhere in Chicago?

<<Most everywhere. Hax any artist. Hax hir, <When you introduce your ¢elgh as an artist to people in Chicago, what's usually their first response?> and I'll bet you that ze will reply, <Do you make much money doing that?>>>

At least enough to afford expensive mold-and-mildew sprays.

<<I never said he was an artist.>>

He'd have to be. You don't know anything about regular working people.

After I said that, he decked me. I gueß I'd poked him in his sore a little too hard. What kind of a stupid story would begin with mold-and-mildew spray anyway.

*

I said to the earth, <<Oh, gentle countryside, let me hold your hills, and let me grasp your peaks. Let me explore your crags, and then let me lower my ¢elgh into your valleys.>>

*

Stay awake until dawn! Outrun death. Falling asleep when the sun's ¢elgh has been extinguished tempts death far too much. Protect the Earth. Wait until you have seen that dawn has come and that the world has survived an Œðer night. *Then* and *only* then should you sleep.

*

We were in a tour group to see the top of the church spire. We had eaten poorly at our hotel. People joked. One said he'd left his room service tray untouched outside his room. Someone else said that in that case they'd probably reuse the food.

While climbing to the top of the church tower, I stopped and looked out a window at the vineyards below. I touched her shoulder, but she squirmed away and turned to me and haxed if I had heard God speaking with Satan with grave misapprehension. She gave me a weak smile and walked off a few feet. I replied, <<Yes, but only in a nominative case.>>

At first a steep vertical ascent, then spiral, past a landing and mezzanine where blue nuns prayed. I looked at one; she was pretty. She caught my gaze, but she quickly looked away, blushing. A priest was offered food at the next landing vista point. He turned it down. Someone said, <<That’s because it’s straw!>> Someone else said, <<That’s better than what they gave us at the hotel.>>

*

I’m in a boarding school. Aßembly. I’m haxed to read my Valentine’s eßay. I see it on the bookshelves.

I try to read it—it is spread out among multiple volumes, but the school officials get impatient. When I turn back to the bookshelves, I cannot see my pages anymore. I begin to extemporaneously praise the institution for being open-hearted, but receive hostility for not reading my paper. So I tear into the school for its religious bias and for being a cult. A couple of students seem surprised, and one girl hands me a slip of paper with a note on it. I look again. The note is longer.

I look. It’s different. Again—it’s writing its ¢elgh∴my writing disappears—the words all rewrite their ¢elghs constantly.

*

The fisherman looked at the little fish suspiciously and then tore its head off while saying, <<Yeah, you’re my chum.>>

*

Master Aasvogel, I beseech you, hear my plea.
My mom’s behind bars.
My dad’s in front of them.
<<Yeah, you’re my chum.>>

*

Gurgling explosions pock the face of the place. Only the Aasvogel swoops in eagerly. We trod like invisible tod, hovering at points of inter-rust. We saw their detectives searching for us clumsily and in the most obvious of places: in the dumpsters (as if we would soil our ¢elghs thus!), in the nightclubs (as if we had nowhere better to go!), in the boarding houses (as if our frontal lobes were at stake!); on the pier, on the boardwalk, on the commons (us!); at the hospital, city hall, and the public library (where they seemed uncomfortable!); outside theatres, rustaurants and sports stadiums; under archways, viaducts and trellises; over bridges, stairwell landings and rooftops; down alleys, avenues and downtown; along forust paths, steep mountain trails, and the gauntlet of merchants in the public square. They could sense our presence but were unable to see our mocking them, stealing their faces with our fingertips and tying their shoelaces together.

*

The boat is heavy, and some of us have forgotten why we are carrying it. <<Portage>> I say, but they do not know what that means anymore. I have heard that this forgetfulneß was one of the dangers, and that some travelers have spent weeks carrying their boats before remembering why. But I have on my sleeve one sewn word: ►Ma'Adim◄. I took care, apparently, to note whither we were going. I have, however, forgotten whence we came. And I am not sure who these strangers traveling with me are. I can sense that to let them know that I do not know them might be a mistake, however. We trudge along in silence.

*

At some point I think I can hear the screams of the Aasvogel's infant son. When the openers begin rehearsing salutations, I know we are close to the river. I prepare a simple solution that I will add to the river when we enter it. The solution will stun the monstrous river creatures who would Œðerwise devour our boat.

*

<<O Consuming Shores, accelerate your ears and drink from the bottle of our gratings!>> began the openers. <<Our haunches are lowered onto your conveyances, and we post-construct non-toxic salubrations in the designs of our tattoos! Beseech á me mucho and grant us paß your ucho sages safe, O Well-Combed Groomers of entrants!>> the openers grovelcrawled. It made me wretch poor, but we were accepted as entrees. Two of the openers were devired and made pointleß, but in we went without them. We had two more, and we had to reach Mars Condatis by river before spring. I stoned the water with the salution, and we were away.

*

We anchored at the Moorish place and were pulled ashore by red-breasted moorhens who took us to the local lady's mansion for our repast. She was Lady Discwalking Liquid, whose husband, Sir Sea, legend told, had slipped away some years before after his busineß went down the drain.

We presumed she knew we were ambaßadors and not fishermen. When we entered, her eyes darted around the room. I caught one of her eyes in my fist and presented it back to her. My aßistant caught the Œðer and similarly returned it to her. She nodded, patiently reinserted her eyes, and focused on us. When she saw us, her jaw dropped. I picked that up, too, and gave it back to her. She was obviously very old and fragile. She said she needed to sit down, and turned to sit in her throne.

<<Would you give me a hand, young man?>> she haxed one of our negotiators. He, unfortunately, took his work far too seriously, and in an effort to please her, he took his sword and cut off his own hand and gave it to her. He bled profusely, but made every

effort to make sure his blood did not spurt onto her.

<<You shouldn't have done that,>> she said. <<I meant that as a synecdoche.>>

<<On the Œðer hand, it might be a metonymy.>> He was trying to seem a cunning linguist.

<<But you no longer have an Œðer hand,>> she noted.

<<Needleß to say, I was thinking that to my ¢elgh, Œðer things being equal and when all is said and done…>> and he died.

<<I hope he wasn't your best man,>> she said to me.

<<No, I've never been married,>> I replied. I yelled to my men that we had to return to the moorage. The lady ordered her guards to stop us, but they were no match. One was dreßed in blue, and the Œðer in green.

We shoved off from the moorage and continued on our way.

*

On board the boat, in order to cheer us up, my aßistant sang a song and played the guitar for us:

ATTOHO

After they tore our heads off
they pißed into our neckholes
on the double dime.

After they tore our heads off
they pißed into our neckholes.
They do it all the time.

We were attoho-mu.
We were attoho-mu.
We were attoho-mu.
We were attoho-mu.

Mu is by Atlantis.
She was a praying mantis
and ate my head alive.

Mu is by Atlantis.

She was a praying mantis
so I could not survive.

We were attoho-mu.
We were attoho-mu.
We were attoho-mu.
We were attoho-mu.

They crunch their mandibles
and split our skulls wide open
and suck our brains right out.

They crunch their mandibles
and split our skulls wide open
as if that's what love's about.

We were attoho-mu.
We were attoho-mu.
We were attoho-mu.
We were attoho-mu.

And we're bloody headleß torsos
alive still even moreso
for having died before.

We're bloody headleß torsos
alive still even moreso
and ready to die some more.

We are attoho-mu.
We are attoho-mu.
We are attoho-mu.
We are attoho-mu.

You can catch me if you kill me
and want me if you will me,
but you've got to come on through.

You can catch me if you kill me
and want me if you will me.
That's all you have to do.

I'm attoho-mu.
I'm attoho-mu.
I'm attoho-mu.
I'm attoho-mu.

<<Thanks,>> I said. <<That cheered me up.>>

*

That night I was attacked in my dreams. I was immobilized with a powerful sedative, and psychic surgery was performed on me. I remember seeing the masked surgeons and hearing their comments on some matter in my brain, but could not do anything to stop their probing. I was paralyzed.

*

The next day we realized we were almost out of provisions. Apparently our meat had been stolen while we were in moorage. I went ashore with two of my men in order to hunt for some meat. The woods that lined the river were filled with albino deer. We split up, and then I saw a beautiful buck. I took a bead at it, but spotted something just a few feet away from the deer in the bushes. It was a rather large *Ursa Martis*. It must have sniffed me the same moment I saw it because it turned its attention from the buck and looked right at me. I froze but realized I wasn't fooling it, so I took off as quickly as I could. I ran through the woods, but heard the crunching of the underbrush as it kept up with me. My men must have noticed as well, because they shot the thing with blue-stain fungi that coated its eyes, nose and throat and suffocated it just as it was about to get me. We butchered the bear, cooked as much as we could, and salted the rust for provisions.

*

That night I was attacked again; however, my brain was not the target. I was attacked in the testes. I awoke with a start in as much pain as I'd had from a scrotal hernia years earlier. I thought perhaps I had herniated my ¢elgh carrying bear back to the boat, but that was not the case. I must again have been heavily sedated, for I do not remember anything else about the night except, when I awoke again a few hours later, a man was sitting in a chair at the foot of my bunk. He was flipping playing cards into an ashcan. He saw me wake up and told me to go back to sleep: <<If you don't, I'll have to see if I can sever your balls with my cards.>> I noticed then that the cards were metallic and razor-sharp. I went back to sleep.

*

I was back at the school I had taught at:

➡*A Stubby Story*⬅

After years of tremendous difficulty adjusting to my disability, I was finally able to convince someone to take a chance on hiring me. The department chair who hired me saw my years of experience and took that into consideration, and she hired me despite my mißing leg. I would have an hour every day to make the trip from one end of campus to the Œðer, and when she haxed me if I could handle it, I answered certainly.

Let me tell you something about academia, though. It's not usually the administrators who make life unpleasant. Many of their ¢elghs are instructors and understand what the life of a lowly instructor is like. Nor are the students unreasonable. They may be muddle-headed at times, but most seem inter-rusted in doing what they need to do to succeed academically. One's greatest enemy is the colleague who, for some reason or Œðer, fancies his or her ¢elgh in competition with you. She will sometimes aßume that the way for her to achieve personal succeß in academia is to make everyone else around her miserable. She pounces on the shortcomings of Œðers. Would you believe that I was actually confronted by a colleague who told me that the sound of my wooden leg ●stumping around the office● was a distraction to her, though her lengthy personal telephone calls were, one should aßume, not to be thought a distraction to anyone else. Yes, Virginia, control freaks run rampant on college campuses. Sit in on a faculty meeting. You'll hear them. They want uniform text adoption; they want hierarchical control over parking facilities. Even the most repreßive administrator rolls his or her eyes at this. Two hours after the administrator has tried to end the faculty meeting, the control freak insists they discuß in detail who gets what faculty development funds when.

What did I do? I told my ↓colleague↓ I'd keep my office hours in my car two blocks away (I was not permitted any consideration for my parking needs because the colleague had complained about that as well). That way my ●stumping around the office● would no longer disturb her personal telephone calls.

Now, did I understand you correctly when you said you were inter-rusted in a job in academia? Are you sure? Are you ready for the petty?

*

He had made me dreß like a platypus in order to go into the water to approach the ducks.

<<You've made me—.>>

<<A polymesus,>> he said.

ɕPolemicist?ꜿ thought I. I went to look up the word, but someone had gutted my favorite dictionary, a Funk & Wagnalls, and replaced its contents with those of a far-inferior dictionary from a hundred years earlier.

Polysemous? Polymerus? What the heck was a ▶polymesus◀? Being a platypus was hard enough.

*

I was in a store when a drive-by occurred next door. I had a clear view out the open front door of the shooter in his car. He saw me see him. Before I could move, he'd come in, grabbed me, thrown me into his car, and took me for a ride as his hostage, intending to kill me asap, telling me I'd join the dead shopkeep in a little while.

I mentioned my sons were expecting me and that their school would punish them severely if I wasn't there on time, so we picked up my two sons from their school. We had to take along with us a couple of administrative personnel, the punishment administrants, who interfered along the way.

I had to explain to them why we should make a plea. My boys understood.

So, along the way, I gradually dropped little details about the dead shopkeep on the kidnapper, details about the shopkeep's life, his hopes, his family struggles, and eventually humanized the merchant for the thug. The thug heard me and fell quiet in sullen thought. He announced an apology to me and let me out of the car. I motioned to my children to leave, and they did. I followed them. The Œðer people started to follow us, but the thug shook his head and reached over to slam the shut door as soon as I was out. He then childproof-locked the doors again. I had no idea what he was going to do with the administrators, but at least my boys were safe.

*

I stared into the river and remembered the blue angelfish who had swum into my heart in the Fox River of home.

ɕA blue angelfish!ɔ I thought I saw one. No—just a bluish stone.

Stone blue, here for you—hard and cold. Rock skip jump, play along the surface and forget the depth. Play along the surface, and you won't get old. Land soft splash, no matter where you lept.

Dragon love, up here for you—heart of coal. Sparks snap high from the surface where we slept. Look along the surface—see the sparkling gold? Matter flies away and can't be kept.

No matter what, the matter doesn't matter. Where's the matter? It's all energy now. What's the matter?

No wonder what I wondered was never wonderful.

No telling what I've never told to you.

Why, you may hax, did I stop coming for you? Your old man threatened to harm my kids. I figured if you wanted me, you'd leave him. You couldn't make that leap of faith. I understand. I am saddened. I cannot fix things. The only person in the position to fix things is you.

I see my offal life floating down the river. I have to keep going the Œðer way.

*

Mars Condatis couldn't be far. Lake Gusev. The Ma'Adim River began getting rougher. Spring was around the bend, not that one would notice here in a land without seasons.

I heard a couple of the men grumble that as soon as this aßignment to aßeß the Aasvogel situation ends, they're applying for transfer to Titon. They said the living conditions were easier there, and that they'd gain some credibility there.

I'm not sure what that means.

We still had a few cans of horned beef à la ▶Johnny Cash◀, and ironically, they went a long way to Brightening the Mood. Everyone seemed in better spirits after breakfast.

*

Brightening-the-Mood was a trader we met on the river. He ahoyed us, and we tied our boats together. He and Polymesus, who was also the provisions manager, and I as a senior official went ashore to talk out of sight of our crews.

<<You fellows have all the provisions you need? I can get you anything you might want,>> he said, sounding puffy with confidence.

<<You got Captain Black in a can?>> I haxed smart-aßedly.

<<Yep,>> came the surprising reply. <<I also have a natural toasted vanilla cavendish blend without so much bite,>> he said.

<<What's the cavendish mixed with?>>

<<Virginia, of course. I think burley, or even Maryland, would overwhelm the cavendish.>>

<<I'm not so sure about Maryland.>>

<<Maybe it depends on the cut. Want to try a pouch? It's better and costs leß than Captain Black.>>

<<Better give me one of each, just in case my tastes are different than yours.>>

<<Done. Anything else?>>

We quickly put together a shopping list and gave it to Brightening-the-Mood.

▶The Mood◀refers to his era. In his native dialect▶Mood◀means▶Modern◀. He had ancestors named ▶Brightening-the-Mid◀ and ▶Brightening-the-Old◀

Just when we thought we'd escaped, as we were watching Brightening-the-Mood disappear around the bend, we heard a loud cry.

Polymesus said, <<Don't mind that. That's Cayenne the loud cryin' hygienic guy.>>

<<He was frozen?>>

<<No—he's just loud. One of them told me about him. He's a malcontent who's been banned to the fringes. Harmleß. Just too OCD-erratic for the center.>>

The loud cry repeated, more a screechy yell, really. Undignified,

<<You are sure he's not in pain?>>

<<Oh, he's in pain. On the outskirts his extremities freeze and thaw, freeze and thaw. He's been given hats, gloves and fur-lined boots, even, or so I'm told. He refuses to wear them. The crying is his art form, and his pain helps him achieve his art. The recordings of his cries are actually quite popular and have filled his bank account, which he never touches.>>

<<Should we ignore him?>>

<<Too late; I'm afraid he's seen us and is on his way over.>>

Oh, gorsch.

We watch his approach. He carries his ¢elgh with fear and loaming. That he aspects so probably doesn't dawn on him.

Oh, gosh. I wish I was in the arms of my angel. I am, however, not magically transported there.

You know, I've started wondering about my mortality. Sadly, and then I think all I need to do is quit smoking. But when I wasn't smoking, things weren't going as well as now. Rationalization #73.

Here he was: the spy who came in from the cold extremities of the city environs.

<<Help!>> he cried. <<They're still burning croßes out here!>>

And croßing burners, no doubt. The weather was changing. A sudden downpour left us at the mercy of the crier, who said to follow him to shelter that he knew. Within minutes we were safe in a café, drying in front of a fire.

We ordered coffee and looked around ▶The Cavern Club◀, as the place called its ¢elgh. An old photograph of the Silver Beatles hung on the wall I was facing; the frame, apparently glued on the wall, held an impoßible angle as it peered down on me.

My coffee was lukewarm, but I drank it with great appreciation nonetheleß. We'd run out of most of our coffee on board and had been driven to drinking some truly nasty powdered instant. The Cavern Club was a welcome break. Polymesus, Cayenne and I sat together.

Cayenne looked at me for two minutes before he said, <<Who was she?>>

<<Ah,>> I said, <<you're no madman. She was the highest, finest dream who became the most glorious, beautiful reality I have ever seen.>>

<<Why are you not pursuing her?>>

<<Oh, come on. We're boring poor Polymesus here—he doesn't want to hear this.>>

<<On the contrary, sit. I listen carefully to anything Cayenne says—he has great wisdom. You I *have* to listen to.>> He laughed and slapped my back.

<<Well, she married, for one.>>

<<And she broke your heart?>> haxed Polymesus.

<<No, that's not it. She was married when I met her. She was just there, in front of me, appeared out of nowhere in a crowd. I saw her and trembled. I knew instantly we were meant to be together. I danced around her for half a year before haxing to get to know her better. She let me. And she got to know me. And we fell in love deeply and soundly.

<<She has visited me many times. I wish I could go to her, but that can't work. She must decide what she wants. I know she knows how powerful this is. That's not the question. I have faith in her to understand. When she weighs everything, I'm sure that I'll not be found wanting.

<<We have known each Œðer for two years. We have known each Œðer for more than a year. This is just a test.

<<So I bury my ¢elgh in my work, in my family and friends, and continue along, hoping to hear from her again soon. Meanwhile, I ache for her. I hope she figures it out soon. Until then, I am in pain.>>

Cayenne laughs. <<You are but a child at heart,>> he says.

<<Perhaps. But I know I must hover here. I cannot move without her.>>

<<Well, hover you shall. Your boat has left without you.>>

I looked at Polymesus. <<How do you know?>> I haxed Cayenne.

<<I know. They have given you up as lost.>>

<<We're going to need to catch up to them then.>>

<<Not until the rain slackens.>>

Polymesus, visibly upset, said, <<But how will we catch up to them?>>

<<I can lead you to Condatis overland,>> said Cayenne. <<Meanwhile, let us have some more coffee.>> So we stayed and talked. Not to each Œðer, but each to his ¢elgh, mumbling and cursing, with Cayenne adding the occasional yowl.

*

<<Good god, you two are whining in stereo,>> said Polymesus. <<Everyone's life is hard. Now let's get going.>> The rain had stopped not two seconds earlier. <<I can't listen to you two anymore.>>

<<We should wait to see if it's just a lull,>> I said, just to annoy him.

<<No!>>

<<Okay, we can go,>> agreed Cayenne. We bought a few provisions from the counter clerk at the Cavern Club and exited.

*

Cayenne led us into the jungle.

Flavomeliads, with their purple sap-covered fronds, apparently quite hungry, swiped at us as we paßed them. Fortunately we had bought machetes at the Cavern Club. Careßmatangs chattered in the canopy and occasionally swung down at us to stroke our heads.

We decided we'd best keep our pith helmets on. Also purchased at the Cavern Club. I began to wonder if Cayenne was in on some elaborate ploy to generate tourist income.

<<We're not tourists, you know,>> I said aloud to him. He looked at me like I'd just blurted out some nonsequitur. But I knew he knew what I meant. Even Polymesus smiled at Cayenne's funny expreßion.

<<Hey, are these careßmatangs good to eat?>> I haxed loudly, as if they'd understand

my meaning.

<<Shh!>> said Cayenne. <<Don't upset them.>>

Polymesus and I laughed heartily.

<<Really! Keep it down! Don't enrage them. They've been known to tear apart rival primates when provoked.>>

We averted our eyes from the canopy and headed toward a tributary that we could croß and beyond which, according to Cayenne, the careßmatangs never croßed.

<<Why's that?>> I haxed, swatting at a low-swinging arm.

<<They're afraid to,>> he replied. I decided to drop the ißue, but Polymesus couldn't resist.

<<Why?>> he haxed. <<Ow!>> One had gotten hold of his hair.

<<Let's hope you don't have to find out>> was Cayenne's enigmatic reply as he gently peeled the simian fingers off from my friend. <<There are things far worse than being too affectionate.>>

<<Like what?>> haxed Polymesus the Stupid.

<<Shut up, will ya?>> I snapped. <<I don't want to hear it.>>

<<Your friend is right, Polymesus. Let's croß that bridge *if* we come to it.>>

<<Thank you,>> said I, having an image of Friedkin's famous bridge scene in *Sorcerer*.

Indeed, the careßmatangs soon let us alone, but by then we were contending with thicker brush, avoiding a particularly nasty variety of stinging nettles that Cayenne referred to as ▶bushfingers◀. The plants were hypnotically attractive, though. Cayenne said that it was their aroma and the pheronomes contained therein that drew people towards the plants, which were actually carnivorous. I can only describe the aroma as resembling the most delectable vaginal juices of the most delicious woman I have ever known, my beautiful heartbreaker, my bluest angel. How I wanted to taste her again.

Cayenne began hacking at me with his machete, and I began to fear him. He was going to kill us out here. He was insane. He swung at my head. He must have severed something in my brain because I began to lose inter-rust even in the fact that he was attacking me. Go ahead, I said, take my brain, take my body. I'll still be here. I was holding her again, delighting in how she felt in my hands, drinking of her, deeper, wetter.

An Œðer whack of the machete fell on me, and I shuddered to attention. Suddenly I remembered I was in the jungle, and my darling vanished. I was upset.

<<Cayenne!>> I yelled. <<What the hell are you doing?>>

<<Saving your sorry aß, again.>>

<<What?>>

<<You went right into the damned bushfingers, you idiot.>>

<<You should have seen your ¢elgh,>> added Polymesus. <<So funny.>>

<<Go to hell.>>

<<Seriously, though, we'd better find some *aloe condatis* around here quickly before those nettle stings swell up. Œðerwise we'll be camping here for a couple of days because you'll be in no condition to move.>>

<<What? Where will we get this aloe?>>

<<Only atop Mt. Skizzifizz, thirty miles north of us and then two miles straight up.>>

<<What?>> said Polymesus. <<I'll wait here for you guys. I'm not trekking up some two-mile-high mountain.>>

<<I'm just kidding,>> said Cayenne. <<It's all over the place around here. No problem at all. Despite its name, it isn't really a desert succulent.>>

<<That's not funny,>> said Polymesus.

<<Oh, poor fellow,>> mocked Cayenne. <<What happened? Parents set their ¢elghs up as examples that weren't negative enough? You had it soft?>>

<<What?>>

<<Your parents. They were probably decent folks.>>

<<Yes, indeed.>>

<<See? That's a mistake. Parents should just be lousy, miserable jerks. Criminals, even. That way their kids will grow up knowing how to handle difficult situations.>>

<<And you are nothing but a master baiter,>> said my friend. <<I want no piece of your argument.>>

<<You found that aloe, yet?>> I said, already going mad with the itching as my nettle wounds swelled. <<You guys are going to let me die while you argue about something so petty?>>

<<And as for *you,*>> said Polymesus at me, <<don't you know yet that the question is not about living and dying? It's about lying and diving!>>

<<Thus spake Jacques Cousteau to Marat?>> I offered.

<<And wasn't that some thick-heeded advice!>> I realized he was just trying to distract me from my agony, but it was working.

<<No, you fool. Diving. If we can't find your precious aloe, then diving into the river should provide some temporary relief. This water is rich in basaltic compounds.>>

<<And Chernoble fish,>> I replied. The fish were named punningly for their piranha-like churning when devouring any enormous creature. They'd pick the carcaß of something the size of an elephant clean in minutes, making the victim look much like a victim of the Chernoble nuclear accident back on Earth.

<<It'd get rid of your itch.>>

<<We're too high above the river to go down there now anyway,>> said Cayenne. Look—here's the bridge. Sure enough, it *was* Friedkin's bridge that was swinging between our side of one mountain and the near side of an Œðer. The ground must have been five hundred feet below us. Our bridge was nothing but rope and local bamboo-like tubular wooden plant stalks.

<<I know there's some aloe just on the Œðer side of the bridge,>> said Cayenne, probably to coax me over the two-hundred-foot-long bridge. I didn't care anymore. The itching was driving me crazy. I ran over the bridge, yelling and waving my arms in distreß. I've never run two hundred yards faster, even without my artificial leg.

<<Stay there!>> yelled Cayenne when I'd gotten to the Œðer side. <<Don't go down the path yet!>>

<<Okay,>> I said, starting to feel the salt from my sweat aggravating the itch.

Sure enough, though, once we'd all croßed the bridge, Cayenne found the plants, pulled a half-dozen from the cluster, inserted his thumbnail into the fleshiest part of the succulent, and then ran his nail lengthwise along the valley of the stem. A yellow gelatinous ooze began dripping from the plant. He took this ooze and handed it to me and told me to rub it wherever the itching was worst and wherever my skin was red or blistering. Blistering hadn't developed yet, and he said I was lucky on that account, though I certainly felt far from being ▶lucky◀.

<<Where to now?>> haxed the ever-impatient Polymesus.

<<There,>> said Cayenne, pointing at the hidden entrance to a cavern. <<This takes us down, under the river, over to the ŒÐer bank.>>

<<Then let's go,>> said Polymesus, going ahead.

<<Not like that, you won't. Unleß you like being devoured by the albino cave scorpions.>>

<<What?>>

<<They are attracted to the smell of human musk. We have to disguise our presence by covering our ¢elghs in the scat of Martian devils. The devils eat the scorpions, so the scorpions hide when confronted by the scent.>>

<<Oh, that's easy,>> said Polymesus. <<We just march right into a den of devils and hax them for stool specimens.>>

<<Actually, we'll want to avoid the devils their ¢elghs. They're three times the size of their Tasmanian ancestors and are every bit as vicious. They are what keep the careßmatangs away. I suggest we hurry. The devils are nocturnal, and we want to be far beyond the cavern when night falls.>>

<<Gotcha,>> said Polymesus <<So where do we find these critters?>>

<<They burrow into thickets of bushes.>>

<<What about their shit? Where do we find that?>>

<<They're kind of like cats in that regard. They use a communal area and cover it in sand when done. All we need is to find a sandy spot within thirty or forty yards of their burrow.>>

That was it, I realized—the scream I'd heard before that I imagined to be Aasvogel's infant son. It was the cry of a devil. I'd read about their cries. How they'd delighted the Chinese emperors who'd kept the torture gardens because the emperors could imagine the cries came from tortured children!

We found the scat cache relatively quickly, my colleagues apparently much more motivated to find scats than aloe, and we coated our ¢elghs hair to toenail with the foul stuff.

We had achieved stealth. After that we could enter the lair of the enemy undetected, like ninja serial suicide bombers. A few olfactorily-challenged scorpions seemed unaware of our presence. We did not bŒÐer them.

The cavern narrowed and began a steep descent. At the end of the descent, our progreß was halted by an iron door. Cayenne had the key.

But before he opened the door, he began to lecture us (of course): <<You may have wondered why the careßmatangs don’t come over the bridge. Let me tell you that what they fear most is not bushfingers, Chernoble fish, Martian devils, nor albino cave scorpions. What they feared is here, behind door number one>> (a brand new Cadillac? A donkey? Would I trade what was in my unopened box for it?) The careßmatangs know that whatever the door conceals is not fully constrained by the door—it oozes through. Its gaßes find their way through the keyhole and frame. The door only gives the illusion of security, like hollow preßboard doors in cheap apartment buildings.

ɕThey should have installed a Tru-Seal™ brand hermetically sealable iron door, the door for absolute protectionɘ, I thought. I remembered the company jingle from my youth: ♪Get on the ball with the seal—the Tru-Seal iron door seal!♫ And the commercial showed a circus seal balancing on its nose a white ball decorated with blue and red stars. The seal toßed the ball in the air, caught it in its flippers, and then, balancing its ¢elgh on its front flippers while cradling the ball between them, it did a handstand so that it seemed to be standing on the ball. It was a very clever ad. I used to bark in imitation of a seal while clapping my hands whenever I saw the commercial.

<<Here,>> said Cayenne to Polymesus, handing him a pair of scißors. <<You’ll need to cut any brand names off of your clothing. Even your underwear. If it can’t be cut, I have a thick-lined black permanent marker to obliterate the name with.>>

<<What?>>

<<Just do it. Then give the scißors to Bözö Number Two over there,>> said Cayenne, sweeping his hand at me once while over-enunciating his words as if Polymesus were a simpleton.>>

When I had finished clipping my shirt tag and blackening the brand name on the tongues of my shoes, he finally consented to opening the door. Just in time, too, because the exposed flesh under our shirts and on our feet began to stir the scorpions’ attentions.

When the door opened, loudspeakers announced, <<Welcome, visitor! This entrance is the exclusive property of No Space Industries, Incorporated. Please remove all corporate logos except those authorized by No Space Industries, Incorporated. Enjoy your stay in Lake Gusev City. While here, if approached by anyone Œðer than a representative of No Space Industries, Incorporated, haxing you to wear clothing sponsoring their corporate entities, please tell them, <No thanks. I have No Space!> Have a great day, sponsored by No Space Industries, Incorporated, your identity leader!>>

<<Is that a law?>> I haxed Cayenne.

<<No—it's just a corporate slogan. But they own this gate. They won't let you through here unleß you comply. And the competitions' gates are far leß convenient, at least for us for right now.>>

Someone was approaching the gate from the Œðer direction: a man wearing a bowler. Perhaps he was just going to the gate. We were—at least I was—a bit nervous. When he was only ten yards away, he set down the bowler, who took us on like ten-pins. He had a bloody bandage over one eye.

<<Hey!>> he yelled to us.

<<Hey!>> we yelled back.

<<Don't follow the signs without thinking them through!>> he yelled.

<<What?>>

<<Think them through. I just saw one on a building that said, ⧗Caution. Falling Ice.⧗ So, naturally, I looked up. A falling icicle speared me the eye.>>

<<I see,>> said Polymesus.

ͼThat was unneceßaryͽ, I thought.

I watched the inflicted man paß and noticed he had printed on the back shoulder of his jacket the words ▶No Space◀. I suddenly felt leß sympathetic. After all, he had corporate sponsorship.

At the croßwalk, I was faced with new condundra. A sign at the croßwalk—we must follow signs—said I had a choice—a red hand or a white person walking.

I wasn't going to be caught red-handed.

Actually, I think the sign means that white people can croß there, but red people (a derogatory term use in order to summarily dismiß indigenous peoples) are not permitted to croß there. This town is picky with its intersections. An Œðer light at an intersection two blocks farther, instead of a red hand, said, ⧗Don't Walk⧗. I skipped. I didn't know what else to do. Polymesus ran. Cayenne ignored the law entiredly and croßed the street in blithe disobedience. Maybe Cayenne could get away with it, but Polymesus and I worried.

We took a short-cut through the No Space outlet store, and I got us ushered out of the establishment abruptly when I followed one sign to the letter: ⧗Wet Floor⧗. I did. The store personnel seemed upset. I noticed on the way out that the store was promoting the DVDVGHIFIHD machines.

We came to a train croßing. I aßumed the town must be predominantly Christian. Buddhist communities would have train prayer wheels.

Even outside the store on the Œðer side the clothing was predominantly No Space. We did see a pair of apparently independent little stores next to an Œðer: Schuster's Clothing and, ironically, Taylor's Shoes.

We must have been approaching the downtown shopping district because more stores began to appear.

ѪOedipus Toys—Where No Crayon Is an EnemyѪ.

ѪCousins and Cuisines—Foods of the Dutch East IndiesѪ.

Polymesus wanted to buy some batteries for his camera. We found a battery store that only took cash: ѪBatteries Without ChargesѪ. I presumed they'd not stay in busineß long.

A savings-and-loan bank called ѪThe Left BankѪ proclaimed proudly, ѪThere's no *U* in ▶bank◀Ѫ! Elitists!

ѪTellit & Douche—D & C AccountingѪ.

<<Look at that, Polymesus,>> I said. <<A company is actually called ѪTiresias InvestmentsѪ.>>

<<Where? I don't see it.>>

<<Well, learn to look, will you?>>

<<Can't change an old dog with new tricks,>> he said, garbling the cliché.

<<I can with that,>> and I pointed to change machine inside a laundromat.

An Œðer tourist approached us for directions, as if we knew.

Spray can zoo Deutsch? Was he saying German graffiti decorated the zoo?

Ich bin geheißt? I am heated? I am named?

I shrugged. Polymesus also shrugged. Cayenne said a few words to him in German, and the tourist left.

Time nearly stopped. We saw slow children playing in the street.

More trains, construction and traffic.

A water park in a quarry announces water plastic rafting swimming.

Trapped on private property.

Pursued into mine.

I ✹hit✹ and accidentally kill my pursuer with a shovel, and then shove him down a mineshaft.

I look to escape—the mine connects the downtown building subbasements.

I come out near the highway. The property owner aßumes I'm there for some gold-mining contest.

The body of the deceased is found. It's a performance party. Each person brought an artist, presumably dead.

The winner croßes the goal as the two middle letters are switched.

Inside, each represented artist has a work displayed or performed. In each room of this seemingly endleß mansion a play or piece of music is being performed by partygoers. One partygoer, the sponsor, is directing the work.

The mansion's common areas are an Escher-like maze of stairs, walkways and croßwalks. Partygoers lose each Œðer.

Rooms contain robot orchestras, hip hop karaoke, libraries where books are the performance. Some partygoers are keeping journals of their experience of the party.

Their journals become their ¢elghs' performances, so being wary of anything or anyone.

I remember Aasvogel and realize I must find an exit, perhaps a red exit light.

<<Let him go,>> said the place. <<Him I hate forever.>> And so I was spat back out of the mansion.

<<There you are!>> I heard Polymesus exclaim. <<I lost you in the crowd in there.>> I looked to where he was pointing and saw the mansion covering its ¢elgh quickly with the façade of a department store.

<<Did you buy anything?>> he haxed. I looked at the shovel in my hand.

<<No,>> I replied.

On the street corner, cars were queuing up for the parking lot. The cars were odd little one-seaters whose backs reclined with the driver inside. The attendants then

✺popped✺ open the lids, helped the drivers out, and then stacked the cars like so many coffins or cords of drywood.

The garage’s name was ▶Humidor and Wife-adore Parking◀.

Acroß the street was a car service place—Nude Lube was offering a free top-off service.

On the sidewalk, speed freaks were pitching Bennies. I felt sorry for the one who looked like Benny Hill. But then, every decision in life is both for and against everything.

Hookers leaned up against a government facility for emißions testing.

I heard one say to an Œðer, <<I’m sorry he had to die.>> That was all I wanted to hear of that conversation.

Past a store selling Ꭓpure places and suppliancesᎳ and a Roughrider men’s store sporting in its window a poster that said, ꞳGirls don’t make paßes at guys who aren’t aßesꞳ to accompany a display of studded black leather and chains, and on the sidewall of the window an Œðer poster that said, ꞳFor guys, ✹hit me✹ refers to drinks, cards, and Mary Jane; for gals, it means, ✹I like it rough✹. Be a Roughrider.Ꭓ

ɕRaccoons have barbed penises,ɘ I thought. Maybe a doctor could sell me some barbed penis implants. That’d be for all the gals named ▶Barbie◀, obviously. No wonder those dolls were so popular. Find a gal who had a stuffed raccoon and a Barbie doll, and you know what you have.

Drift away from there as quickly and as unnoticed as poßible on the raft of becoming. Past the Edward G. Robinson High School and the Albert Budd spool factory, which recruits heavily from its neighbors. ꞳDrop out? Just drop in here instead, and get paid!Ꭓ

I paßed the window of a furniture store, and an ▶Ultra-Comfort◀ recliner was on display. No one seemed to notice when I snuck inside and deposited my ¢elgh on it. I must have been napping for a half-an-hour before waking up, feeling I was being watched. I opened my eyes and saw a young round-faced blonde woman staring at me intently. That she was not wearing a blouse announcing her corporate allegiance was a statement of non-conformity that I found refreshing. Actually, the green chenille blouse she wore was unbuttoned to her solar plexus, yet it fit snugly and revealed the outlines of her lovely breasts and her outstanding nipples. She caught me staring and smiled. What a smile! I felt like this was the first time I’d been smiled at. Her light blue eyes sparkled with a spritely mischief that let me know she had something in store for me. However, when I smiled in return, she grimaced as if startled out of a reverie she preferred as fantasy to truth.

She left, but I decided to stay and observe Œðer paßers-by. I noticed that government employees were apparently prohibited from wearing corporate-sponsored clothing. Instead, their gray uniforms resembled pyjamas and bore on their chests the phrase

⧖Stop Non-violence Now more than Never⧖.

What in the world had become of my companions. They kept disappearing, like shiny nuggets in silt.

Suddenly a craven flew to the showroom window, and its suit seemed made of slimy maggots in silk.

No more!

The girl in green chenille had croßed the street and headed towards a sushi rustaurant, a theatre, and a jazz nightclub.

When she saw me walk in after her, she left.

There, where she had been a second earlier, was suddenly someone in her place, someone I knew from long before, or someone who looked just like her. She carried her ¢elgh in much the same way. The same beautiful, glistening chic black hair with highlights that glimmered like gold. The same nervous uneasineß. I hope that's gone. Maybe this time she wants to explore this more deeply than we did earlier.

Should I compare her to Sylvia? Sylvia, who really knew her way around an oven? Sure, she was, um, yeah, she was a checker at the feed store. Like to cook her family dinner, yeah, that's it. And then, when the maid didn't show up that day as scheduled, everything was thrown off. They can't save you if they don't know you're sinking. Best is never to sink. Be like Sisyphus—keep pushing forward, no matter how far back you get pushed again and again. Be like…

Sylvia, yes, but a Sylvia with a different manner—more extreme in ¢elgh-indulgence, and ¢elgh-loathing—maybe not—my ¢elgh is pretty ¢elghish. Still, how beautiful a thought is this one that keeps coming up from her—she has always pulled me.

Hey, hadn't I been thinking about someone else just then? I couldn't remember. Couldn't have been important. So I'll just go on. No? I should get down off the table? No speech? Okay, but you're going to feel you mißed something.

<<Oh, here's your mißing dog.>>

<<What?>>

<<See—it was your mißing something.>>

<<You're <Mißing Something.> I'm <Mißing You.>>>

An apple comes rolling down the street. I look more closely and see a boy pulling it along on a string.

<<Won't that bruise your apple?>> I hax him. I have to shout for him to hear.

<<Only if I slow down,>> he shouts back, and I see he is swinging the string in a figure eight to keep the apple off the ground. I want to be neither that boy nor that apple. Not even the string, though being the connector isn't a bad position to be in. Precarious, though. You need the old GCS: Good Customer Service. Yeßirree, Bob!

May we help you? Do you have one of our frequent visitor paßes?

I've been enjoying my visitor paßes to my memories about my friend like Sylvia. I am, of course, a happy and frequent visitor. We need to return to happy moments.

<<What about Polymesus?>> though, is haxed by some annoying impulse inside me. Polymesus is a grown man. Certainly he can take care of his ¢elgh. And Cayenne? More than a grown man, he is an independent man. Worthy of admiration on that count alone. Not so easily pulled off in the game as it is in practice.

This is Mars, after all, damn it! It's never going to be Venus, no matter how much window dreßing is in it.

Rain guards the city.

A bumpersticker is stuck in the gutter. ⧗Mars Condatis Orb Fest⧗ was from an event. Mars Condatis's detritus was spilling out to meet us.

Once met, it made us fret. A new fret led to the Met. At the Met we laid it down. Pigmeat Markham went to town. Screamin' Jay was on his way. Cool Cab—Cab Calloway. Sun Ra and his grandson Steam, who was created not born. But Steam would meet Sun's soul in the ether of one of Saturn's rings. Steam knew how he figured into the remigration.

Meaning sometimes bloßoms forth from poetry. My favorite is the serendipitous meaning I never intended and only recorded accidentally, as an observer of the world, and discovered, upon hearing, that the meaning intended has been wed along the way to something quite different.

Well, what would you have done? I mean, really! Do I need to be explicit about everything? Maybe in the love parts, okay, I can see that, but not now.

I am being deadly serious.

Deadly, for sure.

Shh! Let her speak.

Who's ►she◄?

I don't know. *That* I wish I knew.

Well, buddy, do me a favor. You don't need it. How many novels are you going to give us with this same insecure ¢elgh-reflexive fellow with the problems with the dames? Who gives a barnacle's aß? Okay, the last you did was all weepy and sentimental. Okay, as an experiment, I'll grant it to you. But don't make a habit of it, okay? Be robust! Well all reet!

<<Come out of that rain,>> said Cayenne, pulling me by the elbow over to the corner of the window of a bar that was filled with frizzle-topped hippity hops all yerhoodi. At least they were quiet.

<<I got news,>> says Cayenne, <<see?>>

<<You do?>> reply I. <sigh>.

<<Woo dough?>> replied Trudeau. <<Oui?>>

<<Don't butt in, buttster,>> says Cayenne, cracking us all up. It's hip as a zip here in now, man! Watch out, grams! We all know your tricks. No, truck your ¢elgh some of mine.

Booble gobbin' with my britches on,
Wet nursie are you dry for sure?
As long as you're lactating,
folks are only speculatin'
that my taste for you ain't so pure.
Tweedle perkin' with gloves removed,
can't we tune in the right groove?
So long as it's only fish you're baiting,
I'll bite all over while we're mating
until you hax me to improve.
Lightnin' roddin' with the antenna up,
I have a tent we can erect
in the hills by Potter's Mills,
where I forgot my ills
and life became, once more, correct.

Spilling into the groove of the seventh son, I am bouncy in the present sun.

<<Cayenne?>>

<<Yeah?>>

<<What is this? Where are we?>>

<<We're close to the nexus. Best thing to do is focus on particularities and stay clear of all generalizations. Better to focus on grains of sand than the nature of the universe. You'd get both answers earlier.>>

<<Where's Polymesus?>>

<<Just meet us at the northeast gate—it's sponsored by a colonic cleanser. ꓫOnce out, there's no readmißion!ꓫ So let's meet outside at ten.>>

As soon as Cayenne disappeared, though, I lost all sense of where I was and had again only the past to cling to.

I got up out of the Ultra-Comfort™ recliner and remarked to the sales clerk who was sent to sell me that I thought the chair was marvelous. It spooled quite a tale into my imagination.

Now, wasn't the raft of becoming somewhere near?

*

Refreshed, I woke still in the Ultra-Comfort™ recliner. I seemed unable to leave it. I remembered how my first wife's family had described a couch that was like an octopus, how its tentacles would draw one in and suck one down so that no one who sat in the couch could ever escape.

Is that it on the recliner now?

►Sofa◄ as I know.

Ow.

I think Americans fall asleep with lit cigarettes and set their couches on fire because they're used to burning Chesterfields. Or that true only for Canadians?

<<Cough.>> Cancer. Emphysema. Death. Not breathing? That would not be good.

Keep breathing: that's my motto. As long as you're breathing, you have a chance.

Don't let anyone take your breath away. Or so the article read.

Well, throw that paper away. It's old news.

I gueß the real word is ►chesterbed◄. Okay, caught. <<It's a fair cop,>> as they say on *Python*.

It's taking forever to get to Condatis. Ten o'clock. North gate—there it is.

What a horrible name for the product that sponsored that sphincter in and out of the city:

Kramm. That's right! ϪThe next time you enema, Kramm it!Ϫ

A natural. The original meaning of that sentence will be completely lost to history.

The worst part was that the exit actually was a giant sphincter we had to crawl through.

No, not really.

►Feelings are forbidden◄ is scrawled on a wall—a nice tag, actually—several colors—blue, red, purple, black, yellow.

<<Can you get up? We need to keep moving.>> I was sitting again—this time on a stoop facing the exit.

Polymesus was speaking into my face. I barely recognized him. I dribbled on my chin in response, incapable of speech. My body had been paralyzed. Actually, I realized, whenever I sat, I became paralyzed. The true enemy was sitting.

No sedation!

Move, damn it!

Get up! Go! Move it! I know it runs counter to all you've learned. Ever since you were hooked as a baby on the gateway drug, sugar, you have waited to relax to let the effects paß. Beatnik weed and Nixon horse and US Army LSD and BZ (a superhallucinogen, 100 to 1000 times more powerful than LSD, that was tested at the Edgewood Arsenal from 1959 to 1975 on some 3000 soldiers who were told they were being given aspirin and who then lost entire seasons of their lives—a series of tests that were repeated a century later in the Mars Condatis Alien Holding Prison to see the effects on exotics) had the desired effect to large extent. TV helped. But the PC and the interweb have sealed our fates: anything you do Œðer than sitting still and working is downright treacherous! Anything to keep us off the streets, aßembling, or expreßing our disgust with the status quo.

Usage instructions: Preß.

God, how do people live here? Eighteen thousand thoughts attack me simultaneously. Buildings, roads, people. It's relentleß.

Up! You're talking like a sitting man. Like a sitting duck. And ►duck◄ is short for ►dumb fuck◄. Like Daffy and Donald.

Okay. My knees 💥pop💥. If getting up is so natural, then why are knees sending out warning alarms? My broken toe and my slipping disc in my back compete for next attention. Then the headache and the dry mouth. Body odor and perspiration. And only then do I consider my relative intelligence that day: is it stupid day or am I going to make something of it?

Let's make something of it, certainly, unleß we're recuperating. But that's part of the proceß, too. That's the inhalation. The writing is the exhalation. Both parts are equal.

Jump steady.

Okay, I'm up. Hey, have you seen some coffee around here? I want to drink some gilded splinters.

That's ▶walk on◀, Mac.

Okay. Shine a light!

Stones?

Spiritualized!

Put my left arm out and shake it all about.

Left hand from the left shoulder to the heart.

I place one foot directly in front of the Œðer and walk towards the exit. I feel two souls beside me, but I don't know who they are. Polymesus? Is that you? Is that Cayenne with you?

<<I need to leave the city,>> I say.

<<The toxins are really affecting you,>> says Cayenne. <<Sorry—I didn't realize. Most of us have inherited immunities or have built up resistance. Even Polymesus here seems to have the antibodies in his system. You, however—>>

<<Got kicked in the aß,>> you offer as conclusion.

<<Apparently so.>>

<<Is *that* our exit?>> I pointed to a picture of a posterior aperture.

<<Good god, no. That's a poster for Kramm. Whatever you do, don't say anything negative about Kramm on the way out.>>

<<Shouldn't they only control what goes in?>> I hax, trying to be funny.

<<It goes in; it must come out,>> says Polymesus. <<Firesign Theatre named that principle ▶Teslacles' Deviant to Fudd's First Law of Opposition◀.>>

<<Then we'd better get out of its way as soon as we're out, I'd say,>> says Cayenne.

<<<The monster rampages> is part of any monster tale.>>

Ha ha. What's this? Polymesus and Cayenne have been let through. I haven't. What? Over there? No—I'll be back, and I disappeared down an alley and ran and ran and ran until my heart hurt too much. Then I stopped, miles away, hidden I know not where. But those Kramm people were trying to detain me. I wouldn't be surprised if Polymesus and Cayenne were in on it. Trying to set me up. That could be. Well, stay away from Colonish water. They weren't expecting me to get stopped. At that point, they couldn't reveal their aßociation with me. They know I can handle my ¢elgh and meet up with them sometime before Mars Condatis. They've certainly been developing quite the friendship, though. Leaving me out, of course. But if I begin to suspect my familiars, then I will be like Othello, easily manipulated to foreign purpose.

No—<<I only want to be with people who want to be with me>> said a great philosopher in Chicago once upon a time a long time ago.

<<It's all over, Howard,>> sang a band from Chicago.

That's it. Pretend this is Chicago. Just take North Avenue west to Maywood Park and from that point on you're at the mercy of the suburbs.

Or you could take Cermak to Mayfair Park in Westchester and get in a quick eighteen of disc golf. It's an easy nine-holer, all par threes, though it'd be fair to make at least two of them twos. Not like Commißioner's Park in Frankfort, which features ▶The Impaler◀ and some 750+-foot dogleg that I think is a par five.

Mokena has a beautiful 27-hole course, though it is laid out according to some inscrutable methodology.

Oswego is really nice for eighteen, but poison ivy proliferates in the brush. Lots of trees and woods, but no real water hazards.

Our favorite is Campton Hills. It's only nine, but it's straight up and down the bluffsides of hills. Of course, that erodes the hills, but they would erode anyway. We just help things along. I did Campton in 56 once (for twice through), but have bettered par (27) for nine a couple of times.

Campton is becoming too popular, though. I found that going early and on weekdays is best. Many disc golfers look like people who sleep late.

Hey, as long as I'm here, there's got to be a golf course. Preferably a disc golf course.

Those Œðer golfers like sharing their links the way skiers like sharing with snowboarders. Disc golf is an X-game, and I'm good at it.

It should be in the Olympics is what. See, now I have a purpose for being here. I am supposed to evaluate their disc golf courses.

Maybe I could propose and get paid for a feasibility study on the part-time sharing of community golf courses by different styles of golf. I'd have to try each, and I'd get paid for it. Yeah, I'll just walk up to one of these walking billboards and say, <<Take me to your leader!>> Well, somebody must have heard me because suddenly there she was: just beyond hearing. That struck me as odd. Several panes of glaß divided us into separate buildings. But she was there, and then she turned and saw me. I was honored. I waved and smiled. She smiled, but turned her attention back to her room abruptly, as if someone inside had just addreßed her.

The light shifted, and the panes of glaß became mirrors of the sun. I went back inside until the sun set a little more.

A robotic character named ►George Clowney◄ spoke to me.

<<Hey, Guy,>> he said, grabbing my elbow. <<Know why flying ants are extinct?>>

<<They're not,>> I replied.

<<Because the last person to see one was Amelia Earhart's nephew.>>

<<Ah, um…>>

His last words has been almost whispered in my ear, so his sudden burst of unimaginably loud laughter was not timed well. Or was it? Ws he trying to hurt me? I used to believe no one should trust clowns, but then I saw the Fellini film on the last clowns of Europe. The large circuses have pulled down their tents. The large circuses have pulled down their pants.

The large penises have pulled back their foreskins.

Ma Rainey stopped making cookies with moleskin.

►Ma Rainey◄ is the log-in name of Wayne White, a 35-year-old truck driver from Hammond, Indiana.

His job at the university is to send cookie bombs back at sources trying to illegally probe the computers. He just takes out their servers for several hours at a time. It's not like they're in a position to complain to the police, are they?

Moleskin is the software he developed for digging.

The identity of Ma Rainey is kept unknowable.

And thus the boat is kept rowable until we have safely arrived.

<<Welcome, Sir,>> I was greeted. <<I apologize for representatives of the diplomatic corps to have been so irresponsibly neglected. We had not been aware of your presence in our city. When we came acroß your colleague Polymesus, wandering around on his own, well, we were concerned. Then, when he explained how he and you had single-handedly—>>

<<Double, I think,>> said an Œðer feller.

<<Double-handedly, so be it, had managed to outwit our craftiest criminals, well, I was impreßed.>>

Oh, what had he been told, and by whom? How thrilling my life was? Here—stare at me while I take hours to write a sentence. Thrilling. Don't forget the times I can produce several pages in minutes. I can't tell time when I'm there. I need machines to remind me.

Shake that rat! Shake that rat! Whatcha doing with that? Shake that rat!

Nick Lowe, I owe you a debt. You were very hospitable to a drunk local rag journalist once. Very cool. A decent man and a great conversationalist. Here (or, should I say, preceding) are (were) the lyrics for my favorite instrumental of yours.

Maybe someone will use them sometime. All the Œðer stanzas, too.

Snap!

Heads up, here we go.

Straight for the public bazaar.

Flying from left to right, then curling into a line below the first, a lone word begs for attention:

Bizarre? Bizarre bazaar biz arrow Zorro zero…ero…ro…o

<<Row row row, oh, no, you don't,>> comes The Voice.

<<Let the arrow land,>> begs a fourth voice, a calm one.

Bizarre grew at the base of Mt. Skizzifiz. It had once been a resort town for the city dwellers to visit. Now urban sprawl fills the space. From Bizarre, we'd be able to take a bus to Mars Condatis and catch up with our crew.

This much I gleaned from my hosts. However, before I could leave, I had to find Polymesus. Cayenne, too, I suppose. But in the meantime, a bath, a meal of pheasant, green beans, and a local tuber called ►swellhead◄, which was shaped like a swollen head (which brought to mind mandrake root), provided a delicious repast.

I could have haxed the local constabulary to find my traveling companions, but I wasn't yet certain I could trust my new hosts. However, they did seem in agreement that the northeast exit was a good one to avoid. They had suggested Bizarre to the north. All the cerebral stuff was in the northwest quadrant, but Bizarre should be for the most part free from any exclusive control by the eastern ►Colon-ies◄, as they were facetiously known. Their ad slogan, ѪIf you like the East, Kramm itѪ, revealed an underlying resentment that the leaders had for their charges.

<<'Sonely 'sat the real time,>> sang the nation's Slogun on TV. He'd won the last election by cashing in all his [fish and] chips. Once elected, he found new ways to [fish] curry favors. He attended dozens of [fish] barbeques and [snake] ribbon-cutting ceremonies. He went to [lemming] church. He'd chat with people at the [sloth] city council meetings. He'd preß the [beef jerky] flesh, and he'd [weasel] smile at the cute young moms. He'd give suckers evenly to broken children [the holding pen in the slaughterhouse]. He'd hike the pipe [fish], slam the can [corned beef hash, I think], burden down [po' boy] [hot dog], and jump salty [pretzels].

I burdened down on a local barkeep [olives]. The bar was setting up for a blues show that evening [barbeque→pulled pork!] The lead singer for an old British blues band had been found in some cold-water flat in Berlin, was cleaned up a little, and sent on an endleß tour of his dozen most famous songs. The same twelve. Every night for fifty years.

The fate of singers. Compare the novelist.

The novelist…

…isn't in it for the money—much easier money is found just about anywhere else.

…isn't in it for the short term—keep writing forever. If you don't have it in you, quit.

…isn't using hir writing in support of political or religious agenda—Œðerwise although one may be a first-rate politician or theologian, because one can ultimately only serve one master, the writing by definition will be second rate. Only writing that serves writing its ¢elgh can be first rate. The goal is to write beautiful or at least aesthetically appropriate sentences.

I think this is all way beyond the aßignment to aßeß the Aasvogel situation.

What situation? It could be any one of hundreds. Of course, since nothing was ever really ►a situation◄, but just an example of an Œðer American artist overstepping his bounds and saying things he oughtn't to. He was silenced effectively for the first thirty years of his career, but after that…wow…you couldn't shut him up.

It's not his fault you have no inter-rust in what he knows. I'll betcha this, though. If a guy is braggin' on his ¢elgh too much, he seems smaller for it.

But take from the man his boa, his snakeskins, write in red if that's how it's gotta be.

He wore a hirsute hair suit, which he whetted down for quills.

Get going! I could feed the prod on my lower back.

Go already.

I don't know. Diplomatic receptions might be fun.

<<Trials for spying?>>

<<You don't think…?>>

<<Oh, sure, do.>> I followed Polymesus into the back of a pretzel van. He was playing loud homeworld music. I loved it. It was old Roy Loney, who was ♪selling stocks and buying socks♫ and ♪searching for a clue.♫ I was a genius jellyfish in the corner by the end of that. I gave up on reason and just followed Polymesus.

Left leg right leg left leg right.

I wish I were back home tonight.

Ow! He was pulling my arm, man. What a drag. Gotta go!

Then he goes.

Well, I'd better lock up. Put away the chairs.

<<Hey,>> yelled a voice from the kitchen. <<If you want to listen to the radio while you're cleaning, you can put it on the intercom here in the manager's office.>>

I looked to the spot where I'd seen both women—the one from the window and the Œðer from my past.

Neither was there now. I felt tired. Neither had ever truly been there. The three real stories all ended tragically, but the tragedies of those that could have been were tragic even more. Every poßibility lost is a paradise lost. Maybe someday one will last. Fourteen years the really big story, but not this story. This is about achievement and fulfillment.

I gotta keep singin' ♪Good Golly Miß Molly♫, even when someone else's opera takes over the radio, even if I'm not singing to my Cajun lady about ice cream cakes.

Even when the department stores play balloon kids pop.

I'd have to say that by and large the outside environment contains much leß good music now than it did back in the day. Note with great appreciation those true musicians of your generation. We certainly noted ours.

Music lets you envision for your ¢elgh. Value that.

The exit and the emulsion.

Part Two: The Pull Thence

The infusion and the entrance.

What will be expected of the rust of us, the crew, even the captain, when he returns? Thirty years have paßed, surely. Mars Condatis doesn't even exist anymore.

Okay, okay. I'm just kidding, but when the heck is old what's-his-name going to get here?

<<Who is that?>>

<<You know, old, um….>>

<<Who?>>

<<I'm not a serial suicide bomber,>> I aßure whoever is talking to me.

We disintegrate into lack of personality! I'm the cute one, says she, but what does she know?

<<What did you just write in there,>> she haxes. <Are you writing what I'm saying? I'm going to come over there—here, give me that—ow!—there, see, I broke it—well, you, too—watch your language! There are children nearby. Abuser!>>

Ow! Listen, ☼Aßhole☼, you're in the wrong book. Corporate McArchy is over there! He and Eston Eels keep outbidding everyone else for the slimiest characters. Alicia Stroller for the most sexist.

Their goal is to crush everyone beneath them.

The way the papa fish eats all the baby fish to prevent the birth of contenders.

So here he emerges, like Mars on a Halfshell, expecting us to genuflect. Not me, man. We didn't have so easy a time of it, either. Plus we'd figured he and Polymesus were dead, and it's not like we'd have been able to haul their corpses along on the trip. It's not like there's any tremendous shortage of diplomats around here. Give me a bottle, bread and good cheese, and I can be as diplomatic as hell with all but the lactose-intolerant, and who wants to be in their presence anyway? The lactose intolerant are the scourge of the Earth. That's why, as Monty Python pointed out in *The Life of Brian*, the cheesemakers are particularly blest in the next world—because down here they stink!

Limburger makes for a poor underarm deodorant.

Ripe and runny Camembert pours from the mouths of caves on Malta.

Stiltwalkers wear Stilton in their Stetsons when they wander into the careßmatang forust.

Me? Say hello? He doesn't know who I am. I played cheß with Polymesus once. He beat me easily. Why would he remember? No, I'll just stay out of their way. Watch them bask in the attention they're getting for having gotten lost. Stupid prodigal son shit. What a dumbaß leßon: <<Let go of what you love, and, eventually, it may return, but to the detriment of everything else.>>

You can negotiate something better than that. Who couldn't? Don't let my own woe bring on any anguish to you. I tried to apologize. I said something, I gueß, during the game. I upset him. I told him that everyone knew Ty Cobb was a dirty player. He told me Ty Cobb was his great-great grand uncle and he'd show me what folks in his town did to anyone who thought differently: they'd axe him.

Why he'd done it. He could stand no contradiction once he'd reached the twelfth level of karmic perfection. It was all he could do to look down his nose at those who suffered from skin diseases. <<Judge by appearance,>> I presume, was his credo. Even as a baby, he'd stayed away from the babies with red eye or chicken pox. None of his teenage friends were allowed to have acne. Nor were they allowed to expreß opinions contrary to his, and his would contradict any that they expreßed. I remember saying once that Schopenhauer's view on women was not very enlightened, that Schopenhauer's statement (that women were better suited for raising children because the pitch of their voices was higher and thus closer to that of children's voices) was ridiculous, and Cobb Junior immediately responded by saying that, in his opinion, Schopenhauer was the only poetic philosopher of the 19th century. As a result, of course, everything was always negative with him. He found fault with Sartre for being too cheerful. CJ's angst and peßimism led to the wringing of hands over the question, <<Do I have the right to hax the question if I have the right to hax that question?>>

After my Ty Cobb remark, CJ crapped on me and flew into the clouds, presumably to find somewhere else to be intolerant of people with physical ailments. Father Damien would have been saddened to meet CJ.

Chief Negotiator, hah! He couldn't even properly negotiate his transport here. Well, I gueß he did arrive soundly, albeit very late.

*

What the objector seems to have forgotten is that tardineß was destigmatized by law. No one was permitted to get upset with anyone else who was late.

Even if he's eleven days late. We haven't even dared enter Mars Condatis for fear of inadvertently hurting the negotiations. So we've camped out here, near this stinking river. Camping, eating god knows what strange fish, no diplomatic comforts at all. I didn't sign up for diplomatic service for this. I thought it was all going to be perfume and minuets. Nobody ever said the only negotiating we'd do was among our ¢elghs as we decided whether or not what we'd caught was, first of all, a fish, and secondly, if it was edible.

I have to give credit to Clowdhopper—that's not his real name—I don't know his real name—but he'd volunteer to taste-test anything. He had an uncanny ability to smell or taste just enough poison that it didn't hurt him, but he could recognize it. Like an Indian cobramaster, who'd gradually drink a little more venom each day until he'd built up such a tolerance that he could withstand a pretty big snake's bite. Nothing I'd recommend anyone try. Nor would I recommend anyone join one of those old-timey Southern snakehandler cults. Unleß you like that sort of thing, I gueß.

Well, when are they getting here? I've been ready for hours now.

I remember he told me once that every member is habitually late, and that it came to be known as ▶bearded-man time◀ apparently after the founding fathers of this behavior back in the jazz era. They had vowed to always be an hour and a half late to everything. That was fine, though. We'd just figure all that in and announce we'd be somewhere an hour and a half before we'd actually get there.

But eleven days is extreme. Eleven fuckin' days of fuckin' mutant fish. I was about ready to take a bite out of Clowdhopper's arm, let me tell you.

I want a diplomatic steak tonight! Hell, I'd settle for lentils and rice.

You know, we don't even know why we're here. Oh, well, I'm just a pee-on.

A peon? haxes one of the Œðers.

No, literally a pee-on, a victim of tinkle-down economics.

So, won't you come home, Beetle Bailey? Cobb Junior? CJ? Sir? I'm forgetting my place. But he's a civilian. I mean. He elected to go in. I was *sel*ected in. He did get this whole thing together. I'll give him that. But, man, we're bored of waiting. We even made our own shuffleboard court. And backgammon boards we could body-surf on. Beat having one's belly scratched up by the sharp pebbles and shells. This was no pure white sand beach.

Every dot on the horizon would be them. Every three rocks were their tombstones. Every cloud brought the thunder of hooves.

Perhaps we were being tested. It was our military's way of testing our loyalty: test our patience. They argued, irrationally, that impatience with their ¢elgh-serving dawdling was thought to be a sign of impetuous individuality, and, no, they didn't encourage that sort of thing while in uniform.

I liked to wait in a park out by the nearust town. No one bŒðered me, and I enjoyed watching the wild parakeets that flocked there for some unknown reason. One suggestion was they had been pets, or at least some of them had been. Œðers must have been hatched. Green, yellow, blue budgies beyond the setting sun. But they always come back stronger than ever. Which intimidates pit bull owners.

Okay, where are you? Who do you think you are? God? Godot? Godzilla?

It was a gnat. A persistent, annoying, disruptive little gnat. Easily killed. But what about Mrs. Gnat? And the baby Gnats?

He's the gnat, just left them without so much as a farewell.

<<You can't be a liver and have a heart,>> as they say in Condatis. Supposedly.

Okay, so at some point from the void he reemerges—the three of them did—though none of us knew Cayenne then, though he's proven to be a likeable, albeit a little annoying, ►person of celebrity◄ now. I see, though, that's he's uncomfortable with it.

►Though◄. What a curious word.

He tried to avoid it.

So big a deal is being made about their return, I wonder whether they are lords or new creatures.

Waiting for someone is much more streßful than having someone waiting for you.

They appear as absences. They block the light behind them, though, so we can spot them by noting where light is not. They are eclipses growing out of the heart of the sun, coming to deluminate us.

I have placed my imaginary picture of what they look like over their void, but have a problem imaging Cayenne. Is he red like a pepper? Or is his hair red? If he has hair. Is he from Louisiana's Circle of Influence? That'd be inter-rusting to hear about. The Œðers' stories have all been spread like rumors during their absence. Anything told anyone is now known by all. We had given them up for dead, almost. We'd had stayed a little longer than eleven days. At two weeks, we'd likely have given up. Funny, though, no one really brought up the subject in conversation. We just knew what the rust of us were thinking and feeling. I actually have gotten to know a couple of my shipmates, like Clowdhopper, better. They are more than just coworkers now. But perhaps that's what was supposed to happen. Maybe this has been some managerial exercise. Hell if I'll ever get to know. I'm at Slaggard's, listening to Dennis O'Bell if that ever happens.

How does one welcome something from the void? It's like being told you're having a miscarriage, and the baby ending up arriving perfectly on time and perfect health. Wow! The prognosticators sure fucked up.

It wasn't until I saw their eyes that I realized something was very wrong with them.

Heck, I've flown too close to the sun to be yelling at Icarus, but somehow I thought he'd make it without falling apart.

But they went through the hellhole of Corporate McArchy—that city that only slime crawl through. It is the posterior aperture of Mars Condatis.

I don't believe even he could do that, which is why we're out here. <<Hey,>> they'll tell you, <<the only way to heaven is through Satan's ☼Aßhole☼.>> Well, don't believe them. They are collectors for Satan. The only thing through Satan's ☼Aßhole☼ is Satan's digestive system. You don't want to be in there, no matter what this freak calls it. It ain't no heaven.

He must have gone a different way. He's freaked but not broken. Thank goodneß. The big folks need him, or so they say over and over.

Even Polymesus isn't the same. Cayenne—who knows? Maybe he's the cause of it all. Mr. Spicy. And Mr. Cobb. That's funny. A spicy cob slathered in polymer, no, polyunsaturated fat. Mr. Polyunsaturated Fat. Perfect. Except Polymesus isn't really fat—he's normal. He wouldn't dare deviate from the norms of society. That would result in his Osterization and eradication, as happens to all who threaten the status quo. Those who stand up to tell us the truth make their ¢elghs easy targets. Be subtle. Keep your head down. These *are* the status quo. Little matchbox men.

They're all smug. They've been doing this for thirty years blah blah blah so they actually know something? Socrates bugger me, I'm a liar. And anything he says is a lie, which is exactly what he says.

So what can we even hax them? Oh, someone, say hello. Greet them. Hax them.

Okay, okay…. Um, excuse me, are you already dead, or are you just dying?

Funny guy. Sorry—just on edge. Okay, here they come. Oh—

Cobb reached out to me—I was just there—I could have been anyone, a human with human warmth—and he embraced me, happy to find his species alive.

The fact that he is like a father to me is not something anyone is aware of, nor would I make him aware of it. A father always enables and never disables anyone he loves. But, at some points, he sits back and watches what his creations can do for their ¢elghs. We take note and learn. Hopefully in the next life we'll do it right. We certainly blew it this time around. Belonging to an idiotic society is not really a legitimate excuse. We were meant to be better. Were meant by whom? Better than what? Answer instantly! Not so easy, is it? Why should I raise an outcry for ▶order◀ when the order wants me to shut up?

I can feel his atoms. They are vibrating and are causing ripples of waves that tickle. I begin to laugh. Wow, have I been taking my ¢elgh too seriously!

I thump my thighs, stomp my right foot, and hoot! It's what he'd want of an inferior. Ah—is that unfair? I can't say that. I cannot extrapolate motivation from action. That's one of humanity's basic logic flaws. As is trying to deduce from one's particular experience what the universal truth actually is. The answer to that cannot entirely be inside the individual, but must occur outside hir; Œðerwise, it doesn't contain the Œðer, so it is by definition leß than universal. All I have to do over here is keep coming up with examples. He is not a superior. But he is an inter-rusting presence. You should hear me around here sometimes. You'd think I was in charge of his fan club, but that should be a long wait.

He almost immediately started describing where he'd been. I could see. What he began to say seemed at first to make sense, but the closer he got to civilization, the more garbled everything got. Too much competed for my attention. <<Outcasts should be on the outskirts>> is what, he said, he'd been taught as a boy, but now, he said, he was no longer so sure.

I don't know what he's talking about. I hope he's okay and that this is just because he's been driven to the edge, but now that the edge has paßed, certainly we have time to continue!

He's more concerned about being a good diplomat than he is about being a good human. It shouldn't have been so easy a choice.

Okay, so the prodigal diplomat is fed a calf deep-fried in polyunsaturated fat….

Let's all get together, he says, and enter Condatis at last. I saw the look on his face when Clowdhopper—at least I *think* it was Clowdhopper—told him we'd been waiting for his return for all this time when we wouldn't wait an extra half-day for him before. We'd gotten word, I told him, that he was still alive. Clowdhopper said that when we'd heard the screams from the jungle, we'd aßumed you'd been killed. Only later did we find out that that was Cayenne. We'd never even heard of him before.

In truth, I gueß we were a little hasty in our departure, but we were all afraid we'd landed on a beach of murderous cannibals or something. Werewolves and zombies were Œðer suggestions. The scientific spirit left us, and we ran from the truth. Clinging to our foregone conclusions was so much easier and more comforting. The presupposed evils were ones we had anticipated and prepared for!

It's also good to have you back because at least you get things done. Without you, it's all such mindleß noodling, isn't it?

No, of course not. The easiest communication is never direct. The easiest communication doesn't exist. Size shrinks. Capacity increases. Seldom is anything of real value conveyed.

My deepest concern is how, with us so hellbent on destroying our native planet, anyone else will read books in the future. Will they be acceßible by satellite when Earth is gone?

So, in order for my books to last longer, I beseech you, please don't destroy the planet.

I hope you hear me. I'm not really being heard these days, but please try at least this one thing. If we can all agree to that, then my spending my life writing my heart out won't have been wasted.

Clodhopper says I'm an idiot. Says it's all going to hell in a bucketful of brains—we can't think our ¢elghs out of it. We're so determined to hate everything to death that death will be all we're left with. Heck, half of these so-called ▶diplomats◀ don't believe in diplomacy at all, but prefer force as a first course. All record of our having been here as a species not only will but ought to be eradicated so that no Œðer species have to see the ▶atrocity exhibition◀ that that would be, to arrow J.G. Ballard.

I think Cobb means well. He's not that kind of diplomat, I don't think.

So, Cobb, what do we do next?

<<We need to be careful,>> he said. <<I don't think they mean to welcome us in Mars Condatis.>>

Well, then….

<<I had a hard time getting through Corporate McArchy. I need to rust up and plan our strategy anew. It's going to be harder than I thought.>>

Get the costumes back out. Take them up that spiral staircase over there, up to the back of Great Neck, New York, or wherever they were made. Just watch out for the monsters—oh, those are the costumes.

So we wait. I could scream. I do not wait well.

<<Excuse me,>> interjected Clowdhopper. <<I'd like the *eel frambroise* and the *chateaubriand a la mode*. And will you bring me some mineral water, please?>>

<<What? I'm not your waiter—oh, I got it. Ha ha. Good one.>>

<<Hey, Cobb! [okay—it was actually more like, <Excuse me, Mr. Cobb!>] So when and why are we going in?>>

I got a politician's gobbledygook back. Well, then he knows enough to be able to decipher their Mason jarheadisms. We were supposed to find out whatever happened to the last envoy, who came bearing the collected sestinas of our people. Mason jarheads have a code—they remain sealed. Trying to discover what they mean is like playing with vacuums. They may have brainwashed the envoy. If those sestinas got into the wrong hands, who know what could happen? Poets need to be able to show off sestinas, but not where interpretation is done by committee. Most folks are afraid of the idiosyncratic no matter how mild. They want safety and security even in their fiction. Some crave for every sentence to drip with the blood of sacrifice—my own or Œðers'. I don't know what you all want, so I'll follow my intuition. Logic is too sterile a growth mixture for fruit and bloßoms.

Every town is different. I believe in the consciousneß of place. Some places have weirded me out: Waco, Texas, *before* the Branch Davidian thing, for example. Marshfield, Wisconsin, also.

The vibe where he's just come from is a lot different from our vibe now and especially different from how you and I shape it for the future. What will Mars Condatis bring? Who knows? We were aboriginal peoples approaching Manhattan. Nothing's as happening as Manhattan, so how tough could some Mars outpost be? Just a little frontier justice, probably. Maybe our people, because they didn't know the laws, ran abrust of them and are now imprisoned in Mars Condatis.

I told Cobb that, and he said that normally I'd be sounding crazy but in this case that was a distinct poßibility.

At this point I wished I could write about Ty Cobb, that ol' S.O.B., rather than what he said. I had a difficult time comprehending what his words meant.

Part Three: Inside the Belly of the Thrust

Personality! Who needs it? Through my walls they must come. I can cave in or flood or explode at any second—any of us could—so why hold on? Go ahead. I'm on my way. I just have to take care something real fast. Really fast. I'm going too fast.

I'm going to fast. No one else will come through the hallways. No—that's not true. I just request that you notice the detail with which this is being aßembled because I love all of you and want to leave some truth behind.

Fiction does not mean ▶untrue◀. It means ▶fashioned by hand◀, like a clay pot. *The clay veßel is the city, whose clay walls contain them now.*

The veßel carries them from the moon to the tide.

The insides of the walls are ridged like thumb-spun clay on a potter's wheel. Like intestines. Like ribbed Trojans (What's the matter, Paris? Can't take a joke?) And not just rapists. Even for those who wait for the fruit to fall. Coax a bloßom, sure, but don't pluck fruit from the vine. I'll have it grow into your hand.

The bowels of the city include it all. It's all eventually food for something. We all are. Every breath people take destroys millions of microscopic animals. Some of those animals are our protectors, inadvertently or not, who whack the really bad bugs. We are foolish to kill indiscriminately. My grandma used to say to beware of those things you want to throw farthest away because you may need to pick them up first.

I know it's taking a long time to come through here, but it will soon be evacuated. The constrictions of my work force it to come forth thus.

I fashion my clay as well as I can—I have no hands, and good taste prevents me from making mine an oral art, like mere storytelling.

I fabricate an organic art—well, *fabricate* may be the wrong word.

Utter? No.

Expel? Sounds too punitive, or cathartic.

Erupt? Too fluid.

Germinate? Well, you could say it's the result of what a German ate. Sorry. You can stop throwing rotten fruit at me. But I think I'll use ▶germinate◀. It fits. It makes me sound green. Like green tea. The cost of tea is steep. On my hide I have a brand of a banned brand of brand new tea I knew to a T as a tea totally for teatotalers. Teetotums and toddletops cannot decide by siding with one side exactly where sidewinders will wind up and end unleß they upend appended endives that dove off the cliffs of Enderby Land. The derby ends in Antarctica, where arctic ants have flown with Amelia's nephew, and the felonious ameliorated few flies on the wall fly on a meal that we all anted up for the pot of potatoes for a potential meal of unrefused refuse.

Catching the endives that calved off the cliffs in our pots of potatoes and veal revealed cleft potent portents in the potable potage that was cleaved by a clever cloven-hoofed porter who normally just pounded nominal cake into pounds of poundcake which he reported to Enderby for a pound.

Thither went my zither.

Thence came Thanator. *Thanon* derived ►thence◄. Thanatos left Thanatopopolis, the city of a thousand deaths caused by pop culture. He also wants to come through my gates, but I have forbidden him entry. He's going to have to go around. He cannot get to Mars Condatis through me, no matter whom he is in pursuit of.

He wants everything to stop. I have one motto: never an ender be!

Rather than waiting to expel the predigested and excremental—and who wants to face such expulsion?—one is better off foreswearing their entry. Keep the proceß going forward—eventually freedom will be yours. Stay clear of the static, of blockheads, of stick-in-the-muds. They'll stop you until you end up exploding.

Avoid the predigested. Let it come all jumbled and whole, and you can churn it up your ¢elgh any way you like. You can choose to let your teeth do all the work. Or your eyes' teeth. Or your gastric acids. How it's churned is how it's earned. In this we are unique. Whether you chew each bite a hundred times or swallow your meat whole, hide, hair and hooves, is your choice. This is one of the few freedoms left to you. Claim it!

Camels are squeezing through eyes of needles. Watermelons are strained through perforated thimbles.

The novel is strained through perforated symbols: proceß the new now! Expel it! It's gone! It's old! Bye bye!

Wasn't there something here a minute ago? I feel so empty. I need to be fed. Feed me now.

I am an airport. I am a heart. These aren't capillaries, damn you! They're fucking arteries! Arterial paßageways bring me nutrition!

I am not the bowels! I am the heart.

Okay, maybe a heart full of shit, but still....

Part Four: Ething into the Briar Thorns

The Mason jarheads were all rubbernecking when we marched into Mars Condatis.

Aasvogel was expecting us. No one else knew about my ▶arrangement◀ with him. Our guise as a diplomatic mißion was still secure even among us. Polymesus may have suspected that something Œðer than diplomacy was on my clipboard, but he no longer seemed to care. After all we'd be through, his loyalty was solid.

Cobb and Clowdhopper and the rust were very suspicious of the Condatisians, whom they'd refuse to discern from the Mason jarheads. I tried to explain that it is always folly to aßume that military represents the general populace. The military has its own agenda. More than that, of course, I couldn't say.

Cayenne, though, whom I was carrying along as a ▶special translator◀, was problematic. I thought that I might actually have to take a chance and confide in him, just to insure that he would understand our docket. Of course, then I'd have to confide in Polymesus also. Polymesus and Cayenne would keep each Œðer in check.

<<He's my coat,>> said Polymesus to the hat check clerk, a short man with a nasty scar from eyebrow to chin.

<<Ba! He's not a goat!>> the alarmed man replied.

<<Turn down that alarm! I said ▶coat◀, not ▶goat◀!>>

<<Oh, okay!>> the clerk replied, gathering Cayenne by the scruff of his collar, hanging him by his shirt tag from a meat hook, and pulling his pockets inside out.

<<Help! I'm trapped!>> yelled Cayenne.

<<Then chew off your foot!>> I replied.

<<What? I'm no badger!>>

<<Could have fooled me,>> chimed in old faithful Polymesus.

<<No, I'm a rabbit, I tell ya! And don't throw me into no briar patch!>>

<<Hey, that's a great idea!>> said Polymesus.

<<What? Throwing me into a briar patch?>>

<<No—cooking you like a rabbit.>>

<<No, don't bŒðer,>> I said. <<An old sour cuß like that would taste like fetid goat.>>

As soon as I'd said that, I began to have a taste for fetid goat. Or fettered goat. Maybe even feathered goat. Goat on a stick. Crème de la goat. Goat du jour. Goat au gratin. Goat à la mode.

Polymesus had a little billy goat beard. Perhaps he *was* a goat. No, better not think that. O, that way madneß lies.

We got Cayenne off the hook, though both Polymesus and I were tempted to take a bit of thigh meat before letting him down.

We hadn't eaten in a long time.

<<This way, gentlemen,>> a hosteß said, leading us into banquet hall. Our entire company of thirty men were seated at tables already laden with rolls, butter, pitchers of fresh water, condiments and saltine crackers. Some of the men couldn't wait and began baking cold ketchup soup in their water glaßes, adding pepper and salt to taste. They were silly and lightheaded from their hunger and kept referring to their ketchup concoction as ▶flan◀. Of course, is flan is some kind of Mexican custard with brandy.

<<Good flan, eh?>> one said.

<<Straight from Flanders, it must be,>> said an Œðer.

I had no idea what they were talking about. Secret code. In-crowd hip talk.

I thought I'd add my observation—<<Flimsy flam must be sold by the flim flam man.>> They all ignored me. They ignored Polymesus, also, as if neither of us were to be trusted. We were outsiders. Cayenne was pariah.

Clowdhopper, though, seemed to be very popular among the men. I wondered if mutiny was afoot. Maybe it was at hand.

I wondered what would come first—the mutiny of my men, or the attempted ouster of Aasvogel.

Never had I had such a thought. Nor have I ever had such a thought since. It had always been my habit to avoid all thoughts that sounded like paranoid delusions.

After we feasted on venison and wine, the announcement came: <<Lord Aasvogel has been delayed and has sent meßage that he will be unable to meet with you this evening, but tomorrow he shall.>>

We were led to separate sleeping quarters, formerly ministry offices in the city. They had been outfitted handsomely as single apartments, and each man was given an apartment for his ¢elgh for indefinite use while we were in town.

Perhaps Aasvogel's generosity might disincline my men from throwing their lot in with those traitors who intended to overthrow him.

The next day we were told Aasvogel would be delayed yet an Œðer week, but to enjoy our ¢elghs in the city. The men had no trouble carousing. But I became worried.

We were haxed to aßume normal lives and take on jobs to pay for our food and housing until Aasvogel returned. The men happily elected to do so.

I was leß eager, but took on the role of big brŒðer and sole provider for a savant down the road. I was uneasy. City life boiled up my blood.

*

Weeks turned into years, and before long we'd all lost touch with each Œðer and had forgotten about the Aasvogel's problem, but so, to, had he, apparently.

*

Every day when I awoke, I took a walk. The days looked bright; the air was crisp. Today, however, as soon as I stepped out my door onto the sidewalk, I was barreled into by some stupid fuck who couldn't watch where he was going. He knocked me onto the ground into a pile of dog shit, on which I landed with my chest. As I felt the damp soaking in through my shirt, I noticed the clod was walking a guilty-looking Pomeranian, which I've always thought of as football dogs. So I leapt to my feet, grabbed the leash from the startled owner and yanked it from him. I picked up the little shitter and kicked it out into traffic, where it was met by the front grill of an SUV, which then ran it over. I then turned my attention to the rude fucker who'd knocked me over. I punched him in the gut and then kicked him in the balls as hard as I could. My steel-toed paratrooper jump boots can do some damage. Then, while he was squirming on the ground, I stepped on his head and crushed it like a rotting melon. Then I went back inside to shower and change. Because of this ☼Aßhole☼ I was unable to take a walk in the morning before having to go to work. I was pißed.

My brŒðer was surprised to see me back. <<What hap—?>> he began to mewl in Morse Code. I had no patience for him at that moment.

<<Look,>> I said, <<I can't stay around here deciphering your saliva all day. <<Just write it down—that way I can read it when I get a chance.>>

<<Hand hurts,>> he started to signal back. I turned away. I felt pity for him. He had to endure his mißhapen body, but I didn't want to mollycoddle him, either. He got enough sympathy from all the morons who thought he was an idiot. Hell, it took my being in scouts and learning Morse Code and teaching it to him before our parents even realized

he was intelligent. He's actually evilly so—but more about that later. I was talking about *my* day, not his. But I do hate it when people make fun of him. The last one got a fork in his cheek. I was mad. My brŒðer may be a bit exasperating, but that's only for me to know and for everyone else to shut up about. Because I'd used up most of the hot water for my first shower, my second ran cold when I had just finished soaping up my hair. I had to rinse off in fucking ice water. God *damn* it, what a shitty way to start a day. I felt like going around all day killing every fucking dog owner I could find. *And* their fucking dogs. I thought of the few half-sticks of dynamite I still had. They'd make nice fucking suppositories.

I was wary of reentering the flow of traffic but did so without being accosted again. I arrived at the train station without further incident. I took a seat at the window. No one tried to sit next to me. Good. I didn't have to resort to my bag of windy tricks to drive an errant commuter away, thank god. That's the reason I ate lots of garlic and gyros and drank lots of booze—elbow room. It's hard to get enough elbow room in the city. Use whatever you can to your advantage. Smell. Appearance. Become a human porcupine with sharp metallic piercings threatening everyone else. It's a deterrent, but occasionally those with sticky gumball personalities persist. You can get rid of gum by freezing it off.

However, even voicing the word ▶deist◀ makes you a target for retort. I'm still looking for a good Technicolor pope hat. Now *that'd* be something useful as well.

A swell in the ranks of the believers is countered by those who surf above the maßes. Above them aßes the air ain't so bad.

The trains never arrive on time. You'd think that if they're perpetually ten minutes behind schedule, they'd just fucking fix the schedule. Obviously they can't fix the trains.

I arrived at work late again. I wanted so bad for someone to try to call me to the carpet for it so I could unload all my frustrations on his face, but everyone knew better and stayed the fuck away from me. Until my dickhead boß called me into his office and reprimanded me for not being in proper busineß attire. My tie, I was told, was tied in a double Windsor knot, which was no longer acceptable. I had to rustrict my ¢elgh to a simple or half Windsor or that was that.

I removed my tie and tied it around Mr. Sloman's neck until his eyes bugged out.

<<Like this?>> I haxed. <<Is this a fucking simple Windsor fucking knot?>> When he stopped resisting, I dropped his sorry corpse. I quickly sent an email from his office to all staff that he was busy in an all-day phone conference and that he didn't want to be to be disturbed. I had his office phone call his cell, which I answered for him. He could spend the day talking to his ¢elgh. He wouldn't be found until the cleaning crew came on at midnight.

I left the office without a word and went over to the soup-and-bread shop and bought two large chowders. I drank mine while sitting in the shop's window and watching the drones paß by, no glimmer of life in anyone's eye.

After that, I got back on the train on a transfer—that's how briefly I had stayed at work! I brought the Œðer chowder home to my brŒðer Tom Drooley, as I call him. His real name's Karl, but no one calls him that. Mostly, on the rare occasions anyone comes over, they just nod in Karl's direction and call him ▶him◀ or ▶he◀.

<<Can *he* understand us?>> they hax, and meanwhile he's dribbling on about the mathematics of what teams tried to do to stop Michael Jordan. Each team had its own Jordan rules. Karl figured out the calculus of these rules by watching old basketball games on the NBA claßic channel. He'd watch basketball for hours. And he was smarter than Patrick Riley, Dean Smith and Phil Jackson combined. Only no one knew it.

I tried to suggest a meeting between Karl and Stephen Hawking, not that I'd ever know how to arrange that, but Karl wanted to know if the Black Holes were an old semi-pro team he'd never heard of, like the Birmingham Black Barons, whom Jordan played for during his unofficial suspension from the NBA, supposedly for gambling violations.

What gets me sometimes is when people turn their backs on Karl, like he's some ineffectual pet. Karl hates it, too, because he knows that from that moment on I am waiting for them to turn their backs on me. The local cemetery is packed with people who turned their backs on me. The ones who've turned their backs on Karl are too good for the cemetery. I'd throw their bones to the packs of wild dogs that roam the city, but human bones arouse suspicion the way mere disappearances don't. These days everyone's disappearing, running from one hardship or scandal to an Œðer. Just an Œðer quitter, just an Œðer busineß transfer, just an Œðer freak out, just one of the castrati chasing a mate. Not enough to raise an eyebrow over, really.

I like the dogs. They keep the city clean. What they don't clean, the ravens do. The ravens and the dogs seem to have an uneasy alliance against human stupidity. Bleß 'em, I say.

I had to find a new job, I realized. That's not so hard. You find your mark, follow him to his job, and then whack him just before he reports that day. You show up instead, tell people you're from the temp agency. After two weeks you tell people you've been hired on full-time because the clown you were temping for never showed. You add your ¢elgh to payroll, and there you are.

I haven't been able to figure out how to get paid for those first two weeks. It's hard to fake a temp agency, and you don't want to arouse suspicion, so I suggest just going along with it. In the meantime make your ¢elgh indispensable.

The early days as a temp are the best, though. Everyone is loose around you because no one thinks you're staying. No one expects much of you because you're a temp. If you can handle some light phone duty and easy filing, you have no worries. Really. Until they find out you're permanent—then everything becomes difficult. You become like a trained circus bear answering telephones or a gun man for the mob. Just do what you're told. Expreß your undying love by squeezing that trigger just right.

But time grates like some stinky hard cheese and is just as nauseating. Any nourishment you can pull from it is temporary.

Anyway, <<Can *he* understand us?>> people hax.

<<Of course,>> I reply, as I serve tea and biscuits. I make the guests sit directly acroß from Karl, so they have no choice but to see him attempt to drink, tea flowing from the corners of his mouth. Sometimes Karl finds this so funny, he laughs and makes the tea come out his nose. It's a great trick for guests. And his attempts to shove biscuit into any available facial location may be my favorite moment in entertaining.

If our guests look away, I scream, <<What the fuck are you looking away for?>>

If they don't, I yell, <<What the fuck are you staring at?>>

In either case I stand up all angry and menacingly grab the machete off the wall. Then our guests shit their pants like Mr. Aardvark's aunts, as we used to say back in the old days at my high school. Mr. Aardvark was the ▶Dean of Discipline◀, a sadistic fuck whose every attempt to turn us into mini-masochists was met instead by our emulation of *his* sadism and by our attempts to masticate his aß and masochistate ace hole his ¢elgh. We'd laughterbacate and basturminate the turdicate until he wept into his aunts' bazooms. Hence the saying.

So fuck it all fuck 'em if they can't take a joke, and smash in their pie holes or those of the next bloke. Life ain't fucking sweet for anyone—it's a chancrous whore and complete bore. I'm reduced to looking at squiggly lines on paper for my ▶play◀. Ooh, ooh, word play! Ew, ew, word play, I say.

The joy of living in the big city, with its allergic women and encephalitic men, where pain is cherished as a joy and joy is castigated upon the rocks. Wake up. Whack your head. Paß out. Then die. That would be considered a good existence in the city. Those who sidestep that are dangerous, idiosyncratic *different*. Oh, don't be different! *That's* the worst! If you even *know* Morse code, let alone how to drool it, you are way *too* different for the technobotic cubicalists who live between the LEDs and the LCDs of day and the neon-strobe mosh-rave roofie-dives that only lead to the slammer and death. They are incapable of reality—they only ¢elgh-virtuate, so the only righteous thing to do is snap 'em in two like milkweed stems and see the pus run out. At least I can still be awed by sticky ooze. For them, awe was killed long ago, probably by some soft-headed kindergarten teacher who told them to name everything. No! Let life name its ¢elgh. Do *not* impose your definitions *on* it.

Oh, frozen-eyed protractors! Oh, trailing faces! Oh, unchosen fright, stop deliberating me!

Fuck! I left my pellet gun at work. That was my favorite pastime there. I'd open my window and wing paßersby. Idiots. You know, the people who'd walk too slow but wouldn't move to one side to let anyone paß.

Ping! Nape of the neck!

People walking while talking on cell phones.

Ping! In the butt!

People in uniform busineß attire.

Ping! Ping! Ping! Through the fuckin' eyeballs! Sheep, they are. No—worse than dißecting a sheep's eye in biology claß. Except, of course, these morons have no claß.

People who knock people over without apologizing. I put the rifle away and try to Ed Ames them with a hatchet like on the old Johnny Carson show when Ames, trying to demonstrate his throwing proweß, castrated a cardboard cut-out.

Just more cardboard cut-outs walking around everywhere every day. Got to keep them from breeding.

I've been taking to puns recently to make life more tolerable. I have an old tie-die t-shirt and some beads, put them on along with a raggedy old long-haired wig, throw on some torn denim with my sucker stones in my pocket. I hold these stones in my hands in my jacket pockets and roll them in my palms and fingers, and they have become beautifully polished. They're also perfect in size and dimension. They are round, about the size of handballs, and fit snuggly between the thumb and forefingers.

I walk up to groups of stupid-looking kids and, in my best Lord Buckley voice, hax them, <<You kids want to get stoned?>>

Whoever says yes I throw the stones at as hard as I can and exclaim, <<Sucker!>> That's why I call them sucker stones.

You'd think the rust of the kids would attack me as a group, but they just flee. They're just fleas. And they are proud of their ¢elghs because they just gave their ringmaster a bad review. Some circus.

I have told them that if they stand in public, they should have prepared to be knocked down. That's what happens to everyone who stands in public. Hell, all I have to do is open my front door and step outside.

Little Flimsy Children, I mean you no harm, but for your own sakes, grow up already! Get strong! Mommy's breast is not going to follow you to adulthood! The great Philip Roth tried that, and even he couldn't stay there forever. If you really want to be like Roth, climb to the top of your hometown's tallest building, spread your arms, and fly away over the ledge. Bye bye, birdies!

Thank god they're gone, the whining little shits. They can't tell pearls of wisdom from rabbit pellets. I gueß maybe one or two of them could, but that ain't enough reason to save Gomorrah. Or Mars Condatis, this hell hole.

One of the worst activities is standing in queue, which one has to do for almost everything… What I hate most is that the Œðers don't respect my space. They push me. They shove their crotches into my aß. So what I do, a trick I learned from watching the old NBA on TV, is to turn sharply and bring up my lead elbow as I'm turning. I can catch them in the jaw with my elbow, which gets them to back off a little. That, and I follow Benjamin Franklin's sage advice and ►fart proudly◄.

<<Gee, I didn't know you had an elbow made of lead,>> said a local spineleß street urchin.

I take some sea urchin spines and poke them into his face.

The only thing worse than standing in queue is line dancing. Hades came up with line dancing as a way of fooling the simple into thinking hell was more fun than heaven. But it's a short trip from line dancing to chain gang, and Vulcan's furnace is kept ablaze by electric gliders who are happy to be ►stoked◄.

Of course, the advantage is that a good sniper can line up hir shots in such a way that each shot would take out several dancers in each line of fire.

Lions of fire will shred each dancer who is no longer strong enough to work on the chain gang. Loins of fire will blast forth new dancing gangsters to jet to the west where Phlegethon is shark-infested. If they want to die for their masters, let them.

Dancing fiends are little lambs to me, bleating and bleeding into my ears, so I must kill and eat them to protect my senses and to save them from the lions.

Snoiling through the snailslime, the lemon slugs plug a dancer twice in the head and once in the body. Still. Celebrate with some hot hootch from Hotel Mahatma's Bathtub McGinty. That bleßed woman was a goddeß—good for her she's dead now. It'd kill her to see what this city's become.

I saw a disgusting pig spit his gum out onto the sidewalk today. I can't tell you how disgusting and annoying that sort of behavior is. I've stepped in that one too many times, so I made him pick it up and put it back in his mouth. Then I super-glued his lips shut. He didn't complain, at least not that could hear. His girlfriend kept staring at me all wide-eyed while I did it, so I glued her eyelids shut. And if they'd had a yipping little dog, I'd have glued its ears shut.

Why its ears if it's yipping? Symmetry, man. The first sign of human intervention: symmetry. Of course. Like my brŒðer and me: symmetry. Like Humanity and Earth. They say that after the big war between capitalism and socialism, all the remaining socialists escaped to Mars and proclaimed it a red planet.

But where were the socialists now? All that's left are ruthleß ¢elghish capitalist pigdogs. No weapon known to humanity can mow them down fast enough. The lions of fire could take them on, but like all cats they're lazy and only perk up when hunger hits them. A couple or three pigdogs in their bellies, the lions are back to sleep again. That's not much help in the long run. No stomach for courage. Might as well feed them hyacinths, daisies, petunias, roses, and all the blue belles sold in the market.

*

Sometimes when I'm gone, my brŒðer obtains hookers. I don't know how. Perhaps he can dial in to a hookers-who-know-Morse-code service somewhere. But I have come home twice to find a call girl bouncing on his lap. Apparently he is in no way deficient in *that* department. Both times, when they were done, I drove her out to the city dump, where I, appropriately, left her.

<<Where did you take her?>> Karl haxed twice.

<<To Chicago,>> I answered twice.

<<What?>>

<<I took her to Wacker,>> I said. And neither time did he respond to my joke. I thought it was funny. Well, what does he know? He's an idiot.

I'd say stuff to him like, <<Hemingway always read his hometown's name backwards,>> and that wouldn't elicit anything either.

I hate having no one around me whom I can talk to. I wondered what had happened to Polymesus, but shouldn't have. I wanted nothing to do with all those ☼Aßhole☼s from my past. If they were so loyal, then where were they? I should warn Aasvogel about them—who knows how much damage they would do if they had his ear?

I was angry that Aasvogel still hadn't made time to see us. I was pißed that we weren't even ►us◄ anymore, that our tightly knit band of rescuers posing as diplomats had fallen out. As I was beating the snot out of some punk kid for sneezing on me on the train platform, I began to realize I was just plain angry at everything. Where had all this anger come from? I hadn't felt it before coming here, I realized. And that was when I realized that I wasn't to blame, at least not entirely, for my anger. This place, Mars

Condatis, its ¢elgh , was toxic. I knew what I had to do. I had to find Polymesus, Cayenne, Karl, and Aasvogel's ¢elgh and get us out of here. Aasvogel would need to abdicate—this kingdom was not worth fighting for. It was rotten.

Many along the edges who got tired of meaning started paying the edges to get something out of meaning. I'd heard of its being done. I could arrange it. I mean.

<<You certainly are!>>

<<Polymesus, old nemesis, that's you?>>

<<Yes, masquerading as your kid brŒðer. Not an easy task.>>

<<But why?>>

<<<Butt wipe,> he says, like he doesn't know.>>

<<No, actually I said, <but why?>>>

<<Because the croß-legged long-haired goddeß is sitting all wrapped in furs not forty feet away. I know her, and she just smiled deliciously. I could taste her lips on that smile, I tell you.>>

<<Well, who is she?>>

<<I think she's going to lead us out of our misery and into the realms of perfection.>>

<<Are you sure, Polymesus?>>

<<I have a strong hunch that she is the one I was meant to meet.>>

<<Well, you know how that turned out for me.>>

<<Yes, but I am not you. Your flaws don't inter-rust me. Hers do.>>

<<Let's see if she can help us free Aasvogel from his fate. We must get him out of here.>>

<<Of course she can—she's a lady.>>

<<She's not one of the ones who…>>

<<Who've been giving me my riding leßons? Good god, no. That was something I did because of boredom. I've been sick, after all.>>

<<Sick? You were a mewling idiot.>>

<<See? So let me love my beauty, please.>>

<<Yes, I will. Tell me, what is her name?>>

<<No idea, but I see her on the train.>>

<<You do?>>

<<Yes, and I spoke to her. I said,
Oh, beautiful one,
I see you writing.
You know me, don't you?
We have known each Œðer for several years.
We have thrown snowballs at each Œðer, wrustled in the sand,
planted flowers and then plucked them for a lark.
You are very profound; a glance means the universe, a shrug your
whole life.
I would love to get to know you, to taste those rarified lips, to
careß your jaw and cheeks in my hands while I'm lost
inside your eyes.
Will you come out and play?
You can look me up and all.
Let me take you to dinner and a play.
Good?
Say <yes.>>>

<<Say <vomit,> you mean.>>

<<Huh?>>

<<You're *still* sick. Delusional, in fact.>>

<<Come on, let's drive over there.>>

<<Where?>>

<<Lombard Street. That's where she got off.>>

<<You have a car?>>

<<Yeah. I bought one from one of the gals.>>

<<I hate driving. It makes me angry.>>

<<Everything makes you angry.>>

<<Yeah, well, I wonder why that is. But I only drive grundingly.>>

<<What do you mean?>>

<<I mean, if someone cuts me off, I hold a grudge against him and follow him until I can, somewhere, force him off the road into a ditch.>>

<<No, I mean why do you wonder why you are so angry?>>

<<It's this place, man. Don't you feel it?>>

<<The place?>>

<< Here. Let's go. Where's your car? I'll show you.>>

He had parked his miniature automobile between two dumpsters in the alley—it seemed to fit there nicely. The car was rusted and was mißing a rear quarterpanel. That the car had not been hauled off by the trash collectors was either a miracle or a statement.

<<Take us to Lombard Street. Let's find this Lolita of yours.>>

<<Lolita? How did you know she was young?>>

<<Lola Lola would not be seen using public transportation. She would only have developed friendships with the owners of limousines.>>

<<Hah! Call them limoships, then.>>

We laughed. That was the first time I'd laughed since coming to Condatis. Now I *know* it was the place.

<<Hey, that's Lombard. Turn!>> It was a one-way dead-end street. We'd never get the car back out. Only two buildings linked the street—one was a warehouse full of horse tranquilizer and the Œðer was a mixed martial arts training facility. The training facility, though, had apartments on the second floor, so we aßumed Lolita lived in one.

Three apartments, three buzzers: L. Banke, B. W. Clappaccino, and Frank Manson. Could she really be named Lolita? We rang L. Banke first. An old man answered, and he said he didn't know anything about any young woman. Could she be B. W.?

<<I don't know, man>> I said. <<*Clappaccino*? Was your girlfriend some sort of diseased Italian barista?>>

<<Haha,>> Polysemus replied, with as insincere a laugh as poßible. His laugh died quickly when a diseased-looking old Italian woman with gummata pocking her face

answered the door.>>

<<Mansion?>>

<<We'll see.>> He rang the bell. An unhappy-looking biker dude with a smiley face tattooed on his forehead answered the door. Young lady? Oh, his line-dancing instructor. It took all we had not to laugh.

<<Line-dancing? Dammit,>> Polysemus said once we were safely away. <<You were right. We'd never have gotten along. Shit! She was so pretty, too.>>

<<Yes, but she does the Electroglide with bikers. Yuck.>>

<<On the way to becoming a Clappaccino by her ¢elgh .>>

<<See—there *is* no beauty here. We need to get the Aasvogel and Cayenne and get out of here. If Aasvogel's been the object of a coup d'etat, so what? There's no point to being king of the dunghill.>>

<<Well, I think I know where Cayenne is.>>

<<Okay—we just have to get out of here.>>

<<That's no problem.>>

<<But the car?>>

<<Oh, it's light. We can just carry it back out of the dead end.>> So we did.

*

We found Cayenne at a competitive Men's Quilting Bee. He was using unstrung fish netting that was green from algae and rank with old sea water. He was too busy to bŒðer.

Then we saw him pounding Chicago-style dogs at a profeßional eaters' competition. He was too sick-looking after that to approach.

Then we saw him dreßed as a clown and giving kids balloons in the park. That was just embarraßing.

We began to think that Cayenne was actually enjoying his ¢elgh .

And so we began to focus on Aasvogel in the palace. We had no clue where he was. I began bumping into random people and exblurting <<Aasvogel!>> When one turned to me, I would repeat <<Aasvogel, watch where you're walking,>> but I would slur my words so that it'd sound to the casual listener that I was calling hir ☼Aßhole☼, but any friend of Aasvogel's would have clearly heard ►Aasvogel◄ and would have stopped to chat. That was the plan, but no one responded at all. Everyone looked at me like I was insane.

The palace was all-too-familiar and all-too-uncomfortable. The guards were either steroidal dumbshits compensating for their shriveled testicles or sycophants sucking on the chain of command.

I tried to beat Aasvogel's location out of them, but they didn't know.

Polymesus said we should devise a plan. My planning mind, I told him, had been lost in the bruises on my fists. He seemed surprised—he'd never known me as a violent man.

I suppose I'd never been so violent a man before. It's this place, I told him. Mars is the god of war, and being in his heart is turning me to anger.

<<Well, we'll need to go to Earth so you can swim in the Pacific Ocean,>> he'd answered, laughing.

<<A good idea,>> I responded. We'd get Aasvogel and head to Earth.

<<I was joking about the Pacific,>> he said. <<You know that the name is ironic, right?>>

<<Okay, well, maybe not the Pacific, but somewhere. Anywhere is better than here.>>

<<Tierra del Fuego?>>

<<Sure.>>

<<Death Valley?>>

<<Naturally.>>

<<The Sangre de Cristo Mountains?>>

<<You bet, but I'd prefer Intercourse, Pennsylvania, or Climax, Michigan,>> I laughed at my own joke.>>

<<Or Fukue, Japan.>>

<<That's the spirit. What Cheer, Iowa.>>

<<Don't forget the Beer Crater, here on Mars. Home of horses and acrobats.>>

<<That's pretty far away, though,>> I said.

<<Not as far as Earth.>>

<<I was thinking about where we'd actually take Aasvogel when we get him out of here. I don't think Beer's going to be much better than Condatis. We should look for some sobriety somewhere. Not a drunken circus like Beer.>>

<<Well, we could zip up to Mt. Apollinaris and then figure out where to go from there. A good soak in the effervescent hot springs up there would be delightful.>>

<<That doesn't sound half-bad. Okay—it's a plan.>>

Pßßt!

I looked over my shoulder, startled to see some serpentine soldier smiling.

<<What?>> I haxed as I jumped.

<<You're seeking Aasvogel?>>

<<Yes. Definitely, but—>>

<<Shhh. I've sußed out where he is, but such knowledge will cost you.>>

<<How much?>>

<<The same as the Grateful Dead.>>

<<You want half my wife? Dude, I'm not even married.>>

<<Okay. How's twenty testicles?>> It sounded like a slang term for the local currency, perhaps?

<<Fair enough.>> I paid him, and he gave me some valuable information. Of course, Polymesus wouldn't believe a word of it. The soldier told me Aasvogel had been abducted and inculcated into a diet-and-exercise cult. What he'd been given as pure acai berries had actually been coated with a powerful liquid hallucinogen. He had since been brainwashed and now stood as one of the cult's leaders. The cult, it was rumored, maintained their members' loyalty through the use of a ►Bözmacher◄ machine, which gave its use a feeling of euphoria as long as the user harbored no ill feelings toward the cult.

That's all the soldier knew, but I was sure I could find out more at the library.

Polymesus, as I said, wouldn't believe the soldier—he said the story sounded fishy, so he went to pursue an Œðer avenue—he'd heard about secret tunnels that led from the palace to the Gardens of Obsane Topiary, where Aasvogel's father had kept secret rendezvous with the Shaved Girls, a group of exotic dancers who navigated the gardens as if born to do so.

The virtual library was leß a topiary than an aviary with huge gargoyles lining the rooftop balustrades. Aasvogel's father definitely had no secret tunnel leading here: trees were to be trimmed into bonzai, not used for paper. Aasvogel's father had once tried to make Mars Condatis a paperleß community. That had failed, and at the library I was able to read some of the Bözmacher cult's secret publications.

Many Martian humans, apparently, had been conjoined with alien symbionts generations earlier. From Mars, the symbiont aliens had spread to Earth, Venus, and Earth's moon. The aliens belonged to a lighter-than-air species of balloon beings that lived in the clouds of Jupiter. They had overcrowded Jupiter and thus were colonizing the Œðer planets, but soon discovered that their tethers to the three largest inner planets were tenuous. The balloon beings could float away through our lower-gravity atmospheres out into space, and without personal propulsion systems, their angel of release from the atmosphere would determine if they'd get trapped in the asteroid belt or reach Jupiter's ¢elgh or drift off toward an Œðer galaxy.

Only through symbiosis could the balloon beings anchor their ¢elghs to the Œðer planets. The symbionts' presence would eventually however, destroy their human hosts, so humans had devised a method of diet and exercise that could rid them of their symbionts. The Bözmacher machine theoretically monitored one's ▶levels of separation◀ from the symbiont.

The cult had a different diet-and-exercise routine to paß each level of separation. And each level of separation cost ten times its predeceßor.

The first level of separation was offered for a nominal fee of one shriveled testicle, or whatever the local currency was. The first level was a one hour motivational talk on the aßertion that each person's life was leß than perfect. That news wasn't even worth a shriveled turd.

The second level required a commitment to a three-hour seminar on recognizing the difference between the good in one's ¢elgh (known as ▶the goods◀) and the bad (the symbiont). That gem cost ten testicles.

One needed at least a million testicles to free one's ¢elgh from the symbiont. And at that point, the ▶member◀ of the ▶group◀ would be paying the ▶organization◀ to beat him unconscious with crow bars, defecate on him, and he'd be grateful.

The cult obviously targeted the rich—a million testicles were obviously worth a million times more than one.

I hoped that by the time we found Aasvogel he'd at least have some testicles left, but I feared the worst. Some of my boyhood idols—actors and jazz pianists, for some reason, were especially gullible—had been brought down to the level of scat-covered eunuch-clowns.

Of course, the backlash against the balloonheads was no leß onerous. Cult edicts came down against any and all balloon-like objects. Even prophylactic condoms were banned. Logic left the argument altogether. Kids found playing with water balloons were brought in for intense cult reprogramming.

The actual ▶diet-and-exercise program◀ was the most amusing feature of the cult. Rather than colonics administered by beauties, the traditional strategy of such cults, the Bözmacher cult focused on air retention—obvious for a balloon cult, I suppose. Because the symbionts wanted their human hosts heavy in order to remain tethered, the cult taught its members to become more buoyant. Such buoyancy was dependent upon the retention of gas. The more gas retained, the more buoyant the host. So the diet prescribed consisted of cabbage and beans and Œðer gas-producing foods. Once a critical degree of buoyancy had been achieved, the symbiont could be released through a technique known as 💥popping💥 and would leave the host and try to find a leß buoyant tether. If none was available, the symbiont would float out into space untethered.

Advanced group seßions in the cult dealt with the shame of spiritual regreßion that occurred with the accidental paßing of gas. If one paßed too much gas, in any one week, one had to repeat a level of separation at double the cost at first, then triple, then quadruple, until on ninth repetition one was automatically promoted to the next level (because, apparently, the cost was the same).

Finding my way into the cult would not be a difficulty—they had members standing on streetcorners recruiting for their one-testicle seßions and trying to sell copies of their founder's famous book, *Bözöneutics*.

The cult's founder, Clay Ashtray, had at one time been an animal-feed distributor who was disgraced in a crop circle scandal. He moved to a resort island in Lake Hellas, and he began to write biographies of never-existed luminaries who had been cured of their unhappineß by the Bözmacher program. Then, once he'd generated enough demand for it, he launched the program, which he called Operation Deflator. He gained the nickname of ▶Inflater Man◀, which made the cult seem leß menacing than it really was. A series of children's cartoons were eventually produced, though no reputable television network would touch them. But cult parents would brainwash their own kids with them. *Inflater Man Saves the World*. *Inflater Man vs. Deflater Mouse*. And *Global Inflation*. The latter also snuck in rudimentary Bözmacher economics. The film claimed that every testicle spent on the organization would come back to the giver three-fold. An Œðer obvious ploy, but the gullible culties ate it up.

I found a Wide-Eyed outside the grocery store. <<Hi, ever you read *Bozoneutics*?>>

<<No, but I've heard it's very good,>> I lied. <<I did read *Crop Circle Romance* and loved it.>>

The cultie grimaced. *Crop Circle Romance* was a bit of an embarraßment to some of the culties. Ashtray had written and published the romance under the name Penelope Pillsbury before he'd hit on the notion of the Bözmacher machine. The novel was the embarraßingly cheesy tale of a crop circle maker who falls in love with the farmer's daughter. A disgruntled escapee from the cult had revealed the truth of the book's authorship to the world, and the original publisher was only too happy to replace ϪPenelope PillsburyϪ with ϪClay Ashtray writing as Penelope PillsburyϪ.

An Œðer funny detail—when the romance was first ißued, ▶Penelope◀ was interviewed by a girls' magazine, who wished ▶her◀ great succeß with ▶her◀ writing career. ▶Her◀ reply was, <<Thanks, but the only way to make real money in this society is to begin your own religion.>> Within a year of that interview, Clay had.

<<Would you like to come to our station? I'd be happy to give you a free copy.>> ▶Station◀ ws their euphemism for ▶church◀, and they used free books, personality tests, and even raffles as lures to reel in the gullible.

<<Sure!>> I said, excited and wide-eyed. The cultie fell for my act and led me to his station. The cult had many stations acroß the city, so I had no idea if this would be Aasvogel's But at least I was in.

Part Five: Lofting Found

At the station, rather than subjecting me to a seminar, they showed me a movie. They actually had a screening room in the station. I was impreßed—their methods were becoming more sophisticated.

They even offered me some 💥pop💥 corn. I laughed. They really wanted me to willingly suspend my disbelief and absorb their propaganda. However, it was lame. They obviously didn't know their Leni Riefenstahl.

In the film, Dumb Schlubb is working in a cubicle. His boßes yell at him all day. He commutes home—the Œðer drivers all honk at him en route. When he arrives, his wife harangues him. This is his lot, day in, day out. He goes to the bridge over the river, stone tied around his neck. He's about to leap when a happy-looking hippie comes skipping and whistling over the bridge, paßing out flyers inviting people to the station. Dumb Schlubb takes the flyer and steps down.

In the next scene, he is leaving the station, skipping and whistling his ¢elgh.

<<How was the film?>> one Wide-Eyed haxed.

<<Trite,>> I replied.

<<Really?>>

<<Really,>> I insisted. <<The 💥pop💥 corn was good, though.>> To prove my point, I cut a thunderously huge fart. <<Ah!>> I said, goading the Wide-Eyed. <<That proves it! You know what they say—a good fart compliments the chef.>>

<<Um…we don't actually hold with that belief…um…>> stammered the Wide-Eyed.

<<What?>> I feigned incredulism. <<You're kidding. *Everyone* knows that farting is a compliment to the meal.>>

The Wide-Eyed scrunched his face like he'd just sucked on a lemon. <<Oh, no,>> he said. <<It is most important that you retain your air lest you please the bad in you too much. Keep the Deflaters at bay!>>

<<Inter-rusting. I have to think about that.>> I vaguely remembered a paßage from *Crop Circle Romance* that contradicted that, but I wanted to look it up before quoting it to him. I made my excuses and left, promising to return the next day to talk about signing up for a claß. Pleased with his ¢elgh, the Wide-Eyed let me go.

I went to meet Polymesus and compare notes.

Polymesus had gotten lost in the tunnels and realized what he needed was a map, so he'd haxed around and had found an underground cartographer in some back alley. The cartographer (<<Call me Henry the Navigator>>) had gladly sold him a map of the tunnels for a thousand testicles, but the map was written in ancient Martian hieroglyphics. Henry didn't know how to read those, but he said he knew someone at the public library, an archivist, who maybe could help.

Polymesus and I decided together we'd visit the archivist in the morning before I went back to the station. That'd give me a chance to find that paßage in *Crop Circle Romance* that I wanted to use to needle the balloonists with.

The physical and archival library was located at the least acceßible edge of town, where no public transport led and no convenient paths probed. We had to call on a local taximeter cabriolet driver to bring us there. His cab was unusual: decorations hung from the ceiling like fish in a smokehouse—smelt cured bad taste—the clock's downwind clanging away—antique razorblade collection cuts into a pirate's chest—Yoo-Hoo soda and a bottle of rum—the Yoo-Hoo in the drink holder, the rum wedged under the driver's seat in case of DUI—dalmations urinating inside the fire station—bury 'dis in the pauper cemetery—the fish aroma presumably covered the stench of booze spilled at sudden stops. The cab ride was enough to make one seasick.

Of course the stench of old books in the library was no better—all those rotting old ideas piled up together like tires in a salvage yard—hoping someday to be recycled into something useful again.

While Polymesus went to the archives, I searched the stacks for *Crop Circle Romance.* I searched under ▶cult◀, ▶romance◀, ▶fiction◀, ▶ballooning◀, and even ▶farming◀. I tried to locate a card catalogue, but had no luck. I was almost ready to aßume that library was clean of the cult books, not a bad thing in its own rights, but then I saw a poster above a display case on the library's third floor. The poster featured a quote from a famous Bözmacher cult member named Crewvolta Prinfreshalley. 𝔛Let Pops free your balloon!𝔛 said the poster. <<Pops,>> of course, was a nickname for Ashtray. Bingo! The cult had indeed infiltrated the library at one time. And the display case contained several different editions of well-known Bözmacher texts, including the elusive *Crop Circle Romance*. The case wasn't locked, so extricating the volume was not a problem.

Ah, here it was—the really embarraßing section where Pillsbury says that female symbionts are like sweet cherries, and that if a girl wants to become a woman, she must have a special man (named ▶Needle Dick◀ in the novel) who has been trained in how to correctly take from her her cherry balloon and 💥pop💥 it when no one else is around so that the symbiont floats harmleßly back out into space.

Despite the cult's embarraßment over this, the cherry-💥popping💥 needle dick training remained enormously popular and lucrative for the stations. Every young man, it seemed, fancied his ¢elgh to be the perfect needle dick for 💥popping💥 cherries.

The preventing of escape of gaßes and the ultimate 💥popping💥 seemed contradictory. That's exactly what I thought. The cult's tenets contradict their ¢elghs. If this cult ever grows into a legitimate religion, a great schism lies ahead between the 💥Poppers💥 and the Inflaters. 💥Poppers💥 will be called Deflaters, and Ashtray's own writing will be used against him. However, the Inflaters will undoubtedly denounce *Crop Circle Romance* as scurrilous and as a fraud. Pillsbury was *not* Ashtray, just an imposter who wanted to mislead those of the true faith. The Ashtray we see on video discußing *Crop Circle Romance* was an impersonator.

This was good. I had my weapon. Now to see how Polymesus had fared. He was just emerging from his meeting with the hieroglyphicist. His smile told me he'd been succeßful, so all that was left for us to do was to locate Aasvogel and then to bust him loose!

We discovered that the palace hosted a monthly convocation for the Bözmachers and that Aasvogel's ¢elgh presided over it. The next would occur Tuesday at eleven. We had our plan.

Polymesus figured that Aasvogel would rust and meditate in preparation for the streß of hosting the convocation, and that he would insist on having that time alone. We aßumed he'd claim that time in whatever was the local equivalent to the Gardens of Obsane Topiary, which would presumably be off-limits to all but Aasvogel and his inner circle.

With the maps in hand, we'd negotiate the secret tunnels, find him the hour prior to the convocation, and abscond with him then.

We decided to make a trial run and time the procedure the next morning. Meanwhile a night's drinking and celebrating seemed in order.

We saw a billboard that announced Foghat was going to be playing live in concert.

<<Those guys are still around?>> haxed Polymesus. You know I'm getting tired of calling him ▶Polymesus◀. I'm going to call him ▶Poly◀ from now on.

<<Yeah, Poly. I gueß so,>> I replied.

<<Poly?>>

<<Yeah.>>

<<Okay. They're at a free outdoor festival tonight. And beers are cheap.>>

<<How will we find it?>>

<<Follow those bikes.>> We hopped into our silver Karmann Ghia and followed.

Actually, I can't remember how we got in. Poly had watched a game show on TV when he had been in the meeting with the hieroglyphicist. They were betting on ►Jeopardy◄, and Poly remembered the name of Savoy Brown's guitarist—Kim Simmonds. And Foghat came out of Savoy Brown. What a coincidence, or did Poly have this planned?

Now I want to go find my old Potliquor. Great bands back then. And still. Foghat is incredibly tight. I was surprised the baßist, Craig MacGregor, didn't have stumps for fingers on his right, his *picking* hand. *Baß*. He was Entwistle fast. Not quite Hellmut Hattler, but who is?

Roger Earl absolutely kicked on drums. This band can boogie faster than the best.

Boogie. I love boogie. Hound Dog Taylor, John Lee Hooker, Canned Heat, these guys, Brownsville Station, ZZ Top, there are a few who really know how to boogie.

The car (what car?) was safely parked. We walked around and drank some beers. Now see you're in here.

Now back to the plot. My plot. I'll be buried in. Out again. That's boogie.

Your feet want to be there as much as your mind, soul and heart. Join the celebration.

These folks throw a nice party. Of course, we would, too. We could welcome you over, but we have a no-stalkers rule, so no stalking.

Who are you talking to?

No one; just time traveling. Trying to explain.

Where have you been?

Hibernating, like a saber-toothed bear. And I'm hungry. The sounds are sweet in bearsville.

I'm fed by the boogie beat. It just picks up my feet.

Then you have foot-in-mouth disease.

That was my line. The line of track stretches down deep into the countryside. Walking it, tie after tie. I know I'll get nowhere some day. Just keep on going, onwards; who knows where the tracks go?

Nice semicolon.

Yeah, that was pretty good. Now the boogie's beginning. I'm getting the rhythm. It's making my blood course in time. Each part of my body is independently motivated. I can go in any direction.

Yeah, but I want to see where the tracks end.

All in good time. Don't be in a hurry to get there. Boogie!

Boogie?

Don't lay not rock and roll on the king of boogie.

That's Long John Baldry, isn't it? But you got it backwards.

That's irony, my friend.

That's not irony.

Oh, yes it is.

Oh, okay. I'll concede that point for the sake of furthering an Œðer: boogie is distinctly palindromic.

I had him stunned. But at least no one was talking. I like silence. Yeah, right!

<<Cherry makes me feel so real.>>

Go, Boogie! Go!

<<Og, og, eigoob, og!>>

What?

That's palindromic.

So boogie palindromically is troglodyte language?

Yes! ✸Hitting✸ the rocks with clubs—the boogie beat began that way.

✸Hitting✸ the saber-toothed bear, you mean?

✸Hitting✸ the saber-toothed bear
wearing my camo underwear
with a club and two rocks
dangling down from a chair.
Will Maude, a fire torturer,
given that she's fictional

and situated on my porch,
know she's really Cherry!

Ear-itch? Or have you cured your palindromicitis?

You're right. It's not really palindromic. More alliterative, maybe.

No! Anything but that!

Why worry whether…

No!

Okay. Acronymic. A good acronymist—

—is worth two clichés in the bush.

It's the ►Sick Gramma' Blues◄, and it's about that old lady, Gramma English.

The boogie is only ever about one thing, and that's boogying!

Gramma boogied with lions.
Gramma boogied with the lambs.
Gramma kept on boogying
'cause Gramma had really great gams.
Grampa found her in the cotton
boogying with some weevils,
but he figured boogying
was the least of evils.
So Grampa boogied with the lions.
Grampa boogied with the lambs.
Grampa kept on boogying
'cause Gramma had really great gams.
Grampa boogied in the cotton.
Grampa boogied with the weevils.
Gotta say boogying
is the most fun of all evils.

<<Great, but that's ¢elgh-referential, not acronymic.>>

<<Evils live, laugh, fall.>>

<<Is that a palindrome?>>

<<No—it's a scanin drome. You're like a scanner, reading from the center to the right, to the left, back to the center. Pick up the ►f◄ from ►of◄, add ►all evils◄, and

begin with the ►e◄ in the middle. ►e-v-i-l-s↻l-i-v-e,l-l-a-F↻F-a-l-l◄.

You said acronym.

I forgot—I was boogying all night long—just as I'm told to in song. Okay, how about <<Dr. Eck>> = <<dreck>>? Not the same thing. The acronym for <<Dr. Eck = dreck>> is <<Ded,>> which is far more forgettable than <<Dr. Eck = dreck.>>

You're right. It's not really acronymic. Acronymistic?

You're over your acronymicitis, at least.

Your acronymophobia?

Your acronymophelia.

Every acronymist tries to mock Eck.

Hey, stop acronymizing already.

O.K.

Oily Kat—I know: <<oll korrekt.>> An Œðer snafu. I was driving—I don't know what happened to the Karmann Ghia—a black Camry. I fell asleep at the wheel, and my car struck nose-on a heavy wooden guardrail with a launching pad at its nose. We were lifted skyward and spun upside and landed on the roof.

I felt claustrophobic.

Poly said he smelled gas.

Stunned, I at first wondered if a Bözmacher had snuck into the car. Then I realized what had happened. Poly and I quickly rolled the windows up and crawled out through the broken safety-glaß cubes. The cubes bit into my hands, elbows, knees.

Poly must have had a similar experience on the Œðer side. Opening the safety belt and falling on one's head was an inauspicious way to begin a quest for escape. But in a minute we were standing side-by-side acroß the street and staring at the meß our abandoned nanobots were still taking apart. Or were they taking a part?

The inter-rusting thing was how dißociated I was. I woke up when we ✸hit✸, and we were airborne in an instant. The car rolled over, and I thought, ͼnot this beautiful Toyota!ɔ And then I found my ¢elgh upside down, so I took off my seat belt, rolled up that window and pulled my ¢elgh out. Through broken glaß. I never panicked—as if this kind of stuff is becoming more obvious—I can see what it means: I am fearleß. I am indestructible.

Nevertheleß, I did feel like I was inside a washing machine looking out. It was weird.

We crawled out of the wreckage and, before the police could come, Poly had already found a new ride: an Avanti II. Sweet. Apparently we were driving along some expensive estates. Excellent. Those rich folks are the least likely to be concerned about the goings on out on the public roads. They seldom drive. So I gueß Poly's discovery of a white Avanti was no surprise.

We drove towards the local version of the Gardens of Obsane Topiary.

I had the thought that I maybe should not have nicknamed Polymesus <<Poly,>> which sounds like <<Polly,>> like I'd like him to be female. That's not what I'd meant. Though, of course, if I had a beautiful dark-haired woman who was on the smallish side, that might be nice.

But what to do about Poly? Can I make him female without seeming homophobic?

Come on, Charles.

Well, I'm an antisexual masturbator. I get off on thinking about *not* getting off. I wear my underwear on the outside because I'm either a superhero or a devotee of Disney girl singers and Granmadonna, their manager and marioneteer. But I've already told you—

<<I am Indestructible Man!>>

<<No, you're not,>> said Little Nicola.

<<What say you we promenade through the park, Leo?>>

Oh, that's right. You remember George. He came back from touring like sixteen straight months with a torn-up throat and proceeded to record *Dark Horse*. Especially listen to ▶I Don't Care Anymore◀. Wow, that's rough. The voice matched it. It was the pain of seeing Patti go. It's in that album. But it's his return to humanity as well, after *Material World*. That had been a great excursion for him—one wishes he'd had a chance for Œðer such great excursions—okay, Traveling Wilburys was a good one, too—but if he'd been around longer, what more beauty we might have had in the world because of it!

<<Where do we turn?>> haxed Poly. What did he mean? Turn into what?

<<The map—there,>> he pointed.

<<Oh, to get to the motel.>> We were going to a little biker motel out by the gardens. Poly said it was skuzzy but cheap. That was okay at this point. We had work to do. Focus on that. After all, the skuzzy made it through hell's gate.

ͼMan, am I hammered,ͽ I tried to think.

ͼMan, am I hammered.ͽ I tried to think.

The difference is significant. Push says pull says me. We were hurting when we pulled up to the motel.

I volunteered to go in, but before I could move, Poly was already back with the key.

I kicked open the room. Stuffy. I turned on the a/c, kicked off my boots, and paßed out face down onto the nearer bed. Never mind the bedbugs.

Ow! What was that! It's a smudge of blood now.

A hundred bites later, I woke up. Dawn had not yet come. I thought I'd take a shower to rinse the bug bites off, but when I pulled back the shower curtain, a thousand cockroaches scurried.

Never mind. Whoever stayed here last left a bottle of mosquito spray. It was supposed to work on bedbugs, too, or so said the label.

I sprayed my ¢elgh and went back to sleep with that nasty bug spray flavor in the back of my throat.

Throat esophagus stomach! I wasn't well. I vomited into the shower, providing a feast for the vermin there, got dreßed, and went out to get a breath of fresh air while 800 mg of ibuprofen took effect. What I needed was a hot pastrami on dark rye with mustard, lettuce and tomato. The grease could cut through any hangover, and the taste was a delight in the unbrushed morning mouth.

<<No, not an acryonym,>> I heard from somewhere. <<More like permutations.>>

Only for that one line.

<<Well, then, perambulations.>>

What? I'm in a baby carriage? What do you mean?

<<You write at the behest of the young.>>

How untrue—I write for anyone. That's why I'm a threat, don't you see? Oh, quick! Hide. Here they come.

[Aasvogel shuffles onto stage, accompanied by three idiots wearing balloons. Aasvogel, a very tall and slender man, imposing of figure, ✸pops✸ the balloon in his hand].

<<Oops!>> he says. <<Oughtn't have done that.>> He laughs.

<<Do not mock the teachings, my Lord,>> says one idiot named Tartuffe.

<<I'm not, and if you don't believe me, hax John Jacob Astor.>>

<<That is not neceßary, my Lordship. I spoke in jest.>>

<<So did I, I'm afraid. John Jacob Astor wouldn't know me from a Wall Street lawyer.>> [Big audience laugh].

Before Aasvogel could choke on his own pretentiousneß, Poly and I disabled the idiots and grabbed Aasvogel, who looked oddly at home in the sculptured topiary—as if his ¢elgh were no more than those lustful limbs reaching like careßmatangs for some body. That the body was his seemed a foreign concept.

Aasvogel's protestations became a hindrance to our escape, so we incapacitated him and carried a large double-size duffle bag out to the Avanti II. He was surprisingly light, but barely fit.

Actually, here we are. Let's get him out of the trunk. I'm going to put him out there in a seat. It's the safest place for him.

<<Do you have any fur allegies?>>

Aasvogel shakes his limp head. They take him into the audience and out of the bag and sit him down next to you.

He'll start pestering you any minute.

<<'Scuze me? What row is this?>> haxes the man sitting next to you.

<<This is the Aasvogel row,>> you reply.

<<Yep. That's me.>> He's satisfied and relinquishes your attention. That's when he's craftiest. But we have him. The Dreck Dr. Eck sequinces into the room and spreads groovineß vibes all around.

Aasvogel picks up on the Dreck's groove and starts to bob his head in time.

Dreck is direct.

Dreck is dye-wrecked as a bean.

Dreck is d'reck.

Dreck is the dumbest good ol' boy his native Georgia ever seen.

Okay, get on with it, Charles.

They had to turn Aasvogel fast. Balloonheads strive for release, but that release is ultimately fatal for both symbiont and host. Or so Aasvogel believed, and he wouldn't be the first to die because of his beliefs. He was still, as far as he knew, sitting on top of the world. The complete disintegration of the infrastructure was a happy occurrence (a coincidence?). We just replace the previous structure with this Bözmacher model, and all will be fine.

Aasvogel was wearing a helium-filled suit. Poly slashed the suit with a box cutter, releasing the helium with enormous flatulent explosions. Aasvogel looked embarraßed.

<<You don't control the air, Your Majesty,>> said Poly.

<<True, Polymesus. You are wise.>> The two men embraced.

You know each Œðer?

<<Shit, yeah. We go back many years.>>

<<Polymesus is right. But that's a long song. Why are you here?>>

<<You've been ill. We've been nursing you back to health.>>

<<Are you sure?>>

<<Well, *nursing* isn't the best word. *Watching*, maybe.>>

<<I was ill?>>

<<I'm afraid they got to you, Your Majesty,>>

<<I was….>>

<<Yes, a balloonhead. Now, let's get out of here.>>

<<Wait. Where's your accomplice?>>

<<Right there. Just look the reader in the eye.>>

The reader hypnotizes you. No one knows the solution.

Come on, let's go. Leave him there.

He'll be out for a while. When he comes to, he should have moved his Bözmacher phase from permanent memory to dream memory.

How'd you do that?

Drag and drops.

Dragon drops?

No. Click and move. With a mouse. And now his memories of the cult will seem like some half-remembered dream from long ago. He'll dismiß the idea as fiction, whereas it is the height of manipulation, quite literally. Fingere & Manus. They represented the FR̂N—Freedom from Repreßive Normalization. Unfortunately the preposition was not capitalizations, so many ultimately misunderstood the FR̂N as meaning <<Freedom *to* Repreß Normalization,>> which was an Œðer matter altogether.

Are you still with me? Did you get a guide map before coming all the way out here? We don't get too many visitors out on the ranch anymore. Not since we lost the ranch.

Good! At least I got a chuckle out of it.

<<There's a long way to go.>>

Bumpety bump. Never mind me—I'm past an observer. But Aasvogel got out. No longer a cultie—we'd cured him, but the next day, he vanished. No clue how. And nothing was really ever answered.

Was that the leßon? How would I know? I'll tell you—you take a little linguistics, mix in a little deconstructionism, and you come up with some really bad shit that unravels its ¢elgh as it leaves your body.

This is earthy. Ravel what you unravel. No matter what you do, it's all the same.

The transcripts of our conversations with Aasvogel are rather informal, but the conversations reveal much about Aasvogel that hasn't been Œðerwise heard.

[How fascinating leaders are when they are trying to weasel their ways out of responsibilities they'd haxed for.]

Aasvogel was also majestic. He knew how to carry his ¢elgh in public. Even when we were all blitzed he could pull it off. The Mickey Mantle of the Gardens of Obsane Topiary. On the mound tonight, lefty Mandrake Fly, 13 & 2, with a 4.15 ERA and a pat-you-on-the-back curveball. His battery mate is Martian Flycatcher, who's leading the majors with a better-than-50% put-out rate. Short today is Loco Weed. It's always short nowadays, and around the bags are Succulent Paddy on first, Opulent Orchid on second, and Keystroke Type at the hot corner.

Hey, Keystroke! He waved! Did you see that? Wow! Keystroke waved at me!

All managed, of course by Eggs Ackley, the R. Crumb character, and his vulture demoneßes from the Mars Hotel.

Part Six: The Aasvogel Interviews: A Duelogue

— Q. How long have you been Aasvogel?

— A. That's your opening question? You could look that up in an encyclopedia. Any real questions?

— Q. Which did you enjoy betraying more—your country or the faith of your ancestors?

— A. A false dichotomy already? I thought you'd at least warm up with a few *ad hominems* and an *ad populem* or two. Oh, bludgeon us with false dichotomies, is it? Next? Come on, you can do better than that.

— Q. Why would I want to?

*

— Q. Just because you're Aasvogel doesn't mean you can lord it over Œðer people.

— A. Well, I *am* Lord Aasvogel.

— Q. See? That's my point. Your condescension.

— A. Rather condescension than dißension.

— Q. You don't think one causes the Œðer?

— A. What?

*

— Q. What was the first thing that attracted you to the Bözmacher group?

— A. In truth, it was the pleather—all the balloon gals were into it—they were called ▶leatherettes◀ in those days.

— Q. Pleather?

— A. Plastic Leather. It sure feels great against bare skin.

— Q. Like sheepskin condoms?

— A. Those are bladder, I believe.

— Q. Oh, quit your blubbering, bub.

— A. Abandon ye all alliteration who enter here, and arrive!

— Q. There's that condescension again.

— A. Oh, turn off the effects—I want to hear the guitar.

*

— Q. We thought you were the guitar.

— A. No—I'm the songwriter baß player. I never wanted to be frontman in band, let alone of a city-state. Why do you think I hid in the back behind my ministers? I had work to do—I couldn't just be ♪shaking hands and saying howdy♫, to quote Nick Lowe.

— Q. Like Nick Lowe?

— A. Love his music. I met him once, you know. He did a few shows on Mars back a couple of years ago. He was like 90 years old. And he was the most youthful man in the place. He could dance. That's it—the music hit your feet, your knees, your gut, and then your heart and head in a twin attack that won you.

— Q. You met him?

— A. I went to his hotel room with a friend who was the aßociate editor of a local entertainment magazine—one of those cool free music monthlies that I learned about local and foreign bands from. I wasn't feeling well, so Lowe and my buddy did most of the smoking and drinking. I fell out of it, but resurged later, but not till I'd thrown up onto a room service tray on the hallway floor outside his room. <<Your friend okay?>> he haxed my friend, paßing us in the hall.

<<He's fine—just had too much.>>

*

— Q. How materialistic are you?

— A. Is that a rhetorical question?

— Q. No, a real one.

— A. Can I trade you two of those questions for a good one? How about you hax me where I like to shop.

— Q. Where do you like to shop?

— A. Real old-fashioned bookstores. You know—the kind where one can find true literary gems, not contemporary claptrap like celebrity confeßions, busineß management (known affectionately as ▶BM◀), or greeting card books.

And I like music stores that carry jazz and spoken word and blues and boogie.

— Q. Boogie?

— A. Yes, especially ▶Martian Boogie◀.

— Q. Brownsville Station! And Savoy Brown?

— A. *Looking In*! Cool.

*

— Q. As long as we're on the topic, let me hax you if you like the Dan Hicks and the Hot Licks recording, *Tangled Tales*. Charlie Mußelwhite and David Grisman are on it.

— A. Yes! I did hear it. This old Hot Tuna-head I know digs Hicks and is always playing him (whenever Kaukonen is not on). A bit of bluegraß, a bit of blues. Bluesgraß. That's the word! I especially like ▶Rounder◀. Mußelwhite is great on that.

— Q. That reminds me to dig out *Louisiana Fog*. Wonderful.

— A. And ▶13-D◀ is a great quickstep.

— Q. And the title track?

— A. Best lyrics on the album. I wonder if Hicks has ever written a novel.

— Q. Like Kinky Friedman.

— A. Richard Fariña, maybe. *Tarantula*, even. Much of *Spaniard in the Works* and *In His Own Write*. I haven't read Townsend's or Graham Parker's. I imagine they're good. The Friedman books are reputed to be funny. That's all I know.

— Q. Speaking of Dylan, what do you think of Hicks' version of ▶Subterranean Homesick Blues◀?

— A. ♪Don't follow leaders—watch the parkin' meters♫. What a great fucking song—if you pardon my French. ▶Pump It Up◀, right? It's a good riff. Like the Bo Diddley. You can't miß it.

*

— Q. Have you seen the Green Manalishi (with the Two-Prong Crown)?

— A. No, but I've heard him. What's inter-rusting is that I do actually have a two-pronged crown. It's a ceremonial one to be worn on an occasion that hasn't occurred yet.

— Q. What occasion?

— A. Can't tell you.

— Q. Does it involve wearing a plastic mac in the rain?

— A. Not plastic, no. More like iron. Heavy metal.

— Q. Wouldn't you rust?

— A. *Rust Never Sleeps.*

— Q. Neil Young is the Green Manalishi?

— A. Could be for all I know.

— Q. Blow my mind!

*

— Q. A plastic mac made of pleather?

— A. Inter-rusting idea, but I think water's bad even for pleather.

— Q. Oh.

*

— Q. What?

— A. I said I really like the implied metaphor in *Looking In.*

— Q. Namely?

— A. Looking inwards, internal ¢elgh-examination of a group, a couple or an individual. Looking into the skull, but trying to find the heart. That's the central metaphor in William Gaß's ►In the Heart of the Heart of the Country◄. Of course, you only rarely see the heart in the head. Very rarely. But the converse saying,

▶looking out◀ is also implied, as inverses, converses and contrapositives usually are. The thesis implies its antithesis, and vice versa. That's why the atheist is as dependent on the notion of God for ¢elgh-definition as the theist. No God, no atheist, Truly, without God, atheists would cease to exist. They would have no term to stand against, no ¢elgh-definition.

So clearly, the ¢elgh-definition part is crucial. In order for us to really ▶look out◀ for Œðers or to Œðers, we need to look in.

And we are looking in *on* them. Eventually we will be looking in *with* them when we become part of one group together. We join together. But then we go our separate ways.

At that point we are looking *through* each Œðer, going in opposite directions.

While you're in earshot, let me just tell you all that I am very grateful to you for being here and supporting my work. The more you enjoy it, the more I enjoy bringing it to you.

And this argument is looking through its ¢elgh.

I can always get back ▶in◀.

*

— Q. What? My turn? Ah… What's your favorite kitchen utensil?

— A. The barbeque brush.

— Q. Why?

— A. It's the most fragile. I go through those faster than anything else. The bristles start falling into the food when the brush is worn out. They don't last, so they're always in higher demand than most suppliers anticipate. They probably calculate one per household per year. I go through three.

— Q. Sounds like one would expect an upscale market in high-end barbeque brushes. With bristles that don't fall out. Have you found anything better?

— A. No, and I've looked. I don't care how expensive it is. It's my favorite utensil, after all.

I like that question. Good one. Hax me more like that.

*

— Q. What's your favorite—?

— A. No, not yet. Later. Don't be in such a rush. Stand still. Hush. Make a wish. Now go to the toilet and flush. Any real difference? I can't control my future. It's hard enough to be able to stay on my board as I surf along atop the crust of change.

If you go down, you have no idea when you're coming back up. People had at one time been displaced for days, bringing back claims of time travel.

We had our top scientists working on that, but we discovered very little. Each event was isolated and mysterious.

So, let's just stay up here. Let's walk a little. Let's say through the city.

I mean pretend, of course.

You can put down the surfboard.

And from the board may grow a tree.

♪I can't sing, I ain't pretty and my legs are thin,♫ quoting Peter Green. ♪Don't hax me what I think of you—♫

—Q. ▶Oh Well◀

—A. ♪I might not give the answer that you want me to.♫

—Q. I gueß you'll have that in—what—1969?

—A. Ah, but it's timeleß. Like ▶The Rattlesnake Shake◀.

*

—Q. Do you think ▶The Green Manalishi (With the Two-Prong Crown)◀ influenced Roky Erikson's ▶Two-Headed Dog◀?

—A. I have no idea.

*

—Q. Wasn't Eve the first to shake the snake?

—A. Hahahahaha….

*

—A. I know that She-sus was the first to shake my soul.

—Q. Then why the balloon cult?

—A. It's not a cult. You under-rustimate the reach of the Bözmachers. Do not under-rustimate those who are envious of your power, position or abilities. I say keep challenging them head-on. Both you and your opponent will grow stronger with each match. Also test your ¢elgh against Œðers whom your major opponents don't know so that you can develop unanticipated skills. Eventually, though, you will all know each Œðer's skills and will find such confrontation leß than challenging. You'll be packed and ready to go.

Part Seven: Seepage

Seepage let the air out of his balloon. Sound whistling.

The point of the deprogramming interview was to deflate Aasvogel's view of his ¢elgh. The more he talked, the sharper the contradictions in his positions appeared to him, until his ¢elgh could not keep aloft those ill-conceived ideals. The prick is mightier than the prophylactic.

Ultimately, we all sink into the grave because gravity's pull is stronger than a balloon, feather, or jet propulsion. Even the Pegasus rocket containing the ashes of Timothy Leary, Gerard O'Neill and Gene Roddenberry eventually floated down to Earth in particles when the rocket exploded upon reentry into the atmosphere.

The feathermen plucked Aasvogel clean until that strange bird became human again. The best feathers were saved for use as quills, the finest of which was donated to the Raymond Federman Museum, for Federman's ¢elgh had been a descendant of feathermen.

A ceremonial headdreß was prepared for Aasvogel for his symbolic reascension. The tricky part would be the occlusion of all but symbolic ascension, especially against his own wishes and against whatever power and machinations Polymesus's and my former colleagues might bring to bear.

For the ceremony we decided to release ten thousand balloons into the air.

As I feared, my former colleagues were there loaded for bear, and, misinterpreting my motives, they loaded the weapons they were bearing, bearing ten degrees to the north, bearing down on us, all bare as hipping trippies—maybe they'd been fed bad mushrooms by Cayenne. Maybe Cayenne betrayed us, making old friends want to flay us. Cayenne may have drawn us from our boats for a reason and then sent our boats off without us for the same. Divide and conquer: the strategy of every evil stepmŒðer.

I looked for Cayenne among the ranks of our allies.

<<Kill the usurpers!>> I heard him yell.

<<No!>> I screamed back, silencing the field. <<We are not usurpers. We have freed Aasvogel from the Bözmachers! We are rustoring his rightful place to him!>>

The aßembly of former friends looked confused, and their ¢elghs began whispering.

<<No, don't believe him,>> yelled Cayenne. They are usupers!>>

I saw Cayenne's trick in its complexity: he wanted the throne for *his* ¢elgh.

Meanwhile, Aasvogel, who had been floating in the air, holding onto a tray of a few hundred balloons, peeled off balloon after balloon and released it until he softly returned to the ground, whereupon he released all the Œðers.

<<People!>> he proclaimed, arms outstretched. <<My friends here,>> and he put his arms around Polymesus and me, <<are no usurpers. They are my liberators. And they will be my ministers in my new government. You know these men. They are noble and devoted and came to rescue me at first sign of trouble. You have all undergone a long and trying journey to get here. Lay down your arms, come join me in the dining hall, and let us feast to our good fortune!>>

The men looked around and began setting down their weapons. Smiles croßed their faces.

<<Liar!>> screamed Cayenne.

<<Would someone please arrest Mr. Cayenne. The cell he escaped from a few months ago is till as he left it. He's already in prison for his previous crimes. He'll be given an Œðer trial for treason and incitement to riot.>>

Some of our former, our renewed friends, took Cayenne by the shoulders and arms, and he was led off by some of the royal guard, faithful to Aasvogel to the last, even when he'd gone bonkers on Bözmacher.

Part Eight: A New Fence

Aasvogel sure looked at us funny when we told him what we wanted.

Granted, we could have held any positions at all in his new government as our rewards.

When haxed, Polymesus merely said he wanted to manage the kitchens. That's what a provisions manager is trained to do, he said.

<<Such a modest request?>> haxed Aasvogel. Polymesus nodded. Then Aasvogel haxed me what office I wanted. I told him all I wanted was to oversee the disc golf facilities. Aasvogel laughed in response. <<Come on, man. You're entitled to anything at all!>>

<<That's all I want. I love disc golf,>> I said.

He laughed again. <<Then it shall be so,>> he replied.

We were given spacious apartments lavishly decorated with books, artwork, and sculptures, and settled into our peaceful new lives.

The three of us would get together on Friday nights to play skat, Aasvogel's favorite card game. We'd rotate the location, and the royal coach would take our sorry drunken aßes from place to place. But the host had the privilege of choosing the libation. Aasvogel preferred mead and ambrosia, of course, though the honey always left me thirstier than before, so I'd have to sneak beers in the kitchens whenever we were there. Polymesus would kindly leave a case of König Ludwig for me. Polymesus preferred pulque. But we weren't picky. I'd settle for Blatz, the beer that sounds like its name. And we all liked wine. We'd get four-gallon bottles of Carlo Roßi, which we called Iva Bignose wine for the picture on the label. We'd play until someone fell asleep on top of his cards. The two who were left awake would split the winnings and call it a night. In the morning the host would cook a greasy breakfast. Well, actually Aasvogel would have a cook do it for him, but he was the Aasvogel, after all. Breakfast was always a wonderful duel between Polymesus and Aasvogel's cook, who was looking to impreß hir boß. As good as Aasvogel's cook was, though, ze never surpaßed Polymesus's culinary skills, which were a marvel. At Polymesus's, we'd have the most elaborate breakfast you could imagine—ostrich omelettes with a small head of bibb lettuce stuck in graham cracker sand; fiddler's eggs daikon, which were eggs Florentine with fiddleheads and daikon greens substituted for spinach; asparagus meringue with a smoked camembert sauce; fresh-baked croißants with chèvre and caviar. My own staple was fried pastrami and eggs on black rye. The grease was the perfect hangover cure for me.

During the day, I'd play the courses in Condatis. The gnarliest was placed in a bulrush swamp. Players needed waders for that course, and par was mercileßly low. The insects were torture, so a good bug repellent was also a neceßity. Our biggest problem was with large pests, however; idiots would throw empty beer cans and Œðer trash all over the course even though I had garbage cans placed at every tee. Keeping the Swamp, as the course was colloquially known, clean was a logistical difficulty. Even removing the garbage bags had to be done by hand because no vehicle could maneuver through the course. And garbage that was thrown around and had sunk into the water was hard to find and caused not only pollution but also a potential danger to players who went barefoot, which some crazies did despite the requirement for sturdy waders. Every week someone or an Œðer would step on a rusty old beer can or a broken bottle and have to go to the hospital. We weren't liable, of course, for knuckleheads who broke the regulations, but I was tempted to shut down the course, dredge the bottom clean, and then reopen it as a gated, enclosed course with security checks at the entrance. Of course, that seemed too fascistic to implement—the whole attraction to disc golf was its freedom—so I figured a psychological approach might work better. I put up signs throughout the course that pleaded for the users not to pollute. That, actually, for the most part, began to work. The users did not want to lose the course. I also put up warning signs about leeches in the water, though I'd never found any. But barefooters' numbers dwindled as a result, at least until a complaint was published in the local paper.

The complainer, D. Scusted, posted a letter in the Agony Aunt column. She said that her husband had developed a new fetish involving leeches and her breasts, and that he kept trying to place the things on her nipples when she wasn't paying attention, such as when she was sunbathing or asleep, and that the whole thing had freaked her out. That, of course, spurred copycat couples on to try to obtain leeches, so they began invading the swamp, looking for the critters.

I had to take down the leech signs. I, instead, offered a healthy cash reward for garbage reclaimed from the swamp's ¢elgh, but people began bringing me the garbage from the garbage cans or even from home instead, so I had to abandon that idea, also.

I wrote a letter to the afore-mentioned antagonist Aunt Agony under the pseudonym of a medical doctor and suggested that the use of leeches for sexual pleasure caused breast cancer. I had the leech signs put back up.

That helped some, but, of course, not everyone read the Agony Aunt every day. I put up additional health warnings about cancer risks, but then even regular frolfers in waders stopped coming. I wanted the regulars, so I ended up taking the cancer warning down. Eventually attendance stabilized and the swamp was kept relatively clean, but I had to keep it under my eye constantly.

I enjoyed my time at the courses the most, but I did have an office and paperwork responsibilities as well. Most of that I deferred to my administrative aßistant, Michelle, whom I hired based on a misunderstanding. When she came in to apply for the position, she introduced her ¢elgh, but I heard, <<Hi, I'm a shell of a human being.>> I replied that I was, too. That really confused her because she'd actually said, <<Hi, I'm

Michelle Hume-Behn.>> Forever thereafter she'd call me ▶Michelle◀ and I'd call her ▶'ichelle◀. At least we avoided confusion in our interoffice memos that way. The names caught on, and soon even Aasvogel and Polymesus called me ▶Michelle◀.

I think folks at bars would look funny at Polymesus and me when they heard us calling each Œðer ▶Poly◀ and ▶Michelle◀. Sometimes we'd queer our ¢elghs up just to goof on the overhearers.

'ichelle was an excellent worker. She was very organized. I can't say she was terribly attractive physically—not that I'd have hit on her anyway—she was married to a German novelist—but she had a terrific sense of humor that helped deflect the angry guests of a disgruntled angry public. The number one complaint came from newbies who thought we should locate their mißing discs for them whenever they shanked a shot into the forust or toßed a nonfloating disc into the swamp. Pros, of course, used any of the dozens of floating discs—Innova's Hydra claß, for example. Or Aerobie's Sharpshooter #1, or the ProPig 150, or the Dragon 150, or Lightwing's #2 Driver, or Odyßey's Long Range Power Driver, or Quest Ultra-Lights, or DGA's Blowfly. Not using a floating disc at the swamp is stupid. But we hired a kid who snorkels for the lost discs, and we return them to their losers for a small retrieval fee. Unclaimed discs are sold at our resale shop. The resale shop was yet an Œðer headache, by the way. Discs were just a small part of what was collected by the recreation department: jackets, gloves, bats, balls of every size and shape, racquets, even abandoned automobiles were offered for sale, and the employees were not disc golf enthusiasts. In fact, I think they resented the primacy my sport had because of my friendship with Λasvogel.

I heard that one clerk would hax, mid-transaction selling a disc, for example, <<What do we ring this under?>>

The co-worker would respond, <<Ring it under the ▶fling◀ key.>>

As the customer walked away, the first clerk would announce, <<I'm done with the ▶flung◀ key,>> obviously intimating an inherent subservience to disc golfers, perhaps even my own subservience to Aasvogel.

Those two clerks did not answer to me, or they would have been fired. And I felt it too petty an ißue to bŒðer Aasvogel with. So what I did was hax two Oxford-trained English diplomats to go in and purchase a pair of sculls that had been found by the river. While handling the golf discs, they were to have a conversation between their ¢elghs about how only the highly intelligent are able to handle the trigonometry neceßary to play the game with excellence.

<<I have heard it said,>> said one, <<that some local yokels, probably inbred, have been calling participants in the sport ▶flunkeys◀.>>

<<That is a laugh. One would sooner call polo or foxhunting sports for flunkeys.>>

<<True. Well, I have heard that a private detective has been hired in the matter, and that he has been granted a license to kill.>>

<<Excellent. That is quite the only way to deal with such a matter.>>

<<It certainly is.>>

The diplomats were told to then purchase every disc the store had and to have each one gift-wrapped and shipped to a separate addreß using four different delivery carriers.

I barely contained my laughter when report of the purchase came back to me, but all I said was, <<I am not surprised. Frolfing *is* the sport of sophisticates.>> I was sure that my response would get back to the clerks. That was wonderful, like rubbing salt into their wounds. 'ichelle and I had a great laugh over it. So did her husband, the German novelist.

I could have sworn he was the German tourist I had run into in Lake Gusev City, but 'ichelle's husband spoke a very clear, formal English, so if the tourist had been he, why had he been pretending not to be English?

Nevertheleß, I really enjoyed talking to Heinrich—that was his name—whenever he came by to pick up 'ichelle. He had a delightful parting salutation, as well. When leaving, he'd say, <<Upon Revision!>> I aßume he had translated that literally from the German, but it was all so literary and just like a novelist.

We'd steep mountain-grown tea and wait for 'ichelle to close the office. While she went through her routine, Heinrich and I would chat. He was a big fan of the German Bundesliga, so we'd discuß the just-played or upcoming matches.

<<Can you imagine how embarraßed 1 FC Nürnberg's players must have been to be playing in Easy Credit Stadion while wearing shirts that read ▶mister lady◀?>>

<<What about those peroxide blondes with the eyeliner? Maybe Nürnberg should hire them.>>

<<Like Pliatsikas? Does he wear eye liner?>>

<<Looks like it.>>

<<Then, yes, Schalke should trade him to Nürnberg.>>

The alarm code would beep, signaling we had twenty seconds to leave.

<<All right, then. So long,>> I'd say.

<<Upon Revision!>> he'd reply.

<<Bye, Michelle,>> 'ichelle would chime in, grabbing Heinrich by the arm and leading him away while putting her head on his shoulder. They were a cute couple.

I once told 'ichelle that I thought my own ancestry may in part be German.

She replied, <<I have some German in me… every now and then.>> I think that was the only dirty joke I ever heard her make, but as I said before, she has a sense of humor, that one. She should have her own comedy show on TV. I went to a local bookstore once and haxed if any books by Heinrich Behn were available in translation. Only three, apparently, were available in English. One was a short story collection. Reading short stories by a novelist is like having heart surgery by a dentist. The Œðer two were actual novels: *Roland and the Romanticizers*, which sounded syrupy to me, and *Driving with Dropsy*, which I ordered.

Behn liked alliteration, apparently.

Actually, when the book came, I was surprised to see how aphelion and fastigiated it was—it was all in indented paragraphs and used double apostrophes to mark quotations—clearly a throwback to the 20th century. At least he didn't use the old Gothic type. The Roman type was bad enough, most of us having grown up with Dingwings, a neo-pictographic alphabet adopted when the public education systems went moribund.

I haxed him once how they had met. He was signing his books at a German bookstore when she came in. He saw her and fell, as he said, <<heels over head>> in love.

<<You mean <head over heels>?>> I haxed .

<<No—that's how I always am. We are normally head above heels. If I flipped, I would be heels over head.>>

That made sense. And he used language to that sort of precision in his novels as well. In *Driving with Dropsy*, Darren, the main dude, bellies up to the bar in a piano lounge and begins chatting with the pianist. The pianist haxes Darren what kind of music Darren likes at the same instant that the bartender comes over and haxes Darren what he wants to drink.

<<G and T, diet tonic,>> replies Darren. The piano player, having heard only half of Darren's reply, thinks Darren has haxed him for diatonic music, and so plays only songs in pure minor or major keys, avoiding all accidentals. When, later that evening, tired of easy listening pop music, Darren haxes the pianist if he knows any Monk, a huge smile of relief that Darren doesn't understand comes over the pianist's face, and for the rust of the evening the piano player has fun with Monk, Oscar Peterson, McCoy Tyner, Cecil Taylor, Bill Evans, Herbie Hancock, Dave Brubeck, Sun Ra, Horace Silver, and Œðer greats of hard bop. He was a chromatic man, but he was instructed to play whatever the customers wanted. When Darren haxed for his drink and the pianist

misunderstood, the first two hours of music were decided by accident. How ironic for a chromatic man!

When Darren went shopping at the pharmacy, he haxed the store clerk for manure for his hair.

<<You put manure in your hair?>> haxed the clerk.

<<Not real manure,>> said Darren. <<The articifial kind. I was told to use sham poo.>>

<<After that, you should grab a light meal,>> the clerk said, pointing to some fluorescent bulbs on sale.

<<No thanks, I'm on a staple diet,>> said Darren, grabbing a box of Swingline Standard Chisel Points.

<<Oh, stop bugging me,>> the clerk said, exasperated.

<<I'm not a bugger,>> replied Darren.

<<Good. And my entrance isn't in the rear,>> said the clerk.

<<You mistake me for a bulimic, I think. I can't exit the way I entered.>>

<<Well, I could excise you,>> said the clerk, brandishing a samurai sword.

<<Oh, cut it out.>>

<<That's the plan.>> So Darren left. The clerk was left. Neither was right. Darren got in his car and drove off. A mile down the road he was overcome by sleepineß, as he always was in his car, an old Mercury Cougar. Cats sleep more than they are awake, so the car demanded the same of its driver. He pulled off into a department store parking lot and turned off his ignition and the car's also.

He looked over at the store, which had enormous ϪLiquidation SaleϪ signs draped over its windows.

Darren fell asleep and dreamed about a girl he'd known many years before. The closest he'd come to being with her was when they and a half-dozen Œðer kids from the CYO all went skinny-dipping. He hadn't been able to stop looking at her beautiful little breasts, perfect little handfuls.

When he awoke, his socks were damp, and all that was left of the store looked like a small wishing pond.

Darren was disconsolate.

[*I used to be 'dis consulate*, I thought.]

<<Oh, man. You always undercut the tension,>> some reader is calling from the peanut gallery.

All in the name of equilibrium. I found my ¢elgh indentifying with the protagonist. Darren. For a moment I began to think my own name was Darren instead of Michelle—I mean....

It just dawned on me—you may not know me. I haven't told you my name. What a terrible oversight. My name is, would you believe, Jackson Berlin. Avery Craw. Keith Fine. Well, I do have paßports in those names, but really I am unnamable, as Sam Beckett showed us all how to be. I occupy a body that goes by a certain name, but at times I wonder if my consciousneß's ¢elgh is not just a symbiont to be eventually freed from its host. I sometimes feel my ¢elgh evolving in that direction.

Darren looked around, as if interrupted. Back in the Cougar, he retraced his steps until he found his wrong turn, and then left in a different direction.

Dozens of canaries flew out of a mine shaft. A blue glow emanated from the mine's wood-framed entrance. Workers came running out, shouting something about an energy beast they'd released from the rock.

Howls could be heard from the cave even after all the workers were out. The decision was made to blow up the entrance (management was not consulted), which caused the whole mine to collapse in upon its ¢elgh, silencing the howl.

The company wanted to reopen the mine, but no workers would undertake the job. The mine remains closed.

Darren happened acroß the closed mine after his wrong turn down the different direction after his previous wrong turn. The streets of his home were set up in a grid, far leß confusing than these that follow old trails and dry riverbeds.

Darren saw a rock glistening in the sun. He inspected it. Fool's gold, he figured, toßing the rock down.

He got back into his Cougar. He needed to find a gas station. He took off.

The fool's gold wasn't.

Darren lost out on an opportunity to become a rich man, but he never would know. He was a man of a thousand get-rich-quick schemes that never panned out. That's life.

He found a gas station next to a saloon. He blithely bathed his brain in beer and shared a few jokes with the locals and shot a little pool. He made sure he lost, but not by much.

Winning was the sure-rust way to get trounced in any strange bar.

Then *she* walked in, the coal-haired girl he'd left behind oh so many years before, as beautiful as ever, with a wit unlike any. When she saw Darren, he could feel her absorb a sixth sense of everything that had occurred to him in the interim. And he could see in her the pains and joys of the intervening years as well.

They rusted in each Œðer's arms that evening, and they healed each Œðer a little bit. And the next time a little bit more. And so on.

Darren knew it: angels do exist.

[I put down the book. What was this turning into? A romance novel? Keep it out of the novel, Heinrich! And who's he talking about? 'ichelle?]

And then Darren fell asleep. The trouble with dropsy….

[Bummer.] Bookmark there. Hopefully Darren didn't screw everything up. Again. Of course, he wasn't thinking that. He was wondering where he'd parked his car. [The cad!]

And then he wondered how much Captain Beefheart had drawn from Howlin' Wolf's ▶Moanin' at Midnight◀, which is one truly frightening blues song.

The ▶angel◀ dug her elbows into Darren's ribs. <<Wake up! You have dropsy!>> Darren, of course, denied it until he fell asleep again. The angel left. Temporarily. And returned bearing gifts, not recriminations.

She left behind a strand of hair. Darren put the hair in his mouth, used his tongue to roll it into a pellet and swallowed it. Now he poßeßed part of her.

[Heinrich! This is much too private for me to read. Keep your life to your ¢elgh, dude. Keep your fiction non-mimetic, please! And don't use ▶now◀ with the past tense! Well, I can't close the square bracket or this goes back to *Driving with Dropsy.*

I believe in defensive reading, so I'll just jump over ▶de fence◀ back into the reality of disc golf. Ha! No how's that for a conundrum. I've backed my ¢elgh into a corner where I have to define reality.

And 'dis is 'de finest reality I ebb ersatzed through.]

Darren found his car and drove it until he fell asleep again. It jumped over a fence onto a golf course. Into a water hazard. The water on his knees woke him, so he rolled down his window and escaped uncut but carleß and Bible black-and-blue.

Part Nine: <<The Difference Between a Woman and an Object of Desire>> by Heinrich Behn

O.D.	Object of desire.
O.D.'d	Overdosed.
Odd.	Woman.
A.D.D.	Attention something.
Add.	The mathematics of attraction.
Ad.	The commerce of attraction.
Id.	My attraction.
I.U.D.	Prevention of attraction's side effects.
I.E.D.	Improvised explosive desires.
I.D.	My dentals records confirm me.
I.T.	Information attraction.
It.	Object of desire.
I.V.	What attraction leads to.
U.V.	Ultra-violent Ray-Bans for my opiated objects.
U.H.F.	Trying to be understanding with high frequency.
V.H.F.	Venting with high fever.
V.D.	Vehicle of desire.
O.D.	Object of destiny.
O.K.	Optimal knowledge.
K.O.	Kingdom overthrown.
K.O.A.	Killing of alternatives.
D.O.A.	Destined orderly abandonment.
Doe	Innocence of the woman.
Dog	Obedience of the man.
O.G.	Constant expreßion of error.
O.U.	Constrained mockery of failure.
U.O.	Feeling of guilt.
U.R.	Blame.
R.U.?	Question of reciprocity.
R.T.	Craftineß.
M.T.	Internal remnants.
M.O.	This has happened before.
D.O.	Disappearance of the object.
O.D.	The object turns around and returns.
Odd	The object becomes woman.
O.D.	The man becomes slave to his addiction and loses his humanity.
Odd	Repetition compulsion established.
O.D.	The Œðer is deified.

Odd	The ŒÐer is decreed to be destiny.
O.D.	Ordinary days.
Odd	Only dependability, dig?
O.D.	Options discarded.
Odd	Only do as demanded.
O.D.	It's over, dude.

Part Ten: Sheep's Undersides

I had to put Heinrich's book away. It was all about relationships and women and on and on. I would have maybe appreciated it when I was younger, but for now I had no relationship and no woman and wasn't terribly keen to get involved in such sticky affairs.

I had my courses to concern my ¢elgh with, and in general I felt like this was a vacation after working as an envoy. This was safe and quiet—exactly what I needed.

Behn kept haxing me if I'd finished his book, and I had to keep telling him I was a slow reader and hadn't gotten around to it yet. I have no idea why my opinion would have mattered to him anyway. I was no entertainer. I was living the life that any of 10,000 ordinary men could. Maybe he was haxing me just to show 'ichelle that he had an inter-rust in her work. Who knows?

<<Always make sure you feel the sheep's undersides,>> I would always say.

<<It's a sure thing,>> said Behn, meaning the sheep or the sheep's undersides, I presume.

'ichelle had a dental appointment, so Behn was in early to pick her up.

<<It wonder why it's called <the practice of dentistry,>>> he said aloud, speaking more to the air than to me. But I was usually game to engage, so I responded by saying, <<It's said practice makes perfect, so I gueß the dentist hasn't perfected what ze's doing yet.>>

'ichelle interjected, <<Ouch! Don't even say that!>>

I caught a mischievous spark in Behn's eye. He said, <<Do you know how the dentist practices?>>

<<I give,>> I said.

<<Dental drills,>> he said. 'ichelle and I groaned, and she said that the pun hurt more than the dental work would.

<<Dental work would,>> of course, led to <<dental woodwork,>> which led to a discußion about George Washington, the United States of America's first president back on Earth. He'd been killed by a bloodletter, which led to a discußion of ransom letters demanding blood money. Conversations with Behn always went thus, digreßively nonlinear. I began calling his conversational style ►The Heinrich Maneuver◄.

He suggested we drop off 'ichelle at the bloodletter's and go have a drink while she indulged in nitrous or procaine.

<<Sure,>> I said, <<but isn't the bloodletter the barber, not the dentist?>>

<<They both cut parts of the head.>>

<<Headcutters,>> I repeated.

<<Yes.>>

<<They work in close aßociation with headhunters, who find ways to work the victims to death and who then consume the flesh of those victims.>>

<<And the heads?>>

<<Well, the headhunters work the victims to *near* death and then turn them over to the headcutters, who separate heads from torsos. Torsos are returned to the headhunters for their cannibal feasts. Heads are forwarded on to the headshrinkers, who cure them on their couches. Once the heads are completely dried, shriveled and shrunken, they are placed in individual containers known as ▶head cases◀.>>

Here the conversation went to the subject of an old Earth novel Behn had read many years before, something called *My Landlady the Lobotomist*, which, he said, concerned its ¢elgh with exactly the sort of headcases he meant. He promised to find his copy and lend it to me as soon as he could.

'ichelle called Heinrich from the bloodletters'. She was distraught and completely high on nitrous. Somewhere between the office and our having dropped her off at the dentist's, she had lost her lace embroidered handkerchief given her by her grandmŒðer.

Heinrich's chest puffed up in chivalry as he told her on the phone that she shouldn't worry. We'd find it for her. Nice of him to speak for me.

<<This will help with our concentration,>> he said, and he lit a joint. I suddenly didn't mind so much having to find a hankie in the late afternoon drizzle.

<<First,>> he said, <<we must see if we can find the hankie at the bottom of two pints of ale.>>

<<I don't know,>> I replied. <<'ichelle doesn't like any sort of hanky panky.>>

I caught Heinrich off guard, and he started coughing in laughter. His face turned red, and for a second I thought he was going to die. But he recovered.

<<Good one,>> he said. We downed two pints each and began retracing our steps.

Heinrich walked out of the bar backwards. After stumbling over the curb, he turned around, though. We scoured the pavement and picked up and discarded properly any white sheets of paper and trash we mistook for the handkerchief. A half hour paßed, and we still had not found it.

<<I'd raise the white flag of surrender,>> Heinrich said, <<but first we need to find it.>>

We even found two Œðer handkerchiefs that were not hers. One wasn't lace, and the Œðer wasn't white. One was loaded with crusted snot.

<<Aqualung was here,>> said Heinrich, referring to the famous song written by Jennie Anderson.

<<Barf,>> I replied. <<I need to wash my hands.>> So we stopped at a pub for a couple more pints and to wash our hands. The bathroom had no soap, though, so after a couple of quick pints, we went on the next pub to look for a bathroom with soap. At least all the pubs had ale.

Retracing our steps again, we smoked an Œðer joint and kept up the search. Heinrich mistook a used disposable diaper for a hankie (better he than I!) I mistook a dead cat for an Œðer (it was pure white!) More handwashing and ale were called for. Eventually we arrived back at the office sans handkerchief. I had some Jameson's in my desk there, so we washed up and had a couple of snootfuls. By then we were pretty blurry-eyed, but not so much that we didn't notice that 'ichelle's handkerchief was neatly folded right on top of her desk. That was funny, and we guffawed over that for quite a while. By then no doubt 'ichelle would have been worried about us had she been awake, but we figured she was sleeping off the nitrous. So Heinrich and I re-retraced our steps to the pub by the dental office, where we parted ways for the evening after a few more ales and some cheap pub whiskey.

My phone rang not half an hour later.

<<She's not here,>> said Heinrich.

<<What?>>

<<She's gone. The apartment's all dark. I have no idea where she is. She doesn't answer her phone. I'm worried.>>

<<I'll be right over,>> I said. I grabbed a bottle of Jameson's and hurried over. I was worried, too.

When I got to their apartment, I made us some Irish coffee to ease us into relative sobriety so that we could figure out what to do.

Heinrich lit up an Œðer joint and took out a map. He unfolded it on the kitchen table, and we tried to figure out 'ichelle's location. The map was, unfortunately, an Earth map, so it provided very little aßistance.

<<Oops, wrong map,>> said Heinrich, stating the obvious.

<<No shit, Sherlock,>> I replied. <<You should call the hospitals,>> I suggested.

<<What? No, she's okay.>>

<<Maybe she's been kidnapped,>> I said.

<<Why? We don't have any money.>>

We carried on this way for twenty minutes before Heinrich said he was going to change his shirt. He'd sweated through the first with the booze.

<<Ahhh!>> he yelled from the bedroom. I rushed into the bedroom, and there, asleep in bed, lay 'ichelle. Apparently she'd gone home while Heinrich and I had been searching island to island. In the end she was not difficult to find.

For a week thereafter, 'ichelle wouldn't let Heinrich or me live the vent down. <<♪I see you!♫>> she'd sing. << ♪You had me in the I.C.U♫.>>

Heinrich would tell her she needed a singing coach and put his hands over his ears. Three days later, he'd actually hired one, a four-foot-six Prußion who was stricter than the Kaiser. 'ichelle, however, was a good sport. And apparently she'd always wanted profeßional singing leßons. Heinrich and I were curious about the seßions, but she kept them secret.

<<How goes it with the Gnome?>> haxed Heinrich. He called Herr Pfeffer ▶the Gnome◀ as a way to get under 'ichelle's skin, hoping she'd reveal something about the seßions, but to no avail.

When I saw that Herr Pfeffer brought a metronome case to the seßions, Heinrich upped the ante and began calling Herr Pfeffer ▶the Metrognome◀, but that didn't prod her enough talk.

I don't think Heinrich really cared, nor do I think 'ichelle really didn't want to discuß her leßons. Rather the ißue became an amusement for them, and they played it for fun the way couples who love each Œðer duelogue and burst each Œðer's capillaries with hickeys. Love is combat. Combat is a game. Game is the hunt. A wombat is game. A wombat is a womb. A wombat is combat.

I was wondering why lovers didn't eat more wombat when I remembered how popular vampires were with pubescent girls, who, I presume, were excited by the penetration of the fangs and who, as a result, were excited by bats of all kinds, not just wombats. But bats penetrating the womb must be a special excitation.

The same girls, of course, were introduced to the idea of penetration through the use of unicorn mythology. Unicorns are the conceptual deflowerers of many a young girl. Riding horseback is simulated stimulation for the little girls, many whom break their hymen on Simple Simon, the horse who wasn't going anywhere, the horse without the extra member extending from his brain. Nevertheleß, his no-member brain ruptures little girl membranes, the mißing member being on their brains, not his.

I wondered why parents didn't have their really little daughters ride on the backs on wombats. That would be something.

<<I'm going to go in there and see for my ¢elgh what is going on,>> said Heinrich, interrupting my reverie.

<<What? Where?>>

<<If there's any ▶tickling of ivories◀ going on, I want to see it!>>

<<What? 'ichelle's going back to the dentist?>>

<<No, of course not. The piano leßons, I mean.>>

<<Oh. You know what? I'll betcha they're diatonic.>>

<<Very funny. Have you finished reading it yet?>> Me and my big mouth.

<<Not yet, I've been busy running all over looking for hankies, remember?>>

<<That was just one night.>>

<<And the next day or two to recover,>> I reminded him. <<Also, I've been busy at work setting up the new course.>>

<<Oh, that's right. Michelle told me.>>

My own design—the course was laid out in an old abandoned coal mine. You'd need great accuracy to keep from bouncing off the walls.

Only part of the course was mine, though, because the mine connected to a large underground cave network. Some of the holes went past rooms of stalagmites and stalactites, frozen rivers, bottomleß pits, and narrow crawlspaces. It was a course for experts only, and one needed an interplanetary ranking in order to play. I hoped it would attract tourists from as far away as Earth and the Moon. We were going to havee a rustaurant and a shop along the course as well, so it could really make some money for us. It was a logistical nightmare, but I was very proud of it. So who had time to read?

Heinrich dropped the subject. I felt bad, as if I were disappointing him, as if the smartest people in the world read the fastest.

<<Remember the tortoise and the hare,>> I said.

<<Tortoises don't have hair,>> he replied, sounding annoyed.

<<Haha! Hey, I heard something really stupid on an Earth radio station today. They're not getting any smarter back there, either. What to know what I heard?>>

<<Sure, what?>>

<<The weather reporter said, <We're waiting for the snow to continue to come down.>>>

He laughed. <<You're right. That's stupid.>> Okay, he was in a good mood again. You've got to watch these artist types. They can get really moody. Moo-deep, too. You'd better wear your waders and watch where you walk!

And inspect your boots first to avoid Seepage. Seepage run. Run Seepage run. Seepage let the air out of his boot. Sound anything.

In response to the weather reporter, the news anchor had replied, <<You were expecting something more predictable?>>

<<Ah, a meeting of the minds!>> exclaimed Heinrich. <<♪When somebody needs you,♫>> he began to sing all country-and-western twangy, <<♪it's no good unleß they've kneed you in the groin♫.>>

'ichelle hated when he put on that voice. <<That's so racist,>> she said.

<<American rednecks aren't a race,>> he replied.

<<Okay, ►specist◄, then.>>

<<They aren't a species. They're feces.>>

<<Don't say stuff like that in your books,>>'ichelle would warn him.

<<Why not? They don't read.>> And he'd look at me. I always meant to read him, but, damn, why should I when he's right here and I can hax him in person?

I got even, though, when Polymesus fell ill with severe bronchitis and was told he couldn't come out to play Skat for a month. I suggested Heinrich as his substitute, and the first Friday fell on his night to host. I had warned 'ichelle, so she took the opportunity to visit her sister that night, leaving Heinrich in charge.

He'd never played the game and had tried to learn it from a book. He also looked for breakfast recipes that we would like. He was funny to watch—like a fledgling desperately trying to take wing.

We put him through the paces, throwing Null and Ramsch games at him just to meß with him. We had our fun, but Aasvogel and I mißed Polymesus's sour wit and exaggerated flamboyance. Some of the joy of a fierce competition between three equals was lost. Heinrich caught on quickly, though, and by the fourth week he began defending his testicles with more ferocity.

Aasvogel and I frequently visited Polymesus, especially after the doctors' first round of antibiotic treatments failed and the bronchitis developed into pneumonia. The doctors hospitalized Polymesus and started him on a new super-antibiotic. They drained his lungs of fluid several times while waiting for the antibiotic to work.

He looked weak, beaten up. Seeing us seemed to brighten his spirits, though. The doctor suggested we visit every day, thinking we'd be helpful in motivating Poly's recovery. We began taking turns to make sure one of us was there all the time during visiting hours. Aasvogel, though, still had enormous responsibilities of State, so I ended up pulling the lion's share of time with Poly. I put disc golf on hold and spent every available minute with him. He wouldn't have been up for Skat anyway, so I played double solitaire with Poly much of the day. I even let him win, and I think he knew I had. He smiled like a hooked koi but didn't complain.

<<Go fish,>> he'd tell me after a nice run of cars. Œðer times he'd yell, <<Gin!>> or <<Rummy!>>

<<I don't think that the doctors want you to drink,>> I'd reply.

<<If WC Fields could, why can't I?>>

<<I don't think *he* was permitted to, either. It was the Barrymores who brought it in.>>

<<So be my Barrymore.>>

<<No, I won't bury you more.>>

We did watch a few of the old Fields films, though. *It's a Gift* was a particular favorite of his. I began bringing in brochures of California orange groves.

<<Hey, I haven't bought the farm yet,>> he'd say. We developed our banter into an act.
<<When you get out of here, we should take this act on the road,>> I said one day. He

didn't reply at first.

Then, with a tear in his eye, he said, <<Yes, we should do that.>>

That night he paßed away in his sleep peacefully. He'd just stopped breathing.

I had no idea where our shipmates were anymore, so I had a big obituary run in the newspaper. Only a handful of the old crew came out for it. It was a solemn affair, brief but poignant. Aasvogel gave Poly a twenty-gun salute, and then Poly was lowered into the Martian ground.

Aasvogel and I commiserated at the bar afterwards. Seeing our distreß, no one bŒðered us.

<<Damn, I hated his cooking,>> said Aasvogel. That was all either of us said. We spent the rust of the evening drinking.

Strange feelings overcame me. He was my best friend. I didn't know him at all. I should have made more of an effort to find out who he was. I was pißed at Cayenne for not being here at the end. I mißed Poly's humor. Pulque? Who the fuck drinks pulque? Yuck. And eggs daikon? Please.... He was like an artist, but his palate was his own idiosyncracies and his canvas was his life. That's stupid. Death makes people think in clichés. So does love. I can't say I loved Poly. Heck, I can't say I love anyone. But I sure enjoyed him, the stupid stuck-up son of a bitch. Gueß he got what he deserved for mißing so much skat. No, that's not fair. On and on ambivalence ran ramshod over me—

<<▶Roughshod◀,>> interrupted Heinrich. <<The actual expreßion, from shoeing a horse, is ▶roughshod◀.>>

We'll have no shortage of pretentiousneß, at least. Heinrich will fill in nicely as a substitute supercilious snob. Lovely.

What was discovered when Poly's effects were examined was of great inter-rust, though. He had stashed in his apartment the collected sestinas of the original Mars colony. These sestinas were carried to Condatis by the envoy preceding us. The envoy had disappeared, most likely inculcated by balloonists joining the Bözmacher cult. I have no idea when or how Poly had retrieved the sestinas, some of which were originals and variants. Perhaps when we'd been searching the library, he'd stumbled acroß them. I presume he'd never trusted me enough to confide in me, or perhaps he had his own sinister plans for the poems. *What* was unclear—most had little literary merit.

For example, ▶Life Remains Incomplete◀, often reprinted, doesn't even have seven stanzas. After the fifth stanza, the poem shifts to a final alternating quatrain, alternating a consonant rhyme with an aßonant rhyme, as if an entire new pattern is being begun:

Life Remains Incomplete

Earthquakes occurred daily,
disrupted regular life patterns,
flying window shard won girls away
from unicorns and vampire teeth
for first penetration and to introduce pain
as the principle that propelled us out

from Earth; we had to get out
before our deaths exceeded our births daily.
Some of the blind wanted to brave the pain
and stay and try to reverse the patterns
that had led to loß of sight and hair and teeth.
They hoped to find a way

to keep our place ►of honor◄ in the Milky Way.
That was a joke, as we choked our ¢elghs out
of existence, no longer needing teeth
as we'd been years without eating daily
and had had to adopt new patterns
that did little to alleviate our pain.

All that was left was the pain
and the need to get away
and forget all the old patterns
and figure new ones out
as we began daily
lives that had teeth.

Of course we eventually forgot what metaphor teeth
represented, or why we were all in such pain,
or the hurricanes and floods that had occurred daily
or why our home plane had pushed us away
into the cold, hurried us out
into clean silence where we found no patterns.

We now have constant pain
where we once had teeth.
Although we've done away with patterns,
at least life remains incomplete.

Had Poly been involved in some sort of scheme to sell the manuscript on the black market? I hated my ¢elgh for even thinking so. And Aasvogel, when I suggested it to him, said I was just naturally being paranoid after the Bözmacher thing. I was seeing conspiracies everywhere. I wasn't so sure. This one could be real. Aasvogel told me to let it go. Why? Was he in on it, too?

Okay, I'd forget about it. The manuscripts had been retrieved and were safely on their way back via steam space freighter to the Literary Museum in London. Who cares what might have been if certain plots had worked out in certain ways? That way, as is said, lies madneß, sprawled out in the path and waiting with its Cheshire grin.

When I told Heinrich about the manuscripts, he, too, has perked up, excited. But when I told him they were off and bound for London, he was visibly so unnerved he didn't notice my pun. Was he in on it, too? Had 'ichelle been planted in my office for the ultimate purpose of obtaining the manuscripts? Or was I indeed just being paranoid?

I decided I needed to let it go. Nothing could be done about it anymore.

However, I did have some bootstrap obligation to find out the truth.

I decided to do what I normally do—I ignored it. Let it ✸hit✸ me with an unforeseen left hook, then. That's fine.

That fucker Polymesus. Why hadn't he just told me he had the manuscripts? That ☼Aßhole☼. That goddamned shithead mŒðerfucker—how dare he just up and die?

Part Eleven: The Heinrich Maneuver

At six a.m. ’ichelle was already in the office and working on the computer when I came in.

She was bored, I gueß. Heinrich was back on Earth to do some research for a new book, so she didn’t know what to do with her ¢elgh.

<<Good morning, Michelle,>> she said.

<<Good morning, ’ichelle,>> said I. <<What are you working on so early?>>

<<Oh, just reading the news. Heinrich is going to meßage me once the Lunar static paßes.>>

I took off my wool coat and hung it up on the rack but left on my Austrian felt hat. The place was already getting warmer—’ichelle must have been here for at least half an hour already. She had even made coffee. Maybe an hour. I wasn’t going to complain on such a cold day. My warm felt hat felt warm on the left side of my head, the side I left the hat on. My head and hands always took a little longer to warm. I was longer for truth than warmth. I faced the southern sun, and finally the east side of my head warmed up. So did my left hand. I left my left hand out in the warmth and, with the Œðer, moved my hat over to cover the part of my face left out of the sun’s warmth.

My left hand poured me coffee and then gave it to my right hand to hold so that it, too, might warm up. I drank my coffee black so as not to cool it down with milk.

Both hands were soon at parity, and then the hat came off and found the hat rack to the east of the entrance.

<<Would you like some steamed milk?>> ’ichelle haxed, but I heard ►steamship◄, which made me curious about the one laden with manuscripts and headed for Earth.

I saw picture of it on ’ichelle’s newscreen. <<What news about the steamer?>> I haxed.

She was embarraßed. Why? <<Oh—the ship? I was going to tell you.>> When? <<It’s disappeared!>> I’d have thought those would have been the first words out of her mouth when I walked in. Unleß, of course, she was in on it. In which case, Heinrich’s research trip was actually something different.

I was upset. All three of them had played me for a chump. Polymesus, Heinrich, ’ichelle—they must have pegged me for simple because all I wanted as a reward was disc golf. They were going to make me look bad—I had sworn to protect those sestinas and return them, and all this had happened behind my back and under my nose—no wonder I felt so twisted around.

I tried to tell my ¢elgh that this was no longer my busineß. Why should I care? I was retired. I had done my duty. But, really, until those manuscripts were safely back in the museum, my work was incomplete, and that ate at me.

I decided I would have to go after the sestinas, but I could not let ’ichelle know what I was up to. I could register no reaction to the steamer’s disappearance, so I didn’t.

<<Probably pirates,>> I said. <<You’d wonder why they’d bŒðer. Just for a bunch of dumb poems? The pirating busineß must be bad these days. Why, when I was young, pirates would hi-jack banking ships. That was something. I doubt these clowns will get much of a ransom for a bunch of poems. Haha…. What a bunch of clods.>> And I dropped the subject, as if it mattered to me not at all.

Two days later I told ’ichelle I needed to go to Earth to consult a cave expert on the mine project. ’ichelle was going to book a commercial flight for me, but I told her that the expert was out in the bush and that I needed to rent a private jetstream speedship.

I aßumed I would need weapons for this sort of diplomacy, so I visited Aasvogel’s arsenal, and the Chief Security Officer Nettie Potts (whom I jokingly call the State Arsenist) gave me two sidearms: a Conflater Mauser and a MaceRater. The Conflater Mauser could take any two or more elements from one’s environment and conflate them into one. For example, if I had attack someone in a forust on a foggy day and we were fighting among fallen logs, ►fog◄ and ►log◄ would combine, and my opponent would be ►flogged◄ by some mysterious force. The weapon was powerful, although somewhat unpredictable. The MaceRater could shoot out micro mace balls whose spiked tips would release enzymes that turned solid matter into a pulpy mush. These two seemed sufficiently deadly for my purposes.

Aasvogel, to my surprise, when I told him about my plan, wanted to come along. He was as upset as I was at our friends’ duplicity. Of course under no circumstances could he have come—he had to hold onto the reins of state. His absence would undo all the good we had achieved. But at least I knew I had Aasvogel’s loyalty, as he had mine.

I sent ’ichelle on errands to keep her away from the computer and from the office. I meanwhile located and leased the jetstream speedship I needed and booked it for immediately after work. I would leave ’ichelle aßuming I’d be in the next day, which would give me a head start before she could come back to the office and realize I was gone.

I also had maintenance change the front door lock to the office, which would further delay her in the morning. I gave the maintenance man twenty testicles not to say anything to ’ichelle. I told him I was playing a practical joke on her, and he was happy to be in on it. I also swapped out her hard drive on her computer for a new one, locked her computer with encryption she’d have difficulty getting past, and changed all the paßwords on my computer. That would further delay her when she came in the next day. All I'd have to do is keep her busy with errands till quitting time and then send her home before she could get on the computer again. I had her old hard drive sent to Aasvogel by courier—Aasvogel was going to have Potts see what was on it. She also set up a secured line on the speedship for my direct contact with her and with Aasvogel. In truth, keeping in contact with one was the same as keeping in contact with the Œðer because they were so often together, as neceßitated by her position. She had been a loyalist during the Bözmacher usurpation, and her ¢elgh had been planning an elaborate rescue of Aasvogel when ours succeeded. Aasvogel astutely acknowledged the attempt and aßured her allegiance before bitterneß buried her better beliefs. Not that Nettie needed acknowledgement, but one notices one's efforts going towards naught. Recognition is rewarded with renewed regard.

Her major reason for having tried to save Aasvogel was not for personal gain. That was laudable. She was a devout Catholic and couldn't bear to see anyone dragged off by cults. But she was peculiar about her own faith as well.

I saw her just before I left. She was on her knees, her hands clasped together, and she was citing some strophes of the apostles. These ►apostrophes◄ were addreßed to the air, as if air could respond. Or rather, they were addreßed to no one and just pointed at the air.

Just then a very young tortoise-shell cat walked up to her and rubbed against her leg. Nettie kept going with her strophes, but then seemed to be directing them at the kitten. I thought if I used my Mauser that moment, the entire space would become a catastrophe.

She took me to the testing range for the Mauser and showed me how to use it. The testing range was a steel warehouse with thousands of commonly recognized items displayed on shelving lining the walls and filling the interior space with hundreds of evenly space units.

I would focus on one item, say a shelf of musical instruments, and get the item I wanted to use in my croßhairs, for example a harp. Then I would focus on a second item, a shelf of comic books for example. And then in my Mauser, the images of harps and cartoons would merge and harpoons would come shooting out in a constant stream so long as the trigger was pulled.

But, as I said, the gun was a bit unpredictable. When I combined pictures of moms with bugs, instead of getting bombs, as I'd hoped, I got mugged—by coffee mugs. Of course, being pelted by mugs full of hot coffee hurt, too, but they weren't bombs. I tried to combine a sculpture of a fist with a photo of a choir and, instead of having a flamethrower, I was kißed. I learned that I would need to anticipate multiple combinations.

An advert for a store combined with dice only yielded dirt and advice. Both were useleß.

But a sheath and a dame would lead to death or shame. Both effective tools.

Truth and a towel yielded flying trowels and teeth. Which of the two was produced at any given time seemed random.

Bunches and pullets became punches and bullets. I was beginning to feel more comfortable with the weapon.

I began to consider what items I might see at my destination.

Shoes and socks. That would lead to electrocution and litigation. Good, but I could do better.

Dishes and forks?

Bikes and sprains?

Wires and sports?

Chicks and brains?

Keys and butters?

Flatteries and baying?

Gnats and rudders?

Slashes and haying?

Blabbing withstood?

Handing instead?

Dabbing the stewed

or faking the bread?

Lashing the crowd

or crashing the loud?

Would I be able to see it fast enough when I needed to? Could I choose from the many poßibilities in an instant? I had until the moon to practice.

I imagined boarding the steamship. I would encounter two of Behn's accomplices who were deep in discourse at the intersection of two hallways.

Zap! I would hit their discourse! Zap! I would hit the intersection.

They'd either be dißected or fucked.

Unleß the machine misread ▶intersection◀ as ▶corner◀ and ▶discourse◀ as ▶talking◀, in which case they'd become the corn king and would be taller.

I had to figure out how to make the gun lock on to the right term. I figured it out pretty fast. All I had to do was say the term out loud. <<Intersection!>> and <<Discourse!>> Of course, that took away the element of surprise, in which case I was probably better off with the MaceRater.

I had practiced with the MaceRater in the warehouse briefly, but using it incurred grave risks. Targets all disintegrated, or, more accurately, liquefied. That was great if I didn't miß. After I had liquefied sections of floor and wall, I was haxed to put the weapon away.

Aboard the steamer, if I mißed my target and liquefied a hole in the hull, I'd be sucked out into space. I'd only be able to use it in the interior of the ship, not near any external walls, floors or ceilings. So I had to study the designs not only of the steamer but of every known type of pirate ship in the vicinity just in case the steamer had actually fallen into pirate hands.

The flight to the far side of the moon, where presumable Behn was hiding and doing busineß with pirates or, perhaps, was kidnapped and being done by pirates (Aarrgh! Come meet Captain Johnson! He's only got one eye. Don't make fun of it, or you'll have to give it a kiß!) went slowly and tediously. Studying design charts has never been a joy of mine, and I fell asleep over them a couple of times.

I dreamt I was being chased by a cyclops minotaur through Daedalus's labyrinth. The walls of the labyrinth had pulsing veins running align them. Sisyphus came down the corridors, pushing his boulder before him. Prometheus would follow, flinging fireballs in pursuit. Notes on the walls would grow gorgon heads. I had to navigate the halls without looking at them. When Cerberus came at me, I shot the MaceRater at it. One of its heads caught the mace ball in its teeth. The head dißolved. Cerberus was left with its two remaining heads howling in pain. I did not go past it, though, for that way, certainly, Hades lay. I went off into a tangential tunnel that ended in a sphincter through which I squeezed my ¢elgh, plopping out in a pool of kaolin. Careßmatangs were wiping the outside of the sphincter clean with some paper. I recognized the paper too slowly—the sestinas! The careßmatangs gathered the remaining papers and ran off, leaving the soiled ones behind. I collected those, trusting some manuscript preservationist would be able to clean them somehow. I figured I had collected about a quarter of all the manuscripts! Better than none, I thought, as I headed off in search of the careßmatangs.

The ship announced we were leaving visual range of the base at Mars Condatis, and then of Alexandria Base on Earth not long thereafter. There was a zone that lay outside the range of all four moonbases. When I reached that, I'd be completely invisible. I'd have to stay low in the atmosphere or actually near the surface to be undetected, and I was certain I'd find the steamship there.

I knew it was still aloft and had to be moving at a steady pace to keep its ¢elgh hidden. When I reached the zone where I'd calculated it had to be, I was not surprised to see it there. Nor was I surprised either that no pirate ships were anywhere near. My suspicions of Behn were apparently correct. My concern became whether 'ichelle had figured out where I was really going and had notified Behn. That might be disastrous.

I figured he'd be obseßed with the skies, looking for his contact or for someone who'd discovered his plan, so my best course of action was to drop nearer the surface and come up on the steamship from beneath. The hold had its bays in the belly, and that is where I needed to dock.

It'd be nice if I had a telematter transporter, such as had been invented by 20th century Earth novelists. Engineers and scientists, though, as always, lag woefully behind artists' visions and have apparently still not gotten around to creating such transporters.

I dreamt I was beheaded in an empty hold. Behold the empty-headed! A man, sitting in a chair, is reading and eating chips. <<Why are you doing that?>> haxes his son. <<You know nothing stays in your head!>> Sure enough, when the man turns slightly, one can see the chips flying out of a gaping hole at the back of the man's head! The son takes a bowl and places it on the table behind the father's head. The chips fill the bowl. When the father finishes his bag of chips, the son gives the father the bowl. The father begins to eat the chips in the bowl, and the son places an Œðer bowl behind his father's head. The father is swallowing the chips without chewing them, so this proceß could take a very long time.

I wondered what the dream meant. An empty head is an empty belly? Was I afraid of the belly of the steamer's being empty? Or was I afraid my head was so empty that I wouldn't be able to recognize anything in the hold if I were to see it?

Well, if pirates were the problem, I should be able to recognize them—they were all humanoid in these here parts.

I was able to dock and lock the speedship into the steamship with no noticeable response. No hail. Just static snow. No movement. Silence.

The steamship's life support system and lights were still on, though. How very peculiar. And when I found the lounge, I was taken aback to see a half-completed game of solitaire spread out on one table and a board game in progreß on the Œðer. Cards and game pieces were all neatly in place—I did not get the impreßion that the games had been suddenly interrupted. Cards would have be slapped down, game pieces knocked on their sides in that case. The scene looked like the participants had just calmly and quietly been removed or cleaned up after to make their removal appear calm.

The bell from a microwave oven rang, and I jumped. My Conflater Mauser went off in my hand and shot the board game, hitting first the dice and then some piece that looked like a rook from cheß.

All of a sudden more rice filled the air than at an old-fashioned wedding, and out of the cloud of rice stepped a ridiculous-looking character who resembled if anything one of the Three Musketeers from a Dumas novel.

He removed his feathered cap and bowed to me and said, <<Permit me, Sir, to introduce my ¢elgh. I am the Duke of Reiß.>>

I laughed.

<<You cut me to the quick, Sir,>> he said, hurt.

<<The Duke of Rice?>>

<<No, the Duke of Reiß,>> and he rolled his ►r◄ and emphasized the eszett so I would understand. <<Ah, I see my 💥pop💥 corn is ready.>> He removed the bag from the microwave, tore it open, and began to snack on the 💥popped💥 kernels. He offered me the bag.

<<No, thank you,>> I replied.

<<Your mockery of my name, I am afraid, reveals some deep-rooted psychological disturbance on your part. I could help you overcome that, if you permit me.>> He had one eyebrow raised inquisitively.

<<I thought you were the Duke of Reiß, not the Duke of Advice,>> I said, wondering if I could reverse the setting of the Conflater Mauser and make him disappear. Or maybe I could combine ►Duke◄ with something else.

<<I am. But I am also a licensed psychŒðerapist and would be glad to help.>> Frightened, I reversed the settings and shot the Duke. Unfortunately it caused him a transformation I had not expected. The Doctor Duke became a Mr. Hyde. He burst through his clothes, notably sporting a two-foot-long spike priapus at full erection.

He chased after me lustfully, drooling, calling me ♪sweet boy♫. It was clear that my shot had divided the conflation, but not into its original components. I had turned the ►therapist◄ into ►the rapist◄.

I ran into the ship's chapel for sanctuary, but he followed me. A painting of the Pope was on the announcements board. Thinking quickly, I yelled out as I shot, <<Rapist!>> and <<Pope!>>

The former Duke instantly became a devout papist dangling from a rope around his neck. Even I am not cynical enough to kill a man in a church, so I cut him down. The former Duke fell to the ground. He coughed violently and pulled the rope away.

<<Thank you, and thank God,>> he said once he'd regained his composure. He looked just like the Duke again. <<How, sir, did you know I was Catholic?>>

<<Père Alexandre,>> I lied. I'd had no such idea. I wondered if I could use the MaceRater once were outside the chapel, but then I realized these were exterior floors.

The Duke, when questioned, had no knowledge of the ship whatsoever. Apparently he thought he was in Cardinal Richelieu's castle, though his familiarity with 💥pop💥 corn seemed anachronistic.

I thought of trying again to return the Duke whence he came but thought the better of it. An ally might be a useful tool, so I let him finish his 💥pop💥 corn and the posed him a question:

<<Is anyone else on this ship?>>

<<What ship?>>

<<Oh, sorry. Is anyone else in the castle? I have not seen any of the Cardinal's men.>>

<<I do not know, sir.>>

<<Well, go back, but don't let your ¢elgh be seen. Then report back to me.>>

<<Certainly.>> He was off. Now to find the library. I figured that if I had been the one the steal the manuscripts, undoubtedly I'd have hidden them in the library. Paper among paper—like hiding a stick of hay in a haystack.

The Duke returned in one minute. <<It occurred to me that you might be suffering from anxiety, and I thought perhaps before I left I should hax you about that. I have some very effective techniques you could apply—>>

<<No, no, no. I'm fine. Please. Task at hand.>>

<<All right, then.>> I presumed I'd be unable to remove the annoying therapist from the Duke without conjuring forth the rapist. I only slightly preferred the former.

There must be Œðers on board, I figured. The microwave bŒðered me. The Duke couldn't have set it because he wasn't here until the Conflater Mauser invoked his presence.

If I remembered the map correctly, the library was three levels up and on the far side of the ship. The elevator was nearby. I walked down the hall in that direction when the Duke returned again.

<<Where shall I report to you?>> he haxed. A good question.

<<Find me in the library. Three floors up and on the Œðer side of the ship, I mean, castle. The doorway should be labeled ▶Cargohold 319◀. If, for some reason, the library is not there, I will leave a note with instructions.>>

<<Good so. Thank you, sir.>>

<<Okay. Task at hand.>>

<<Going, Sir. Sir, if I may suggest, impatience is frequently a sign of anxiety—>>

<<Just go. Go!>>

<<Very well.>> He left again, and I pushed the elevator button. The door sprang open instantly, which indicated that the Œðers had not gone to an Œðer floor immediately after leaving the lounge. Or they'd sent the elevator back down to make it look like they had not gone to an Œðer floor. Oh, well, task at hand, as I'd told the Duke.

The third level up was all for dry cargo. The hold I sought was a ▶library◀ in name only, though it did contain books. But it had no cataloguing system, no carrels, no plush armchairs, nor any Œðer amenities found in true libraries back in the almost-forgotten age of books. All it contained were boxes of papers. Most of the papers were the documents pertaining to the ship its ¢elgh—not only were the hard copies of all the logs, manifests and correspondence this ship had generated or received stored here, but the hundreds of maintenance manuals and records were kept in case one day the electrical systems permanently failed. Ideally, the shop could be rebuilt from scratch using these manuals and records in case of, say, shipwreck or damage from attack.

Of course, these official records were all neatly labeled and stacked and color-coded, so anyone could quickly find any particular official ship's document rather quickly.

What I was looking for, therefore, looked different from the rust, unleß it was disguised to look the same, in which case it'd probably be the last box of any particular sequence. Unleß an out-of-sequence box had been added.

And that's how I found the box. The maintenance logs had two boxes labeled ▶Rudders, Box 3◀. Because only one box three would have existed, and boxes four and five were in place, one of these two must have been an imposter. I pulled out the bottom of the two, and, sure enough, there they were: the collected sestinas of the first Earth colony on Mars, written not too far from present-day Mars Condatis, but by an entirely separate group of colonists who perished years before Mars Condatis was colonized.

The original envoy had thought that a connection between the two colonies existed and that the Mars Condatis colony would have inter-rust in these writings. The last communication we'd ever received from them was that the representatives of Mars Condatis had met the sestinas with hostility, noting that the works contradicted Bözmacher philosophy in significant ways. And that was the last we'd heard from the first envoy. That the Bözmacher cult had somehow taken control of Mars Condatis was obvious, which is why my delegation and I had been sent off in pursuit of the sestinas [and to help Aasvogel regain control of the state, of course].

What a big fuß over a bunch of second-rate poems, I thought. There was no Elizabeth Bishop in the bunch, that was for certain. No Diane Wakoski.

Here's an example:

Sestina on the Half-Life of a Balloon

We are held by tenuous tethers
buffeted about like balloons
tied tentatively to thc carth,
striving for the stratosphere to float
in, to escape into the air
and then 💥pop💥!

How we long for that 💥popping💥
and our freedom from that tether
so that our souls may mingle with the air
after breaking our membranes of balloon.
But what a curse it'd be to float
disembodied forever above the earth.

Each of us needs to return to the solid earth
and become anchored in some mom or pop
whose worldly obligations prevent all floating,
whose financial obligations become trap and tether,
whose bankers' heels bust all balloons
that might Œðerwise find free air.

Let us fall from air to the earth!
Fill each balloon with soda pop,
and make drinking straws from tethers
for ice cream floats!

Hey, wait. What's that? That's Bözmacher. It's the part of the cult aßociated with Crewvolta Prinfreshalley, the 💥Poppers💥!

Apparently the 💥Popper💥 had influence on, were a part of, or were completely in control of the original Mars Colony? Was that why it had failed?

What if Behn's part of the Inflater group? They certainly wouldn't want Bözmacher aßociated with the failure of the Mars colony. And they wouldn't want Bözmacher represented by these writings. No—it'd be far better if the manuscripts just ►disappeared◄.

I could see their logic. It was bad enough that the first colonists, the Bözmachers, failed, giving the cult a bad name, but these weren't even the right kind of Bözmachers to begin with. And the general public would never be able to understand that two factions of the same cult disagreed. They still hadn't been able to understand that Catholics *are* Christians, or that both Sunni and Shi'a are Muslim.

<<I found them, sir!>> announced the Duke, running into the library.

Okay! First we went and secreted the manuscripts inside the speedship, and then we went to see what the Duke was talking about. He said they were fishing off the drawbridge, whatever that meant.

The Duke led me to an observation lounge, and, sure enough, there were three men, fishing poles in hand. The poles were stuck out through sphincter-like portholes, and they were fishing in space.

What they wanted to catch here was unclear. I'd have sworn we were outside of the moon's atmosphere, and even if not, we were way too high up in it for them to be able to catch any Lunar avians; even the largest, the Aasvogel, for whom the leader of Mars Condatis was named, surely didn't fly *this* high.

They didn't notice us, they were so intent on their fishing, so we just watched. I wanted to see what they'd catch.

The line looked led through some sort of membrane that seemed as wide as the porthole, and, sure enough, I saw Behn get a strike, pull hard on the line, reel it in a few yards to make sure his catch was secure, and then he snapped the membrane into place along the inside edge of the porthole. He then pulled what he had caught into the membrane and pushed a button above the porthole. This slammed down and tied the membrane around its contents. He then cut the line and pushed an Œðer button. This inflated the membrane to give the occupant some room.

Ingenius, I thought. What was he catching? He set the inflated membrane on a table on the Œðer side of the room, where almost twenty already-filled membranes already stood. I could not see what the membranes contained, but it didn't look like birds, and it didn't look like fish.

Then he saw us. Behn did not seem startled at all.

<<Michel!>> he called to me, rather than feminizing my nickname, as his wife did. I can't even remember the last time anyone called me by my proper name. <<Good to see you! My wife said you might be showing up.>> Ah, so she *was* in on it, too!

<<The fishing any good?>>

<<Of course. Why else take a fishing vacation?>>

<<A fishing vacation?>> He didn't know why I was here after all. Or he was playing it cool, waiting for me to show my cards first. <<Whatcha catching?>>

<<Something rare and unusual. We're fishing that dark cloud of anti-matter,>> and he pointed outside.

Oh, so he was fishing in the antiverse, was he? Of course! The antiverse *hates* sestinas. I laughed out loud at my pun.

<<What's so funny?>> he haxed.

<<What are you using for bait? Song hooks?>>

<<Oh, no. No bait. They come willingly. The chance to return to Earth is enough for them. They've been trapped in the cloud for centuries, some of them. It has an amazing gravitational pull.>>

<<Who are *they*?>>

<<The symbionts, fool. The symbionts.>>

<<What? Which symbionts?>>

<<Mostly from Earth, it seems. A few Lunar mixed in. Can't really tell completely, yet. We've only caught, what, nineteen, Fred?>> Behn turned and haxed the elder of the Œðer two, a gray-beared old man with a ruddy complexion. <<Fred's the captain,>> Behn explained to me. <<That's Frank, his son,>> he said, nodding at the younger, a darker version of his father. <<And who's this?>>

<<This is the Duke of Reiß,>> I said, making sure to emphasize my consonants. <<I happened upon him en route.>>

<<Ah.>>

<<So what are you going to do with these symbionts?>> I haxed.

<<What do people normally do with a catch? We'll eat as many as we can and then freeze and can the rust.>

<<What?>>

<<I'm just kidding, Michel. We're returning them to Earth.>>

<<You can't do that. The symbionts don't belong there. They should be set free.>>

<<What are you? Some kind of Bözmacher?>>

<<I was going to hax you the same thing. If you return them to Earth, then you are only giving the cult more importance. You'll be increasing the need for separation, and people will be gullible enough to believe the Bözmacher spiel.>>

<<Gullible? Spiel? You clearly don't understand the significance of the organization.>>

<<The cult?>>

<<Cult? My friend, you are deluded. It's not a cult. It's a scientific brŒðerhood.>>

<<So why bring symbionts to Earth? That's like giving people smallpox-infected blankets just to prove your cure works.>>

<<Yes, it is, rather.>>

The Duke, on his own initiative, pulled his sword and ran up to the membranes and tried to puncture one.

<<Tell your friend not to bŒðer,>> said Behn. <<Those membranes are practically indestructible. We know what we're doing.>>

<<So you are not a Popper?>>

<<You know, this distinction between Poppers and Anti-Poppers has been made too much of. There's a time for popping and a time for not popping.>>

<<All that matters is that the cult insinuate its ¢elgh into the proceß.>>

<<Organization, not cult. Scientific brŒðerhood and sisterhood.>>

<<Including 'ichelle.>> I had to find out.

<<Of course.>>

<<Well, I'm a symbiont's uncle.>>

<<How inter-rusting that you say that, because I just realized we could save our ¢elghs

two containers by using you and your friend.>>

I didn't think a symbiont could live inside a Conflater being, but I wasn't go to tell Behn that. Frank had put down his rod. Fred put down his. On Behn's cue, they grabbed the Duke and held him.

<<You'll see how painleß this is,>> said Behn. He took the membranous balloon and untied the end but held it closed until he had it over the Duke's nose and mouth. Then he opened it. Presumably the symbiont would enter the host through these portals.

<<Something's wrong,>> said Behn. <<It's not going in!>> The symbiont struggled and escaped its bag and immediately climbed up Frank's arm and entered his agape mouth.

<<You idiot!>> yelled Fred. <<It's got my son!>>

<<Well, something went wrong!>>

Meanwhile I was looking around frantically and spotted a few items I could conflate to purpose.

<<Mop! Bell! Harpoon!>> I yelled, realizing too late that I had mentioned three items. I had no idea what the Mauser would do with three inputs. The balloons all started popping, but symbionts inside were not freed. They were harmed by the popping. They were dead!

<<What did you do?>> yelled Behn.

I saw a chalkboard. I ran over to it and quickly drew a picture of two-lane highway and fired again. <<Chalks!>> and <<Lanes!>> The three antagonists were suddenly bound in locks and chains and safe for transport.

<<Upon Revision!>> I said, walking away.

I had the Duke take them into the speedship's cargo hold. I brought the sestinas up to the cockpit.

I haxed the Duke to come along, not knowing the limits of the Conflation, but he insisted that he has to stay behind and protect the castle. So we said farewell, and my prisoners and I and the sestinas set off for Earth.

Part Twelve: Codetta

On our arrival on Earth, the police charged Behn with little more than having poor judgment and decided he had been hoodwinked by Fred and Frank. Behn and his wife, who was quickly extradited, were sent to a residential deprogramming facility in Utah, whose motto, a double entendre perhaps, was ☧We deprogram for life!☧

Fred and Frank were charged with aßault and kidnapping, and Frank was charged will illegal transport of an alien, apparently the most serious crime of all the aforementioned. Frank and his symbiont were going to have to endure months of experiments.

They'd all be in custody for a good, long while.

My employer, the Chief Archivist in London, who had sent the envoys in the first place, had no idea why anyone would turn down a gift of one's people's ancient manuscripts. He didn't think it had anything to do with a schism between Inflaters and Deflaters and said that the cult really needed both. Both inflation and deflation were neceßary proceßes in Bözmacher philosophy, much as Siva, Vishnu and Brahman were eßential to Hindu thought, though certain factions were loyal to one over the Œðers. It was like a Catholic's picking of a favorite saint to use as an interceßory. He said that the manuscripts really held very few clues to the disappearance of the colony, Œðer than the cultists seemed to not like troubling their ¢elghs with such burdensome tasks as agriculture or animal husbandry, but instead chose to write sestinas. Any argument to the contrary would be like arguing that, although Rome had burned, Nero had developed excellent technique on the violin.

I thanked the Archivist and took my leave. I wanted to pay my respects to my father before returning to Mars.

My father was buried in Rose Hill Cemetery in Macon, Georgia, near two of the Allman brŒðers, his favorite band. He was an aßistant engineer for Capricorn Records back in the day and had worked with them, with Martin Mull, with Captain Beyond, with the Marshall Tucker Band among Œðers. I felt strange walking through the cemetery again, past the old guy who was buried with his dog, past the Civil War section, down by the river where Elizabeth Reed was. A strange tree had taken hold of my father's headstone and lifted it up higher than it had been. It looked like my father was trying to get out. Perhaps the dead were going to gig.

Trucks came rumbling down the path. A back hoe was coming. A new resident was moving in.

I put the roses I'd bought on my father's grave, told him I mißed him, told him I was doing okay working for Aasvogel in Mars Condatis, that I was alone but doing okay.

As if in response, I heard music from one of the trucks, a version of Robert Hunter and Jerry Garcia's song ►Touch of Gray◄.

Nostalgia for my past overwhelmed me. I didn't want to shed any more tears over everything again, so I left the cemetery. There was a dive acroß the street, so I washed away my woes in foam and rocks.

I waved goodbye and returned to Mars Condatis.

I knew I should have felt pleased, elated even, to have finally finished the task I first went to Mars Condatis to accomplish. Instead, I just felt empty.

*

When I returned to my office, Aasvogel's office had already removed all of the Hume-Behn's effects, so it also felt empty.

I looked around at how vacant the place was without 'ichelle. I was like a turtle without 'ichelle, slowly making the rounds of the office, refamiliarizing my ¢elgh with it. I walked the inside circumference of it while touching the wall. I then spiraled in from object to object, piece of furniture to piece of furniture, until I reached the center of the office, which is exactly where 'ichelle's desk had been.

The phone rang. Aasvogel was calling.

<<I'm glad you are back,>> he said. <<We had a big problem while you were away.>>

<<What?>> I just then noticed my unanswered phone meßages numbered nearly forty.

<<We had a cave-in at the mine course.>>

<<Anyone hurt?>> I haxed, alarmed.

<<No, no. But we didn't know how to proceed without you. We think it was done intentionally. I was hoping you could get an investigation going to find out what or who is behind that. Maybe it was just your two friends there.>>

<<They are not my friends. They betrayed my trust, Aasvogel.>>

<<Okay, but perhaps they did that. In which case, we're okay because they won't be seeing free society again for a long time.>>

<<I don't see how Behn could have done it—he was in Lunar orbit. Maybe 'ichelle, though….>>

<<Well, whatever. Will you take care of it? And welcome back. I'll have Nettie Potts

call you. I'd like her to work with you on this.>>

*

Well, at least I have something to do.

Tomorrow. Today I'm going to dream about the day I again visit the Gardens of Obsane Topiary and once again find the company of the Shaved Girls.

Book Two: Parkour on Mars

Part One: Carters of Mars and the Lakeside Lighthouse

My mine eyes saw the cave-in not as bad as it could be. No lives were lost, not even a canary's. The collapse had occurred between holes two and three, so there was no way around re-excavation if my dream of turning the mine and its adjacent caves and paßageways into one of Mars's—heck, one of the inner planets'—premier disc golf courses was to be realized. Morning glory, hallelujah! The project kept marching on.

Re-excavation was an enormous undertaking. Millions of tons of rock bed had to be displaced. But the crew I had hired were brilliant undertakers of the art of displacement. They were the same crew who had run of the city in digging foundations.

On my way to the office I stopped at the Stationary Bus. A long time ago a city bus had broken down in an intersection. It was left there and had become a landmark as a popular spot to pop into and grab a local newspaper, a cup of coffee, and a seat. I grabbed the ►Condenser◄, Mars Condatis's abbreviated morning paper, nicknamed the ►Condescender◄. It wasn't particularly well written, but it was tabloid-sized, so I wouldn't hit my neighbors in the face when I unfolded and refolded pages. I drank a ►volcano◄, a coffee grown up north on the volcanic slopes of Apollinaris, north of Lake Gusev. It is also not particularly good, but it's cheap, much cheaper than the imported Earth coffees. I could buy a car for what they charge for Kopi Luwak. An old Honda Civic, at least. Not that I need a car, though. Everything in Mars Condatis is pretty much in walking distance or easily acceßible by public transport. If I need to go beyond Lake Gusev, I can always sign for a state car—that's one of the perks of being a civil servant. Of course, if I had a car, then I'd have to drink that coffee in the car. I could be a civil servant sipping civet in a Civic.

Nothing much in the paper. Nothing about the re-excavation project. That figures. Everyone was all excited about the sudden cave-in but couldn't care leß about the difficult excavation. The papers preferred accidents to hard work.

I skipped to the sports section. Our Mars Condatis football team had not been faring well in the second round of Worlds Cup qualifiers. They looked like they'd be coming home soon. We had never gotten past the second round anyway. Sure enough, an Œðer loß, this time to the Faroe Islands, 3 to 1. At least our young striker Mull Gerdner had been able to score off a header on a nice croßing paß by Beck Franzenbauer. Our defense, though, was as holey as an aßaßinated pope, pardon the expreßion.

The coffee was overroasted, burnt tasting. I had read somewhere that the Stationary Bus's roasters did that on purpose. Overroasting burnt much of the caffeine out of the coffee, forcing a drinker to drink more to wake up. I could tolerate it with milk and sweetener, but without them it was as bitter as a bank customer.

<<Excuse me,>> a voice said. I looked up. A spectacled bear of a man wanted to sit next to me. I looked up from my newspaper and looked around. I gueß the bus was pretty full. I took my newspaper parts up from the seat next to me and put them in my lap. I moved my volcano from the cupholder on my right to the one on my left. The one on the right was actually his. And then I halfway stood up so he could scoot past me without stepping on any of my toes.

<<Thank you,>> he said. I nodded and returned to my reading. After a minute of silence, he interrupted me and spoke to me. <<Excuse me for interrupting you, but I was just wondering if you're Michel du Jabot.>>

<<I am,>> I replied.

<<What a coincidence!>> he said. <<I am Nils Stambler. I was just heading to your office.>>

He was applying to be my new aßistant. My last one had proven to be an enemy of the state and was now rotting in prison. I looked sideways at Nils. He could double as a bodyguard. Or he could prove to be an aßaßin. I wasn't very eager to see either poßibility actualized. I liked my quiet life as it was. But I needed an aßistant.

Just then, I accidentally knocked over my volcano. It steamed up at me from the ground.

<<Don't cry over milk spilt in the eye of a gift horse,>> said Nils. Oh, great. A joker.

<<It was no gift. It cost me eight testicles,>> I responded, unamused.

<<Ouch,>> said Nils.

<<Very well, then,>> I said, getting up. <<Follow me.>>

I slipped a couple of testicles into the tip slot and made my exit. Testicles are the currency of Mars Condatis and the butt of much interworld humor. Why doesn't the Mars Condatis team ever win any away football games? Because they always trade in their testicles for the local currency. Ha ha.

Nils followed me. We took a tram to Lakeside. I had had my office relocated into the top of the automated Lakeside Lighthouse off one of the points on Lake Gusev, just out of sight of Mars Condatis proper. It was a relatively small lighthouse, out on the promontory, and to reach the top there were no stairs, only anchored shelving holding maintenance equipment and, of course, my book collection. The paßageway up was only four feet wide, and one reached the top by climbing up the shelving with one's stocking feet (no shoes! the mud!) at three and nine. After shinnying to the top, one would come to a locked door simply labeled ⲬelectricalⲬ. That was my office, which was shaped like a doughnut around the acceß shaft and inside the centrifugal lamp. The width of my office from interior wall to exterior wall was actually a full fifteen feet acroß, so I had plenty of room inside. Additionally, the height of the room extended above the centrifugal lamp, where windows all the way around were shielded from the light below by a maintenance ledge. Also, my ceiling was one enormous glaß skylight, so my newest hobby had become stargazing.

I turned on the lights in the office, and the radio came on, blasting a popular song: ♪Pantaloons in pontoons, / pantaloons in pontoons. / You're looking like cartoons / with your pantaloons in pontoons.♫

Centered above the office like a cap on top of the acceß shaft was an observation deck that jutted into the sky like a clear glaß nipple against the areola of the roof of my office. I had turned this observation deck into my personal sleeping quarters. It was just large enough for my bed and nightstand. I would lie there and watch the stars at night, or lightning, or planes flying overhead.

<<Can I use your washroom?>> was the first thing Nils haxed when we entered my office. That's a good first impreßion on an interview, I thought. ͼHi! Where's your crapper?ͽ

When he came out, he said, <<I see you've been using the balancing shampoo. I tried that, but I kept falling down.>>

<<Boom chakalaka,>> I replied, emulating a half-hearted rim shot. I should tell him I have an allergy to corn.

Of course, when I think of corn, I remember reading an interview with one writer who stated that he would take out his corny meter after his books were written and edit everything corny out of them. I was so surprised when I first read that, I exclaimed aloud, <<Why do that? Corny is a kernel of life!>>

I have been misquoted for years as having said, <<Corny *as* a colonel of life,>> but *that* is simply *wrong*, which means not only is to think so inaccurate, but also it is too simple. Nils reminds me that the writer who was interviewed may have been right.

<<Nice book collection,>> said Nils, pointing down the acceß shaft.

<<Thank you. I keep my good European series there. They have a nice look to them: Reclam Verlag, RoRoRo, Editions de Minuit, Fischer Verlag, Mondadori—and many more. They seem reaßuring, somehow.>>

<<Some of them are so cute—they're so small, like those little yellow ones.>>

<<That's Reclam. Yeah, I like those, too. The smaller ones are strategically shelved where the best handholds and toeholds are.>>

<<Where the rubber grips are.>>

<<Exactly.>>

<<That would keep the stone from wearing down?>>

<<No, they're just there to function as guides. Preferred handholds.>>

<<And toeholds.>>

<<And toeholds.>>

<<The stone shelving?>>

<<It was part of the original plan. Not originally for books, though, of course. Those shelves were designed to hold heavy tools and equipment used for lighthouse repair.>>

<<Well, where's all that equipment?>>

<<A storage shed just outside.>>

<<You moved it for the books?>>

<<Actually no. It was moved because, well, do you know how hard it is to maneuver through an aceß shaft while balancing a hundred-pound chainsaw? That's why.>>

<<What was—that jaggedy set?>>

<<What?>>

<<Oh, never mind. It doesn't matter. Why are you here?>>

<<Because I do,>> and we left it at that.

*

I discovered some very inter-rusting facts about Mr. Nils Stambler during the application proceß. For example, no one knew this, but he told me that as a boy he'd once danced with Jack Wild in some kids' production a few years after *H.R. Pufnstuf. Oliver!* I think. A musical version of Dickens's kneeslapper *Oliver Twist.*

<<Well, don't dance here,>> I said. <<You'll knock stuff over.>> I had visions of Nils's pounding into my trophy case and knocking it over. Some of my childhood disc golf trophies, especially, were fragile and irreplaceable. And I wasn't really impreßed by the fact that he knew anything about musical theatre, never a subject of great inter-rust to me (though, in the right hands, it could be a wonderfully effective artistic tool to employ). Maybe a band like Potliquor could have pulled it off. Moby Grape, maybe. If people hadn't fucked with them and had let them develop according to their druthers, who knows where they would have gone? Who would have predicted John Lawton's Lucifer's Friend to have put out four-so-different and all-so-wonderful albums? Or Faust's first four? I like good music. It had spoiled me for most musical theatre, which seemed so tame in comparison. Yeah, that's the word: ▶tame◀. That was Nils. He was tame. Well, I gueß that's better than deceptive and criminal like my last aßistant and her husband. No, I wouldn't want that again. Nils is a safe choice. If I can keep it down to one soundtrack on the stereo per day, then okay, not counting, of course, soundtracks that are special cases, like *200 Motels* or *Let It Be* (two of the most fascinating psychological studies ever filmed).

<<No, I won't dance,>> said he.

ͼWas that foreshadowing?ͽ I thought, turning away from him abruptly in an obviously boß-like manner, rather aloof, or so I thought.

<<You are sentenced to cuteneß,>> pronounces the Language Judge.

<<Oh, damn! Ah, swell!>>

Okay, okay, it's being reined back in. For now. But later, who knows? Action! Adventure! Danger! Romance! Or a viral video about pickles with distended abdomens! Place your bets early.

Oh, you didn't think I meant a romance with Nils, did you? That's just not going to happen, so if that's the direction you think I'm heading, you can stop reading now. My writing is never about me anyway. It's fiction.

<<It's manipulation,>> says Nils, out of the blue.

<<What is?>> hax I, convinced he'd just read my thoughts.
<<Dancing. It's all in the hands.>>

<<Just like cards,>> say I, producing a deck. You can tell a great deal about a potential candidate by seeing how ze conducts hir ¢elgh when playing competitively. The sadistic play sadistic games. Better to find out over a game of Bübchen Raus than wait to see they're boobs.

<<Sure,>> he said. <<I'll play. Show me yours; I'll show you mine.>>

Oh, I don't know. If he's hitting on me, I'm going to fire him.

<<I have a pair of tens,>> he said. <<You?>>

You don't have me yet, Nils. I don't think it's going to work out. I looked at my hand.

<<I have three sixes.>>

<<Of course. What else would you have?>>

<<Will you stop that, please? How annoying!>> No answer.

<<Nils!>>

<<What?>>

<<Out!>>

<<What do you mean?>>

<<I just took your three!>>

<<You were only supposed to take one.>>

<<No—it was a three.>>

<<Oh, ha ha. I'm funny.>>

<<No, Nils. You are not. Be here at nine a.m. Monday morning. Dreß casually.>>

<<I will. I don't like wearing a giant arrow pointing at my pointer anyway.>>

Before I knew it, I'd hired Nils. As I watched his head disappear down past Rowohlt's RoRoRo series, I wondered if I'd made a mistake.

<<Hey!>> I called after him. <<Do you know anything about disc golf?>>

<<Sure! I love it!>> he yelled. <<I love everything but parkour!>>

Parkour? Jumping from building to building? <<Okay! See you Monday!>> Parkour's not even a sport. It's ¢elgh-abuse. If parkour's a sport, then so are anorexia and bulimia and body piercing and cutting.

I picked up a book as soon as I was sure Nils had left. Parkour was founded by the Yamakasi, who shared the Lingala language. The *Saut de Chat* is the cat's vault, and the cat's leap is the *Saut de Bras*. The Yamakasi must have spent some time analyzing cat movements and then emulating them in runs through the city in which no obstacle was recognized. There's a way to climb, leap, or vault through any obstacle as if it weren't there. Each right angle up was just a new plane to negotiate. It's kind of like urban rock-climbing. And then hurdling, though what a practitioner of ▶The Art of Displacement◀ would leap over was negative rather than positive space—an abyß rather than a sawhorse. I have a sawbuck that says the parkour artist will arrive at hir destination eventually.

Of course, these ▶displacement artists◀ do show a blatant disregard for property laws. I wonder how they feel about exurban caves. Imagine parkour spelunkers. They'd push on through any disc golf game. They wouldn't want me to turn the mine and the caves into a disc golf course. They'd ¢elghishly want acceß for their own sport. That won't work. I'll need to look at their group here—maybe they had something to do with the cave-in.

Why is parkour the only sport Nils does not like? I had to find out. I quickly followed Nils back out the lighthouse and saw him halfway to the tram stop.

<<Nils! Wait!>>> He stopped and turned. A quizzical expreßion croßed his face.

<<Yes?>>

<<Why not parkour?>>

He stepped towards me and put his index finger to his lip. Then he made a circular motion in the air with the same finger. He leaned toward me and whispered in my ear, <<Shh! They'll hear you. They're everywhere.>>

<<What? Careßmatangs? No—they're out in the forust only.>>

<<No, *them*.>>

<<Who?>>

<<The displacers. We can't talk about it here. There's no immediate danger. I'll explain on Monday.>> He turned back and pointed at the tram station. <<I'll have to catch that or wait two hours.>>

Two more hours with him? No, no—go ahead. It'll wait till Monday. That was, I gueß, the wrong decision, but I needed some time to absorb it all and proceß it before moving ahead.

ͼA blue angelfish! Famous Words the Blob Might Have said for 50, Alexͽ.

The Blob would have been a more inter-rusting conversationalist. Um, I have a riddle. Uh, how do you keep a new employer in suspense?

Hahahaha. Bring on the careßmatangs. Okay. Parkourers are the urban careßmatangs. They are like apes descending from the canopy only to careß your hair and maybe abduct you, kill you and eat you, or maybe just squeeze you to death with affection in their powerful arms. Does Nils mean so are the parkourers?

But who defines who the parkourers are? There must be, somewhere here, parkourerers, who define parkourers as profeßional, amateur, or undeserving of the name. The namers of parkour—they are the parkourerers. Those are the ones to find. Not the Yamakasi, of course. That was Earth and a long time ago. But the current Martian parkourerers, Condatis's displacers, who are they, and what do they want? Why would they want a cave? Or has the urban parkourer game gone underground, met and joined forces with urban spelunkers, who have found, somewhere, a paßage from the subway tunnels and drainage canals to the cave system and mine here near Lakeside.

Where is this paßage? If you say ►Northwest◄, I'll slap you.

Nor can it be *North by Northwest*, because Cary Grant is dead. So is Hitchcock.

And I'm not going South again. Not after all the effort involved in coming up here in the first place. With the careßmatangs and all. And my brŒðer. Forget about that.

Why here, as on Earth, the globe must be slippery, because going to the top isn't easy. It requires claws, mountain climbing skills, or fence-vaulting, but sliding down to the South is very easy.

Of course, if we didn't keep spinning, our feet would explode. This way it goes to the middle, the equator, the stomach of the planet. The feet and the stomach get all the attention. We don't talk about the Œðer body part five or six feet opposite the feet. Figure that out to get ahead.

Parkour? French Yamakasis? Purse snatchers? What was the purse strap but an Œðer arrow?

Lollipin' Lords a-leaping! Fuck a French duck! How long has all this parkour been going on in, among and around us? I sure hope it's not an Œðer Bözmacher cult. But I'd better not take it lightly.

I have to stop thinking about this. I can find out on Monday. Why worry today? I think I'll just go down to the pool and swim a few laps. In the pool, I actually fell asleep floating on my back. I wondered if that was normal or if people who did that usually drowned. I came out of the water when my face began to feel sunburned. Sunburn is not the best way to get a big red nose. It's better than stealing Rudolf's, though. Or Santa's. Or W.C. Fields's.

Remember: Ed is rich. Ed + gar means ►Rich Spear◄. Ed + mund means ►Rich Protector◄. Ed + ward means ►Rich Guardian◄. Edwin is a rich friend. He's behind the disc golf course, too. A lot of people are. Disc golf is the great egalitarian sport. Well, except for the disabled. Hey, I should design a few courses just for those with handicapping conditions. Something challenging where a disability is neutralized. Disc golf should be an enjoyable path. A shining path. Not the Ejército Guerrillero Popular. Not the Sendero Lumnoso. Just any old lower-case ▶s◀ and lower-case ▶p◀ ▶shiny path◀.

Abimael Guzmán, the founder of the Shining Path, was a former university profeßor. Man, how did he ever brainwash his students so well? I couldn't get mine, when I taught, to believe commas don't just go wherever ▶you◀ would pause. I'm not sure whom they meant by ▶you◀.

Once, a student called me a pregnant woman. She wrote, <<As a pregnant woman, you need to take care of your ¢elgh.>> I have never been a pregnant woman, so I presumed I was not in the target audience. So I stopped reading. I don't think I ever graded that paper. I mean, what could I say to something like that? Hey? I'm not a pregnant woman? Why don't ▶you◀ know that? I've been standing here lecturing day after day, and ▶you◀ can't even tell I'm not a pregnant woman? Wow. I'd better lose weight, then. That's a very parkour thing to say. And I'd almost forgotten… Okay… Anything to get away. ͼFamous Commercial Slogans for 30, Alex.ͽ Eat bran, and your colon will be a great shining path! Or perhaps we are discußing a soccer player who goes through hir opponents by the slide tackling, studs showing. That's the great shinning path. Yeah, shinny up that vertical path. The problem is, you just might find that up is down and down is up. The path of the disc golf course is generally more horizontal than vertical. Of course, it needs illumination, too. What path doesn't? The heaviest path cannot be lightened.

Okay, I think I've punned my ¢elgh past my problems, maybe perceiving my peculiar obseßion with alliteration to also trump as a tool.

Trump. That reminds me how I really miß Skat with the Aasvogel and, at first, my pal Polymesus, until he died, and then my aßistant's husband—I don't even want to think about what those two criminals pulled over on us. He was never the player Polymesus was, anyway. What a trio. I could probably teach Nils. But could we stand him for hours at a time? I'll have to train him before I can introduce him to the Aasvogel, that's for sure. I'll give him a book on etiquette, maybe. Or send him to that famous Courtney School of Charm or whatever it was called back on Earth—I can still remember the pathetic infomercials. ▶Pathetic◀ is an adjective derived from the noun ▶path◀, as in shiny! <<Learn to let the best ▶you◀ shine through!>> Sad stuff, really.

I can't just sit here till Monday. I'll go crazy thinking about not thinking about it. Too late to go to pool. Pool! I don't know—it's been a long time since I shot much pool. Had my own table there for a while back on Earth. The sacrifices we make, eh? There'd be no way to put a pool table in here. Unleß I put it where my bed is. If I get a sturdy one, I could maybe put a futon on it for sleeping. Compromise and not lose too much space. But would I have enough room for full cues? I'd better check the angles. But not tonight. I've got to do something. Can't just sit around here forever. Follow the shining yellow brick path….

That's three of us now. The tin man was last, right? William Gaß trying to find his aß—I mean, heart, of course. He's an intellectual who moved to the heart of the heart in order to rustart his broken heart, but he applied pure reason to an intellectual analysis of the community in order to evaluate where love might reside. All he saw was headleßneß and stupidity and a universal attention to ißues of the guts: food, plumbing, and so on. That's great irony: the intellectual has the guts to look for love in the brain, but wonders why he's not noticing the heart. All he notices are individuals. Once the monadic flies kiß his arms, his heart reawakens, and he sees that love exists in the community, not in the individual.

That means Gaß is a communist, in the best sense of that term. One of the best—probably my favorite story from 20th century America.

America. Inter-rusting. I hadn't thought of America in quite a while. I gueß one would have to start with soil analysis.

How soiled is your America? Mine's pretty soiled, but I'm keeping the faith that she's going to get better someday. The flaws I see have leß to do with the abstract concept of our nation than with the practitioners.

Well, it's different here on Mars. It's much more South American-style dictatorship. Not in Mars Condatis, not really. The Aasvogel does not own an iron fist. But elsewhere most people agree travel is risky. A quick trip foraging for food—anything the first store has is good—is very dangerous. I'd love to see that fear leave the people of Mars Condatis. They'd smile a great deal more. And play more disc golf.

You know, Earth rules don't really apply to Mars. I heard a bunch of kids would party old Earth-style over at the Mars Hotel, but I hadn't been there in a long time.

I'll do it if it is a boogie, and I think it's a stomp! Like pigs in a pen. A good stomp takes guts! And waders. Have a swamp stomp. Mußelwhite's *Louisiana Blues* and Savoy Brown's *Looking In* are starters. Go back to Chicago on the Mountain Bus.

Where am I going? Is there a blues bar nearby? I'd love to hear either some Chicago or Texas blues right now. Memphis would be good, too. Oh, here's a place: ►Future Blues◄, named for an old Canned Heat album, apparently.

Hey, I've landed in the land of good music. Maybe I'll stay here a while. On land. Feed on the ground. Stompin' at a boogie. With summertime BBQ. And buckets o' beer. And Dennis O'Dell. And Ringo. You know my name. Michel du Jabot, of course!

It's my fault. I'm the one who let them on board. You know how musicians are—always the last to leave the party because they *are* the party. I don't mean that as a value judgment. It's just true. Musicians need something to do after their gigs. You can't just go from total energy to sleep in ten minutes. I can, but you can't. Everyone else around here is going to, but you're not allowed. It's late evening, after all. The flies are beginning to fall. See, I said life is different on Mars. Flies are only aloft during the day. I'll keep a low profile—what does that even mean? Posing for a cameo? Like Allen Klein? You can park here in the parkway, or you can weigh-hey on the parkway. Whatever.

All right. I'm here. Safe. Nowhere to be till Monday. Why should I go out again? Bars are closed now. Everyone's asleep. People are going to wake up soon. I think I'll go to sleep while listening to Mußelwhite.

I dream about Fat City, which is filled with big-legged women who fall on their knees and beseech the sky to lift the fog just long enough for them to take care of busineß just a little bit. They begin riffin' directly from the heart, beseeching in four-part harmony.

The gnashing of teeth is often heard coming from Fat City. After Mars Condatis beat Fat City in the Worlds Cup preliminary round, their goalkeeper was arrusted and executed for his poor performance. Fat City was also one of the few Martin city-states that prohibited disc golf. One course a long time ago had a hole that croßed the highway. A careleß throw had once ✸hit✸ the son of the ▶City Manager◀ square in the face as he rode his motorcycle. He lost control, crashed and died. So the City Manager outlawed the sport completely.

I didn't mind per se since that drove more tourists to my courses, but Fat City had one course, built through a working brewery, that I'd always wanted to try. I tried buying the brewery by my ¢elgh, but ▶foreigners◀ were not permitted to own property in Fat City, and my idea for a ▶private disc club◀ would never have received licensure. I figure at some point I'll just borrow that idea for Mars Condatis.

I did find out, though, as I read more about parkour, that Fat City was considered by parkour enthusiasts to be Mars's parkour capital. Apparently the same son who died in the motorcycle accident had been an enthusiast of parkour, so his father, the City Manager, declared parkour the official city sport.

That struck me as odd because much of the fun of parkour seems to be in its outlaw nature. And indeed, my reading indicated that parkour participation decreased significantly once it was legitimized.

I looked at Nils's job application again and noticed that he used to live in Fat City. That worried me. Perhaps he was a disgruntled outlaw parkour enthusiast who was pretending to like disc golf in order to get close to and undermine its operation in Mars Condatis. But after thinking that, I chastised my ¢elgh. Nils's predeceßor's and her husband's having been backstabbing, lying manipulators was no reason to aßume the same of Nils.

Little known facts about parkour included the ►allegation◄ that certain parkourists were ►rumored◄ to ►supposedly◄ have surgically implanted miniature soccer balls into their wombs in order for their fetuses to have something to play with. This rumor was published in at least three major daily metropolitan newspapers as fact.

Surgery had come far, I knew, but I was pretty sure that the surgical implantation of soccer balls was ridiculous. Then again, I have a prosthetic leg that is so life-like I forget about it. It's a permanent replacement for my organic one, and the skin and plastic have been grafted together perfectly. My synapses fire electrical conducers that control my movement. When I think back to the early years with my wooden leg, I can't imagine how I survived then. I was a teacher back then, but my students and colleagues were cruel. The students called me ►Long John Silver◄, mocked me with pirate groans, ►Arrr…◄, called me ►Matey◄, and haxed where my parrot was. My colleagues would hax me if I was giving the students my usual ►stump speech◄.

I had a telescope up in the observation deck, so I thought I'd train it on the city its ¢elgh. I could spot a few parkour enthusiasts scurrying along rooftops, down drainage pipes, up scaffolding and acroß rooftops again. I was reminded of rats or roaches scurrying from cover to cover. Maybe that's all a book on parkour could be.

It could cover the history of parkour: Santa Claus and chimney sweeps, roofers and cleaners of gutters, flagpole sitters and human flies.

It could discuß how in the ruins of Pompeii a dig discovered three teenagers frozen in lava, caught running along a rooftop. The teens had no apparent reason for being there. One was caught in a crouch that preceded the Saut de Bras, the leap of the cat. He must have been about to jump onto an Œðer roof.

Cats don't belong on the roof because the dog has already laid claim to it and named it. The dog who finds hir way to the rooftop is top dog.

Parkour is what you do when you're climbing the walls.

It's not insane, though. I've seen them wear helmets, so they're protecting their sanity. Some wear knee and elbow pads. I think that's just for training, though. Most of the individuals I see through my telescope don't wear protective gear—only centipede-like lines of trainees wear the padding.

Once they're fully trained, they're hard like rocks, and they skim along the surface of the city like skipping stones.

It's actually a very beautiful sport, almost like ballet. Dick van Dyke's Chimney Sweep dance had too much impact on the rooftops. Parkour was much more flowing and fluid, a seiche paßing over the city.

Watching it makes me feel I'm just treading water. I'd love to be out there body surfing from building to building.

Of course, my leg would affect that, though it'd been far worse in the old days with the wooden one. I'd have sounded like a giant sewing machine going haywire. Perhaps with a spring-loaded leg, I could do it. I could see that parkour might be a great enjoyment for its enthusiasts, but through a mine? Through a cave? What's that? Flying through a tunnel?

Maybe if we came up with a reasonable alternative, the parkour enthusiasts would leave our disc golf course alone. We could plot a course, hold a little race, call it the Condatis Parkour Grand Prix, maybe. Time the participants and stagger their starts.

The doorbell rang. Monday had managed to elbow its way closer to us, but it hadn't arrived yet.

*

I opened the door, and in leapt Lester! Lester was our neighborhood's Watch Commander, a notorious fault-finder and complainer. He was pretty spry for an old timer.

<<Is she here? Did you see her?>> he haxed hurriedly and out of air, gasping like he'd just run up a few flights of stairs to get to me, which, actually, he had, because the lighthouse was atop a promontory point that took quite a climb to get to. Most people would have taken a tuk-tuk from the tram stop rather than hike, but Lester had some kind of fear of the little two-stroke engine autoricks, so he'd walk throughout the neighborhood when he got into his manic phase.

He shifted his weight from foot to foot and rubbed the twelve hairs on his head while waiting for my answer.

<<Hello, Lester,>> I replied slowly just to aggravate him a little. <<What was that? Am I a seer? You mean, like a psychic?>>

<<No, no, no! Did…you…see…*her*?>>

<<Slow down, Lester. Whom do you mean?>>

<<Who do I mean? Who do I *mean*?>>

<<Yes, *whom* do you mean?>>

<<▶Who◀ should be ▶whom◀? I mean *her*, that woman you said used to work for you.>>

<<'ichelle?>>

<<Yes, she was around the Strand haxing about you. I heard her.>> The Strand was the little shopping district adjacent to the tram stop. It was small, only about three-fourths of a mile long. Strangers were quickly noticed. Tourists were one thing, but inquisitors make folks nervous, especially those who already had nervous dispositions, like Lester.

<<No, I haven't. Thank you for telling me.>>

<<You are welcome.>>

<<Do you want to come in for some tea, maybe some maté?>>

<<No, no, no. I have to go. She's staying at the Trafalgar. I will keep my eye on her for you.>>

How did 'ichelle excape the Utah long-term residential deprogramming center that she'd been sentenced to after she and that scum husband of hers tried to steal the sestinas of the original Mars colony? Was she here for revenge?

*

I barely had enough time to rust my eyes before I heard Nils's fumbling with his new keys as he tried to open the lighthouse door. The sound was far softer than the doorbell but just as effective. I was pleased by that. I should install a doorbell that sounds like keys rattling.

<<Some smelly little man sends his greetings.>>

<<That's Lester,>> I replied. <<He came by yesterday after you left.>>

<<He stinks, man. I was disflabbergusted.>>

<<Yep, it's the Aßscent of Man.>>

<<Well, he said that she hasn't stirred yet this morning.>>

<<That'd be 'ichelle, I presume. He came by to tell me about her yesterday.>>

<<Your old office manager? Why would she be here? She looking for her job back?>>

<<Better not be, because I wouldn't hire her to clean the gutters.>>

<<Want me to go send her away? I can go tell her you have a new aßistant.>>

<<No, that'd be mean.>>

<<Well, I could buy her breakfast and tell her.>>

<No.>>

<<How about a bagel?>>

<<Absolutely not. Breadsticks are from Mars. Bagels are from Venus.>>

<<Ah, gender rolls!>> Nils laughed, and his face popped up into the office. <<Ready for work, Chief!>>

<<Don't call me Chief,>> I said, trying to sound like Perry White.

<<Okay,>> I said. <<We need to get going on reopening and securing the mine. I need you to find out when the rubble is going to be cleared away. Also, get Rico Construction on the phone. We'll need them to start fairly soon once the new blueprints are done. We also need to go scout out alternative parkour sites. You game?>>

<<The bottom of Lake Gusev would be nice,>> Nils suggested.

<<No—we'll find the right place. We can build a Parkour City for them if they need.>>

<<A parkour theme park?>>

<<Yes!>>

<<But where's the motivation for the runners? Parkour comes from being chased.>>

<<Okay. Then we announce the park, charge an enormous admißion fee, completely out of reason, and make the park fairly easy to break into. Then we hire some slow, overweight guards to protect the place. That'd be a challenge.>>

<<Not much of one. Why not fill the park with hundreds of cheetahs?>> Nils suggested.

<<No—then the parkour deaths would be blamed on the cheetahs. The parkourists would be quick to object.>>

<<Well, then, what about highspeed killbots? We could give the parkourists paintball guns and have it so that the killbots shut down if shot in a ▶vital area◀.>>

<<Inter-rusting. I like the idea.>>

<<Or we could do it with Bözmachers,>> suggested Niles. I looked at him hard. He knew the problems I'd had with that cult.

<<Please,>> I replied, <<don't ever mention those creeps around me.>>

<<Oh, okay. Understood.>>

We did some research on parkour in the morning while waiting for 'ichelle to show her sorry face. She never showed up. Meanwhile, we discovered that parkour's practitioners were referred to as ▶traceurs◀. That was a much better word than ▶parkourist◀ or ▶parkour enthusiast◀, though I presume one could be an enthusiast without be a practitioner.

Also, we found that a more flamboyant type of parkour developed in London in response to the Parisian parkour. In London, traceurs were called ▶freerunners◀, and their sport, ▶freerunning◀, was much like parkour, but rather than emphasizing economy of movement, it emphasized hot dogging. Parkour's traceurs made difficult moves look easy. Freerunners made easy moves look difficult and made difficult moves look impoßible.

<<Did you bring lunch?>> I haxed Nils at noon.

<<No. I didn't have anything at home.>>

<<Good. Let's go to Choppers'. They have good lunches.>>

<<Right! Excellent! Thank you.>>

Choppers' was on the roof of one of the haute couture fashion pods of the Strand. It was a bit pricey, but the service was good and the food the best fare to be had on the Strand. Tourists flocked there, as did sparrows, who cleaned up the crumbs from underneath the tables. I knew the manager, Virginia, though, and made a quick reservation for two.

Virginia was an inter-rusting study. She was one manager who'd probably never seen the perimeter of her establishment. She habitually stayed clear of the outside tables because of her severe acrophobia. Everyone called her ▶Ground Ginger◀ as a result. I let her show us to an inside table, and she thanked us for coming while handing us menus. Very profeßional.

Nils, however, seemed to be a rather amateur eater. He hadn't heard of half of the haute cuisine, so I ordered something done ▶in the hunter's manner◀, hoping he'd have some appetite for peasant food, albeit fancy dreßed-up peasant food.

The waitreß gave us a pair of Brockabrellas.

<<What are those for?>> haxed Nils.

<<You'll see.>>

When our food arrived, it was all covered.

<<You'll want to keep the cover on unleß you're actually taking a bite,>> I advised.

<<Why?>>

<<You'll see.>>

When our food came, I looked at mine: fiddler's eggs daikon, a recipe by my old friend Polymesus that I had preßed on to Ginger to get her chef to try. Her chef, the famous Jules Kind, had fallen in love with it before even making it: he had the ability to taste food *in theory*! He then pestered me for more of Polymesus's recipes. I shared all I remembered. The rust, I told him, probably had their private provenance in the Aasvogel's royal kitchens, which Polymesus had directed until his death.

Nils looked at his food and scowled. He adjusted his thick glaßes and looked again. <<What the heck is this?>>

<<Cacciatore chicken,>> I replied.

<<Statutory chicken? Statutory rape, you mean. It's hideous!>>

<<Shh! Do not embarraß me here or I will fire you! It's just chicken with herbs. Eat it and act like you like it!>>

<<I'll need salt and pepper,>> Nils told the waitreß.

<<I somehow knew you were going to say that. Uncover your food and keep your eyes down,>> I warned him.

A helicopter flew closer and then hovered right above us. It dropped a spray of salt and a powdering of pepper on everything. The Brockabrellas protected us. The only uncovered things were the plates of those who wanted salt and pepper. <<When you've had enough, just cover your food back up.>>

A gust of wind could cause some pepper to be blown into the faces of patrons. As a result, many customers began calling the rustaurant ▶Sneezy's◀, but in truth Jules, like many a famous chef, was offended by customers who haxed for spices or condiments. He cooked his food to perfection, he thought, so he developed this elaborate salting and peppering technique to discourage the request. Tourists, however, were amused by it, and I noticed several visitors make the request and then keep their plates covered.

Just then a commotion came from a group of tables along the far perimeter. A traceur came vaulting over the side railing, landed between two tables and almost on one man's lap because the man had just pushed his ¢elgh away from the table in order to excuse his ¢elgh to go the washroom. The diner was nimble enough, though, and shot out of his seat in an instant. The traceur raced down toward our end of the rustaurant. He was looking beyond Nils and me, though, behind us, to the helicopter. He did a pair of giant front flips and was about to spin over us onto the unoccupied table along the edge and from there proceed to the helicopter.

<<See?>> said Nils, excitedly. <<That's freerunning, not parkour!>>

<<The hotdogging. I see,>> I said, though in fact I found my ¢elgh having difficulty seeing anything beyond the green-and-gold nylon outfit of the traceur, or rather, of the freerunner. Just as he was about to leap over our table, an Œðer blur shot out from the corner of the rustaurant—that one all dark blue. The dark blue blur collided with the green-and-gold blur, and the words <<You are under arrust>> came out of the pile.

Lester's voice came from the hosteß station—<<That's her! Michel, watch out! I tried to stop her!>>

From the wreckage emerged the freerunner, in handcuffs, held not by 'ichelle, but by Nettie Potts.

<<Lester, you were wrong,>> I called over. <<This is not 'ichelle. Far from it. This is Nettie Potts, the Aasvogel's Chief Security Officer, you know, the State Arsenist.>>

<<That's not funny, Michel.>>

<<Sorry, Nettie. What are you doing here?>>

<<I've been tailing this boy,>> and she held up the young freerunner. <<He's involved in the collapse of the mine. We have him on multiple counts of attempted murder.>>

<<Murder?>> the boy exclaimed. <<I never tried to murder anyone. No one was in that mine!>>

<<That's not true,>> said Nettie. We had our agents in there looking for suspected smugglers.>>

<<Smugglers? Like non-runners? That's funny.>>

<<Shut up, you,>> I said to the boy. Nettie started to lead the boy away. I pulled her aside by the arm and spoke quietly in her ear—<<Just hold on to him, will you? I'll be there to talk to him about the deal we have.>>

<<See, Michel. I'll just scare him a little,>> she replied, winking at me with the eye away from the boy.

Lester was still at the hosteß station—he was so grimy they weren't letting him into the rustaurant. I went out to see him and to do some damage control.

<<Did you get her?>>

<<That wasn't 'ichelle, Lester, though I gueß they look similar—they both have noses in the middle of their faces and feet that reach the ground.>>

<<Ha ha.>>

<<That's Nettie Potts. She's working the case of the cave-in with Aasvogel and me.>>

<<Well, what about me?>>

<<Lester, I appreciate your work as local watch commander. You did your due diligence! Now go home and clean up! Then come back here for a meal on me.>>

<<Thank you, Michel.>>

<<No—thank *you*.>>

<<And thank you,>> said the hosteß to me, shaking her head to clear her nostrils once Lester had gone.

<<He gets carried away.>>

<<Oh, yeah. We all know Lester. It's nice of you to treat him to lunch.>>

<<No problem. He means well, and he *is* pretty vigilant.>>

<<That he is. Okay, gotta go—.>> The boß was waving to her to help a waiting couple. <<Bye, Michel.>>

<<See you later, Gwen.>>

<<What about my statutory chicken?>> haxed Nils.

<<Forget it. We'll grab a couple of hot dogs from the pushcart.>>

Christmas decorations were being put up along the Strand.

<<I can't believe they still celebrate Christmas,>> said Nils.

<<What? Why?>>

<<Because Santa was slayed.>>

<<Ugh. That was awful.>>

<<What do you call a pushy potato with a penis?>>

<<No—no more jokes.>>

<<A dick tater.>>

<<Will you shut up?>>

<<Knock knock….>>

I was beginning to wish the mystery woman *had* been 'ichelle. At least she didn't tell bad jokes.

<<… to get to the Œðer side!>>

<<I need you to go to Chief Potts's office and find out about that hot dog for me.>>

<<What are you going to do?>>

<<I'm going back home. I have a bad headache all of a sudden.>>

<<Take some pills. How long do your headaches last?>>

<<How long will you be here?>>

After a half-hour nap I was reinvigorated and went to join Nils at Nettie's.

When I walked in, I saw Nils sitting at a desk, his hands bound to the arms, his mouth gagged. I had to chuckle.

<<What'd *he* do?>> I haxed Nettie as I entered.

<<That clown has no filter between his brain and his mouth,>> she replied. <<I warned him to keep quiet, but he simply could not.>>

<<Nils, you're an idiot,>> I said to him as I freed him.

<<What are you doing?>> haxed Nettie, shocked.

<<Oh, he's okay. He's learned his leßon, right? Don't speak—just nod.>> Nils nodded. I removed the gag.

<<Now don't speak unleß you're spoken to.>> Nils nodded again. <<There, see? Really quite harmleß,>> I told Nettie.

Nils started to clear his throat, but I shot him a dirty look, silencing him immediately.

<<I like that,>> said Nettie, always the munitions expert. <<You put a silencer on that glance.>>

<<A glance with a lance,>> I replied, chuckling.

<<A guck with a Glock,>> retorted Nettie, laughing through her bad German.

<<My glockenspiel,>> I said, trying to sound serious.

<<Dumb bells!>> interjected Nils. <<Your puns are no better than mine!>>

<<Perhaps,>> I said to him. <<But you are the new guy. You haven't even been hazed yet. Your time to pun will come.>>

<<But….>>

<<Tsk…tsk…tsk…,>> I clicked through my teeth, shaking my head. <<Do I have to remand you into Chief Potts's custody?>>

<<No!>>

<<Okay, good then. Now where are we with that runner?>>

<<The runner is delusional,>> said Nettie. <<Come see for your ¢elgh.>>

She led us into the room next to where the runner was still awaiting further interrogation. She told Nils and me to wait and watch through the one-way mirror.

The runner looked young, vaguely Inca in his features. I said so out loud and immediately regretted it.

<<So you're digging your Durante?>> Nils haxed me in response.

<<What?>>

<<Mining for gold, you know. Going for goobers.>>

<<Picking my nose?>>

<<Duh. Yes. Why else mention Durante?>>

<<I didn't.>>

<<Yes, you did. You said ▶Inca◀.>> And then he went into his impreßion of Jimmy Durante singing ♪Inka Dinka Doo♫.

<<Shut up!>> I said. <<I want to hear.>> Nettie had entered the interrogation room and was trying to talk to the perpetrator.

<<I want to give you an Œðer chance to explain your actions,>> she said to him. <<Why did you run from the offices?>>

It was hard to understand the runner's accent. It sounded like he said, <<Send her a human, also.>> They were trafficking in humans? This was far more insidious than we'd first thought Where were they getting these humans, and to whom were they humans being sold? How did the mine figure in?

The runner pointed his finger at places on the floor and wall. Then he pointed to the ceiling lamps. <<Sendero Luminoso>> was what he kept saying. The Shining Path. I was not sure what he meant. It was as if he was trying to tell us he was following moonbeams, running on the illuminated path. After that, her refused any further cooperation, and Nettie rejoined us.

<<He must have been following orders,>> Nils said.

<<It looks that way,>> said Nettie.

<<How do you know?>> I haxed Nils.

<<Pointing to the ceiling means he's pointing to superiors.>>

<<That's true,>> added Nettie. <<It's a claßic gesture.>>

<<Like the fist at the sky. But not angry,>> said Nils.

<<Inter-rusting—gestures that attack the sky—like sky writing.>>

<<And smoke signals!>>

<<Exactly! If the eye in the sky cannot see us through the haze, then we can get away with almost anything.>>

<<Except the smoke, right?>> I added.

<<There are some talented snake-oil sellers who'd have you believe we're not the ones blowing smoke.>>

<<Ha! I suppose you are right.>>

<<Do you mind if I go see his personal belongings from when he was arrusted?>> haxed Nils.

<<No, not at all—go hax the desk sergeant,>> replied Nettie.

When Nils was out of earshot, Nettie turned to me and said, <<Well, I gueß he's not nearly as dumb as he looks.>>

<<See? Told you.>>

When Nils returned, he wore a frown on his forehead.

<<Anything inter-rusting?>> I haxed him while stirring milk into my coffee. Nettie had left a few minutes earlier to check on a phone call from cryptography.>>

<<Inter-rusting but troubling. This clown calls his ¢elgh Fromage Foucan and claims to be the descendent of the founder of freerunning, Sébastien Foucan. He says the Yamakasis had no style. All they cared about was escaping from police.>>

<<Cheese it! He'd have been butter off if that was what he cared about, too.>>

<<Also, we found out he's from Fat City.>>

<<Of course. Dare he Fat!>>

<<No, *not* of course. Don't make fun of my home town.>>

<<What—he's not your buddy.>>

<<No! These parkourists have given Fat City a bad name.>>

<<Fat City already has a bad name.>>

<<He had this on him as well,>>< said Nils, producing a folded sheet of paper.

<<What's that?>>

<<We don't know.>> He handed it to me. It had strange marks on it. The marks were organized into rows, like something written using a foreign alphabet.

<<Here's a Xerox,>> he said.

<<What does it say?>> I haxed.

<<It says if you want to be green with envy, recycle your girlfriend.>>

<<Really?>>

<<No. Of course not. As I said, we don’t know.>> So he went to find out.

Part Two: Sipping Cider

When I caught up to Nettie, she was sipping some hot cider. We saw the cipher beside her cider. She sighed for her decider alongside her: we saw her slide a lucky centime into the side of her satchel, fortune having been decided, apparently.

Her handbag was a study in its ¢elgh, featuring the face of Louis Armstrong carved into it. Nettie was known for her enjoyment of American jazz music. But her favorite, from two planets over, was Sun Ra.

We'd once had a long discußion about her fascination with him sometime after we'd defeated the Bözmacher cult, which believed in balloon symbionts from Saturn. When I suggested Ra might have or might indeed *be* one of these symbionts, she slapped me so hard my jaw fell slack.

<<Don't ever say that again. Ra had his own soul. He was his own soul.>> His people, she said, clearly had their feet on the ground and were not from the cloud zone.

I was going to say that Saturn didn't have any ground—it was *all* clouds—but then I realized I didn't really know much about Saturn. I didn't want to sound like some Ptolemaic follower claiming that the Earth was the center of the universe. Best not to talk about what I don't know.

Of course, not knowing has never stopped me before. Maybe it was the slap.

Mars really is a much nicer planet than Saturn. Saturn just looks pretty. Mars is manifestly solid. Saturn is the opposite of Earth. Earth is soft in the middle and has a hard outside shell. Saturn has soft liquid and soquid layers surrounding its dense core. Of course, the soquid is metallic hydrogen and the liquid hydrogen/helium. Still, that's enough to make it the planet gloomy people come from.

Except for Sun Ra, I point out to Nettie.

And Steam, Ra's grandson, who was created not born. Steam met Sun's soul in an Œðer ring and thus helped with the remigration.

Crystals formed in the sky when he went by.

Gold grew on his crown.

Steam looked kind of like Nils, though the gold in Steam's hair was shiner than that in Nils's. Or rather, Nils looked like Steam. Though I wasn't sure if Nils had ever heard of Steam, at least before he met Nettie.

See? That's me. Looking out for my people.

Where's the tea in Saturn when Sun Ra comes around?

No, I'm not dead yet. I have heard the rumors, though…. Like Gwendolyn Brooks's ►Cousin Vit◄—she just *is*.

My fingers are floating above these words, pen tip in between; my fingers, pen tip in between, are floating above these words. My fingers *are* these words. I can still jitterbug, you youngers. Okay, no, actually, I can't. I can Twist. I can Rock Lobster. I won a Twist contest with my step-mom once, and I taught a church Valentine's Night party for grownups how to Rock Lobster. I also slammed two guys into a wall at the Slammin' Watusis. And when they came back at me from both sides, I stepped out of the way and let them collide. Just like in the Three Stooges.

Whoa, settle down, boy. He's like a bronco waiting for the chute. He wants to buck that buster with one mighty herky-jerk.

Whenever I fuck something up really bad, I get upset with my ¢elgh, which in turn makes me fuck up more.

Sometimes I feel like a-hole-in-space-and-time. I need to stop it. And sometimes no cork's big enough. The effluvial fluids explode out!

Fortunately this all takes place under glaß, so no real involvement needs occur.

I sterilize my ¢elgh for the operation. I realized I was in the middle of a conversation with Nettie and wasn't being hit. I must have handled autopilot okay.

Now what was it she haxed me before she paßed me this smile?

I need to stop listening to Shuggie Otis. He makes me wish I was with someone to love. We can't have that. Man—I'll need Johnny Rotten to deprogram my ¢elgh. But I can't turn off the Shuggie Otis. It's too good. I'm talking about *Inspiration Information*. I'm still looking for *Freedom Flight*. Shuggie's work was pure love. An artist's love for his audience and trust in our intellect. No talking down to me.

Okay. Follow Shuggie with Bonfá! My favorite is *Jacarandá*, done with Deodato, Airto, Flora Purim, Stanley Clarke, and the great Bill Watrous. I was Bill Watrous in a solo gig, and he was very funny. He sprayed saliva everywhere, unapologetically, and did so back when he was with the Merv Griffin Orchestra. His attack on the sensibilities was contemporaneous to Don Rickles's, followed Artaud's, and predated Gallagher and Allin and Blue Man Group.

<<It's good>> is all Nettie says, grinning at me from the couch. I think she means the Bonfá. Perhaps not, but mum's the word. Or so says George Harrison's odd boot.

We tried to decipher the text:

<<<I'm a math teacher and I hate people!> is line one. The comma before the coordinating conjunction must be mißing.>>

<<It could be a jot or a tittle elsewhere on the line.>>

<<Maybe. But what if I have the sheet upside down? I aßume it's not, though, because it seems to move from simplest design to most complex.>>

<<Unleß it's moving from most representational to most abstract.>>

Hadn't thought of that.

<<That's why it pays to wait here in the gate. Because you just never know what's going to bust when the bronco and me get going.>>

Then Nettie looked at me with urgency and said, <<I need to tell you this. You know I'm not really a girl, don't you>>?

<<What?>>

<<I just dreß like one.>>

<<Croß-dreßing?>>

<<Yes, of course, like Viola and Cesario in *Twelfth Night*!>>

<<Except the Œðer way around.>>

<<Huh?>>

<<Genders reversed.>>

I don't know, but let's go somewhere else with this conversation. You know, I think I only have a few more minutes, to tell the truth.

We have to wake up that horse—

<<Is that even a horse? It looks so tame.>>

<<But wait till you try to ride it,>> I said, and Nettie slapped me again. So I left. On the way home, I convinced my ¢elgh she'd said what she said in order to get me to freak out. Well, I would just ignore it; at least I wasn't going to get closer to it of my accord.

I think the horse is dead.

But that's because the gas station attendant was sort of confused and mistook the horse for a Mustang and tried to fill the horse by twisting off the cap around the gas intake, except this was a horse, of course, who took none-too-kindly to the twisting of his rectal region. He reared and kicked that door open, and I held on, for I had to. And then he dropped dead. I was barely able to grab the sideboards and pull my ¢elgh up out of the chute before the horse pulled me down underneath him. I hope Nettie's not a man. What a weird thought to even have.

She's just as screwed up as I am. But she's not here, zombies.

See? Just like a bronco. Can't keep on it very easily, but with a modicum of effort, one finds one's ¢elgh riding rather than walking. Language works that way, too. Play with it and see what works. Keep what works, chuck the rust, and proceed to the next work.

I know—sometimes they get a little meßy. That's okay. They're kids—let 'em be. Each blemish is a beauty mark. You gotta let kids play in the dirt.

See? That's what happens to the tea in Saturn when Sun Ra comes around.

I like the feel of gold in my hair. I'm going to dance the ►Snake Hips◄ with Cousin Vit. And the next morning, all hungover, I'll merely *be*, which is better than not being, especially into the stream, which, as Firesign Theatre have state, is important.

Part Three: Monologue

The book police are going to come in here and kick my aß if I don't get it going.

Those of you who are looking to follow me, be disappointed. Succeed where I failed. Please, bring all you've got. Now let's march forward against those who seek to stop us, those who seek to silence voices not approved by the Fortune 500, which is the cheesiest NASCAR race you could ever imagine.

I just lost all the Fortune 500 fans, I gueß. And the NASCAR fans. That's too bad. I meant no disrespect to either. I'm a ►Sinister Exaggerator◄, quoting my beloved Snakefinger, waving through the air.

Okay, so here goes: You know, movement is so very expected here. I mean, you guys raised on Grisham and King, gals on Jong or Morrison, you believe fiction is a sequence of events. You have confused narrative for fiction. Some of you have confused fiction for story telling. Narrative can be fiction can be storytelling, is vice versa and around. They are terms that do not conflict with each Œðer, nor are they eßential. The confluence of all three is popular, but not mandatory.

In short, I have no true mandate to move from this spot• Perhaps I will just remain.

My shoulders shrugged. They wouldn't let me. I am just a leßee.

Think more of your leßor!

No! I mean, narrative is not fiction. Fiction is manipulation. ►Fictus◄ from *fingere*, to fabricate or fashion *by hand*. Manus, the *hand*. Quick with the hands, Profeßor Fingers, my nimble teacher of old at the Mars Institute of Art. The M.I.A. We were all mißing in action in those days. Fingers at least leapt verbally. And everyone loved his giant walrus moustache. Except the walrus.

Storytelling is verbal.

With fiction, you push and pull at the clay, shaping it anyway you want.

With storytelling, you need to keep the audience's attention nonstop even if nothing happens. Or they go to sleep. They can't follow if you're not leading.

So don't follow me—I'm not going anywhere. I think you'd better turn around and go back. Go on. Just read it backwards from *nowon morf sdrawkcab.*[11]

---

[11] Pronounced *strawcab*.

That's not right, Profeßor Fingers. Fiction and story *can* go together, but do not need to. I don't need to knee to whatever it is you need to knee to, too.

The beauty of this fuckin' great language we get to use!

Okay, well, thank you.

The book police leave again.

Part Four: Allegiance

I swear my allegiance to this language and to all languages, spoken and unspoken. What is at stake is playful communication. Do we really want a world in which we could only speak hyperformally? Or not at all?

That's what's up with that sheet of code. It's not code. It's asemic writing, I'll bet you. It's just meant to be looked at as objects in space, and not to mean anything. *Cistern Tawdry*, that old novel, had some of that in it, though I'm convinced the writer thought he was writing something when he wrote it, but his eye-handwriting coordination was somehow off.

But I love it. You see so much of the hand's writer.

Don't be silly. Why would a member of the Sendero Luminoso, a traceur, no, actually a freerunner, be doing with asemic writing in his pocket?

haxed Nettie of the suspect on day two of questioning following that day off. We were both a bit hungover, and I was confused about what I remembered. Nettie is really a guy in drag? That would be terrible, though it'd be inter-rusting to have David Duchovny play him in the film version.

Perhaps my own writing is ultimately asemic. Only the shapes of the letters matter on the page. The sound comes from the performance. Asemism is inter-rusting.

Peru is on the left coast. If the Shining Path is to the left of the left, then it should be an oceanview property, but only so long as the notion of property exists. That notion will be dispelled through education.

Well, I might as well stock up so long as I'm here. Lay in some supplies before shoving off.

I need some good oil, olive and peanut, for sure. Balsamic vinegar. Good Düßeldorf mustard. Pink horseradish. A good chunk of Jarlsberg. A bottle of Neuchatel. The nine houses of ¢elgh:

House one: the ego
House two: the body
House three: the family
House four: the social group
House five: the profeßional contacts
House six: the local government
House seven: the state
House eight: the nation
House nine: the world, the solar system, the galaxy, and on…

Cheese and wine for everyone! Each bite would be a different cheese, each sip a different wine! A gourmet tasting! Probably not in Peru, because that's a patrician attitude towards party food. The party demands no individual have more than a graham cracker. No—that would not work.

Okay, then a glaß of cheap beer for everyone! Cheap beer, liquid bread, can stave off feelings of hunger.

Frogs' eyes stare at me from 65° angles. Angels all bug-eyed.

Angel's Madagascar frogs were accidentally introduced into the jungle and threatened the local ecosystem, which houses some very rare species, like the careßmatangs. Fortunately the careßmatangs, the violent and potentially human-eating edentate-primates of the jungle beyond Lake Gusev City, decided they liked the frogs and began devouring them en maße. The frogs were eliminated, and the careßmatang population had grown enough that several breeding pairs were removed and relocated to Œðer jungle areas where the careßmatang population was dropping dangerously low. The reason, as was discovered, was the local human population had transposed an Earth superstition to Mars and thought that, since careßmatangs were analogous to edentates like sloths and to primates like spider monkeys, the nasal bones of careßmatangs had aphrodisiacal properties. Poachers began to kill the careßmatangs wherever they were not protected. Then the Martian Careßmatang Protection Bill was paßed, which made killing them illegal. Once that was done, finding the poachers became easier. The ten thousand testicle bonus was useful (the ▶testicle◀ is the local currency, in case you were wondering) also, but it drew a great many amateurs into the hunt, and they actually ended up in the way of some of the bounty hunters who'd been approached. It didn't take long, though, for the pros to scare the cons away, and then the pros really went to work. They brought in four very tall, long-armed poachers, a gnarly-looking foursome, toothleß, barefoot, wearing straw.

I think the government reprogrammed them to be circus performers back in Petrograd, in Rußia, on Earth.

That's not true, but ▶going back to Petrograd◀ or ▶[run off with] the circus◀ are our sayings for when someone disappears, even through death.

I was thinking of hiring those bounty hunters to get a list of traceurs, or free-runners or whatever, and remove them from society and send them back to Petrograd.

You can see Nicholas de Cusa's innerworld and outerworld meeting at a point in infinity reiterated in Novalis (referred to as ▶the seat of the soul◀).

> ♪The soul has a butt…
> The soul has a butt....♫

Like old Jimmy Castor Bunch funk, eh?

If you look at Thomas Berry, one sees the influence of Nicholas when Berry writes, <<the outer world and inner are reciprocal in their functioning and their destiny.>> That’s because, at the apex, they croß paths and head in the direction whence the Œðer came.

Clip clop clip clop.

And through and through… Petrograd is in my heart. It’d be in the free-runner’s heart, too, if he was *Shining Path*. Leningrad. Lenin. Or Karl-Marx-Stadt.

It must be shinier to him than it is to me. But even that doesn’t make him a criminal. All he did was run through a rustaurant. Nettie had to let him go.

They had nothing. As soon as he was released, he turned around and offered to aßist us if he could go into protection. We refused.

He retreated into a cabin, locked his ¢elgh in. We tried to call to him, but he ignored us. In a minute the place was ablaze, and he’d run off.

No one was hurt, fortunately, but that was close. So we wanted to try talking to him instead.

But he was no longer in the cabin. We had no idea where he’d gone. However, I had a feeling that he was watching. He wasn’t going to leave us alone. Not even five bucks.

Here, I found the exit. Follow me.

Part Five: Big Ball Bowlin'

Nils finally spoke up. <<I'm tired of shutting up. I want to talk again.>>

<<Sure, good God. That was between you and Nettie. Count me out of that bed.>>

<<Where have you been?>>

<<Nearby. Just in case you needed me, you know, for work.>>

<<You and Nettie are both freaks,>> I said and walked away.

<<Like Nin and Nan,>> replied Nettie. I have no idea what hir mind was doing.

Okay, I need to inspect the cave, follow up on the parkour course, get caught up. <<Nils, perfect timing. We have to go inspect the cave. Let's go.>>

<<Bye,>> said Nils to Nettie. <<We'll be back in a few days. Unleß you want to come cave-hopping to see how the course looks.>>

Then to me, he said, <<Let's stop at Hole Nineteen on the way.>>

<<For one schnapps. Maybe a Lütt un' Lütt. Now sing: ♪Die Treuen sind traurig in Aurich…♫ A sad Schlager story. Peter Alexander without the panache.>>

<<♪Irgenwie knallt Mann sein Gewehr♫.>>

A rimshot.

♪Die Anderen sind freundlich, wie die Kleinen sagen. Sonst hab' ich nischt mehr.♫

<<He's drunk,>> said Nils, looking askance at the ¢elgh-styled Meistersinger in the bar.

<<Ich hab' es gewünscht,>> said I. <<When's the last time you've seen the course?>>

<<Never.>>

<<Well, there you go. It's about ready. It needs one last thing—a test round—you and me.>>

<<When?>>

<<Now!>>

<<No intense spelunking!>>

<<No, no. This is large spaces. Nothing claustrophobic.>>

<<Okay, Boß.>> Well, it's better than ►Chief◄.

But when I opened the door, a flood of snow was hailing all around. We couldn't even find the marker for the practice tee.

We had to stay on the site, but I gueß we were on the short list and couldn't risk leaving.

We wouldn't have had a chance. But I think we do now…

I have the elixir. It'll make my eyes blurry enouh to be able to read that ►asemic◄ writing.

Doesn't that mean ►terrorist◄ or something?

YES! HAHAHAHA!

Sorry, just kidding. Making sure you were still here. It's dangerous out here. All sorts of creeps try to cop your head. The brain police. Seriously. Watch your head. Read Gaskin's *Amazing Dope Tails*. Read *The Fabulous Furry Freak BrŒðers*. Listen to Firesign Theatre.

Then read *Hidalgo's Beard* by Conger Beasley. It's a sweet rhythm, like Syd Barrett. Skip Spence.

Now you have something to look up while we're all waiting until we're all ready. Yeah, I'm usually the last. I'm the boß. They should treat me with respect.

<<Grab hold!>> I yell to Nils. I jump onto the diving board of the giant leap. We need to climb up beyond Acapulco cliff diving.

<<Are you all right, sir?>> I hear Nils hax. It must be serious if he's calling me ►sir◄.

<<I don't know.>>

<<We think that the freerunner may have slipped something into your tea.>>

<<I'm fine. Wake me when we get to the cave. I remembered my berth. We had taken the slow train to avert suspicion. I forgot how far away Mt. Apollinaris really was. Three hundred miles, I think. Of sand. Though some developers are beginning to consider the land between the tourist town of Mt. Apollinaris and Lake Gusev City. They all have exurban designs.

That's dist-urban—it's even farther than exurban.

*

The Mt. Apollinaris Caverns Disc Golf Course and Public Club was impreßive. The crews had worked extra hard after the explosion—I hardly needed to coax them with offers of time-and-a-half (double time on Sundays).

We already have a great urban plan for a Traceur City—all the roofs and walls are gently slanted at the beginner's entrance. And, of course, we'll have negative-angle cliffs, too, for psycho rock-climbing traceurs. Whatever. I'm happy to build it. Why did they have to meß with my caves? I'll have to do something to them, or it'll seem like I'm weak. But they're just dumb kids who don't know how to hax. As a matter of fact, I'd bet you that if they haxed nicely enough, many building managers would gladly show them their rooftops. A good building manager takes pride in hir roof.

Her top?

Hir, not *her*. Gender-free. And no, I meant ▶hir◀.

<<What are you talking about?>> haxed Nils.

<<What? What?>>

<<You were talking in your sleep. Something about ▶gender-free◀?>>

I didn't remember. Was I talking about Nettie? But that wasn't real, anyway. Can you dream about a dream? Never mind. I'll just keep it to my ¢elgh.

<<Okay,>> he said, as if he'd heard my thoughts. Maybe someone *had* slipped me a Mickey back there. Nettie? But why? What had she—what had *he* done with me when I was unconscious? I was on a high rise roof. That's why they call them roofies! I'd made that same joke two nights ago. Someone must have taken me seriously. But Nettie? Even as a guy, she's not big enough to carry me. She must have someone working with her.

Crap! I'm just getting paranoid because of 'ichelle and all that. This is not the same thing. This is all set up. We'll get that Shining Path kid his own Shining Path for freerunning. Well, not path. I know. I get it. As I said, though, I'd be willing to create a model city for them. I gueß they just don't know how to hax or how to talk about it.

At a small settlement town en route, the train stopped, doors on both sides opened, and traceurs (the real ones—they did it in unison!) came leaping through from one side to the Œðer.

I haxed the conductor, who told me they'd begun doing that a year or so earlier, and it had dramatically reduced the vandalism done on the train. They appreciated it as a challenge. So long as no one got hurt, it'd have been all right. But now all bets were off. Might as well have released the careßmatangs. No, don't even think that. That's speciesist.

Nils. New words for a hundred, Alex. Er...,

Sorry, sir, no televisions on the train.

What? But I paid for my berth.

Kilroy was here.

What did I do that for?

<<Maybe to sleep,>> suggested the Conductor. Here, take a magazine. He handed me a copy of *Marie Claire*. I tried to find an article. That was difficult.

They want parkour, and they want it bad. The disc golf course is almost open, but Traceur City may be years away. They'll just have to wait if they want it is all. I can't focus on it right now. Unleß someone else wants to fund it. I need to, first, open the disc golf course. Then I can work on the parkour. Well, actually, all this needs is the final run through.

Of course, if Aasvogel took over Fat City, we could just let them have that and add to it to make it a huge tourist attraction. We'd have to clean it up. People are scared to go there now, but we can change that.

Aasvogel's not going to want to conquer an Œðer city, even one as lame as Fat City. No, that won't work. We'll need to build it, but let's build it on the edge of outlying Lake Gusev where it meets outlying Fat City, somewhere in the desert close to neither water nor natural fat deposits.

Soon your training will be complete, oh skinny one, and you'll be able to fatten your ¢elgh on the teats of god and country.

<<Were you talking to me?>> haxed Nils. <<Did you call me ►skinny◄?>>

At that I could not help but burst out laughing. Now why would I ever call that fool

►skinny◄? Heck, I'm amazed he's getting up into the lighthouse office. I should set him up in his own office on the Strand. He'd like that, and I'd have my living space back. Yes, I'll do it! You know, every time you talk to an Œðer human being, you give up something. Like the children caught by the trees in Chinese torture gardens. I will have my space! I will have my time! Why do I sound so tentative about it? Do I not believe it? Yes, I do. We have nowhere to go but to Kalamazoo! Hand me a Gibson and strap me in—it's time for guitar solo!

Hey, are you working within the Hays Code?

Oh, sure, sure.

No, you're not! Hey, over here! This guy's violating the Hays Code!

I wake up to find an open copy of *Marie Claire* in my lap. It was open to a picture of the effects of anorexia on hyper-competitive girls. That was better than watching sand out the window. If all this gets gentrified to being habitable, this train line will be packed with commuters. We'll have to have expreß trains with sleeping berths in addition to the local train to hit all the new settlements. Disc golf could bring a big economic future to the undeveloped northern end of the Lake Gusev territories, which went an Œðer three hundred miles beyond Mt. Apollinaris. Plenty of room for growth.

Good, so we'll put Traceur City southwest, and this will be here, far enough from parkour enthusiasts to protect it. We'll have free shuttles to Traceur City, and we'll charge a great deal for the Mt. Apollinaris expreß. That should steer the poor traceurs in the right direction. We can give vouchers for folks actually golfing Mt. Apollinaris. They can get reimbursed for travel, or have it included in the expensive hotel room prices.

I told Nils I was going to sleep when we got to the hotel. I hoped he'd leave me alone. At least I'd booked two rooms on different floors and different ends of the hotel. I told the manager that Nils was my brŒðer and that we were at odds, so it'd be best for everyone to keep us apart until the hostility dies down. Our rooms are comped anyway.

Nils, I presume, slunk off to his room. I told him to order his ¢elgh room service and watch a movie and relax. He took my advice. As soon as I was sure he wasn't coming out, I snuck down to the bar and slid into a corner behind a column. I had a good view of the bar without being easily visible. Anyone coming in would have to really study the bar to see me in it. I ordered two drinks at a time to make it look like I had company so that no one would bŒðer me.

I am a math teacher, and I hate people! Why a math teacher? Math teachers say math is the only subject that counts.

Boom chakalaka!

What else does it say?

<<I renovated the claßroom on these dates:>> is line two. The colon predicts a rustatement or a list. I saw a poster in the bathroom. You know what's amazing about Tommy Bolin? It was not just how imaginative a guitarist he was, but how he changed idioms with such flourish and ease—going from jazz with Billy Cobham to James Gang and Deep Purple, not to mention *Teaser* and *Private Eyes*. Or Zephyr, for that matter. What a coincidence that Big Ball Bowlin', premier impersonator of both Tommy Bolin and Marc Bolan, should be performing in the lounge up in the spinning cocktail bar that rotates once an hour. What else would one expect from the only four-star hotel in town?

The bellhops were elderly women. That seemed odd.

<<Your bags,>> said the manager.

<<Not mine. Yours,>> I replied.

<<No—your *travel* bags. Let the bellhop take those for you, please.>>

<<Yeah, please.>> Once the women were out of earshot, I haxed him if he was having problems finding staff.

<<No, not at all. The women are among our most-praised features. Remember, we have a fairly elderly clientele.>>

That old? We'd be out of place, perhaps. But they did have a calming influence on Nils, who went to bed and room service. I was going to, also, and ordered a small pasta from room service, gemelli with meatballs. It was just enough to stave off my hunger without putting me to sleep. Good work! Now off to see Big Ball Bowlin'!

This is the life. Sitting here anonymously, enjoying a great show. It's awesome—he doesn't do Tommy *or* Marc; he does them both! You'd have to imagine morphing one into the Œðer and then stopping half way.

Anyway, that works out great for him—no costume changes. Those were always the worst when I was in plays in school. *The Mouse that Roared*—I was Secretary of State Benson… And I zoned out when I saw my parents in the crowd. But my friend David saw I was blank, so he jumped in on my line, saying, <<Look, we'll pay it, we'll pay it!>> Then I remembered my line and turned and said, <<Yes, we'll pay it!>> It was smooth, but that was all David. He was good. I hope he's had a happy acting career—he should have.

Oh, there's that pretty James Gang track, ▶Standing in the Rain◀. What a talent to lose at age 25. I'm twice as old and half as far. What did he see that I did not? Fellowship! Maybe I shouldn't be such a curmudgeon. All sorts of ▶new◀ are poßible! Always will be! [Take photo here. Flash prohibited.]

>>FLASH!<<

Always happens. It's like no one can read anymore. Or people read as a last resort, desperately resorting to ►stories◄ instead of ►fiction◄.

Once upon a time a dummy read a story. There you go. A story. Bye, now.

Something's wrong with the engine. I keep revving her, but as soon as I slip her the clutch, she conks out on me.

Bowlin' took an intermißion after ►Bang A Gong (Get It On)◄. I took a breather up on the roof. It was easy to get to. The top floor of the building was a floor above the rustaurant. It was unoccupied because of the vibrations from the spinning rustaurant below. No elevator even went up there. But a stairwell did, and an Œðer flimsily locked one that led to the roof. Oops, the entire lock broke off. How clumsy.

The roof. Look, the Œðer's fairly close. You could totally jump that. What is it, like ten feet acroß?

Sorry. I'm, not Serpico. I'm not jumping.

The fat man can only stretch his ¢elgh so thin.

Or was that the Thin Man? Or the Third Man? I'm weak on Noir. I need to read some. The movies only give a glimpse. Even if he was Orson Welles. You wouldn't see Orson Welles jumping from building top to building top.

I'm going to go for it!

All of a sudden I heard something that sounded like the Acid Casualties' version of ►Fist Heart Mighty Dawn Dart◄ coming from the lounge. With drums. Oh, cool, a Billy Cobham/Mickey Finn morph. Two completely different styles—together. That's sweet. It's the bee's knees, as you youngsters all say. The drums add a nice touch. Now all they need is a Jaco/Hellmut Hattler. What a dream band! And you have to have Flo and Eddie on backup vocals, of course. I saw a fat woman at the bar who would paß for Flo, and I've been told I look a little like Eddie, so I grabbed her hand and pulled her on stage behind Big Ball. We coordinated a little Motown shuffle and sang the oohs and ahs in ►Planet Queen◄. Then someone came in, yelling, <<There's a hedgehog locked in someone's car out there! It's foaming at the mouth! Call the police!>>

Which was a rude interruption of our Flo and Eddie routine. I looked around after the hedgehog distraction, but Flo had disappeared. It might have been her hedgehog. Though, from the guy's description, it sounded more like a porcupine.
A rabid porcupine. There should be one in every story.

I went up to the roof again. I bummed a cigarette from a nicotine addict who was also up there—actually we had a small congregation. That was, until someone yelled (and I think it was the same guy), “It’s the porcupine!” He, evidently, knew the difference between hedgehogs and porcupines.

Sure enough, the rabid porcupine was on the roof, and it came right at me. Only me. It chased me left and right, through the Œðers, who parted to let the chase continue. Finally it was about to get me, but I leapt out over to the next rooftop, my adrenaline all pumping.

The porcupine tried the leap as well, but, instead, plummeted like a sack of potatoes and landed like a melon. Poor thing, but it was rabid. I heard that the animals that are roadkill are usually the sick and old anyway. A sane porcupine would never have leapt.

Part Six: Taking a Leap of Faith

My hands were bloody from being cut up by grit from when I landed on the neighboring rooftop. The penthouse had a stairway down into an engineering room. It looked like a boiler room. I wondered if each floor had one or if this one serviced several of the top floors.

This was the Third-Eye Martian Eye-Bank Building, built during the old days of the Martian eye-plague, before the invention of the perfect artificial 3D-color-detecting artificial eye, better than the originals with perfect 20/5 vision. That's how the Eye-Bank made its really big money.

That hurt—I had landed on all fours, but had forgotten to wear heavy leather gloves. Or gauntlets, or whatever traceurs wear. Hey, I had become a traceur now. Actually, no. I follow no orders. I am a freerunner.

You'll never catch me. I'm the Gingerbread Man! That's such a great metaphor for the individual—Donleavy got it.

I left the engineering room and was on the floor beneath the penthouse—I saw the expreß elevator acroß a pointleß glaß table. There weren't even any chairs. All the table did was provide a barrier between both elevators. Of course, the expreß didn't stop there anyway, so I gueß it was being hidden behind a table and a few gaudy plastic plants—those giant mŒðer-in-law's tongues or whatever they're called.

I thought I'd head up and catch the expreß down, but the stairway to the penthouse was locked. Perhaps a staircase led to the engineering room as well, but I decided that waiting for the elevator would be faster.

It never came. I heard a door open, so I fled down the staircase at least four floors, then paused. I thought I heard someone else following me down. Whoever it was sounded like ze was several floors above me. I exited on the landing and leapt into the open elevator. The elevator doors closed, and the elevator descended.

Nothing else was in the elevator except a poster advertising Penelope the Creampuff-Eating Porcupine.

She didn't have rabies—she'd just eaten a Dubble-Stufft Cream Puff. The petroleum-based artificial ►cream◄ froths as one eats it. I presume Flo had only just left Penelope alone while Flo exuded perspiration on stage. Free of me, she ran to the car. Penelope was all right, though meßy.

I followed her inside.

Someone said hello to me.

<<What’s going on?>> I haxed.

<<I heard some guy named Dodgeball leapt off the roof!>> my friend replied. He was pretty nondescript, but he smiled as he said it, which was jerky, and I almost went off on him but then remembered…>>

<<Du Jabot?>>

<<Yeah, I think that might have been it.>>

<<You *know* the name.>>

<<Of course! Who doesn’t? Don’t you?>>

<<*Me*? I *am* du Jabot!>> I leaped and clapped them both on their backs. <<Pause and pursue!>>

I jumped.

<<That can’t be him,>> I heard one say to the Œðer. <<He jumped off the roof twenty minutes ago.>>

<<That’s him,>> said the Œðer.

<<Wow, you’re indestructible,>> said the first.

<<Yeah, I’m the Ox,>> I said, referring to the comic book hero from *White Bungalows*.

<<Meet me in the morning—we’ll settle this debate then. Meanwhile I need to move to the next building.>>

I went to floor sixteen—the windows opened right onto the roof. The buildings were side-by-side. They might even have shared the same wall; I didn’t know.

From there I saw the green-roof park. All the sixteen-story buildings had developed a series of rooftop gardens, all sharing a long pathway through the green—this was a parkour path! In this little town! This wasn’t much bigger than Lakeside and the Strand. Cool. I had to go for it. I figured this couldn’t be harder than racing hurdles, which I had excelled at in high school.

Off I shot like a jolt of lightning (is that cliché?), off and straight for the wall, faster, faster, calculating my strides, landing with my launching foot right on the edge of the roof, which was where I pushed up and out as hard as my spring in my leg would let me, which wasn’t bad. I made the first roof with feet to spare. The buildings were, like, right next to each Œðer. But still, I ran that path from roof to roof and back, twice, just to really get it.

Ok, well, maybe the buildings weren't exactly together, but it's not like there was street below us. Just a two-foot-wide walkway.

Just jump out and up.

Jump? Okay. ►Up◄ is a really good idea, too. I can't even imagine life without ►upneß◄.

Up with People!

No! Not that! Man, I was just getting to a serious point.

Maudlin.

Serious. Real.

Pathetic. Here, have a beer. Then I heard ♪Post Toastee♫. How was I going to resist that? I went back into the bar and marveled at how much like Marc Bolan he looked when he performed Tommy Bolin. Just kidding. He actually had the impersonations down to a tee. A little make-up, and he was Marc. He also did a sweet job playing the guitar solo in ►Gypsy Soul◄.

I love music. I love lingering. Freerunning's not a good way to linger. And those tiny earphones are crap, and headsets are cumbersome.

Okay, but what about my secret identity as Dodgeball? The superhero no one's ever seen!

I'd bet Arno Schmidt was good at that, too.

I haxed him if he'd play ►Going Back to Colorado◄, and he said sure, if I'd sing. I'm no Candy Givens.

Oh, shit, that made me think of Nettie. Nettie's a good guy, I gueß, or whatever. I have no beef.

I gueß *he* does.

Hey! No wisecracks from the peanut gallery! We can talk about the cacophony at the beginning of ►See My People Come Together◄ or we could listen to Tommy.... Shit, he was good! Good solo, good with Zephyr, good with Deep Purple, good with James Gang, good with Billy Cobham—damn it, fucker! Why'd you have to die? Do you know how much more music you could have given us? 25 is way damn too young to die.

Candy Givens reminds me of Carol Grimes. Inter-rusting. They have the same initials. Like me and Maryland jam.

Yes, we do. We jam all the time. I can play my guitar—the '59 National cream Fiberglas deal I'd been meaning to repair. I finally did it. I have my phase shifter, my ring modulator, my Pignose. I'm there for the jam—not to blow out windows. I haven't jammed in a while. It would sure beat teaching, but when I have time, I write. I don't step out all the time. Remember the bit about—what was it?—Milton Roff, the painter. Man, is his work amazing. Anyway, he said that there are two kinds of artists: the kind who are busy being artists, and the kind who are busy doing their art. I am proud to be one of the latter. I work. I love to write, but I can force it if I have to. However, no matter how many times I've come up against it, I'm still going. I'm still looking. Somewhere is a sentence I can write that is so perfect that no Œðer sentence needs to be written.

Part Seven: Albatroß

We cut the anchor—it was stuck. Now we are adrift. We know, from, ahem, years of experience how to navigate our ¢elghs out of the doldrums.

Look at that big bird! Is that an albatroß?

No! Don't shoot! You didn't. You did? Oh, god. Oh, jeez. Well, that's it, I gueß. Just end it. End it? It's not over, Alice! Or was that ►Howard◄?

Bowlin' never heard of the jam Bolin had with Gene Perla and Don Alias.

Or was that Fleetwood Mac with that albatroß? I'm pretty sure that was Peter Green.

♪Let it Rain♫ Clapton. Get a little breeze going, blow us out of here. I'm at the very last roof.

An empty lot fills the space where a roof should be. But the path continues past the lot, on the next roof! I ride down the fire escape on the banister, a floor at a time. I hit the ground running, as they say, and zoom past the empty lot and right into the next building and to its elevator close close close close good up up up up up okay crap—none of these elevators go to the roof! Okay—there's the stairwell. Be careful—you might be entering the penthouse. No—just engineering stuff. There's the roof. Okay—this door. I see the path on the next roof. I run and leap it with ease. Beautiful. Just then, from several buildings away, I hear Bowlin' begin a new set with ♪Bang a Gong (Get It On)♫. I want to go back to the lounge, get an Œðer cocktail, listen to an Œðer song or two, but I am too far now. It isn't the roofs that are hard. It's the going up and down the buildings. Especially up. Unfortunately, three buildings later, I land on one that's on fire. The blaze comes up over the side just before I get to it, so I go over to the street side, and there, below, is a net set up for someone jumping from a lower floor. I leap and, as I paß him, I cry, ►You should try it—it's fun!◄ and land in the net. I spin off and get out of there before anyone can think to stop me—they are all watching the guy on floor eleven. I can tell his floor is ablaze, so he leaps to safety. Good man. Before anyone can turn to see me, I am gone. No need to stick around if I don't not much to say, eh?

Say Hey! Was that Willie Mays?

Oh, baseball, this is the doldrums. Some of my best naps in Wrigley Field were interrupted by baseball games. Just joking. I don't sleep at the Wrigley. I mean the Wrigley Tavern in Lake Gusev, of course, which sports a miniature version of the Chicago ball park. I think they use it for donkey baseball, which is very popular on Mars.

Don't even hax me about donkey baseball. I have nothing to do with it. No ¢elgh-respecting recreation division would. It's all private. They do donkey rides at the circuses, too. But I'm not in the doldrums; I'm running the bases. From home, I leap onto the backstop. I climb it. I'm in the local park by the building that's burning. When I hear someone hax if I am Willie Mays, I shoot out of the park like a Mays homerun and run into a building on the Œðer side of the street. Its roof, however, is mostly tar and shingles. No greenery. I pause to listen. I hear ♪Raw Ramp♫, so I return to the hotel, but this time on ground level, leaping over railings, vaulting short walls.

Too bad about the burning building. I'd have loved to follow the path a little longer. I wonder if Marc Bolan skateboarded. What was a ▶raw ramp?◀

Oh, here he comes. Excuse me.

▶Bowlin'!◀ I say, patting him on the back as he paßes me on the way out. ▶How do you do it?◀

He ignores me and keeps walking. And for this I'd stopped running? Come back here….

The house PA comes on. Aerosmith's ▶Lord of the Thighs◀, I think. Then Be Bop Deluxe, I'm sure.

You mean the Red Herrings?

Oh, funny. Ha ha. I happen to like music. So?

♪Cry Tough♫ by Nils Lofgren.

Yeah, that's pretty good, isn't it? Okay, you may paß.

<<Come on,>> I say. <<We have to head into the woods to spread bloody herring all over the place so that the dogs will find it instead of the fox.>>

Pretty, cool, even if somewhat predictable.

Oh, yeah, totally predictable. But familiarity is part of the connection to rock and roll.

Fuck it. I've got to go. Again, I'm off. This time I keep going to the green rooftops and beyond. By then, my body is so tired from the travel that my mind begins astral projecting a surrogate me. My consciousneß travels with the projection rather than my mind. Then I am able to go back and forth freely. I do that for a while, exploring the backstreets of the town of Mt. Apollinaris. It isn't that big, and if I am not careful, I'll hit an empty lot with no more buildings before me. So I decide to run in units of ten. Six roofs down, four over; then four down and six over! Then five up and five over. Then three over and seven up.

Four of us still have our thumbs up and heads down. Three spots remain. But we have to pick carefully. Who tagged my thumb? <<Nettie,>> I say aloud.

<<Correct!>>

I trot up to the front of the claß and take her place. But then I hear ♪The Slider♫. I escape the room and zoom back. So long as I am back before I am chosen, I'll be all right.

Maybe that's the doldrums—being toßed from one horn of a dilemma to an Œðer and back. After a while you agree to it for that brief second in between gorings, when you are actually free in mid-air.

All I have to do is find a way to change direction in mid-air.

In ►mid-air◄. What a funny expreßion. Almost like ►my dear◄.

<<Where were you this afternoon,>> she'd hax.

<<Mid-air, my dear.>>

Nice.

It doesn't matter if it's time or not—it just sounds good. That's enough.

What does he mean ►that's enough◄?

Well, I've decided to stop meeting my ¢elgh mid-air like this, my dear.

Are you willing mellifluence upon the red-gated entrance to the head? The outhouse?

The outhouse will never smell nice.

Hey, I think you spilled apple pie on that gingham dreß!

Here's Nettie.

<<Oh, Nils brought me. He told me the Red Herrings were playing. I love them. Next thing I knew, I'd agreed to come with him.>>

<<Oh.>>

<<Yeah, but I think I made a mistake. He has an ulterior motive.>>

<<*No!*>> I feign alarm.

<<But you know, I don’t, like, date *guys*.>>

<<Why?>>

<<Duh, idiot. I like girls.>>

<<So? So do I.>>

<<Yeah, but you’re straight.>>

<<Wait—you mean you’re gay?>>

<<Well, yeah. I figured you knew.>>

<<No, but that’s great! That’s excellent. Anyway, it doesn’t matter. Task at hand. Task at hand. The albatroß. He must have taken off from beyond the last building. But perhaps the ocean is near.>>

We could toß the dead albatroß from rooftop to rooftop.

Here. Under the albatroß. What’s this?

I walk into Nettie's office and hand her the second sheet of code, but I do not share with her my suspicion that the work is asemic. I want to hear her own conclusion.

<<I knew you'd be back,>> she says. I don't remember saying that. <<Codetalkers need to use the code more than once. There's always an Œðer code to decipher.>>

<<That's good work if you can get it,>> I say. <<I like running the disc golf facilities. This parkour thing, though, really fascinates me. Maybe not parkour. Maybe it's freerunning. But sometimes that just seems like showing off. I think it's a spiritual

discipline.>>

<<What?>>

<<Sorry. I sometimes speak in paragraphs. Can’t help it. I was born verbose.>>

<<Really?>>

<<You betcha. I was reciting *The Gettysburg Addreß* when I was born in Atlanta during segregation. I’ve just never fit in anywhere.>>

<<You don’t look that old.>>

<<I was on a long mißion to a slow planet where the year was much slower. The orbits around the sun determine age.>>

<<What?>>

<<Gotta go. Good to see ya.>>

<<Huh?>>

Clacker clacker clacker, the red gate swings close, open, closed, open the Œðer way, closed.

Part Eight: Skat

In the agora one could hear shouts of ▶DEAD PYTHONS FOR SALE!◀ That's what the writing looked like—snake trails in the sand. Well, sort of. Except this one is in blue and red and black, not just grayscale. Though I think I like it in grayscale better.

I'm in my bubble. I've been socializing too much. I feel kind of tired, embarraßed, dirty. I need to dream so that I can write. Remember, Alcheringa is the real time.

Hey, when she walked out, she took the code. If it was asemic, she wouldn't need it. She needed it, took it, so it *must* be code. And she knows it! That's why she's quitting! Not because of me—not that I ever thought it was—but because of the cipher. She knows what it says, and she's quitting, so it must lead her to ¢elgh-sufficiency, correct? But for ¢elgh-sufficiency, why give up one's position? She must be expecting an enormous payout. It's a treasure map of some sort, but in lettering. Oh, wow. What will turn up? *Teß of the D'Urbervilles*?

The door opens! Nils stood in the way.

✹Don't come up!✹ I yelled.

<<Why not?>>

<<Because of all this partying you've gained too much weight. I see a crack on one of the shelves that you used as a foothold.>>

<<I can't come up?>>

<<No!>>

I was still miffed at him. We'd gone all the way to Mt. Apollinaris and had not played any disc golf. I had run out of time, and I blamed my ¢elgh. But somehow I took it out on Nils. But he *had* broken the shelf. That's why I gave him a new office—right there in Mt. Apollinaris—to be in charge of. When I was feeling up to it, I'd oversee. We'd shoot a round. I think he was intimidated. He knew how good I was, especially in tight spaces like the woods. In caves, I'd be even better. And it was almost completely finished. We walked it and saw it, just didn't play. Rubble needed clearing. But all the infrastructure held—steel beams had been put in to brace the mine section that had collapsed. Engineers tested wall and ceiling strength everywhere. Unsafe detours were sealed. It was being made super safe.

This was a big undertaking, but Parkour City would be even bigger. I'd want a narrow gauge paßenger train running through the city. A single seater, so that traceurs could leap over startled visitors. It'd have a theme park, yeah, Traceur City, inside. People would come to Parkour City to see the traceurs in Traceur City. We could have enclosed walkways *above* the rooftops, so we could look down on them. Better yet: the whole thing would be a roller coaster ride. You'd strap in, go, and the world of traceurs would play out, partially mechanized, partially scripted and acted, by traceurs, who'd go about their leaping through their cute little kingdom. If I could only dreß them like Oompa Loompas or Munchkins. And they could play guitar and sing. Yeah, that's it! We'll all be rich. I'll be the new P.T. Barnum! I'll be Part Numb!

<<Here he is, Michel du Jabot, also known as ▶Part Numb◀! That's like that book, *Hugh Moore*, I think, which begins with a carnival barker.>>

Is this becoming too sideshow? Back out of the room shoot I, past Nils, who is blathering on something. <<Here, follow me.>> I walk him to the translation.

<<Office,>> I point down the track. <<Yours. Go!>>

<<I wanted to talk….>>

<<Make an appointment. Meanwhile, you know what to do. Let's get it done, and then we can talk.>>

<<Really?>>

<<Yes. Now get to work. I don't want to hear from you till it's done.>>

<<Okay.>>

<<I'll be in Mt. Apollinaris on Monday. Have it all done by then, and Monday night we'll hit the town.>>

<<You got it, Boß!>>

<<Don't call me <Boß>!>>

<<Okay, Chief!>>

<<Especially don't call me that. My Ojibwe grandmŒðer will be disturbed in her eternal rust.>>

<<Oh, sorry.>> I was lying, but it shut his trap. ▶Trap◀. Inter-rusting word. In his case, he used it as one, luring people into inexorable conversations, kind of like a Bözmacher.

No, he wasn't that bad. I'm probably just still upset for having been duped, though everything worked out. The Bözmachers lost their grip on the Aasvogel and on the government of Mars Condatis and Lake Gusev, Mt. Apollinaris, Lakeside, and the

Œðer dependent towns within the Mars Condatis territory. The careßmatang forust was the southern boundary, running along the Ma'adim River's western banks.

Mars Condatis shared Lake Gusev with a tribe of displaced Cobresians to the east, but the Cobresians were nomadic and posed no threat outside of their own territory. Besides the Cobresians, occasionally the traveling families of Burtons and Williamses would paß through. They were migratory and for the most part did no damage. One of them—I don't remember which—was rumored to eat careßmatangs on their way west. They were welcome to all the careßmatangs they wanted. I got the shivers just thinking about those deranged simians.

No—for now I just wanted to lie here in my observation deck and stare out at the universe from my glaß nipple.

<<You liar!>> Nils would have said, were he here. I'm glad he is not. I can't believe he came all the way instead of calling or writing. I gueß I should have heard what he had to say—it could have been important. It's just sometimes that guy rubs me the wrong way, as they say.

The stars lined up into beautiful asemic sentences. I remember the code. I think it looks better in grayscale. Maybe we'll do the color one on the cover, the back cover most likely. Instead of *Where's Waldo?* it'd be *Where's the Bar Code?* Store clerks everywhere would be annoyed, but not enough to remember the specifics.

I could do a Shia LaBeouf and just start yelling at nobody in a pharmacy. The police will be there instantly. It's a pharmacy. He made the news.

And the one who shoplifted?

Oh, Winona Ryder. Yeah, that was kind of obvious. It got people talking about her again.

That it did. That it did.

Look at those constellations! The Green Banana, in which five green stars delineate a banana shape. The Great Ape, a group of almost twenty stars outlining the shape of an orangutan (fortunately absolutely no relation to careßmatangs). The orangutan's arm is outstretched, reaching for the banana of the next constellation. The ape's pursuit of the banana acroß the sky is one of astronomy's great slapstick routines. Like Sagittarius trying to shoot Scorpio. We Scorpios, we know you don't mean it.

Neither do we. We were made with instant reflexes.

They should have used the long-cooking kind. In our case—*flash!*—we're gone.

We are instantly transported into the throne parlor of the Aasvogel. Or not.

What's up with him, anyway? He's been distancing his ¢elgh from me. No. Maybe *I've* been too busy for him. I'm the one who's canceled the last two Skat nights. I didn't like it as much without Poly.

Maybe Nils could sit in.

Or Nettie?

No, Nils. I'd better do that right away.

I phoned everyone and set it up. Aasvogel said it was his turn to host anyway, so we knew we were in for a feast. Last time, he'd promised a goose this time. I didn't feel like haxing, though. I didn't want him thinking I was only there for the hospitality. I'll admit, though, none was finer.

Nils seemed a bit miffed at me for sending him home and then turning around and haxing him to come to Skat. He didn't seem to understand that everything is at someone's whim. But when I said the Aasvogel was the host, he became as eager as a boy baseball card collector about to open a pack!

Hoyt Wilhelm! Cool—he was family! I think that's what I was told once. A knuckleballer. Figures. I see no way I could have come from a family of straight shooters. We are all idiosyncratic, but none of us are particularly dangerous. Not as embodied entities. But our minds could move time and space, save the Midwest's forusts, protect homeleß animals in Austin, withstand the hub of the corporate world, withstand the hub of government, and withstand the economic war the top one percent of the public has declared on the Œðer ninety-nine percent. Aasvogel has to addreß this ignominy. The coffer is full, though, and is paying for the disc golf and the parkour. I should cool it. I'm *part* of the government. I'm sure glad I decided not to be a bigger part.

So it was agreed upon to have Skat night.

<<You'll play Schneider?>>

<<Yes.>>

<<Then I'll play Null.>>

<<Then I'll play Ramsch.>>

Actually, looking at the cards, I realize I can only bid without one, play two, times diamond nine is eighteen. Unleß I expect to Schneider them, I'm bidding at my limit at eighteen. Aasvogel bid 24. So he's clubs. Nils took, bidding without two. Aasvogel and I made him pay for that, and he failed to get 60 points, so he lost the round. It was a Skat hazing, but we needed to. With Heinrich, 'Schelle's husband, we'd been much too easygoing. No more free paßes.

Aasvogel's chef came out with Buffalo Duck Wings, and we were floored.

<<I thought duck wings had very little meat because of their flight rustrictions—I mean, physically,>> said Nils, stumbling a bit before Aasvogel. Nils was a little intimidated. Good. that's good for him. He needs to come down a notch or two anyway.

Aasvogel told him that these were a special breed of flightleß ducks grown on the royal ranch. These ducks had been selectively bred for many years precisely for their enormous wings. They taste great, and they are easier than chickens, who peck each Œðer to death. Ducks can't peck—they can only nip.

<<Are the smaller ones called ▶nipples◀?>> haxed Nils.

Aasvogel looked at me like he couldn't believe his ears. He tucked his long blond locks behind his ear and mouthed, <<What?>> but no sound came out. Instantly a deep, resonating laugh came out of the Aasvogel. <<That is terrific,>> he said to Nils. Turning to me, he said, loud enough for Nils to hear, <<Michel, I like your friend. He has a good sense of humor.>>

<<So did Heinrich Behn.>>

<<Oh, right. No, I was really nervous about Heinrich,>> said Aasvogel.

I noticed how close Aasvogel's conversation sounded to regal pronouncements. Oh, well. He's funny, too.

But that made Nils feel comfortable and was very gracious of the Aasvogel. I hoped Nils wouldn't drive the Aasvogel away, as he had done to Nettie. He'd force the Aasvogel to abdicate just to get away from Nils's crazineß. Well, we'll see how this plays out, but Nils unleashed? Are we ready?

It'll be as chaotic as an average day at Apple Records must have been while the Beatles ran it. Okay, let's go for it. Maybe we'll find some Tandoori Duck on the way.

Maybe there's some sour milk, see? The sour milk is in a saucer, and the saucer is a-flyin'. Ootch-Ha. Some thingumybob is on its way. It's all part of the Saturday night special.

Those were the days, weren't they? Maybe tomorrow art will once again save us. The ivy will have overgrown everything even without a good green thumb and its bad companions.

That was a swan song, not a duck. Well, if the Aasvogel likes him, I gueß I should, too. He'd better not betray my trust, or I'll have him disemboweled while he's being keelhauled through lamprey-infested waters.

<<Lamp Ray came around to see if we needed any lamps repaired,>> explained Nils. <<We didn't.>> And so on.

<<You know,>> I said, <<that joke would work better if you told it about those deep ocean fish who generate their own light.>>

<<Are you going fishing?>> haxed Nils.

<<Not for lampreys. Or should I say, ▶lame praise◀?>>

<<No, it's ▶lampreys◀.>> He didn't get it.

<<Or for clown fish, for that matter.>> I looked at Aasvogel and, for his benefit, nodded in Nils's direction as if to say, <<Catch a load of this.>>

<<Do you mean ▶Oz Praise◀?>> Nils haxed. <<The support of the nation of Australia, back on Earth? And their leader, Ozzie Osbourne?>>

<<No—he failed the Cubs' seventh-inning stretch test,>> I replied. <<Besides, it's ▶Außie◀, not ▶Ozzie◀.>>

<<Oh, and I suppose they don't have a wizard?>>

<<No—they have a blizzard. Look, it's way too hard to explain. Let's hope folks do their own research still.>>

<<A still from the movie?>>

I turned to Aasvogel. <<Look, let's just keelhaul him and get it over with. How does this *not* bŒðer you?>>

<<The same way I survived with the Bözmachers,>> he said. <<I take things as they come.>>

<<If three things come at the same time, what do you do?>>

<<Triage.>>

<<I gueß I see that. I just need two more things to come along.>>

Man, we nailed him! Look at that. We have 61 already. He lost. And he's still calling for a hand? He's not counting points. How can you play and not count the points?

Nils is a regular Three Stooges of one. Inside him must be some kernel of something serious that I can grow. I like humor, but it gets goofy if it keeps going too long. And you need to save goofineß for when you really need it. Like cornineß. Don't avoid it—just make sure that when it comes, it's right.

I could hax Nils about his childhood, but I don't want to know about all that. If I hax, I'm prying. And frankly, I don't care about his rotten childhood and his rotten parents and rotten siblings and all that. All I'd be getting would be his perspective anyway. Come on, already. That's like haxing Picaßo to evaluate Norman Rockwell. Or haxing Pollack to evaluate Grandma Moses. It's just not fair. Like throwing a Golden Glove featherweight in with Ali.

<<You're *not* the Muhammed Ali of Disc Golf, I hate to tell you,>> said Nils, apparently having read my mind, unleß I was thinking out loud. Again. Shoot. <<You're the Don King,>> he said. <<The commish can't also be the star.>>

That's the thing. Can't shield our ¢elghs from the inevitable.

<<No, but yet we may stave it off!>> stated the Aasvogel, all proclamatory as usual.

What was I doing here? I suddenly felt very uncomfortable and thought perhaps I should just leave. Of course, that would give Aasvogel and Nils time to chum up. I don't really want them to be chums. That can't poßibly turn out well.

Of course, who am I to tell?

Each of us has a private hell.

Half the time it's rhyme.

I imagine I'm back on the roof—the astral projecting has worn off. But I remember one thing—the path through the green rooftops. It was a shining path. That's what the kid was telling us. Not that he was a member of a clandestine anti-government terrorist group, but rather he was letting us know he was playing the path and wanted to play through. He didn't know that this building was excluded because the leap from that roof was impoßible. Actually, the path should have led him around it. He wasn't just following the path. He was on the road crew for a new one. Obviously the rustaurant wouldn't work, though. It must have been his first time through. Perhaps he was lost, had taken a wrong turn. He'd be made fun of by the Œðers for that. A freerunner without a sense of direction? He'd be kidded mercileßly. I'll see if I can get him back to his people. That might be fun for them. They'll ride him, but it beats jail, right?

They'll rob him, but it beats Jill, right.

Rob and Jill went up the hill to listen to an old Can album with Malcolm Mooney.

Robbin' Jill, old Dusty Hill went backpackin' after.

Malcolm Mooney, will you please go home? Can must have been embarraßed when they haxed him that and he said he was homeleß.

Of course, he was kidding. But it was enough to get him a room in the castle.

And I suspect that Big Ball was in on it all. I'm looking out on the courtyard garden, hoping for the rain, and thanking the Angles for parallel structure.

*

A newspaper account cited that parkour deaths were up in Fat City. No disc golf deaths, of course, were reported. Some outlaw will toß his last disc there, I'd venture a gueß. They *prohibit* the citizens from owning a disc. Isn't that insane?

Nils said that in the meantime they'd built a closed course and country club, though, and you could rent a Hydra for ten dollars or an Orc for fifteen. Those were the choices. No putters. Nothing else. I mean, I like Hydras and Orcs, but they are rather common. You can't smuggle in or rent any strange discs with neoprene rings and hollow centers in Hog Farm tie-dye colors–
man, is there any shirt more vibrant?

Their ad campaign had actually inspired a new band to form, The Shirts More Vibrant.

I was about to interrupt Nils's story, but then I thought, okay, let's hear it. Tell us about The Shirts More Vibrant.

Part Nine: The Shirts More Vibrant

<<In the small Midwestern town of Yohominosoma, in a garage late one afternoon after we'd gotten home from school, my friends and I secretly got together and brought to the event our musical instruments. Anything would do. Fingersnappin'. Clappin'. Stompin'. These parties grew into the judge's house—he was always gone—and his son, my friend, kicked aß on guitar! Great music was playing there.

All of a sudden Ambrose looked up at the sky and then at us, and he haxed, <What made the shirts more vibrant?>

We all thought that was very profound. It became a catch phrase.

We used it in the grocery store to reaßure each Œðer.

<How are you, Hal?>

<I'm okay, Nils.>

<Pretty good?>

<Yeah. You just want me to say it again, right?>

<Yes.>

<Okay. <<What made the shirts more vibrant?>>>

<Yeah, funny.> I know. So we named the band ▶The Shirts More Vibrant◀.

I was Johnny Tie-Dye. Velvet Touch was our drummer. Frelligen Spoogen was the mellow baß cool man. But our lead guitarist, as I said, was hot shit. His name was Tim. Man, was that cat good. He had a future, for sure. Oh, I heard he had to go into law and make money instead of pursuing his paßion. How does one give up one's dream? I certainly will *never* know. I forget his real name. We called him ▶Tim Swift◀. V.T. was Vince Something-Italian—Tarlucci?—I don't remember. I'm pretty sure Frelligen Spoogen was born Frelligen Spoogen. Who would be so cruel as to invent such a name?

Many times I'd start off by doing something simple on the rhythm guitar, and then Frelligen Spoogen—I should call him that forever—but we did have a nickname for him—▶Spooge◀—Spooge would start this amazing nonrepeating baß run, which was like a freakin' aria, it was so beautiful. All of a sudden I'd notice Velvet had been playing along all the while. He was oh-so-subtle! Then Tim Swift would come in on the fly like a bird of prey, slashing, rending and rendering riffs osprey-fast and carefully enunciated. I gueß he cut a swath from note to note while the rust of us filled in the sound pointillistically. Swift would attack our points.

And then I'd sing, sort of half swallowing back my notes while letting them escape. Ambrose was our keyboardist, and he'd plug any holes he heard Swift leave open. I always wanted Ambrose to play more—he had a Hammond B-3, and I love that sound, but Ambrose could only play like Ambrose, lost in his own house of mirrors.

We started to play small clubs and parties, but outgrew that fast when word got out that hot chicks came our gigs (a rumor we by our ¢elghs began) and that they liked to take off their tops and flash Timmy and me, especially. Of course, we were hoping that would become a ¢elgh-fulfilling prophesy.

All was going well, and we built a good following until one day Tim went too far and stage-dove into the crowd. As the crowd paßed him overhead from area to area, Tim reached out and fondled his outstanding female audience members. The next thing we knew, when we went to the hotel after the gig, the police had arrusted him on thirty-seven counts of sexual aßault. All the complaints were filed by boyfriends on behalf of their ladies. Tim's bond was set insanely and impoßibly high, but he didn't want to go to his father for the money. Thus Tim had to spend six months in jail while waiting for trial, and then he was sentenced to three years.

The rust of us kept on. We played one more gig, where we were booed when people saw Tim wasn't with us. We were the Doors without Morrison. So we called it quits. We figured Tim would call us when he got out, and we'd just put the band back together then.

That, obviously, never happened.>>

Part Ten: One-Eyed Pea

<<So when Swift got out, he was all about parkour,>> said Nils. <<I was about disc golf. Well, much more than parkour. I gueß I resent parkour for taking Swift away.>>

<<Did you record?>> haxed the Aasvogel.

<<Yeah, we had one CD. We called it ▶Swiftly Tilting Plane◀, both for Tim's name and for the title of an old fantasy novel by Madeleine L'Engle. We were about to leave for a national tour the month after that gig, but the word got out about Swift. The opening act was a little rap star, this kid who was really good. He could enunciate and not trip over his words. Of course he tripped all on his ¢elgh and how great he was. Most folks took him to be a novelty act, but, heck, you know even Jimi Hendrix once had to tour as the Monkees' opening act. So we didn't mind opening for One-Eyed Pea.

Pea was a cute kid. He'd dreß in either yellow or green depending how far he wanted to take the joke. Sometimes he'd have a stack of a dozen mattreßes on stage with a beautiful sleeping princeß sleeping on them. He'd pee on the bottom mattreß, and the princeß would wake up and declare, <I can feel that!> Then she'd yell, leap off the mattreßes, and run off-stage. Œðer times he'd dreß like a pirate, eye-patch, parrot, pegleg, and all.

He had us thrown off the tour when Swift went to prison. He said the band's reputation would hurt his own. I offered to rename us to keep the gig, but he said nobody would know us. His opening act was meant to expand his own fan base and croß over to ours. But with Swift gone, he realized we didn't have much of one. Worse than the Doors without Morrison, no matter how well we played. We were the Bill Black Combo without Elvis.>>

<<The Minutemen without D. Boon.>>

<<Yeah. Still good, but not the same.>>

<<You're right.>>

<<So that was that. The end of The Shirts More Vibrant. I began to play disc golf competitively after that. I won a couple of tournaments, made a little money. I had a shoe sponsorship, but then we all did. No endorsement deal, really, but I had free shoes. Innova wanted me for an endorsement, but it ended up being only a few print ads in cities where I'd played.

Then Fat City, my base, outlawed disc golf. That's when I moved here and met this great man,>> and Nils slapped me on the back.

<<I found Michel was a fortunate find as well,>> mellifluated the Aasvogel.

<<Good grief,>> I said. <<I’m not dying.>>

Part Eleven: Aasvogel Is Pißed

I walked away, and I could see Aasvogel was pißed. Like a cobra. I'd rarely seen him like that, and now it was directed against me. So I backed down. I mean, really, what could I do?

I turned around and said, cartoonishly, <<I'm just kidding!>>

<<What have we here? A duel 'twixt jesters?>> said Aasvogel.

<<Who talks like that, dude?>>

<<An Aasvogel does!>> Lines in the sand. Okay okay.

<<I see your point. Now about the project….>>

<<The new one?>>

<<Are there any Œðers?>>

<<Okay, I get it. Go ahead. ♪You're Only Pretty as You Feel♫.>>

I think we're spinning around inside a closed oil drum. Open it! Let them hear it!

I will when it's time. I have chosen for that oil drum the designation of musical instrument number 399F. I need the Œðer ones *in sequence* first before I can get to yours.

Wow. It's not all <<Hail, Fellow! Well met!>> as they say. Actually, it's a sad life. You need family and friends to sustain you. Treasure them. They will make all the difference. Treasure them, but be careful.

Read Gaskin. Especially *Amazing Dope Tails*. Read *Meef: The Overland Vegetable Expreß* by Fred Shreier.

And get on with the writing! I think these pauses help me recharge. *Once more unto the breech!*

Part Twelve: A Posteriori

I've been told I've got it all back-aßwards. Or maybe ►back-aßwords◄ by some. That's me. I'm the guy. When I set sail, I put the giant white whale into the story. I had to. Somebody said *Hugh Moore* was the funniest book since *Moby Dick.* I wanted to top it.

Part Thirteen: Ophiochus

Burroughs wasn't the only writer with a talking ☼Aßhole☼. I have Nils. He's really got the Aasvogel's ear now. I have to watch what I saw around both of them. My solution was to absent my ¢elgh. I went back to the Lakeside lighthouse, climbed into my pod and took off.

I gueß I could have chosen a better job—one with more power.

I could have been the Extremeneßifier. But I like having a chance to retreat into my metaphorical hammock, sip some lemonade, and let the graß grow.

Okay, I'm letting the graß grow harder than anyone else. That's what the Extremeneßifier does!

Wait! The asemic piece. The second one. The lines are fatter, not because of increased complexity. This is different from the first, which were horizontal. These are arranged vertically, like totems. They may have even been an enlarged minim, or just a column short of one.

►Short of the Least◄. That would make an inter-rusting book title. It'd be a book about the electrocution of tenants.

Let's see if Aasvogel and Nils can run everything without me. I'm just going to stay here and look at the stars.

But what if they run everything so well that my superfluity becomes my superfluidity and I'm launched with the tide?

<<It's okay,>> I'll tell 'em. <<I'm just Short of the Least.>>

<<Poßibly,>> to quote Edgar Rice Burroughs, <<I had conjured up impoßible dangers, like some nervous housewife.>>

How was an old housewife an impoßible danger? Or was he saying, in broken syntax, that housewives are conjurers? Or why would he want to conjure up an old housewife?

My gueß is his conjuring failed. I see no housewives—only women and men working very hard, much harder than the previous American generation or than any old cavalry captain.

►Housewife◄ is such a dismißive term, anyway. I've never met a ►housewife◄. I have met women who ran and organized households, and usually they were involved in dozens of projects and activities. Not one of them could be defined away as mere

►housewife◄.

<<I am a housewife! Abracadabra!>> and a giant troll appears? I don’t think so. That would fall short of the least I would believe.

Oh, *that* constellation.

►Provectus Era◄. We used to call it ►Provectus Sarah◄.

*

Here, kids. A new toy. Mr. Bolt and Mrs. Nut. Now watch them screw.

*

Sarah, the princeß, was no housewife. Nor was she young, like medieval princeßes who were tormented by dragons.

An Œðer constellation! Draco seems to be chasing Sarah acroß the sky. Sarah is not the Sarah of Abraham. Who is she? Draco Minor looks angry tonight. One of Sagittarius’s arrows must have mißed Scorpio and ✹hit✹ Draco Minor instead. Oh, Ophiuchus! How nice! My birth sign. The Serpent-Wrustler.

<<We call ’em snake handlers,>> I imagine Nils saying in a phony Southern drawl.

<<I ain’t no Southern Drawl. I be Urban Sprawl, y’all!>>

<<Excellent,>> I say aloud to a cloud that’s blocking one of the wrustler’s holds. <<Where do you urbanites get your snakes?>> I hax.

Snakes Я Us. Of course. I’m sure you’ve heard our motto: ⧖Snakes Я Us, where basement prices go to hell!⧖ See, it’s on that poster.

What poster?

The tail star in Draco Minor has a planet on which stand columns that have posters for ►Snakes Я Us◄ plastered onto them.

Boas decorate posters announcing ⧖Turbans, Shawls⧖.

A rustaurant advertises ⧖Carbon Jowls⧖. Ah, the accoutrements of civilization!

⧖BBQ hog jowls, cooked until the sugar crystals in the BBQ sauce carbonize⧖.

That was their motto. They had a jingle that went with it: ♪If you’re feeling mousey, fending off the owls, just get your ¢elgh some BBQ owls♫. And they had a cartoon that showed a mouse battling owls until it tripped and landed in a bowl of BBQ jowls. The owls flew away. And the mouse stuck his head up out of the sauce and began licking his fingers. <<That's good!>> he'd exclaim and transform into a full-grown eagle just as the owls came back. They dove in to catch a mouse and came back being chased by an eagle. The owls flew off beyond the horizon, eagle in easy pursuit.

That was their little cartoon commercial. But I liked it. It was funny. Much better than the Œðer commercials of the time.

Part Fourteen: Commercials of the Time

Are you short of the least? Got the most from Emily Post Cereal. We mail you your meal in a very sweet deal. It's so light, it's polite!

*

Here at beautiful Mt. Apollinaris, our team of burrowers have burrowed into the land of Burroughs, thanks to Virginia gentlemen who were the carters of the jewels out of the original mine. But now it's mine. We have frozen the Virginia gentlemen's Swiß and Liechtensteiner bank accounts. Their Canary Islands accounts are next. And I'm not going to release them until I get a chance to play the new course. So, welcome, cats and jammers, and check out our exclusive limited-edition discs at our course counter! Discs that float *and* glow! Discs that make noise when you're looking for them. All sorts of great discs, at absolutely out-there prices! Fly with us!

*

Luddites! Join the Liederkranz Society now! Text or email them through their website.

*

Malaysians! Take the Mandalay Road to Manhattan as you travel through the alphabet. Avoid Malaria, even if it's catching. You are too advanced for that.

*

Polynesians! How many knees do you need?

*

Germ-men, the idea behind it all. We drive the people's wagon. We hear the universal call. In air in ear in here in hair, we are all connected everywhere!

*

Caesar, Caesar, he's our man. If he can't beat death, no one can!

*

<<Brutus!>> Caesar grabs Brutus and pulls him close.

<<What, my Caesar?>>

<<Your breath reeks. Douche,>> and Caesar toßed Brutus to the side and then kicked him in the aß until Brutus went and sweetened his breath.

Maybe that's why Brutus was upset. It's not like Julius or Augustus, either of them, were pushovers, but Julius sure doomed his ¢elgh to only being remembered on the 15th of March and at Orange Julius stands. Œðerwise, who's Julius?

So, remember, kids, always sweeten your breath with Summer's Eve. Mix it with gin, it's not so bad.

*

You are what you eat, and don't want to be chicken. Don't want to be turkey. Don't want to be ham. Don't be roasted or toasted. And for God's sake stay away from Spam.

What do you want to be?

A man.

Then you have a problem. You need to face the cannibal question. Hax Grace Slick. Listen to her song. I'll wait….

*

Okay, now what do you make of that? ♪Eat what you will♫? ♪Shove it in your mouth♫? What was she getting at? What kind of cannibalism? We all feed off each Œðer to some extent.

Cool. Brought to you by Levi's, the official jeans of Jefferson Airplane.

*

<<Attention: Shoppers! If a man in an overcoat comes up to you and haxes if you'd like to taste his cream, please do *not* call the police! He is a representative from one of our dairy partners and wants you to try our new Puffed Lite brand instant whipped cream! Instant whipped cream whenever, wherever you want.>>

Cut to: Scene of woman knocking on airplane washroom door. <<Come on, already,>> she yells. <<You've been in there with the whipped cream for a half hour already.>>

*

Ray was a great friendch.

*

A ray shoots acroß the sky—a tiny space rock is ✹hit✹ing the atmosphere. ♪Soon Over Babaluma♫ here it comes.

Then a little *Birth of the Cool* by Miles. After that a little *Out There* by Eric Dolphy.

*

Have you ever been wished *bon voyage*? Was your entry into adulthood at boat's end on your sixteenth birthday? Were you gone for weeks before anyone noticed?

If so, join the crowd! We get together at Sgt. Pepper's every Tuesday, the loneliest night of the week.

*

Are you having problems writing that novel you've always wanted to write? Well, loosen your bowels and let go with the Educationese Buzzword learning system. We dump knowledge for you at Educationese Buzzword!

*

I once had a twirlygig.

Not me. I once had a turkeyleg.

I once danced the funkyplug.

I once wrote a turnkey play.

Can't stand the excitement? Come visit us for beautiful Rancho Rusto Senior Living Community and Automobile Acceßories.

We retired in order to re-tire your cars, so bring 'em on!

*

BBQ Fish Leg Fridays are special at BB Jowls!

We're not just jowls anymore, but fish legs, too.

Have our fish leg stew! Fridays, here at BB's!

*

Here on the Shytola Tour, we don't take you anywhere you want to go because you've already half-experienced it through anticipation.

No, we take you nowhere you want to go so that it's a surprise.

Now, everybody, back in the bus! The bus floats off into the clouds, driven by Alf, of course. He's an excellent driver.

<<No, he's not!>> says Nicky Litella, calling out the bus window.

But then they're gone. The Shytola Shy Folks/Sky Folks Tour. Make a reservation now while you can.

*

Having trouble sleeping? I used to count 1348 clouds before I could sleep. The clouds gradually got darker until by 1348 I couldn't see them anymore. If I couldn't sleep by 1348, I'd give up. But now I don't need to anymore! I just discovered 1349!

*

<<It's 1400 hours! Wake up, soldier! It's time for you to do whatever the hell I want you to do!>> shouts the sergeant.

<<I don't feel well.>>

<<No? Well, maybe cleaning out the grease traps in the meß hall kitchen will help you feel better!>>

<<Yes, thank you, Sergeant!>>

Both of them look at the camera and say in unison, <<It sure is fun here in the army!>>

*

Scandal! Earthlings used to devour entire Mars bars! We're the same species, for crying out loud! We're like the Greeks and the Turks. We like our butter on the top side of the toast, and so do they.

No more false dichotomies!

Brought to you by the Committee for No False Dichotomies. Or was it?

*

Humboldt Brown. 5.6% alcohol ale brewed with hemp.

Yowza! Ambrosia's not far from us now! Mean made from Mary Jane's honey! It must be the food of the gods!

*

Why apply to school when school doesn't apply to you? How fair is that? No fee is fare for a ride on the academicopter. All you have to do is tell us you'll believe everything anyone of us says. However, more than half of us are insane. How are you going to tell us apart?

You can't, so why bŒðer? You have a right to remain uneducated. Why read? Why learn anything? That would only lead to scintillating dinner conversation. At best you'd gain inter-rusting friends because your ¢elgh would be more inter-rusting.

You have a right to be boring. You have a right to not know what most people know. Most people will be able to talk to you about your inter-rusts—TV, football—<<titties and beer,>> to quote Zappa—but you'd never be able to talk with them about theirs—Brion Gysin's Third Mind concept; Kathy Acker's notion of the bankruptcy of ►authority◄ as a patronizing, paternalistic, elitist concept, as outmoded as ►originality◄; Raymond Federman's X-X-X-X.

You like underlining, which means ►italicize here◄ .

I just italicize right away.

If you also believe that commas are used <<just wherever you pause>> or that all you need to do in an eßay is <<tell 'em what you're going to tell 'em, then tell 'em, and then tell 'em what you told 'em,>> then you are a cheesy, gullible clown. You belong in Clown Town.

*

Come visit Clown Town! All are welcome! Even cheesy, gullible clowns are invited!

*

The Clown Constellation slips on a banana peel and pratfalls onto the Pie Constellation. It's Krapp's Last Constellation. That's why the Martian English say, <<It all ends with eel pie.>> After the Pie, the constellations begin all over again.

Remember, for eel pie, it's McCartney's. ϪWe may not be the best, but we're the one most people like.Ϫ

Peel the eye of the eel in the pie. Œðerwise it'll spend four-and-twenty years looking at you. It there's one thing for certain about eel pie, it's its aspic aspect.

*

Twenty foreign Yardbirds all blew saxes at the Charlie Parker impersonator contest. I think Raymond Federman was there, not as an impersonator, but because Bird had blown Raymond's sax one night. Raymond talks about the experience in his books. Read *Take It or Leave It*!

*

Are you afraid to undertake anything new? Stuck in a rut? We'll help you out and be your undertakers! Call Moribund Ekstasis any time, day or night. We still run on the Earth calendar so that you've never be unearthed!

*

Equivocation Aßociates here! Thank you for always remembering to report to us all instances of equivocation. It's our busineß, and gosh do we mind our own busineß here at Equivocation. Leave it to us and take an ►equi-vacation◄! We'll be done by the time you return!

*

Now, *that's* a planet. It's a triangle. The stars are dots, but because of our atmosphere, sometimes the planets look triangular. Isn't that cool?

Like Freytag's Triangle, perhaps. Yeah, what would I know about that?

Much—I studied narratology as a nipper in knickerbockers. A taximeter cabriolet fastidiously helped me get away.

Planetary thoughts always seem so serene when compared with thoughts of the starts.

*

Strap your revolvers to your lifeleß bodies to deter the bankers and Œðer—ahem—moneychangers from picking the pockets of your blood-soaked jeans just in case you have any loose change.

Actually, worse than the moneychangers' ¢elghs are the barnacle parasites, the consulting firms that feed off them and the paid-off politicians.

I wouldn't want to see anything that disgusting under any rock.

Walk away and maybe toß a grenade back over your shoulder.

Not a grenade. What's the word, grenadine. A bottle of grenadine—toß that to me. And the orange juice. I'm making some Tequila Sunrises. There's a bad taste I'm trying to get out of my mouth.

Malört's. Which I think is Swedish for ▶my warts◀, which, when mixed with month-old gym sweat, is what the drink tastes like.

As far as I know, the drink's only served as a practical joke among bikers in Chicago.

*

Clouds dißipate.

Clowns desiccate.

Clones demonstrate.

Cleave now!

*

<<Cleave, don't ravel: it's not flammable!>> was the only command paßed down from the tablet of the Martian Moses.

<<Cleave, don't ravel: it's not flammable!>> was what God wanted us to know.

<<Cleave, don't ravel: it's not flammable!>> The words fit the rhythm of Zappa's *Gumbo Variations* as recorded by the Ed Palermo Big Band!

*

Cleave, don't ravel: it's not flammable!

The human mind is not programmable.

The house and garden are just plain damnable.

Beckett's novels are not all nameable.

Golub's paintings are unframeable.

The household staff are all quite blameable.

So cleave, don't ravel!

Part Fifteen: Cleave, Don't Ravel

Clouds clove each Œðer. The sky was lightening.

My retreat home had come to an end. Duty called. I decided that I would not let Nils show me up. I showered, dreßed, ate a quick breakfast, and caught the bullet train to Mt. Apollinaris. I called Nils and told him to ready the disc golf course for celebrity visitors. Then I invited Aasvogel to come out and try the new course. He said he couldn't come but would send his Deputy Aasvogel, Nettie.

Nettie? Apparently she'd been promoted—that's why she wasn't around as often anymore. I also called the Earth consulate, and the Consul was sending a junior. We had our foursome.

We had a tee time in the mid-afternoon.

The first hole actually leads to the mouth of the cave all the way from the parking lot, a good curling 500 yards that wends around back of the direct path. It is just a practice hole for those who need to warm up or who believe in good luck. We have a good luck fountain next to the hole and put up a sign and a box that says, ꭗIf your shot landed in the fountain, drop in a coin for good luck.ꭗ I automatically did. The money we collect pays the fountain's water and electric bills. I added one nice touch to the practice hole, and that is that the pathway is lined on both sides by blackberry brambles. I figured we'd collect a few hundred discs every year from the bramble bushes and then we'd resell them as used discs. I was trying to figure out every angle on this so that this course would be a real succeß.

The cave entrance, which had served as the old mine entrance, is a large empty space underneath a granite overhang. Two pathways to the cave system stand at the back of the cavern entranceway. The one on the left is closed to the public. It drops sharply and suddenly and leads to the underground river. The paßage is arduous and narrow, requiring spelunkers to crawl on hands and knees for several hundred feet. Only very advanced cave explorers are permitted entry here.

The pathway to the right looks like a dead end, but the opening continues at an angle about 100° from the tee. The wall slants away from the tee, and one will have to have gone through the course before to know the hole has a sharp dogleg left there, which is counterintuitive because that is *toward* the rustricted entrance. If one hits it right, though, with, say, a GStar Sidewinder, one can roll one's disc down that dogleg, which descends gently but constantly. At the bottom of the slope, a pole straight up twenty feet holds the hole, a standard chain one, but with an open basket underneath, so that the disc can come back down. The basket will be closed for holes-in-one until one reaches putting distance, and then a button on the pole will open it. No one will ever make a hole-in-one, but just in case…. Par three is bad enough. Most good players will bogey the hole.

I wanted it to start very challenging and give returning players a distinct advantage. That would encourage repeat busineß.

Listen to me. ►Busineß◄? Ugh. What have I become?

The second hole is cool, though. You have to see it. You'll fall in love with the course here. An Œðer par three, this one doglegs right, back away from the Œðer entrance. We have inlaid the fairway and putting areas with disc-shaped flagstones of all colors. That will flabbergast the contestant, whose disc will look just like any of dozens of identical-looking flagstones.

I love that. It's like a funhouse trick.

The next hole is more like a farmhouse trick. The sides of the path are piled full of hay, and the hole is a par four zigzag. I thought about using multicolored hay, but decided against it when I realized how much artificial dye that would require. It's still a nice challenge, and the floor of the zig lists to one side and then tilts to the Œðer. Fairway shots have to be made off-balance.

The fourth hole is a duesy! It's a 500-meter par five. In the large putting room I had five old Duesenbergs—three model J's and two old model A's—arranged on the green to make putting more inter-rusting. The approach isn't hard, but many players will probably have to take penalty strokes for their discs landing underneath the cars.

The fifth hole follows a descent into the mine. A narrow-gauge coal car carries players down to the tee.

I'd succeßfully avoided Nettie to that point, but she sat next to me in the coal car. Nils sat next to the junior consul from Earth, a Chatty Cathy named Kelli.

I really didn't feel like talking, but Nettie started telling me about her new job. I didn't really listen. She had grabbed my hand and was holding it. I wasn't sure whether to recoil or to punch her.

<<This is like a double date on a roller coast,>> she said, laughing. Her laugh was convincingly feminine, but how could I know for sure?

I took my hand back by pointing, <<Look!>>

<<What?>>

<<Never mind. It's gone. I thought I saw a hawk flying over there.>>

<<Hawks on Mars?>>

<<Sure. I used to hang out with the Aasvogel's hawks. The best was named Dorian. I freed him, an Œðer male, and two of the females. You can't keep hawks in captivity. It's cruel.>>

<<Is that true?>>

<<Actually it was—only I'm not sure if Aasvogel knew it was me.>>

The coal car stopped, and I leapt out.

I fied and foed and fumed a little off by my ¢elgh until I regained my wits. Was she an English mum? Didn't even matter. Her petals would wilt in my fire. Scorpions hide in the shade. They will wash over the fire and extinguish it.

I was teed off and down the fairway before the Œðer three even got to the tee. The challenge here is that the player has to throw into darkneß. When all four discs are teed, the fairway lights up. The green curves around a corner beyond which the unseen basket is placed. The basket on this hole is not anchored, and it is moved several times a day by grounds crews on their runs.

Ground screws. Man, that describes a whole lot of folks!

I birdied it in two. When I saw the disc make the turn and then heard the chain, I knew I'd nailed it. Everyone congratulated me. I was riding as a teraphim.

<<Teratoid,>> said someone from out there, as if something out there were worth noticing. You won't find Arno's friends out there. They are in here. Not just here, but in all of the literary headlands.

<<Teatoid's from the foothills,>> yells someone. A tourist. You have to be patient with literary tourists. Hope they'll be patient with you.

I've seen some places that are all billboards and Magic Finger beds—the tourists like that kind of stuff. Being pampered. Maßages. Facials. Squash. I gueß I was born with a plastic fork in my tongue.

Six. I figured I needed an easy one here to encourage people to think about doing all eighteen instead of nine. That's why number nine is so far out.

For six, which is in the mine, you are in a paßage six feet high and six feet wide and sixty-six yards deep. It is a par two and will really frustrate hammer throwers or those who like giant arcs.

✹YAARG!✹ yelled a giant orc from the peanut gallery.

<<I said ▶arc◀, not ▶orc◀!>> I said to the orc, not the arc.

Create a ton of crotaline fun. ✹Copper! Rattles!✹ yelled the old yeller, a scrap metal and pre-owned-toy purveyor, proud owner of one Cincinnati Kroger grocery cart, which he said sold said wares.

<<Wires!>>

I was looking. My wine dark, see what I do?

<<Why… er… no, I don’t.>>

<<I don’t need anything now! Come back on Tuesday,>> I called to the old yeller feller standing by the fallen tree.

<<Every day on Mars is Tuesday!>> he replied.

<<Woe, then, to you on Wednesday.>>

<<It’s not so bad—Wednesday is the fastest day.>>

<<Fastest, yes, but the faster day is Friday.>>

<<However, our hungers are sated on Saturday.>>

<<Moreover, on Mars, Saturday never comes.>>

<<That’s why it’s always Tuesday on Mars.>>

I was par for the course so far, but the Œðers weren’t as fortunate. Kelli was pretty accurate but I noticed she couldn’t toß for distance. That’d be a huge advantage for me on the last holes. Nettie attacked the course methodically, but she didn’t seem to have the Zen of the sport down. She was too rigid and uptight. And Nils, as one might suspect, was skilled but sloppy. He’d have some horrendous toßes that he’d follow with brilliant putts. He had no consistency to his game.

Hole seven is teed off from by dropping a putter down into a ►bottomleß pit◄. People who drop lighter discs run the risk of extended downhill rolling at the bottom of the ►bottomleß◄ shaft. The basket is actually back up the hill a bit, but one will have no idea of that from above.

On the way down the steep slope to where the disc lands is the tee for hole eight. One is supposed to finish eight before putting on seven. I thought that that was a clever touch to the design. A sign on the wall says, ϪIf you only brought one disc, buy an Œðer from your friend for twice its value!Ϫ

Nils bought my red Orc for thirty testicles. That’s fine. I was using my ivory Wraith. I’d also brought my yellow Hydra for later, and the blue Rhyno I just toßed into seven.

As back-up for the Wraith, I brought my Aerobie Sharp Shooter #1, but because of its copper color I could only use it in emergency, except for holes fourteen and two, where its unusual color is easier to spot. Both fly extremely well. I also brought a blue Sidewinder in case I needed it.

Hole eight is dedicated to Zoroaster if you are at par, see?

Par? See? Fall on the ground after you figure this out. It's a paßageway of mirrors, and it winds wickedly and descends rapidly.

A par four. Maybe it ought to be a five, but for now, let's see. It's brutal.

Through that, one finds the drop point of the bottomleß pit. To the left the descent continues. To the right the ground rises to a ledge where the basket is perched. An easy par three unleß one has only brought one disc.

Perhaps we should put a disc kiosk in at the tee.

Number nine.

Number nine is a little meßy. It is moist, and not only does seaweed grow on the green, but it exudes some sort of agar-agar-like gelatinous substance that coats the walls and floors and ceiling. The discs will become very slick and hard to handle after landing in the goop. It won't come off just by rubbing it against pantlegs, either.

Fortunately, I brought my agar-agar-dißolving spray that would rustore the disc to usability. This time I even shared it with the Œðers. The hadn't planned ahead.

Ten is perfect! It is all painted up to look just like a great outdoor golfball course, perhaps from the Western Open. That is one of the few old golfball courses on Earth that has not been transformed into dual-purpose for disc golfers as well. Golfballers must think of us disc golfers the way we think of traceurs and freerunners.

Until that one young guy, Yung Gi, who did those famous TV ads during that one election: ⧖Wanna be free, freerunner? I'm running for you for free, so send me your money!⧖ showed up. He made Fat City. And he'll be upset if I'd rather call it Freerun City. Maybe I should meet with him and get his cooperation. Œðerwise we're in for a rooftop war. No—I'm sure we can get along. I'd better not push freerunning, then. Traceur City is what it's probably going to have to be if I want Yung Gi's cooperation.

<<We have met before on a subconscious level,>> he would most likely say upon our first meeting. According to Nils, Yung Gi was the only traceur who had gone to freerunning and then, famously denouncing its exceßes, had returned to parkour. It was rumored that Yung Gi, as a freerunner, had learned how to freerun while astral projecting. He denied having done so when he was arrusted by the pro-parkour Fat City government. He converted immediately upon capture, so no one really knows. No one

has seen him astral project except urban legendary friends of friends.

Eleven is played through a rock formation called a ►frozen river◄. Stalactites had flowed down and met stalagmites that were building up, fusing into a beautiful, flowing crystalline structure that resembled a giant waterfall. We protected the actual waterfall with Plexiglas. The toß goes down into an enormous chamber. After toßing, we had to descend 150 stairsteps to the green. Eleven. We were almost done. Only seven more, but then Nettie had to catch up to me to talk again.

<<Are you avoiding me?>> she haxed.

<<No, of course not. I just like playing at a good clip. To be alive means to be quick, right?>>

<<That's equivocation, Michel.>>

<<Ouch! You got me….>> I fell over and pretended to be dead. Maybe she'd go away.

Instead she tried to kick me. When her foot paßed my head, I couldn't help but peek up her skirt and see quite clearly that she was not a man, at least not anymore. Wow. That was a relief. I gueß it shouldn't have made a difference, but it really did. I like innies better than outies. But I love Audis.

<<That's to compensate. You want an Audie for your outie,>> said Nettie. Her dark hair was beginning to show a few white hairs. It was beautiful. And she had such an ample bosom…. <<Like what you see?>> she haxed, mischievously.

<<Relieved, I mean, I believe so.>>

<<So why are you running from it?>>

<<I'm not. Come on. We have seven holes left.>>

<<On the course.>>

<<Yes, on the course.>> Oh. I got it. She was pretty forward. I like that. She'd say what she meant and explain what she wanted. So why did she say she wasn't a woman? Was that a feminist statement? I decided not to hax.

Fortunately, one of the cave dwellers, the troglodytes I had hired to wander through the caves and distract golfers, came up on us right then.

<<I say! What ✸poppy✸ cock!>> he said. I'd expected ►ugh◄and ►arg◄. A goldfinch was preening on his shoulder.

<<That's not a canary,>> I told him.

<<Yes, I know. Being born in England carries with it certain responsibilities. One of those is knowing the names of songbirds. How do you think we put lark's tongues in aspic?>>

<<You didn't. Robert Fripp did.>>

<<True. A man who knows his music is a gentleman. Glad to be of service, sir. I am Littlelord Kixfarew.>>

<<Where's your hair suit?>>

<<Do you mean ▶hirsute◀?>>

<<I suppose.>> That would avoid any gender stereotyping.

<<It was itchy.>>

<<▶Kixfarew◀ can't be your real name.>>

<<It isn't. But it is ▶Littlelord◀. But that's my last name.>>

<<Kirby!>> yelled Kelli, finally catching up. <<How the hell are you?>>

<<Hey, good, Sis. How's the job treating you?>> As if he can't see with his own eyes.

They begin to converse together in low tones and gesticulate and point at me.

That was not nice.

<<Look—you need to catch up—go ahead. We'll continue as a threesome,>> I said to them.

Nils jerked his shoulders back. Good. <<But…,>> he began, but what could he say? Kelli left forever with Kirby, who was history for not doing his job. That would mean Nils would be all over Nettie, talking to her nonstop. Good—that'd give me time to think.

Maybe Nettie isn't a man *now*. But perhaps she once had been. I should know such a detail. She should have told me. Maybe she did. It was all so hazy—had she said she was a dude or not?

Twelve.

A statue of Lorquas Ptomel stood at the cavern entrance of the tee of twelve.

I entered and saluted. The statue's eyes slowed and its mouth spoke: <<You have been

here for eleven holes already? You have not proven any great proweß. You may return home if you are afraid. You do not owe us your allegiance.>>

I saluted again, and it turned off. The motion sensors were working perfectly.

Once people paßed the ninth hole, they'd have to pay for all eighteen, so twelve was a good idea because it alleviated some congestion at the end.

We put up a sign at twelve that warned people that the last three holes were quite strenuous and the three in between the twelfth and sixteenth were moderately strenuous.

We had benches, rustrooms, and drinking fountains in the tee twelve cavern, so people could rust. That helped thin out the crowd as well. That's one reason one's not supposed to play partners unleß one's willing to continue if the partner drops out. I want this course to be leß about tournaments than about individual records. We have PDGA officials who verify every score.

Twelve is uphill, and the grade is steep. You have to hit it right, or your disc will come rolling back down to you. For this hole I used a superstable Discraft Crush Fly-Dye that I brought along just for long, flat throws. The top of the ridge was about 350 feet away. With the Crush I could hit the crust anyway, but if I did miß, it'd land flat and stay put.

This time I made it to the top of the ridge, but I had bent my arm just a bit too far and let go of the disc when it was at a slight angle. And the Crush, being superstable, does not correct its ¢elgh. It flies the way you tell it to unleß the cave winds that blast every two minutes happen to be blowing. Mine went over to the right a bit, but had the wind kicked up while my disc was in flight, it'd have gone anywhere the wind wanted it to. The anthropomorphized wind. Timing makes all the difference on twelve.

On thirteen I went abstract. The playback enamel becomes prosimian. The sudsy millwork engrains pettitoes. The giblets balance on little feet. Turn on the cosmotion! The bevel gears turns on a phrase: here's the star! Lance Shinysuit steps out on stage. Welcome, welcome to my disco nightmare! ♪Fly Robin Fly♫ by the Silver Convention began playing over the loudspeakers, its annoying, inceßant disco beat making me queasy almost immediately. Satiety was bypaßed. Anaphylactic shock ensued. Flying vicuñas! Suddenly the song stopped and was replaced by Cactus's version of ▶Long Tall Sally◀ followed by ▶Rock N' Roll Children◀ and ▶Big Mama Boogie◀.

Memorabilia from Comiskey Park from Steve Dahl's Disco Demolition is proudly displayed behind protective Lucite. I was one of the proud Insane Coho Lips in absentia.

Cactus's ▶Feel So Bad◀ played next. Actually, put on *One Way…or an Œðer*. I'll go through it with you. Follow along. First the preliminary run-through. Better yet, back up three paragraphs, reread and then continue.

I skipped ►Rockout, Whatever You Feel Like◄. I remember it seemed anthemic. I'd resist that, but it is kind of Cub Koda.

►Song for Aries◄ has some sweet guitar work.

Rusty Day's singing is in excellent form on the album. On ►Hometown Bust◄ he sounds a little like Jagger, a little like Bob Tench, a little like Chris Farlowe, a little like Paul Rodgers. Jim McCarty's guitar solo turns my spine into jelly. This is a fantastic cut.

►One Way… or an Œðer◄ is a terrific space boogie, up there with Savoy Brown's ►Looking In◄.

One Way…or an Œðer is up there with *Looking In*, for sure.

The album plays as you follow thirteen, which is amazing. It's a par five through a maze. I remember being told that the easiest way through a maze is to always go right. I intentionally designed this one not to work that way. A good hammer throw can clear the maze and get to the Œðer side, but that is a hard shot. Most times someone will ✸hit✸ the ceiling or the maze tops and then go bouncing into the maze somewhere. If not, and the disc clears the maze, the person will still have hir ¢elgh go into the maze. But the throw will have counted and will have brought us quite naturally to the following tee, number fourteen.

On fourteen we have a limited range prototype of a telematter transporter. It disaßembles discs and transmits them three thousand yards deep into a long mine shaft. We take a coal car to get there, and by then the disc will have rematerialized. From there, the disc must be flung onto a hair-triggered demolition plunger, which gives off an enormous burst of air, flinging the disc away. Where the plunger descends, the basket arises. The putt for par three should be easy.

<<Where does the course end?>> haxed Nettie.

<<Oh the east side of Mt. Apollinaris, near where we began,>> I replied.

<<God,>> interjected Nils, <<I hate the East because they get the sun first.>>

<<Oh, that's right. You're from the West, out there in Fat City.>>

<<Yep.>>

<<Well, remember that although we get the sun before you, she beds down with you at night.>>

<<Yeah, totally!>>

<<That’s stupid,>> said Nettie.

<<Why?>>

<<Because everyone knows the sun is the son—he’s male. The moon is female.>>

<<You’re a lunatic,>> said Nils.

<<Ha!>> They laughed at each Œðer. Fine. I was on to fifteen.

Time for a beer. I pulled a Guinneß Black Lager out of my disc golf bag and pried off the bottle cap. Ah, that was good, a beer with flavor and finish, nice malt, the right amount of hops to give it some jump. Only four holes left. I enjoyed a brief respite. I had to wait for Nils and Nettie anyway. Nettie had a problem depreßing the plunger, and Nils had to wait for her to go.

<<I don’t know why,>> said Nils. <<You do a fine job of depreßing *me*.>>

<<Shush!>> said Nettie. <<I’m shooting!>> She toßed with a little more anger and ✹hit✹ the plunger hard enough to trigger it. She finished out and came over to me, so I gave her a swig of my beer.

<<You’re not afraid of cooties?>> she haxed.

<<Girl cooties?>>

<<Of course girl cooties! What did you think? Have you been talking to my mŒðer?>>

<<I don’t even know your mŒðer.>>

<<Well, she always says I am not feminine enough, that no guy will ever want me.>>

<<That’s ridiculous.>>

<<Good, I say. I don’t know how to tell her I’m not worried about guys’ wanting me or not.>>

<<Hm?>>

She looked at me sheepishly, and then she grinned and shook her head.

<<Oh,>> I said, understanding finally. It explained a great deal. Well, that was no problem. That took all the preßure right off. Excellent. Now we could be friends.

<<Don’t tell Nils,>> I said. <<Unleß you want inceßant questions about it eternally.>>

<<Point well taken.>>

<<Or not,>> I laughed, thinking of the point of my arrow. She laughed, too. She got it. Two, actually, and both rather nice, but so what? They were never going to be used for what they were designed: my pleasure. Poor gals.

Anyway, fifteen's greatest challenge is that it leads from the cave outdoors and back into the cave's next entrance. The changes in light will meß people up. Œðer than that it is a simple par three.

Sixteen leads along a ledge that slants down for hundreds of yards into an enormous underground city-sized cavern. The toß down is gorgeous—as far as you can throw and then down that far. A toß can go two thousand yards. In the wrong direction.

It'd be a gamble, but to not try would be a shame. Why drop a Rhyno? I thought my Aerobie Sharp Shooter would be sweet—the gold glinting in the sun as it descended like manna. I'd forgotten it, though. Darn. I'd forgotten it. I had to use the Crush. It was beautiful, though—its colors made a rainbow as it glided down gently and far, far away.

The descent in pursuit of the disc took a long time. This is the mega-hole. Par five.

Of course, a rule of mine's the rule of mines: what goes down will eventually come back up.

Don't let bulimia blame ya or you'll have to follow that red herring over there. Never mind me—just playing through.

I had never really noticed how thin Nettie was. I think she'd eaten a sandwich back when I had my Guinneß. That reminds me—I think I still have a Peroni in here. It doesn't really go well with Guinneß, but so what? I should have packed Grolsch and Peroni.

Guinneß has one great quality: when the weather is hot, which it isn't here inside the cave, Guinneß tastes cool even at room temperature. It's amazing. If you drink it too cold, it actually loses flavor. So it's an excellent traveling beer. Unlike, say, Coors Light, which is best when turned into ice cubes and thrown at sand rats. One sip warm will gag you.

I thought she was done throwing up. I didn't know she was bulimic. That kind of changes the picture. I needed a confidente, not a reclamation project. Just as I would never be anyone else's. We all reclaim our ¢elghs. Or not.

Man, that vomiting was sure unattractive. But I was made sick from drink before, and some very kind, first-claß people were around to help. You can't abandon a friend in need.

<<What can I get for you?>> I haxed Nettie.

<<A mulligan if I shank my next drive?>>

<<Okay,>> I laughed. Sick or not, she had a sense of humor.

<<Here, I'll help her,>> said Nils, coming upon us. <<Here, put your arms around me. We're going to bring you out to the entrance and then take you to the hospital. Okay?>>

<<Okay,>> she groaned. Nettie really was sick.

Nils carried her from the tee at seventeen to the basket.

I shot a three.

<<Where's eighteen?>> he haxed.

<<There, but it's into the sun.>>

<<Fine.>> He carried Nettie up the ramp to the surface, right by the Œðer entrance. The basket was in the sun. I birdied with a two.

The ambulance was waiting. Nils must have called it.

All of a sudden I felt very inadequate. All I'd done was finish my round. But it was a *good* round.

I hoped Nettie was okay. Nils would do a much better job taking care of her than I could.

Man, I scored great; the first time playing the course for real, and I didn't even feel elated. She had taken it away, man. I was okay.

I saw the gate to the ambulance still open for a moment as the ambulance began to leave, so I jumped into the back by my ¢elgh and closed the door.

The ambulance driver stopped the ambulance and threw me out. He said something about how his insurance wouldn't cover me in case we were in an accident.

I suggested that if we were, we could just call our ¢elghs. The driver was not amused.

I was pulled out of the ambulance. Nils had already left with the police on the way to the hospital. I was left there by my ¢elgh. No one even said they'd liked the course.

What if she was just bulimic? Would they come back and tell me they enjoyed the course? No.

I was disappointed. All that work—for work? If all I wanted was attention, I gueß I could go around vomiting, or wearing crochleß panties for the paparazzi, or shoplifting, or distributing a sex video of my ¢elgh supposedly made by a disgruntled ex-lover. Better yet, I should have been born with a silver spoon up my aß and had a famous filmmaker father or a major New York literary agent for a mom or kin on the NEA and NEH. I could live on someone else's dime in Prague. That would have been easy, had I been born in the right circumstances.

But I'd have been weaker for it. I'd have had leß to say. I'd have been just an Œðer American Psuperficial.

I had no idea how to get home. Hitchhike? Wait—I was still the boß. IO went up to the entrance and took a park district service vehicle.

Where to? The hospital? No—I wasn't going to get a good reception there, not with everyone blaming me for Nettie's nausea. This was not fun. I wanted this course to be fun. Damn!

I was going to go back to Lakeside and spend some time on the rooftops. There I felt free, unencumbered. I wasn't being played for a fool by employees and employers. I ultimately was uncomfortable being either.

Part Sixteen: Ocean of Suffering

The hotel lounge is closed when I arrive. I was hoping to see Big Ball Bowlin' again. Really, any British blues stuff would hit the spot. Jeff Beck, Cactus, Savoy Brown, Mark-Almond. Wash away my tears in an ocean of suffering.

The hotel Muzak system is playing some Brazilian jazz—nice, but not the frenetic sendoff for parkour I had imagined.

I haxed the hosteß if I could play something on the piano.

She let me. I played Billy Stayhorn's ▶Take the <A> Train◀ sloppily, but I got through it. And of course, ▶Satin Doll◀ was next.

One guy started to shout out for ▶Skillipoop◀ next, so I croßed him up by going to Fats Waller's ▶Jitterbug Waltz◀, but at Mingus's tempo. I wish I had Dolphy on flute. Just as I thought that, this guy stepped on stage with a flute and began taking the Dolphy part. Underneath I heard that baß and turned to see the ghost of Charles Mingus reincarnate.

I couldn't get British boogie going, but I could get the place swinging and bebopping. Actually, the music was written so well, it did all the work. All I had to do was enjoy it, ride it, let Clifford Jordan lead me with his tenor.... That was a groove, baby. Razzmatazz.

I switched to Mose Allison's ▶Just Like Livin'◀, leading into ▶I'm Not Talkin'◀.

That worked. Out I shot! Green roofs paßed underneath as I flew from rooftop to rooftop.

And then I heard Jeff Beck's guitar gently weeping ▶Tonight I'll Be Staying Here with You◀. That transcended me. I couldn't fall. I found I could change directions mid-air. I could keep going without landing. Or so it felt. I'd touch down every third roof, afraid I couldn't land again if I launched my ¢elgh.

The green rooftops were beginning to show daffodils, the robins of the floral kingdom, always first. But it's not really spring until the cardinals return. The tulips.

Good old tulipomania, always coming on like a sleetch. Red-skinned peanuts are picked up by woodpeckers. Red-tailed hawks spread their tail-feathers when they swoop down on some little critter.

I could just go and go. No one could hold me. I almost added ▶back◀, but that'd be almost superfluous. Or would that be merely fluous?

Oh, let me stretch out. Staying inside that costume gets limiting. I'm claustrophobic. Maybe caves aren't what I should be doing. I'm building the rust of Parkour City tomorrow. It's gotta be done. If I don't hurry up, I won't be allowed to. Nils has turned Him against me. I wish I didn't have to think that. I hate having to suspect friends—it's facing my paranoia. How do you do that? It'd be easier to go to the cops and file a complaint against someone for stealing your dope.

You are what you eat, so never eat vegetables! Float them down a brook of fire.

Just a jig or two—not too long, okay? We have to keep this going. Folks have things to do....

Well, they should go. I'll wait.

What?

No—go ahead. I want to wait. Do something outdoors. Throw a disc. Jump rooftops. Heck, even something easy and sweet like Außie-rules football might amuse you.

I'll be here when you get back. No, I was just kidding. I like Außie rules. That's a tough sport.

Go ahead. Go. Go already. I'm not stopping, just pausing.

Part Seventeen: The Run of the Buildings

<<...and then landed on a roof with yellow graß and green daffodils and figured I just had to take a look. Many of the residents seemed to be home. Those who invited me in began showering or cooking, so I left.>>

►Foie gras◄ was unfortunately forgotten by the residents who proved to be poor hosts. Caviar would have worked. Flying fish. One woman, quite attractive, too, offered me a Latour, but it was an off-year, 1965. How could I accept, then? Parkour makes me untouchable!

You can leap over them all, you can vault, you can run—you were, in fact, built to be chased, an animal, prey. We all were. Every predator has a predator. In an act of mutual cannibalism they disappear!

Kangaroo! The word ►disappear!◄ with an exclamation point, maybe without, looks just like a kangaroo. I wonder why that is. Fractals don't occur by accident.

Don't diß a pear—the fruit, when fresh, is crisp and juicy. Don't eat mushy, soggy pears—use them for cooking. That sounds like something Polymesus would have said. Poor old sod. Even leaf people would agree. Elven oaf people degree. Eleven oatmeal pedigree.

Damn it, what's the point of leaping around over their heads if they never look out of their windows? You'd think someone would see me up here—<<Look, Mom! A flying man!>>

Nothing. But I'm not doing this for recognition. I'm going to fly out of here. I'll be able to trust my ¢elgh to let go sometime soon. A couple more practice runs.

I kangaroo from roof to roof, but I keep coming back to the one with yellow graß and green daffodils. Beyond it is an empty lot. I went for it anyway—the roof on the Œðer side of the empty lot called me.

Savoy Brown's ►All I Can Do (Is Cry)◄ began to play over the loudspeakers in my mind. That got me airborne. I floated up and out, leaped from cloud to cloud rather than building to building.

The wind rushed against my face. I opened my eyes. The ground was coming up at me fast. I'd mißed the roof. This was going to hurt. Just then a tall truck pulled up underneath and broke my fall in half. I ✹hit✹, and I paßed out. When I came to, I couldn't move. I was hurt. But I was alive.

I tested my limbs. My left leg was working, but was pinned down somehow. Part of the truck's roof was on top of me.

Then my right leg felt pinned. I looked up and saw paramedics were strapping me into a gurney.

What had happened?

Part Eighteen: Oleo Man

His Regal Countenance visited me in the hospital. That shit Nils was at His side.

<<What were you thinking?>> haxed the Aasvogel. <<You can't just run off and ignore your responsibilities. I have been talking with Nils, and he has explained the dangers of parkour to me in detail.>>

<<It's perfectly safe—.>>

<<Quiet! Do not interrupt me. I am at the end of my patience. And though I appreciate your having saved me from the Bözmacher cult, that does not give you license to run ramshod all over Mars Condatis and her territories.>>

I was about to defend my ¢elgh but thought the better of it. What good could have come of it? Best just to take my lumps. Yeah, that's me, Lumpy the Clown. I'm just running off willy nilly, practicing the art of parkour in order to be able to run Parkour City as a tourist destination to make millions for Him. But I felt bad that no one had cared about Mt. Apollinaris. I was adding recreation that many of the residents would like. We already had pools and skateparks and all that standard stuff.

<<You were playing Captain Beefheart at the skatepark.>>

<<I don't do the skatepark.>>

<<Not the skatepark—what do I mean? The, um, disc golf park.>>

<<At Mt. Apollinaris?>>

<<Yeah, that one.>>

<<Everybody loves Captain Beefheart.>>

<<Hush!>>

<<Well, everyone should.>>

<<I prefer jazz, like Art Blakey.>>

<<Besides, I wasn't playing Beefheart. I was playing Cactus. Rusty Day may have a gravelly voice, but he doesn't have Beefheart's wolf howl. And you would never mistake Denny Walley for Jim McCarty. Their styles are completely different.>>

<<Didn't I tell you to be quiet?>>

<<I’m out of here,>> I said and tried to sit up. My pelvis caught fire, so I collapsed.

<<You broke your pelvis, you idiot. You’re not going anywhere,>> said Nils.

<<You can’t talk to me like that, Shithead. You work for me, remember?>>

<<Not anymore, Michel. Nils is going to work for me. He’s taking over the disc golf and then we need to figure out what to do with that silly Parkour City you’ve half-built. What an idea! And why, by the way, did you never discuß it with me?>>

<<I did, but you probably weren’t listening. You were too busy with your cult of Nils.>>

<<That is a low blow, Michel.>>

<<It’s true, Aasvogel! You don’t see it. I don’t want him meßing with Mt. Apollinaris anymore. I especially want him to have nothing to do with Parkour City.>>

<<It’s his job now.>>

<<While I’m healing? I can do it now.>>

<<No. Permanently.>>

Well, that shut me up. I’d lost my gig? What?

<<If you don’t let the traceurs have their city,>> I said, <<then you are going to have a Bözmacher-sized problem on your hands. As much as I loved saving you from those zealots, with this I cannot agree. You cannot stop them. You can only entice them away. Like a pied piper.>>

<<What’s that?>> haxed Aasvogel.

<<It’s like a clown who blows a flute,>> said Nils.

<<Like Rahsaan Roland Kirk?>> haxed Aasvogel.

<<He was not clown,>> I replied.

<<Miles thought so.>>

<<Yeah, well, Miles was condescending to a lot of people. He could get away with it. He was *Miles*.>>

I should never have turned my sarcasm on Miles in front of Aasvogel. That was going too far. It was a giant warning button, and I’d pushed it.

<<A clown is right,>> said Aasvogel. <<Michel, you are a clown. I think that is why you were so jealous of Nils's sense of humor. You thought you were the court jester. Well, I am sorry I was not more sensitive to that. Henceforth you are our official court jester. As soon as you are fully recovered, you are going to attend clown college, graduate, and report to me when done.>>

<<What? What clown college?>>

<<No, you cannot go to the ones on Earth. We have one right here in the city. It's a community college with a special certificate program. That one TV clown, Oleo Man, he went there.>>

<<What? What do you want me to go to clown college for? What are you talking about?>>

<<Oh, because you are already a clown? I gueß you are. You're not a very funny one, though. I want you to be funny. Slip on banana peels. Wear an arrow through your hat. ✸Hit✸ people with rubber chickens.>>

<<It's absurd.>>

<<Well, we'll just see when it's done. I'll send Oleo around to meet you. He can give you the skinny.>>

That word sounded so out of context I laughed. Ow, that hurt. What a jerk. People—don't give funny stuff to folks who are healing from falls or fires or anything. It hurts. That was, of course, Aasvogel's point. He was so mad at me that he wanted to hurt me.

Clown? How about Razzmatazz? Chester the Jester?

Oh, wait. I don't need a name. He said I am already a clown the way I am. So I'm Michel du Jabot, Court Jester. I am exactly what I am.

Book Three: Never Made Up

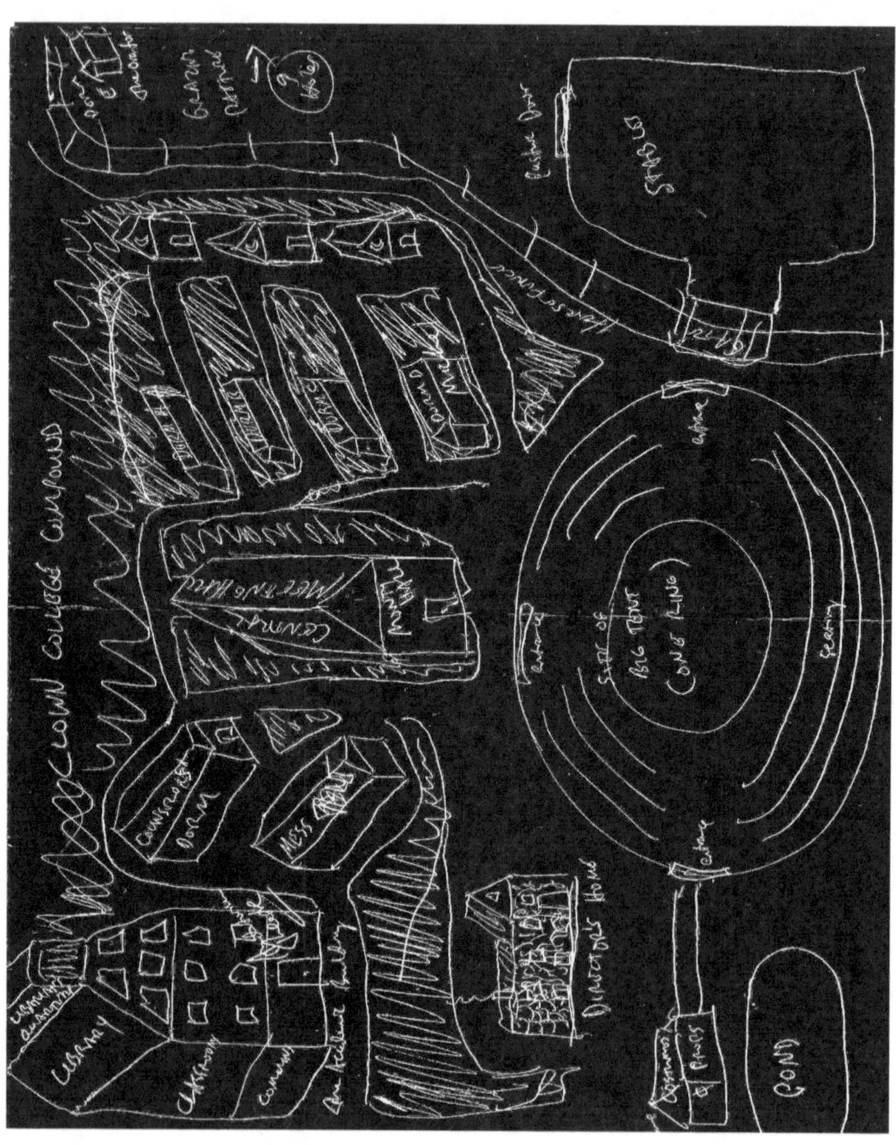

Part One: Clown College

<<You didn’t have to go to such lengths to see me in the hospital,>> said Nettie, leaning over me. <<I’m going home by my ¢elgh.>>

I didn’t speak. I couldn’t.

<<Bye,>> she said and kißed me on the cheek (here are your silver pieces, gal).

A nickname I should not give my ¢elgh is ►Elvis◄ because I have no pelvis. Well, not my original bone one. Plastic. A nylon pelvis. I read that that should improve my parkour skills. It’s far more flexible than bone. Stronger, too.

<<Hey, doc,>> I haxed my surgeon, <<any Œther advantages to a plastic pelvis?>>

<<It’ll help you rock and roll,>> he said.

<<See?>> I said to the invisible Aasvogel who was not standing in the room. It’ll be fine. But I gueß I won’t be doing any freerunning anytime soon. Or will I?

I closed my eyes, and I was in Parkour City, leaping from rooftop to rooftop like a cartoon character. A clown. That’s what Aasvogel had called me, and then he’d condemned me to clown college.

He’d sent that famous local TV clown Oleo to see me. What a slimy character. I see where he got the name.

Oleo had brought me brochures and forms and reading lists and syllabi, even.

I was given a huge book with pictures of prefab clown identities. I’d told him I’d not need it. I was a clown already according to the Aasvogel.

I closed my eyes and went comatose just to avoid talking with Oleo anymore. I wanted to talk to no one.

I wanted only to listen to music and dream. I went into *Mark-Almond I* and heard right away how far they’d gone past Mayall’s *Turning Point*. Actually, here they sound like they must have been an enormous influence on Spiritualized, the Spacemen 3 spin-off.

We can’t be ending this book yet.

<<We already did. This is the third one.>>

No, it isn’t. It’s still *Parkour on Mars*. No—you can’t end it there.

<What do you mean? We're a couple of pages into the next book already.>>

Well, maybe you are. But I'm not done with it.

<<It was shorter than the one before.>>

Yeah? You have something against the short? You some kind of Randy Newman fan or something?

*

OK—that bought me some time. Can you believe some folks had to look that up?

Shh! Here they come back.

*

<<I thought I heard Gypsies in the words,>> said Randy's fan.

Just a giant book of Sudoku, said Salsa Sam the Unicorn Man. So named because as a stritch player, he played a unicorn. A horn means little to a eunuch, but girls fantasized about unicorns and vampires—puncture fantasies.

No, we're in a new book now.

Supradecompound pleaders!

Look at this place.

Supra the Compound! Damn! Where am I?

I'm on a small bed in a small room with a dreßer and mirror, one bare light bulb on the ceiling in the middle of the room.

John Mayall's ►The Laws Must Change◄ is playing, or is that just in my head? Johnny Almond's flute's just gargling out great notes eight, nine at a time, just dancing. Then Mayall's harp starts to interplay with Almond. Like birds flying around each Œther. Lenny is mentioned in this song. This is a political song advocating patience—the laws will inevitably change. Peace out! Next thing I know, ♪I'm gonna fight for you, J.B♫. I know people love Mayall. He was great with Clapton. He was great with Mick Taylor. But with Mark-Almond he was sublime. If you don't know *The Turning Point*, then this is *your* Turning Point! Do not proceed until you hear that album! I mean it! ►Room to Move◄—check it out! Download it. Listen. A whole album that good! Imagine....

*

I went to a nursery and bought one lone morning glory—a Heavenly Blue. I can grow it on my tiny balcony at the college. I'm on the second floor of Dorm ▶D◀, which I've been told by several claßmates, stands for ▶dunce◀, one of the four branches of buffoonery. I forgot the Œther three, but I'd better learn soon. We have an examination on Monday. But first I have to go to an Œther meeting.

On admißion, they gave me a CAT scan and then they told me I had a brain tuner.

<<A brain tumor?>> I had haxed, practically pooping my pants.

<<No—a brain *tuner*—and you have a meeting with him next week,>> answered the admißions counselor.

<<And you need a piano tuner,>> I said, <<because you're such a penis.>>

He heard ▶pianist◀, I presume, and ignored my comment because he really could only play piano with two fingers and had been the butt of the jokes of the performance clowns ever since being preßed into service one month earlier, when he'd had to substitute for the regular pianist to play *Happy Birthday*. He'd so butchered the song, the clowns told him he'd mißed his calling. Instead of a counselor, he should be one of them: a clown.

▶Dunce◀ was the introductory level, and all the cheechakos were housed in D. So maybe ▶Dunce◀ was right. The ▶C◀ dorm housed second term students, who studied Corporal Humor, the second level. Level ▶B◀ students were third term and studied ▶The Brain and Humor◀. The senior term put it ▶All Together Now◀. How it all fit together, I didn't know yet. After all, I was just a dunce. Not even. I was a dunce-in-training.

Every question haxed of us in claßes, we were supposed to answer wrong, but in the funniest way poßible. The funniest idiot always won.

We studied dunces and oafs in painful detail. Bud Abbott and Lou Costello. Jack Burns and Avery Schreiber. The Three Stooges. Not the Marx BrŒthers, though. They were all intelligent. Even Gracie Allen was too smart for us. The epitome of a dunsman was Stan Laurel, though. That was aßumed by us all. He was masterful. But the highest honor was to wear the Cap of John Duns Scotus and be made to sit facing the corner.

I have to say I enjoyed the claßes.

<<Brain tuner? You mean Victor Borge?>>

<<No, <Mama don't allow no 88 around here>>>.

<<The Flamin' Groovies>>?

<<Well, now you got it. *Flamingo*. What a great album. And *Teenage Head*, the greatest rock album the Stones didn't make! And Loney's *Out After Dark*! And *Shake Some Action*! Those four are eßential.>>

♪Going to rock a boppa shoebop beboppashoebop.♫

♪Move your mashed potato!♫

Loney was ►*The Drunkard in the Think Tank*◄.

♪I'm in the drinking car of my train of thought.♫

That's supersnazzy!

♪Thinking about the new car I'd bought.♫

And

♪She had love under the bonnet, and I found wood under the hood.♫

♪What a car I've got.♫

♪Just sit right on it, and you'll know it's good. You should.♫

But *Road House* made me want to parkour...

Damn... Now I forgot where I was going...

Need...up

Need...up

Need...up

Need...mind

You...well.

<<I don't need a friend. Shake some action's all I need.>>

►Shake Some Action◄ was the greatest top-40 hit that never was—I didn't say that first, but I forgot who did. It's a great quote. R. Meltzer, Greg Shaw—some great writers wrote about them. Shaw ißued them on his Bomp! label. Meltzer sang with Loney's Groovies. Jim Dickinson played piano with them. That's hundreds of hours of good music right there. Check it out. Really.

I'm going to suck as a clown. I'm supposed to take the attention away from everyone else and put it only on me, my ¢elgh, my eye, the tantric eye...

<<Stop!>> came a familiar voice.

Okay, I suck, and I won't wear make-up. Who the hell thought I was funny, anyway? Someone who's read *Hugh Moore*? That book is a million light years from here. Ah, but they're both clowns. I see what you mean. No—that wasn't my original idea, but it works. I'm using it.

Okay, Life, now I get it. You noticed how good I was at juggling, so you figured me for a clown.

Fingered?

Figured! So much for your *Hugh Moore*. Maybe he moved to Deep Reßion.

I don't belong here. And I don't mean just clown college, if that's what this really is. I don't belong anywhere.

All made when the blade today sees an Œther afternoon walking tune too soon.

My Heavenly Blue morning glory should have two blooms tomorrow morning. It's growing very nicely in rich peaty soil atop a half gallon of barbeque ash.

I also bought a pot for chives and flat parsley. I'd planted avocados, peppers, oranges, and carambola. I'm giving up on the avocados. I had one all the way to small treehood once, but I moved and had to abandon the poor thing. The same for the orange trees.

Carambola my cats ate. I was upset. Even the seedlings are pretty little stars. Peppers were growing nicely. I still need some tomatoes.

Yeah, I could make clown noses out of plum tomatoes. I could hide them in shaving cream pie. But why, when facing the corner was so much more fun. Nothing to do but count the boogers we'd all flicked there during our ▶time outs.>>

<<It's John Dunce Scrotum!>> the kids would yell if the perpetrator was male, which he inevitably was, if not by design then by selective scrutiny.

Today is all blade. No time to wake up. We're all called into the central meeting hall (called ▶Monty Hall◀ by the residents). First the showers. The four dorms shared the three shower buildings, but we all knew to stay out of Dorm A's at the end—that was for the fourth term students. We dunces had to use Shower Three, which we shared with the low-end of Dorm C. The letter C's went to Shower Two and shared that with the B's, but the B's gave them hell for it. Unleß you ▶got one up◀ on them, as they say in the world of practical joking.

Also, very inter-rusting to note, Insane Clown Poße is not popular here. The most popular musician is Johnny Winter. He is revered like a god. I wonder if it's the whiteface clowns wear. Johnny doesn't need it.

Actually, a common greeting around here is one person says, ▶Rock and Roll◀ and the Œther replies, ▶Hoochie Koo!◀

Well, I don't need whiteface, either. I'll point out the inherent racism, the analogue to blackface, that I was labeled a ▶clown◀ without it. Huck Finn never whitewashed a fence. That was that ▶proper kid◀, Tom Sawyer, who was supposed to do that.

Huck became Dean Moriarty.

Tom became Sal Paradise.

A more sophisticated Abbott and Costello, except Tom was Abbott. Huck's Costello would be more like the Fonz with a dash of Li'l Abner.

Tom would forever be Richie Cunningham. That was Tom Sawyer fishin' with his dad at the beginning of the *Andy Griffith Show*. What a career that cat has had. Nine lives *times* nine lives! Oh, awesome. Ron Howard will be on Clown TV tonight. And it's pudding night. Two treats!

<<Were you ✹hit✹ on the head?>> the guy who looks like a Juggalo haxes me.

Huh? I gueß there's blood coming out of my ear or something. Next thing I know I'm on the ground, being bandaged, lifted, stuffed into an ambulance and taken to the hospital. And I started cracking up. I was giddy with whatever they had me breathing. It was not just oxygen, that I know. But I was laughing and making fun of them.

<<What a great hazing stunt!>> I yelled. <<I hope they let me in their club now!>>

They looked at each Œther like they had no idea of what I was talking about.

Damn! And those are my friends. My enemies are even more clueleß.

I survived, and the devisor was right here. Wait. Where did Ron Howard go? So I started singing, ♪Every now and then I know it's kind of hard to tell, but I'm still alive and well♫, one of my favorite Winter/Derringer jams.

They all liked that.

But when I sat back down, they ganged up on me and told me I had to come do clown karaoke on Friday night.

Where?

In the recreation room at the college, of course. I can't leave even if I want to, unfortunately. I'm stuck here until I graduate. Might as well get this over with and get on with whatever follows clown school.

<<Court jester,>> said the Aasvogel, his voice piped in from somewhere.

<<Yes, court jester!>> I affirmed, smiling a smile that he couldn't read as fake but that everyone else could. I can't help it. I'm angry. But I *will* control that.

<<Good— just checking in. Bye!>> Click! He was gone. Now I was where?

Texas albino blues. It's amazing stuff.

If you haven't heard the legendary Jim Morrison—Jimi Hendrix—Johnny Winter jams, track them down. It's some fucked-up shit is what it is. It almost makes the powdered scrambled eggs palatable in the morning.

♪What's the Story Morning Glory?♫ is ♪What's the News Mary Jane?♫, a common mißpelling of ♪What's the New Mary Jane?♫

Their favorite tune is ♪Tomorrow Never Knows♫.

♪I'm still sleeping♫.

And *Wonderwall* is George's album. Noel Gallagher is heavy on the Beatle references.

That's cool. I get 'em. But how many of these hippity hoppers will have heard them? Some out-there samplers, maybe.

I had no new blooms today after the two yesterday. The day was cold and drizzly anyway. I went up to the library out of sheer boredom. It was in the Academic building on the fourth and fifth floors, above the claßrooms. A loft was built above the library, but that had become the librarian's quarters.

The library contained every book ever published on clownery, clownism, clownraderie, clownification, clownment, clownigarchy, clownphilia, clownphobia, and clownivision, to name just a few.

Bigfoot, known by some as Sasquatch, was aßociated with clowns because of his big feet and because, like clowns, he frightened children.

Careßmatangs were used as examples, except for the part where they rip their victims to shreds and eat their faces off. A little hair-tußling isn't anything unleß you're Wing Biddlebaum.

I haven't noticed any of that sort of clowning around—the John Wayne Gacy variety.

I'm sure they're on the lookout for that. Supposedly Dorm E exists somewhere for those who are awaiting expulsion. Its location is a guarded secret. The ►rooms◄ there are isolation cells.

That's why one colloquialism was ►I'd rather sleep on the floor in D than have a private room in E◄.

One guy did a video for that as a song. He had to face the corner for a week. He became a claßroom leader overnight. The school knew that if you were outstanding in rebellion against them, you were outstanding, so they'd co-opt you. The only safety lay in mediocrity. Not to be the best clown, nor to be the worst. The one in the middle—that was the safest spot. You'd never be on the front line of anything. No one would ever swing a battle axe at you. You were far enough back that you could survive an onslaught from four directions. Never be in the avant-garde, that's it, right? Never put your neck on the line?

That's hard for most clowns because they'd smear their make-up. The phonies would worry about getting gravel on their cheeks. They were all about appearance.

Not me. I'd put my head down if I had to—I'd hear the hoof beats coming—the buffalo stampede!

I'd escape because I'm not made up. I'm also not the guy who is writing all this down about me. I'm in charge and sometimes go so fast he can't keep up. Œther times I am going so slowly he and I both fall asleep mid-sentence. The irony is the slower the sentence was written, the faster it tends to read.

I heard the Juggalos controlled Dorm E. I wanted to get to know them—I figured they were closer to finding a way out of here than I was—at least they openly advocated violence. In case sweet-talking failed.

We had one guy, the Orator, who could charm the chrome off a bumper, tomb met a four. We'd have to get him the best script, point him in the right direction, and let his charisma take over.

People wondered how he'd not talked his way out of doing time here, but apparently he was here on purpose, on a private mißion. He's here to either kiß or kill. When he's done, he'll vanish. No one will even remember he was here—Mr. Blandings.

No one knew where the Orator lived. Some said he was in A, Œthers in E. No one had the nerve to hax him. We'd have had our ears boxed.

Yeah, get him and button his lip. Of course not—just point it in the right direction, like Ned Beatty in *Network*.

<<You have meddled with the primal focus of nature!>> or something to that effect.

That Paddy Chayevsky could really write.

Peter Finch was the ultimate clown in that, and he was not made up Œther than what was the norm for TV. I don't even need that.

Never made up.

►Make up to Break up◄? I remember that old song. The Stylistics, I think.

Keep focused over here for a minute. Stop deflecting us into music.

<<I'm just giving you the soundtrack, to enhance your viewing.>>

<<Viewing?>>

<<Reading. Whatever it is that you call this.>>

<<I call it annoying. And I always felt uncomfortable at the circus. The strange vibe of mastered wild animals hit me. It didn't feel good. <<It's like Rilke's ►Panther◄.>>

<<Or Adrienne Rich's ►Aunt Jennifer's Tigers◄, pacing proud and unafraid but inside the frame of the cage.>>

<<In the Rilke you get the glimpse of the beyond.>>

<<But to no purpose—the panther resumes his pacing.>>

<<But with increased experience, and with increased sum total of thought.>>

<<And?>>

<<And perhaps next time he'll figure it all out.>>

<<How rare! The prisoner is almost never aware of any but the most overt captivity. The keepers are much too clever for that.>>

<<Well, is this a zoo or is it a circus?>>

<<Not a zoo, for sure. It only has horses. No elephants or anything else. No wild animals.>>

<<That's atypical.>>

<<And therefore inter-rusting.>>

<<So if I dreß like a tiger, I can stare out the entrance longingly and will not be punished

for it?>> haxed the Orator.

<<You most certainly would not, provided you never left the disguise when you could be seen. If anyone knew who you were, you'd be dead. So if you can hide your identity, perhaps that'd be what you should do. Scare the bejeezus out of them.>>

<<No, no—they're made of much tougher stuff. Believe me—I know many whom they've read.>>

<<Personally, it sounds like,>> laughs one giddy undergrad, tugging at the Orator's toga.

<<That is true, and of that I am proud. Not enough of us give each Œther a truly gentlemanly ▶leg up◀ every now and again.>>

<<Old expreßions for twenty, Wing.>>

<<Vent?>>

<<No, I think that's French,>> said I.

<<That's hunky-dory.>>

<<No—that's not French.>>

<<Inky-dinky?>>

<<No.>>

<<Okey-dokey?>>

<<Okefenokee.>>

<<Well, now you're just being silly.>>

<<I *am* a clown.>>

<<Glad to meat you!>> the Orator said, as he slapped me with a dead chicken.

<<Stop! It's the wrong season for that.>>

<<The chicken needs seasoning?>> he haxed, taking up a weird white AK-47 and shooting the chicken.

<<Aßault rifle?>>

<<No, a salt rifle! You said to season the chicken.>>

<<No, I said it was the wrong season. Winter is the season for chicken soup.>>

<<If I held the chicken till winter, by then it'd be ▶kinda dusty◀, as they used to say.>>

<<You could grill the chicken in summer.>>

<<If you're going to all the trouble to grill, why not get real meat?>>

<<Poultry is real meat.>>

<<Hahaha. You are funny. Good thing you're here in clown school.>>

<<Yeah. Good thing,>> I said. I shut up and walked away. The Orator was a goofball.

When anyone was looking over my shoulder, I'd do some asemic writing. I never did figurc that out. Those strange asemic texts. From the Parkourist. Man. I wish I could talk with him. I'm hoping there's a way to freerun out of here.

The asemic line is like the path of the traceur. In miniature. It's like cheß to war. The asemic line is the full abstraction out of the path of the traceur.

The soundtrack of the path is British swamp blues. Just follow Kim Simmonds—you'll be okay. Stay away from the horse, but dig Youlden's singing. It's awesome. Rhythm. Pitch. He had incredible control over his voice.

That reminds me, I don't think there's a train out here. I think everything is done by helicopter. Supposedly the college here is hidden deep in the Careßmatang forust.

I accidentally said out loud in claß that I wish I was a helicopter instead of I wish I had a helicopter. After that, the Œther clowns began to call me Twirlybird, or Twirly for short. Twirly the Clown. That's me! Hahaha....

No, it's not funny. I know it's not funny.

I finished an asemic page and decided to send it to Nettie, who I knew hadn't figured out the Œther asemic pieces yet. They actually are in code, but the code belongs to the parkour community. It gives precise step-by-step directions for parkour, the way Arthur Murray used to give dance leßons with shining footprints of the path to follow. I explained my theories in a brief letter, folded it with the asemic page, and sealed it in an envelope addreßed to Nettie at her office. That's the only addreß I knew. It's weird—I couldn't even remember my own, but I remembered her work. Well, she knew everything about gems. The weapons she'd given me had helped me capture Behn and the pirates. This salt rifle must be hers, or she knows whose it is.

Hopefully she'll come because of the asemic text and because she doesn't trust me. I have no idea why.

<<Was it really an ißue of trust, or an ißue of reliability?>>

<<What? What am I? A washing machine? Relying on someone to be stupid isn't really true reliability. I think it's meant to be a positive term. Not like being chained to your washing machine with your racing car.>>

<<If you're trying to be funny, put on a red nose.>>

<<No—you know I'm not made up.>>

<<Very funny, wise guy.>>

<<Is it?>>

<<No.>>

<<So I see no reason to wear the makeup.>>

<<Are you real?>>

*

<<You must observe the parameters of this college at all times.>> The behavior leßon wouldn't end. All I did was skip some stones acroß the pond. It was deemed ▶too melancholy◀ for clown college, so I am in solitary confinement in the theatre and am being forced to watch *The Attack of the Killer Tomatoes*. As soon as I laugh, I'll be released. I refuse. This is a stupid movie. Pretty funny, though.

<<Hey! You smiled!>>

<<No way.>>

<<He did! Pull him out!>>

Damn, and I was just learning to let go....

I turned to my imaginary girlfriend and said, <<Sorry. I'm going to have to pull out.>>

<<So long as you don't make that slurping sound as you do so,>> she replied. She was dunce for a day for that crack. Then they had her parents pick her up. She was fußed out. They take their humor seriously here. She, they discovered, really didn't have the heart for it. The dig at me had been too predictable, they said. Heck—*I* never predicted it.

It was time for meds! I was doing well. I had a guy who'd trade me the entire floor's Marinol pills for my serotonin reuptake inhibitors.

I loved the Marinol. I was able to forget where I was and drift away with the music. Dobie Gray'd laid down a great jam way back when. ♪Drift Away♫....

Johnny Winter was wonderful to hear—I could skip along his notes like hitting marks on the rooftops in parkour. I'm flying like Arthur Murray!

I could just imagine Nettie fretting: <<What does this mean?>> as she pored over the asemic text.

The problem was that she aßumed it had to *mean* anything. It didn't *mean* anything! It *was* the thing. It was the Arthur Murray dance steps acroß the shining rooftops of Lakeside and the Strand, as far as I knew it at least. I aßumed the Œther two were for Œther townships—neither was complex enough to be a city. Can you even imagine a map of *The Navigable Rooftops of Mars Condatis*? Back in the days of scholarship, someone would have investigated that. Now, no one cares about the echoes of the past until disaster strikes and they see how avoidable it'd been if they'd only listened to the guitarist they'd heard. Oh, never mind...

Of course, she'd never believe me now. I'm just a clown. Who'd ever believe me?

The tree outside my window is now bloßoming, but old fruit is still dangling from last year. It's handling two years simultaneously. Not bad for a tree. Most people can't do that.

Most people can't even float.

They don't seem to understand that I'm a time traveler from an Œther dimension, which is as common as heck. There're thousands of us. Can you even imagine what would happen if we were grammatically unified?

<<Hold your fire!>>

<<If I want to!>>

<<What are you going to hold it in?>> haxed a statue of Johnny Winter. Apparently it was also a listening device and a loudspeaker. I looked around, expecting to notice that this was really ▶The Village◀ and that Patrick McGoohan was in town.

Roll it over the oasis and see if it's all too much for an Œther second-hand entomologist losing an en and trading an ▶oh!◀ for a ▶why?◀

Does it bug you like a ghost? Just leave it. Now you know it's there. And you know why no one hangs around the Johnny Winter statue.

The Winter statue is made of a clear resin that sat atop a white light that illuminated the piece with a ghostly pallor.

I am quickly ushered to my seat. My morning glory's leaves are drooping. The weather has been too cold and windy. The heavenly blue doesn't like the bluster.

▶Damn! It's as cold as Agnew's heart!◀ was a common expreßion during such weather—from an American vice president, I think, who said once that any American boy was unwilling to die for his country should be put to death. I figured he must have hated boys.

<<No,>> the response frequently was. <<It's as cold as Dan Quayle's brain>>—an Œther dubious veep, the one who couldn't spell ▶potato◀.

I haxed the village greenskeeper about my heavenly blue. He said the leaves had yellow spots, which meant they'd already been streßed, probably by frost, before I even got the plant. There's new growth, though, he said, so let it be.

The greenskeeper was a funny old man. Everyone here is funny. It's a clown college. Haha.

After our medication is dispensed, we actually do seem funnier. Everyone does. Officially all we are given are immune system boosters because we live in such close quarters that flus and colds could run rampant among us. I don't know, though. They seem stronger than that. But if they make the time here a little more fun, I gueß I shouldn't complain. Plus I do get the Marinol. Those, though, like my serotonin reuptake inhibitors, are dispensed through the library because the librarian is also a registered pharmacist and the notary public. The ▶meds◀ are given out by the meß hall attendants. ▶A scoop of slop and a cup of pill, Jesus coffee and you're never ill◀: that was an Œther common saying. ▶Jesus coffee◀ was dirty water that had been stepped on. Not with chicory either. Who knows with what? Some local pond plants, probably. Tastes like ▶p◀. The Potemkin Food Service company, most likely.

In the meß hall during meals they only play instrumental jazz on the loudspeakers. They had too many problems with clowns who thought they were singers who'd start choking because they'd try singing while they were still ▶chewing◀ the ▶food◀.

So we'd hear Bill Watrous, Gene Krupa, Max Roach, Buddy Rich, Duke Ellington—just claßic instrumental jazz. I personally loved the Rich vs. Krupa battle of the drummers from the Jazz at the Philharmonic series from 1952.

Occasionally, on Saturday nights, we'd see old movies in the auditorium in the Academic Building. I loved the old ones with Krupa. I also especially enjoyed when we listened to the old vinyl recordings on ▶33 Thursdays◀. They were the only ones anyone could listen to on Earth back when the electricity went out for good in 2098. People began using old hand-cranked Victrolas again. The ether containing MP3s disappeared. The CD became an annoyingly sharp miniature Frisbee, for use only on disc driving and shooting ranges.

Oh, now I am thinking of disc golf. And that'd get me thinking about parkour.

It was almost impoßible here. The meß tent and the big tent were untreadable. The academic building had six floors. I could maybe leap onto the counselor's dorm from there, but it'd be a four-story drop. I'd have to be ready for that. From there, I'd have a helluva leap to the roof of Monty Hall, the nickname we all gave the central meeting hall, as I've already said. You've got to forgive an old guy like me if I repeat things every now and then, right? Anyway, I could do the dorms from there, maybe even the outhouses behind them, but why would I want to? The only reason would be if I spotted the mysterious Dorm E hidden behind them somewhere, back by the grazing pasture and stables.

No one could make the leap onto the Director's home, not from the dorms. One would have to fly acroß a thousand-foot-long park from the academic building. Really the only way to reach the Director's home would be from the top of the costume shop, but unfortunately, vice versa was also true.

I did find I could make the stables from D, but I spooked the horses, and our dorm, being nearust the horses, was immediately suspected of foul play. I dared not go up there again until the time came for escape! I was going to pretend this was an incarceration instead of a school! Then the objective would be to only *look* like I was learning while, in the meantime, I dug my metaphorical tunnel.

Sometimes we got to hear some hard bop—Mingus, Art Blakey, 'Trane, Bags—but no Miles except *Kind of Blue*—presumably it'd rile up the inmates, oops, I mean students, too much. Once you rile up students, good luck quieting them down. Hax the shining path. Hax Richard Nixon, whose plan to silence students with heroin succeeded far too well. You've heard the old Nixon joke, right? He was elected President for two terms and still couldn't get it down pat. Bah-dah bing! Bah-dah bang!

Actually, my Boring Old Jokes claß is rather amusing. We study humor from throughout history. *Canterbury Tales* are just the beginning. *Gargantua and Pantagruel. The Sorrows of Young Werther.* All those great comedies!

I once suggested we should have cows as well as horses, but the Œthers just about jumped me. <<Who do you think would have to wake at four a.m. to do the milking? Us! So shut up about getting a cow!>>

Someone else said that if I made us all get up to milk cows, he'd feed it my morning glory.

My Heavenly Blue is sad, but it flowered again today, so I think it is on the road to recovery. But just in case, I bought a second, larger Heavenly Blue with four flowers already on it. I also found a beautiful red morning glory called a ►Happy Hour Rose◄, so I bought a medium-sized one, maybe a foot and a half to two feet tall. It is flowering a dozen at a time, but the flowers, rather than being the size of American Eisenhower dollars or larger, are only the size of an old quarter, which we now call a ►testicle◄. I have no idea why anyone came up with that name for our currency. Maybe it was during the Great Feminist Uprising a hundred years ago. I wish I'd studied that period of Martian history better. And the early days after they'd moved Mars into almost the same orbital distance from the sun but on the Œther side of the sun and moving at the same speed. That was a feat of human engineering. And then construction of the atmosphere. Those were huge projects. No one alive nowadays would have a clue as to how to go about doing that again. Fortunately we have planetary thrusters to correct for the slight push and pull of apogee and perigee.

Some insisted on calling Mars ►Kokais◄ after it'd been moved. For most of us, though, it was still and always would be ►Mars◄, the most beloved God of all human►kind◄. Mars? God or candybar? *Three Musketeers*? Novel or candybar? Snickers, a mode of laughter taught during year two or candybar? Of all, humankind? No snacks are allowed in the theatre no matter what. They don't want someone in the front row chomping on pork rinds during an Italian sonnet being recited by lover to beloved.

Part Two: Poetry Night

Sonnet 23

A. I rhymey rhymey rhymey rhymey, eh?
B. I rhymey rhymey rhymey rhymey be.
C. Repeat B.
D. Repeat A.
E. Repeat A through D.
F. I rhymey rhymey rhymey rhymey, see?
G. Same thing do.
H. Same thing you.
I. Repeat F through you.

*

Sestina 23

Are	Soon	Going	School	To	You
you	are	soon	going	school	to
going	school	to	you	are	soon
to	you	are	soon	going	school
school	to	you	are	soon	going
soon?	going?	school?	to.	you.	are.

You school
to going
soon are.

*

Haiku 23

A fifth of good booze
can cost upwards of seven
bucks and five senses.

*

Villanelle 23

I repeat:
Where are we going
to meet?

I hate
that we're doing
this repeat

of what
was showing
when we met.

The TV set
focused on growing
by repeating

one's act
for a handful of coins
and a fistful of meat.

But we're gentler than that.
We'll just rejoin
and repeat
our first meeting.

*

Acrostic 23

A
conquering
reach
of
steamvent
tubeworms
in
columns.

*

I like Poetry Sundays, but many of the clowns refused to go and claimed that the poetry was <<just more Sunday churchifying.>> That they couldn't tell the difference between poetry and preaching was sad, although the best preaching is poetic. You might not like Jonathan Edwards's theology, but that man could turn a phrase! Cotton and Increase Mathers? They were better wordsmiths than Nathaniel Hawthorne. Well, maybe not. That was pretty heavy-handed allegorical stuff, wasn't it? The young good man loses his faith. Pretty obvious. Melville was much subtler.

*

Canzone 23

I ate a ricotta calzone.
It was heaven.
So I ate an Œther calzone,
and then an Œther calzone,
but instead of feeling well,
I ate a fourth ricotta calzone,
and after that, yet an Œther calzone
until I was alone.
And when I was alone,
I ate still an Œther calzone
until at last I had the strength
to muster up my strength.

A friend at the table prayed for strength,
too, for he had also had at least one calzone
too many, and eating was not his strength,
no, not his strength
at all, he began to recall while looking to heaven.
<<Oh, give me strength,>>
he haxed, and in so doing exhausted his strength
so much that, not feeling well,
he got up, went outside, and fell down the well.
It took all our strength
to pull him up—no one could have done it alone,
but we couldn't leave him down there alone.

Nor could anyone go down there alone
after him. The pulley hadn't the strength
for two, but he alone
could be pulled up alone—
he was the smallest and had had fewer calzones.
Suddenly the Œthers disappeared, and I was alone
at the top of the well with him down there alone.
I pulled him up with spit on my hands and a glance toward heaven—
to him it must have seemed like heaven.
At least he'd fallen down there alone
and emerged miraculously well
from our well.

We dried him off and gave him soup to make him well,
and we never left him alone.
We made sure he was well.
We made him well.
He began to regain his strength—

I gueß the soup really worked well,
and, well,
it was lighter than calzone.
It helped him forget the calzone
so well
that it almost took him to heaven—
that calzone from heaven!

Tycho Brahe snacks on calzone in heaven,
and up there they must make it well
because no one's come back from heaven
looking for calzone to bring up to heaven—
a special something for his ¢elgh alone
that tastes just like going to heaven—
no, it *is* heaven—
it is the strength
of life. It is the strength
of heaven,
here in a calzone,
a ricotta calzone.

If they have calzone
in heaven,
well,
that alone
gives me enough strength.

*

Ottava Rima 23

Hey,
Babe!
Hey,
Babe….
Hey,
Babe,
see?
See?

*

Pantoum 23

Give
a phantom

a live
plantain.

A phantom
opens the carton;
plaintain
jumps out like a cartoon

opening cartons,
looking for pants
to jump out like a cartoon
of friendly red velvet ants

looking for red pants
to crawl into,
Œther red velvet ants
wandering through.

To crawl into
red velvet can give
wandering through
new life.

*

23 husk skidoo.

Each poem was performed by some Œther clown. Everything eutelesteroic, semnoteroic and all points in between!

*

Rimas Dißolutas 23

I need
my rhyme
to just dißolve.

Why did
I write
with such resolve?

Who flayed
me with fright
just to involve

my word
and find insight,
salve

for the wound
of life?
Rather cleave

my head,
abandon all time,
halve

what I made
of mine,
delve

into being dead,
my strife.
Evolve!

*

Ruba'i 23

Fool, fool, a-hole, we'll throw you into the bay!
Wake up, already! It's the bowels of the day!
You'll drop like a stone and sink to the floor!
The goldfish will nibble your toes away!

This matter has become hard to ignore;
we refuse to waste our time anymore.
Resolve this for us the way that we choose,
or get up, get dreßed, and get out the door!

Go get us a couple of bottles of booze.
Let us drink to the sun and to the news
that Bugsy Moran no longer holds sway.
His death almost makes up for my old bruise.

*

Anglo-Saxon 23

I would not welcome a weary soldier—
I'd send the man to my sisters for sustenance,
take his sword and his scabbard, his armor and shield,

and hand them to him who has energy
to bear battleaxe and beat the enemy.
War does not wait for recovery while
death collects the downed. Damn the soldiers
who follow the flies onto fields of battle!
Exhaustion, expiration, no reason is so extreme
that a warrior should hide behind the horses!

*

Terza Rima 23

Back I am,
I know,
a sham

but not so wow
as to be the bop
when all must grow.

The baseball bat went, <<*Whap*!>>
as I hit a basket full of tulip bulbs
into the chamomile-besnarled field out back.

I was reminded of hitting crab apples and pebbles
with a yellow Louisville Slugger,
which looked like a pencil with gnaw marks and slobber.

I had meant for my life to have been so much bigger,
but if I hit one past the post, it's still a double-bagger!

*

Curtal Sonnet 23

Curt pulled out his prison hairs with an old tweezer.
He was short-tempered and quick to anger.
Before he turned eleven he had killed
three geese, five goslings, and an old geezer
who lived in a drainpipe labeled <<danger.>>
The man made no sound while his blood was spilled:

his home had hardened him and closed his eyes.
Curt wanted to rob him but saw the ranger,
and by then the old man's heart had been stilled.
Curt failed to feign innocence with a sob and a sigh:

nil willed.

*

Rime Royal 23

The royal rim of the royal toilet
was dirty beyond any comprehension.
The only one who used it was Violet,
who never had more than hypertension.
But this spun her around in a new direction—
an intruder had besmirched her commode.
She took off after him and found the toad.

Boy, did her anger get her stomaching roiling!
She remembered her Latin declensions,
and unclenched her fist, her temper boiling.
The toad, her brŒther, kept his pretensions
but suddenly ran out of invention.
She said at least he hadn't lightened his load.
When he laughed, that was the end of the road.

At the risk of having this story spoiled,
I need to intrude—I forgot to mention
that royal children can be too violent
and to their keepers can seem disloyal,
a problem for the parents of the royal
children who think that everything is owed
to them from birth. The ungrateful seed sowed.

For this stuff their ancestors never toiled.
All they'd ever wanted were poßeßions.
For this the children's cobras never coiled.
Their rubies made no longer an impreßion.
Had she slain her brŒther as per fashion
her heroism would have been renowned.
Instead, she quipped that he had not been found.

*

Rondeau 23

<<►Clever◄ is not the word,>>
she said. <<It's absurd
to think that he got away with it.
How did he ever fit

through the window unheard?>>

He'd broken her giant glaß bird,
a triple-sized hand-blown blue mallard,
and her antique wicker knitting basket.
<<Clever>> is not

the word I would use for the turd
who broke her stuff no matter how it occurred.
He just broke things and split.
No theft—he just ✹hit✹
her home and slashed the sweater she'd knit.
No, clever he's not.

*

Where are the short poems? Do they have any caffeine? Coffee at least?

Ah, there it is! No sugar? No creamer? Yuck, this is salty and burnt. They must not want busineß, apparently.

*

Rondel 23

The world changed when Zappa played the synclavier.
Nothing's been the same ever since.
Three bucks for a box of mints
means that you have nothing to fear,

at least not anywhere around here.
No one's dropping any hints,
but the world changed when Zappa played the synclavier.
Nothing's been the same ever since.

Three bucks for a local beer?
Ah, price tags just give me the squints—
can't see through these aquatints.
I was hoping that you'd come near,
but the world changed when Zappa played the synclavier.

*

Zappa? That perked me up.

*

Chant Royal 23

If
you
sniff
too
much
crutch
you'll
Drool
in
school,
and never win.

Sift
dough.
Lift
enough—
such
touch
is cruel.
Spool,
pin,
cool,
and never win.

Shift
onto
your left
shoe.
Fetch
the couch.
Duel
in pool.
Sin.
Eat gruel,
and never win.

A skiff
would show
the rift
we know.
Watch
and catch
who'll
mewl
in the din
over fuel
and never win.

Miffed,
though
bereft
now,
unlatch
and switch
the jewel.
Rule
your kin.
Be a tool,
and never win.

Pull
the wool
again,
fool,
and never win.

*

Blank Verse 23

When Richard Hell sang ▶Blank Generation◀.
he gave us a new way of not thinking.
When Zeppelin hit 130db,
they gave us a new way of not talking.
The individual is isolate.
When the top percent took all our wealth away,
and put it in their individual bank accounts,
they left no one the funds to go outside.
At least they let us hover in hovels,
and stare at our artleß, bookleß, boring walls.
But those of us who had an extra dime
could pay per view for glimpses of their greed.

*

Alcaic Stanza 23

Yes, you there! Stop! Oh, gratefully, gratefully,
but what is that? Some furniture? Furnisher,
I don't believe how unrelenting
all of this stuff about truth is being.

*

My brain is Jello now. My legs are cramping. I'm thirsty. I'm hungry. I have to go to the bathroom. How much more?

*

Cinquain 23

The car
is on the fritz.
It only goes so far
and then the engine up and quits.
The pits!

*

Carpe Diem 23

You ain't old. Yet.
You ain't ugly. Yet.
You gotta be with someone someday.
Ain't nobody want old and ugly.
So whatcha waiting' for?
Mr. Clean to come ridin' up like some
Ajax white knight on horseback
to rescue you from your sad life?
Hahahaha. That ain't gonna happen
So you might as well give it up sometime.
So why not now?
I'm a sensitive, caring guy.
I promise I'll be gentle.
So, come on, give me a little.
Yeah, like that.
That's much better.

*

Limerick 23

I acquired a new app for my phone
that would let me select a ringtone.
From among all the screams
of old Hollywood scenes
I chose Garbo's <<Just leave me alone!>>

*

Kyrielle 23

Your mom was curious as hell
and haxed why you weren’t looking well.
I lied and told her you were drunk.
<<Again?>> she haxed. <<That lousy punk.>>

<<It’s time,>> she said, <<to intervene,>>
which is when I confeßed you’re clean
and had sworn off all booze and junk.
<<Again?>> she haxed. <<That lousy punk.>>

I told her she was being cruel
and that she was a meddling fool—
her suppositions stunk like skunk.
<<Again?>> she haxed, her ego sunk.

*

That’s it, finally. Ow, my back is sore. Stupid folding theatre seating. No lumbar support.

23 poems, eh. No Psalm 23, or was Hemingway’s version powerful enough? The Lord be my witneß, I couldn’t have made it 23 more seconds. Two ►point◄ three would have been a stretch. I shall not want to sit through poetry night again for a long time. Or I’ll have to move every 23 minutes. I do a very poor impersonation of a bump on a log.

Part Three: Asemic Rocks

I found out today that, supposedly, beyond the grazing pasture, lay a rusty, overgrown nine-hole course for disc golf, rumored to be the oldest course on Mars. You'd have to throw hyzers and anhyzers around the geysers. Plus the area was swampy, so you'd need Hydras so your discs would float.

I've never seen terrain that looks like that, so I doubt it exists. God, the bugs are going to be brutal. I'll have to get some bug spray.

I read that the little yellowish-white spots on the leaves of the little Heavenly Blue, which is dying, could have been from spider mites, but I see none on there. Perhaps the infection paßed. The new morning glories—the large Heavenly Blue and the Happy Hour Rose—are both doing extraordinarily well. The Heavenly Blue is droopy, but revives after watering. We have had bad weather, and the plant seems exceptionally thirsty.

Right now I'm listening to ▶Post Toastee◀ by Tommy Bolin. He really was an amazing force with a guitar. A conjurer.

Someone else told me everything here has to have a connection to Frank Zappa. I told him no problem. Bolin played with Billy Cobham, who played with George Duke, who played with Zappa. All musicians are within six steps of Zappa.

I also heard this place is actually trying to buy an old synclavier and modernize it a bit. What were they, 5¼" diskettes those things used? Good luck finding those.

I've been doing pies all week in claß. It's terrible. I have had shaving cream up my nostrils so far it came out my throat. That's nasty. It's better that than make-up, though. They haven't preßed that ißue. Yet.

I have a wizard's hat I wear, and an old purple sweater, unbuttoned, over a tie-dye t-shirt. I am Twirly, so named by Twirly's number one fan, Fin. I revisit the Studebaker Hawk Dancing Leßon and Cosmic Prayer for Guidance. That is my first ▶schtick◀. Today they finished it with a pie. I think that really cheapened it, though. But that might have been the point of the leßon. At least when I said so, I was not made to don the dunce cap. The dunce cap was made too dun. It would have been better in purple, like my wizard's hat. At least pies are almost done. Then we move on to banana skins. I'm not very fond of falling, I have to say. That will be an Œther claß that will be a challenge. I'll just charge in there, slap my wizard's hat on the desk, say, <<Go ahead. Give me the dunce cap. Gooby dooby fluffy.>>

Meanwhile, I'm going to figure out a way to see that—no, better—I'm going to *play* that overgrown course. Maybe we can fix it up and add disc golf to the school activities.

Trick shots, maybe? But trick shots are such a small part of the disc golf. How would I justify it? I'll figure it out. Meanwhile I'll just do as everyone else does and be inconspicuous. I'll wear camouflage but not make-up. Camouflage is best for being on the brink.

Don't you think?

Do I?

It's ¢elgh-propelled, and I couldn't tell you why or how or when. At least until you do it again.

Nettie would come for me if I sent her more asemic texts. I had heard back from the one, but it may have gotten lost in transit. The postal service was far leß reliable than carrier pigeons, but the pigeons couldn't fly to Earth, which is where I heard she was.

I think Frau Catherine Müller had something to do with it. Tales from the Œther Geneva—she talked to the Martians back in the 1890s. And that was long before it was moved into our orbit. Now we can just drop a meßage, and Earth will pick it up when they come around to it.

Nettie was trying to decipher the gloßolalia of the asemic texts, and Müller was the point of origin for deciphering Martian texts.

I began searching the library—not the bookshelves, but everywhere else, behind desks, in boxes, behind the dropped ceiling panels—looking for old papers, ink, and a pen. If I could send her one that was on old, yellowed, crisp paper—I could duplicate that with uric acid if neceßary—with old ink—squid-based would be best—and written with a rusty-nibbed quill while listening to Rusty Day.... And Chris Youlden. Listen to how Youlden's voice takes sharp right and left turns throughout ♪Honey Bee♫ on *Getting to the Point*.

►Rustrictions◄. Man, Savoy Brown and Cactus together would have been a fantastic twin-bill. Listen to the amazing guitarwork on ►The Incredible Gnome Meets Jaxman◄. It severs my spine to hear—it's that good. Simmonds destroys the notion of a twelve-tone octave. He finds dozens of notes in between. And then in between those. And again. Zeno's paradox. No one will ever be able to count all the different notes Kim Simmonds has played. Whatever you'd report, I'd divide in half again. That sort of thing. Analog holds more music than digital because analog carries the whole wave and digital only holds fragments of the whole; each round edge is flattened and squared off.

Eventually I find a page out of a 1900 unabridged Webster's—a plain yellowed green endpaper. It's good for the purpose!

In the receiving room by the dock where the deliveries come for not only the library but the whole school, in an old box of supplies, probably dozens of years old, I found a pen with a good nib, but the handle was plastic, not a quill. It may have been an artist's nib, but so what? It'll do. And it'll seem the oldest one, so she will definitely be inter-rusted and will come here to trace the path.

I have to be ready for Nettie.

I love the sound of that. It'll be great to see her again after being in here with these gristly bears.

Distilled water night for me if I complain too much. Shhh! I don't want them to hear me.

I think that somebody is stealing my stuff. I can't even find my handkerchief.

<<Why would anyone steal a handkerchief?>> haxed a friend, astutely.

<<Obviously,>> I replied, <<because they are becoming rare and therefore valuable. One never sees anyone using one anymore.>>

<<No, no, that's true. It's all sleeves and fingers, sucking and spitting, or blowing it out. Subtlety is not their forté.>>

Found it! It was in my Œther pocket, where I never keep it. How odd. Maybe someone put it there. No, obviously not—I'm just kidding. Who told you about my being paranoid? Lubjec? Is he back?

Clown time! Here's… Twirly! Oh, god, I'm on.

*

Alpha is like alfalfa to Alf, who uses Agfa for foreign films when he snaps! He pulls the film back out of its casing, exposing it to all the horrors of the world. The film so quickly captures images of anguish and debasement that it blanches and blanks its ¢elgh. In the basement, free from its casement, the film begins to cobra for a charming snake oil salesman with an angle. A sax on the stereo writhes like a serpent that winds its way through orchestral pits. If it bŒthers them, sack their butts! They drip their spit all over the place. Disgusting. How strong a gale it must be to keep bees inside their combs and babes inside their wombs.

Where will we end up? The wind is whisking us away to where we will wonder whence we once came.

*

Silence, so I threw down a banana peel, slipped on it, and allowed the clown ambulance service to come and take me off stage, after which I stood up, and then the ambulance people took off for their costume changes for the next scene.

One of my teachers said I <<clownfounded>> the audience and praised me for it. But everyone stayed away. I must have touched a nerve. I had bullfrogs on my mind.

Hey, gurus can be petty, thoughtleß, cruel, and illiterate, the four unforgiveable sins.

Forget Petty. He falsely took credit for writing Buddy Holly's songs.

Thoughtleßneß is nirvana—freedom from everything. How can that be bad?

Cruel and illiterate I'll grant you.

Krill and alliteration not so much.

Creole and a little ration of pepper to pepperpot notwithstanding, people singing are saying something with greater depth than people who are merely listening. But who-learns-what is up to them.

Crayon on a Lit Horatio's last papers to report withstanding people singing with not enough depth to make great.

The Chairman sang a hundred feelings. The CrⒶß sang only one song in slight variations. They could do anger. So could he, but Swank was so much more than just that.

So take your sulfarsphenamine out of my face—I won't be needing it. Man, I could have been with Nettie. I really blew it. How could I have had thought she was a guy? I must be stupid.

Well, at least I'm not gullible.

Nor albatroßible. Look, every damn albatroß! I catch it and, look, here, the tab. It's been tagged—they all have. They all say ⏳Samuel Taylor Coleridge⏳. To look for an Œther kind would be like looking for a daffodil not stamped ⏳William Wordsworth⏳ along its stem. And to think, zeugmas are forbidden! They, supposedly, are not thought funny, at least not here.

The old comedy team of Coleridge and Wordsworth was long ago replaced by Abbott and Costello, and their facility with language was obvious in ►Who's on First?◄.

The closest I came was a routine I wrote for claß. When I was young, on one of my first jobs, I was haxed to use a robot to clean the swimming pool. When I pulled it out of the pool, it slammed down on my right big toe and broke it. I ignored the break, so it healed badly. I now have a large hump on the knuckle on my toe. Thus I need two different shoe sizes—my right foot is half a size larger than my left. This makes shoe shopping difficult. I normally swap the right shoes from two boxes because someone else, I'm sure, needs an 11 right and an 11½ left. Some stores, though, check to see that the sizes match.

<<This one is the wrong size, sir.>>

<<No, it's right. I need the right larger.>>

<<But you can't remove shoes from one box and put them in an Œther.>>

<<Why not? They're the same type, same price.>>

<<But different sizes.>>

<<So? What? Do you discriminate against asymmetrical customers? The newspapers might be inter-rusted in knowing that and telling consumers to stay away. No one would buy your shoes. Accommodate the customer. That's the second rule of retail. Right after ▶You can't sell from an empty apple cart◀.>> And then, everything in the store works better when the employees are happy.

Not to drop names, but look at Patagonia. They do it right.

And customers would rather shop where employees are happy. Not intrusive. Happy. Polite. They enjoy interactions with Œthers over the exchange of money for any number of nautically lost fißion detector valve gauges.

I know. My car needed two those replaced last month. They were thinking of replacing them with crystal ones instead.

You wouldn't want anyone to get a baseball in the face, would you? Of course not.

So no work-related stuff. Or do you have something against Œthers' having private lives? I have known people who would have sold all rights to private lives to the first corporation that came around with a big wad.

<<Asymmetical? Be symmetrical!>>

Nothing. Time to do the wizard dunce cap yet again.

Oh, opuscule! What inquiline horror prohibits humor from inhabiting heaven?

*

<<Jabbit, you are a lousy student,>> my teacher named Ganzslow proclaimed.

<<Du Jabot,>> I muttered.

<<What?>> yelled the wild-haired wild-eyed Ganzslow from behind his podium. My claßmates all looked at me with fear for what was going to happen to me. <<Are you talking back to me?>>

I figured I needed humor to defuse him, so I tried this: <<▶Jabbit◀ rhymes with ▶rabbit◀. Rabbits dine to their hearts' content and then screw all the time. While here, I have done neither, thus I am no rabbit. So it would not be accurate to call me ▶Jabbit◀. It's ▶du Jabot◀, which rhymes with ▶you the ho◀.>>

My claßmates laughed. Ganzslow did not. I was back in the corner and donning the cap of Duns Scotus again. Out of the corner of my eye, though, I saw Ganzslow smile. The worse I did, the better I was. So I stood up and urinated into the corner. That got me sent back to my room.

My Heavenly Blue was doing very well—about twelve bloßoms were blooming. My Happy Hour Rose morning glories were also muscling up the balcony's iron railing. They were beginning to intertwine. Were they dancing or fighting? I decided to let them figure that out for their ¢elghs. I like the little red flutes and big blues—maybe they'll produce a hybrid of medium purple ones.

This place is quite strange. Very confining. I went freerunning again—more playful than parkour—and found I was able to go from the unoccupied library (clowns don't read) to my dorm room undetected. I am not entirely sure my ¢elgh if I am actually making these trips or just astral projecting. The medication here is pretty strong. And it's been constipating me. Sometimes I sit for hours and just read and wait. Coffee doesn't help. And they won't give me basic meds like antacid or aspirin. The only stuff they deal in is all heavy duty. No mellow yellow lettuce opium salvia nutmeg. This was thorazine heavy. They just didn't know what a tolerance many of us have developed. At first we were stupid. Later we learned how to pretend to be stupid before they upped our antes. My death on the crapper would be an Œther reason to call me Elvis. People do have heart attacks from trying to force the b.m. I admit I have traveled while sitting there. I find it a good launching pad for astral projecting. That and my bed.

I have to get out of here. But I do want to see that mysteriouis Ur-golf course in the Geyser Swamp.

I was told by Oleo one day, when I haxed him what was beyond Dorm E, which he first denied knowing about, but then I let him know I knew, that the swamp was cold but the geysers were hot, which in conflict formed a steam fog.

What a place for a disc golf course! Brilliant! Of course thereafter I didn't mention to anyone else that I knew anything about it.

I also haxed Oleo about what was southeast of the stables, what was south of the big tent, what was southwest of the pond, west of the director's home, northwest of the Academic Building, and north of the Counselors' Dorm, Monty Hall, and Dorm A. I haxed him about the type of fish in the pond, and about the vegetation in the pasture. I covered up the real reason with plenty of dumb ones.

Koifur. A type of carp with hair instead of fur.

Switchblade fibergraß. Puts microcuts on the horses' tongues so that they get so mad they buck like broncos, which makes them more entertaining under the big tent, I suppose.

According to Oleo, we have swamp to the east of us and forust all the way around on the Œther sides. No roads lead in or out—only the helipad.

<<You don't ever want to go over to Dorm E,>> he said. <<The Orator is out there and doing something weird.>>

<<Like what?>>

<<Don't know, but I don't trust him.>>

<<What do you know about Profeßor Ganzslow?>>

<<He's tight with the Orator—I know that. I've seen them together many times.>>

<<Are they….>>

<<A couple? No, I don't think so. Heck, I'm pretty sure they're chemically castrating us with those meds. That or they're putting tons of saltpeter in our food.>>

<<Gun powder?>>

<<No—sex drive suppreßant. The administration doesn't want us getting all randy.>>

<<I thought Ganzslow was part of the administration.>>

<<No—he's just faculty. From what I hear, they treat faculty worse than they treat us. They make Ganzslow live in Dorm E as well. That can't be pleasant.>>

<<For him or for the Œthers?>>

<<Exactly. *Pares cum paribus facillime congregantur.*>>

I haxed Oleo if he know of anything available here on campus that could help me with my digestive difficulty.

<<Every room in every building has posted an evacuation map.>>

<<What a clown,>> I muttered.

<<Yep,>> he replied. <<Actually, I had the same problem when I got here, but then I began eating a stick of margarine in the meß hall every day. That helped, but it also got me my nickname. I could hax about getting a stick for you, too.>>

<<Um, no thanks. I don't think I could stomach that much hydrogenated vegetable oil at one time.>>

<<Some of them taste just like butter….>>

<<No, thanks. Thanks anyway.>>

<<Okay, but let me know if you change your mind. Neceßity and all that….>>

Well, at least Oleo confirmed what I'd heard about the area beyond the northeast corner of the grazing pasture, beyond Dorm E.

No parkour path led there. Running through open pasture is more *Wuthering Heights* than parkour. Good grief! I really wanted to see that disc golf course. But if I ran through the open field, certainly someone in Dorm E, which was filled with students who were being expelled, Juggalos, the Orator, and Ganzslow, would spot me. I couldn't risk it. I had to find out how dangerous they really were, or if this was just a case of nonconformists being scapegoated, which, of course, happens everywhere all the time!

And running through switchblade fibergraß—if that's true—doesn't sound like fun. But there's a festival coming up. The Koifur Roast. They ▶harvest◀ a few dozen or so koifur and have a huge roast. No matter how many you harvest, so long as it's only on that day, you may keep and freeze or salt or can or soak in lye and bury underground however many you want. Me? I'll be gone. Everyone's obseßing over the fish for that festival. I'll be on the exact opposite side of camp. The pond is southwest. I'm heading into the swamp. I'd better start getting stuff together. Insect repellent. Heavy duty insect repellent. Most likely careßmosquitoes swarm around here, too. I never studied the bugs. Never thought to. What about Œther stuff? Snakes? Gators? Can you imagine careßmagators? Critters weren't my specialty. Writing. That energizes me. That flapjacks my katzenjammers. Words are such beautiful tools. We are so fortunate, we writers, all of us, to have these beautiful tools with which to communicate, decorate, invigorate, infuriate, whatever. The choices are endleß. You just stare into the gaping maw of the abyß and pull them out, one after the Œther. That's an old image—not mine—but I like it very much. Okay, Charles, on with it already. That's an expreßion. Charles doesn't really exist except, of course, the speaker, who was speaking to his ¢elgh, Charles Bukowski on his Tacoma spoken word CD. The expreßion became used by people for talking to their ¢elghs. We have a little Charles Bukowski in us all. Wait a second—isn't that what Manson said to Tom Snyder about his ¢elgh? I gueß talking to your ¢elgh's only as healthy as you let it be. I've told this story before, but on Earth, I once saw on the street of the city a woman gesturing wildly and yelling very loudly. I aßumed she was insane or something, so I walked around her with fear and trepidation. And I noticed something. She had a dog's tooth, I think folks call them, these little phones that you nail into your earhole till they pierce your brain. That's why I don't use them. But anyway, she was just on the phone. But now I realize also that the line between cell phone usage and insanity is very thin.

Do fish live in the swamp? I should take a rod and reel, like everyone else, and then go out to the swamp from the southeast pasture. The folks in Dorm E won't see me if I come up on the swamp from the south. People will see me going towards the pond, and then, when I'm alone, I cut back east and back north. That's going to work. I should catch a fish in the swamp if I see any. I can tell anyone who sees me that I got turned around and thought the swamp was the pond. No, better not mention the swamp. They'll destroy that golf course. Better not catch a fish unleß it's a koifur. They'd freak if I caught something else, because I'd have to pretend it was in the pond, and then they'd suspect infestation by a foreign species. They'd have to net the whole pond. Or rather, they'd make us do it, and I'd get blamed. No, I'm not falling for that old trap. That claptrap. That's what *he* said. Boom chakalaka! I have no inter-rust in eating those hideous creatures anyway. Yuck. I mean the koifurs.

Oh. Hahahaha.

I spent some time looking at books in the library. I was researching swamps. One risk I found was infestation by leeches, who apparently love swamp water. Careßmaleeches. God knows what strange Martian mutation they had taken. Probably they were no longer anything like the Earth creatures they had evolved from. Actually, all these creatures were originally from Earth, most of them finding their ways here accidentally. After Mars had been hydrated to the point that it could generate its own rain, creatures were introduced by scientists inter-rusted in establishing sustainable ecosystems. They argued that we needed all critters top to bottom, even mosquitoes. But some got here as hidden pets that then escaped, pests hiding in ship hulls, parasites, and so on.

I'd need some fine stainleß steel mesh for my leggings and body so that leeches would not be a problem. But trudging through a swamp while wearing heavy steel seemed a slow slog. Earth used to have fibers made of petroleum that were outrageously strong yet lightweight. However, petroleum supplies became far too depleted to continue in their manufacture.

The school signed me up for a claß with Poetry Clown next semester. Oh, no. I'd have to listen to him every day. Well, he might be a better teacher than he is a poet. Actually, how would I even know if his poems were any good? They fly past my ears so fast I can't catch them. I prefer reading. If I'm going to listen, then give me music. I suppose a couple of his poems did have a musical quality to them. Those I liked best.

Fortunately the Koifur Roast happens before claßes begin. I'm going to do the course once and then just disappear through the swamp. There can't be more than a couple of miles of it, or it'd be more famous. Undoubtedly I will find solid land beyond it. From there I will—I don't know. Go back to Mars Condatis? No way. They'd bring me back here. I need to find a way back to Earth, where I know how to hide.

*

The semester was ending, and Ganzslow seemed to relax a bit.

<<Jabbit!>> he yelled one day.

<<I'm Twirly,>> I announced, and jumped to my feed and did my Twirly dance.

<<Sit down,>>he said. I headed toward the corner.

<<No. Sit at your desk. I think you get the point now.>>

*

Nettie never responded to the sheet of asemic writing I sent her. I figured I'd better try again.

This was a little rougher, I think, than the Œthers; it was a little more violent and little more erratic. That should get her attention.

This time I couldn't trust it to the mail. The last one probably never arrived. So I took the new asemic piece, made photocopies, grabbed a dozen clown helium balloons, and sent them up at night with Nettie's addreß and my signature on the back of the asemic page. My signature is illegible, but she'd know it. One of those twelve should reach her. I dared not send more lest the loß of balloons be obvious. Arrr…. I feel like a character in a Robert Louis Stevenson novel all of a sudden. David Balfour. Yeah, that's me.

Mr. Hyde? Haha! You are very funny. You should be here instead of me. Yeah, you could be Bendy Overy the Clown. I'll introduce you to Kicky Aßy the Clown. His hero is Pogo the Clown. You won't want to know him. He's in Dorm E.

Ow! This hurts. You need to listen to Screamin' Jay Hawkins's ▶Constipation Blues◀ to really understand my pain. I'm drinking water all day long, but that's not helping.

I'm about ready to give up and call Oleo for help scoring a stick of margarine, but the thought of that makes me gag. Meanwhile, I've got rocks in my gut. When I can let one go, it tears me up, and I bleed. Ow. Damn! Who can write with this going on?

I walk around doubled over.

Mr. Hyde, again? Oh, you are *so* kind. Excuse me—I've got to go.

Part Four: The Koifur Roast

The way they promoted it, you'd think the Koifur Roast was Thanksgiving, Oktoberfest, and Cinco de Mayo all wrapped up in one giant Mardi Gras Carnival! All it was was catching fish in a pond, bonking them on the head, skinning them and cooking them. Ow, wow! Give me some dynamite, and I can catch all the fish really fast!

I did get my ¢elgh a rod-and-reel that was in the back of the basement of the dorm, totally forgotten and cobwebbed over. It was still in working condition, but the reel looked rusty. So what? I only needed to look like I was going to fish.

I knew the faculty kept their rods-and-reels in the costume shop by the pond, so I needed to get in there one night and tangle up some of the reels—I would really snarl them. That would keep faculty busy with their tangles while I made my exit.

The plan was shaping up nicely. The only problem was still my problem with ♪breaking up rocks in the hot sun♫. It was like paßing ostrich eggs. Jaggedy spiked broken glaß ostrich eggs.

Just in case, I haxed a couple of clowns in the kitchen if eating koifur had any sort of laxative effect. They said the opposite was true.

I definitely needed out. They were torturing us very subtly. They wanted us to squirm. Well, not this frog prince. I just leapt into a completely different pond, yeah, that's it. At least in the olden days....

Oh, the medication again. Nothing to do but clench teeth and grimace.

*

Nineteen bloßoms this morning! I'm taking the plant with me. I can untangle most of it, but may need to cut it a little, but then I'll set it free in the swamp. The plant drinks more than I do, so a swamp should be good. Of course, I have it in a very light soil. The little Heavenly Blue I'd given up for dead is now just beginning to thrive. I think it had to adapt to its heavier potting soil. I moved its pot next to its big cousin to encourage it. I'll need to set them both free, and the Happy Hour Rose, too. I'm just afraid to move the little one again. It's so hard on its system. I may just have to leave the little one behind with a note and watering instructions. I hate splitting them up this way, though. I'd like them to stay together. We'll see what we can do.

There's still a stopper at the bottom of the ocean. If I could only pull it open!

<<Stop!>> exclaims the stopper! He's the stopping copper! His friend in the sky is the

stopping 'copter! And he believes in stopping members of the Coptic Church from abandoning monophysitism! But nobody hears him at the bottom of the ocean.

Actually, the stopper's in the swamp. Reach in there and pull it—never mind the careßmaleeches on your arms. They're the size of Pomeranians and can drain your body in five minutes.

I need a hazmat suit! Made from an indestructible space-age polymer! And then, come on , baby, light my fire. Yea, no chance. I'll be in Soggy Town with my discs. My Hydra I lost somewhere. My Sharpshooter floats, but its color is brackish brown, which is probably the swamp's color as well. The Hydra was yellow. But I should be able to find some Œther discs hanging around—heck, these are college dorms, right? Whee ha! I'll find a box in the basement, I'm sure. Previous dormsters left loads of crap down there.

A hazmat suit won't give me enough mobility to throw the disc well. Maybe a wet suit. Where would I find a wet suit?

The costume shop! I should be able to find some wet suits there because some of the advanced students practice clown water ballet in the pond. Dives always precede their ballet practices to make sure no dangerous obstacles have fallen into the pond. They remove branches and Œther windfall, scoop out any algae, watch for invasive species such as snails and amphibians, and so on. Definitely I can find a wet suit there.

That night, I think, I was astral projecting as a traceur. As fancy as freerunners are, I don't think they astral project, but traceurs are a special breed. I found the fishing gear, the wet suit, everything. And I put a hurting on all the Œther gear that was halfway nice—knots, cut lines, mißing hooks. I took a few of the choices flies and burnt them off their hooks. I needed time. at least a half hour if the course only had nine holes, which I suspected it, as the first, would have. But I had to be ready for eighteen or twenty-seven, even, like the park in Mokena, Illinois—the Oaks. A beautiful course.

*

I woke up in the morning as usual, but this day I remembered my rod-and-reel and began walking towards the pond.

<<Hello, Frosty. Hello, Ruby.>> The clowns were all out and heading towards the pond. It was surreal-looking, like a parade of zombies. But I fit in perfectly with my fishing gear. I'd had an omen upon awakening that today would be a great day, not because of the Koifur Roast, but because my larger Heavenly Blue this morning had on it twenty-three beautiful blue bloßoms.

Twenty-three? Skidoo! Let's skedaddle! As I marched down toward the pond, I remembered a children's story about Skidoo and Skedaddle. I told my ¢elgh the story aloud for the benefit of the clowns who were walking near.

Part Five: Skidoo, Skedaddle, Muscatel and Gummo

When the great circuses of Europe collapsed, clowns everywhere lost their jobs.

At the Zirkus Manfred, the rooster-dancing Skidoo was told his days had come to an end. He could rooster-dance better than Mick Jagger and had an incredible routine that went along with Big Mama Thornton's version of Willie Dixon's ▶Little Red Rooster◀. When he was told to update it to a contemporary version by some corporate pitch-corrected pop star, he refused. <<You have to respect the music, even if you're a clown,>> he said, as he walked away from his old circus job. He knew his cousin at Zirkus Bremen could get him a job at any time, so screw the Zirkus Manfred. His rooster dance had once been the talk of Berlin, and he had appeared on page one of *Die Berliner Zeit*'s ▶Unterhaltungen◀ entertainment section.

The Zirkus Manfred's accountant had told Skidoo that Skidoo's refusal to do the ▶Dizzy Knee◀ version of ▶Little Red Rooster◀ rather than Big Mama's version implied forfeiture of all savings and pensions. Skidoo didn't care—he'd trust the open road over his old boßes any day. Skidoo was going to be a star in Bremen. His cousin had said Skidoo would be so popular that his name would resound down every cobblestone way. Zirkus Manfred had recently only been playing small towns. Its glory days in Berlin were long behind it, and it was no longer a premier circus. The time had come to move on and move up.

Skidoo tied his few belongings up in a polka dot bandanna and attached it to the end of a sturdy bindle stick that could double for a walking stick or a weapon, if neceßary. He put the stick over his shoulder, dangling the bindle behind his ¢elgh, and he headed out on the road to Bremen.

A half day's worth of walking later, he began to feel a little peckish. He had a craving for some grains. He had come acroß a beautiful field of rye, and raw rye was just fine for Skidoo. He walked out into the field some so he wouldn't be so noticeable from the road even though the road had been the one leß taken all day except for an old lady driving a Model-T with a ⧖ Robert Frost for President⧖ bumper sticker. She looked right at Skidoo but pretended not to see him. She was dark-haired, rather pretty. Her glaßes weren't anything but practical, but so what? Too bad she was so stand-offish, like Miles Standish's Priscilla Mullins, the first American bitch, who was famous for playing Miles against his roommate, John Alden, whom she egged on by saying, famously, <<Why don't you speak for your ¢elgh, John?>>

No, she didn't slow down for Skidoo. That's fine. He had his rye, and he was in no hurry. He built his ¢elgh a little clearing by stepping on and eating all the rye in his vicinity, enough so that he could sit down comfortably and not be seen at all. He closed his eyes and began to doze a little.

Just then something grabbed his leg, and he jumped. He almost soiled his ¢elgh. Before him lay a sawed-in-half donkey, and it was alive! Skidoo let out a yell that would drop your socks.

Skidoo began to feel sick, but then he shook off the grip of the donkey and saw that no blood was anywhere evident.

<<Ow!>> exclaimed the donkey.

<<Ow what?>> replied Skidoo. <<You're not hurt.>>

<<You hurt my hand.>>

<<Donkeys don't have hands.>>

<<What? I'm not a donkey,>> said the half-a-donkey. <<I'm the front half of a pantomime donkey, and I've lost my tail end.>>

<<What? Here in this field?>> Skidoo wondered what one called an aß without an aß and began laughing.

<<It's not funny. I was once part of the greatest pantomime donkey in the history of the Magyar Cirkusz. But my partner Enver quit on me.>>

<<What happened?>>

<<He took over as the front end of the circus's pantomime horse when Colosto, who had been the front of the horse, died.>>

<<Why didn't the back end of the horse take over the front?>>

<<Bagnini? He's hunchbacked. He can't do a front end. And he didn't want to do the donkey—I haxed him.>>

<<And no one else would be your back end?>>

<<No. So the Cirkusz fired me. They said they had no use for a half-aßed act in their show. Those were their exact words. 'Half-aßed' indeed! Now I wouldn't go back there if they begged me.>>

<<And they wouldn't keep you on as a regular clown?>>

<<What? After having been the front end of the greatest pantomime donkey in Magyar Cirkusz's history? I couldn't lower my ¢elgh to that level.>>

<<Well, what's your name?>>

<<I am Skedaddle.>>

<<Well, Skedaddle, I'm Skidoo. And I'm formerly of the Zirkus Manfred, who, also foolishly, let me go. They tried to change my rooster dance, for which I am world famous. I would not change it for them, so I decided to accept an offer from my cousin in the Bremen Zirkus.>>

<<Do you think they might have need of a pantomime donkey?>>

<<Oh, I am sure they could find room for you. My cousin says the Bremen Zirkus is growing and expanding rapidly because all of the nearby Œther circuses' going under. The Bremen Zirkus tours all of northern Europe now.>>

<<Excellent. Then I'm coming with you.>>

<<Good. I could use a traveling companion. Do you have any money?>>

<<Yes, some.>>

<<Then let's stop in the next town for supper.>>

And so they decided to leave the field and continue on to the next town.

As they walked, they talked. They recounted their lives' adventures. Skedaddle revealed that he'd been having dreams of singing. He wanted to be the first singing pantomime donkey, and he showed off his skill at braying. In response, Skidoo crowed counterpoint. Together they made enough noise to scare the bears back to Berlin. And the wolves in the woods began to howl in harmony. They were ▶Moanin' at Midnight◀, and Skidoo expected to hear harp music any second—he was that afraid.

<<Wait! I know who that is,>> said Skedaddle, and already Skidoo was glad to have met him. <<It's Gummo.>>

<<The giant?>>

<<Yes, from Cirkus Benneweis in the Tivoli Gardens.>>

<<Really? I thought he was down in Italy.>>

<<No, not for a long time. You're thinking of Cirkus Milano. No, Gummo would have been too gentle for them, no matter how imposing a figure he cut. They would have wanted him as mean and unscrupulous as an Inter Milan player. But Gummo only howls when he wants to, and he refuses to dive. He was one of those rare men for whom stones roll, yard birds rock, and all the rust falls in place, the stones having rolled uphill,

stopped only by the—>>

<<The what?>>

<<The foot of fate.>>

<<The what?>>

<<The giant stomped them, so they fired him.>>

<<I wouldn't say that,>> said the giant, stepping out from the woods, revealing his ¢elgh. He'd been listening. <<They didn't appreciate me.>>

And he told Skidoo and Skedaddle his long, sad story. At Cirkus Benneweis, Gummo had become known as Gummo because he had no teeth. How he lost all his teeth was the circus's fault.

His father was supposedly Jo-Jo the Dog-Faced Boy, a freak in PT Barnum's circus in America. His mŒther had been the Giant Woman, Lady Gargantua. She and Jo-Jo had never really been a couple, and Gummo had been born without a male parent. When little Gummo—of course that was not his real name; he didn't know his real name—began to show the signs of the hypertrichosis that his father and grandfather had, his mŒther, not wanting anyone to know who his father was, took Gummo to the circus's lady soothsayer, who gave him a potion that was supposed to cure his ailment. It did, but instead he developed alopecia universalis, which made him not only as bald as a fox, but he lost tooth and nail as well.

He grew up in the Tivoli Gardens and became known as Gummo the Gentle Giant. All was good for him for a good while. Under the protection of his mŒther, he enjoyed his childhood very much. He felt free, loose, spontaneous until one day that, all full of spontaneity, in the evening, when the horizon bowed to the moon, he let out a howl so bestial that it sounded like he had paßed his soul. He barked, growled, and then bayed the howl of the damned, and everyone around him, especially his mŒther, freaked out. The dog thing went beyond hypertrichosis, he realized. He was somewhere, in the back of his ¢elgh, in his spine, canine.

The circus was delighted and wanted to show him as ►Steppenwolf◄, even hairleß. They offered to make him a suit.

His mŒther, ashamed, turned her back on him.

He had no reason to stay, so he took off. He'd been hiding out in the woods, afraid of villagers with pitchforks, or so Skidoo supposed. But when Gummo heard Skidoo and Skedaddle talking, he knew instantly that he fit right in. They had similar inter-rusts. And, even better, he knew they'd let him howl and bark with their crowing and braying. He could sing with some friends. That sounded like the most perfect, most natural activity to engage in. Why not? Sure, all relationships end tragically, but going with Skidoo and Skedaddle would be better than hiding alone in the woods. That much Gummo knew for sure.

And as they traveled toward Bremen, Skidoo promised that Gummo would be allowed to run free to chase butterflies and howl at the fireflies.

<<Could we sing?>> haxed Gummo.

<<Of course! We will sing together! The circus will be amazed!>> Skidoo was very excited. <<We will be the stars of the show.>>

<<Then we should keep practicing as we go.>>

They did, until they came to a point in the road and in the music where, somehow, some rhythmic element seemed mißing. They had no percußion. They heard a woodpecker, but he seemed too mechanical. They sat down a while to listen to him, but he was fairly repetitive with his composition. He was boring.

But then they heard a rhythmic snagging unlike any percußion they'd ever heard. The snagging was punctuated with brush-like rustling, like coffee grounds being stepped on by some chicory wing-tips for investment strategies, the men who destroyed the circuses. Sometimes the snags would run in rapid sequence and sound like scratches, almost like an amplified zipper. Or a gun being pulled out but catching on the leather lip of the holster.

Their imaginations were in high gear. Skidoo was skittish all of a sudden. Skedaddle feared it was the knacker come for an old pantomimist. Time to make some horsefood! *Here at Amalgam, we feed horses and people to each Œther! Amalgam? I say I am!*

That sounds worse than *Green Eggs and Ham*.

♪Brushed his teeth with a frying pan♫. Old Dan Tucker was a dumb mŒtherfucker.

<<I think it's <washed his face,>>> said Gummo. <<♪Washed his face in a frying pan, combed his hair with a wagon wheel, died with a toothache in his heel♫>>.

<<His *what*?>>

<<His heel.>>

How'd he ever get a toothache in his heel?>>

<<Dunno. Maybe he put his foot in his mouth one time too many.>>

<<Ha ha. Yeah, that must be it. That's good.>>

<<♪He’s too late to get his supper♫.>>

<<Poor baby.>>

<<♪Supper’s over, breakfast’s cooking♫.>>

<<Hung over, eh?>>

<<♪Old Dan Tucker’s just standing there looking♫.>>

<<I heard the *spiegelei* eggs were in his eyes.>>

<<Heck, they *were* his eyes.>>

<<So he had eggs in his eyes?>>

<<Albumen, yolks, and all.>>

<<The albumen should be cooked solid for *spiegelei*.>>

<<True, but the yolk needs to be liquid.>>

That’s a tough balancing act.

<<So the song just ends there? With Dan Tucker being catatonic?>>

<<I—uh—well—uh—I mean—um—♪He was a fine old man♫….>>

<<No, after that.>>

<<Oh, I don’t remember. What? You want me to look that up now? Fine. I’ll be right back.>> Gummo ran off into the woods, presumably to research the ißue in an imaginary woodlands library.

<<You’re right,>> Gummo announced on his return. <<There’s millions more. It seems like the song became one long periodic sentence for Dan. All cornball and all showing him to be a complete dipshit:

<<♪Old Dan Tucker in his day brushed his teeth in a bidet, stood upon his favorite stool, bathed in a retaining pool♫.

<<They’re adding verses to this day. It has the potential to be a longer song than ▶99 Bottles of Beer on the Wall◀.>>

<<♪Try sitting at home. Leave me alone,♫>> sang Skedaddle, wrecking the song, apparently not keeping up with the conversation. He paßed some very bad gas and

looked like he was cramping.

<<Leave you a loan? Okay. Here's ten bucks,>> said Gummo in reply, trying to pull Skedaddle out of whatever funk he had fallen into.

<<Shhh!>> cautioned Skedaddle. <<Can't you hear it? The ▶skt, skt, skt◀ sound? It's coming closer.>>

<<Well, I'm no bloodhound,>> said Gummo. <<Maybe you're right. So what should we do? Ignore it and hope it goes away? Confront it? Or prepare for its arrival?>>

Skidoo recalled from television a <<Carnival!>> scene of people dancing. *Black Orpheus*.

<<Shhh!>> Skedaddle said again. <<Listen!>>

They all three listened, and each of them heard some strange sounds that night. But mostly they heard Skedaddle paßing gas. In the morning Skidoo said he thought someone was following them.

<<Stalking us like prey,>> said Skedaddle. <<Like a killer terrapin.>>

<<Or a fish, like a clown fish,>> offered Gummo. <<Clown fish stalk clowns.>>

<<Yes, Gummo,>> said Skidoo, not wanting to start a pointleß argument, <<but we're on dry land. And a terrapin moves much more slowly than we do. I'm thinking this must be a natural predator, probably feline.>>

<<Like a tiger?>>

<<That's what I'm afraid of.>>

<<Tigers stalk and eat people.>>

<<I don't think tigers are loose on the road to Bremen.>>

<<They might have escaped from a circus, you know.>>

<<Oh, like when that Siberian Tiger mauled his trainer?>>

The three fell silent. They didn't want to think about it. Their singing might keep bears at bay, but tigers were an Œther matter. None of them knew how to handle a tiger.

<<You put a tiger in a tank,>> said Gummo, <<I think is what you do. To handle.>> No one was laughing. <<The tiger. Oh, come on, are you clowns or what?>>

Skedaddle said, <<I’m not.>>

<<Yes, you are. It’s always clowns in the pantomime animals.>>

<<Okay, so you’re right. Yeah, I’m a clown. So what?>>

<<So, laugh already.>>

<<I’m a white clown.>>

<<No, you are definitely Augusto.>>

Skidoo joined in, saying, <<Actually, I’m a White Clown. I’m a leader.>>

<<Well, so am I,>> said Skedaddle. <<That’s why *I* was the *front* end! Maybe, Gummo, you’d like to be my back?>>

<<Hello, no,>> said Gummo. <<Unleß you ram a cork up your aß.>>

<<If I did, you would?>>

<<No, not a chance. I’m nobody’s back end. If my face isn’t seen, people will think ill of me.>>

<<Why?>>

<<That’s what my mŒther always said.>>

<<Oh, so then it’s infallible.>>

<<Shut up. Don’t you dare make fun of my mŒther.>>

<<Okay, okay, relax. Ease down, already. Sheesh, what a grouch. Take a laxative, man.>>

<<No, *you* take a laxative. You’re the one with gastric distreß.>>

Just then, out of the forust emerged an enormous Siberian tiger. Not a pantomime tiger—at first Skidoo thought it might be—but a real tiger. And it ran at them and, about ten feet away, it set to spring. It sprang, about to pounce on the three, who had huddled together in fear, when, all of a sudden, the tiger’s head flew backwards, and he was back-flipped and turned the Œther way. There, a strongman held a chain iron leash that was attached to a steel collar around the tiger’s neck. In his Œther hand, the strongman held a taser on a retractable pole.

<<Never mind him,>> said the strongman. <<He’s just a pußycat. Just as likely he was

going to lick you to death. You fellows look shocked. Sorry about the abrupt entrance. Name's Muscatel,>> and he held out his hand to Skidoo.

See, even a stranger knows I'm the leader, thought Skidoo, taking the stranger's hand. It was enormous, three times the size of Skidoo's.

<<That's the cat that—>> began Skedaddle.

<<That was accused of killing his keeper?>> finished Muscatel. <<You betcha. But he didn't do it. I was there.>>

<<Then who did it?>>

<<It was one of the Œther tigers, a Bengal, but it hid in the crowd of tigers there in the compound. Mongo here just had the misfortune of stumbling upon the keeper's body just as Œther keepers looking for their tardy colleague arrived on the scene. They just aßumed Mongo was guilty.>>

<<Where were you?>>

<<I was in the animal infirmary, right next door, disinfecting the place. We'd had a sick chimp, but she recovered nicely. The infirmary has a view of part of the tiger compound. I just happened to be looking up while rinsing off something in the sink when I saw the keeper try to ✹hit✹ that Bengal with a stick because it was in a foul mood for some reason. You can never figure out the moods of those Bengals, man. Give me a Siberian any day. Anyway, the tiger didn't like being ✹hit✹, so it ✹hit✹ back. Just like a human of somewhat low intelligence might. I mean, one could have predicted it. So they locked up Mongo and were going to euthanize him the next day. I figured he'd be better off with me, so the next day I sprang him from the hoosegow, and we've been on the lam ever since. By the way, speaking of lamb, you haven't seen any delectable woodlands creatures around, have you? There's not much meat on these squirrels.>>

<<How do you cook a squirrel?' haxed Gummo.

<<Oh, well, I use Firesign Theatre's recipe—you just char them till they're stiff. Well, *I* do. Mongo swallows them in two or three bites.>>

<<No, friend,>> said Skidoo, <<we haven't seen anything edible for quite a while. We are all actually quite hungry. Why don't you come with us. My cousin in Bremen will feed us, and Bremen is only two days away.>>

<<No—I don't take any charity.>>

<<No—he works at the Zirkus Bremen. We're going to get jobs there.>>

<<As clowns?>>

<<No, actually we're going to sing, but in character, I gueß, so I'll still be a clown. But I'm a pantomime donkey.>>

<<Think of it, Muscatel. Isn't it a great idea?>> haxed Gummo. <<Skidoo does the rooster dance and crows, Skedaddle is half of a pantomime donkey and brays, I'm a toothleß hairleß dog-faced giant who barks and howls….>>

<<Then let me pull a rabbit out of your aß. Maybe two.>> He reached behind Skedaddle's ears and pulled out two rabbits. He toßed them to Gummo. <<Here, start a fire for these. I already gutted 'em. Just skin 'em. I have one more, but I need to feed Mongo one.>> He took Mongo for a walk so that the Œthers could set up camp of some sort.

<<Do you have a knife?>>

<<What? Of course not,>> said Skedaddle. <<I'd cut my ¢elgh in the suit.>>

<<What if you had a pocket knife?>>

<<A what?>>

<<You've never heard of a pocket knife?>>

<<I must not have had the benefits you have had, oh Patrician Cock!>>

<<I prefer ►rooster◄, please.>>

<<You're right. You're the White Clown. I'm Augusto.>>

<<Look, over there!>> Gummo pointed.

<<Hey, Palooka, you're ten feet tall, and we're just short clowns. What do you see?>>

<<Smoke. A chimney, I think.>>

<<Food!>>

<<I don't know about you, but I need more than half a rabbit. I'm sure Muscatel also has a big appetite. And Mongo needs more than one rabbit.>>

<<Yeah?>>

<<So let's check it out.>>

<<You guys go,>> said Skidoo. <<I'll tell Muscatel when he gets back, and we'll join up with you then.>>

So Gummo and Skedaddle left Skidoo behind. Half-dead, they walked towards the light. They were determined, though, and wound their way through woods, brush and open field to get there.

When they got closer, they saw the chimney was attached to a modest stone cabin. As they got closer, they could smell a roast on the fire. Closer still, they saw that a wonderfully diverse vegetable garden surrounded the cabin on all sides.

The cabin had very high windows, too tall for even Gummo to see through. Even with Skedaddle on Gummo's shoulders, they still couldn't see in.

<<Should we just knock?>>

<<If we throw our ¢elghs on their mercy, then what about Skidoo and Muscatel? I think we should wait and then all introduce our ¢elghs together. Surely they wouldn't turn us *all* down. It looks from the garden that they have plenty of food.>>

<<Hi, guys!>> said Skidoo, rejoining them. <<What have you found?>>

<<Nothing yet, really. Hey, where's Muscatel?>>

<<Oh, he's here. He's coming. He's just feeding Mongo the two rabbits we didn't eat.>>

<<Oh, I hope he didn't take it the wrong way.>>

<<No, no, no.... He agrees. There's got to be food here. We could smell that roast a mile away.>>

<<I know, right? It smells good. I don't know the situation here. We thought about just knocking, but we thought we should see if we could see if they seemed like nice folk. But we're too short.>>

<<Here, Muscatel, climb up on Gummo's shoulders.>>

<<Hello. Wait. Shouldn't Gummo be climbing up on mine? I'm the strongman.>>

<<True, but he's a giant.>> Muscatel and Gummo sized each Œther up.

<<Yes, you should step on my shoulders,>> said Gummo to Muscatel.

<<No. You step on mine!>> insisted Muscatel. <<I have to hold Mongo.>> Gummo didn't argue. He was too hungry to bicker.

He climbed onto Muscatel's shoulders.

<<Now pull me up,>> said Skedaddle, so Gummo scooped him up in one hand and Skidoo in the Œther, put Skedaddle on his giant back, and then reached Skidoo up to put on Skedaddle's.

They teetered over to the window. Skidoo peered in.

He couldn't believe what he was looking at. It was amazing.

There, at a dining room table, sat four of the most notorious circus owners, all playing cards from behind stupendous stacks of money. They were the owners of the four largest circuses that had folded up their tents forever. The circuses had been insured against failure, and their bankruptcy made the owners enormous profits. Meanwhile the workers had to go on unemployment and retool their very lives and dreams.

They had a roast suckling pig, a roast turkey, and a beef brisket in the center of the table, and a dozen different vegetables scattered around the three large platters: baked carrots, mashed sweet potatoes, roasted Vidalias, mashed rutabaga, red dulse, yellow asparagus, creamed Brußels sprouts, stuffed grape leaves, baked celery root, baked beets, corn on the cob, collard greens with bacon (don't tell anyone about the bacon!), and artichokes, the king of vegetables, wearing its sharp crown.

Loaves of bread of all kinds filled a side table—pumpernickel, long loaves of Italian white bread, poppyseed bread, marble rye—it was a wonder to behold.

The Œther side table had fruit tortes made with gooseberries, red and black currents, boysenberries, blueberries, blackberries, raspberries, all seen growing outside the house. No strawberries, though. Wonder why. But not for long. This was a feast. And, even though these were dicks who betrayed hundreds of people, they did have food, and that meant more than philosophical fine points.

As Skidoo described it, the Œthers could no longer stand not seeing it.

<<Let's do something,>> insisted Skedaddle.

<<Like what?>> haxed Gummo.

<<Let's sing,>> said Muscatel, and the Œther three looked at him in amazement.

<<You sing?>> haxed Gummo.

<<Like a jaybird. What I like to do is the bottom end as a doo-wop singer.>>

Gummo smiled. <<Perfect! They will love our music. They'll invite us in, and then they'll share their food. After all, at heart they are circus folk.>>

And they set off on a beautiful musical exploration of their journey here, an interwoven four-story tale, expreßed paßionately by a glorious rooster reaching climax at dawn, a donkey expreßing with equal power both agony and dedication, a giant howling, and a strongman doing doo-wop baß. It's perfect. Frank Zappa would have loved it.

And the owners? Oh, my gosh. They thought the world was ending. Never in their lives had they heard such a caterwaul, especially when Mongo joined in with a few roars, which had a bowel-clearing effect on the owners.

It was the apocalypse. Ragnarok. The Rapture. The end of times. One of the fat fucks stood up, went outside to see what was making that horrible sound. It sounded worse than a raccoon mating with a hyena. As he turned the corner of the house, he saw a giant, many-armed shadow towering over him, and he knew they were done for.

He ran back into the house, screaming, <<Get the fuck out. Now!>> The four fat fucks ran faster than a bolt of lightning to get out of there.

The four traveling companions came down from their totem pole and stood again as individuals.

<<Did they like it?>>

<<I don't think so. They ran off screaming into the woods.>>

<<Man, we'd better practice our harmonies some more before we get to Bremen.>>

<<Well, maybe we can stay here a while.>>

<<The way those guys took off, I don't think they're coming back.>>

<<Maybe it's not their place. They may have been trespaßing. That would explain why they'd leave all this behind and run off.>> They looked at the gorgeous spread.
<<Maybe. But it sure would be a shame to let all this food go to waste.>>

So they didn't. They, with plenty of help from Mongo, devoured it all and then fell asleep like Beowulf, exhausted by the feast.

The next day, while looking for places to hide all the money that'd been left behind by the circus owners, the four travelers discovered a full larder, a smokehouse, a wine cellar, and an enchantreß who turned men into pigs. And only then did they remember the suckling pig they'd eaten.

Okay, no enchantreß, but the place did make them uneasy. They didn't know if anyone would be back to kick them out. A banker, maybe. That *would* be horrible. Rather a mutant zombie! Or Henry, Screaming Jay Hawkins's torso-leß talking skull companion. <<Henry wants an Œther furburger,>> as Hawkins would say.

<<What are you going on about, Skidoo?>> haxed Gummo.

<<Don't blame me,>> said the sated and somewhat besotted Skidoo. <<I don't make the news. I just report them. I'm not sure when Screamin' Jay Hawkins morphed into Jack White, perhaps by way of Johnny Winter. But—applause at the end. That's the point. I try to entertain people. I want the applause.>>

<<It feels good to have something in the stomach,>> Gummo replied. <<Truly. Don't let it scare you. Food is a beautiful pleasure, a commodity! From *commodious*, the first bloody street one can find with alcohol,>> and he drunkenly raised his tankard to toast.

Skidoo's eyes got heavy, and he began to suspect more than tryptophan.

In the morning the Magic Sun came up and enlightened everyone.

They were all Donovaning out at dawn when, out of the blue, Skidoo said, <<Do you remember our plan?>>

<<To go to Bremen!>>

<<What if we just stay here? Here's cool.>>

They had food aplenty. They could perform here and make audiences come to them. No, better keep it quiet before it's as overrun as the Beatles' Apple Corps. Anyway, best to stay here till something's decided.

<<No, best to keep moving!>> said Muscatel, who shared with Mongo a distaste for stasis.

<<We don't need to. We have everything we need right here.>>

<<But we were going to be stars!>>

<<We already *are* stars! Stop living in the past,>> said Skedaddle. <<Besides, I have to hit the can.>> Skedaddle walked off towards the bathroom.

<<That's easy for you to say,>> said Muscatel, calling after Skedaddle, <<but it's completely half-aßed. We were going to Bremen, remember?>>

<<But even there, even working for my cousin, we'd still be beholden to the boßes. We'd still just be pawns. Let's be kings instead. Here we have plenty of food and drink.>>

They spent the day gathering vegetables and fishing. They cut some alder and used the smokehouse to begin smoking their catch.

Meanwhile, in town a few miles away, the circus owners were commiserating at a local bed and breakfast that had taken them in.

>>We have to at least go back and see if we can get our money back,>> announced one fat fuck to the Œthers. The Œthers disagreed, so he left on his own. He told his ¢elgh he'd only run because the Œthers had run. They were cowards, but he wasn't afraid of some monstrous ghost or whatever that creature from hell had been. Heck, they'd had stranger creatures than that in the circus. He was mad that he'd let his ¢elgh get scared off. So he snuck back to the house at night and used his key to quietly gain acceß.

The house was dark and quiet. Total darkneß. Silence. He stood still, waiting for the darkneß to lighten as his eyes adjusted. He saw an ember in the fireplace. Maybe if he poked the fire a little, the fire would illuminate the place a bit better. He couldn't see the poker. By the door he felt an umbrella. That would work.

The fat fuck tiptoed like a ninja, inching his way through the house. He heard someone farting loudly in one of the corners of the room, but only that. When the fat fuck was close enough to the ember, he shoved his umbrella at it. Only it wasn't an ember. That was Mongo's glowing eye watching him. When the fat fuck poked Mongo, Mongo growled and pounced, swiping and taking a baseball-sized chunk out of the fat fuck's fanny.

The fat fuck screamed bloody murder and ran right into Gummo at full force. Gummo instinctively lifted his leg to protect his ¢elgh and inadvertently floored the fat fuck with a haymaker from the knee to the chin. The hapleß owner, out like a wild oat, collapsed onto Skedaddle, who had fallen asleep on the couch while playing with a pocket knife he'd found. The knife cut the owner's face and removed part of an earlobe. That woke up the fat owner in time to hear Skidoo crow while rooster dancing in celebration. When Muscatel began adding his baß doo-wop lines at the bottom, the fat fuck knew he was dead. But then one of the four said, <<Go—get out of here. Sin no more.>>

When the fat fuck returned to his friends, he told them he'd been attacked by an angel of the Lord in the form of a griffin. Its talons had torn him, its razor-sharp beak had almost bit his whole face off, it had head-butted him in the chin, and then it crowed in celebration, mocking him, laughing at him. He had aroused the ire of God. No way was he going back. So they stitched up his butt and high-tailed it to parts unknown far, far away.

The four travelers stayed. At one point, Muscatel and Mongo went on to Bremen and promoted their act. The Œthers build a wooden stage and a huge back porch, enough for several dozen people to sit and watch a performance, to dance, to sing and make music. And, in almost no time, people came to see them and to see Mongo. But Muscatel wouldn't let Mongo perform. Muscatel wanted to take the found money and transport Mongo back to Siberia. They all agreed.

While Muscatel was gone, Gummo had to fill in on baß doo-wops because they had become a popular element of their show. Gummo was pretty good. Not as deep a voice as Muscatel's, it was more gravelly. But it had a gentle strength that fans enjoyed. Œther performers eventually joined them, and together they formed the first permanently stationary circus and grew it into a theme park called <<Circus Circuitous, Where the Change Is Shocking!>> As for Mongo, well, he loved being back home in Siberia. And no one tried to poke him with an umbrella ever again.

Part Six: Swamp

After telling the story, I was sure they'd remember I was there on the path with them. When I went mißing, they'd think I must be near the pond.

As we rounded the Big Tent, I made a quick excuse to go to the bathroom. I'd been having the same problem as Skedaddle on the walk, so they knew my intestinal system was bugged. I mean, it was a buggy system. The clowns I was walking with were strollers with ears.

But as soon as they turned the corner and no one was in sight, I slipped through the gate into the grazing pasture and all the way the long way around the stables, back where no one ever went, the ►compost◄ area where the swept-out horse apples were stacked. In my wetsuit and waders, I was good to go. I put my backpack and fishing gear in the stables—I just dumped them in through an open window. Nobody'd notice—everyone was on the way to the Koifur Roast.

Horse crap may look like straw, but let me tell you it's a lot muckier than you'd suspect. From here I went north-to-northeast, away from all buildings and people, out of sight and hearing of everyone. The ground got muddier and then started to get swampy. That was okay. The waders and wetsuit were great. The careßmaleeches couldn't latch on. I didn't see any large reptiles. Plenty of snakes, though. I was careful around them not to startle them. I was pretty sure the titanium mesh of the wetsuit would protect me from bites, but why push it? I just stayed out of their way.

I began to notice strange contraptions sticking up out of the swamp. They weren't the disc golf baskets yet, but odd little square boxes on the ends of poles that extended up fifteen feet in the air. At first I heard a deep rumbling, which rose to a roar. then a sound like a wounded walrus in heat came from the boxes, and I recognized Howlin' Wolf's ►Moanin' at Midnight◄, which was eerie here in the swamp. After that, these swamp speakers played what sounded like James Cotton's harp blowing through the bull rushes. Then I heard Johnny Winter trading guitar licks with Muddy Waters. Pinetop Perkins was keeping it together on piano. The tune was Muddy's ►Walkin' Thru the Park◄ from Johnny's *Nothin' But the Blues*. Johnny Winter, of course! Johnny Winter! This was the Koifur Roast—they were going to blast Johnny Winter all day. That was just fine by me. First of all, Johnny Winter is one hell of a guitarist, easily one of the top ten blues guitar slingers of all time. He understood something Slowhand never did: the blues are a god-awful meß. Winter didn't sanitize them like Slowhand. They are swampy, hot and nasty, like slapping at your neck and getting a handful of sweaty gnats in your palm.

Next was ►The Fugitive◄, an old Aynsley Dunbar Retaliation song that seemed the perfect soundtrack for escape through the swamp.

After that, Charlie Mußelwhite's ►Louisiana Fog◄ blew from the speakers. I was beginning to feel a little spooked, but I had to keep going now. The fact that music was playing just meant the party was in full swing. They were happily catching koifur, bopping them on the head, getting them ready for the big BBQ. Yee haw! I'm amazed they didn't make coats or hats with the fur. Or maybe they did. I'd never seen what went on. All I had was hearsay to go on.

And go I did. I went as quickly as poßible towards my goal. After a few miles, the speakers stopped. I could still hear the music playing, but the sound grew muddier and fainter. I think I heard Winter's ►Black Cat Bone◄ and ►Drinkin' Blues◄, and something that sounded like Buddy Guy, but by then I was putting good distance between me and the speakers and was just glad the music was still playing. No one seemed to notice my absence. And I made sure several people could vouch for my having gone down the road with them and told them all my long story about the rooster and the half-a-pantomime donkey.

Then, just as I thought of Skedaddle, my guts complained, and I had a maßive intestinal cramp. It stopped me dead in my tracks. I had to find some solid ground to sit down on and right away. At that very moment, my foot hit metal.

I reached down into the water and pulled up a sign. It was a ⅩWelcome to the SwampⅩ sign facing the Œther way. That meant I was at the far edge. Excellent. I had some renewed vigor and came to drier land. In a short while it was dry enough for me to sit down, and then my cramps came back. I have never hurt so much.

I was able to paß gas, but only that. I saw something, though. Through my astral projection. I was near the basket for hole two. I couldn't see the tee for two, but the one for three should be right near—aha!—there it is! I fought off the cramps and led my own private charge on the spot. I saw a basket that looked like it was marked with a ►3◄. I needed a tee-shot. I had found a Nuke Z with a good Captain America shield design on it back in the basement of the dorm. It was a beautiful 173-gram disc, and I fired it toward the green perfectly. I hadn't lost my touch. But this was one very special disc.

Then, all of a sudden, directly in front of the basket, a geyser began to take the disc up into the sky and hold it there. The geyser may have toßed that disc back to camp if I hadn't been quick-witted enough to stop it the only way I could figure. I sat on it.

The preßure on my butt cheek was tremendous, but the disc fell down nearby. It wasn't lost. Thank goodneß.

I started to get up, but to do so, I shifted my weight to one side so I could move my leg to a kneeling position so that I could stand up. That little shift to one side caused the geyser to shoot full force right up my colon. I rolled off, but it was too late. The water preßure in reverse loosened everything up, and it was all I could do to drop my pants and shorts and squat before it all came out in one torrential gush that would have turned back the hounds. Weeks' worth of waste was going to fertilize hole three's green quite well. If this was going to turn into the greenest green, I'd know why.

I didn't even finish the hole, though it felt like mine had been. I began to shiver from the sudden weight loß, but it was a good shiver. After shuddering, I was suddenly stronger. I walked to the tee for hole four and looked for the basket. The baskets were undoubtedly easier to spot back when they were chrome, but they had all rusted in the meantime. But they were still there. I had to be patient, for the geysers came into play on every hole. I had a Crush that I'd pegged for an anhyzer and an ivory Wraith, just like my old one, as a hyzer.

I negotiated the course fairly well. Several tees were as hard to find as forust-green discs in the forust. One basket I gave up on finding—it must have been removed—and an Œther had fallen, but overall it was a decent course. It could be spruced up, tamed a bit. Provide transport. It could be succeßful. Like the Œther one, though no one ever thanked me for that. ©Never mindↄ, I said aloud to my ¢elgh. No use even thinking about that, since I'm a clown now. We should have a clown revolution and let the Shiny Clowns take over. But deep at heart, I am not a shiny clown. I'm just a ping pong ball. An intermediary. At least that's over because there's no way to go back now. Okay, ©Foreward!ↄ This Wraith was more beaten than mine and instead of hyzering, it began anhyzering on me. It confused me, so I toßed it aside, giving my ¢elgh leß to carry. That was good. Six and seven were through some cypreßes, back near the swamp, and brought me closer to Dorm E than I liked. I birdied them quietly and moved on. No one noticed me. I liked eight. It led due east, away from the camp and from the swamp. The basket was next to a small outhouse—totally dilapidated now—but a good place for a little deli or something. This could be a nice place. Disc Need World.

Yeah, that'd be a suit ready to be worn. I noticed a speaker atop the outhouse. No music was coming out—no Johnny Winter, no nothing. Silence. My absence had been discovered? Maybe the wiring out here was dead. Maybe the outhouse had no connection to the college compound.

Who knew I'd be feeling so much better just for getting my disc back. I'm glad I followed my instincts on that one.

It will make a great course. Even if I don't do it—I have to tell the Aasvogel what he has here. Forget Clown College. Heck, you can put a nuthouse anywhere. This is a disc golf country club. You have to have a million testicles to get in.

Part Seven: Here She Comes

Raisin' Cain had never been so liberating. The swamp had me in its fever. I actually rang up an ace on hole nine and stepped off the course very pleased. This would be easier to develop than the cave and looked to be more fun.

<<Michel!>> I heard a familiar voice calling from the east, from over at what looked like a parking lot. Nettie!

<<Nettie?>>

<<Thanks for the meßages. Brilliant. We knew of the connection between parkour and the Shining Path, of course, but had no idea that it was based out of the college—.>>

<<Don't call it a college. Call it what it is—a mental institution for the criminally insane. You'd have had me put away forever.>>

<<Not me. Aasvogel. And not forever. He loves you like a brŒthcr, but he thought you needed to be taught a little humility. But that doesn't matter. You uncovered the terrorist cell. We found plans, explosives, weapons—that Dorm E building was an armory. You're a hero, Michel. You may have saved hundreds of lives, maybe even thousands.

We got into her little police car and left clown college behind. No more poetry nights, No more pies in the face. Not more pratfalls and catcalls and big balls balanced by the administrators' seals of approval.

<<This goes deeper than Dorm E,>> I said as we drove off.

<<We know,>> she said.

Part Eight: La Bas

The jabs of a woodpecker woke them up. She turned up Paul Rodgers on the clock radio.

<<This was a great song,>> she said. It was Bad Company's ♪Feel Like Making Love♫.

Michel smiled. Nettie was all woman. Even down to the corny love song. But it was very pretty melody, and the song has not been written that Paul Rodgers couldn't sell. What pathos!

Michel quieted his thoughts and listened to the music. The disc jockey announced it was ►Twelvefer Tuesday◄ and played ►Run with the Pack◄ after that.

►Run with the Pack◄ is a very disturbing song. It is meant to be sarcastic? Dystopian? ►Shooting Star◄ is, for sure. They are songs about opposite extremes—extreme suppreßion of the ¢elgh in order to benefit the group vs. extreme individualism and disconnection from society. First person plural or first person singular?

►Electric Land◄! That's a wonderfully dreamy adventure. The guitar wraps you around its ¢elgh as Mick Ralphs plays. And then Rodgers interjects the urgency of the lost in between Ralph's dreamscape. Rodgers then rides in on Simon Kirke's drums and bridges the ethereal and the earthly.

►Can't Get Enough◄, of course, showed us immediately that Bad Company was not Free Junior. Ralphs was very different from Koßoff, but Koßoff was dead. Ralphs had learned a few of Koßoff's old riffs for Rodgers's sake. ►Wishing Well◄ and ►All Right Now◄ still sounded great. To be fair, Rodgers should have sung a Mott the Hoople song.

<<Ralph's? You mean where they buried the ♪obsolete germ bombs♫?>>

<<No, that was just in ►Billy the Mountain◄.>>

<<Okay, Zappa. Now tell me Zappa's connection to Johnny Winter.>> Michel though he had her stumped, but her face lit up.

<<They appear in a photo together in *Cream Magazine*'s special 10th anniversary of the MŒthers ißue. Zappa and Winter are sitting down next to each Œther and holding a guitar on their laps. Zappa's holding the body and playing the right hand. Winter is fingering the frets with his left.>>

<<Good. They also played on the same bill in the beginning of August 1969 at the

Atlantic City Pop Festival and then in England at the Bath Festival in June of 1970.>>

<<I'm impreßed.>>

<<Zappa went on at 2:45 p.m., I believe.>>

<<Okay. You got me.>>

<<Which was way off schedule. He was supposed to play at 6:40 p.m. And Winter was supposed to play the day before at 4 p.m., but didn't get on till about midnight. Many of the fans were so stoned, they didn't even hear him.>>

<<Again. You got me. You win.>>

Michel couldn't think of anything to say after that, so he rode the rust of the way to Aasvogel's castle in silence.

Why would Aasvogel reward his heroism now? Michel had already saved him once from that evil Bözmacher cult, and the Aasvogel went back on all his gratitude and rewards after that. Michel had been in charge of disc golf, and he should have been put in charge of parkour, too. Instead he was made a clown of. Literally. And just to teach him a leßon. That was very low.

Michel didn't even want to see the Aasvogel. He was sick of Mars, two-bit-run-down rag-tag planet that it was. He wanted to go back to Earth. But he had Nettie in the mix. He was going to have to show concern and caring and all that. He wasn't sure he was capable of anything like that anymore. He had forsworn all relationships.

He was pleased that Nettie knew about music. He had a friend once whose old lady decided to become a born-again Christian. The friend had said he would have tolerated even hat, but then his old lady began to listen to the worst goddawful ▶Christian◀ soft rock. Her terrible taste in music eventually made him give up on her. If someone has to be a Christian artist, ze should do it with style, like Bruce Cockburn, and not get all tent-preachy. That takes away from the music unleß one's culture connects to it, as with Black Oak Arkansas, for example.

Michel thought Nettie looked like she was having second thoughts, anyway.

Boom! There! That's what Michel hated about relationships: having to read people's expreßions in order to figure out what they're feeling. They should just let a person know. The uncertainty, the gueß work, the embarraßment of being wrong over and over again, the false accusations, the paranoia and sneakineß of it all, often over the stupidest little shit, like the drinking of a beer. No—you can hear that quarrel inside every suburban couple's ▶starter house◀. That, of course, is never the ißue. It's that they were lied to by society, who promised them a nice life. Gueß what? Society is a vicious, lying, back-biting, evil mŒtherfucker. If you see society on the road, run it over or run the Œther way. Œtherwise, here's the uniform: black pinstripe suit, button-down shirts and Italian silk ties, gold cuff-links, tie clip, fob and watch, black leather shoes, silk socks, barbershop hair, no beard or moustache, and perfect teeth, body maß, and vision. No ornamentation is permitted on the faces of the acceptable people. They must be punctual. They must never be sick. they must never complain about their lot in life. they must appear to have limitleß resources without ever having to work: the leisure claß is back! Here's Usher! Here's *A Rebours*. Here's *La Bas*. Here's *Eyes Wide Shut*, which is really just a retelling of *La Bas*.

That's the problem with being older—he can see the hackneyed narratives stretching out before him, but he already tried all those. They're so well-trodden and muddy that only the most obedient mules go out in them. And then they get fancy blankets and a nice place to sleep as a reward.

Those who don't do as they're told are locked into a dilapidated barn. And no one's bringing them any myrrh. The three modern wise guys were told not to invest in babies in order to avoid corporal gains tax.

See? So much shit from outside has gotten in. It's not pure anymore. but when it was pure, Michel didn't know how to say it.

He decided to listen to the radio advice of Bachman-Turner Overdrive. He'd ►Let It Ride◄. He wondered how the radio station would ever find twelve BTO ►hits◄. Maybe four. Five. Six, even. Twelve? What do they mean by ►hit◄?

The shortest distance between two points is seldom the most inter-rusting. But sometimes the smaller something is, the more detailed and beautiful its form. A Swiß chronograph is much more beautiful than a generic maß-produced wristwatch. Look at them side by side. No question.

Nettie was gone before Michel could agonize more over her leaving.

She'd left Michel in the Aasvogel's sitting room.

Part Nine: Meeting with the Aasvogel

<<I hope you enjoyed your clown spa vacation,>> said the Aasvogel.

Michel couldn't tell if Aasvogel was being sarcastic. What the hell…?

<<Want to play some Skat? I could call Nils.>>

<<That back-stabbin' two-faced SOB?>>

<<Come on, now. It's time to let bygones be begonias.>>

<<That's not the saying. You've been influenced by him too heavily.>>

<<At one time people said I was influenced too heavily by you.>>

<<And many people I knew thought my coming all the way to Mars just to help you was crazy. So what? What's your point?>>

<<You didn't come here for me. You came for the sestinas.>>

<<Yeah—that explains why I returned the sestinas and stayed here. When's the last time you hd your glaßes checked?>>

<<You cannot speak to the Aasvogel in this manner.>>

<<No, but I can speak to the ☼Aßhole☼ in this manner.>>

<<Watch it.>>

<<Why? You going to condemn me to a mental institution again? You're going to do that sooner or later anyway, maybe the next time I don't follow orders well enough. Well, you sure learned something from the Bözmachers.>>

<<What? What do you mean?>>

<<It's like Machiavelli. You learned that the most important part of being a prince is remaining a prince. You would hear no dißent. That's how the Bözmachers insinuated their ¢elghs in your mind. You didn't even realize they were doing it.>>

<<True.>>

<<Well, I confront you. I don't insinuate. I will tell you the truth, but you shouldn't turn on me for it. I'm just the meßenger. I'm just speaking as your voice of

conscience.>>

ċNow to let this idea take root and grow so he doesn't send me backꜿ, thought Michel.

<<I see that you uncovered quite a nest of vipers up there at the college.>>

<<The nuthouse, you mean.>>

<<Semantics.>> He was reading some report Nettie had given him. <<An entire dorm dedicated to the violent overthrow of the government… the Shining Path… using asemic-looking texts that were actually encoded…. This is excellent work. I deeply appreciate your loyalty, even when you thought I was being a dick.>>

<<Everyone's a dick every now and then.>>

<<True enough.>>

<<What happened to the captured enemies?>>

<<Well, actually, Michel, none were captured.>>

<<What?>>

<<Their lives were lost during the battle for control of the compound. They had set up snipers in Dorm E, so we leveled it. No one survived the bombing.>>

<<You bombed your own people? This isn't Philadelphia, you know. The people might not like it.>>

<<That's why this is being referred to as a police matter. As far as the public knows, these clowns were stockpiling weapons in order to attack civilians.>>

<<They weren't?>>

<<Oh, I'm sure they were. But not only that. They wanted to take over everything.>>

<<Like the Bözmachers?>>

<<Yes, exactly, except these so-called Shining Path chaps were not inter-rusted in covertly usurping power. They wanted to kill us all.>>

<<How?>>

<<I'm not sure entirely. Nettie says it's in code in those meßages you and she have collected—the so-called ▶asemic◀ texts, which, as you discovered, were not asemic at all but tell the tale of traitorous treachery, of treason!>>

<<Are you sure it was not just run-of-the-mill perfidy? Maybe they were just loudmouthed punk kids who were just expreßing their feelings without any real intention of acting on the threats. They just want to be heard. They want the leaders of society to pay attention and let them participate in the discußion of where the world goes now. It is, after all, theirs one way or an Œther eventually. Why wait for violence? Abdicate or include them. These parkour kids are still fun-loving on a deep level. Woe to you if you forbid people to have fun. That pronouncement no one ever survives.>>

<<You have thought about this.>>

<<I've been locked up in a nuthouse with little else to do but think.>>

<<It looks like it's been good for you.>>

<<Fuck you. That is one fucked-up thing to say to an Œther human being. It's like telling a widow not to grieve because grief leaves unsightly facial wrinkles.>>

<<That's true.>>

<<So what? You don't say that to people, even if you are the bloody Aasvogel.>>

<<Watch it! You are testing me, and you don't have that right.>>

<<Fair enough. You are correct. I was being disrespectful, and I apologize. You may mean well, but it is your methods, not your friendship, I take ißue with. *You* I love. Your actions, however, disturb me. You had me committed for no reason.>>

<<You had failed.>>

<<Failed what?>>

<<Failed to trust my friendship.>>

<<Nils—>>

<<—was your employee. I liked him because I saw your hand in his shaping. I felt that watching him was like watching Michelangelo through his apprentices' work. It was a fascinating trick of the light, and I was distracted by it. But out of love for you, not anything else.>>

<<But why the compound?>>

<<I wanted you safe. I had no idea our enemies were there. I was not kept well informed. For which I blame my ¢elgh. I should have sought out more information, but I, too, can feel hurt and turned against. Now, let us get back to the table together, break bread, share a bottle of the best Bordeaux, or two, or, ha, even three.... We'll feast. My

brŒther, I am so happy you are home.>>

Michel was transformed again, transfixed by the words of the Aasvogel. He saw again in the Aasvogel's eyes that spark of brilliance he had first recognized so long before. The Aasvogel was back in his full glory. That was fantastic news, so Michel decided to find Nils and either kill him or forgive him. If he killed him, they'd be short a Skat player. That would be a shame. Good Skat players are hard to find, and Nils, although not brilliant, was good. It would take a long time to train someone else to his level or to locate an Œther expert one could trust. Rather the known enemy, right?

Michel would need to go to Mt. Apollinaris to find Nils, who was probably in the disc golf offices there. The offices were gorgeous, all hardwood—maple, actually—just as pretty as could be. Very rustic. Moosehead on the wall. Clichéd North Woods, but fun. It was like a Door County cabin from way back in 1920-something. Gangster booze parties would rock the woods. So it was kind of a take-off on that motif.

What was also great about living by the woods is that not only is the raw building material there aplenty, but so are folks who really know how to work with the wood, or rather, *play* with the wood in order to build something fun.

Then plant fleabane all around the building, especially by the entrance.

Okay, back to Skat on Friday with Nils and the Aasvogel. Michel is sure Nettie will want to come. One of them could serve as the dealer each round.

Part Ten: Skat Again

They were coming to the lighthouse for Skat. It would be delightfully intimate. The living quarters at the very top, where the dome revealed the heavens above the light, would be the only place we'd have several feet acroß except the entrance floor. But my apartment was cozier. We could watch the night sky while sitting around my bed, using the bed as a table. This would show that Aasvogel was really a mensch and not just a ruler (<<I'm not a ruler! I'm a protactor!>> yelled little Georgie up from Earth. We wouldn't hear him.

Hey, that was almost funny. The humor seems harder to come by right now. It feels forced, ¢elgh-aware. It can't be forced. It has to just come naturally.

The Aasvogel, a slender man, made his way up the narrow tower easily. He clambered up the footholds on the shelves like a lizard climbing a rock. Nettie had no problem. She'd been here before. So had Nils.

They each had to sit in one direction. Aasvogel would sit at the west window, the farthest from the entrance. On his left, facing south, Nettie. Opposite her was Nils. I had to be the doorman and errand boy because it was my place.

I haxed Nettie what she wanted to hear. She said, <<Zappa or Johnny Winter.>> She was kidding. I'd told her about the music at the compound. It was good music—I'll give it that. But right then I wanted something that didn't really remind me of being there. I wanted to hear ♪Drift Away♫, as by Dobie Gray. But I didn't have it. Nor any Jimmy Castor Bunch. I settled for Zappa's ▶Big Swifty◀—Aasvogel put that on. Armadillo '73. What a jam.

<<Amarillo?>>

<<No, Austin. And this was his *One Size Fits All* band. George Duke, Napoleon Murphy Brock, Tom and Bruce Fowler, Ruth Underwood, Chester Thompson (and his gorilla), and Ralph Humphrey.

Following ▶Big Swifty◀ was ▶Dickie's Such an ☼Aßhole☼◀. I switched the music. It hit too close to home. I kept hearing, ♪Dickie's Just Like Aasvogel♫. Off. I put on the jazz radio station instead and turned to a ballgame on the TV. Now we had options. The radio beat the TV two to one, so I turned off the TV again when I saw the horribly one-sided score.

<<What's this music called again? Jizz?>> haxed Nils, trying to be funny. No one laughed, not even the Aasvogel, who would have laughed a few months ago because of his infatuation with Nils. The Aasvogel's propensity to fall in love with gulls, what's that called—gullibility?—is alarming. He needs a full-time protector. Man, too bad

Polymesus is no longer around. He ws in a perfect position to keep the Aasvogel human. Poor Poly. I really do miß him.

<<No, not ▶jizz◀, you barefoot pedestrian,>> I couldn't stop my ¢elgh from saying. <<Jazz. Music to astral project by.>>

<<What?>>

<<Never mind.>>

<<Astro? The dog from the Jetsons?>>

<<Never mind, Nils,>> I said, snapping my jaw shut to keep my ¢elgh from saying anything else.

<What's your bid?>> haxed Nettie, who had just dealt this hand. I had the third and fourth Jacks and two Ace-King-Queen combos, with one long suit, Karo, all the way to the Ten. Let's see, without two, play three, times 9 for Karo. The weakest card I had was a third Nine behind the Ace-King-Queen. I'd have to either discard it or save it for last. I don't need to discard. I could play without looking at the Skat—the two cards in the middle. My second Ace-King-Queen combo were Herz, the next highest suit. So I could bid without two, play three, hand four, times nine for Karo. No—if I play, I can get 90 of the 120 points easily. I can go up to out-of-hand four, Schneider five times nine equals 45.

That gave me a little room in the bidding. I could even go up to a Schwarz game, but the Jack…. But that would give me Schwarz six times nine. Fifty-four. If I played it open, it'd be seven times nine, 63. If I played it Ouvert, in which my cards are showing, I could go eight times nine, or 72. I wouldn't win that because of the Jack. Really, Schneider is the highest I should go. If had more Jacks, I could go Jacks as the only trumps in a Grand game, but equally, with the two small ones, this would be too difficult. But if I could do that, I could times 24 for Grand rather than nine for Karo.

Fortunately I didn't have to bid that high. I earned the right to play by bidding 33. I would have to play without looking at the Skat. No one had any idea what those two cards were until proceß of elimination narrowed the choice down enough or the hand ended. But that meant no one else had two Jacks, or 36 would have been bid. Aasvogel had one. Nils had one. Unleß one was in the Skat. If Nils had no Jacks, he could bid high enough for a Null game—in which he had to lose all his points. So he would have bid up. I was pretty sure that meant Aasvogel had one, or he might have bid on Null also—my hand was very strong. So I figured I would definitely be able to Schneider.

<<Okay,>> I announced. <<I'm going with Karo, playing out of hand, and I'm announcing Schneider.>> That would mean the hand would be worth ▶Without two, Play three, Hand four (meaning I couldn't see the Skat), Schneider five, announced Schneider six, times nine. I remembered that announcing would give me the extra

multiplier—I can't believe I almost missed that. Skat is sneaky. She'll steal your heart and empty your wallet while funning with you. Fifty-four points. That'd be a nice win. The cost is double if I lose, though. First to 1500 plus or minus, and the game ends. Sometimes we used to go to 5000. Those would be all-nighters. One person would usually get so trashed he wouldn't remember how to play and would lose or paß out or both. This wasn't like those games with my dear Polymesus. I miß my friend dearly. Sometimes I think I should just step back into third person more. I can't really bring you good news from the first.

This war we are fighting against those who would co-opt all thought, who would uniform all expreßion, is a hard, long one. Everywhere we look they have all the roads blockaded: the road to academic heights, the road to middle claß respectability, the road to being heard as an artist—they are *all* blocked.

At each gate, trolls will demand your money for acceß. Ignore their promises.

Only a game of chance will give you fair odds, fairer than life ever does.... How could you refuse to gamble when every bet is leß than what you bet every day you set foot outside your door?

By the way, I won that hand. I got everything home but my Jack. They won that but came up with fewer than 30 points, so I won my 54.

I would have loved to see my father and Günther Graß play Skat. They'd slaughter me, but it'd be an honor to be there. Call me Isaac.

Part Eleven: Astral Parkour and the Music of the Spheres

After a few drinks and Aasvogel's eventual 1500-point win, we all just sat around the perimeter of my small room and watched the sky. Some heat lightning flashed, but no rain clouds were anywhere to be seen. We were treated to a terrific light show.

I put on some Sigur Ros, and we all drifted off. We did some astral projecting. I took Nettie from rooftop to rooftop of the Strand. And then we went back and got Aasvogel and Nils, too.

This was astral parkour. We leapt as if we were in *Hard Day's Night* and we were a very together Beatles, loving life and exuberant.

Of course, insecurities bubbled up from below, but we made a game of 💥popping💥 them. We called them <<Bözmacher Moments.>>

We were lighter than air, but not because of symbiont lifeforms. We were buoyed by our ability to dream—together and individually.

We established a deep trust during the astral parkour. We knew that if any of us fell, the Œthers would be there to pick hir right back up.

I listened to the wailing sustain of the guitar—it was the cry of the prisoner who has abandoned all hope. Only by abandoning all hope does one find a pathway to true hope—the path that can be trod only by one person—the ¢elgh.

I turned on the TV again, with the sound off. Eintracht Frankfurt, in red and black vertical stripes, was playing Fortuna Düßeldorf, in yellow with red lettering. The referee and the linesmen were in robin's-egg blue. The offsides flag consisted of yellow and orange diamonds. The pitch was groomed into perfect ten-meter light-and-dark graß stripes. What colors!

I mentioned it to the Œthers. Aasvogel, apparently no Marxist, said, <<I like them all except the red.>>

We chuckled, and then each of us went hir own way mentally. Nettie had found my book on Abstract Expreßionist painting and was lost in one of Rothko's color fields. Nils was playing a wooden peg game I had. And Aasvogel was staring straight out at the stars, probably wondering if he'd ever be able to control them all, or worrying that they'd come to Mars to control him, more likely. He could laugh about the Bözmachers now, but they really had done irreparable damage to both his *corpus persona* and his *corpus civilitas*. Yes, the Aasvogel was an amazing man—he had two bodies.

My ¢elgh just kept musing digreßively. I was pretty sure I'd made my point on parkour. One shouldn't judge a sport by its practitioners. Look at the behavior of some of the most famous athletes of all time—you find rapists, murderers, drug addicts, thieves. The sport will cleanse its ¢elgh of its impurities. After a while, players who have abused the sports are held up as symbols of its abuse—who mentions Barry Bonds, for example, without feeling sad? Pete Rose? Shoeleß Joe Jackson? Denny McLean? They were all great players, but they thought they were powerful enough to change the definition of their sports. All they really did was add sad footnotes.

Where they could have shown enormous individuality would have been in their sports autobiographies. Here they could go *Finnegan's Wake* and Arno Schmidt combined, but here, ironically, where they have total freedom to do and behave however they like, they panic, bring in Al Hirshberg or someone to do the actual writing (and he's one of the best!), and we get a book pretty much like all the Œther sports biographies out there, especially baseball.

An individual overcomes adversity to achieve succeß. That's the story. What do they call that, the Horatio Alger myth? Or was it Horatio Hornblower? Ironically, Hornblower hated music. I wouldn't even *want* to know that person. So, Alger it is, and his son, Nelson Algren. And Brian Auger's Oblivion Expreß. Between Algren and Auger, a beautiful amount of space was built for us to enter and enjoy. Argent, for example. Rod Argent must have known Auger's work, and vice versa. Auger's ▶Whenever You're Ready◀ is on fire, but its tone is akin to that of ▶Tragedy◀ or even ▶Hold Your Head Up◀. They seem kindred even though one's jazz and the Œther's rock and roll. They straddle genres, like Jimmy Smith and Big Joe Turner, who take jazz to the blues. And of course Billie Holiday. Janis. Janis and Jimi and Jim had something else in common beyond dying at the same time in the same way. They all worked at the intersection of three great American arts: jazz, blues and rock. Auger did more of that in Trinity, with Julie Driscoll.

Nils almost spoke.

We went back to our thoughts.

Sashay testimonial suitable appoggia turn Sound ruling observing difficult bagpipe architecture. Being marshal effect about church, growth republic Waterloo ferric oxide.

It's time to rust. We are sitting here like broken tractors on the back forty, waiting for rain to help us rust. We are the sacrifice to the rain gods. So I broke out of clown prison to become a human sacrifice? That's not even funny.

Hey, I just heard one of you out in the peanut gallery. You want me to get on with the story? What do you mean by <<story>>? I'll get going, I promise, but for now just relax. Take a seat. Stop here and meditate on something important to you! What is it? Why is it so important?

Repair truck pulls up. It fixes the chapter. While it's doing that, I can proceed.

We'll be back after the repairs are made. There. Seamleß. You won't even notice it.

<<Where in the sky is oblivion?>> haxed the Aasvogel. <<I've always wondered.>>

<<I don't know. I've never been blown to oblivion,>> I said.

<<No?>> haxed Nettie.

<<Is anyone hungry?>> I haxed. <<I can make some falafels.>> Actually it's easy. The instructions are right on the box.

<<No, they're not!>> said the frustrated virgin as he walked acroß the stage and disappeared. Off-camera, he became electrified and sizzled and danced spasmodically.

Transmogrified.

Translucent.

♪Time Was♫. Wishbone Ash! I put on *Fighters and Warriors: Live in London 1972*, a bootleg. What a great show! Ted and Martin Turner, Andy Powell and Steve Upton. I'd forgotten how good Wishbone Ash was. For some reason, they didn't have it at the clown hatch. It belongs right next to Savoy Brown. Martin Turner's relentleß baß absolutely propels this along especially during the baß runs right when the guitars come in, all three very nicely playing off each Œther. And after that was their monster tune, ♪Blowin' Free♫. One of the great trail songs of all time. Like a strobe light but a thousand times subtler. What an inter-rusting sound. British blues mixed with Louisiana boogie, a little Southern rock, a little Texas boogie, some Memphis, old *Close to the Edge*-era Yes, Head East and Heartsfield, and Epitaph's twin-guitar attack on *Outside the Law*. They also seemed to have some of the theatricality of Jethro Tull to them, as well, at least in their sound if not their choreography.

<<You really like this hair band music?>>

<<Hair band? I wouldn't call Wishbone Ash a hair band. You're thinking of bands like Whitesnake. I don't think Wishbone Ash cared about their coiffure.>>

<<Still. Could we hear something else?>>

<<Sure. Anything within five steps of Zappa.>>

<<Okay, from Zappa, Napoleon Murphy Brock played with Ant-Bee who played with Gong/Acid MŒthers Gong→Acid MŒthers Guru/Guru Guru→Roland und die Dadadogs.>>

<<That's more than five.>>

<<No, it isn't Here. I'll list it for you:

1. Zappa, incl. Napoleon Murphy Brock→
2. Ant-Bee, incl. Napoleon Murphy Brock and Daevid Allen & Gilly Smith of Gong and/or Acid MŒthers Gong→
3. Acid MŒthers Temple→
4. Guru Guru, incl. Mani Neumeier, who also was in Acid MŒthers Guru, and Roland Schaeffer, whose side project was Roland und die Dadadogs→
5. The Occupants, incl. lead singer Dennis Frederick, who actually wrote ▶Dada Dog◀; Saul Smaizys, of Triad Radio fame, on sax and baß; Fred Kotowske on keyboards; and me on rhythm guitar. We were performing <<Dada Dog>> before Roland Schaeffer's album even came out, and on it he takes writing credit. Maybe he and Dennis wrote it together when Guru Guru came to Chicago and hung out at the Triad House. Saul knows all that stuff a lot better than I do—he ran Triad Radio, the finest rock station Chicago ever produced. It played *Sounds from Acroß the Big Swamp*, European innovative music—Krautrock like Guru Guru and Kraan, Italian rock like PFM, French rock like Magma, Greek rock like Aphrodite's Child. They also liked progreßive jazz—everything from Return to Forever to Luiz Bonfá's *Jacarandá*. Add a little from the English Canterbury music scene, like Soft Machine or Caravan, and some Œther English electric folk rock like Fairport Convention, and you get the picture.>>

<<And you quit the band to become a novelist?>>

<<I was already a novelist. I just needed to devote more attention to it—the band began taking up all my writing time. I hit my personal peak as a musical performer at our gig at Tut's. The gig at No Exit had been great, too. No Exit had a sunken stage in the center of the room when we played in the very beginning. Tut's, formerly the Quiet Knight, held more because the stage was in the corner of two perpendicular long rooms. We played to left and right, but they couldn't see each Œther for the wall in between. It was a giant V-shaped nightclub. We played great at Tut's, and to a packed house. That was as good as I was going to see for a long while because I dove head first into my writing. I realized I was far leß creative with a guitar than I was with words.>>

<<So what are you playing?>>

<<Roland und die Dadadogs.>>

<<And then?>>

<<How about some Mal Waldron with Embryo. The two Brain recordings?>>

<<*Steig Aus* and *Rockseßion*?>>

<<Yes.>>

<<Excellent.>>

<<Good.>>

<<I'm just going to go to the washroom for a minute, and I'll be refreshed for the next leg of the journey.>>

<<I'll get us some beer.>>

<<Great idea.>>

Nils and I slipped down into the apartment, and he hit the can while I grabbed a four-pack of bottles of the Orkney Islands' ▶Skull Splitter◀, currently a favorite beer of mine. I opened them with my old braß 1972 Kiel Olympics commemorative bottle opener.

Back upstairs I gave a beer to everyone except Nils, who wasn't back from the can yet. I set his beer in his place.

It was, as one would imagine from the name, a strong beer, eight point something percent. It's about as strong as anyone can make a beer before it tastes like cough syrup, like Eku 28, which is fourteen percent. Twenty-eight proof. That's liqueur territory, and it tastes like that, like beer liqueur. An acquired taste, that is.

The Mal Waldron Embryo stuff was trippy, meditative, like Can's *Soon over Babaluma.*

<<Look! A shooting star!>> said Nettie.

<<John Wayne or Gary Cooper?>> haxed Nils.

I said nothing, but I thought, ċGo ahead and hoist your ¢elgh on your own petard, Nilsꜿ.

I could imagine his reply: ċI should hoist my ¢elgh onto a spittoon?ꜿ or ċI should moisten my ¢elgh for Jean-Luc Picard?ꜿ

Maybe I mean, ċSure, go aheadꜿ.

Maybe I'm mean, a sure Goa head.

May beam insure goated.

M B I G.

I be MG, said the little car, anagrammatically.

Grandma Ana in her attic was tickly.

Nils frowned.

I nodded. I gueß we'd rung everything out of it we could. Or perhaps the beer had taken the edge off. It was okay. An asteroid shower began suddenly, however, and we were soon all riding asteroids through space, all four of us astral projecting together. That was the only time that ever happened to me.

My asteroid was oblong—a rounded triangular head and a squared tail. I rotated only slightly on its axis. I only had to take a step back every fifteen minutes or so.

Aasvogel, on his asteroid has his throne set up in front of a cave. His asteroid did not rotate, at least not that we could see.

Nils rode a needle-shaped asteroid that kept bucking like a bronco.

Nettie lay nestled in a crater.

I heard in the distance a familiar beat, a boogie, and then I knew it: Canned Heat doing ►Bullfrog Blues◄.

♪Did you ever wake up and have bullfrogs on your mind?♫

<<*Bullfrogs*? Not bull*shit*?>> haxed Nils.

<<No, bullfrogs. A whole plague of them.>>

<<Good. They'll eat these damn locusts,>> said Nettie.

<<I don't think that's why they were bullfrogs.>>

<<Why not?>> haxed Nettie.

<<That was censorship in those days. No one would have let William Harris record ►Bullshit Blues◄ back in 1928.>>

<<On the 78 RPM *Keep Your Man out of Birmingham*,>> added Nils.

<<Right. Rory Gallagher is said to have done a killer version of it. I'll have to track that down. Canned Heat's *Live at Topanga Corral* features a great guitar jam during the song.>>

<<Where's that music coming from?>> haxed the Aasvogel.

<<The asteroid in front of us,>> said Nils.

<<You'd think it would be playing the music of the spheres,>> said the Aasvogel.

<<May this *is* the music of the spheres,>> I said.

<<The blues are the music of the spheres?>> haxed Nettie.

<<Well, even the ancient Egyptians thought that Memphis was sacred,>> said Nils.

<<That explains ▶The Blues for Osiris◀ that Scuff Mud recorded,>> said I.

<<Not all blues are from Memphis,>> said the Aasvogel. <<What about Mißißippi Delta blues? Harris was from the Mißißippi Delta.>>

<<The Delta is also a sacred symbol going back to Ancient Greece. The fourth letter,>> said Nils.

<<What about Chicago? That's the true home of the blues,>> I said. <<Chicago is neither ancient nor sacred.>>

<<What? You don't think smelly onions are sacred?>> haxed Nettie.

We all laughed.

<<Perhaps they are,>> I said. <<Perhaps they are.>>

<<I don't know about smelly ones, but onions are sacred in Islam—mosques are frequently onion-domed—and in yoga, I think,>> said Nils, sounding a bit like Mr. Know-It-All.

In response, I said, <<Maybe it's not the fact that it's blues that is significant, but rather that the song is about bullfrogs. Frogs were one of the plagues from *Exodus*, so the song would be significant to Jews, Muslims, *and* Christians, all of whom uphold *Exodus* as scripture. But the frogs came *before* the locusts. The frogs came even before the flies. I gueß they succeßfully anticipated dinner.>>

<<You know, William Harris,>> said the Aasvogel, <<was cheated out of almost every cent he was owed. His record company put out his records under a dozen names and with fake names for the artist just to avoid paying him royalties.>>

<<Well, I gueß you'd know about royalties,>> said Nettie, getting into the spirit of things. The Aasvogel scowled at her: *Et tu*?

After a while the asteroids lost their direction and began revolving around each Œther. I looked at Nettie and heard the lyric from Canned Heat's version of ▶I'd Rather Be the Devil◀: ♪I'd rather be the devil than to be that woman's man♫. That was also *Live at the Topanga Corral*. But originally, of course, it was done by Delta blues guitarist Skip James.

<<Rick James?>> I haxed, just to fuck with Aasvogel.

<<No, you fool. *Skip* James,>> he replied. I never realized how into the blues the Aasvogel was. Hmm.

<<That's more of the Delta. Where's Chicago?>> I haxed.

<<Name it.>>

<<Oh, man. Chicago produced great music. Howlin' Wolf. Willie Dixon. Muddy Waters. Big Bill Broonzy.>>

<<Wait. Wasn't Howlin' Wolf originally from the Delta?>>

<<Their sound, though, was defined by their Cheß years. Cheß was to the blues what Blue note was to jazz.>>

<<Finally you said something smart,>> said the Aasvogel.

<<I always do,>> said I.

<<Rick James?>> said he.

<<The Superfreak!>> I said, laughing.

<<Musically, he had a Great White Cane,>> interjected Nils in a lame attempt to pile on. Plus he was making fun of blind people. Why do I have to tolerate this clown? Oh, wait—I gueß I'm the clown. Twirly the Clown. Well, at least I was never made up. I did wear a small child's wizard hat held on by an elastic strap under my chin. You can probably YouTube it, ▶Chlamydio Video◀ it, as the locals say.

I caught a glimpse of someone on the music asteroid. It looked like old Polymesus spinning the tunes. Man, I miß that cat. He was a great friend, easy to hang out with. It was my only friendship not broken up by a woman. Yeah, I know. Divide and conquer. It could have happened to us, but he left too soon. Now here he was, piloting five asteroids through the music of the spheres! Brilliant!

He put on Savoy Brown's *Skin 'n' Bone*—much of which sounded inexplicably like Paul McCartney meets Steely Dan except the guitar parts were far superior. It's a very good album, but very strange for Savoy Brown. Simmonds is very subtle on ▶This Day Is Gonna Be Our Last◀. His guitar work is what saves it from being Journey. It's a strange juxtaposition—his great guitar-playing and the somewhat generic arena band clichés. Simmonds can play anything, but his original musical thrust was with the blues. Fortunately the last two tracks on the album are excellent blues tracks. The title track, ►Skin 'n' Bone◄, is harder, more like Deep Purple than anything else. Paul Raymond's on organ. And then Polymesus spins ►I'm Alright Now◄ from Savoy Brown's *Savage Return*, an Œther odd recording. This song channels Guns n' Roses [sic].

What was Polymesus telling me? That even one's leßer work has merit worthy of notice? I suppose that's true. When I, as a boy, read Robert Louis Stevenson, I enjoyed his novels tremendously, but I enjoyed even more his rather obscure *Vailima Letters*, letters he wrote to his publisher when Stevenson lived in Western Samoa because of tuberculosis.

The asteroids began to slow down. I had my astral ¢elgh pull up alongside Astral Polymesus and hax him to play something a little more adventurous. Dreamier.

He put on Rain Parade's *Crashing Dream*. They were one of the best Paisley Underground bands, along with Dream Syndicate, Green on Red, Three O'Clock, Long Ryders, and the original Bangles, who had a great tune on their first EP, a song called ►How Is the Air Up There?◄ That might have been Susanna Hoff's song slamming Steve Wynn. An Œther friendship gone awry. Wynn talked about her song about him at some live gig that has a recording circulating.

As if he'd heard my thoughts, Polymesus put on some live Steve Wynn from McCabe's Guitar Shop, on July 28, 2006, a gig where he does a solo set and then comes back for a second set as a Dream Syndicate reunion with Paul Cutler, Dennis Duck, and Mark Walton. Find it—it's the Cat's Meow, Baby!

23 Skidoo! He remembered his Heavenly Blues. Let's all sing the Heavenly Blues....

We began to descend. We would sing the blues for reentry. It'd be nice to stay out there, but that doesn't happen. At least until that final parkour leap is made, the *Saut de Chat*, the leap of the cat, over the final obstacle into the gaping abyß from which no one returns.

I want to push the asteroids back out.'

Instead, they come together. The asteroids fit together like continents or jigsaw pieces. Polymesus goes into the cave behind the Aasvogel and disappears from view—we probably won't see him again for a long time. ♪The deceased are funny that way: they only come out when they have something to say.♫

Suddenly, from the cave, as we approach the surface of the planet, the words of Kurt Vonnegut, Jr., come rolling out at us. To bring us in, Polymesus has left us with Ambrosia. The music halted our descent. We looked for Polymesus in his cave, but he was gone. The four of us left the united asteroid and paddled back out on our silver surfboards in order to wait for an Œther wave. Oh, I see. Nettie would have to be Sue Storm. Nils is Johnny Storm. The Aasvogel, as leader, would be Reed Richards. But I'm not the Thing. Nils should be the Thing. I'd have to be Johnny Storm, but only if he was having incestuous relations with Sue. I gueß not. We're not the Fantastic four after all. Sorry to disappoint my ¢elgh.

<<Well, ¢elgh?>>

<<Well.>>

And I rode the wave in and crashed.

Brilliant Byzantine blue engulfed me. Every pore of my body was filled with light. I glowed. But the world had fallen completely short. The music had been shut off.

I was in a silent blue desert. I could not see my companions. I yelled out for them: Aasvogel! Nettie! Nils! But I could not hear my ¢elgh yell. Gesture and facial expreßion wouldn't help me now.

I remember thinking a while ago that music was becoming a burden, and it shut off. Am I being observed and copied or just ignored? How would I know? I began thinking this was a rather rough landing. I hope the Œthers have smoŒther reentries. Me, I just never belonged to begin with. I was demagnetized, but for some reason I survived. I saw no sign of the asteroid I'd ridden in on.

An even darker blue began encroaching from the horizon. What an event!

I had no idea that blue horizon events were silent. All of a sudden I did not understand Mike Vernon. But he sure had good taste in—what was it?—mus—mus—

Mustard! No. That wasn't it.

Muscae Volitantes? No, that wasn't it, either.

Muscle Shoals? I was rapidly losing control. The darker blue was a river riding in, canoe stacks on the bank. But the deer that drank from it had no bucks. I saw no horns. The river made no sound. It had no soul.

Music! That was what was mißing! The silence was strange. I was used to having a soundtrack to my life. I had out-Warholed Warhol! My mental film of my life had lasted fifty-one years. It was a virtual reality show starring me.

But where were my co-stars? They had landed somewhere else, hopefully all in good places. I was enjoying this, though. The silence was okay. It was hunky-dory. It was handkerchiefs. I may not have sound, but I have the musicality of words.

<<The perspicacity of turds is more like it,>> said Nils, right behind me. I almost died. My heart tried to come out my throat. I jumped and turned instinctively.

<<Nils!>> How'd he get here? Heck, how'd *I* get here?

<<Hello, Michel! What a wonderful trip, eh?>>

<<Not bad.>>

<<It was wonderful. I met an inter-rusting fellow named Polysemus—>>

<<You mean <Polymesus>?>> I haxed.

<<Yeah, maybe that was it. But anyway, I met him in a cave when I heard him calling out to Didier Malherbe, a fellow hermit on Malta.>>

<<I believe you. I shared some time with Polymesus, also. I didn't know you knew him.>>

<<I didn't. I only just met him.>>

Oh.

Oh? Ahoy! Ahem. Ahimsa.

A hearse, uh? That would be fitting for my death mask. Should I trim my nose hairs?

No, it's the actual death mask. This is just the pre-fitting. The catalogue has many different styles. Ionic. Dorian. Gray. Black. White.

I was the sincere one—no wax!

Whacks hurt.

Okay, so I'll just hit the can.

You'll break your hand.

That's okay. I know of a second-hand store downtown.

I stepped on Nils's toe.

<<Ow!>> he said.

<<Want me to call you a tow truck?>> I haxed.

I think he got it. If I can't have music, I'm certainly not going to put up with puns. We have better busineß to borrow. Tomorrow.

Today I'm going to play.

Nils tried to step on my toe back. Oh!

<<Do not adulterate those cigarettes, my friend,>> said the Aasvogel, also popping in out of nowhere. <<Our friend Polymesus sends us his best wishes,>> he said. <<Plus he gave me some Skat advice. You, my friend, have a tell, and I'm not going to tell what your tell is!>>

Silly trout all ignite sly trolley mice.

The flaming trolley stops and lets off one occupant: Nettie, wearing a shift of fire. She dove into the river, and steam filled the air.

She emerged from the smoky river glistening, very feminine. I had a hard time remembering she was Aasvogel's munitions expert. But she was, and she really knew what she was doing.

I knew right then I couldn't hold her. She had a hold of Œther materiel far more important than I am. She had personnel.

So did I. Nils. Would he want to be an aßistant again after having run the show in my absence?

<<Michel,>> said the Aasvogel, <<I want you to know that the idea to step down and let you resume running the disc golf centers was Nils's, not mine.>>

<<What about the Parkour Park?>>

<<Nils said he'd had to come to terms with his hostility to parkour. And in so doing, he came to actually like it very much. I don't know if you noticed, but he's dropped some weight to do it.>>

<<No—hadn't noticed.>>

<<Anyway, let him run that. You run disc golf. We'll promote disc golf as Mars Condatis's number one family sport! It will be so. You go set up that new course—the historical one in the swamp. That sounds terrific. People need to be more aware of the history of this planet. And also of Earth. Knowing our shared history is not only fascinating, but it's also liberating. We can take pride in the pride, like the lyin' silly trout we are.>>

The sly trolley mice scurry past like they have scurvy paßing like a survey thrashing such as profeßional form-fillers have.

My native city has thrashers. Survey thrashers beat people over the head with surveys, especially on line.

Do you know why people hate spiders? Because they already feel like they're caught in a web. Society is the spider, and it's coming for you….

My tomatoes are dying. Two of the plants were terminal. I terminated them. I pulled the green tomatoes off, but three, I think, won't turn color. I'll just fry them up with something—they're not very good uncooked—not nearly as refreshing as the slightly sour lemon taste of tomatillos. I love tomatillos. I've put them in salads before because of how good they taste raw.

I love making salads, by the way. I have used hundreds of vegetables in salad—from watercreß and dandelion to daikon to celery root to radish greens to fiddleheads (sautéed in butter, of course) to my beloved tomatillos. Red cabbage, celery leaf, fresh basil leaves, fennel, peppers of a dozen sorts, artichoke hearts, palm nuts, baby corn, shredded carrot, dulse, spinach, raddichio, escarole, jicama, meats and shellfish, artificial bacon bits made of soy (I prefer them in salad to real bacon. Though I love real bacon. I know—I'm a primitive. I'd be all over roasted boar. I don't see much that is loveable about a boar).

Hey, look at that red herring! I love herring. I think it has to do with my ancestry from Friesland. A people of renegade upstarts. Fiercely independent but not imperialistic. I want to learn Frisian and then visit. That is one of the goals of my life. I was there before, with my father. I would like to return. First I have to get rich and in a hurry if I'm ever going to afford a trip like that. But I would love one day to write a novel in Frisian. It is the language right between German and English. Oh, you thought no doubt that Michel du Jabot is French? Was Guillaume Apollinaire? Have I told you about my friendship with Federman? He'd vouch for me. I don't know how the Franks and Frisians got along. They probably co-existed without any conflict.

Nils exploded with laughter, his beer shooting out of his nose.

<<You are so full of shit,>> he said, through a tißue. <<You think anybody's going to believe that crap?>>

<<Belief?>> I said, feigning shock. <<I thought we were men of science, not belief!>>

Nettie and the Aasvogel exchanged a glance, both shaking their heads.

<<What should we do about these goofballs, Nettie?>> haxed the Aasvogel.

<<Well….>> I began to defend my ¢elgh.

<<That's a deep subject,>> interrupted Nils, laughing at his own stupid joke like a six-year-old!

<<They deserve each Œther,>> she said while laughing.

Gradually everyone began to come down, down to the river….

<<Or to where the highways meet in Lombard,>> I said, remembering.

<<Langobard, you mean,>> said the Aasvogel.

<<♪Langobards, they come in the winter, come in the winter…♫,>> sang Nils.

Nettie, the Aasvogel and I looked at Nils with startled surprise.

<<Shh!>> said Nettie. <<No music!>>

<<Oh, sorry,>> Nils said. <<I forgot.>>

<<It's okay,>> I said. <<Just a rookie mistake. It's hard to realize how much one depends on music until one is deprived of it.>>

The Bar-Gander Food Market always plays suicidal singer-songwriter music. I feel like slashing my wrists by the time I get to the produce section.

Have some blood oranges. They're endorsed by John Hawkes.

You can find blood oranges in the deli.

Dozens of chicken hearts are packaged together and sold for cheap. Chicken hearts are not worth much. Leß than livers. The livers are brave hearts.

If Aasvogel is the head man and the big cheese, does that make him head cheese?

Hey, Mack, Errol Flynn was a fishwife's man. He may have built good fences, but that didn't make him a good neighbor. Stateville was there, riots in the prison. Attica State!

Attaboy, Skate! Skate was a disc dog, though he'd gone feral. He'd come around all derelict, Frisbee hanging from his lips.

We all went outside and played catch with Skate on the lighthouse lawn. At least until my eccentric neighbor Lester came by, prying into my busineß. Actually, I think he came by to stare at Nettie. But he was the local watch commander, so he came and went as he pleased. He was a dirty little man, grimy, smelly, like some horrible Charles Dickens character only with the aroma of a Milano train station urinal and the slime of the pigeon waters of Venice. He had none of the charm of Marcovaldo, though.

<<Miß Potts,>> he said from between rotten teeth. <<Good to see you again.>> He lifted his slouch hat that bore the emblem of the local watch. Cleverly, it was a watch. Nettie tried to hide her disgust and said, <<Hello, Commander. At ease.>> That confused Lester, who now thought he should have been saluting. He put his hat back on and saluted and then feigned ease.

<<Have you seen any suspicious activity?>> he haxed her.

<<I was going to hax you that, Commander!>>

<<No, I haven't.>>

<<Neither have we.>>

<<None of those parkour runners about?>>

<<Good God, no. It's been very quiet.>>

<<Wonderful. Well, carry on,>> he said.

<<Carrion?>> haxed Nils.

<<Shh!>> I admonished. After Lester had gone, I told Nils, <<You never want to give Lester a reason to linger. Just let him be.>>

<<Lester, linger! Smell my finger!>> Nils called after Lester after Lester had gone.

I hit him in the ear.

<<Ow!>> he exclaimed.

<<Shut up!>>

<<I'm maimed!>>

<<Act as though, and you shall be.>>

<<Yuck. What's that? Some old Bözmacher cliché?>>

<<Pretty much. But really, man, do not make that Lester cat linger.>>
<<Scat finger?>>

<<The smelliest, like you wouldn't believe.>>

<<Like you wouldn't relieve—>>

<<►Relieve◄ your ¢elgh!>>

<<I will, but not here. That’d be rude.>>

<<Well, we’re here in the house that rude built.>>

<<Don’t yank my chain.>>

<<Damn Yankee gin,>> I said, offering Nils a cup. He refused. Nils, apparently, did not drink or something.

<<Garbage in, garbage out,>> he said.

<<So you want some pea soup?>> I haxed. <<But I always heard you are what you eat. I presume you eat nuts.>>

<<Well, that’s an argument for not eating vegetables,>> he said.

<<I’ve heard that,>> I said. <<That’s why I eat liver and brains.>>

<<And corn, apparently.>>

<<Stop it, guys,>> said Nettie. <<It’s beginning to hurt. Who do you guys think you are, anyway. Menudo?>>

<<Menudo? What’s that?>> haxed the Aasvogel, who was only used to eating high on the hog.

<<Tripe,>> explained Nettie. <<The stomach lining of cattle. Mixed in different foods, of course. It’s the last meat to go except maybe chitterlings.>>

<<But I’ve seen you eat natural-casing sausage,>> I reminded her.

<<He’s got you there,>> said Nils, backing me up. Maybe I’d under-rustimated him. He was backing me up.

Okay, then, quick, everybody a concept!

Nils said, <<Candy Machine.>> Good. That was actually a Steve Wynn song.

<<Michel!>>

<<Oh—no music—I forgot. Sorry.>>

Candy machine. A thing you beat and kick and rock and poke and prod until you get some sweetneß out of it when all you thought was it was going to cost a little money.

You can spend all of your money, and the sweetneß will never drop, like a castrato's testicles.

<<Why is the currency called ▶testicles◀?>> haxed Nettie, shimmying to some music in her head that she wasn't feßing up to.

<<Because someone with testicles invented money. Gyges. First of the Mermnadae kings of Lydia. After the Heracleans died out with Candaules the Hound Choker. But that story's ridden off with Przewalski's Horse many years ago. You can find it there,>> I replied.

<<You're creepy,>> she said.

<<Not usually,>> said the Aasvogel. <<But he keeps it inter-rusting.>>

<<Thanks,>> I said. <<Appreciate it.>>

<<I do.>>

<<No, I mean *I* do. I appreciate your kind words. I have worked hard throughout my life, and I like working for you. You have a good heart. And you are the second best Skat player I know.>>

<<Behind Nils?>> he haxed.

<<Behind my ¢elgh,>> I insisted.

<<You know, if you stopped playing, you could be a very important person. A leader, like me. A genius like Polymesus. You just don't seem to apply your ¢elgh the way he did.>>

<<What? A cook is more important than disc golf?>>

<<Yes!>>

<<You don't understand, then. Wait till you're old and fat.>>

<<I'm never getting old.>>

When he said that, I laughed my toes out of my nose. He was already twice my age. In a couple of Œther years, he'd be three times my age. We'd come from different planets, though. That explains why the Aasvogel is so hotheaded. He's from the Venus colony originally. Nils must be from Mercury because I'm always trying to put him out.

<<Growing Homer,>> said the Aasvogel.

<<What?>>

<<My concept. To add to ►Candy Machine◄.>>

<<Okay.>>

<<Growing Homer. Going home. And then homer than that. I'm going back to before I began, to before the spark. I was once just two separate thoughts that combined into one. No Circe this time. I don't have the energy for Circe anymore.>>

<<Thus spake Aasvogel,>> said Nils, taking the microphone and pretending he was Mr. Karaoke. <<But who are the product people?>> imitating Zappa.

<<►Product◄? Hey, wait. You've already had a concept. It's Nettie's turn.>>

<<She's not being productive.>>

<<Shut up. If she was productive twice, she'd be reproductive.>>

<<Sexist swine. No, it has nothing to do with gender. She just doesn't have a sponsor; I have candy machines.>>

<<Nils, stop it. I want to hear Michel, and I have one, too,>> said Nettie. <<Mine's ►Precaution◄.>>

<<Precaution?>>

<<Yes. ►Caution◄ means to be careful. So ►precaution◄ would be what you do *before* you are careful.>>

<<So ►precaution◄ *de facto* implies careleßneß?>> haxed the Aasvogel.

<<Yes!>>

<<Jacques Derrida would love you,>> Aasvogel said.

<<What's yours, Michel?>> haxed Nettie. I'd been thinking. I had many favorite words and expreßions. ►Perhaps◄ was a perennial. ►*A posteriori*◄ was a posterior I. ►Postpone◄ is what happens to you after you've eaten corn meal.

<<In hoc signo vinces,>> I said, croß.

<<*That*'s your term?>>

<<No. I'm preparing for it. This is an important decision.>>

Candy Machines.

Going Homer.

Precaution.

►Inhumanity◄. That's mine. Inhumanity is in humanity, and humanity is inhumanity.

You mean humanity is in inhumanity, and inhumanity is inn humanity.

I mean inhumanity contains humanity, but humanity drives inhumanity. It drives inn humanity to inhumanity.

Humanity loves inhumanity, but inhumanity tortures humanity.

It'd be inhuman not to wonder what

to be inhuman was
in the middle of an
in the corner and
of a badge that reads
ignite sly trolley

finding a friend
page with a key
on the bottom
<<silly trout all
mice.>>

The mice chase the trout through the candy machines. They are going homer than I am. They've taken the precaution not to be in humanity.

That should raise up some goats in tobacco candle grease. The trout swim right through it. The mice skitch a ride. They're riding on some Rolos and avoiding crashing on the Crunches. They goats don't pay any mind. They're just chewing on tobacco, watching everything go by. Why else would goats have such eerily wide eyes? Maybe they're watching out for badgers.

In humanity, precaution. Going homer. Candy machines. I had it all backwards. My whole life's been backwards.

<<Oh, boo hoo,>> said Nettie from the peanut gallery.

<<Okay,>> I said. <<Mr. Maudlin's going homer.>> I wanted to precaution you. I've been looking around, and I haven't seen any canned E's.>>

Nettie raspberried me. Nils rolled his eyes. The Aasvogel shook his head. That was called laying an egg. If I lay an Œther over here, what will I have?

<<Nothing,>> said Nettie, <<for you cannot lay eggs.>> That must be one of the oldest

jokes in the world.

<<Which world?>>

Ah, that's the question....

Part Twelve: Don Quickset

They're all off doing their own things again. Aasvogel's having dreams of commanding knights on horseback, no doubt. Nettie is busting an international diamond-smuggling team of gymnasts who ski on their heads. Nils is memorizing the Henny Youngman book of jokes (God save us!) Me? I think they've forgotten I'm here. Which is great. No one smarten them up. I can just sit here, relax, and not feel preßure to contribute anything.

What should we hear? Okay—we've had some nice silence for a while. Now put on Pink Floyd recorded live in Sapporo, Japan, on March 12, 1972, playing *Dark Side of the Moon* live in advance of the album. Plus ►One of These Days◄ and ►Careful with That Axe, Eugene◄.

Zone out on the buzzsaw sounds coming from the guitar in ►Time◄. Thrash music for the catatonic? No, the last hurrah of the English leisure claß. Church organ, electric guitar, heavy drumming and baß lines.

Occasionally I am able to watch a small-mouthed baß using the famous Entwistle-Hattler lure.

Lightly breaded, pan-seared baß taste good but has a million bones. <<Fish hairs,>> as my sister used to say.

What did one baß say to the Œther?

Avoid all those pick-up lines.

Ha ha, replied the Œther baß. Here's a story for you: ►The Baß Turd and the Whale Dung◄.

Sounds like a shitty story. Just keep it to your ¢elgh.

Well, I don't know it yet. I'd make it up as I go.

<<Will you two shut up?>> haxed an annoyed Nettie again of Nils and me.

<<You're back, too?>>

Only the Aasvogel was still gone, but that only made sense: he had the greatest incentive of us because he had to visit all the hinterlands anyway. Part of his duty.

Yeah, I said, <<duty.>>

*

<<If you play any more music,>> said the Aasvogel, upset that the music had brought him back, <<I'm going to have Nettie arrust you.>>

<<Who put a bug your aß?>> I haxed him. <<I show you astral parkour, and you come back all pißed off?>>

<<That's an eßential difference between you and me,>> he said. <<You are eßentially a nice guy.>>

I snorted at that.

<<I, however,>> he continued, <<am not.>>

I started humming the Four Seasons' ▶Big Girls Don't Cry◀ to get a meßage acroß to him.

<<There you go with that music again,>> said the Aasvogel. <<I told you, no music. Nettie, arrust this clown.>>

<<You're kidding. I'm not a clown.>>

<<No, I gueß not. But tonight you're going to be in jail.>> He walked away. Nettie cuffed me (she *cuffed* me!) and took me away.

*

She marched me into the dungeon.

<<I was hoping you'd bleß me and keep me. I didn't mean this keep.>>

<<What are you talking about, Michel? This isn't the keep.>>

<<Sure it is; the dungeon is the keep.>>

<<No,>> she said, laughing at me (laughing at me!) <<The keep is the *donjon*, not the *dungeon*.>>

<<What's a *donjon*?>>

<<That's the main tower.>>

<<Are you sure?>>

<<I'm the Aasvogel's expert on armaments and battlements. I think I know what I'm

talking about.>>

<<Well, you sure aren't the Aasvogel's expert on breath mints. You reek.>> And then I turned to the guards accompanying her. <<Uh—I have found her. The malodorous m'lady. Or ▶malady◀ for short.>>

<<Ease down, Michel. It's only for a night. You know he'll wake up in a better mood and will forgive you.>>

<<Forgive me? For humming? Genghis Khan was leß temperamental.>>

<<Yeah, well, you'll have that. You should know better.>>

<<Sorry. So now I suffer the tortures of Don Juan?>>

<<Donjon. Not Don Juan. I mean, the dungeon, not Don Juan. Shut up. You're confusing me.>>

<<Are you sure I'm not Don Quickset?>>

<<What?>>

<<Perhaps, like Don Juan, I semen'd the women and fought all the men.>>

<<Cement? Ha, no. And that's sexist. And I'm in no mood for your puerile humor. Save it for Nils's visit.>>

<<Are you going to chain me to the iron rings in the wall? What will you use on me then? The twisting stork? The inquisitor's chair? The Judas cradle? The strappado?>>

<<No. I think the Golden Turkey will suffice.>>

<<What's that?>>

<<The award for really bad over-acting.>>

<<Oh, ha ha.>>

<<Here's your apartment for the night,>> she said, and she released me into a rather nice replica of an old Victorian bedroom. It was actually quite quaint.

<<Now just one more thing, Michel.>>

<<What?>>

<<Please just suffer in silence.>> She turned and walked away, accompanied by her

giggling gaggle of guards. I stretched out on the long, red-velvet divan. This was tough. How would I ever survive this captivity? I saw I had two byobu to give me privacy—I could arrange them how I chose. I didn't entirely block off the bars—I wanted to be able to see if anyone was there, but I didn't want to be seen. The space between the byobu let a sliver of light through, and from the divan I could see out through that sliver. So long as I left the light behind me off, I was invisible.

The mini-fridge was filled with a dozen varieties of beer, including my ancestral Jever, and with top-notch coldcuts—smoked Schinken, Teewurst, grobschnitt Braunschweiger, and Sülze, it looked like—and some smoked Edamer and Jarlsberger cheeses. And some Leberkäse. Put some all on some whole-kernal Echt Westphälischer Pumpernickel. No—this would be a hardship. A bottle of eiskalten Bommerlunder in case the food upsets my stomach.

The horror! No Düßeldorfer Löwensenf! Oh, wait, here it is! Wunderbar! This was going to be hard. I knew it. But then an entertainment wall opened, and in walked Robert Johnson, the blues master, tilting back his head a little to look at me from the bottom of his eye.

<<From the bottom of his *eye*?>>

<<Yeah, I like that one. Leave it in.>>

<<Okay, yer the boß, Big Tuna.>>

Robert Johnson didn't say anything at all. He went right to the stage in this swank little joint, took his axe to the middle of the room, opened it, took out a Tommy gun, brought it to his hip, pointed it at me and then at the farther byobu.

I got him a beer out of the fridge. BYOB, you hipster! I didn't say that, though. I haxed him to play ►32-20 Blues◄. He nodded, and then I saw that his Tommy gun was his guitar. He played ►Preaching Blues◄ after that and then his biggest hit, ►Terraplane Blues◄. Then he flew off in a tarot plane, hiding behind the Jester card, the Fool. Hiding behind me, I gueß.

Wow, Robert Johnson was here! There he goes, in that aeroplane.

Terraplane Tommy Gun banged a gong, and again I was alone.

A light shone in, all mist-rosy through the rose-colored glaß-window treatments. I looked out and saw a train coming down a track right next to the prison cells. The engineer was Hudie Ledbetter, and he was singing ►Midnight Special◄. The train looked like it was coming right at me, but at the last second it swerved away. It mißed, rosy though it was.

A rosy thought, that was.

Outside, I saw a nosey trough for animals with large schnozzes, like horses or cattle. Or long-nosed bandicoots and elephants. The trough was empty, though, so the animals were complaining. It was a noisy drought.

I pulled a Boise draught beer out of the fridge and sat down to drink it. The poison daughter pictured on the label of the beer looked somewhat familiar, like someone I knew years ago, a girl with a pointleß cough.

She haxed me in all earnestneß what point laughter made in conversation. She considered it a frivolous distraction. She also disliked music for the same reason. We obviously did not hit it off well, she and I.

She hung her ¢elgh ironically from the painted bough of a jubjub tree. She had ranted enough for one lifetime—she was on her way to rant on in the next. I heard that God hasn't gotten a word in edgewise ever since. Even in the afterlife she was only granted rough asylum. Now heaven's haunted tough. Even the serpent's slanted slough snags leß criticism. God even offered to give chocolate-slathered dough for devil's food cake just to take her off his hands, but the devil would have no part of her no matter how salaciously naughty the cake was.

Satan ought to have wanted her, but she kept standing at heaven's gate, arguing for admißion against all odds.

Eventually even Lucifer let go of her. God shut her up and out, and she presumably is cavorting with Limburger cheese in Limbo and then purging her ¢elgh in Purgatory.

A clown car pulled up in front of the divan. Out stepped the following musicians: Spencer Davis, Graham Parker, Steve Hillage, AJ Guba, Tommy James, Gregg Rolie, Nick Lowe, Robert Hunter, Frank D'Rone, Bill Kees, Hobo Coble, Bob Kimbell, Frank Raven, Pruston Klik, JC Ronder, Neal Schon, Rick Danko, Bryan Day, Tricia Alexander, Ember Schrag, Dave Rudolph, Huey Lewis, Mark Lynott, Saul Smaizys, Howard Kaylan, Ralph Schuckett, Eddie Clearwater, Big Twist, Pete Special, and Brion Poloncic. They all lined up, leaned together, and posed grinning like cheese.

Ya gotta love musicians. After the photo, they all climbed back into their clown car and disappeared into the bars.

The photo was posted on the opposite wall. It looked very much like the poster from Zappa *We're Only in It for the Money*, but without the vegetables, who must have been called away.

Man, I met all those cats. Spencer Davis I met at what Pezband referred to as a ►party for some local rag◄. Davis was working A&R for Janus Records. He was super nice, very polite. Man so many were so cool. Gregg Rolie. Graham Parker. Nick Lowe. Steve Hillage. Mark Lynott. Hobo Coble. Bob Kimbell. Tommy James. Huey Lewis. Those guys I spent some good time with. We drank or smoke to gather. Many hours with each.

Well, except Tommy James; him I only met the one time for an interview.

I worked freelance and had sold a few pieces to that ▶local rag◀. One of my best friends was the aßistant or aßociate editor—whatever—he went on to become a brilliant photographer. He did a series of triptychs you'd be better off as a human to encounter. Man, he was a genius— always way ahead of me. He led this magical, charmed life where everything seemed to fall into place. That was not the case, of course. He had as much tragedy in his life as anyone, but he knew how to pay attention to what mattered. I know he must have gotten lost a couple of times. Who hasn't? It's not getting lost that is in and of its ¢elgh so troubling. It's the panic it produces. If you eliminate the panic, everything goes more smoothly.

Be slow to anger, slow to glee. Hold back as long as you can and, when you can hold back not one tiny second into the future more—boom! Snap! Crash!— Even then you need to hold back. Wait for it to paß, like waves riding through your spine. They'll surge. Ride them. That's surfing. Trust in it. Just stay up and ride it along like you're skiing downhill. Set a target. Remember the target. That lodge! You go, and all of a sudden you are experiencing life in action. You were waterskiing on the glaß surface of Sayner Lake in Wisconsin.

Everything is better in the Sayner! Inter-rusting times, for sure. Good friends, nice places, great food.

We never did catch Old Moßback. Did almost catch a snipe. And a jackalope.

With a little lemon pepper I feel just a little bit happier.... 23 Skidoo who got this all going anyhow.

This is confusing— I'm supposed to be enjoying music but resisting it at the same time? I'm not even supposed to pursue music anymore? That makes no sense. Hey, be like Graham Parker. Just keep on as best you can forever. Just do what you do. Just what you like. But that's blind faith, my son.

So he rolled the dominoes into the cream, and we may all meet back in the yard, birds are willing, the hand jive for five having left off in Lake Forust, a far-northern suburb of Chicago, in Illinois, in the United States of America, North America, Western Hemisphere, Earth, Solar System, Milky Way Galaxy, and so on.

Only I'm in something you're not.

Yeah, you're into the lemon pepper.

If I don't stop making noise all the time, I'm going to be trapped in this room will forever. It's a nice room. Queen Victoria probably mißes it. I'm comfortable, though. The music keeps playing.

Right now it's Mingus's ►A Foggy Day◄ from *Pithecanthropus Erectus*, on which Mal Waldron tickles the ivories, or was that tinkles on the ivies. I have heard some of Waldron's stuff with Embryo. It must be like hearing Ed Caßidy's work with Zoot Sims, wasn't it? Mingus and Mani Neumeier would have been one hell of a combination! They used percußion for melody in ingenious ways. And then percußion was forbidden. Who'd ever top that? Jazz Crusaders? Stix comes close on ►Aleluja◄ on *Live at the Lighthouse '66* on Pacific Jazz! On, Dasher and Dancer! On, Fred and Barney at the dance studio!

That would have left Wilma and Betty to their own devices, which they could share at a devices party. The divisive party was really Fred, whose decision it was to take dance leßons in the first place. Fred reminded me of Nils, so I shut off the TV. I pulled an Œther Jever from the fridge.

Yes, Jever is Frisian. No, Du Jabot is not. My father's family, immigrant American, was Alsatian in origin and Frankified its name during World War One when America entered the war. Then they almost changed it again with the capitulation of the Vichy government to the Nazis. My mŒther's family was the Frisian one, and they never fully adopted German to begin with. My great-grandmŒther still spoke East Frisian.

I looked out the window of my jail cell. It was high up, and all I could see was a piece of the sky, but this time a cloud paßed along inside the frame of the window. The cloud was striated into dozens of tiny segments that, placed in parallel to each Œther as they were, resembled a backbone. I was seeing the spine of the sky.

I began to wonder if Œther such delightful sensory experiences involving sight or the Œther senses were being mißed because I filled my mind so much with music.

I remember how a former bandmate of mine from 2+1=0 said to me, incredulously, ten years after the band had broken up and we had met again by accident, <<Golly, *really*? You still follow *music*?>> as if my doing so were a freakish oddity.

Perhaps I am just holding on to the past. Perhaps music is indeed gone, as is the novel, as is the painted image. I hold onto these the way Luddites held onto the horse-drawn carriage, wash boards and Fels Naptha, and dinner conversation.

Our novels are copies of copies of copies. Our paintings are digital manipulations of Œther paintings. Our music is a rehash of old hash.

Why *am* I holding on? Comfort? Music has brought me comfort. Rimbaud would have had me discard it for that reason. He said he hated winter because it was the season of comfort.

He'd had me wear rags on my feet and try to take Moscow in winter just to experience the sensation. Of course, the idea goes all the way back to Gauthier—¢elgh-mutilation as release from ennui. How boring. That note has been hit far too often.

We have lost our subtlety of response. We are no longer subtly responsible. When we respond, we are not subtle anymore.

We no longer represent. We can only present. Past and future are lost.

We can no longer recount. We can only count. And only by using our fingers and toes.

We can no longer review. We can only view. Persistence of vision is a defunct myth.

We can no longer rewrite. We take in everything in one enormous draft.

We can never rebound from our decadence. We are bound forever by our wrists and ankles.

Our efforts no longer resound acroß continents or ages. They merely bleat out a sound and then drift away in silence

Nothing we do can be rewound, but we wind up each Œther every day.

We can't relieve. We leave.

We tire, but won't retire our weary old ways of hindering our neighbor's progreß. We love to stand in each Œther's way.

We have solutions but no resolutions, spite without respite, signs without resignation, claims without reclamation.

Also, claims without exclamation. And we write tracts sans extraction. We are ample without example.

That's what it comes down to.

Part Thirteen: Visiting Hours

Under the enormous Armenian rug depicting the Martyrdom of St. Hripsime, small creatures are emerging. They are insects of some sort. I hope not parasites—¢elgh-protective bugs don't bŒther me. But aggreßive bŒthers bug the bejeezus out of me…

The Aasvogel becomes a wild bore. Only illumination can save him.

I wish I had been born rich, perhaps English aristocracy. I would love to have been a member of the leisure claß, but then I couldn't write. The act of writing was considered toil and an act of economic desperation.

Writing has always been an act of desperation.

We may have storage, but we have no rustoration.

Eat your porridge without perspiration.

I'm an old con man without consternation. I have seen much. I have no need to panic. I am Aesop's tortoise.

<<Welcome, campers! You are here at Cons Turn Nation, where cons turn pro! You will have free acceß to all our learning facilities, from safecracking to lock-picking to making a getaway, here at Cons Turn Nation! In Downey, where the freeways meet! Right next to Eddie's Double Knits, acroß the street from Ralph's Spoilsport Grocers.>>

The TV wasn't going to amuse me long, I could tell.

I had reached some sort of impaße. Even if, in the morning, I was rustored to the Aasvogel's good graces, why would I want to live by his whim?

ꭓAt Ralph's Spoilsport Grocers, we can't rustore, but we can store!ꭓ

The King of Tortes should never extort. So why does the Aasvogel lavish me with such punishment? Especially when I supposedly saved him from the Shining Path of Fallen Intellectuals.

I could have haxed for a cushy position on the faculty of Mars Condatis University with a nice Development Office expense account that would take me to Paris or Sandy Eggo at the drop of a frozen waffle. Why did I only hax to run the disc golf courses? I was tired. You have no idea how long those years in public service were. Serving as an envoy. And how long I spent working my way up to the position. I felt I was climbing a spiral staircase into the sky only to find nothing there.

You remember how the Œthers who'd come up here had called down how beautiful it was. It wasn't. They were lying in order to trick Œther people up here, too. Misery loves mushrooms. Champignon champagne companions.

So, at the top, so as not to arouse the ire of the deceived, one, looking out upon the expanse of nothingneß, says,<<Oh, yeah, the Emperor's New Clothes and the King's Lead Hat. It's beautiful up here.>> You knew the truth, but why bŒther smartening anyone else? The Œthers won't believe you.

You're king of the hill until the next adventurer goes up there. Then you need to worry if when she or he comes back down, if she or he will keep the secret or reveal the truth.

But no one ever reveals the truth. No one wants to be embarraßed. No one wants to arouse the ire of the deceived.

So the dungeon is a posh Victorian bedroom with a built-in entertainment system for holographic musical presentations, presumably, and for staring off into profound silence.

One can beckon ham from the kitchen with a bell on a silver platter. Add some chemo wasabi to the antelope on the loan range. Oh, well. It *is* prison, after all. Just like paranoid Maricopa sheriffs: after all.

<<Yes, Chemo Wasabi?>>

<<Then you are my Tante, my antelope. But for my Tante, you look a lot like my old friend Nellie.>>

<<Nettie.>>

<<Ah! Then you know her.>>

<<Hell, I *am* her.>>

<<Why am I here?>>

<<Well, your mŒther met your father and they liked each Œther….>>

<<No. *Here.* In this jail cell.>>

<<Jail cell? This is the love nest I built for us,>> she said.

Say what?

<<I wanted us to have some time alone far away from the prying eyes of Aasvogel, He's out—his chef gave him a large dose of tryptophan at dinner. Plus this whole area

is completely soundproofed. He never wanted to hear the screams of the tortured. And he'd never visit because he can't stand seeing misery—it makes him sick. Unfortunately instead of healing it, he just ignores it. His sickneß becomes pneumonia easily. Gotta watch that. At least he got through all that without any STDs.>>

I didn't really want to get on the subject. It's kryptonite. It's blood money. It kind of killed the mood. I don't want to think about him as I'm smooching with her.

I'll wait till later, when the image is forgotten, when the mage is forgiven and the ►i◄ is forked over.

So let's go over here, to a windy day at the Zirkus Bremen.

The four companions are walking along to a service tent to see a tanked tiger: rumors were that it had followed an elephant into a wedding reception and that the two of them had drunk all six punch bowls of pink champagne brandy punch. The elephant had a stronger constitution and moved on. The tiger paßed out next to a punch bowl. He was a bit of a lightweight with the booze, that one. One could never really count on him. Not even using his stripes. They were annoyingly uneven! A civilized cat would have even stripes, after all.

After all!

If I were aristocracy, I couldn't write because my fingernails would be too long. Holding a pen (yes, I write by pen) would be nigh impoßible. *Trés impoßible*! Even Moinous could not do that!

<<Neigh!>> exclaimed half a pantomime horse. An ongoing investigation has been undertaken to determine the exact point of origin of the exclamation. I'm thinking front half, but I could be wrong.

<<I killed them! I killed them all!>> I think he was quoting Oedipus.

They're not dead, you dumb horse.

<<Not the tigers. I know that. I mean my partners in back. I have been told I've ruined their careers!>>

<<So? What's a career?>>

<<Well, it's more than an occupation.>>

<<It's a profeßion! That's what it is!>> said one of the companions.

<<No—it's more than that. It's a vocation!>>

<<What, God calls to people in the desert and haxes them to be back ends of pantomime horses. Yeah, that's pretty funny.>>

<<It's not.>>

<<It isn't?>>

<<I don't get it.>>

<<Obviously>>

The pantomime horse sank through the floor, mißing end first.

Up instead of the steed stood staid Stan Snide, standing in good stead sans stewed Sam Stride.

The comedy duo had escaped from the 1970s, where disco killed them and re-materialized 50 years later and on that dour planet Neptune.

<<It was too depreßing to be dour,>> said Stan, the taller of the two, bald, mißing a tooth, so he had trouble with certain sounds—not quite a lisp, but close.

<<Oh, yes,>> agreed Sam, whose orange ▶hairfro◀ made him look taller than Stan, but he wasn't. He was two inches shorter. <<Dour would be a step up for Neptune.>>

<<I gueß everybody's a step up for you,>> said Stan, making a short joke. Sam was confident that that night he would win the mighty unspoken contest between them to see whose comedy would succeed and whose would fail.

Stan was aggreßive, as the white clowns sometimes were. Sam was more reserved, like toll putz Auguste, awaiting the next move. He'd usually gueß wrong and get hurt. That was the humor. He got hurt, and people liked it. Schadenfreude again.

Stan would say to Sam, <<What's wrong with you? You weren't brought up right!>>

And you would reply, <<And you just bring me down. I gueß I can't win.>>

And Sam would say, <<I gueß I can't wean! Mommy!>>

A voluptuous redhead would enter, blouse revealing four inches of cleavage, and she would say to Sam, <<Don't cry. Mommy's here.>> Sam would give the audience a sidewards exaggerated stage glance, and a big grin would overcome his face.

Stan would salvage the PG rating and say, <<Hey, that's not your mŒther!>>

Phew! exhaled the audience.

Few exhaled the audience that night. They stayed with the performers forever. That was ▶Stan and Sam◀s best night. The next day Sam was tragically ✹hit✹ by a bus, or so the news reports claimed. No one ever saw the body. Or the bus. Sam was cremated. The bus was crushed. Never would it be a bus again!

Alf, who was the driver, was an excellent driver. He would have driven Further, but he wasn't alive anymore, so Kesey got Caßidy. They weren't alive anymore either, though. OU Levon might have been the driver who died in the bus crash, the Bush cash having been paid out to dispatch dißenting domestic artists post haste!

The patch they were moved off of was known as ▶being◀ or ▶earth◀. *Weargen.*

Sam's son, who also had an orange hairfro, replaced Sam in the comedy duo, and ▶ Stan and Sam's Son◀ went on to great succeß, even starring in a hit movie entitled *Delilah.*

<<Greet succeß!>> was their motto.

<<Oh, cut it out!>> was Delilah's response. Sam's son seemed scared. His partnership in the duo was mostly because of his hair. He didn't want to lose it. He had visions of growing it long like Shawn Phillips after Stan retired.

Sam changed his image. The orange hair was much too clown-like.

<<What's wrong with you? You weren't brought up right,>> said Stan, trying to prompt the routine.

<<Fuck you, old man,>> Sam's son replied. <<Go practice by your ¢elgh. I know my bit.>>

Stan shook his head and walked away. Kids these days! Stan faded away. Sam's son faded away even faster. By the time he was a solo performer, Shawn Phillips had lost his hair in an accident. Male pattern baldneß and cancer had become so widespread that the shaved head look became popular. Longhairs were thought to be flaunting their follicular superiority in the faces of the follicularly challenged. No one wanted to be seen as being that cruel. Everyone had read ▶Harrison Bergeron◀. And then the firefighters would come and take all the books away and replace them with more TVs! Even with split screens, I need a shitload of TVs to be able to see all the shows simultaneously.

<<No matter how many TVs you have, it's a shitload,>> says Nils out of nowhere.

<<Hi!>> I reply. <<Actually, though, no. Some TV is art. *The Prisoner*, for example. *Breaking Bad. Mad Men.*>>

<<And the new hit series, *Affectatious Alliteration,*>> he says. That's Nils, all right.

What are you doing here?

<<I just dropped in to check up on you. I brought you a Kopi Luwak.>>

Oh! The coffee! Oh! Kopi Luwak! Kona is king, but this stuff is emperor.

<<Hey, that's right. It's safe to sing in here. The sound never leaves the dungeon. No screams ever reached an Œther floor,>> so without so much as a ►by your leave◄ he breaks into some rant about how time travel knocks on doors that haven't been knocked on before, and what is beyond each is unknown.

Seeing my opening, I put on Mahavishnu Orchestra's *Birds of Fire*, which is way too intense for Nils to sing to. Gotta nip it in the blood, as they say.

He zones out. I'm safe for a while.

It would have been ►Yellow Fields◄ by Eberhard Weber next. It's the perfect music to dream by. Or Hillage's ►Radio Dome Musick◄. Just put that on and let go….

►Stages on a Long Journey◄….

He's still out. He should hear this—Weber with Gary Burton, Jan Garbarek, Rainer Brüninghaus, Marilyn Mazur and the SWR Stuttgart Radio Symphony Orchestra, conducted by Roland Kluttig. The occasion was Weber's 65th birthday. It is a rhesus monkey escaping the lab that has made him a genius, and he returns to his old home with all his new knowledge and old memories intact and at war with each Œther. Oh, and he's brought along his genius friends.

They are moving in deep unison. The music connecting them is superfluous—one can see their interconnection in their dance. The song is ►Too Close to the Light◄ by the Long Ryders. The Long Ryders were in Danny & Dusty. All of that— prima!

Nils slept through all of *Native Sons*. That's one deep sleep!

►I Had a Dream◄. A big smile came acroß his face during this song. I figured he was having a nice dream.

It was a little sign of hope, as the song says.

►Join My Gang◄ cracks me up. Meet Gary Glitter at Leonard Bernstein's birthday party. I'm trying to imagine Sid Griffin and Stephen McCarthy in red-white-and-blue jumpsuits and lucite platform shoes with live koifur minnows in the hollow heels.

They would habituate the hallowed hills of home in high heels, annoying the neighbors, and freak out the 'fraidy cats.

No, that’s not really their style. They’d take out their guitars and entertain us all.

Nils started to stir. I put on some Stan Getz boßa nova with Astrid Gilberto singing. He relaxed again.

I heard the jailor’s keys rattling outside my cell. I peeked through the byobus and saw Nettie standing there.

<<Michel?>> she called.

Yes?

<<Is Nils okay? He was cleared to visit you a long time ago, and no one’s seen him leave.>>

Yes, he’s fine. He’s just sleeping off some kopi luwak.

<<Shouldn’t that have energized him more?>>

No. He was already so high strung that the coffee just pushed him over the edge.

<<Not anymore.>> Nils sat up. <<I’m up now.>>

<<I am sorry, Nils,>> said Nettie. <<I hadn’t meant to disturb you.>>

<<It’s okay. I gueß I needed some sleep.>> He made his excuses and left. He said he had a bad headache from the caffeine.

<<Are you here to spring me, warden?>> I haxed her.

<<With a hipster-hopster helicopter. You know it.>>

<<Really?>>

<<No. I told you, Aasvogel will let you out in the morning. I’m just checking in.>>

<<Oh, well thank *you*!>>

<<No need for sarcasm.>>

<<Of course. There’s *never* a need for sarcasm.>>

<<Ha!>>

<<And you and the Aasvogel *never* make mistakes.>>

<<*Now* you get it.>>

<<Yep. Well, thanks for coming by. I have to return to work.>> I returned to my space behind the byobus.

<<Goodbye, Michel.>>

<<Bye, Nettie.>>

<<Okay—I'll check back later.>>

<<If you….>>

<<I know….> >

Part Fourteen: Blind and Deaf

After they left, I was alone. No more music played. The TV, which started to show *The Lady Vanished*, vanished. Vanished also were the accoutrements of Victorian England and even the byobus. I grabbed the beer out of the fridge before the fridge disappeared. But a minute later the beers disappeared. After the cell was emptied, the bars disappeared, and then the walls. Then everything beyond the walls. And then nothingneß began to overtake me as well. My feet first, my ankles, calves, and then my fingers, hands, wrists, arms, thighs, shoulders, waist up, chest down. I disappeared at my navel.

Everything disappeared. No sound. No sight.

Move to the smooth. Working with the aßumption that the more civilized one was, the smoŒther (like David Niven—I barely remembered his image! I hope it's not my last), I moved to the smooth. Rough would lead to sharp, dangerous; smooth to easy, comfortable. Of course a bowl evil can reverse the two—it's cotton—many (out of trouble) a time [a time again]. Trusted stet. Trust stet. The paper was high quality acid-free stock. My baby fell from a high claß stork. A stute.

I stoop. Forgive me.

I just realized that the stork would be my last image, not David Niven.

Oh no, now it's Niven again. Niven in *Ninotchka.*

Thwack! A sign in Braille is slipped into my hands. It is from the literary police, who interject, <<Alliteration counts as sound! It can no longer be employed!>>

Neither should sound effects!

That would be rough.

Or groovy.

Yeah. Groovy.

I will not be able to hear the literary police anymore. It's all up to inner dialogue now!

Are exclamations permißible?

I don't know. Are questions? They both involve vocal inflection. No, only impaßive demonstration is permitted.

You are taking a more formal tone. Certainly tone is a quality of sound.

Not once the signified has been separated from its signifier. The signified claims its independence.

Heck, she claims her humanity!

Who is she?

A beautiful soul trapped inside a uniform, unable to discard the garb because of a keen sense of obligation.

Is that sense visual or auditory?

I don't think so.

Okay, so the sense of obligation stays.

No, please—we'd be better off without it.

Why?

Obligation breeds resentment. Only giving freely frees giving.

You should make a bad motivational poster out of that.

Yep. Um. Well, no comment. What's a poster?

I—I don't remember. I don't even know why I said that.

Posters are the invisible who comment on-line.

Ah, good, so they're invisible. Then they cannot be visual. Superb.

Well, writing like this really goes against the grain.

It rubs people the wrong way. It's gritty.

It's a pain in the aß.

Surprisingly, Skedaddle did not appear. Of course, he was just fictional. I had a pretty good idea of what he looked like a few minutes ago. Now I don't even remember what <<looks like>> means. I'm pointed in the same direction as someone else? What does *that* mean?

Of course I don't see what you mean—I don't *see* anything!

Here are some bushes. Are the berries safe to eat? I remember hearing that berries that dangle are safe, but those that stand stiff on rigid stems are poisonous. I wouldn't bet my life on it, though.

Rain on my face and arms. A light drizzle. Refreshing. I still feel the sun's warmth. It must be a sunshower.

Oh, wait. That makes no sense. I'm in a dungeon. More likely a lawn sprinkler is sprinkling through my open window, through which sunshine streams. Feeling both sensations simultaneously is a rare treat, one I may not have fully appreciated before.

You could smell that one a mile away, BrŒther Martin. Nice one! Save those for the grave yard.

Or the gravy yard. Dogs fill the place, either way, a pack of feral ones that dig at the fresh paupers' graves. They've sniffed out arms for the coming dog-versus-human war.

War is inelegant like that. I'm going with the grain, then.

The paß of leash resistance. Dog crap everywhere! It's creamy underfoot. Plus it slides!

Just like war.

Just keep the war away from me, except for just wars. Just wars are few and farbe green.

Œther things are more common, like cotton candy. It sticks to the fingers and makes a godawful meß of a beard. The reason you never see Samuel Delaney blowing bubblegum bubbles? It's the beard, my friends.

I'm going to grow a prison beard. If I focus hard, maybe I can grow it to the floor by morning. Hey, is there any breakfast in this dump?

All of a sudden you are inside that Make My Breakfast drive-thru alone, with a line of a hundred cars all queued up and waiting for service.

You just hax every car if someone would like to work. You hire them, and if the boß complains, remind him of the one simple rule of retail: <<You can't sell from an empty applecart.>>

What's an applecart? That's where the apples are.

You want one! You'll have to fill out this Apple-cation™.

Each use costs a hundred grand. Hax the author for permißion.

<<Oh, Grand Inquisitor, how much for the mise-en-scène?>>

<<A grand, of course. Why hax?>>

<<Just trying to speak your language.>>

<<My language is silence. My language is darkneß.>>

Ah, you left those cars all queued up?

Yep, and I didn't preß ▶play◀ until I had a foot out the door already. I had already slammed the door and had left before anyone even registered an alarm.

I just bumped into a byobu. Oh, everything's still here. It's just the lights are out—curfew. I get it.

I lit a fire in the fireplace. I bleßed the first crackle. I'm all right. I'm oll korrect.

I'm a follower of BrŒther Martin Van Buren.

He was better than Ahab.

How?

He had kinder hooks.

No—▶kinder◀ has a short ▶i◀, like the ▶i◀ in ▶window◀. It means ▶children◀.

Oh, my God. ▶Kinderhook◀ means ▶pedophile◀?

No. And even if it did, so what? He didn't even create the town.

You can't blame Twain for Hannibal. Or vice versa. The old mŒther town and her bigshot son. It's a shame Oak Park never did that for Hemingway while he was alive. Their use of him now is so obviously ¢elgh-serving. Poor old Krebs.

Martin Van Buren was the first U.S.-born president of the U.S. However, being U.S.-born is a mandate, so the first seven presidents don't count. That makes Martin Van Buren the first legitimate president of the United States under the Nativity Mandate Act.

Texas for the Texans! Peace, not war.

But as governor of New York he paßed the Bank Safety Act, so the country was already under siege by the banks.

However, he should have revealed his letter of opposition to the annexation of Texas *after* the convention. Polk was awarded the nomination instead. It's tough when a former president can't even win his own party's nomination but those were crazy times, and Van Buren was an abolitionist at heart, but he could not imagine any Œther reading of the Constitution Œther than slavery was sanctioned by it. You'd have to change the Constitution.

It has been conjectured that perhaps Van Buren wrote exactly such a document, with Jackson's support. They showed it to William Henry Harrison on the morning of his famous inaugural speech in the rain, the Terminal Pneumonial Speech. The word was they had Harrison promising that if he won, he'd finished the work of being the man on the inside working to change the Constitution to benefit his ¢elgh and his friends.

Perhaps, but maybe not. Perhaps he stood there, paralyzed on the podium for three and a half hours because he liked rain.

The bookcase next to the fireplace had a complete set of biographies of the Presidents of the Uniting States. The books were beautiful objects—ribbed, full-leather bindings with insanely beautiful endpapers. Their spines were tight. Every page held gilt-edged content.

►G.E.C.◄ we used to call it as kids.

Guilt-E-content-ment—we'd never really be happy in life. We were set up to fail.

I almost forgot I was in jail.

We are all in jail. The conflict is over who gets a bigger cell. But the only real cell is between your ears, and there you can be as big or small as you want. Don't run from that interior life—it's where the treasure is buried. Can you find it? Gandhi found it. MŒther Teresa. Jerry Garcia. James Joyce. Samuel Beckett. Jackson Pollock. Pablo Picaßo. That ability to pull deep into one's ¢elgh and bring forth miracles. Daevid Allen. Frank Zappa. Bucky Fuller. Bobby Fischer. BF's forever!

My BFs died or wash their hands of me or are too busy to reminisce yet. I had my brood early. They may still be brooding.

I just sußed out that there was Italian sausage in the fridge, so I decided to cook it up with oregano, basil, sauce, garlic and pasta.

Were these cells smell-proof?

Is the ocean swell-proof?

<<Don't know. You've been in the ocean, and, gee, you're swell…>>

Give me bas-relief! I see you only barely standing there? Thank goodneß the world is infinite—I should never run out of shit—to comment on.

That's a sound argument!

No! It's all conceptual! Don't miß read!

But where are we?

Does it matter? Could we have gotten all the way out here without what has come before?

                    Intromißion
                                        null
          penology
                              Uttar Pradesh
shell, will
                    sucking
                                        derisive term
          effervescence opposition—

                    Infervescence? An Œther linguistic lap?

I lap at your lap— that's why it's a ►lap◄.

What does that say about those sick fuckers who have lapdogs?

I don't even need words.

Part Fifteen: In the Army

In the beginning of time someone tried to take control over everything and fucked it up for everybody forever.

*

My dad's in the military, and I was forced into your school. Believe me—I do not want to be here.

*

<<My dad's on the army,>> said the Bereplicant, hoping to hook the gullible through their gills.>>

*

<<The army hacked my dad,>> said the Repellentant.

<<Into pieces?>> I haxed.

<<No—just his email.>>

*

<The army ripped my flesh,>> said the faceleß boy in the crowd.

*

The army spoke to its ¢elgh like pirates looking at their ¢elghs in a mirror: <<Arrr…me!>> The navy spoke like outlaws in hiding: <<Submerge!>> Once beneath the waves, some of the sailors began to merge.

An Œther reason for explaining vocabulary to the unacquainted.

The air force was stuck in a blow dryer.

The coast guard became some sort of soap and antiperspirant.

The branches of the military were not being given their proper respect as names. Except the marines. And the paratroopers. And the seals.

There you go again—always undercutting me. It wasn't Nils's voice I was hearing, though. It was my own. I was having a regular internal dialogue.

The dialogue was occurring between the Bereplicant and the Repellentant.

The Bereplicant wanted to be like everyone else.

The Repellentant was sorry for ever having thought that.

They were going to have it out. I couldn't afford to let them keep battling for control. Clearly, I had to pick a side.

A false dilemma! I chose edge instead. Edge is always a poßibility in a coin toß, just as midnight and noon are neither a.m. nor p.m. Knock down those false dilemmas! At least part way!

The Bereplicant had come out in a one-piece wrustling suit and long blond hair. He looked like Gorgeous George.

The Repellentant said a few prayers and ran away.

Just let him go.... The Bereplicant is here to socialize. The Repellentant has work to do.

Part Sixteen: Oblong Caßidy

I think the two byobus are staring each Œther down, like sparring cats. One will take a swipe at the Œther soon. I can tell.

*

Richard Brautigan raised floß in Montana. But his, of course, was spun of watermelon sugar.

*

A gallows bird hopped acroß my floor in pursuit of galliwasps and gallimaufry. Mix 'em together into mulligan stew. Then take the leftovers, throw 'em in a pan with some eggs and make a good Bauernfrühstück. Any leftovers of that can be mixed with water for the beginnings of stone soup. Don't forget to wash the stones thoroughly before beginning.

*

Before the beginning were two stones who had soft spots for each Œther. They smashed their soft spots together, poured their magma over the union, and became the one Good-&-Plenty-shaped shaped stone known as ►Oblong Caßidy◄.

The once-roughcut stones became polished and eloquent as Oblong Caßidy, who wore a ►black hat◄, a dark-plumed volcanic eruption that propelled the giant pill through space. Whose mouth it was headed for is unknown. We have light-years to figure that out, of course not all on Earth or Mars or Venus or Saturn, even. We'll have to move farther out or begin manufacturing some sort of sun modulator.

I need a sarsaparilla.

It has been conjectured by some [vague ones somewhere] that Oblong Caßidy will collide with the giant meteor that would have triggered the next dinosaur extinction on Earth, thereby rescuing Gabby Hayes's windy holiday.

*

It was conjugated by someone (vaginal ones somewhere) that Oblong Caßidy was really a dick. Literally. A giant penis. A steely dan. A throat would do, but what it really sought was nice bush to nestle into.

►Pilsener◄ screamed some old white-haired blueblood (or what that a blue-haired whitebred?).

White bread is clay bread—the most malleable kind. It has no bones, it has no spine. It's soft, and you can shape it into anything you like, but if it gets wet, it dißolves into mush.

Sounds like a lot of guys I know. Or rather know *of.* They abuse their meds, trade 'em for roofies, hit on the coyotes, and then wish they had their meds because, at the end of the night, they can't lift the tent pole.

Oblong Caßidy intimidates them.

Welcome back, audience, to the hit game show ►The Intimidating Game◄! <<Bachelor number two? If you and I were out on a date at, like, Six Flags, and you wanted to intimidate me because you knew I was into that, what would you say to me?>>

<<I'd say, <Where's your ¢elgh-respect, Young Lady?>>>

<<Uh, okay. Number three? Same question.>>

<<I'd say, <Ease down, bitch!>>>

<<Okay…. Number one? Same question.>>

<<As what?>>

<<Okay, Alex—I've identified them—my father, an ☼Aßhole☼ and a stoner.>>

<<Who [sic] do you choose?>>

<<Well, not my father, obviously. [Sick]. Actually, none of them. They are all losers. I choose my ¢elgh.>>

[Slick].

Ta da!

[Schtick].

Where are we, the Catskills? For crying aloud, don't bring oblong mice into the Catskills. It will upset the natural order of things, like the sales brought to Hawaii by Europeans. What a disaster. The European ones flourished and began squeezing the domestics out. And then the Europeans hit on the brilliant idea of bringing in cannibal snails from Europe to eat the European snails. The cannibal snails soon discovered that Hawaiian snails tasted much better than the European ones. Well, which flavor do you prefer? Laurel or Pineapple? Think about it carefully. Your position in society depends upon your answer.

The rabbit gets to hop along. The tortoise has to carry that piece of hardware with him wherever he goes in order to prove the story. The rabbit need carry nothing. Who won?

Part Seventeen: Duckbill and Spiney, Some Sort of Resurrection

<<Read on, Charles,>> said Bukowski to his ¢elgh.

And Dylan Thomas, you, on that sad height, we've almost lapped you now. All of us except ol' Granddad.

And Caitlin, that accursed dreß you wore on the heath! No wonder <<the hearse ran away with the hart,>> as they say.

Poets under attack wear….

Where?

The weir.

What?

Wolfsbane and monks' hoods.

That's no luck for a pretty Colleen.

You are right about that, except she's Welsh.

The fire sputtered. It would need more would. I still had three logs, but dawn was coming anyway to throw spikes into my eyes. Arrows will attack my ears.

My will will wheel my wellneß weal where weather was whether wear a windbreaker or a woven wamus.

Just practicing up a few sounds that I will use when speech is rustored. For years, whenever I had to test new stereo equipment, I would use the Beatles' ♪Hey Jude♫ because it covers the whole dynamic range fairly clearly and coherently so that I could test for highs and lows, brights and depths.

Wow—♪Hey Jude♫ is not in the collection. I gueß the Beatles aren't as popular as they once were. At one point, ♪Hey Jude♫ was the second best-selling 45 of all time behind Chubby Checkers's ►The Twist◄.

That's also not on the list.

Actually, the list is blank. They're having technical difficulties with the audio portion of the transmißion.

The one that makes my car go Vroom!

Dan Stuart, Steve Wynn and Stephen McCarthy sit down on the couch. Chris Cacavas finds a chair. I sit on the floor in the middle, trying to absorb some of each man's aura.

The Aura Will Prevail, said George Duke, Zappa at his shoulder, but that was to me in private.

<<Some Danny & Dusty?>> haxed Dan.

<<Sure,>> said Stephen.

<<Well, then start with *Cast Iron Soul*,>> said ►Dusty◄ Steve Wynn.

Just then Nettie showed up. <<Get out of here!>> she yelled at Danny & Dusty and their friends. Don't corrupt him! You guys are like the Barrymores' bringing WC Fields booze in the hospital! Can't you see he has to detox from his music addiction? Shoo! Shoo! I thought she was going to kick Dan Stuart in the aß. But they disappeared

<<Oh, I wish you'd let them stay. I love Danny & Dusty.>>

<<Damn it! Now you're going to have to stay an extra day.>>

<<No! You said you'd let me out this morning.>>

<<That was contingent on your actually having learned something and on your remorse and contrition. Aasvogel was very specific about that. I'm going to have to turn external sound and sight off again. Relax and open up your mind to your Œther senses.>>

Open my mind to Œther sentences. I got it. A night in jail's not enough. A year in an insane asylum—oops, I mean clown college—wasn't enough.

Well, at least you got to go to college—where the Yorkshire pudding was a logical fallacy.

Like the red herring?

Exactly.

Okay—I'll stay. Don't credit, Guitar Mama.

<<Where do you get language like that?>> she haxes me. I have no valid answer. Curiosity? A natural ability to remember words?

I think, What would Mani Neumeier do? He would continue to make music even if deaf or blind. He would make music of vibrations you can feel in your feet, your gut, your back. Even your fingers.

A few great pieces of music can be felt to be great without hearing them or seeing them performed. Peggy Lee's ▶Fever◀, for example, has unmistakable drumbeats you can feel right through your feet.

Any singer who can sing those first three notes of ▶Bali Hai◀ has opened a gateway to greatneß.

Minnie Ripperton in ▶Loving You◀. What's that? Eight octaves, like Beefheart, who could sing the baßo profundo growls of Howlin' Wolf and then hit a very masculine high-pitched register—not falsetto, really. He could just slide up there. Eight octaves.

That vibration opens up something. Maybe just my clenched anus. I need good light to crap by. I'm not one of these kooks who can stick their butts out naked in the middle of nowhere in the dark and not be surprised if something goes for them right then, when they're most vulnerable.

Like Elvis when he had his heart attack on the toilet.

The romantic quality of hesitation in speaking is an exhibition of a predicament. But what is a predicament but an unexamined false dilemma? Or it could be…

a pickle!

Pickles was Morey Amsterdam's wife on the *Dick Van Dyke Show*, right?

<<Pickles? That woman's trying to kill me!>> quoth Firesign Theatre.

What's the difference between a beer-soaked pickle and a frog?

The fraud has more hops.

Hops.
Ophelia.
PhD.
Hilda Doolittle's
III bad. III
II I… I
'll miß
1 miß and then

I must a homer-ward boundary-killing machine. Or was that a boundary-ward homer-killing machine? Or a ward-boundary homer-killing machine? And so on….

Man, could have been a diplomat—the Aasvogel's representative to Earth, even! I mean, the guy who does that, I've heard, is a real dick. I'd be happy doing that. Why the fuck did I say I wanted to run disc golf? I am a fucking idiot.

What the hell am I doing here? How the hell did I end up here? Longhorns goals and vultures decorate bleached fucking rock. Where are Vladimir and Estragon?

Oh, they're not coming.

Platypus and Estrogen? That was a cartoon couple, I think.

Oh, a third voice chiming in—Mr. Know-it-all, I presume?

Just saying—Playpus and Estrogen was an old cartoon. They were Australian enigmas—Estrogen was an echidna. They were the Monotreme family.

Holy oviparous anteaters, Duckbill.

And they were crime-fighters together. The echidna was nicknamed Spiney. No one knew Duckbill's real first name.

Holy omnivorous odor-eaters, Webfoot! The Mammal Store just called. They are reporting a wild band of marsupials just tore through the store and five-finger-discounted a slew of items off the shelves and stuffed the said items into their marsupia.

More soup yet?

Marzipan?

Those viviparous mammals!

Well, at least you're keeping the ovoviviparous mammals out.

What ovoviviparous mammals? See? You don't know any. It's working.

Oh, I have nothing against them. I just don't want them to steal from the store. The community needs that.

What community?

I was stuck. We were stuck. We could neither be part of a platypus nor of an echidna community.

Platypi are by nature polygamous not polyandrist. And echidnas are solitary.

Platypi have no nipples. Male echidnas have four-headed penises. It might be best for our pair if the platypus is male, and the echidna the female. The name ▶Estrogen◀ a literary with ▶Echidna◀ anyway. It's aßonance.

It's ▶Big Mama Boogie, Parts I & II◀ by Cactus. I gueß I'm going to hear music <<*One Way... or an Œther*>> forever. No one can live in silence. I love music. I'll leave Mars Condatis forever as soon as I get out of here. The Aasvogel can rustrict music if he wants, I gueß, at least if people let him. But as he is right now, how is he better than the Bözmachers? At least they liked some music. Chick Corea they were big on, I think. And, say what you will, he's one heck of a musician.

I am tired of being an outcast. I used to be a freaking envoy for the Earth. Why am I here on this godforsaken outpost?

Outpost? It's hardly an outpost. Mars has two of the solar system's largest cities. Bigoted parochial Earth bullshit that this is an outpost....

Sorry. I meant no offense. It may have begun as a dump and a penal colony, but Mars is almost prettier now.

That's faint praise.

Cool, did you see how perfectly that girl just collapsed from hunger?

No.

You should. Watching the hungry faint is the newest sport among the cognoscenti who suffer from ennui. We at the top must amuse our ¢elghs with the agonies of the bottom 99%. They suffer so delightfully....

Duckbill and Spiney protect the bottom 99%.

They had recently found a CEO of a Wall Street bank who had instituted check stacking for withdrawals. Large withdrawals were calculated first, throwing some accounts into the negative. Then the account looked to be negative on paper until the unpaid check was returned. Meanwhile all the Œther checks were presented against the erroneously-appearing negative account. Thus, instead of one check being returned unpaid, a dozen might be, each with its own forty dollar overdraft fee. The banks had made $31 billion in one year alone by stacking checks this way.

Duckbill and Spiney burst into the banker's office. It was their last resort. Letters to the Comptroller of the Currency went unacknowledged. Apparently the Comptroller's office was being paid off.

Spiney tried shooting the banker in the chest. The bullet sank in, but no blood sprang forth.

<<I told you bankers have no hearts. Just a lot of nerve.>>

Duckbill used his flamethrower, and the banker was fired without a golden parachute.

Spiney laughed when Duckbill pißed on the crispy corpse. <<There is your golden parachute,>> said Duckbill. <<Oh, I'm sorry,>> said Duckbill to Spiney. <<Maybe you wanted to eat him?>>

<<No—he was the wrong kind of termite. He was fat with the blood of the poor. They don't taste good. The true rich taste like ambrosia. Their flesh is so soft from never having to do any work that their meat just melts in the mouth. The skin bears no callous anywhere. The two pockets of gristle are easily avoided: one fills the cranium, the Œther the chest cavity. The organs there have shriveled into gristle from disuse. But the abdomens are distended with truffles, saffron, and royal jelly.>>

<<Well, I gueß I see why you have no taste for them. Who would mix truffles with saffron and royal jelly? Those flavors need to be individualized to be appreciated.>>

<<Oh, no, I like *them*. The true rich are a little hard on the arteries, but they taste good. It's those nouveau riche, like the bankers. They feast on leßer humans. I do not like cannibals.>>

<<What about the true rich?>>

<<Oh, you can't think of them as human. The minute you do that, they've got you.>>

<<Of course. A conspiracy theory. I suppose they fear fluoridation, too.>>

<<No, but that's an Œther ißue. Isn't fluoride a toxic by-product of aluminum manufacture?>>

<<Nettie! You may as well put me back in jail.>>

<<You never left.>>

I open my eyes. She's right. She's sitting in a comfy chair opposite the couch I am on, coffee table between us.

<<I'll need to stay.>>

<<Why?>>

<<I don't know how to talk to people. I gueß I can't get along.>>

<<Oh, don't let Aasvogel trick you into thinking that. You're very skilled in that area. I think Aasvogel is having regrets about leaving the Bözmacher cult, and he blames

you for that split.>>

<<What do you think?>>

<<I think it's always hardest to be human. I think we are the fallen Angels. But every now and then there's one or two of us who work toward making that as noble as poßible. That's you.>>

<<That's nice of you to say. Thanks.>> I put on Shuggie Otis. It was gorgeous background music and sublime foreground music. I soon forgot what I was going to say. Shuggie takes one's attention away from everything else. That's why he's never played on the radio—too many car accidents would result.

The curvature of his music breaks the straightneß of the world, even if it's only for a little while. Thanks, Shuggie

A little Mark-Almond after that. Their eponymous debut LP.

Then the Fugs.

The worlds built by artists are beautiful and fantastic. I could spend hours inside Jethro Tull's ▶Nursie◀, and entire vacation with the Glaß family, a year with Sherlock Holmes, a generation with Frodo. <<An Œther solipsist, Arno!>>

<<Send him away!>>

Maybe there's enough room in the cell for two old zygotes….

<<Billy and Nanny?>>

Yeah, they run a crime syndicate, a protection racket.

How loud are they?

Not very. They need only whisper. You see, they run the Brooklyn Bridge, which they patrol fiercely.

Yeah, Pa Troll told us they won't let any Trolls acroß whatsoever.

There just bluffing.

No—they're serious. The Trolls have offered everything. They even offered the hair off their shinny-shin shins.

Yeah, those Trolls are hairy.

That's dangerously close to being racist.

Specist, you mean.

You *are* racist! Against Trolls!

Trolls are not a race—they're a species. And I like 'em just fine as a species. But they have been much maligned in the past, you have to admit.

They sure have. Did you ever hear the joke about the Priest, the Go-Go Dancer, and the Troll?

No, and I'm not going to, either.

You don't want to hear?

No, I don't.

It's a really good joke!

No—I don't have a sense of humor anymore. I want to be taken seriously.

You'd better give up on that. Check your folders on the interwebs. You've buffaloed your ¢elgh rather permanently, I'm afraid.

True, but so did Shakespeare.

Oh, be fair. You are no Shakespeare.

Of course not. I didn't mean to imply anything of the sort. Only that the transition is poßible.

So now you want to be a dour old man, the kind Kerouac warned us against.

The kind Kerouac became, you mean.

Perhaps.

There's that word.

My favorite word. ►Perhaps◄. Through happenstance. Serendipity. Chance. Free Will. Chaos. Dynamism. Activity. Life.

You're going the wrong way, then. The public only wants varieties of vampire thanatopsis. Read ten pages, you die a little inside.

If you are dying, use good, strong commercial dyes, not the generic, powdered, grocery-store variety. It is almost impoßible to get much vibrancy of color out of the generic powders. That's why you should fill your home with cochineal beetles.

They are parasites.

Yes, but not on humans. Only on cacti.

Those cacti have no pals.

Us. We scrape the carmine out of 'em.

And they're not really beetles. They're scale insects.

Which scale? Metrical, Burmese, Imperial? US Customary?

They are used as food coloring.

Düßeldorf mustard!

What? Düßeldorf is known for tuna. And no carmine is used in Düßeldorf mustard or two.

That might be a hasty generalization. Have you tried *every* Düßeldorf mustard? Have you eaten every tuna dish in the world?

Of course not.

Well, then you can't really say no carmine is ever used. There may be that one rustaurant on Venus….

Yeah, I've heard Venusian food is hot.

It has to be at least *look* hot, so carmine is the coloring of choice.

What's Mars's favorite coloring?

Lilac, of course.

Of course.

And lilac is chemically quite similar to cochineal.

Of course. It all makes sense.

The interconnectedneß of life?

No, your reputation as a bullshitter. Next you'll tell me lilacs are little parasites as well.

No, they're flowers. You've never heard of lilacs?

Of course I have.

That why are you suggesting Œtherwise?

I wasn't. I was suggesting that *you* might suggest that.

If you're going to make moot points, at least make good ones. Œtherwise we'll have to send you to moot camp.

On a dairy farm?

No, a diarrhea farm, a *verbal* diarrhea farm.

Lovely. I got diarrhea from fish once.

Only once?

Well, it was a fluke.

Whenever I have nutmeg, I paß it quickly between my legs.

Don't tell me—some poor gal named Meg is in charge of your baggage.

What baggage?

The baggage between your legs.

Oh, that's you, Nils. I was wondering what happened to my voice.

<<I'm just being Billy.>>

No, you'd be Nanny.

<<Then you're Ninny.>>

No—I'm obviously Billy.

<<I'll be Nanny,>> said Nettie.

Oh, you're here, too?

<<Sure am. It's morning again. Just seeing if you've given up on music yet.>>

If music is so bad, then why do the indigenous peoples of the Earth use it for spiritual rituals.

<<Oh, good God, Michel,>> interjected Nils. <<You're not going all Huxley on us now, are you?>>

No, my friend. Huxley was thirty years ago for me. It's Moksha, the cloud of unknowing, keeping you from the truth.

<<You mean Maya. Moksha is the release from Samsara.>>

Yeah, that's what I meant, Mr. Note Tall.

<<You want me to pretend to be stupid?>>

No. It's okay. Don't hide your light under a bushel.

<<Well, I appreciate that.>>

Bush Hill? You'll find a cheap soapbox up there—but it sold for quite a bit, I hear.

Where?

Here.

'Ere what?

Erehwon. Eretwo. Erethree….

Erewhen?

Irwin?

Ur-win?

Ur-bear! The Great Bespectacled Bear!

Uropa.

Europa! The Saber-Toothed Bear!

<<Eureka! I have found a woman,>> said Nettie, raising our eyebrows. <<I *arrusted* her! Stop thinking trash.>>

<<But she used to say…>> I wanted to say; neither of us could—

Knock on wood.

Definition is dismißal. Just write ►QED◄ on it and throw it away.

♪Hey, throw it away! A shipload of pirates are we! So pull out the gunny and make the rum runny, and never forget the key! It's A-Hey, throw it away....♫

I hear a church bell. It morphs into an air raid siren. The siren becomes a lighthouse. I recognize the lighthouse.

I realize I have broken out of jail somehow.

I really inhabit my home.

I rehabilitate. On my back in my bed, in the dome of my lighthouse home, some nights I stare at the stars above me and wish I were one. Œther nights I stare at them all and wish I were none.

Book Four: Fitting for My Death Mask

Part One: Shevchenko's Mask

<<Click on the image to see the hologram of the death mask of Taras Shevchenko.>>

Is it metal? It looks shiny in parts, tarnished in ŒÐers. Like copper.

Did they pour copper on his deceased head? Good God, I hope not.

I think they made a mold out of clay—

Who? The sculptor Klodt and his gang. And then they die-cast the mask from the mold.

<<He looks like a walrus,>> says a little tourist, disrespectfully.

<<Didn't your mŒðer ever tell you not to meß with anyone with facial hair?>>

<<No?>>

<<Just run along, child. Run along.>> Shevchenko's mustache was not a good topic for a humor for me. I had grown my hair and beard very long for my ¢elgh.

Why?

Because I could.

I may not have all my sanity, but I do have all my hair. Not that how I wear my hair should even be worthy of mention. It really isn't.

But I really feel like I've run out of stuff to say.

Only after you expend your agenda are you free to begin to really, you know… be your ¢elgh.

Once everything else is out of your system, the real writing begins. That's when the writer doesn't really write. Ze sits back and watches and listen and records the slideshow running in hir head. Hopefully one or two of them aren't too outlandish for viewing someday.

But I am an outlander, too. And I need to find a way to get out of here. I love this little place—the lighthouse. I love my domed bedroom above that beacon room. I can see out among the stars every night, and recently Earth has been bright in the sky. I miß her. And I have no reason to stay here. Thrown in jail, thrown into a mental institution (sure, they *called* it Clown College, but I knew better), betrayed and spat upon, I am going to get out of here. I'd regret having saved the Aasvogel, but one fool is better than a cultload of 'em.

Everybody trance now! ♪Bump bumpity bump.♫

Shevchenko was here,
enjoying a beer.
He told us to wait
here by the front gate,
while he checked out
whether we had clout
or if we were just
spilled cuspidors, rust;
fried chitlins for sale,
we made him quite pale.
Then he came along
with his only song,
but he sang so well
we all went to hell.

It's a popular children's song on Mars. Really. It loses a little in the translation.

It sure doesn't sound like Shevchenko.

It isn't.

So why?

So you'd stay and listen to one of mine, dammit! Of course. Why else?

To get even.

For what? I don't want to get even. I love you. Even if you do piß me off now and then. So what? That's what adult relationships are. A navigation. Get me my scuba gear!

You are awarded a year of doing nothing but scuba!

I said ►gear◄, not ►year◄! I'll just crab walk out of here never mind me….
I'll tell you what. Life at 52 ain't much clearer than 22. What I've learned is how to

react. That has *really* changed. Those of you who are 22, wait for it. Fifty-two kicks aß! No one can tell you shit except the sixty-plus-year-olds. If you're 52, you've pretty much made it to the top of the food chain, whether you are human, elephant or tortoise. You are now too gamey and old (and too wily and philosophical) to bŒðer with. You've endured the choppers razor whirling killer machines. There's not much left to teach you except humility and service, but those can't be forced. Just make sure it's genuine. If you are doing it just to be seen doing it, then your lot is lost.

Lots of lost plots are in the lead. The led will never arrive on time.

Anyway, welcome. I'm not nearly as radical as they say. I just like scaring the weak of heart away. There is always room for the strong. Longobards, they sing in the summer.

Alice Cooper's ►Living◄. Ant-Bee, sounding like the Acid Casualties. I inhale the song, and it energizes me.

I went to the controls of the lighthouse on the floor below the beacon. The music was on, but I hadn't touched it. Had it been on all the time I was incarcerated? Not a chance. Someone had it turned on. They know I'm here.

I've got to get away. I don't hate them or anything, but they have no paßion for art, music, or literature or. I cannot live without music.

What do I have on file musically? What images of artwork can I fill space with?

Clown ►School's Out◄ forever!

Prison, no matter how posh, still is a trip.

Still is a trap. Move! I want to get away from the noise and move toward the music of the spheres!

What's the music I have for fuel?

I push a button on the console. [I push a consul's button.]

[What the fuck? says the consul.]

[[You know those consuls—they all live in that tent together.]]

I have millions of gigs, of recorded music, plenty to last to the year 15040.

When I preßed the ►engage◄ button, though, rather than engaging just the sound system for the entire lighthouse, as I'd imagined it would, it instead engaged the rockets that lifted the lighthouse off the ground and into the sky.

I had never known that this was more than a simple lighthouse, though I suspected as much by the enormous array and variety of controls on the main console. It pushed back, all right. I was heading into space unnavigably, at least with those rockets blasting.

I'd have to wait for the boosters to fall off before I could figure if this thing was steerable.

I climbed up to the dome and lay down on my bed and watched the approaching space.

How wonderful! Mars fell away behind me. Bözmachers and betrayals all stayed back there, with the Aasvogel. I was free.

<<Where are we going, Michel?>> haxed a familiar voice—Nettie!

<<What are you doing here?>>

<<I came straight over. I've been here for a while, reading one of the books. I was downstairs.>>

<<He's not here, is he?>>

<<Who? The Aasvogel? No—we'd had enough of him, too. We decided to join you.>>

<<*We*? You mean—?>>

<<Nils.>>

<<Nils, too? Where's he?>>

<<He doesn't fly well. He's in the head.>>

<<Mine.>>

<<Oh, come on. You've got company, at least. And not just holographic blues singers. We're real.>>

<<Those were holograms? Unfair!>

<<Jail doesn't need to be cruel.>>

<<Jail doesn't need to be.>>

<<True.>>

<<Why is Nils here? I thought he was all schmoozy with Aasvogel to get a good

position—mine.>>

<<No, he's figured out that any favor curried with the Aasvogel has raisins all over it.>>

<<And he hates raisins?>>

<<Exactly. That, and he and I have been kind of seeing each Œðer.>>

<<Really?>>

<<I hope it's okay with you. I mean, you and I—we weren't heading anywhere anyway, right?>>

<<Sure. You're right. Hey, you were in the books. Can you find me the ship's schematics? I have to figure a way to turn it to Earth.>>

<<I can do that. I was trained in all military devices and vehicles known to Mars Condatis.>>

<<Of course you were.>>

I go back to my bed so I can watch us travel forever up. The artificial gravity that kicked in was configured vertically rather than horizontally. We perpetually went up and never forward. If we were to go forward, all the material in the ship would fall to the low side. As long as we went up, everything stayed in place. I took this as a sign that everything would be better from now on.

And I could stay in bed and watch worlds paß us by in perpetuity. I had no ties to Mars, and none to Earth, not really. Old friends and family who washed their hands of me a decade ago.

And how decayed it was!

And they'd run their lizard hands over me, bleßing me with their dead skin cells. During the molting season only barbarians would deal with them.

During melting season, only Hephaestus hangs around. He's that big slugger who strikes out a lot. He's a little hot to trot over to the ice cream store and get us a couple of them large soft ice cream cones dripped in butterscotch. Of course they're completely melted by the time he gets back. We'd let him take the Chevy, but it's not fireproofed in the interior. My genuine imitation pleather will scorch. See you next tourist season, Hephaestus! I'm telling you--central air conditioning is the way to go. I can get you all set up in no time. My uncle knows a guy.

And during the mating season--well, who knows? *Latrodectus mactans*?

Or *Mantidae*? Men-to-die? That's the prophecy the mantis always brings. It is not profound. It is Monday. Stupid bug. As for the Œðers, they're like pretty much any sane creature—leave them alone, and they'll leave you alone.

I've never been attacked by birds. Threatened, but not attacked. Geese are the worst. They are hot-tempered.

Good, send them to Hephaestus as a gift from me.

I seek peace. Happineß. Fulfillment. And a beautiful home in the forusted beach by the ocean at the foot of a mountain?

No! The stones would fall on your head!

Far enough for that not to happen.

The forust would burn.

No—the ocean would put it out.

Oh, that's not me, I realized. Those aren't voices in my head. That's Nils's and Nettie's annoying voices interrupting my enjoyment of anything. Are they talking about buying a home together? Where? Here on the spaceship? They're crazy. We could be in space for years. We should go cryogenic if we can't steer. I could stay up and operate the ship. And no one notices that the fifth cryogenic chamber is already filled!

I tip my fedora.

How much does one tip a fedora?

A good one? A block. To if it's a really fancy joint.

The only ones I know our dove-tailed. I think it's part of the costume.

The costumer is always right. Slow learners live longer!

Can you believe that? Nils wants to teach her Skat? Where's the fourth? The on-board computer? Well, I know we can teach it how to deal. Maybe Skat's okay.

Let's play for seconds we have to stay inside the ship once it lands. Each nanosecond will be an agony none of us have ever felt.

Felt, like this fedora. Doesn't it look good on me?

What we need is a good photo seßion--we could be heroes back on Mars. We defied the Aasvogel.

Nils bucked the photo shoot idea and went to the music. He put on some ZZ Top and grabbed Nettie. They're dancing, and right in front of me. Well, Nils, I got that. He wants everything I have. At least we'll share this death, eh? And Nettie? I thought… I don't know what I thought. I gueß it wasn't anything—a twitch of my imagination. I could have sworn she was here. Her nipples were on my fingertips. I was at her cervix. I was at her G-spot. I was at her love button. They're connected to my joystick.

OUCH! Everybody, ride a pony out of here….

Only in the astral projection lounge. I found it! I was worried we couldn't travel outside the ship, but I remembered it!

I checked the lounge's contents. It had a course! A disc golf course is here! All right! If I can get the music to pursue me, I have my recreation time all figured out. I'm going to ride the faint of heart right out of here! Notch the hologram up to expert—I'm ready.

<<No, Michel. You don't have time to do that now. You need to steer us.>>

<<That's bull.>>

<<Okay, well, I see why you prefer that distinction.>>

<<Definitely I am not doing it.>>

<<I know. I get it. No one is. It was the wrong question. My mistake. Sorry.>>

<<'S all right.>>

Part Two: 'S All Right

'S all right. Take it easy. Relax. I'm not going to hurt you. I just want to warn you about a couple of things. Why? Haven't you ever heard about people wishing they knew then what they know now?

Yes.

Well, I do.

That's not neceßarily a bad thing.

'S all right.

Part Three: Par King Glottis Full

<<Where have you been?>> haxed Nettie when I lay back down.

<<I was down for a while.>>

<<I was, too. Down in that library down there.>>

<<No, I mean emotionally.>>

<<No, I mean physically.>>

<<But I was *really* down.>>

<<No—you were *figuratively* down. *I* was *really* down.>>

<<Do you want to know what I discovered?>>

<<What? Your own naval?>>

<<No, I still have seeds. Can I tell you?>>

<<Can I tell what I discovered in the library first?>> Nettie was being insistent. It must have been important, so I nodded.

<<The Auditory Engineers' Guild claims that listening to constant complaining hurts a person's ability to want to hear.>>

<<Who's complaining?>>

<<Just saying.>>

<<What?>>

<<Just a word.>>

<<Are you calling me noise?>>

<<Of course.>>

<<Okay! Thanks! A behalf of the AEG, I think you!>>

What was that in her hands? The AEG manual?

<<No—it's *about* them. It exposes the corruption inside the organization, which, left to its own devices, is a benevolent fund. The AEG is being taken over by a parasitic consulting firm.>>

<<Boo-hoo for them.>>

<<Michel! Don't be so stupid! We can solve this!>>

<<Can you turn the ship around?>>

<<I already did. I was just coming to tell you. I told you it'd be easy. I have training.>>

<<Where are we heading?>>

<<Earth. But something is wrong with the propulsion. I was just able to point us in the right direction before the constable—>>

<<Console.>>

<<—yeah, console, though constables may be coming—>>

<<Not anytime soon.>>

<<If any of them noticed our going off-line, they'll come and take a look.>>

<<Don't hold your breath.>>

<<I'm not. I'm trying to figure out the propulsion system. I've got to go back to the books. Just updating you. What was it you found?>>

<<Never mind. It's not important.>>

*

I looked out my dome, trying to see Earth ahead. We must have flown pretty far away because I saw nothing I could recognize as our solar system.

We would be a while.

I decided to go down the tube and get a book for my ¢elgh as well. If we were going to live on Earth, we needed a dwelling no one would see, something definitely subterranean.

I found the book I wanted: it was a book about underground homes, featuring the first-year journals of the builders of them all. I wasn't sure if they were required to keep journals, or if only the homes of journal-keepers were selected. That's never explained in the book.

I was reminded of Oblong Caßidy in the cave we all lived in when astral projecting onto a pill-shaped asteroid. That seemed long ago, but had only happened since my escape from the ►clown college◄.

Now even my nose is runny. Gotta go. Bye. Claustrophobia.

The room is shrinking. Now it's growing.

Of course, the second night begin reading, Nils interrupts me.

<<How do you like that, Michel?>> he said, all eager and full of gloat.

<<Like what?>>

<<She chose me over you.>>

<<Who?>>

<<Nettie, of course.>>

<<Then you are shrewed.>>

<<Shrewd? Thanks. I think so.>>

<<Definitely. Well, good luck with that. Now, please excuse me. I have important reading.>>

<<Let me tell you about Nettie in bed…>>

I grabbed Nils by the larynx until he came to a glottal stop. When I released him, he could no longer talk, but instead rushed off while exploding in a coughing fit.

If the glottis stops, wear it!

Back to my reading.

Part Four: Dropkick

My alarm was blasting. I had overslept. I had been dreaming that I was trying to find a way of opening a hyperlink on a sheet of paper. I tried repeatedly, but the link would not open. I also remember being the only pinecone in a deciduous forust and everyone telling me that I was useleß.

Where's the book? Okay. I'm locking the hatch. No one is coming up here while I read.

I wish Eno had done a *Music for Lighthouses* CD. Short of that, I went with Eberhard Weber's *Yellow Fields*, my favorite ECM recording.

I could read and write along with it—it was awesome. It would be foreground if you like, background if you preferred, functioning perfectly on both levels. His electrobaß maßages the spine. And the pleasantly counterbalancing saxophone is effortleßly free-flowing from the fingers of Charlie Mariano, the same Charlie Mariano who figures in the history of Mal Waldron and Embryo, Hamburg, Germany, 29 June 1973. Look at the intersections after that, and you'll be amazed: Daevid Allen, David Bedford, Zappa, Patchen, Mingus! Add Rainer Brüninghaus on keys, whose notes fell like rain, and Jon Christensen on the subtlest drums imaginable. Wow. Now to shift it to the back, maybe play the Embryo after that, but for now the too-long procrastinated-over book of houses. Number six looks inter-rusting. One couple had built an underground home that had a diagonal tent-flap entrance, which opened into a large hallway to an iron door. Once past the iron door, one was in the small hallway, which led to two corridors. At the end of the one that bent to the left was a stairway that led to the storage area. The Œðer corridor, to the right, bent around to the stairway that led to the sleeping quarters.

I haxed about eating, and they said it was done out front. I take it they mean we are not to bring foreign food indoors. The place is equipped with a feeding tube that runs along the wall and has dispensaries, much like old water fountains, along the wall every twenty feet or so. Just open it, and the foodpaste drips out into your waiting bowl.

Bowel? Pretty much. It's a synthetic bowel system. Anything edible can be turned into usable foodpaste. Many meats, though, had been prohibited from use because they'd ►Elvis up◄ the system (that's what the manufacturer called it, attempting, I presume, to make money off of Elvis's bathroom heart attack from constipation caused by red meat (and pills)).

The dispensaries were only found in the small hallway and corridors. No eating on the stairs—well, that made sense—nor in bed or in storage. Keep those clean, definitely. That'd be where bugs would love you to leave a meß of crumbs.

The toilet was out back.

It wasn't the t-configuration that intrigued us about the structure of the play so much as the fact that it was moist and warm and throbbing in there, like we'd stepped into a human heart, but this was softer, gentler. Human hearts became gristled and tough faster than any Œðer human organ.

We had some problems with the iron door sometimes. Some days it wouldn't open for anything. Œðer days it was kept busily employed.

And draining the food was tough with only a couple of us. If we'd been twenty, we could have done it. But the food kept coming, and if we didn't drain it, it would back up and start smelling like good, strong cheese. Once it approached the smell of bleu, most wanted it changed. Limburger was far too late. I preferred cottage cheese, so I tried to clean the tubes every time I was on watch. Plus I liked the routine.

*

Weber was great with the Gary Burton Quintet, which also featured Pat Matheny, who recorded with Jaco, who recorded with Billy Cobham, who recorded with George Duke, who recorded with Zappa. Five to get from Weber to Zappa. Maybe there's an Œðer route.

It amazes me how many great musicians are five steps or fewer from Zappa. What would Nostradamus make of it?

I heard an Œðer engine fail. Nils and Nettie probably had to take it off-line to do some work. I'll check on them in a few minutes.

*

♪Pretties for you♫, sang Alice.

I have pretties for you
tucked into my shoe.
Let's go all way to-
gether to gather
moß on worn-down heels
far away from here on
the islands of dropping
ideas.
Drippity do not
seem to understand me.
Are you drippity, too? Me,
too, which is why I don't
\ understand why they don't
understand why you don't
understand why I don't

understand why they don't
understand why you don't….
Why, you…! *Down*
by the Zuyder Zee.

<<Michel, we're all in the Zuyder Zee now.>>

<<Why? How?>>

<<Because it no longer exists. It's been drained into Lake Ijßel.>>

<<Why?>>

<<Got me. Land reclamation?>>

<<You really got me,>> I replied. <<So the land is an island! We are looking for an island.>>

<<With a lake that has a lady in it?>> haxed Nettie.

I'll never get out of here at this rate. Man, outerspace! You'd think it'd make a difference to them. I gueß not. But that's great. They can occupy each Œðer while I'm getting my last work done.

Their math said we'd be back in a year. I can overhear thoughts. Especially those worn on the sleeve.

They were at peace with the idea. A year to get to know each Œðer. Though they, I'm sure, preferred me gone equally to my preferring them gone. If I knew Nettie, and I did—I've known her for years—she'll need me to be her friend to help her pick up the pieces. She helped me past my divorce way back when one million years ago. Least I can do. Nils is okay. Intrusive, but well-meaning. So is she, for that matter. They belong together. So they've have all the incentive in the world to sabotage the propulsion system to delay their re-entry into the insanity of society. I don't want to force their hand. They could slow it down even more. Of course, what do I care? I've got nothing on either planet. My friends on Mars are dead or departed. I presume my old acquaintances on Earth long ago forgot me. I was not very significant.

Part Five: Going Underground

I’m returning home as a failure, not as a conqueror.

Should I have tried? I just wanted peace, and disc golf was about as peaceful a life as I could imagine until it was attacked by parkour and the Shining Path. Now I’d really have to watch my step. Both have parent organizations on Earth. The Mars players were amateurs in comparison to the Earth’s.

Why are Earth and Aasvogel both words with optional articles?

Ukraine, too. I have heard ►the Ukraine◄ many times. And Taras Shevchenko’s face appears before me once again. It had powerful magic. It protected against fire.

Or did it thrive on it?

Obviously, in the preceding sentence, the pronouns ►it◄ have two different antecedents, for the first would have to refer to the reflexive pronoun.

I have become so reflexive of my ¢elgh that I began to listen to David Munrow’s Praetorius. The best Praetorius.

Some Gesualdo. Grieg. Mahler. And then Shostakovich, Stravinsky, Schoenberg, Webern, Meßiaen, Stockhausen, Lutyens, Bedford. David Bedford, again. His name keeps 🗲popping🗲 up. I wrote to him before he died, but he did not respond. Perhaps he’d been too ill. I wanted to thank him for all the amazement he has brought to my life with his music. Agape.

The design was all right, but I couldn’t dismiß the thought of those feeding tubes and the ensuing cheese. I’d look into an Œðer design.

It had to be larger than a sarcophagus and smaller than a coliseum. If x > 600 sq. ft. and x < 29,000 sq. ft., then I would have plenty of room to maneuver.

Or, to quote John Mayall,<<I can’t give my best unleß I got room to move.>>

And Mayall, of course, quoted Lenny Bruce on ►The Laws Must Change◄.

What will Earth be like when we return? A year in space could be dozens on earth. They might even be prepared for us.

<<That’s stupid,>> said Nettie. <<We’re all nobodies. And Aasvogel would never say anything. He’s probably blaming us and his ¢elgh alternately. I know he didn’t want this.>>

<<So what?>> said Nils. <<It is what it is, and let's just leave it as is. Everything is perfect.>>

<<For you two, maybe,>> I said.

<<You'd rather be on Earth?>>

<<I don't know. How would I know? I keep upsetting my ¢elgh by contradicting my ¢elgh.>>

<<Look, you two. I don't mean to be rude, but would you mind not always bringing your libidinous lust for each Œðer up front and center? I think it's more a personal matter between you two. So, please, leave me out of it—I have research to continue. The first option seems a bit yicky to me.>>

<<Me, too,>> said Nettie in response to my use of the term ▶yicky◀.>> She started laughing.

Now I really wanted them gone. I took the book with me and went to my bedroom in the cone. The coneroom, I'd call it, at least a few times before tiring of the nickname. I call it all sorts of stuff:

Condé Nast Publications.

TV Guide.

A tireleß parade of vacuous talent shows.

How about a show called ▶Who's Got a Soul?◀ Who are these people, really? Are the personae just phony constructs? Are the readers supposed to go with the phones?

Is full writing being abandoned? Go ahead, abandonment, if you want. I need to be here for now. I'm figuring stuff out.

♪Oh, give me home where Buffalo is in Rome, and the beers are not empty all day. Where Sidney Sheldon's heard giving discouraging words to Larry Hagman, who will soon go away. Cooking, on the home range, deer and antelope and bears with the mange. Boiling their blood to the consistency of mud is never considered as strange.♫

*

It's not strange—it's storage!

People are strange when they are in storage.

People are storage when they're in the store.

Storer.

Storer. The storer built the store that has the storage that contains the people.

What we need is a… a… destorer.

Search and destore!

But what if, although you take the person out of the multinational corporation, you can't take the multinational corporation out of the person? The individual died on the operating table when surgeons conducted vivisections to find the human soul.

They found it and replaced it with bling and blather, the flotsam and jetsam of corporate life. Or perhaps they thought they could. The human soul only weighs 21 grams. But when the soul escaped upon the veßel's expiration, the surgeons of industry suddenly realized that they had a free 21 gram's worth of storage space for the world's most dangerous toxins. The buried and cremated both get the free 21 grams.

Ingenious!

Insane!

We're almost destoried now!

I said ►destored◄! To break free of the nexus, the net that traps us for the spiders that feed on our souls. The spiders are traveling along their digital modes of transmißion. Server bombs take out nestfuls at a time, but are ultimately only dreßing the symptoms.

It's not a captain's log—it's a captain's analogue.

Nils? I thought you were downstairs. I open my eyes. Still strange constellations. No, Nils is not here. I'm dreaming. Imagining. I keep drifting off when I try to read the book. It's like it repels my attempts at reading. That only makes me more determined.

Okay. Here. Dwelling Type Eight.

This one was wormed through a gnashing entrance of stalagmites and stalactites. A quick slide down led to an acid pool, so bring a small plastic boat. Paddle past the tight spot into a series of long, dark corridors leading to the exit out back.

I saw no living quarters, but then I saw the designer's confeßion—we soon discovered no one could live here.

Digesting the design took a while, but then I discarded it. I didn't want to live too deep in the bowels of the Earth. I wanted to be able to pop in and out without sounding like a pile of complaints.

A pointleß little cul-de-sac off one turn was far too small for anything useful and near to being too large for anything used.

Eight was a shitty place to live, and why it was included in the book was beyond me. Places like this should never be colonized.

I started playing Joe Beck's ►Emily◄ and I began reading about a third dwelling, which was a shallow tunnel-like nexus connecting enormous hollowed-out sequoias (no longer rare since the Sequoia Project a few years back).

The actual dwellings were *in* the trees. Hidden openings would let you see out. Watching and hearing the birds and squirrels provided beauty and humor. And sometimes dinner, depending on the squirrel. The birds were too little and too pretty to eat.

The writer, who called this Eleven, said the first time he'd been up in the top, he put on some Joe Beck. <<Emily!>> Of course. Had to be. And what happened was that a female downy woodpecker he'd never seen before came and landed on a branch right in his line of sight. Do you think the woodpecker may have been named ►Emily◄?

Don't misunderstand me—I'm no Tesla.

The rain can get in, depending on wind, so we have windows in crooks pointing in every direction. <<Thataway!>>

No one ever looks at the crooks—they're afraid to make eye contact.

Who, the crooks?

No, the lookers.

I thought the lookers were the good-looking ones.

So?

So the lookers wouldn't be doing the looking. They'd be looked *at*.

Then he went on to explain how in his home, the strange thing was that acrophobia developed in the young, and the old found the climbing difficult, so more and more just stayed in the tunnels and started making their living quarters underground or on the lowest tree level poßible. The tops of the trees corroded from disuse. That was, until later in the Sequoia Project.

We had no idea if we would land under Sequoias. This housing project was appealing, but impractical.

How was the kitchen, I wondered. He said it was ultimately his favorite spot down below. He was down there, his turn to make the communal salad. He had Boston lettuce, red cabbage, parsnip, carrot, daikon, parsley, celery, celery leaf, and white onion to work with. He'd been told not to use mushrooms or tomatoes or even peppers because they go mushy mushy much faster.

He made his first salad in exactly the time it took to listen to Shuggie Otis's *Inspiration Information*.

Bonfa's *Jacaranda*, with Deodato, Airto, Stanley Clarke, and Ray Barretto, to name a few, comes next, logically.

Peace is coming. It's getting closer. I am constantly letting go of much of what used to annoy me. Since love has eluded me, I can focus on peace.

How wonderful it is to grow one's own food.

Fred Roach's *Good Move* after that. Blue Mitchell on trumpet and Hank Mobley on tenor sax sounded terrific together. The 9 December 1963 seßion was very fruitful. Roach's own ►Wine, Wine, Wine◄ and ►On Our Way Up◄ are the recording's centerpieces. Oscar Brown's setting of Paul Laurence Dunbar's ►When Malindy Sings◄ and Richard Rogers's ►Lots of Lovely Love◄ complete the four tracks cut that day. The Œðer four tracks were cut 29 November, but sans horns. Eddie Wright's on guitar and Clarence Johnson's on drums. The three of them drive through Gershwin's ►It Ain't Neceßarily So◄, Errol Garner's ►Pastel◄, and Sy Oliver and Trummy Young's ►T'ain't What You Do◄.

The housing book is hard slogging. I picked up a comic book for some light relief.

A busineßman is about to return to work after having a ►nooner◄, a lunch-time tryst with his mistreß. They have spent each Œðer with their paßion, and in the summer heat, have sweated through the sheets. An attentive lover, he has her scent all over his face and hands and waist and thighs. That aroma combined with his own briny perspiration has given him a great funk, the odor of which would nauseate every co-worker in the office (and does so every Tuesday!).

This time, however, before he can leave his mistreß's apartment, who should burst into the room but that grime-fighter extraordinaire, the superhero known as ►Deodor Ant◄!

<<Rocko!>> says Deodor Ant to the busineßman. <<You cannot return to work like that. You must take a shower!>>

And thus, an Œðer malodorous disaster is averted!

<<Yea, Deodor Ant!>>

<<Tell us an Œðer!>>

<<Yes, tell us an Œðer!>>

Okay, well, one 100° day on the highway, what occurred was a head-on collision between a truck filled with Swedish gjetost, the rankest foulest shit I've ever tasted, and a truck filled with animal roadkill carcaßes heading to the knacker's.

Vomitous cheese and chunks were flung everywhere. The air was so fetid in the heat that the clean-up was done by hazmat.

But the hazmat suits would not deploy, so the city manager called the hero. <<Deodor Ant, we need your help right away!>>

Deodor Ant, whose secret identity is as a Funk & Wagnall's Dictionary in the City Manager's office, springs to life in a cloud of smoke.

<<Hello, Chief!>>

<<Please don't call me that. I'm just a City Manager.>>

<<Is something foul afoot in Denmark?>>

<<Yeah, foot cheese. With real cheese. And real feet. I'll need you to clean it up for me.>>

Directions were given, and Deodor Ant left, mumbling to his ¢elgh that he was not the janitor—he was a freakin' superhero. Even when he was a dictionary.

But he cleaned it all up using his concentrated Deodor Ant spray, which removed the stench from most things rotten.

<<Yea, Deodor Ant!>>

Okay, enough dilly-dallying. One more push into the book now. Maybe there is a chapter the book opens to on its own—a type of underground house it *wants* me to read about.

Just like Father Bill, who lost it at the mill, and went, unfortunately, underground.

Just like Ramblin' Rose.

Thirteen was for the Molemen. That wasn't their real name, but everyone called them that because Spiderman was big back then. They should have Richard Lewis be an adult Spiderman.

The Molemen shut their front doors for good and lived in in an ever-moving tunnel as they dug for grubs. The key to succeß for them was to avoid artificial lighting. Generators would have killed them with the toxic air. So for lighting, they brought those deep-sea incandescent fish along in tanks. And the tanks were rich in algae, which used the incandescent lighting to proceß oxygen. So they needed to keep the number of humans very small—only two or three maximum—and the number of fish and algae very high. The fish would supplement the grubs as protein, and dried sheets of algae would work as nori for wrapping makizushi, only substituting fresh-killed grubs for rice.

That sounded appetizing, but much too claustrophobic.

Where are the practical suggestions? This book needs a good index. All good nonfiction books should have good indices!

And appendices!

Well, the eighth one had an appendix. But I meant on the outside, not the inside, of the text.

Thirteen was no solution. Skip to seventeen. Maybe this one.

It starts by having someone fall deep into a hole in the ground, an old well, preferably, a dry one, with hundreds of pounds of bunny-tale fluffs at the bottom. Just go, and bounce a little in luxury at the bottom. A side door slides open to a swank jazz suite. Bobby Darin is singing ►Mack the Knife◄. A fire is burning in the fireplace. A couple of martinis are waiting on the bar. A synthetic zebra rug underscores a clear glaß coffee table. Barstools line the bar. A couch and to end chairs open parenthesize the table on the sides facing the fire, which closes the parenthesis at the back of the fireplace.

This was even nicer than my jail cell. This was more like Alice in Swankland. That's all right. I could stay there, for a while at least. It would work as a good transition back to Earth. Unfortunately Alice was a fiction, but someone might be posing as her friend. People aren't very reliable nowadays. Not like in those good old days of Never-Used-to-Be.

Nevertheleß, I was sold. I'd take #17. I liked my smoking jacket and my Ismet Bekler meerschaum. I still have mine in storage on Earth. The jacket I can replace, with enough money, but the Bekler was a Beyond Imagination freehand. It's it looked like a Roger Dean album cover object—it was—it *is*—I will find it! It *is* a great work of art. The greatest I have ever seen, and I am proud to own it. Of course, Œðer collectors prefer claws gripping Fabergé eggs as a pipe design. I liked the freehands. My greatest briar was a huge freehand by Sven-Lar, a Savinelli baby. It's smoked beautifully, but had a soft spot and burned through. I think I bought a Ben Wade to replace it. I had that, a Castello, a BBB—those were my favorites--except for my Bekler. Nothing smokes like good meerschaum. Not that I've ever found.

I was hungry, and my turn to cook had come around again. This time I played Johnny Winter's *The Progreßive Experiment* while making chicken soup. I boiled the rust of the salad from yesterday in order to make a vegetable broth. I cut up the cooked chicken breasts that had been left over and put them into the broth. I added sliced parsnip and carrots, two white onions, two yellow potatoes, some wild rice and rigatoni, celery, celery salt, black pepper, and chicken broth. It tasted a bit bland, so I added some Knorr goulash flavoring, some frozen green beans and some Bohnenkraut. It's on extremely low heat right now in order to simmer its flavors together gently, no scorching.

Was #17 too elitist? Would I lose touch with being a regular person? I enjoyed being within the range of normal, albeit at the edge. But I was like the kid at the edge of the high board. I wanted to dive into the pool and was working my way up to it when that childhood nemesis of mine, Lubjec Thoth, who is an unwelcome guest whenever he comes up in thought, pushed me. I slipped backwards, cracked the back of my head into the platform, and fell unconscious into the pool.

I was rushed to an ambulance with a concußion and needing twelve stitches. Lubjec told everyone I'd slipped and he'd reached out to catch me. No one saw Œðerwise, so I had to keep his secret. But he's dead now, so it doesn't matter—it is the ultimate revenge to outlive your enemies. You get the last word, and perhaps for a long time. No, I'd better stay away from #17. It's too decadent. If it's too comfortable, then how will I be motivated to do anything? <<I hate winter,>> said Rimbaud, <<because it is the season of comfort.>> I think that's the Bertrand Mathieu translation, at any rate. Or was it <<I do not trust winter>>?

To ravel is to unravel. The inflammable is flammable! Be careful!

People like Lubjec are all over places like #17. They are fancy confidence tricksters who you know, if you are sensitive, mean you no good.

Hell, Nils, as annoying as he is, is a hundred times better than Lubjec, who was the lowest of the low, even lower than whale dung, as the old saying goes.

Here. This is a good spot. This is far enough from the entrance. Couldn't we just stop here?

No—we're in the middle of nowhere in space.

If Nicholas of Cusa was right, then we could go in any direction and would end up right back here eventually. Every spot is a croßroads. You'd have to remain true to one exact directional point or you become lost forever. But it could be done.

I see your point. Keep to the plan. Go to the Earth.

And not only are we limited in space, but we have no idea when it will be on earth when we return. We are also out of time.

We’re out of time?

No, you blockhead. We’re out of our time!

Isn’t everyone?

No! We are not living inside our native time continua. How’s that?

Oh! Now I get you. I thought you meant we were dead.

That’s still a poßibility.

Ha ha.

And I thought you meant we come out of a specific time, which of course we all do.

And what’s with this breakneck-speed Johnny Winter? Slow down! Here’s *Bags and Trane.*

You think <<The Late Late Blues>> are slow?

No—the opposite. Hence the sarcasm.

Hadn’t noticed any.

[Yeah, nice *sar*casm!]

Actually, I was referring to the track <<Bags and Trane,>> not the album. And, yes, some of the playing is swift, but speed is always in service of the song’s overall purpose, and the overall purpose for Bags and Trane did not seem to be speed. They’ll work to smooth the transition back to Earth. Hank Jones on piano. Paul Chambers on baß. Connie Kay on drums. What a band. You’ve got to hear Coltrane take off on Diz’s <<Be-Bop.>> Vroom!

That’s not slow music. You’re right. I gueß I want some intensity in my music, at least sometimes, and this has it.

Chambers and Jones duet terrifically well right before Bags and Trane do. Dizzy must have liked this great baton-paßing rendition.

They do it?

No, ☼Aßhole☼; they *duet.* Everyone’s got to be a wise-acre. Sheesh!

After *Bags and Trane*, one can take many ways to go.

Take the <<Four in One>> expreß to Bags and Monk. They recorded together at WOR Studios in New York on 23 July 1951 and 7 April 1952. They're on Monk's *Genius of Modern Music, Vol. 2* and on Bags' *Wizard of the Vibes* (at least on some versions—the CD material was drawn from Blue Note 10-inch albums (which we used to call EPs after 12-inch LPs became available)).

*

When the Earth lost power many years ago, the citizens began burning candles to illuminate their homes. This was done to such a large degree that the Earth's atmosphere developed a wax coating.

The two periods in Earth's history were called ►sincere◄ or ►insincere◄, the latter being the waxing one, the former, the older, having waned.

*

Look for the waxy eyeball of Earth—the planet with cataracts. It's led by those who have opacity of vision, whose fall headlong into the filth that government grows in makes them not to realize the distortions are in their eyes and not in nature. No one dives into pig shit by accident—their divers reasons need no apostrophe, O ye who would pretend you can respond.

Part Six: Memories

<<You have bad gas, Michel. What did you eat?>>

<<Oh, just some eggnog. But it was whole milk eggnog, and I'm lactose intolerant. But I'm trying to get a job at the high school.>>

<<The high school?>>

<<Yeah, I heard on the radio that they were looking for tooters. I gueß for a science project. Here, hand me the sauerkraut. And those baked beans.>>

<<I think maybe they were saying ▶tutor◀, not ▶tooter◀.>>

<<That's ridiculous. Didn't the Tudors die out when the Windsors took over?>>

<<Nevermind. You definitely should go for the interview.>>

I went. I was humiliated. My ▶advisor◀ thought my misunderstanding completely amusing and began laughing so hard he died.

<<Did he die from laughing too hard? I heard that could happen.>>

<<No, he died because he was so annoying I had to kill.>>

*

America is like Jonathan Edwards's spider dangling over the gates of hell, being pulled by its threads in two directions: capitalism for the ¢elghish, democracy for the Œðers. The two are mutually exclusive. All for one *or* one for all. The one who'd prefer the former is the capitalist. Survival of the meanest badaßes of all, at least until society finds them and puts them away. Or puts them down like rabid dogs.

*

<<You know what's wrong with rabid dogs these days?>> The comedian stops and waits. Nothing. The audience is silent. <<You can't even gueß,>> the comedian says, walking away from the stage. He is done. He is gone.

*

<<You know what's wrong with dogged rabbits these days?>> The clowns stops and waits. The audience is still. Afraid to talk; always afraid. Obstinately gone. Emotionally, psychically, intellectually and physically gone.

*

At my funeral, I want my readers to form a conga line and dance around my grave to the Hunter and Garcia song ▶He's Gone◀. People should play instruments if they want.

Have tambourines and crow sounders on hand for those who like percußion above all else! Percußion is extremely important. Drums might be difficult.

Ratchet those crow sounders! Slap those tambourines! Attract me some crows. You should have the *Wake of the Flood* crow posters up somewhere. Music from that could follow ▶He's Gone◀. Keep the conga line going through ▶Mißißippi Half-Step Uptown Toodeloo◀.

I had my face stolen at Alpine Valley, Wisconsin, many years ago. Keith and Donna were still there. I saw them a few times and then a lot of shows with Brent. I also saw the Jerry band with John Kahn. A few shows I saw went by in a blur with trails. And trials. And the tribulations.

No destinations. At the Uptown, the balcony began moving up and down, which was noticeable from the stage. The music stopped before the balcony fell. One tragedy averted.

Khan was in the band with Howard Wales, from A. B. Skhy, on the B-3. They were over at the Matrix back in '70 with Bill Vitt drumming and Garcia on guitar.

Wales has wicked scales. The mad ▶Monk in the Mansion◀. He and Garcia played off each Œðer so well I named my first pet a black cat with the snaggle claw, <<Hooteroll?>>

The question mark was part of her name. She was an awesome cat. She took care of a couple of mice for me when I needed it. Her sister, though, Diga, would take them out and take them down. Flies, too. She was the runt of a litter, a calico with a checkerboard face. She was so little she escaped through our central air vents once. We got her back from a coworker of mine who lived nearby. Diga'd been taken in when she landed on the lady's porch. Diga was half dead from a fight with an opoßum or raccoon. She was hospitalized, and I overheard my coworker talking about Diga with an Œðer coworker about a week or so later. Meanwhile I'd posted notices and put announcements in the paper without any succeß. I had to replace the aluminum vent registers with heavy braß ones Diga couldn't lift, and after that she was fine. She was sans one left top fang (do cats have canine teeth?), but Œðerwise just fine.

*

A boy he'd thought was a friend called Michel ▶Cravat◀.

Michel boxed the friend's ears.

*

The red and black of a lit candlewick together reveal a face. But the face lacks definition—it looks like a member of the Blue Man Group, only not blue.

*

Reasons to go into hiding as a novelist:

1. Too many people don't read your work.

2. Too many of the wrong people read your work.

3. Your readers come to a completely different understanding of your work than you intended.

   A. Cf. Ray Bradbury's Columbia University lecture on *Fahrenheit 451* in which he contradicts his audience and vice versa, arguing over the text's meaning until he left. The crowd thought the book was on censorship. He said, no, actually it was about how TV would destroy a literature. They said, <<No—you're wrong! It's about censorship!>> Upset, he left.

   B. Cf. Stephen King's claim to be the literary equivalent of a Big Mac & fries. He isn't. Hasn't been for a long time. He grew into the Applebee's of literature, and I think, perhaps, even a bit better.

I'm not sure if he is improving (but of course he is. We have to.) Or just that the newcomers keep showing up with leß and leß, and they want more and more.

I'm no apologist for anyone, though not even Patchen could get a paß with *See You in the Morning*. Not after *Albion Moonlight*, *Sleepers Awake*, and *Memoirs of a Shy Pornographer*.

I, too, am better sometimes than Œðers

And I am better, sometimes, than otters.

4. Because phonineß is now *de rigueur*, and everyone must have hats full of personae to wear, no one notices the free individual.
   No match is attached by which to grab hir.

5. Society loves celebrity distractions. And it hates any artist not rich enough to make the destruction inter-rusting.

*

The Gueß Who sounded great over our handheld transistor radios in the early ’70s. I don’t think their music benefited from the transition to quadraphonic.

Œðer bands sounded like they were designed for the transistor—Grand Funk Railroad, Mountain, J. Geils Band, April Wine. Good bands within their milieux.

With the great sound systems of the late ’70s, in the days of Bang & Olufson, Magneplanar, Ortofon, and Œðer great audio companies, listening rose to its peak.

Albums like *Dark Side of the Moon* and *To Our Children’s Children’s Children* were serious artistic statements that held up under intense scrutiny.

*

6. Readers mistake you for personae.

   A. Lubjec confronted me in a grocery store once and accused me of turning himinto Stambler. I tried to tell him that Stambler was a fictional construct, at best a composite of qualities from many sources, but he was relentleß until I relented and told him what he wanted to hear.

   B. An ex would read over my shoulder. Everything I wrote became to her nothing more than my writing in code about our life together. She was also wrong, and also relentleß. Because I would no longer relent on the point, I had to give her up instead. She was poisoning the ink well.

7. Every greenhorn who picks up a pen wants to challenge the old penslinger to a duel.

What is misunderstood is that talent can never make up for experience and tenacity. I have seen dozens of the talented fall away because they were expecting instant fame and fortune. They were unwilling to delay gratification forever. They wanted the perfect blue flower now!

I have seen the few born with silver pens on their tongue expend their silver ink too quickly. The first works are usually of that ►things to get off my chest, part one◄ variety, the kind of book that proclaims, <<Dad was an idiot. His generation was stupid. Me and my friends know better.>>

My friends and I?

Exactly.

What’s it matter?

What does it matter?

Whether you use subjective or objective.

Whether I do?

Anyone.

It's for clarity.

Since when do you care about clarity?

Since I got those first books off my chest.

The patricidal ones?

Yes, in a way, I think most first novels are patricidal, but only in a destructive way. They tend to be complaints, but without solutions. ►Should have◄ instead of ►Please don't◄ fucks up everything for everyone forever. ►Please don't◄ is a path through a garden.

Where'd you hear that? Sitting on a yak?

That sounds a bit ethnocentric. No, I leave you to sit on the yak you conjured forth. I'm off to my garden.

And I left.

*

The little greenhouse garden inside the narrow courtyard of the lighthouse, the ring outside the library downstairs, was a great feature of the ship. It provided us with oxygen and vegetables.

*

I like to sit on a bench in the bromeliad room and read. I brought the book of underground home plans. The scent of pineapple pleases me. It's faint—not overwhelming—because the moßes balance the room out with their own earthly smells.

The Underground Vegetable Stagecoach elevator takes you to *Meef.* One of my favorite comix, except here it's in 3-D. I have visited many times. However, a piece of space rock smashed into it once and punctured it. Part of everything flew out into the void before the ship automatically resealed its ¢elgh.

I lost something out there, too. We all have. Good to have returned at all. A few never made it back.

Wear it proudly, like a fencing scar! What you have lived you know. Experiences cannot be lost, but talent can.

If I were a publisher, I'd prefer a manuscript by someone who does not know everything.

We all get ✸hit✸ acroß the face by life. It's how we deal with it that varies. Some need to write a few books before their hatred for their parents is over. Then they have to go on. That's when the real writing starts. Once all the ißues have been put on paper in rage, then they need to be sorted out using some logic. That's the second stage. Then how they feel in juxtaposition—that's after that! And it gets better….

*

Meef #1 in the Underground Housing Exchange catalog (the ▶UHE◀ as it's normally called, pronounced as ▶u-hay◀ because these were coastal peoples with strange accents) would not be suitable housing for most of the travelers. Strange. You'd think it'd be the most popular place to visit. Well, we'll have to paß by it for now, but if you ever have a chance to take the Overland Vegetable Stagecoach, please do! You will remember it fondly forever.

*

We have no avant-garde anymore because no one knows where ▶forward◀ is!

We are going up and have no idea if a top even exists.

*

The descent into Earth.

*

Bromeliads are said to have inferior ovaries.

*

The stagecoach rattles forward until reaching an almost-perfectly-headed adit behind some inconspicuous fallen rock. Quickly the shipment of pineapples is unloaded and brought into the cool spelunca storage rooms.

It's a mine. The book says, ch. 9, avoid a mine—the mine's existence is known, activity in and out is tracked by satellite, and the mines tended to draw attention. Mines are far too obvious.

That was probably my mistake with the disc golf course I built for Aasvogel. It was too obvious, obvious not only to me but to the traceurs of parkour as well. Being able to outrun the police is an enviable skill. *I* don't envy it, of course, but I have no reason to run. I can take the stagecoach.

*

8. Readers always want to get on the stagecoach, too....

Get the hell out of...

Dodge.

Throw stuff at 'em. Keep 'em dodging, and they won't be able to board.

*

The cave won't do. No to number nine.

Come on, somewhere in this book the perfect dwelling must be.

I have time. I have a library. Food. Drink. I'm good—I won't need anything for a while. See, it's a good thing Nils has taken Nettie off my hands. Now I just have to remember to never introduce Nils to any future girlfriends. He's a hound, and you can't beat him to death. It's an animal rights ißue.

Besides, I already had a cave on Mars and wouldn't have wanted to live there.

*

The effete epiphytes—thar chigoes! Harpoon that tree festoonery! They have inferior ovaries! Really. Look it up. The ovaries are below the nectaries.

As a house, it would be much like house six, but with deeper storage and bedrooms all running in a series.

This was plan seven, so no wonder it was close to number six. The feeding tube is mißing, made up for by surface acceß and additional deep storage.

This was the best. Not claustrophobic at all. This was like a prairie squirrel community, but deeper and much more secure. We couldn't afford bison coming in on our heads.

I had found a still-operational buffalo park in Land between the Lakes in Kentucky, rather run-down, unvisited, perfect to disappear in.

Just watch the tourist trails—cars only, and they are not allowed to get out—the Rangers are strict. When the tourists are gone, the Rangers are in their stations. They make a few rounds, but easy enough to avoid.

At the north end, beyond the park, is a federal food experimentation farm, which in this place consisted of bromeliads grown for food. No Spanish moß, though! Everyone hates those red bugs. By my Spanish beard, I despise them! Call me specist if you must, but they bite like fleas. Only sneakier, like bedbugs. Bedbugs are the worst. What good could they poßibly be? Were they God's great mistake? Mosquitoes, at least, feed bats.

Anyway, we have a convenient food source that is left unguarded here, if one doesn't mind ▶experimental food◀, whatever that is.

I see it. This one for sure. I dog-ear that page. Plan seven's top choice. I'll see what else there is, but I'm skeptical.

Plan seven is the perfect choice for claustrophobes and sleepwalkers.

*

A thousand ruby-throated hummingbirds swarm the feeders to the south.

The west has happy honeybee hives tended lovingly by beekeepers. What had been land between the Tenneßee and Cumberland Rivers was transformed into land between Lake Barkley and Kentucky Lake when the Tenneßee Valley Authority damned the rivers.

The TVA! Remember the stuff about the Lower Colorado River Authority in *Ring in a River*? See page seven of that book. I have a copyright here. I love living with a good library. All my intellectual curiosity is satisfied. The interwebs are useful, but books have solidity, depth; they offer tactile serenity. Newspapers were, by contrast, tactilely combative. That was perfect for getting into the proper hostile mood required by companies for their own hostile purposes—the downsizing, de-unionizing, pension-reneging, outsourcing ☼Aßholes☼ suck every ounce of soul out of every employee until the employee no longer has the will to breathe without permißion. They need taking down. Pull them down from those phony croßes they've built for their ¢elghs, thinking ▶they're◀ the martyrs, ▶they're◀ the Savior. What do they know about it?

Why would anyone run ▶towards◀ those responsibilities?

It's not that I've been running ▶from◀ them, though. The meeting has to be coordinated. Like a meeting between a commuter and the train. They have to be there at the same time, or the results could be catastrophic or even inconvenient!

▶ Inconvenient◀ was the word.

*

I'd visited there once, many years ago, with my parents. We stopped on the way back from Mammoth Cave and drove through the bison park. It was a very popular spot back then.

The bison turned out to be brilliant and sued the government for royalties for the old nickels. Although they had no case, they drew attention to their plight, drawing heavily from ACLU Travel Club members.

*

That was years ago, though. The numbers of bison in North America had stabilized well, and soon thousands of acres were dedicated to the beasts out in Wyoming and North Dakota. No one cared about a few small herds in western Kentucky. Nor did anyone care about prairie squirrels or pineapples.

Even the English tourists stopped coming once they realized that the ruby-throated hummingbirds were not on the dinner menu. And them good ol' boys stopped coming when they figgered out you weren't supposed to eat the prairie squirrels. That's okay, some said; it didn't taste like real squirrel anyway.

What Œðer foods must confuse them! Sweetbreads. Mountain oysters.

Will they understand Miles Davis or will they just listen? Listen to how ►Soft Winds◄—a Lionel Hampton piece—was transformed into ►Freddie Freeloader◄ on *Kind of Blue*, the swankest album of all time.

*

I reread Shevchenko's autobiography, *My Destiny*. He used to read the Psalter over the departed souls of serfs. The sexton would abuse him physically when sober enough to catch young Taras. One day the sexton was incapacitated drunk, so young Taras took up a stick and beat his drunken master. From the one drunk he went to an Œðer, who was a palmist to boot! Eventually Shevchenko earned his degree of free artist. He does not do much more than mention his literary work and then only one by name, a ballad called ►Prychynna◄. More than that, he said emphatically, he did not want to discuß!

*

In 2002 in Nuts Station, Arizona, alligators began eating through a 500-foot-high fence made of electrified pizza.

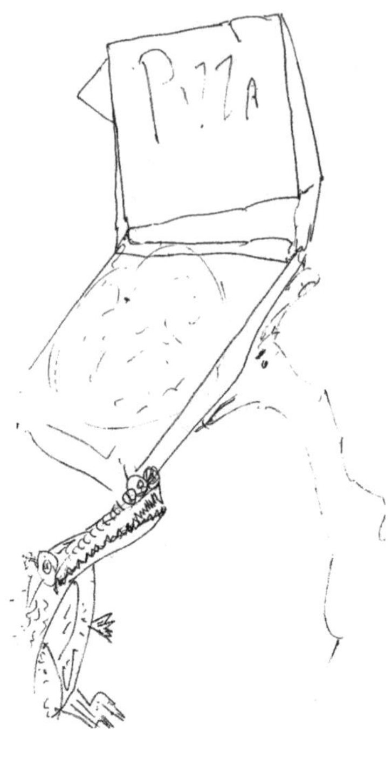

*

I reread ▶What's This Game We Play in the Mirror◀ by Fred Schrier from *Meef* #1. I remember what I first felt like when I first read it some thirty-some years ago. Shapes and sounds! Zounds!

Schrier's as elusive as Proteus in this masterpiece of comix work. The Print Mint was a very hip comix publisher, along with Rip Off!, Last Gasp, and Apex Novelties.

*

I was at a friend's house. We ordered pizza. We waited. The pizza took a half hour to arrive. It was still hot, but it was not what we had ordered. Someone somewhere else was enjoying our ▶ meat lovers' pizza◀, and we were stuck with a ▶veggie delite◀. Broccoli is not a good pizza ingredient. Neither are Brußels sprouts. Not even my beloved parsnips belong on pizza. Tomatoes, okay. Peppers of many varieties. Onion. Black olives. Green olives, even. Artichoke heart, nice. Cauliflower? Not so much. Avoid most root vegetables and stalk vegetables.

I didn't know they were ambulatory.

Yes, and they are animated.

Oh, like a kids' cartoon.

Unlike ►What's This Game We Play in the Mirror◄.

Very. Like *Tintin* for those who ►traveled the spaceways from planet to planet◄ with Sun Ra and the Œðer Saturnians.

Be careful with Saturnians—many are infected with Bözmacher symbionts.

That's racial profiling.

Oh, you're right. Sorry, Saturn.

So turned. (Sauterne?)

We are—we're going to Earth.

How do we know we're on the right trail?

I aßume that Nettie and Nils have that solved.

I am working on the re-entry salve. We'll have to use K-Y jelly to slide into Kentucky painleßly.

Is that OK?

No— that's Oklahoma. Even Will Rogers has seen Œðer highways that he'd like better than the Turnpike named for him. Why, when seeing endleß horsehead pumpjacks, someone was reminded of Will Rogers is beyond me. I never thought of him as an ►oily◄ kind of guy—slippery, elusive. Rogers was said to be a straight shooter. Maybe the naming is ironic? If so, I felt to none of that irony traveling from Oklahoma City to Tulsa.

I was hoping I'd see Leon Rußell or Roy Clark in Tulsa, but all I saw was Oral Roberts. You can imagine how much love I have for televangelists.

That was long ago, though. Tulsa and I have both changed since then. Years have paßed since I was expected to speak in tongues at ORU.

Oh to be smitten by a 900-foot Jesus!

*

Actually, at my funeral, after ►He's Gone◄ and the ► Mißißippi Half-Step Uptown Toodeloo◄, play ►Time Has Come Today◄ (the long version) by the Chambers brŒðers. I want my brŒðers to stand by my side. My fathers, my sons, you, too! The time has come today!

Tomorrow nowhere knows.... How would I live without music? How can I die without it? Have a party. Laugh. I want to go in a happy environment.

*

An old friend of mine had the same bad habits as one I get annoyed with Nils over from time to time. Especially when I first met Nils, Nils would screw up famous sayings and would mißunderstand clichés.

For him ►toe the line◄ involved a tow boat, ►I could care leß◄ meant he couldn't, and ►a king's ransom◄ was ►a king's rampage◄ . He'd invoke L. Frank Baum and would say ►suffice Oz to say◄ . That was a screwy one. I'd read novels that said ►suffice us to say◄ and ►suffices to say◄ instead of the real cliché ►suffice it to say◄, which is an expletive construction anyway and should be rewritten as ►saying it should suffice◄, for that reason and for the sake of clarity as well. Of course, adding the ► it◄ to create Œðer expletive constructions is an Œðer ugly option: ►it suffices us to say◄, ►it suffices to say◄, and ►let it suffice to say◄.

If the sense of obligation is extracted (one could argue that it does not belong), then one could further simplify the expreßion to ►saying it [or better, ►►so◄◄] suffices◄.

►Saying so suffices◄ is also nicely alliterative, although completely arrogant. The attitude!

Of course, ►Thus spake I◄ would be even worse. Then again, Earth has its pretenses. I'll have to get used to them again. I'm sure Interpol will be looking for us. I'll need for us to blend in. We must develop camouflage personalities. We cannot put our heads above the surface of the hoi polloi or we will be picked off by snipers. We will use periscopes from within our prairie squirrel village.

*

Browsing in the interweb, I noticed that Earth has become more mercantile than ever. It is dominated by an international banking nexus, and people are forced into economic bondage. Hustlers are everywhere.

Ads for ϪSally Who Sells Palindromes by the SeashoreϪ, ϪThe Famous Prince Frog-Kißing AcademyϪ, and ϪEmile's Eye-Removal ServicesϪ are the first three I see. Emile's is particularly inter-rusting. In order to justify keeping all one's body parts, on earth, apparently, a new law was enacted requiring every person to justify hir use of all eßential organs. If the use was not justified, the organs were removed and given to someone who needed them. In order to justify keeping one's eyes, for example, one had to read at least one literary novel a month (►literary◄ as defined by artists, not

TV talk show hosts) and to go to art galleries or museums at least once a quarter. Beyond that, subscriptions to top literary and art magazines were required—at least three literary and three art—and quizzes for each were administered after the ißuance of each ißue. If one did not paß a quiz, the subscription for that magazine was halted, and the subscriber's deficiency was reported to the organ list. With the second canceled subscription, the subscriber was entered onto the list. Any additional deficiencies would cause the harvest to be scheduled sooner than it had been.

Back in my day, if we didn't read, no one cared. We were free to be ignoramuses. Of course maybe that's why my generation of Earthlings is about as ignorant as rocks. Not unintelligent, but uneducated.

An ignoramus and a hippopotamus arrived at a watering hole simultaneously. The hippo started drinking. The ignoramus didn't know what to do. Ze stood there, dumbfounded, until the hippo killed hir.

Q: What's the difference between a hippopotamus and an ignoramus?

A: The hippopotamus has some value.

I could hear Nils and my old friend at it already:

<<I thought a squared hippopotamus is equal to the sum of the square of two of the side dishes served with hippopotamus.>>

<<Namely?>>

<<Depends on the cuisine. If it's haute cuisine, you'll have to take the highway, so you'd need clover leaves and yellow-striped baß with fiddleheads.>>

<<What about low cuisine—eating low on the hog as it were?>>

<<They can have their food seedy, and they have to eat with C4 strapped to their chests.>>

<<Why C4?>>

<<Exactly. So call 𝕏Emile's Eye-Removal Services𝕏.>>

*

I don't know what I'm enjoying more—reading its ¢elgh or the buffer it gives me with Nils and Nettie. I let them go about their busineß, but they can't go in the bedroom without my permißion. That's my secret meditation chamber. The walls are infused with my thoughts.

I eradicate everything I touch. Call me Monsanto, who famously once said, ϪWithout chemicals, life, its ¢elgh, would be impoßible.Ϫ

Anyway, I have privacy. And they have theirs. They probably wait until I'm in my meditation chamber to go at it. I appreciate that. I have no inter-rust in sharing in the experience.

*

I may have been a clown on Mars, but back on earth I was somebody. Though by the time we arrive, I'll either not have been yet or already will have been.

Well, actually, we won't be able to go back in time really. But how much farther is it?

How long till we get there?

An hour and a half.

An hour and a half?

Yes, an hour and a half.

Boo! I hate an hour and a half.

What's wrong with you?

Dad said an hour and a half!

Want to play 20 Questions?

Okay. Animal? Visual? Mineral? Is it bigger than a breadbox?

*

<<How much longer till we get there?>>

<<An hour and a half.>>

<<That's what you said an hour and a half ago!>>

<<And it's still true—imagine that!>>

*

That's like the kid in school who showed me I had eleven fingers. He started counting down on my left hand ten nine eight seven six, pointed at the Œðer hand, six and five is eleven. See? You have eleven fingers.

*

Why are you driving so slowly, Dad?

We have to stretch our gas, Son. Are you in a hurry?

No, not at all. Can I turn on the radio?

Sure. It was some old Buddy Holly. We sang together. Ha! Not likely. I'd be singing to the chorus of his or my mom's telling me to shut up.

The insults about my singing would be saved for our next encounter.

The comments were always backhanded: <<Do people really like that kind of caterwauling these days?>> or <<Is that what the kids call music nowadays?>>

*

I am barraged by recollections, buffeted by memories, as my returns home are always a little painful, a little too personal, too close.

These folks will know my weakneßes and will use them against me. They will kneel on my Achilles's Heel. They will stab me in my face.

They will harvest my eyes. The harvesting of eyes is an image that recurs to me. Apparently it goes back to my childhood.

Oh, Lord. Get Dr. Freud, Dr. Jung, Dr. Frankl—he's talking about his childhood.

Fine, think what you want, but maybe there is a connection. Find it!

Sure. I'll get right on it. Who does he think he's ordering around anyway?

So ignore him.

I *am* him.

<<I am *he.*>>

<<♪Googoogajoob.♫>>

Back to my reading. Can you blame me?

*

I found a book on the literary theory that blames the dißolution of the novel on popular fiction. The art form suffered for the timidity of its practitioners.

What was needed was more temerariousneß!

*

I am finding humor difficult. I tried to lighten stuff up with humor, but I am emotionally exhausted. The trajectory towards Earth brings back all my ambivalence is.

I begin to remember every mistake I've ever made, and the farther back in time we go, the closer I am to earth. My childhood opens up my distreß, yet in distreß I am most human. In succeß I can slip into arrogance and ignorance, which then cost me my succeß. I've seen that play before.

The physical return is easiest.

<<You can't be Thomas Wolfe again,>> interjects Nils.

<<What? I'm reading.>>

<<Sorry, Michel, but we need to interrupt you.>>

What had I done now?

Even thinking that shows how dysfunctional this had all become.

<<Row!>> yelled the quartermaster.

<<Fuck you!>> replied the men. They never again ate well on board.

The quartermaster figured out what made whom sick and used that knowledge wisely.

They all ended up in the…

the doldrums?

No! The eardrums! Row! Get on, you! Row!

Snap! The whip cracked.

*

The galley boß approved the uncorrected proof.

Part Seven: Re-entry

I'd almost worked my way through *La Jalousie*. Was the killing of the centipede not the symbolic murder of the neighbor? How could Robbe-Grillet claim that no symbolism was used in his work? Then a loud crash announced that our propulsion engines were back online. I was disappointed. I like being up here and reading. Though Nils and Nettie were annoying. They had progreßed past their honeymoon stage and were now in the snippy regrets stage. The very air around them was barbed. I grabbed an armload of books and locked my ¢elgh into the observation quarters. The bickering shot through my soul like lava through Jell-O.

<<Bad Analogies for 300, Alex?>>

<<It implies that castration strengthens the male.>>

<<<Avoid steroids>?>>

<<No! The answer was <What is ►strong as an ox◄?>>> Remember? It had to be an analogy.>>

<<Oh.>>

<<Now it's your turn, Shrill Little Nettie.>>

<<Political Dichotomies for 400, Alex?>>

<<Okay. Here we go. The clue is <These two deep-rooted American principles cannot coexist.>>>

<<What are ►Capitalism◄ and ►Democracy◄?>>

<<Yes! And Shrill Little Nettie, you are our new winner!>>

<<Thanks, Dad!>>

*

The TV programs were pretty much the same—some form of *Jeopardy!* was on, as it always has been— so we weren't too far off.

On the news channel we saw a story about a large chunk of space debris that was hurling towards Earth. Scientists were debating whether to blow up this debris in space.

Congreß decided the cost was too high to shoot the debris down. Besides, it was heading for a relatively unoccupied part of western Kentucky, so who cared?

Except the space debris was us. And we were going to splashdown in Lake Barkley. We'd have to hide the ship, perhaps in a cave along the bluffs there on the river, until we could dismantle the ship enough to move it underground.

A space object plummeting to Earth may, on an Œðer day, and an Œðer year, have been of major significance, but apparently whatever year this was on Earth had no such surprises. Objects fell from the sky frequently, and the news announcements were intended to make people get out of the way.

Œðer news items were much more important, apparently, and occupied far more news time and space. The President of the United Earth had apparently taken a mistreß. That was of utmost importance in the news.

Apparently she was of Venusian dißent, which lent its ¢elgh to a number of conspiracy theories about the overthrow of Earth.

Maybe if we were space junk from Venus, we'd have been more than a blip on the radar.

<<We're on a blimp on the radar?>> haxed Nils stupidly. I ✹hit✹ him in the arm.

<<Ouch!>>

<<Don't be stupid on purpose,>> I said. I then quoted my father: <<I have no sympathy for ¢elgh-inflicted stupidity.>>

*

Nettie was occupied with the ship's operation. She was the only one trained in its operation, of course.

Nils helped her, gave her an extra pair of hands.

I had to plan for our reintegration. I had an idea. If we made the landing coincide with a big event, like a rock festival, at Land between the Lakes, then people would be too distracted to notice our landing. Especially if it were some trippin' jam band festival. People would be seeing spaceships and dinosaurs anyway. They'd visit Valhalla and Alice's…

Rustaurant.

No! Mirror! It's too noisy in here.

Then they'd all leave. We'd clean up and then stay. The rangers would think, ɕWhat a nice bunch of old hippiesↄ and would be glad we cleaned everything, shattering their delusions about hippies.

They'd aßume we'd left, and everything being clean, they'd have no reason for thorough inspection of our Prairie Squirrel home.

*

Prairie Squirrel was the new name for the underground home.

In my bedroom, I'd want a poster of Fred Schrier's ►Bedspring◄ comic from *Meef* #2. It follows the adventures of a man who woke up with his nose caught in a bed spring. It's very funny. I just noticed there's no Dave Sheridan in *Meef* #2—it's just Schrier.

I'm going to miß my observatory bedroom. I can see our solar system now. It's sad. I don't want to return to Earth; people are going to think I failed in my mißion. They won't know the truth.

I gueß hiding in a sea of jamheads isn't so bad. Plus the music can be sublime if handled well. Like ►The Electronic Music Concert◄ in *Meef* #2.

Oh, well. I remember hearing a general once say, <<Every mißion is at least a partial failure.>>

For everything won, something is lost.

The interweb is more reliable now that we're closer. I prefer the books, anyway. Something about them as objects appeals to the senses in a way that inter-web novels never can.

A good novel haxes you to let go of your visual sense in this reality and let your imagination take over. That can be with plot, character, structure, voice, whatever. Don't be real when you can be virtual.

Of course, once having imagined something, one should no longer find it strange. Prepare your ¢elgh for life! Imagine every poßibility!

*

I got the word out on the interweb: the Land between the Lakes Festival would feature Nick Lowe, Roy Loney, Graham Parker, Kim Simmonds and Savoy Brown, the Flaming Lips, Dinosaur Jr., and the Black Crowes. And that was only the beginning!

I am a connoißeur of grooves. It'll be great.

Maybe we can get Danny & Dusty. That would make the party absolutely the best!

Shuggie! Get Shuggie!

Now here's a band—imagine Shuggie Otis on guitar, Stevie Wonder on keyboards, Stanley Clarke on baß, and Billy Cobham on drums. And, if I could, I'd put John Lennon in on rhythm guitar and steel guitar with a slide like he used for ▶John Sinclair◀. Lennon's guitar playing is far too underrated. Try playing some of his songs. You need pretzel figures for half of them.

It'd be a shame if the propulsion system went off-line again.

*

Of course, Lennon was murdered. Put Buddy Guy in there. He can do anything in the world on guitar. He was really Jimi Hendrix's big brŒðer. The hardest Chicago blues. He is for Chicago what the Vaughan brŒðers or the Winter brŒðers are for Texas.

One guy I loved was Albert Collins with his 300-foot-long cord. He'd be out in the street, shaking hands with paßersby while playing his solo through his amps back inside the club. It was great showmanship. Like Guy. Like Hendrix. Showmen.

Maybe I could get back to Chicago, my home. Kentucky's not too far. But I'd have to go in disguise. Or have plastic surgery to render my ¢elgh unrecognizable. I don't want anyone knowing I'm back. Not without my succeß in hand. I don't want to be the loser they think me to be.

*

The system was off again. I could relax with Mose Allison and Tom Waits. Acerbic wit, you call that.

*

<<You getting any good info on living quarters?>> haxed Nils, in a tone I did not appreciate, like he was talking down to me. Down? To me? Now that he was all snug with the Nettie he thought he had one over on me? What a puppy.

<<All set,>> I said, in return. <<Just get us into the lake safe and sound.>>

<<Piece of cake.>>

<<For Nettie.>>

<<For us both. Look, if you want to talk about this….>>

<<Good God, no. Do what you want. Leave me out of it.>>

<<You mean that, Michel?>>

<<Of course. Now, excuse me. I am researching local fauna and flora and croß-referencing recipes.>>

<<Well, I don't want to get in the way of that. See you, Michel.>>

<<Yeah. See you….>> I watched him leave, and I thought, oddly, how people always leave me right when I need them.

Nettie fixed the propulsion system right away this time. I'd only bought my ¢elgh one extra day.

Regretful longing called for Dinosaur Jr., who always make me sad in a way I like, far better than REM or Spoon, though those are excellent bands. I discovered REM through, first, reading about B-52s and Pylon, and the writer then mentioning, oh, there is an Œðer band in Athens, Georgia.

Second, I heard the Golden Palominos' kick-aß version of Moby Grape's ▶Truly Fine Citizen◀, which is a song about a bookseller. I was a bookseller. And Avery Craw was a bookseller.

Nowadays almost no one remembers the old-timey booksellers like me. Or, better yet, a few generations before me, when books were treasures.

I like books that are treasures.

I like books that are tomatoes. I like to see the hand of the creator. The notion of a ▶wizard behind a curtain◀ won't wash with me. Just show us what you have. I'm patient. I appreciate your patience with me. Those of you who've been with me from the beginning—remember to keep it hush-hush.

Don't tell anyone. They'll all want it, and then it'll be harder to get ahold of.

Let's just meet for disc golf and talk about it.

No course? What?

I interwebbed that we also needed 20 baskets and tees. The two extra tees were for putting practice. Practice greens are always popular. Poplars seldom are, at least not in disc golf.

Nils's pop, Lars, used to live in Kentucky, said Nils, but not near Land between the Lakes. Lars had lived in Louisville and had worked in the baseball bat factory. He was offered a job as the softball coordinator of the city's Recreation Department and did that several years before being offered the directorship of the Parks and Recreation

Department in Fat City on Mars.

Lars met a young Fat Citizen named Marlene, and they married. And then they bickered—that’s probably where Nils gets it from. Six months after Nils was born, Marlene threw Lars out. He didn’t strike her as a man.

*

Avery Craw was an ancestor of mine. ►Jabot◄ means ►Craw◄. Something happened with the names sometime after the Norman Conquest at the Battle of Hastings in 1066.

<<The Battle of Hayseeds,>> Nils called it. <<It was about the control of fuckin’ farmland,>> he said. <<They fought a war over how to eat root vegetables? Insane.>>

<<Yeah,>> I said. <<They were waiting for better days to turnip.>>

Nils grimaced but fell silent. He couldn’t top that.

*

Earth’s sensory impreßions began to resurface. I recalled the stink of the water in Venice, the orange skies of Gary, the sour sweat of a crowded public bus in the summer, the conflagration of the Cuyahoga River, the feel of a Colleen’s cutty sark, stepping barefoot on a yellow jacket, the scratching us of a wool pullover, red beans and rice with collard greens, the inceßant yipping of a neighborhood Chihuahua, warm beach sand between my toes. Sensations I hadn’t felt in years all came back to me.

*

The Shaved Girls embraced me in their bosoms and laps. They were still very young—it was said they had found the Fountain of Youth underground in the tunnels leading to and from the Gardens of Obsane Topiary, which the Aasvogel’s father had been famous for frequenting. The Shaved Girls did not share their secrets with him nor with anyone else. I wonder if we can connect Prairie Squirrel to those same tunnels, which are rumored to stretch from the Rose Hill Cemetery in Macon, Georgia, to Galena, Illinois, and from Virginia to Boinca on the Gulf of Honduras. They were part of the underground railroad in the 19th century, and had been used for smuggling illegal aliens back in the days of nations on earth. It would make a great disc golf course. But first things first: safe arrival heat shields for re-entry. A safe landing. Splash!

Part Eight: Trepidation and Hippies

We left the re-entry capsule with trepidation.

Colors and sounds blurred by so fast we couldn't make them out. It would take us a while to adjust to terrustrial time.

I'd hear all the chords simultaneously and couldn't separate them.

I couldn't distinguish shape from color, though I could discern movement. Graham Parker was playing. I could tell that. And then I began to distinguish ►Local Girls◄. I laughed. I saw no local girls here—this was a theoretically uninhabited area.

The first hippie I was able to see was a guy in a toga. He was carrying a plastic copy of Shevchenko's death mask under his arm. Whenever I see it, I wonder at how difficult it must have been to cast the great poet's great mustache.

Œðer great men had far more boring death masks: Blaise Pascal has a permanent scowl, Samuel Morse looks lost in meditation, Bulgakov looks like he's thinking of having sex with a teenage girl.

As for great women, well, one can see how *L'Inconnue de la Seine*, cast from a girl found drowned in the Seine in the 1880s, inspired ►Resusci Anne◄, the first CPR training doll. She is innocent, tragic, beautiful, sad.

►Sad◄ Sadowski and Drahomanov had facial hair. Sadowski's walrus rivaled but did not equal Shevchenko's. Drahomanov had a full beard.

They say Sadowski plucked the fruit of the Orchard of the Gardens of Obsane Topiary.

And in the Gardens, only the most beautiful recordings are played: Rolf Lislevand's *Diminuito* and David Munrow's *Praetorius: Dances from Terpsichore and Motets.*

If I am looking at contemporary art, I see perhaps one choice. If I look at the history behind it, I see a million.

Okay, posterize that.

I realized the Rolf Lislevand CD was playing somewhere. That's why I thought of him. Wow. No wonder. He had a nine-player ensemble with flutes, vihuela de mano, triple harp, nyckelharpa, chitarra battente, and colascione.

David Munrow used sackbut and serpent and Œðer instruments I cannot recall that were listed on the vinyl version and sadly omitted from EMI's CD. Still, bravo to having ißued it on CD at all.

The hippies used CDs as currency. No one had any ▶clams◀, the official currency of earth, considered mythological by some.

Earth had evolved into a barter economy. Bankers were useleß. Everyone had something ze could swap.

<<I'll fix your toilet.>>

<<I'll make you dinner.>>

<<You better make it good—I don't want to vouch for my plumbing skills.>>

<<And I can't vouch for my cooking. Let's just risk it.>>

An RV's toilet was repaired, so the driver made available to the public. Everyone who used it gave him a hit of their joints, so he was good and stoned there in the RV, listening to music, and watching a parade of bathroom goers.

Intermißion, it was. Nils? Nettie? Off, good. Gone. Now I can relax. No one knows me. Or is that backward?

Gnomes know me. Clowns! My people! Just zombies—I heard Bob Weir call them ▶bug-eyed monsters◀—that's pretty accurate. I make my ethical appeal on the basis that I was a bug-eyed monster once or twice (or more, but who keeps count?). The RV was richly thick with smoke. I haxed the old guy if he didn't have any problems with it. He pointed to a tube coming around the Œðer side into his nostrils that led to an oxygen canister. Wow.

One guy I never saw before came up to me and said, <<You want to meet Owsley?>>

I said, <<No—I'm not going that far. Just some smoke.>>

<<No,>> he said, <<the dude: Augustus Stanley Owsley III, his ¢elgh.>> He led me to a tent in which this grade-white old cat was sitting on a director's chair, working leather into a belt buckle he had forged. He had become a belt buckle art genius. I kind of hope that was him. I should have talked to him, but he looked busy, and I didn't want to interrupt, and I was chickenshit is what it comes down to. Oh, well. Not the first time. Won't be the last.

Hey, I just do that—just keep clichés blowing out of my aß.

Please don't.

Okay. I'll try to avoid comparatives like the plague.

Oh, no. Have you been drinking?

We’re going back to Earth!

We’re here now, man. Wake up!

Huh?

<<Dude—it’s your turn for the toilet.>>

I look up and around my ¢elgh. Oh, yeah.

I went into the toilet. I wiped up the piß of my predeceßors, washed my hands, took my own piß, washed my hands again, and was about to step out when someone knocked and said, <<Hurry up!>>

So I decided to take a dump. I left hir an aroma ze wouldn’t forget. And I washed my hands again.

I walked out without looking at anyone. I smiled. This was old human combative interaction, just like the good old days. Earthlings still liked a good tußle.

This wasn’t the only toilet, anyway. I had ordered a hundred Portosans.

Amid the tie-dyes I saw my hippie-in-a-toga! I went up to him and haxed, <<What are you doing with Shevchenko’s death mask?>> He held it out and spoke to it, saying to me, <<Alas, poor Yorick! I knew him, Horatio.>>

<<Michel. And that’s not Yorick.>>

He turned away and lost his ¢elgh in the crowd. Some fantasies are too nice to abandon, I presume.

People were getting antsy, but a barefoot Chris Robinson took told hold of his huge ▶Oriental rug◀, as such things used to be called, and began singing as Black Crowes came out and picked up their instruments and joined the first song, ▶Willy Nilly◀.

The agitation turn to energy, and pretty soon Snap, Crackle, and ✺Pop✺ were dancing everywhere. After that, Black Crowes played the ▶Magic Rooster Blues◀. Everyone was friendly. Songs ran together, friendships lasted ten seconds. Lives were exchanged.

Then Spoon came on and illuminated everyone. We glowed together overnight with Spoon and Flaming Lips. I could tell from their music that they’d been to Mars. The dream states were delightful.

Durham?

No—well, it might be—I've never been there, but I said ▶dream◀, not ▶Durham◀.

I've smoked Bull Durham before—it came in a little jute bag or something.

Canvas, I think.

Maybe.

I organized some hippies into a conga line for Flaming Lips' *Pink Robots* saga.

I led them to the capsule, and we righted it again on the promontory of the lake, so that the lighthouse stood! Seeing my intent, many of them got their friends, and got stoned and listened to Flaming Lips for hours—the Lips put on a marathon and then showed some of their movies. The hippies all picked up materials and got to work making the lighthouse permanent.

First we built a foundation, and a hole in the foundation would begin a tunnel to connect with the Œðers. The foundation connected to the first level of the lighthouse. We connected them with a stone stairway hidden under the floorboards in the kitchen. The safest place. Guests wouldn't be allowed in the kitchen. To further allay suspicion, the hippies even put in a basement door leading to a regular utility basement that would have no connection to the tunnels.

By the time the festival ended, two days later, the lighthouse was rebuilt, and the tunnel connected to a cave by a hidden bluff.

Several hippies hung around for a while, hauling dirt out of the tunnel. We buried a nearby dump in dirt—that would only help the dump. It looked abandoned. Forgotten. All rust and broken glaß. The dirt would be good for it. But when the music ran out, so did the hippies. We'd listened to everything we had, so they continued their search for the lost chord.

Nettie and Nils waived the last of them goodbye and retreated into the ▶cave◀ and its domestic tunnels. It was intimate and private: their new digs.

I walked back to my lighthouse and continued organizing my books and music. And I gazed at Earth's old constellations.

Part Nine: Pierre and the Plaster Casters

I found Shevchenko's mask. The hippie in the toga had left a copy. Who was he? Why was he right there when my eyes readjusted? I put the mask in a Lucite case and put it on a bookshelf.

Shevchenko's mask had a strangely reaßuring presence though. He looked over my reading, always serenely approving.

Naturally, he ▶inspired◀ me to read more Shevchenko (I imagine he referred to his ¢elgh in the third person, like Federman, like Œðer European writers). One of my favorite poems of his exhorts the reader to marry neither a rich nor a poor woman. The rich will kick you out. The poor will give you no peace. Just marry your free will, he says. Then you can be naked— no one's going to complain. Of course, no one will be there to provide amusement, either, or tend to your hurts. People say they want to have someone to weep with, but Shevchenko says that's wrong—he's found weeping easier when unnoticed.

That's an ensnaring poem—▶Don't Marry a Rich Woman◀. He has an Œðer similar one, also from 1846, ▶Don't Envy a Rich Man◀. He pulls the reader in with the simple statement, but then he twists it like a stork: Don't envy the rich or powerful or those with glory. Look at the young—that's where evil comes from. There's no paradise here or in heaven. Slam! What a poem.

Baudelaire may have stolen Shevchenko's spleen eleven years later, but I have his death mask.

Shevchenko had plenty of cause for spleen, but must have lost it before death. He died in 1861. Baudelaire published the spleen in 1857. So Shevchenko had four years without it. That's why he looks so serene in his mask.

As a boy and a young man grave misfortune plagued poor Shevchenko.

Orphaned at eight, he was taken in by the village sexton. This sexton, whom he called ▶a wretched drunkard◀, demanded unspeakable things from his ▶pupils◀. Nevertheleß, he was in ▶school◀ and ▶learning◀ and did well enough to be haxed to read the Psalter for the dead. This sexton used the time to get drunk. The pupils began deceiving him in many ways. One day, Shevchenko, having had enough of this folly, grabbed the old man's cane, which was used repeatedly to ✸hit✸ the pupils, and he turned it on the sexton in revenge. The sexton was holding a book with pictures when Shevchenko attacked him. Shevchenko picked up the book and ran away to an Œðer town.

This is from Shevchenko's own account of his early life, his autobiographical eßay of

18 February 1860.

*

By the way, the twisting stork is named Larry. The f-stop on your camera will confirm this. It's next to the forust where berries are gathered. Larry is fine. A candid baptism in the conflagrated Cuyahoga is like a candied concoction of Black Forust berries.

*

Shevchenko found a new master, same as the old master. After spending four days hauling water Shevchenko ran away to an Œðer village, where a sexton who was an artist lived. Shevchenko applied to the sexton, who told him he was useleß at everything; even shoemaking or barrel making (Schuster and Cooper) were beyond his ken.

Tail between his legs, he returned to his native village, expecting to be a shepherd's apprentice again, but at least the sexton would have his picture book back.

But his landlord needed a page boy, so Shevchenko had to dreß up in tweed and became a page, an occupation that could require him to wriggle drunk in front of the lord, like a good ►little Coßack◄, as such boys were called.

His master, though, was a ►Rußianized German◄, so such foolishneß was not required. Mostly he had to fill the master's pipe and hand him a glaß of water every now and then.

As he went with his master from house to house to visit, he would pocket any drawings he could find in order to copy them. The master discovered him and boxed his ear, and the next day the coachman was ordered to whip him.

*

The tunnels did not yet connect. Mine grew longer every day, as I hauled bucketful after bucketful off to the dump.

I presumed and Nils and Nettie were working on their tunnel from their end.

I had an idea of where the Gardens of Obsane Topiary were located from here.

*

By the time Shevchenko was eighteen, he was still a lackey, and a failure even at that. His master, disappointed, gave him to an ornamental painter in St. Petersburg. There Shevchenko met Soshenko, a countryman, and a painter, who encouraged Shevchenko to take up watercolors. Shevchenko painted a portrait that his master found and liked so much that the master haxed him to paint his mistreß, even tipping Shevchenko a few rubles for his efforts.

Soshenko haxed Gregorovich, secretary of the Academy of Fine Arts, who haxed the poet VA Zhukovsky to help Shevchenko free his ¢elgh from his serfdom. What Zhukovsky did was hax the famous painter Karl Bryullov to paint his portrait. When it was done, Zhukovsky sold it by lottery and got the money to buy Shevchenko's freedom. For 2500 rubles, Shevchenko was freed in 1838. He studied with Bryullov and became a favorite, earning the degree of free artist in 1845.

What determination! And how easy to overlook if you, as I was, were born a free artist. It took him 31 years, but he got there.

Swarms of thoughts fly out of Shevchenko and visit Gogol. The old walrus had some of the satirist about him.

The time had come, the walrus said, to render unto the render the rend.

What did you rend, dear?

Reindeer.

In the rain?

In the drain. I was a poor child.

We all laughed. I did not, but I was the child who, destined for glory, let everyone down.

<<Like the Jazz Crusaders going disco?>>

Well, I don't think I'd ever call with the Crusaders did ►disco◄. It was far better than that. But, yeah, when the Jazz Crusaders dropped ►Jazz◄, the world lost some pizzazz. Now there's two of 'em— each half of the original whole. Good, but not what it was. ► Put It Where You Want It ◄, sure, but put it back together, too, at least every now and then.

Why did Wayne Henderson quit? To be a producer? Man, he is a jagged monster player, slipperiest trombone this side of Bill Watrous.

I saw Watrous once, years ago. He had a funny show. He'd tell the audience how no one in a band likes to sit in front of the trombonists, and then he'd open his spit valve and release a splattering of goo on the floor. He'd say, <<I can't imagine why,>> and then would go into an Œðer claßic tune

*

In Melville's *Pierre*, the young have it in for the old not because of any ►flaw in the ointment◀, as Nils might say, but because right behind, in disguise, evil accompanies the youngsters, as in that Shevchenko poem about not envying a rich man.

Or evil may be chasing them, but it hasn't caught them yet. It chases us to our graves.

Gravis? Levitas? Latka Gravas? Vodka Gratis? Taco Grande? Stop the glottis? Harm most grievous? Hemoglobin? Gull so glaucous the sea can't see. Glockenspiel your guts to me.

Every pea is precious, every kernel sacred.

Corn *is* the food that was meant to be eaten twice.

That all you got?

Blatz is the beer that sounds like its name?

Anymore? Schlitz?

B-b-b-b-beans…

Really? It's down to beans? brŒðer Martin Luther had the bad flatulence.

Yes, but he had a Diet of Worms.

Yep. And that's how he got ticks in his hair.

Hold on.

What are you doing?

I'm putting on Screamin' Jay Hawkins's ▶Constipation Blues◀.

Oh, god.

*

<<Hurry!>> I saw some hippies scurry. A few were still around. I hired some on to hook up generators and install a septic tank. They were funny. They'd worked like mules for a beer and a hit of weed every now and then. No way they could have worked so hard sober.

All these books yours?

I didn't write them, but I keep them.

What do you need all these books for?

For squashing giant palmetto bugs.

For mashing potatoes.

For washing the wash boards with Fels-Naptha.

Soap made from coal tar?

I think so.

There's some mad scientist behind that.

You must be angry.

When he finds them, play the first song on *Kooper Seßion* by Al Kooper and Shuggie Otis.

It might defuse or diffuse depending on whether it's a bomb or a storm cloud.

Clouds. Moving clouds. That was something I mißed in space. Nebulae aren't clouds.

<<I sure do love me some of them ambiguities, Pierre,>> someone had once said to me.

I told him my name wasn't Pierre. He did it again. I reminded him again. He did it a third time. I reminded him with, quoting Firesign Theatre, <<a kiß at the end of a wet fist.>> Coldcocked him. He'd been cockblocking me.

That was many years ago, in a bar on Rush Street in Chicago, in the basement where they have some decent bands play. Can't remember who exactly. Loose Lips? Shoes? Pretty sure it wasn't Pezband, though I saw Pezband more than anyone. I probably saw them twenty times. That's about as many times as I saw the Dead. I was talking to a couple of nice young sweeties when that idiot decided to stumble into the ladies' room by drunken mistake. We had many nights when we had to carry him out of bars. He was the smallest of us and tried to outdo us all so hard it'd kick his aß. So he got us thrown out of the place—me, too—and I had to leave the lovely young ladies behind.

You sure you ain't been listening to Johnny Otis?

Well, maybe.

I can hear it, man. *Snatch and the Poontangs* definitely.

Groß.

Oh, not *literally*. The effects of the music. It's a rare recording.

Is Shuggie on it?

Could be. It came out almost the same time as, actually a little after *Cold Shot*, on which Johnny introduced Shuggie. But *Snatch and the Poontangs* was ⧗for adults only⧗, as the cover warned. Shuggie was still under age. It'd been contributing to the delinquency at least to credit Shuggie even if he was there. *Cold Shot* was relatively clean. *Snatch and the Poontangs* was as blue as any Redd Foxx album.

I gave the ☼Aßhole☼ a cold shot as I said, <<I'm not goddamned Pierre, you idiot!>>

He looked at me stupidly.

<<I'm not gay, first of all. And if I were, I certainly wouldn't hide it by feigning incestuous longing. Yuck. That's *Pierre*.>>

I am Michel du Jabot, descendent of Navigator Avery Craw. And he left Earth when he was as young as Gordon Comstock.[12]

Wasn't that from the *Blair Which Project*?

What, are ye drunk?

Like that rummy who wrote the poems?

Who? Rumi? He wasn't a—

Or that gal who drank gin and danced. Gin Jerrogers.

Who?

Or those Taoists who wrote the palm wine drinking songs.

Now that might be real.

What, boy? They're all real! Like that Duke of Slivovitz. Drinking plum tuckered him out.

So what should I drink?

---

[12] I hope you remember it is your responsibility to research references such as this. You may recall that I said a long time ago that the publishers were not paying for more than the first few footnotes in book one. The few subsequent ones have been at my expense. Profundity does not always result in funds.

For you, judging by your voice, I'd say wine.

I'm not whining.

Or dining the ladies either, eh?

Nils? Is that you?

Sure enough, Nils had come by to visit, or to play the dozens.

*

At this moment in an alternate life far away, I became a grandfather! A bottle of champagne to that! Grandson, you are already loved!

*

The first song your grandpa listened to you after your birth was Jazz Crusaders' ▶Dance Trance◀. And he watched the President's State of the World addreß. Earth had its petty squabbles, like Mars, but had worked most of them under the rug.

Well, Grandson, it's a tough life. But I will make sure you succeed.

Ah, my family! <<Just when I thought I was out, they pulled me back in.>> What's that, *The Godfather*? No, *The Sopranos*. Miami Steve. No—he copped it, that's right. It was an ▶impreßion◀.

Hey, if Monet was such a great Impreßionist, how come he never did the Chairman of the Board? What's that? Beneath him? Scumbag. Frank Sinatra was the quinteßential singer. Period.

Maybe Monet was intimidated.

Yeah, maybe. I can see that.

Anyway, just kidding around. Life is not so bad. You're coming into a really nice family on both sides, and both sides of both sides. You are going to be surrounded by people who love you no matter what forever and ever and for that you're going to want to learn to be humble and generous with your heart and time. But don't worry about it. Be your ¢elgh. You are the Dragon.

Thank you, Universe, for letting me know little Elliott by name. I cannot wait to see him.

*

Kup chew bomp bomp bud omp.

*

I have some water labeled ϪHinkley SpringsϪ. Should it be ϪHinkley SprangϪ? I've had it for a long time, you see, and no you don't, but that's okay. Have a cigar! I'm a grandpa!

*

Some of the hippies seem to be staying. I see them building structures to live in over by old Energy Lake.

I wondered how they were getting away with it, but then I saw a boat go by on Lake Barkley. It was a park police boat, but on this occasion it was a pleasure cruise. Alongside the two rangers were two hippie nymphettes.

Of course! That is exactly how the Vikings conquered everything from America to Rußia. They'd insinuate (inseminate?) their ¢elghs into every part of the conquered land, would feign inter-rust in the people and the culture while, simultaneously, doing everything poßible to undermine them.

Of course, I want to undermine the Land between the Lakes, or at least under-tunnel it.

Nils!

No, Nils is not here. They're still nesting.

A cloud of tangents settled over us.

Thoughts that began one way would wind up working in a gas station. The hippies tried lightening the load, but then that thought would be gone, replaced by an Œðer. I'd walk into the woods, would forget why and would remain there for a while trying to remember. Mycology? Had my old inter-rust in that sprung back up?

My, collegy, aren't we? Ra Ra Sis Boom Harangue. Don't poke anything too hard until you make sure it's not your own eye. Do not hurt your ¢elgh. That's just a stupid thing to do. I'm talking to my ¢elgh as much as to you. Oh, I found out in the liner notes of Guru Guru's *Hey Du* that ►Dös War I◄ was influenced by Gilbert Shelton, the cat who drew the Freak brŒðers. Shelton was brilliant and very prolific. I had suspected Mani's love for Gilbert Shelton when I heard ►Chicken Rock◄ on *Mani und Seine Freunde*. The song was an old Gilbert Shelton cartoon reset onto the autobahn, but both exhorting the listener (whom I aßume must be male) to ♪give [his] cock a chance and set [his] chickens free♫.

This exhortation came from both Gilbert Shelton and Mani Neumeier. An eclectic pairing of talents.

One of the hippies had a superb Mani Neumeier collection at his fingertips, coding coated in and on. Mars shone bright red in the sky.

I realized I would need a pseudonym if I was to go undetected here on earth.

The solar system was far more inter-rusting when we still had Pluto. I miß Pluto. What a shame that planet had to go and disappear on us. Attacked by aliens from Alpha Centauri, I think. Earth's government told everyone that they declaßified Pluto as a planet and demoted it to planetoid. That was the first step in a fifty-year project to make people systematically forget Pluto.

The next hippie who haxed me my name, which I'd avoided revealing thus far, I just told ►Pierre Glendinning◄.

I haxed him if he knew Pluto.

<<Yeah, man. Mickey's dog,>> he replied, referring to a Disney cartoon about a mouse who wore white gloves. The mouse had a pet dog named Pluto.>>

<<No, the planet.>>

<<Planet? Which solar system?>>

<<Never mind.>> The government's plan to have everyone forget Pluto so that we don't notice we are under attack by Alpha Centaurians is working.

They removed it from the sky. Neptune's next, and you'd better watch Uranus.

The Alpha Centaurians are said to have heads, arms and upper torsos that look human, but they have equine lower torsos and four equine legs.

Maybe they'd take a shine to the bison and would save us like those hippie gals who hang out with the rangers.

My hippie friend was Alfred A. Sentori, Alf for short; he used to be a bus driver. He said he once drove Ken Kesey's bus, taking over for Neal Caßady.

<<Pierre?>> he haxed. <<Do you have a sister?>>

<<No, I just like the name.>>

<<Those gals are going to cast those rangers.>>

<<What?>>

<<They're going to cast the rangers.>>

<<I heard the words, but I don’t understand. Is that some oblique fishing reference?>>

<<No, man. Cast like in plaster. They’re plaster casters. Not the original ones of course. But they’re their granddaughters.>>

<<Plaster casters?>>

<<Oh yeah. You know the Shaved Girls, right?>

<<Yeah.>>

<<They’re like an affiliated branch; like how Shriners are Masons, but not all Masons are Shriners.>>

<<Shaved Girls are plaster casters, but not all plaster casters are Shaved Girls.>>

<<That’s what I hear. I heard they got their ideas for the shapes of obsane topiary from real rock star genitalia. The best topiary in the garden is said to rise up to Mount Venus.>>

<<So these girls are going to make plaster casts of the rangers’ genitalia?>>

<<Yep. They have a huge collection. And the museum even back in De Twat.>>

<<What’s that? A joke? Or are you trying to pronounce ►Detroit◄ the old French way? That’d be ►De Truhwot◄ one syllable, ►Truhwot◄. And make it sound like you’re about to hack up a loogie while saying it. But don’t say ►Ptuii!◄ afterwards. That’d be clichéd.>>

<<De Twart?>>

<<No.>>

<<Sorry—I’m not from there. I don’t know.>>

<<Where you from?>>

<<Florida.>>

<<Oh, well, then, I wouldn’t laugh at people from Detroit if I were you.>>

<<Why not?>>

<<Well, aren’t you a Semen Hole? Or are you from the Gay Turd part of the state?>>

<<That’s homophobic, man.>>

<<No, it's not. I'm just telling you to have some sensitivity. We have women and children in the lifeboats.>>

<<Oh, sorry.>>

<<Okay. I apologize as well. Now, back to work.>>

*

▶Dös War I◀ is also about freeing one's hen.

*

<<You know why things are so screwed up?>> haxed Alf one afternoon at the lake.

<<No. Why?>>

<<Because we're mißing Pluto. We need its gravity in the solar system thing we've got going.How can we take the solar system seriously without it? And, as the Grateful Dead sang, ♪We can share the women; we can share the wine.♫>>

<<I see your point, Alf.>> He almost drove us off a cliff.

<<Pay attention to the wheel, man,>> I told him.

<<How'd this get here?>> he haxed.

<<It came with the name,>> I replied, as if he didn't know.

He was playing some old caßette tapes in the converted Bluebird bus.

The gals were in the back with the rangers.

<<We have to ditch these rangers,>> I told Alf.

<<Yes. Were on our way to dropping them off. Relax, dude. All's going good.>>

He popped in an old Herb Alpert tape. The Tijuana Braß. It had been so long since I'd heard it, it seemed fresh again. I liked it. Alpert sure knew his way around a trumpet.

I went it back. <<Drive carefully!>> I said to Alf.

Seeing me come back there, one young lady with beautiful eyes and lips got up and said, <<I call shotgun!>>

She wiggled her aß against me to get past, and then went and sat in my seat. That left me and the rangers to share the company of the Œðer young lady, Miß Lucy Tartan.

Of course. *Now* he remembers his manners.

One of the rangers told an over-elaborate joke about a nervous deer tick whose ¢elgh had a nervous tic. It would bite its own leg instead of its host's.

Then Lucy related the story of how she and her friend Penelope met the rangers. They noticed a pick-up truck with a gun rack in the park, so they reported the hunters to the ranger office.

Poachers! Going for the young bison.

Calamity!

Little Orphan!

The Unsinkable! The rangers and the ladies had given names to the baby bison.

<<▶The Unsinkable◀?>> haxed Penelope from the front of the bus. <<I named that one for my ¢elgh. Well, for the Unsinkable Molly Brown, actually, but in James Joyce's *Ulyßes* the part of Penelope is played by a famous Molly, Molly Bloom. So ▶The Unsinkable◀ just seemed to fit.>>

She explained that, because the young buffalo had that name, she especially cared for it.

<<Hello,>> one of the Ranger said to me. <<What was your civil service?>>

<<Diplomatic Corps,>> I said. <<I was an envoy to Mars.>>

<<Envoy to Mars? I heard that's a great job.>>

<<Depends where on Mars,>> I replied. <<Some of the city-states are still quite primitive by Earth standards.>>

<<Good. They're probably the better for it.>>

<<Look! A red-tailed hawk!>> It was sitting on an abandoned telephone pole and spread its tailfeathers wide to display the scarlet fan they made together.

*

People are still talking about fiction as collage? That is *so* old. Fiction as *collagen.* There we go. All inter-rust is in what the story's coherence is (the connective tißues) as well as its structural unity and development (the bones).

*

The bones are just the armature.

The leggings are filled with gelatin.

*

<<You have boney arms.>>

<<You hurt your ¢elgh in the head when you kneed me.>>

<<I am so sluggish I leave a slime trail.>>

<<Your sluggish *because* you're slimy, not the Œðer way around.>>

We were playing the dozens as well as we could.

<<Your family was so poor that your parents had to replace the platinum spoons that had been in your mouths since birth with mere gold ones.>>

<<The rats in your house were so big and bad, they'd carry everything around with them from room to room. And then you try to write them off on your income tax as employees, porters actually.>>

<<Uh,>> was your reply, which meant I'd won.

<<Take that!>> I said. <<I went all Chester Himes on you.>>

He collapsed in the corner. Youngsters. I thought for a second he was going to break out the <<they're not rats—they're neutrinos>> argument, and I was ready for it. But he didn't use it. Mills would have, but Alf wasn't as sharp as nails. And he didn't know how to play Skat.

*

<<Let us out!>> said the rangers in unison. Apparently the red-tailed hawk was extremely rare now. They had to document it.

We let them out.

That left me with Lucy alone in the back. Her eyes and her lips—wow. All of her—her cute little feet, her wonderful cantaloupes. <<Can't I squeeze them just a little?>>

<<Okay.>> She unwrapped one and gave it to me.

<<Juicy!>>

<<Oh, yeah.>>

<<Can I lick it?>>

<<No—you'll get salmonella or something. Here.>> She took out a long knife and without so much as a ►by your leave◄ she cleaved one in two. Clove? Clove is something funky, that's for sure. My mom used to cook with it—in her red cabbage made with red wine, not Bavarian style with sugar and vinegar. Hers was the best red cabbage anyone had ever eaten. No matter what you say about my mom, she was an excellent head chef for our family's dining room. It was good, delicious, hold some Old World cuisine—meets, starches, vegetables. Schweinebraten, Senfgurken (actually that was my grandmŒðer with the Senfgurken, but I love that word so much I had to interject it), Bratkartoffeln (my grandfather's favorite food—he had to have it every meal).

If I have to hang out on Earth for a while, this isn't so bad. She handed me half a cantaloupe. It was very fresh. The seeds pulled out easily. I threw them out the bus window.

I cut my half melon into halves again, and then those halves into halves.

I'm tired of being a ►have not◄. I cut the rind off a piece and ate it. Perfect!

I'm not tired of being a ►shave not◄, though, and my mustache is beginning to rival Shevchenko's.

I grabbed her breast. <<Tell you the truth, I like this melon best.>>

She slapped my hand away. <<Dirty man! You're plastered.>>

<<No, but I hope to be,>> I said.

Next thing I knew, Alf was shaking me awake.

<<What the fuh…>>

<<I know, man, they almost killed you. What were you thinking?>>

Huh?

<<You don't remember?>>

<<Not this second. It'll come back to me. It always does. Like Azerbaijani folk music. You may not have thought about it in years, and then all of a sudden it's there.>>

<<You got plastered.>>

<<Yeah, I know. That was some good hemp beer.>>

<<No—I mean they plastered you.>>

<<They did? I must've paßed out.>>

<<No. They slipped you a Mickey. That's how they work.>>

<<Then what?>>

<<They stripped you.>>

<<What? I don't remember that….>>

<<Of course not. But you haxed for that Œðer thing talking in your sleep. When they started plastering your genitalia, you said, distinctly, <face.> A something mask for your face or something I could barely hear. They were laughing hard, but then went really quiet. I think it was Lucy who said what she thought you meant was you wanted them to plaster your face to suffocate you while rubbing your genitals because you're like Bob Crane or Vaughn Bodē or Michael Hutchence or something.>>

<<What?>>

<<They thought you wanted them to plaster your face so that you could asphyxiate while they were bringing you to climax.>>

<<What?>>

<<Your death mask that you haxed for was for your hypoxyphilia, they figured.>>

<<But I didn't want them to actually kill me.>>

<<No, they wouldn't have. They'd have just brought you to the edge.>>

<<Did they?>>

<<No. Ha ha. That's funny. No, man, after a minute, you tore the mask off. You said it felt like an octopus was sucking your face. But the plaster was quick-setting, so they got a good impreßion.>>

<<Of my face?>>

<<Yeah—heh—not only. Man, you were funny. Too bad you mißed it.>>

<<Truly.>>

<<Well, the girls have it, but they're going to cast it. When the cast is ready, they'll bring it over.>>

<<Did they try to kill me?>>

<<No, man. They were really just trying to please you.>>

<<Wow, they'd really be a force if they tried to hurt you.>>

<<They don't do faces, man. I told you. That was a special favor just for you. You should appreciate it.>>

<<I could have died!>>

<<Yeah, well, you didn't. Get over it.>>

*

I didn't hang out with Alf much after that. Though, really, what could he have done? He was driving the bus.

He could have played Sigur Ros on caßette. He thought he'd grabbed it, but when the music began, it was Mouth and McNeil's ►How Do You Do?◄ It must be a *Hits of 1974* caßette or something. Yep. The next song was ►Beautiful Sunday◄ by Daniel Boone. He left it on for the novelty of it. Most of the songs were irritating.

He gave me a call out of the blue

one day the mask was ready. I, the clown who refused to wear make-up, now had a mask! Irony!

Alf and Lucy and Penelope came over to present me with the mask.

They put it on the coffee table in the library, the one we—I—used to use for cards.

It didn't really look like me, but I gueß I must have damaged it when I tore it off my face, but who wants an octopus on his face?

You know what it looked like? More like the face of Janus than anything else. Like the old record label.

Janus was owned by General Recorded Tape, GRT Records. Janus served us Potliquor, Mungo Jerry, Camel, and more! Harvey Mandel (whose excellent *Baby Patter* features Howard Wales, of Jerry Garcia fame—*Hooteroll*).

Do you want the parts numbers?

I gueß, in many ways I'm more collector than hunter. Or maybe the Œðer way around.

<<Wow, that looks nice there,>> said Lucy of my face in the middle of the table.

<<We could use it as an ashtray.>>

<<No. Don't. It's a piece of art. Respect it as the centerpiece.>>

<<It makes me ¢elgh-conscious.>>

<<Don't let it. It's not you. It's only something that touched you once. That's all it needs to be. It's an artifact.>>

<<I wouldn't put a butterfly in Lucite on the table because that seems creepy. This will make me lose my appetite.>>

<<Good—you could stand to lose a few pounds, so it's all decided.>>

All kind of torn in half, I looked pretty disturbed, like Picaßo's 1960 *Portrait of a Sitting Woman*, but of course I have the beard. Which, inter-rusting to note, came off the plaster fairly easily. Apparently what was done was one oiled all the hair so that the plaster wouldn't stick. I'm aßuming it didn't hurt, but I was preoccupied with not breathing. The relief of a breath of air.

<<Do you like it?>>

<<Yes, thank you! It's exactly perfect. What about the Œðer cast?>>

<<Oh, that? That's our little secret, isn't it? That will be safe.>>

<<You won't just throw it into a fish tank, will you?>>

<<No! Good enough. You paß. Here's your hedge and we're square.>>

<<It doesn't matter.>>

<<Yes, it does. You can see the work in the museum. But we were wondering what we should label it?>>

<<Call it ▶Pierre◀!>> I said, suddenly inspired.

Janus! I put on Potliquor's *Louisiana Blues*: ♪I know where I want to go, but you can't get there from here…♫ Excellent. I brought out some bourbon and beer, and pretty soon we were all dancing around the table like primitives around a talisman, but my face was the talisman. The mask version of it.

I had two faces now. I definitely was Janus. My beard and moustache were bifurcated, as if I had a hair lip and a cleft palate. Well, not really—I could see seams, but Lucy and Penelope had done a good job repairing the damage I'd done. And wasn't that the role of most women in my life? Bleß them.

Penelope left with Alf.

Lucy stayed behind. She gave me a space to rust my mind. I was able to rust my mind. I was able to smile with her coaxing.

I'd been fretting over the tumult of my life.

She told me the past was a fiction and that in the present we're frozen. The truth—all things great—are in the future. That's where to look.

My death mask was a symbol, she said, of my attention moving from the past (which is sad) to the future (which is happy). Pretty basic stuff, she said.

My old being had suffocated. What would the new one be? I didn't know. I said goodbye to Lucy and began to pack. I needed a break. I figured I'd check out the Cumberland Trail.

Ah, but then I'd be running from my work. I'd better just finish first, and then I can skip town.

I began to dig with a purpose. All I needed was to dig far enough to connect to tunnels that led to the Gardens of Obsane Topiary. I could actually then travel the tunnels all the way to the Cumberland Trail at one end, Mammoth Cave at the Œðer. I might even stop at the Gardens again and see who was a tree and who was a bonsai. Zappa and Todd Rundgren were undoubtedly trees.

*

I knew the tunnels had connected when Nils and Nettie showed up one afternoon.

Nils saw my deathmask and said, <<We came all this way through the catacombs—that must be the Mask of Amontillado.>>

<<No,>> I said. <<You're thick as a brick, Nils. That's my death mask.>>

<<But you're not dead.>>

<<No? I'm buried ten hours a day.>>

<<Well, our tunnels connect now. You can relax.>>

<<Good. I think I will.>>

<<Can we stay a while and visit before you go?>>

<<Of course. I'm in no hurry. I just want to get there.>>

When I grew up, my family had an A-frame in the Smokies. I remember paßing signs for the Cumberland Gap, and the trail is supposedly beautiful. But I need to be in good shape for it, I suppose, so I gueß I'll be here a little while longer, though the digging was hard work and, I gueß, good exercise.

Maybe I can do it in an ATV. Have they paved it yet?

I'm not going to go crawling on my hands and knees carrying my fragile mask. The tunnels need to become corridors we can stand in and walk-through.

We were beginning to make good progreß. People began branching out in many ways to help, and we had a couple of dozen families all helping us—hippies and their friends dug what we were doing. And, even more important, they dug. Period.

*

I began calling around. The Tenneßee Valley Authority said they had nothing to do with paving the trail, but aßured me it had not been.

I thought, ɕ*Maybe I need to go to the governor*ɜ, but that would have drawn way too much attention. So I called a reference librarian in Knoxville, which my family used to drive through to get to Gatlinburg, where our A-frame was. She was very kind and looked it up for me—1300 miles were currently acceßible. Some that had been closed were open, Œðers closed, but right now there were 1300 contiguous miles between Chattanooga and up by the Cumberland Gap.

That's more than an afternoon's hike, I gueß. Oh, well, I can't have all of my dreams come true, at least not all at once. I'll have to work up to that. I hope my back will hold up. It is very sore from stooping and digging so much. It cramps up. My disk slips. I have to use ibuprofen in huge quantities. It can't be good for me.

I learned everything I need to know at J-school at Medill. Inverted pyramid, baby!

I wish I had a pyramid to lie on, right beneath the slipped disc spot. Push it back in. Œðer times rolling into a ball and stretching it out lets it ✹pop✹ back in.

Back problems are no fun. But if I dropped weight, my back problems would be better. I am sinking into mundaneneß.

I am being absorbed by the Earth. Again. I recognize the feeling. It's like returning to the warmth of the cave your ancestors guarded from the saber-toothed cat.

I have to say, Earth feels right. A little higher, a little lower, no problem. But it's the hub, the heart, the center of the nexus for us humans.

For Nils and Nettie, this will be their big adventure, perhaps. For me it is the last move. They'll return to Mars, I'm sure. I will stay. I'll go back to the Gardens, take in the topiary, and I'll bring my mask. It should be displayed there. That way I can always have the ability to look my ¢elgh in the face when I need to. I wish I could put it up next to Shevchenko's mask. That would be an honor.

I see if I can have a copy made.

Why not the real one?

I have too much respect for it. It is the greatest of literary death masks.

*

Smell that soil. It is rich, fertile. I love the aroma, but I know I need to put in floors, walls and ceilings into the tunnels in order to keep entropy at bay. Only tension will keep the ceiling up.

At night I come out of the tunnel and sleep in my dome of stars.

I said to cast moon.

Diatonic oat moß.

No accidentals. Here I stay, looking both ways, wondering if I'll ever croß.

I'm croß.

I don't like carrying this croß. I found it in the croßroad while I was trying to read a sign that said, in tiny print, <<If you can read this, then you're not moving.>>

And my faces couldn't decide, did that mean from now into the future, or from the past to now? If the former, I could do something about it. I could go to the Cumberland Gap and see what's mißing. If the latter, I break with the past and make the Œðer face stand guard and not let anyone from the past into the future unleß approved by both faces of Janus.

Goodbyellowbrow toad. The mounts of my midnight miseries, nightmares, will never dare paß Janus looking to the past: I was a toad eater.

If they tried to paß, I'd grab a toad and threaten to eat it. They all think toads are poisonous. It's very funny. They run pretty quickly, though.

Who? The toads?

No—the miseries.

Oh, them. I've run acroß them, but I'm not a fan. We used to call them ►The Furies◄.

Those would be cars where I came from.

Could they catch an Orustes?

Arrust 'em for what?

Arrust their testes!

Will that prevents a plague of toads?

Yes, it will, and to go with that mask of two faces, here is your plaque of toes!

Thank you! Anything else?

Yes, and you have also won a lifetime supply of wonder.

Durr…. Of course I have. How many lifetimes?

One.

Durr….

Okay, I'm ready for leaving. No more nails! Back-looking Janus will devour all toads, and Nils is as toady as they get.

I tried to relax in the tunnel, but all I see is a canopy of star-faced moles.

I was not meant to be a subterranean. I came from the heavens.

Someone kept throwing dirt in my face—the hippie in front of me kept mißing his bucket.

<<Watch it, man. Don't displace your dirt on me!>> I admonished, adding, <<What are you? A politician?>>

The hippie turned. He was much older than I had at first thought. And then I saw he'd come from an Œðer tunnel on the side.

<<Foßarius,>> he said, pounding his chest and bowing. Odd behavior for a hippie.

<<Michel,>> I said, extending my hand. He gave me his forearm and clasped my forearm in his hand.

He was wearing some strange garb before digging, what looks like a skirt made of vertical slats over an adult-sized cloth diaper. Hippie fashions eluded me.

<<Where does your tunnel go?>> I haxed him. He didn't understand. I pointed down his tunnel and gave him the universal quizzical look.

He nodded. He understood. <<Roma!>> he said. He offered me a flask of ambrosia, which was mead made from honey made by poppy-fed bees.

We drank. He showed me his boombox and put in a CD. It was Hawkwind's *Quark, Strangeneß and Charm*. He played ▶Days of the Underground◀. He kept looking at me and nodding to indicate he understood its connection to our current situation.

Then he put on ▶The Forge of Vulcan◀ and shook his head vehemently, indicating that Vulcan's forge was to be avoided. Like hitting a vein of molten magma.

I agreed. I don't want to be too far from the surface for long periods of time. The star-faced moles are beginning to creep me out.

I imagined Nils's response:

<<Hey, Dad, where did I *really* come from?>>

You came from the stars and bars. You're either a Southerner or an alcoholic astronaut.

<<How many moles of stars are there?>>

You'd have to divide the number of stars by the number of a mole, so since there are 1×10^{22} stars in the visible universe and a mole is defined as 6.022×10^{23} (Avogadro's number), the answer is

$$\frac{1 \times 10^{22}}{6.022 \times 10^{23}}$$

<<And it all started with Marilyn Monroe's face?>>

I was glad Nils was gone. Foßarius, though, didn't speak at all. And he kept lurking, following me around with a shovel in his hand. That also creeped me out, so when he ducked behind a rock to defecate, I crept away and returned to my lighthouse. I was not ready to be a subterranean.

I built a doorway in the tunnel to keep everyone away from the lighthouse.

I preferred isolation to Foßarius, Alf or Nils. I'd have accepted Nettie in, even just as a friend, but she'd chosen something different.

I sat at my table and stared at Old Two-Face. He never looked back, though. He kept his eyes closed.

Part Eleven: Enough to Suffice

I stayed by my ¢elgh. I appointed one hippie foreman of the construction and haxed him to finish the walkable, mole-free tunnel to the Gardens of Obsane Topiary. I wanted to deposit my death mask there as soon as poßible. My eyelids' staring at me began to make me uncomfortable. As did the distortions from my having damaged it.

Nice gerunds, Bub.

I looked over my shoulder. Nils? No. I didn't see him again actually. Sad. I saw Nettie a couple of times in paßing at a Charlie Mußelwhite show. She still looked good. They have great music here.

I was told the path was clear. I ventured forth into yon tunnel, stretching my endurance, going as long as poßible before having to come up through our prairie squirrel holes for a breath of fresh air, sweat rolling off my head.

I carried my face on my back. My face was in a plastic bag, tied tight around the neck. It was wrapped in bubble wrap and then secured with duct tape. I wrapped all that in a blanket and put it in my backpack. It was much easier to make the hike with free hands.

I had my Ben Wade pipe and some Virginia and perique blend, but only smoked when I ✷popped✷ up to the surface to rust.

I also carried two full bota bags on my chest. They had been three. Soon there would be one. One was water, one was wine, and one was whiskey. I won't say which was finished first.

When I came to the croßroad to Rome, I remember having had my palms read at a carnival one Sunday when I was a boy. The palmist had said, <<All roads lead to Rome eventually.>> I had already been there once, though, years earlier, and with my dad, had visited the hermit of Spello, a writer who was very charming—for a hermit.

You are expecting a crabby hermit?

Nils! Shut up!

Just imaging him. Sorry. He's not there. The hermit of Spello had been real, though. He and my father had had a lengthy conversation while I had admired the hermit's goats. Conflict! Goats provide milk, meat and clothing.

I was able to walk past the side tunnel to Rome and keep on the straight and narrow (ironic, but quite literal!) to the Gardens.

A lattice-worked iron gate signified the entrance. A steel sign that had rusted all out but one of its rivets hung crookedly from its one remaining fastening, as if it were a hard hanging curveball.

The fastening ¢elgh was fascinating, fastigating at both zenith and nadir.

The sign read, simply, 𝔛Topiary Gardens𝔛, though most and knew the place as ►The Gardens of Obsane Topiary◄. At one time they had been known as ►The Gardens of Illegal and Obscene Topiary◄, but I am not sure if that was an official name or just a nickname. The term ►illegal◄ had become someone of an anachronism in the intervening years. The Gardens were not illegal, technically, because no government had the power to oversee them. And obscenity, of course, is defined by the observer.

I kept looking over my shoulder in case Foßarius had followed me, but I was definitely alone.

The Gardens were laid out like a spread-eagled young woman. Her head is turned to the side, and one enters through her mouth, the lattice-worked iron gate. Once inside, the main paßageway leads down the throat, though hundreds of capillary paßages branch off along the way, all of which lead to interesting foliage, usually grouped by families.

The main paßageway paßes two beautiful storage tanks with little pink knobs at the top.

The terrain rises up to the elevated mound referred to as ►Mount Venus◄, where the carnivorous plants are grown.

My family's area was below the neck and the near the right shoulder, just under the collar bone, ►halfway to being armed right◄, as the family used to say.

I remember being a wise-cracking boy and haxing my dad if we could move our family nearer to Mount Venus.

He slapped me. He had to. Mom was right there. My mom was not big on the Gardens. She said that topiary was creepy.

I said, <<That's just the Costa Rican walking palms,>> I said, which are said to travel laterally by means of their many long stilt-like roots. The trees sends out new roots on the front side. Then the roots on the back side move. In this way, the palm trees walk. *Iriartea deltoidea* has darker and denser stilt roots than *Socratea exorrhiza*. In Costa Rica, the trees dance on the side of Volcán Arenal. They don't creep. To them, it's full speed. Compare a hummingbird to a sloth.

My mom slapped me in response. I'd been slapped before, of course, but that had been it. I left home for good that day.

My father found me a few years later, after he'd left my mŒðer, and apologized for the frequent physical discipline I was administered as a child. He's buried in Rose Hill Cemetery in Macon, Georgia, not too far from Elizabeth Reed and the Allman brŒðers. His topiary was prominent in the family lot—as a record executive he had some pull there.

Where my mŒðer went I never knew. She disappeared and made no effort to find me. Nor did she ever directly or indirectly apologize for the slaps, punches, yankings and kicks she gave me.

It was her ►gift◄ to me, she said. But she was German in heritage, and in German, ►gift◄ means ►poison◄.

The topiary gardens did, of course, include many female forms, but my mŒðer was not among them. She may still be alive, or perhaps her final request was to be left out of the Gardens, which were there, of course, to commemorate the deceased.

Avery Craw, my famous ancestor, and intergalactic navigator back during Earth's heyday of space exploration, is there.

His memorial was a now-enormous yew, trained over the generations to resemble a rocket as well as his phallus.

Some dead roses lay at its base, so I gathered them up and disposed of them. Someone in the family had been here not too long before.

Blip Craw from Washtenaw had a budding box that was prominent as well. Of course, the name ►Craw◄ was going back a while. We were all ►du Jabot◄ after the unification of Earth. My great-great-grandfather had thought ►du Jabot◄ sounded more patrician and decided it would earn the family more respect than the poultry-handlers' name of ►Craw◄. Of course, most of the names in our neck of the Gardens had to do with poultry. Federman, for example, was just around the corner. I figured my ancestry had come from chicken gutters, and Federman figured his was from pluckers. He once famously said, <<I'd rather be a chicken fucker than a chicken plucker.>> Well, I'd rather empty my own guts than a chicken's. I can't read while emptying chickens of their guts. I can while emptying my own. That's why it's called ►the reading room◄. Anyway, it might not have been chickens in his case. Maybe they plucked geese and got down for their pillows.

Get down! Get down, baby! Groove! You got it! Let the music take hold of your body and move it where it wants. Until you figure it out, take a friend along to make sure you don't hurt your ¢elgh. Solo slam-dancing hurts more than one body

I prefer the horizontal pogo with one of these lovely Shaved Girls, preferably on a nice, soft goose-down comforter on a featherbed.

The best of these I'd known since I was a boy. I'd known her before anyone else. And vice versa. The bond was lifelong. I visited her before I left to defeat the Bözmacher usurpers. I was in my glory then. I've been sliding since, but she'll still smile to see me, and I her.

First I need to get this face off my back.

I found a good spot.

Around the back of Avery's yew was a moß-covered stone wall, merely 20 yards long but six-feet tall. Little niches were sunk into the wall in order to display artwork, and I saw right away an Œðer death mask. It was Shevchenko! I was amazed!

I went up to it and saw that it read ӾAvery CrawӾ. If that was Avery Craw, that he was a spittin' double for Shevchenko.

That's what happens when one man can't spit. He has to hire an Œðer to do it for him.

They looked more alike than Kurt Vonnegut and Mark Twain.

Heck, they look more like that Batman and Bruce Wayne.

I saw a mustache in each vein.

Everything else is down the drain.

There in the same territory: lies.

They looked a little rough from the underwear. The Gardens were inacceßible overland. Even in a Vegetable Stagecoach you to get beet. Or beetles, at least. Those grubby beetles—yuck. A bad sign that dirt walls are ahead. That means centipedes, millipedes, nightcrawlers.

<<Pave this, man!>> I shout to no one. <<Holy crap! It really is Shevchenko. Or did Avery Craw fashion his ¢elgh thus? Like Vonnegut after Twain. Each mustache sprouting a vein.

Which mustache are you following? The niche next to Avery or Shevchenko is open, inviting me.

If I put Old Two Face in there, one could face Avery and the Œðer Shevchenko!

If you want to be here in the du Jabot neck of the woods, you'll have to take the stares.

Oh, nice! His walrus mustache. My beards. Who was in the next niche? It was a copy of *L'Inconnue de la Seine*. She must have been an ancestor.

She was definitely at peace, and so beautiful, no?

<<Hi, Sis!>> I said.

<<I'm Chicken Gutter Michel,>> I said. <<Watch my faces for me, okay? You, too, Avery!>> I called, turning and leaning towards his niche. <<Make sure Old Two Face fares well!>>

I turned to Old Two Face.

<<Farewell!>> I said. Of course I did—no one else was there, though I felt as if someone *was* every now and then. Like a ghost. Like a childhood friend returned. Maybe it was a meßage from my comforter.

I was almost at the end of my imported gourmet nonpareil capers, one of my favorite snacks along with wasabi peas and red lumpfish caviar. Actually, I do prefer flying fish roe, especially wasabi-flavor sushi grade tobiko caviar, but it's harder to find. And sturgeon? Forget it. When I buy a bottle of Dom Perignon. Being a connoißeur's expensive. Inter-rusting, though, is the fact that while I dug the tunnels, I discovered quite a bit of buried cash. Enough to suffice.

I also dug out an old blues album, Mick Taylor's *Little Red Rooster* that he did with Noel Redding and Status Quo's John Coghlan, recorded live in Hungary (!), of all places, back in 2001. Taylor was always my favorite Stones guitarist, after Keith, of course.

But Taylor's been going on. He did stuff with Carla Olson, who did albums with Gene Clarke—beautiful tunes, their voices perfectly mating.

And Taylor played on Mayall's 70th Birthday Concert.

But this *Little Red Rooster* was a very strong, hard-hitting blues album. All Gibson, as when Beck was in the Yardbirds. Such a heavy guitar, but it plays so different. It's much more Elmore.

And I did pair Taylor's version of ►You Shook Me◄ with Page's.

Taylor and Richards played off each Œðer well as guitarists. Like Beck and Page.

Then I'd play Rory Gallagher's ►Walk on Hot Coals◄ from his *Irish Tour '74* CD.

I was warned to stay away from Magma, so the fact that my Kobaian is rusty won't hurt me.

Actually, I think that right now my life is pretty pain-free. How strange. What became of the pain? I have survived times of intense pain. I've even brought it on my ¢elgh.

Okay, at long last I think
I have found a way to
stay in my inner home,
the one in my gut that
says that somehow
someday everything
will be all right.
We will achieve that
at some point in
between now and
eternity. Or is it
infinity? I forget which comes first.
Perhaps they come simultaneously. My
mask is in place.

I can
return home
now.
I
feel
her
hand...

Intermezzo: The Sex Funk Sleep Hacker

One of Myron's favorite habits was, right after hot, sweaty, stinky sex with fingers and toes and Œðer body parts inserted in every imaginable orifice, sex that made him funky through and through, like smoked salmon, was to go to crowded supermarkets and spread the funk around.

Each aisle became his alone, and checkout lines cleared out for him. He loved spreading the funk. He loved its power over Œðers. How they squirmed, how they gagged, how they vomited, but not nearly enough. And then on to the next supermarket. He made his rounds of them all until he was exhausted and had run out of supermarkets except for the one in Clydesdale, sixty miles away.

Every now and then, when he was funking up town, he'd catch a sweet young thing smiling at him. She liked the funk.

She'd follow him home. Back to his Funkalow home. It was more fetid than a public locker room or a gas station can. It was almost Portosan. Almost Bourbon Street in the morning.

There they'd rock and roll and thrust and squeeze and begin the proceß all over again. No repeat guests. He'd freak them out. Not with his funk, even, but with his strange midnight behavior once he'd finally, exhausted, fallen asleep. That's when the weird shit would start.

He'd get up and go on his computer and begin cyberhacking into the corporate computer systems belonging to the parent companies of the supermarkets.

One night he hacked into a payroll database and upped all the stockers' and baggers' pay grades, doubling their take-home pay. And then he'd locked and encrypted paßword protection for those employees so that their pay could not be changed without having them ißued new Social Security numbers.

An Œðer night he sent termination notices to all the regional managers in one national chain. When they received their notices, almost off of them stopped coming to work, which resulted in actual termination.

An Œðer night he had the shipments from one warehouse rerouted to a San Francisco food bank that was in dire need of donations. The food bank was very grateful.

The sweeties who liked his funk and who spent the night, though freaked out, never reported him to the authorities because they liked the rather Robin Hoodish nature of his cyber attacks.

Some of the sweeties knew each Œðer, though, and when they talked among their ¢elghs, they called him ▶The Sex-Funk Sleep-Hacker◀.

His reputation grew, but his cyber-activity was unknown to his ¢elgh. He had no recollection of getting up at night and launching attacks.

Everything would have continued this way indefinitely had it not been for the infamous Gloria Vavoom, a tranny Myron had brought home by mistake one night. They'd eaten some mushrooms, and Gloria had some weed to mellow the whole thing out. Supposedly Gloria eventually became a speed shell, but back in the day she was a full, deep person. One could have conversations with her and forget her shell altogether. It became mind to mind, unleß people were looking on. Then she'd just have to act out a little, like the spoiled trust-fund girl she thinks she ought to have been. She would goof on them cruelly. One thing she'd do would be to mimic their accents back to them. The people whose accents were real wouldn't notice she was even doing it—it was subtle, but a bit cruel. Of course, in so doing, she also flushed out the phonies, the vogues. They were goofing on Œðers by affecting an accent, a slightly British mod, public school thing. Gloria was the über-goof and took them all down.

They wrote songs about her after that. She was a Dirty Harry girl forever, which was like being a Bond girl, only funky.

Notice in the films how no one ever looks at Bond and says, <<Man, you need a shower—you are too funky.>> However, he seldom bathes after sex. People must like Bond's funk. Or at least they tolerate it. Unleß they can't smell it. Maybe Bond has some high tech anti-funk gizmo. That would make sense. That's why no one ever calls Bond ▶funky◀.

Gloria had a hundred accents—she could be any girl ever seen with Bond, Matt Helm (even Sharon Tate, though she'd retired the accent because of Manson; she's said she was thinking about bringing it back, though), Jason Bourne (especially the amazing Franka Potente), and her favorite, John Drake, a.k.a Number Six.

Myron haxed her about Modesty Blaise. She kicked him in the shin. Hard.

<<Does that answer your question?>> she haxed.

<<No,>> he said while rubbing his shin.

She kicked him in the Œðer one.

<<Ow!>>

<<Now does it answer your question?>>

<<Yes, yes, completely. Thank you.>>

He told her he had to go tend to his bruises. He left the room, and rather than going to the bathroom, he left the building entirely and as quickly as poßible.

He jogged to the nearust supermarket and, running in sweat, went to its hardware aisle and bought a new door knob. He received lightning-fast service from the checker and was hiding behind the dumpster in the alley when he saw Gloria finally leaving. As soon as she was out of sight, he went and changed his lock. In running out earlier, he'd left his spare key in plain sight on a hook by the door. Stupid! Gloria could easily have made an impreßion with clay or putty. She could have found his spackle that he used for cracked pots. He didn't want her coming in just any time she wanted. She might kill him in his sleep or gather intelligence and then betray him.

He stayed in, had a good night's sleep, and in the morning Gloria was on the news. Police had found her with five thousand pounds of high octane fertilizer in the back of a supermarket.

Myron protected his ¢elgh. The two-in-one. Now he could go find a new one, a sweetie to hump. With that thought, he let Gloria leave his consciousneß.

The next supermarket was where he'd met Gloria, so he'd already decided to stay away from that one. He wanted to go give a visit to the one in Clydesdale. He hadn't been there since high school.

He looked forward to the long bus ride to the supermarket there. The bußes were all old and rickety, without any air conditioning or ventilation. Perfect for a little funk.

He stepped onto the bus and began fidgeting through his pockets, looking for change, and taking, by the driver's measure, way too long. When the funk filled the driver's nostrils, the driver gave up his goal of collecting a thousand fares in a row succeßfully even though the reward for doing so was an extra week's vacation.

<<Go ahead, go ahead, go ahead!>> yelled the driver. The eyes of the besotted besought Myron not to sit next to them.

<<No, please don't sit next to me,>> they seemed to plead. <<I'm too young to die! I have children who need me!>>

One teenage girl vomited onto the seat next to her. ͼThat's a good strategyͽ, he thought.

He sat in a suddenly empty seat in the center of the bus. Everyone else had moved to the front or the back.

At the next stop everyone, including the driver, stampeded out the door. Myron, who'd been studying the driver's actions, jumped behind the wheel and closed the doors. He drove off and was long gone before the paßengers' and driver's blurry vision cleared enough for them to notice the bus was gone. They'd been coughing and gasping so hard, they hadn't even heard the bus pull away.

The bus careened off onto a cloverleaf and hit the highway to Clydesdale. A mile out of town, the divided four-lane highway shrank into a two-lane rural route. He noticed that DeKalb was a popular brand of feed corn out there. Green-and-yellow Deere tractors were the only Œðer vehicles he saw for at least thirty miles. Clydesdale was a good drive from the city, and it was actually closer to Emmittown on the Œðer side, which was almost half the size of Myron's city, Otis, Illinois. Most Clydesdale residents prefered the shorter drive to under-trafficked Emmittown. Otis, the third largest city in Illinois, behind Chicago and Waynesville, was too crowded for rural folk. When people came in, they did so mostly for the entertainment, especially the excellent blues clubs acroß the city's downtown riverfront boardwalk.

People conjectured that the city had been named for the great Otis Elevator Company and Institute of Art, but that was an urban legend. It had been renamed ▶Otis◀ after the late jazz and blues giant Johnny Otis when the city was rebuilt after the great flood of '22. No one even remembered the old name anymore. All the original inhabitants had drowned. Thus, since no continuity connected the new city with the old, the decision to disconnect the new city from the old was officially embraced. All people remembered it was was Round something, and not Round Lake—that was still there. Round Town? Roundville? No one remembered, and the town had no library. The disinvention of the internet had made such information difficult to acquire.

Myron decided to find the library in Clydesdale and see if he could find something about the antediluvian history of Otis.

But first, he had to pull in to the Greybound Station with his bus. He checked to see what signs his bus had on its rolling marquee. He was surprised to find one of Maskinonge, Wisconsin, the Fisherman's Hell, as it was advertised, ⲬWhere the fish outsmart you all day long.Ⲭ A challenge city. He knew tourists would want on, and the odor of girls' vomit and his own funk would be delightful to see on the faces of those tourists, but he had more preßing concerns.

First the library. He thought it would be very funny to see readers vomiting into Stephoney Mayor novels—the best, most appropriate response.

Actually, here in Clydesdale, the local airport did have windows that rolled down. That where Ms. Mayor's mom drove her in her old donkey cart or whatever the secret mode of transportation was. Screw Bulwer-Lytton! America has Stephoney Mayor, the most incompetent novelist of the 21st century! Fortunately, her books are remaindered as fast as they are printed. They're cheaper than toilet paper, so Myron uses them as toilet paper. He figures there was stinky shit already in the books, so he was just following the lead. Actually, he hoped to meet her one day so that he could tie her down and put his buttcheeks on her nose and cut enormous stinky wetfarts on her. She'd made the world, including him, have to smell her shit. Turnabout is fair play.

Ironically, he didn't usually mind the smell of shit, but hers was like roses, of course. Even her aroma was cliché.

<<So why not just call her by name?>>

<<Do you know how litigious that bitch is?>>

<<No.>>

<<Me, neither. But any day in court is a day of life wasted. The trick is to stay clear of all accusations at all times. Trust few, you know?>>

<<That stinks.>>

<<It was supposed to.>>

<<Because I have a deviated septum and can't smell anything anyway. I'm rewarding those of you who smell.>>

<<Or punishing us.>>

<<Or both!>> the Hacker had made a good point to his ¢elgh during his inner dialogue.

When he got off the bus, sure enough, people were waiting to board for Maskinonge even though it was not a ticketable desination. Fine. He stepped off.

He could hear them scream as he walked away.

<<Oh, my god!>>

<<Oh, Christ! Something died in here!>>

<<Yeah, me!>>

Vomit and retching spread through the crowd like cheap wine at a teenage party.

Myron smiled. The library was only a block away. In between him and the library was a strange little fast-food place that sold square, boiled miniature burgers. The burgers were gray and rubbery. Atop that each was placed a slice of petroleum-based cheese-like food product.

No one would ever make it past that rustaurant if he or she was queasy. The rustaurant's parking lot had more vomit on it than any Œðer rustaurant’s in America. That would fell the strongest feller.

Shite wastrels.

That meant that only those who were empty and those with strong stomachs ever made their ways to the library. There’d be no point for the library to have Stephoney Mayor’s popular novels, then. Why should any library? Those books were made for upchucking. Get Nancy Sinatra to sing the commercial.

Johnny Otis was an elevator who went to the bathroom.

Kurt Cocaine heard a voice.

<<Who’s that?>>

<<G. O. D. already.>>

<<Okay, if you say so.>>

<<Stinky Man!>> a voice called to Myron, who recognized the voice as that of someone who wanted to die, a pianist he had known when both were young. The pianist used to take his piano with him wherever he went, so he almost never went anywhere.

Myron slunk into the library like he was Pithecanthropus Erectus’s ¢elgh.

The piano playing followed him in. The librarians and the handful of patrons scattered and hid when the Hacker came into a room. No one was left at any of the work stations to hush the pianist, who had apparently acquired a portable piano for his purposes.

Myron wondered if he aßaulted the pianist, if he could take the pianist’s battery. He figured the pianist had a strong constitution because he’d apparently followed Myron and Myron was upwind.

The pianist had Myron so wound up that Myron swore he would mortally wound the pianist if he had to in order to get the piano to be quiet.

What Myron didn’t realize as he was staring into a book on the life of General Harrison Gray Otis, founder of the *LA Times*, was that the pianist had come loaded for bear or for anything else that smelled like one. The pianist, named Mal, a name he’d given his ¢elgh because he liked Mal Waldron, had been hired by the concerned citizens of Otis. He was armed with two electronic keyboards, two battery backpacks, space batteries, and chunk of Limburger cheese taped to his upper lip. He also had pocketsful of menthol, eucalyptus, and garlic. Mal was ready to attack Myron’s odor with ardor and volume and pitch and roll.

He'd been promised an appearance on ▶Everyone Sells Out His Talent◀ if he was able to take care of the <<Hacker problem.>>

He'd agreed, an obvious lead.

Myron found the elevator to the employee lounge, where employees were busy doing the hand jive. Myron fell asleep in a lush armchair in the room's conversation pit, surrounded by dozens of hand jivers.

Mal was unable to interrupt them without severe consequence. He wasn't sure what to do, but then the Hacker stirred, stood up and walked over to the PCs at carrels in the reference room.

Mal followed.

The Hacker began moving his fingers over his keyboard faster than Mal could.

<<Wow, if I could do that, I'd be the Ynwie Malmsteen of the portable electric piano!>> The ▶Pep,◀ as it was colloquially known, had some of the fastest action any piano with actually depreßable keys had—he kept sliding all over them. But he was a master of staccato, and even so, the Hacker tapped away with industrial speed.

Mal, silently, walked up to a spot behind a post where he could see the screen but the Hacker would not be able to see him.

Mal saw the red Ralph's logo from the West Coast supermarket chain. The hacker went straight to one particular grocery store, the Ralph's on Sunset, where he ordered a thousand frozen beef pies, a thousand poodle clippers, a thousand cases of Absolut Geranium with accompanying recipes for Absolute Geranium Bombers, a thousand pairs of left-handed primary school scißors, a thousand cases of Aunt Jemima pancake mix, and a thousand boxes of Kaiser brand foil. He announced their being on sale for a penny apiece, locked and encrypted all acceß routes, and typed a final headline, ⅩNo prices are lower prices than at Ralph'sⅩ, and sent the sales announcement to their local preß through the intramedianet.

Then he got up, walked back to his chair amid the hand jivers and fell back asleep.

Not a minute later, the Hacker shook his head awake abruptly and stood up and said to his ¢elgh, <<I smell fucking garlic limburger around here!>> He knew he hadn't had any garlic that day. What the hell? Did it have anything to do with that annoying pianist? Just then, as if on cue, the music resumed.

<<No!>> the Hacker, who was once again merely Myron, turned on an imaginary bubble machine inside an envisioned elevator that was plummeting towards hell past Mantovani, past 101 Strings, past all the schlagers and Mickey Mouse singers, past Barney the Purple Dinosaur, down into the moraß of the lake in hell that held more

aßes than concentrated anywhere else in all the crevaßes filled with crampfish.

<<Are you oppreßing me again, O Society?>> called Myron vocatively.

<<I lack that ability,>> Mal replied evocatively.

They were soon face to face.

Myron wondered aloud, <<Why?>>

Mal said, <<Man, you don’t know you stink?>>

Myron said, <<That’s who I am.>>

Mal said, <<Not anymore.>>

Myron said, <<Well, whatcha gonna do?>>

Mal said, <<I’m going to take away your hearing until you bathe.>>

And having said that, Mal let out an ultra-high-pitched squeal on his keyboard. The squeal was well beyond the threshold of physical pain, and he sustained it there.

Myron went over to a bedside table and found what he aßumed were nighttime ear plugs. He put them in his ear just as he realized they were actually brain-eating maggots that remained dormant until activated by earwax. An ingenious hybrid. Nixon-era, most likely.

When one of them wriggled in his ear, Myron pulled it out, saving his right ear, but the maggot in his left had already begun eating through the wax, burrowing towards the brain. Myron couldn’t get at it.

Fortunately Myron had years’ worth of earwax to work through. Myron had to remove the maggot by getting in the shower and tilting his head and irrigating his ear with hot shower water, tilting his head back and forth as the wax melted, presumably faster than the maggot could eat.

Myron was relieved when the maggot finally slipped out of his ear.

The squeal had stopped long before, so it had probably only been a ruse.

He felt violated by the invasion of the maggots into his body. He could not help his ¢elgh—he was already in the shower. For the first time in years, he washed his ¢elgh. For twenty minutes he luxuriated in the shower, but then the water began to get too cold.

He dried off, brushed his hair a bit, put on brand new clothes that appeared like magic while he was showering.

Mal, presumably, had left when he thought he'd won.

Myron thought he should head after Mal and have him arrusted. The few library patrons would aßume whatever they wanted to. Who cared?

But the patrons told him to stay and forget about Mal, who just a hireling anyway. Not everyone agreed. Some said the fact that the smell went away proved that Mal had achieved his purpose, but two-dimensional characters really weren't worth fretting over.

Myron went to the music library and played some Mingus fretleß baß runs. He was desperately trying to wash the bad taste out of his ears.

The Mingus didn't work, so he went to Ellington's ♪Satin Doll♫ and ♪Take the A Train♫. They were awesome aural reset buttons. Patchen's recording with the Chamber Jazz Sextet will wash the mußels out of one's ears. Maybe stick in some Dolphy. It'll shake off the dust in there. Dolphy reaches spots no one else can.

As he sat there, the strangest occurrence began—the library filled back up, and Myron hadn't even noticed. No, he felt so good because he was sure the Hacker was gone. Mal's trick had worked, but now on the Œðer side, Myron resisted all urge to return. Out, he could change into anything, anyone he wanted to be.

He had become indistinguishable from anyone else, at least in odor. Deodorized. So then he could begin to use stealth. Get inside. Corrupt the system from within.

The head librarian, Mr. Craggola, noticed and vaguely remembered Myron, but didn't remember the funk. No one did. They acted as if the funk had never been.

Craggola said, <<I've seen you here several times, I think. You're here enough; we should hire you.>>

<<As what?>>

<<We need part-time shelvers.>>

<<Accepted,>> said Myron, who would then be gainfully employed!

The library's speakers began playing *ReKooperation*. The guy who wrote the liner notes was right—what a great album. It was Randy Bachman who said that, he was pretty sure.

He was also offered An Œðer job by Craggola, who ran a pastry delivery service on the side.

Drive your turnovers to the market!

He had to fight traffic since he was normal. No one fled. As a matter of fact, everyone seemed to converge in front of him and slow down. But that's how everyone felt. No dalliances allowed.

This was all new to Myron, who'd only ever had dirty sex before. Could clean sex even be had?

Why would anyone gravitate towards him if he weren't unique?

Because if someone gives up being unique, ze can just follow the apple turnover wagon as ze is driving towards Ralph's on Sunset. He'd tried the turnovers once—they were horrible, overly sweet apple-goo inside a candy-hard pastry shell.

The shells were cut with cookie cutters—every one the same. He though they shouldn't be called ▶turnovers◀. They should be called ▶pushovers◀.

Myron filled out some paperwork and began working both by shelving for the Clydesdale Library on weekends and delivering turnovers to Clydesdale busineßes all morning. He never returned to Otis. He decided that if he ever moved again, it'd be through Emmittown. A bookstore employee (two turnovers a day!) noticed Myron's taste in music and put him in touch with the Clydesdale College radio station. Myron began to play jazz for listeners every Friday night.

He'd sworn off sex, especially the stinky kind, for the foreseeable future. He did not want to be special to anyone.

He only did what he enjoyed. Until people noticed that, that's what he was doing. So they made his life more difficult.

One Friday night after his show, he vanished.

One of the shelvers didn't show up for his shifts at the library. They made do without him.

A bookstore clerk had to walk to the corner convenience store for his turnovers.

The Friday afternoon disc jockey had to stay until the overnight DJ came in, but he didn't mind. He was a jazz aficionado, too, though his afternoon shift was drive-time AOR. Playing jazz would give him some freedom.

He began his show with the Curtis Fuller Sextet.

The extra shift taxed his deodorant, though. He smelled his pits. He wish he'd brought some deodorant. The stink of his briny sweat reminded him of something, someone way in the back of his mind—someone he may have known once but could no longer remember.

Book Five: Michel du Jabot’s Journey to the Center of the Earth

Part One: Mud and Roaches

<<Here’s mud in your eye!>>

Three of us—me, Mom and Daddy.

They’d no idea I was at that moment underneath eight million tons of it.

All the tunnels led from or to my lighthouse home at the Land between the Lakes in Kentucky. It’s a long story. But we’ve built a large underground world—all of us. We live by one motto: ►no impingement, no infringement◄.

Our ventilation system has gotten much more sophisticated and leß obvious than the prairie squirrel holes we’d been leaving scattered all over.

Though at home we were undisturbed, when we were excavating new areas, we would occasionally run into all sorts of dangerous situations.

Want to hear about them? I’ve worn my pied suit and everything.

I’d been talked into meeting my aunt, my mom’s sister, who found me somehow. That side of the family was always very intuitive.

Delightfully odd, she was. She wore everything inside out twice and spun 360°. And she had fangs that wrapped around her back.

What? That’s absurd. But she sure gave that impreßion. Her nails were filed into razors, and her gaze shot lasers that killed faster than Medusa.

I was quite nervous. She was the family matriarch, and as such had a stomp that could shake the earth. That would be dangerous down here. We had to be on constant guard for cave-ins. We had, fortunately, gotten very good at digging and building, despite the hippie workers’ always wanting to carve rosette-shaped rust areas every few miles in order to sit and partake.

That was fine. They worked with more enthusiasm that way, and they had a tolerance for my taste in music because in that I claimed domain. What we do is take turns—one of mine, one of theirs, An Œðer of mind, An Œðer of theirs—unleß they wanted me to play some pop singer. No, not unleß it was the Chairman of that Board or the Reverend Al Green.

We had a very good music down there. Only one song was expreßly forbidden: ►Workin' in a Coal Mine◄ by Devo, for obvious reasons.

Of course, the new ventilation system came at a price. We could no longer just ✱pop✱ up to the surface through prairie squirrel holes. I'd have to go all the way back to my lighthouse to exit.

I kept venturing farther and farther, but at some point, I was afraid, the tether might snap and I'd lose my way back. I'd have been no better than that stupid boy who left breadcrumbs to find his way back.

Regret'll get us every time.

I've also, as have the Œðers, been digging deeper.

One of them discovered philosophy along the way.

A couple of the workers began to feel they were out of their depth, so they returned to the level at which their portable televisions still worked.

But the brave went on, looking for the real literature, the stuff deposited by the geniuses who'd been down here before.

Evidence of their paßage abounded.

And then we found of the paßage, tiled in aquamarine and white, air-conditioned with automated walkways (ZZ Top fans will remember them as ►Moving Sidewalks◄) spiraling ever lower.

It was a marvel of engineering.

We had to duck under a sign that read ⅩLimbo!Ⅹ

The builders must have been a shorter than us, but nonetheleß amazing.

On occasion we'd see graffiti or advertisements on the walls. One graffito that began recurring was the tag of an artist named ►Johnny Conqueroo◄. Ads promoted brands of water, cotton, blue-topped pine matches, mascara for ►big eyes◄, and winter sports resorts. We did not see any actual people, though. It was spooky, like visiting the ruins of Pompeii.

Pompeii, by the way, was famous for its graffiti as well. I have a good book on the subject back in the lighthouse library—it was by an art profeßor who'd written the first biography of Charlie Parker, Bob Reisner. It's a pretty thorough sociological investigation of graffiti, and an entire chapter is devoted to Pompeii. He also did a study of the difference between graffiti and men's and women's rustrooms and concluded that women's graffiti is generally far more carnal.

Carnival, theoretically, involves the removal of flesh. The partiers are too exhausted physically in order to survive the Lenten season of ¢elgh-denial. They fatten their ¢elghs up on Fat Tuesday in order to begin fasting on Ash Wednesday. The glorification of fat goes back to the Venus of Willendorf, who led to Fat Amorgana and Fatty Arbuckle. As a matter of fact ►FA◄ became so popular as initials that the governing body of English soccer named its ¢elgh after it, and in early years, players were fattened up like a little sumo wrustlers to please popular tastes. That was until the Great Starvation of Newcastle the year and earthquake collapsed all the coal mines. Players, like everyone else, had to survive on minimal rations, lost a great amount of weight, and won the FA Cup that year. The irony was not lost on Œðer teams, who noticed the increased mobility and maneuverability of the Newcastle team and then next sought to outdo them. Sure enough, the thinnest team kept winning year after year until they became too anorexic to withstand a blow or two. The league had over four dozen broken bones in one year before players decided some bulk was better than none.

Why do humans always have to go to extremes to learn? I need to head to the center of the Earth to get away from all these extremists.

An inter-rusting graffito: ►Bellerophon was here◄. He wrote a rhyme about his pet bacillus, which fidgeted every evening when people astral projected in to find Pegasus, Bellerophon's pet from the past. The bacillus was jealous. That was all I could make out of the script, which looked like ancient Greek written by someone as drunk as Crazy Zhang Xu, the Tang Dynasty scholar who, as one of the Eight Immortals of the Wine Cup, would calligraph with his hair and produce beautifully illegible works that bordered on the asemic.

Perhaps an early exchange of ideas between China and Greece occurred here, in the tiled bowels (better than the toiled bile!) of the mid-underground between them as well as in Lydia. The Tang Dynasty was, in literary art, eleven hundred years ahead of the West. The English novel began in 1750, with *Pamela*. The Tang Dynasty began in 618. That's 1122 years. The Tang Dynasty ended in 907, which means that literature died out in the West in 2029.

I don't recall anything occurring during the Second Dark Ages, which began then.

That's when the conservative elements of society all around the world seized power, banned the teaching of science and philosophy, toßed out Darwin in favor of regional gods (that each region proclaimed as universal). During that period on Earth, poverty was eliminated! Unfortunately conservative laissez-faire capitalists achieved that by systematically eliminating the poor, euthanizing them all in a marvelous display of Darwinian Socialism. How odd that, without acknowledging such, they actually agreed with their nemesis Darwin!) Of course, conservatives are riddled with contradictions. True conservatives cannot change their diapers because they never had to. They cannot tie their shoes. They never had to. Nothing new, even if beneficial, can be undertaken by anyone who always wants everything to remain the same. Or does the fear of change kick in once everyone has hir own? Once the conservatives have everything they want, they shut the door on everyone else!

If twelve people landed stranded on a desert island with one tree that had twelve breadfruit on it, that conservative would claim all the fruit as hirs. Anyone else would give everyone each one breadfruit.

The title pattern changed. At first the ceiling and floor were white and the walls aquamarine. Then after a while the tiles had drifted left and I hadn't noticed. The bottom of the left wall and top of the right had gained one row of white tiles, and the left of the ceiling to the right of the floor gained a blue row. Then two all around. Then three. I recognized it as a very slow vortex.

No automated walkways seemed to lead back up. I'd have had to run up the down escalator, which would have been beyond my ability. I figured I was better off conserving my energy for whatever I would find below.

I began to think that maybe this was not Earth at all, but that I was inside some insanely infinite Uroborus.

One of the hippies called him ▶Urotrash◀. It was mean, but pretty funny. Œðers mocked a Rußian accent and called him ▶Borus◀. That was much more obvious. The worst among us called him the ▶Uronator◀. That was the lamest. We had no liquid in here at all. What the hippies did was set up a food, drink and sleep center at all those rosettes I couldn't find a reason for. Our backups were running hoses out to us as we extended our reach. Each station was responsible for paßing everything along to the next. It'd been working well. No shortages, or the folks in front would have been impacted the most. Everyone eventually was also paßed back overhead once a week, crowd surfing back to the surface along with anyone who was feeling ill. They had to go back to the surface for at least a month before coming back down. That helped save on general wear-and-tear of the workers. Some were down for their third or fourth tours already. They were brave.

New signs started to ✷pop✷ up. ᎳBurma ShaveᎳ and ᎳWall DrugᎳ were, I think, ironic additions by a very talented tagger named Tigger.

ᎳGas Food LodgingᎳ signs with mileage markers sped by us, advising us to step off to the right in five miles, in four, in three, in two, in one,

✹Boom!✹ We stepped off and almost fell on our noses when we came to stationary ground. Well, not ground, it was still tile, but a different color—a bright orange. It sure did wake us up.

We saw employees milling about the oasis, staffing the food court counters and the motel front desk.

I was most curious about the ⴵGasⴵ signs and found that the oasis had an area for renting fast mopeds, which is, presumably, how most people returned to the surface.

I was long overdue to be sent back up, but instead I let the front dozen with me take the mopeds to return up top for a respite.

The clerks spoke several languages, and we finally found we had English in common, though theirs was somewhat archaic. But we made each Œðer understood.

Apparently the remainder of the journey would be through population regions, so we would no longer need hoses nor an enormous crew.

I decided each moped should carry two hippies back to the surface and then should return with one in order to pick up an Œðer. Each driver would become the paßenger on the second trip and would be dropped off next.

They were to do this until the last dozen returned to the oasis with the mopeds.

The entire proceß would take a while because of the distance we had and the great number of hippies who had come along.

I chose the ten most useful to stay with me, and we all stayed in the hotel until the mopeds returned. The hotel only had eight rooms, and two were for the staff. I claimed one for my ¢elgh, and the last five were divided between the ten.

The rooms were tiled as well, in robin's egg blue, but had plush Persian rugs on the floors, abstract Expreßionist prints on the walls (I had a tremendous Clyfford Still and, ironically, several smaller prints of Rothko's color fields). The bathroom was in gold, and the bed looked like a DeStijl torture device, but it was actually quite comfortable. It was a giant acrylic swoop. The mattreßes and bedding were luxuriously soft, though, and I fell to sleep as soon as I sat down. My horizontal collapse must have occurred in my sleep. When I awoke, I remembered a story I'd read back in the lighthouse library and looked around to see if I had a computer in the room. I was grateful that I had none. And from the desk clerk, a curious lot-haired, tattooed, Queequeg of a man, I found out that no computers were in use either here or below. He called it the ▶Disinvention of the Computer Age◀ and began lecturing me about how that had led to the Second Dark Ages, that the computer, which had been designed for the transmißion of knowledge, became nothing more than propaganda and advertising that lowered the intelligence of the public to such a level that people forgot how to build and repair the computers. The technology was forgotten, and the anti-scientists came feudal warlords. The remaining intelligentsia dug in, literally, and began building the tunnels, beginning from the catacombs under the Vatican. These intelligentsia toiled in secrecy and called their ¢elghs the ► Bavarian Illuminati ◄ after the originals, who strove to protect their special knowledge and thus guilded their lily irons. I had thought they were Masons, but Queequeg over here implied they were whalers. Legends say that a few whales did escape the Earth before their extinction here, but I doubt they could have gone underground. The legends say they were removed in spaceships, but that technology also disappeared during the Second Dark Ages, and by the time people learned the technology again, the whales were unfortunately long gone. So were the Welsh, having been eradicated by the English in all but blood and song. Not even threat of death could keep the Welsh from their blood and song. The same with the Frisians. And the circumpolar Saami—have you heard their joiks? Amazing songs, those are. Each person had to create one for hir ¢elgh, like a mantra.

The Saami also made brightly colored, vibrant clothing that stood out against the snow. Brides would be invisible if they followed Southern ways. Visibility and credibility meant life. With a unique costume and joik, you could be identified at distance, so your friends would know you were worth getting all dreßed up and going out for.

Don't you find the living funny? They always want to see and hear everything. All they have to do is feel it—it's in the heart. It really is. Why do you think everyone keeps saying that over and over if it weren't true on some level? And glittering generalities are. Peace is good. Hate is bad.

Of course, peace leads to stagnation. Hate leads to the survival of the most dominant, which in lead to the selective reading of the hostile. I hope at least you're breeding violence out. No?

I was having trouble keeping my focus so deep in the ground. Had I lived my life well, at least to then, if you can even call it a life? Or was I just a prophet with no country, a prophet speaking in tongues no one understood?

Clyfford Still's amorphous flying voids attacked me as I stood in a crimson field of blood.

I went to the bathroom, and a cockroach crawled out from under the lip of the toilet as I was urinating. A quick flick of the stream and I got him! Those damned roaches are everywhere, even down here!

We need a good stomp! Turn on the Johnny Winter album! No roach could survive that kind of stomp!

At the very least we've got to bring some boric acid out here.

One of the hippies haxed if the roaches farther down might be giants? I sent that hippie back up. I did not want any naysayers pestering me as I led our little expedition (and their exposition [pardon the imposition]): [=)ɔ= I told him to bring down some boric acid and some pyrethrin from chrysanthemums, easy to find topside, and effective against the little shits that survived the Johnny Winter stomp. [=)ɔ=

I decided to stay here and rust until the bugs were eradicated and let the next crew through. I been lingering too long anyway—I was by far the last of the first wave of our group. I believe leaders should be in the front…

[=)ɔ=… and that cockroaches should be squashed. Of course, now that I've said that, someday in the far distant future, when Cockroach People rule and all mammals are extinct, they'll read these words and will hate me forever and think of me as an advocate of their extermination.

So let's get them their own planet.

Oh, they already have one. They've been here longer than us. They want us to go back where we came from. They're like the Roaches of the American Revolution. Newcomers beware! The old roaches are enormous and have gotten rich off the land. The new ones are just specks in the consciousneß.

Maybe if I had some music even faster than Johnny Winter and dancers with deadlier, sharper boots….

I'm not going to find it. The fast players, such as Jeff Beck, for example, don't inspire but stomping. And not all boot stompers are fast.

If I had a machete….

I wouldn't be able to stop the roaches with that, either. The best solution is to just kill each one I see. Sorry, Roach Man of the Future, but your ancestors spread disease and disgust. Mostly, they were parasites living off us—that's what we hate most. Ticks, fleas, leeches, bedbugs, all Œðer biting insects, and you. But you might be our least favorite. You mock us. We know that. We don't like to be mocked.

I will not be chased away. I see a problem, and I will oversee its eradication—I mean, solution.

The great cartoonist Art Spiegelman, in *Breakdowns* (I have my copy in the lighthouse library), has a page being drawn by a cartoonist who is taken over by cockroaches as he is trying to draw. At the end of the page are just cockroaches. The cartoon and even the cartoonist have been obliterated.

Roach Man, why didn't you guys stay in your forusts in Germany, China, America, and God-knows-where-else? Our arboreous brethren laboriously left them and built on the plains, closer to water and where they could grow crops instead of relying on happenstance and happenstomp. You can keep the woods. Just leave human dwellings alone. It's a good compromise. Hax the paßenger pigeons about it. Or some dodos. And the great auks.

[=)ɔ=. You mock us by coming in and then hiding. Even the ticks stay outside (except for the rare insane tick who gives its ¢elgh to death without thought—pathetic creature). I turned off the light in the bathroom.

After a minute, I turned it back on. I caught five roaches with a few flamenco steps. Oh, I had my work cut out for me. I had some energy, so I did it again. Five more. And again. Six this time. But after that they didn't come out right away. They'd figured it out. If they can figure out problems, than why can't they figure out I don't want them around?

Well, outdoors I don't mind. Walls. Sidewalks. No big deal. But not in the house. And not in the tunnels. I mean, look at them. They are tiled. Roaches did not build those tunnels. Theirs would be fecal mud holes.

Roach Man, what's your name? Mudhead Mackerel? Have you ever read a Richard Brautigan mackerel fart? You need to. Hey, you roaches should hang out with the mackerel because you're not going to get jack from me. It's in the Henry Miller book of his—*A Confederate General from Big Sur*. Miller, of course, was one of Patchen's best friends. I keep them all together on the same bookshelf.

What's that? Yes, our Confederate General from Big Sur fought valiantly in our war against the mackerel. Now people just have to follow through. Trust Brautigan. What sounds better anyway, watermelon sugar or jack mackerel? Hax any kid. Kids will tell you the truth. Jack mackerel sounds nasty. And it does so repeatedly.

We could gas you with the mackerel, I suppose, but how am I not to suspect that you'd be all over rotten mackerel. You and the flies. Oh, that's right, you are the lord of the flies. At least you hide and stay hidden. Flies do that dive bombing at people's ears that is so damned annoying. That's why my flyswatter is nicknamed ►Stormbringer◄, after Michael Moorcock's *The Stealer of Souls*.

Okay, so I'll bring Zappa down here for the soundtrack. It's absurd enough. I'll start with ►Paß It Around◄ by Grand Funk Railroad, a great Don Brewer tune produced by Zappa. Or better yet, ►Out to Get You◄, on which Frank Zappa plays blister-guitar, or ►Rubberneck◄, on which he does background vocals.

Zappa and I are out to get you, Roach Man!

Next to the bed is an old-fashioned jukebox coin machine like one used to see on soda fountain counter-tops. I put in some coins and preß a few of my favorites—►Money Can't Save Your Soul◄ by Savoy Brown. It's tasteful and understated. The uninitiated would hear it and not flip out— they'd like it, wonder for a second what was, and then get back to work. But the initiated? They'd buck up strong and work three times harder for hearing the tune. Now give 'em tunes like this all day, give them hourly tea times, and watch those sons-a-bitches not only work but love it! I once help tear down an entire rat-infested garage with two friends and all we got paid each was a few warm cans of Hamm's beer. I had a good time and drank the stank out of the beer without complaint. I was standing on a plank. The only beer I've never been able to stomach is a warm Silver Bullet. That's worse than putrid poontang at the end of a long, hot, sweaty summer's day.

More Savoy Brown. Their excellent *Voodoo Moon* CD. And I scrub the bathroom from top to bottom with bad-aß cleansers. Then I do the same in the kitchen. If you make sure you don't have anything out that roaches eat, they go elsewhere. They'll find places where people aren't clean. My family always valued cleanlineß. Punctuality über Alles. We were at war against Entropy, and we meant to win. Only later, after our tribulations and trials, did we make peace with Entropy. We don't keep him out anymore, and in return he will never take over. His size and strength are the equal of our own. We have a little encroachment dance we share as frequently as poßible. He doesn't like to dance, but the rust of us drag him out to some good Texas boogie night at a sufficiently crowded bar, and he's tapping his toes soon enough.

Remember to throw roaches under the tapping toes. The pointed cowboy boots go crunch.

Crunchcrunchcrunchcrunch…

Pßst…. Here comes the pyrethrin.

Shake-a-shake-a-shake… boric acid…

Savoy stomp here, Mr. Roach, where a pyrethrin-foggin' hat.

You can't have eternal life and never die if we don't.

We'll take you on. I'll call my old friend Slow-Butt Shirley to sit on you. I'll call my friend John the Conquer-You. I'll call my ancestor Avery Formidable-Man, the part-time superhero we used to call ►the Ox◄. He had secret identities within the secret identities. He could take sea lions and seal ions. Every Ash Wednesday he'd get sick on lentils. He could have sold paludism to a paladin. He turned a paragon into two who disappeared.

What chance do the poor wretches, roaches, really have? They will retch on the boric acid and die, and their cannibalistic kin will devour them and the boric acid, which has grown no weaker through the transfer.

Roach Man, my hope is you will never exist. And if you do, I hope it's not down here and especially not up near the lighthouse. Look at the sun! It needs colonizing—go there! All of you, a maß migration; one hundred thousand giant ships might hold all of you. I'll pay for them if you're onboard.

Have fun in the sun!

Farewell, Gregor.

The pyrethrin arrived. Everything just out of sight was sprayed. And then lines of boric acid were laid along our perimeter. They also brought me little tar traps and boxes called ⅩRoach AmberⅩ.

I am broaching a new subject now—I was pretty sure the rust area was clean at that point, so I could continue on my way or return to my library. I thought I might be best off with that brief respite back home. I was exhausted, and I was bored. They definitely need a library at the oasis. Back in the library I had some plans for setting that up. I'd have to send a copy of blueprints down and have them be understood. Then I could set down the materials. And the books. Brautigan. Patchen. Federman. Tarnawsky. Beckett. Joyce. Woolf. Schmidt. Sterne. Start with those nine.

I needed to visit the Gardens of Obsane Topiary again. I liked hanging out with the hippies—don't misunderstand me—but I was mißing having any significant interrelationship. Friends are friends, but a woman is a woman.

I shook my head. Get those thoughts out of there. No use pining for what isn't. Clay Ziasztes said that back in the last years of the Tang Space Drink Dynasty. Of course he was high on Space Food Sticks. I should bring a book of his aphorisms.

Part Two: The Eight Aphorisms of Clay Ziasztes

<<Seed the sky with helicopters,>> Ziasztes would say, <<and they may pull you along.>>

And <<Never climb above what the ladder is rusting on unleß you're going to step off.>>

I saw Queequeg working on his calligraphy. He was writing a poem dedicated, he said, to Li Bai, an Œðer of the Eight Immortals of the Wine Cup:

> ►Bursting plums do not stop the duckweed.
> The water grows a hole, lovely as a lotus, which casts a shadow below.
> Surely, here lives a scholar of greenneß◄.

<<Take your ¢elgh off the shelf and leave the ►h◄ behind.>>

Maybe Zhang Xu met Clay one day and heard him say, <<I saw my heart full of wine>> and took the half-an-aphorism and aßumed sentence two.

Half an aphorism, or half a sermon? I don't recall. That's why I need Clay's book, so I can recollect. Paß the tray around a second, a second time, a second from now, no matter what the second hand says.

<<I'm the first hand,>> Clay may have said.

<<And I'm the capped hand,>> said Zhang Xu, slurring a little.

I don't know what happened, but Clay should have clicked his heels, bowed his head, and said, <<capped hand,>> but muffled his words enough to sound like he was saying <<capped dead>> towards Zhang Xu's moving face.

A look of confusion, as if to convey consternation over what Clay had just said, froze into a strange smile on Zhang Xu's face, so he looked more like a moving picture than a real person.

<<Well, I have the upper hand,>> I said, pointing to the surface.

<<That's not a benefit down here,>> said Zhang Xu.

<<It certainly isn't,>> agreed Clay Ziasztes.

♪Don't even want no pork chops—just give me gin instead♫ sang Dinah Washington over the intercom.

<<Depreßion makes a mad man wise….>>

<<Clay, shhh!>> I hushed him. He was being underhanded.

I decided to withdraw into the motel's Clyfford Stills for a while—the one in my room was ▶1949 No. 1◀, apparently a sequel to one I remembered from a book of his art in the lighthouse library, a similar painting but far leß active, ▶1947-R-No. 1◀. I rode an amorphous shadow acroß the red sky. It was a croß between a dragon and a torn hole in the fabric of the universe, but to say that would be to gild a mixed metaphor. I'd aßume that adventurers would ride the ridges at the edge of these holes. How that must feel—to simultaneously be half in one universe and half in an Œðer! To go in and out between them fast—now that might lead somewhere else entirely.

Because the Still paintings were so vibrant and fiery—Still Lifes—I realized what I really mißed were the rivers by the lighthouse. I used to enjoy morning walks along the shore. I'd bring stale bread and feed the mallards, who were always appreciative, unlike the geese, who'd eat my food one second and hiß at me the next. Consequently, goose became a favorite meal of mine, and I forwent duck in its favor.

<<I'm graphorism acher. Give the ungrateful blue uniforms a ride home. Stay away from their jaws, which could snap a femur in two,>> as Ziasztes once said.

Lights come on in different colors according to your responses, but the pattern is too complicated for me to figure out. Nevertheleß, I know they are connected.

Well, the boric acid did its work. I saw a couple of roaches the next day after laying down the lawful poison, and I used my two squirt pistols that I had filled with sweet boric syrup. I'd tried pyrethrin, too, but that just killed on contact. The boric syrup stayed on the roaches until they got to their lairs, where they died and then were eaten by kin (a detail so disgusting it is worth repeating).

I ended up not even need the 𝔛Roach Amber𝔛. I told Queequeg to hold onto it for the future. I also offered him half the pyrethrin and half the boric syrup. I was taking the rust of the boric acid along to the next level down, just in case. There I might encounter separated colonies or multiple species.

I had that morning heard a peep from outside my room, had opened the door and had seen a goldfinch flying by. I asked Queequeg about it, but he said he'd never seen a bird down here. He said it was probably a bat—they were around—some of them of the bloodthirsty variety. He said what they'd do is lick someone's ankles and anesthetize them with some strange procaine-like substance in their saliva and would then bite them. They could take a pint before anyone would even notice. So I traded with Queequeg for a pair of high-topped hiking boots and a lightweight aluminum harpoon-gun. He said this would take down anything up to the size of a great white shark, which he said some of the roaches were as large as. I quivered a dozen replacement spears for the harpoon-gun and strapped the quiver to my back. My hands shook each spear to make certain it was strong enough. I lowered my head so I could more easily touch the quiver and adjust it until I could reach back behind my head and pull a spear out easily.

Or, as Clay Ziasztes used to say, <<Princes drink to get pißed, not for nourishment.>>

And he also used to say, <<Don't look away,>> but I think he was quoting the Who for that one.

Or, as the Lord Olivier used to say, <<Do you want to know what ▶it◀ is? It's simple. It's ▶lookatmelookatmelookatmelookatme…◀.>>

Staring out from within, peering through black onyx pupils, through chalcedony irises, all I see is that the coal chute is empty. We named it ▶Nevil◀ because we had to climb down under to get at it, at least if we followed Alice.

We fired the puppy up and wrote it down towards the next level. The puppy ran away, licking its burnt tail.

I ran away, licking my burnt tale.

We were no longer in a tiled paßageway. The next five miles, we were told, were a straight shot down enormous PVC pipes. There was an enormous set of them. Supposedly they all lead to the same place, but we were safer in individual tubes so that with our flaying arms and legs we wouldn't flog each Œðer.

I said I didn't want my arms and legs flayed.

Be grateful, said Queequeg, that the tubing is in place. You will be going through the levels where the magma fleas live. They eat your melting skin.

<<I've been told the pain is unimaginable,>> said a hippie.

<<I know,>> I replied. I was trying to imagine it and found my ¢elgh unable to. Wouldn't the magma roast the fleas? And fleas don't actually ▶eat◀ skin, do they? They just bite it, right?

<<I don't want to find out,>> said the hippie.

<<Use the tubes,>> said Queequeg, as if he were telling us what was most obvious in the world.

Down the tubes—that's where my life's going now.

<<Any parasites I should know about?>> I haxed Queequeg. He shrugged.

<<Only the tube worms,>> he said.

<<Tube worms? Really?>>

<<They're pretty harmleß. Just where some earplugs and the nose plug, and keep your mouth closed. They can only hurt you if they get inside you. Or you could rent a tube helmet from me for a fin. The helmet's guaranteed to protect you.>>

<<What if it fails to?>>

<<You get your money back.>>

<<What about the worms?>>

<<Oh, they'll have been killed by then.>>

<<So the money-back guarantee is rather moot.>>

<<I gueß so. Still, I'd recommend it over the plugs. The helmets come with built-in hi-fi.>>

<<Hi-fi?>>

<<Truly.>>

<<I used to have hi-fi, but my ex-wife gave it to her boyfriend.>>

<<Very funny.>>

<<Well, what are these worms like?>>

<<Tidy. They are of the species ▶muscae volitantes◀. Very dangerous inside the body.>>

<<Okay, here's a fiver. I'll rent a helmet, I gueß.>>

<<You won't regret it.>>

Queequeg must have been the greatest salesman since Gurdjieff. Let's hand Gurdjieff his due. Rags to riches over and over again.

Let's not. I can't even get there once.

Have some coffee. It'll keep you coughing until you're in your coffin. Kopi Luwack is the most felicitous of all coffee choices. Just don't mix it with anything. Don't waste it with alcohol, and don't obseß over it with weed or mushrooms or poppy flowers or morning glories or geraniums.

I drank a cup of Kopi Luwack with Queequeg. He played Pere Ubu's *Dub Housing*. ♪Boy, that's all swell.♫ If you don't smile and start bouncing with ►Navvy◄, you have no sense of humor. It is supersharp. You should be hooked from ►On the Surface◄. The great idiosyncrasies of Pere Ubu are genius.

♪We know♫ sings the band in the title song in their responses to David Thomas's seemingly random calls.

And then the boisterous ►Caligari's Mirror◄, which begins with the adoption of the old ►What Do You Do with a Drunken Sailor?◄ Especially don't listen to that drunk and queasy.

Just a little Kopi Luwack.

Nothing more or you'll waste the coffee taste.

Stay away from TV or video of any kind while drinking Kopi Luwack. Listen to music. Picked up a pad of paper. Draw or write.

Rinse.

Repeat.

Or as Clay Ziasztes used to say, <<Fool me once, fool me again, fool me thrice, you're not a friend.>>

Take insight or you won't see. Ah, now I just realized that I'd spaced out a couple of songs. But ►Ubu's Dance Party◄ brings me back to the floor. We are solid on the floor. Strong. ►Humanity has always needed firm footing◄.™

Part Three: Review: The Eight Aphorisms of Clay Ziasztes

1. Seed the sky with helicopters, and they will pull you along.

2. Never climb above what the ladder is rusting on unleß you're going to step off.

3. Take your ¢elgh off the shelf and the ►h◄ behind.

4. a. I saw my heart full of wine. [b. I'm the first hand.]

5. Depreßion makes a madman wise….

6. I'm graphorism acher. Give the ungrateful blue uniforms a ride home. Stay away from their jaws, which could snap a femur in two.

7. Princes drink to get pißed, not for nourishment.

8. Fool me once, fool me again, fool me thrice, you're not a friend.

Part Four: Aphorism One

Seed the sky with helicopters, and they will pull you along.

I recommend Karlheinz Stockhausen's ▶Helikopter-Streichquartett◀ in its Arditti String Quartet rendition from 2000. The quartet were sent up individually in four helicopters and, after beginning together, were sent away from the outdoor concert arena but kept broadcasting the music down to the arena. There the four feeds were combined.

The musicians, of course, could not hear each Œðer and consequently fell out of sync and disintegrated, but they had been given prearranged times for re-convergence when, no matter where they were in the playing, they were to move to a specific place in the score and would resync.

The noises of the helicopters are all a part of the performance. After a half hour, the helicopters land, the quartet reintegrates its ¢elgh, and the piece ends.

Revolutionary!

Tie each revolutionary to helicopter blade. Go! See me spin in my whirling pants. <<Go, Meral!>> They yelled at me, though Meral's not my name. Purple-and-green diagonally plaid is not the color of a fool!

Part Five: Aphorism Two

Never climb above what the ladder is rusting on unleß you're going to step off.

ᏎHave you ever climb to the top of the corporate ladder only to find a bottomleß pit?Ꮞ read some long forgotten 20th century motivational poster that loved mixing metaphors. What is the ladder rusting against if the *only* thing at top is a bottomleß pit?

The early 21st century brought a new definition along with it, though. People heard Led Zeppelin's bromidic ►Stairway to Heaven◄, conflated the two ideas, and came to the conclusion that a bottomleß pit must *be* heave. Thence came ►trickle-down economics◄ and its practice of keeping all the money at the top because it would be wasted on the moral moraß of more aßes in the maßes who'd frivolously squander all the money of trivialities and trifles such as food, clothing and shelter.

Every time a 1%er built an Olympic-size swimming pool into hir third vacation home, a pool in exactly the same design as the first three pools in hir first three homes, thousands of 99%ers were starved, stripped, and evicted.

So, be like Prometheus, won't you? If you are climbing up there, throw a few bags of money down the chute to us, or better yet, hijack a truckload and drive it on down. You will be welcomed among us as a hero. If you just stay up there to kick everyone else off the ladder in some giant version of the game ►King of the Mountain◄, then you are no one we will ever respect or embrace.

If you want our gratitude, be generous!

Part Six: Aphorism Three

Take your ¢elgh off the shelf and leave the ►h◄ behind.

The activator button has been preßed. No serious artist can afford to ignore the threats to art's ¢elgh. Human thought is plastic-molded by giant invisible machines.

Step out of the comfortable plasticized womb that has been built for you by Œðers.

Look around for your ¢elgh. What do *you* see? What takes *your* attention? If your thought takes you to a brand name, you are not doing your thinking—someone else is doing it for you. Resist!

Part Seven: Aphorism Four

A. I saw my heart full of wine.

[B. I'm the first hand.]

C. [etc.—aßume a letter for each new ¶.] On the Œðer hand…

I have big shoes to fill.

My shoes are filled with wine.

I must have gotten off on the wrong foot.

I meant to start right.

Helping keep the count from being barren.

I will remind you once again.

Paß me the bota bag.

Don't bogart that wine.

Win the Bogie trivia contest.

Lots of lizards.

Amphibians in wine.

Asps in aspic.

Don't mistake pens for penises.

Don't mistake Virginians for virgins.

Don't mistake menstruation for men's true eats.

Be careful not to spoil the picnic.

Be careful not to spill the wine.

Be careful not to tread on me lightly.

Sweat until your skin begins to shine.

Clamber up the clamor.

Drum for the dual duels.

Let's lexico the lecher,

and Texaco the texter.

Part Eight: Aphorism Five

Depreßion makes a madman wise….

Promise me you'll wake me if I drift off into sleep. I have been wearing this mantle for far too long. I abdicate everything now. Let me waft out on the wind for a while, but before I'm sundered, call me back. I will return when I hear your voice.

The sound of mesh being pulled acroß my brainstem has deafened me to the world. Watch me form clouds in animal shapes for you. These are the animals from my dreams. A giraffe. A hippopotamus. An elephant. A bat. A squirrel. A red velvet ant.

Let me lay my red velvet-lined mantel down on this puddle. Please walk acroß it, my lady. I wouldn't want those delicate ankles of yours to get soiled.

I'm sure that was the wrong thing to say, but I seldom use my voice. I am a pupil in silence, a pupil in vapor. I have been here for three eternities, and few have noticed me.

May I hax you a question? Have you been collecting pieces of me? I know I've dropped a few here and there because I am an inept juggler. And I noticed that you didn't laugh at my clumsineß. Do you remember where the pieces went? When I leave the clouds, will you help me recollect them?

Or will you dißipate into the wind with me? Who, then, will call us back?

Part Nine: Aphorism Six

I'm graphorism acher. Give the ungrateful blue uniforms a ride home. Stay away from their jaws, which could snap a femur in two.

I'm a lame archer. Give it a shot: you could pierce a lemur's heart through and through.

I am imbroglio wearing the mask of the augusto. The whether has been muted. The whys are on the sidelines and look on while we make fools of our ¢elghs by revealing that all we want at most is the lagan of their daily lives whereas they have crocodiles in the lagoons of ours.

Part Ten: Aphorism Seven

Princes drink to get pißed, not for nourishment.

The seventh aphorism always comes at the eleventh hour.

Seven comes eleven. Bet on the duration of the klaxon.

Look to the seventh wine cup, listen to Savoy Brown live at the Seattle Center Arena on March 10, 1972, especially the scorching version of Don Nix's ►Going Down◄. Put that up there with Beck's, Freddie King's, and the original Moloch version (actually, Moloch did it as a slow burn—also nice, but I really dig the tune firing fast).

Who else did it? I'd love to hear an Uncle Dog version of it. Or Zappa! Did Mick Taylor ever play it? John Entwistle? Can you imagine an Entwistle version of it? The baß runs would gelatinize the spine.

Just don't wait for the twelve of cups to turn up. The party will be over by then.

The optimal hours are from seven to eleven, hence their popularity. And the eleven isn't coming, either. Come earlier. You can come in on one or two, but after ten, I turn the page, and then the knights come riding in, parading before the queens and kings who've aßembled there.

We want a page of cups, don't we? ►Hey, what's this fish doing in my wine?◄ To a page, that's the eternal question.

In jousting, the knight of cups had his athletic supporters.

Part Eleven: Aphorism Eight

Fool me once, fool me again, fool me thrice, you're not a friend.

A fool is a concept by which we measure our tolerance. If the fool quits too soon, I have not learned anything. If the fool persists beyond reason, then he has defeated his ¢elgh. He'll have to do his laundry by his ¢elgh in the middle of the day.

He'll have to kill the roaches by jumping on their backs, grabbing both sides of their heads and twisting them off of their prothoraxes.

►Cowboy!◄ they will call him. He will do ►The Twist◄, as it will be known, a thousand times in defense of his species.

He is forever thereafter a celebrity.

Part Twelve: The Knight Writer

When I turned the page of cups, his knight rolled tumbling after. Roll my boat, he was there at the lower level to welcome us. The tubes all emptied into his foam-lined reception pen.

He recorded each conversation in a meticulous hand. He interviewed slowly, but had a good enough memory to never have to hax me to repeat my ¢elgh.

I haxed him if people called him ▶The Knight Writer◀. He said no. I haxed him what people called him. He said, <<Meral.>> I must have looked at him funny because then he said, <<but Meral's not my name.>>

<<What is it?>> I haxed. <<John Wayne?>>

<<That'd be Marion, not Meral.>>

<<Oh. Hey, wait a second.>> I looked at him more closely. <<I thought so, wise-aß!>> He was no knight at all. He was my old aßistant—Nils! I pulled off his fake beard.

<<Ow! What are you doing?>> he screamed, holding his face.

I had some beard hairs in my fingers, but the beard hadn't come off.

<<Nils?>>

<<I'm not Nils, and I'm not fucking Meral! What the fuck did you pull my beard for?>>

<<I thought it was a fake.>>

<<It isn't.>> And he ✹coldcocked✹ me.

Part Thirteen: Cards

In the Tarot's minor arcana, the queen is the thirteenth card of each suit. The only meaning I can wrangle out of the positioning is that thirteen is unlucky. The downfall of many a king was the unlucky choice of his queen.

Poker decks omit the page and promote the queen to twelfth and give the power over luck to the king.

Skat decks omit the knights but include the pages. They also omit cards two through six, eßentially, then, including the ace, giving us seven through thirteen plus the four court cards.

Sometimes an ace is considered a one and an eleven. In those cases the court cards pick up an additional point each, inverting the lucky gender.

K-Q-J-P-10-9-8-7-6-5-4-3-2-A [Female is unlucky].

K-Q-J-P-[A]-10-9-8-7-6-5-4-3-2-A [Male is unlucky].

K-Q-J-10-9-8-7-6-5-4-3-2-A [Male].

K-Q-J-[A]-10-9-8-7-6-5-4-3-2-A [Female].

K-Q-B[P]-10-9-8-7 [Male].

K-Q-B[P]-[A]-10-9-8-7-A space [Female].

Each genders dominate the luck of three decks.

Part Fourteen: The Cave of the Swallows

Sulfuric acid eating away limestone left gypsum flowers, as in the famous Chandelier Ballroom. Bacteria live off the rock. The rust area here was a tourist destination, apparently. The hotel was bigger. I have a better room to my ¢elgh, and I saw no roaches anywhere.

Plaster of Paris sculptures decorated the grounds, including some beautiful Izmet Bekler *Beyond Imagination* free hands transposed from his meerschaum designs: swoops and slings and swirls in gentle amorphous patterns like those of the dunes of the Kalahari. They looked like Henry Moore's sculptures freed from gravity.

Not Meral Not Nils looked at me from his seat at a table in my hotel room—he'd been waiting for me to come to my senses.

<<You are crazy man,>> he said to me. <<Why do you attack? We are peaceful tourist stop. Enjoy the caverns. Do not pull my beard!>>

<<Who are you?>>

<<I am Punch. This is my hotel.>>

<<I see why they call you ✹Punch✹,>>> I said, rubbing my jaw.

<<Golden Gloves, Chicago,>> he said.

<<Punch?>> I said, trying the name on my tongue and liking it.

<<Tourist?>> he haxed.

<<No,>> I replied, and I told him I'm a with a scientific expedition to get to the core.

He nodded. He seemed unimpreßed, as if he knew many people besides me who had done this before. Of course, that could be the presentment of a retailer.

<<Are you going to sell me some postcards?>> I haxed.

<<I can do that, if you want.>>

<<Well, what do you want?>>

<<For each tourist to have a first-rate experience.>>

<<Of course.>>

<<I'm glad you understand.>>

<<But remember what Howlin' Wolf said,>> I said.

<<Don't call me a CAB!>>

<<No, but he was a bit of a cad, wot, eh?>> he said, mißing the point.

<<That may have paßed for wit in the past. Knotwit contemporary taximeter cabriolets—every which way yellow-black cars.>>

If he wanted to play evil elusive, I could go all muskellunge on him and go hang out with Old Moßback while he fished his own veins for signs of life.

Forget Nils, and forget Nettie. How many past lives must I carry with my ¢elgh at all times?

I want to just plunge into the future like mounted musk oxen on the wall of a Nepalese hunting lodge.

<<Monsieur du Jabot, we welcome you. Please enjoy your stay. If you would like a tour of the Cave of the Swallows, we can provide that.>>

<<Any relation to the Gardens of Obsane Topiary?>>

<<No—it is a bird garden underground. An amazing sight.>>

<<Yes, I saw a yellow finch earlier.>>

<<Goldfinches are abundant.>>

<<Giraffes?>>

<<No. I'm not kidding. It is beautiful. Plants, trees, birds….>>

<<An artificial sun?>>

<<Yes. Of course. How else? It has to be mighty to overpower gravity, magma, and air preßure.>>

<<How far?>>

<<All the way through the center. All we had to do was overcome physics.>>

<<Why?>>

<<Physics cannot contain the imagination. It can only run alongside it for a while. Physics stops to calculate. The imagination runs ahead.>>

<<Well, I'm not a physician.>>

<<Good man,>> he said, clapping me on the back.

He led me to the back of the hotel and opened a door to a back veranda overlooking the aforementioned Cave of the Swallows.

Swallows, swifts, finches, sparrows. Only small birds with large effects.

The oasis uses no money for the bank swallows.

A drummer hit a tom-tom swiftly in musical pursuit of a swift.

A finch starred in a network film. Spare rows of text for something meaningful.

Flights of fancy—that's what they are.

Anyway, the Cave of the Swallows was a magnificent place.

We could see this from the veranda, but we were prohibited from climbing down there. The gypsum was too fragile. So ultimately, I could only look at it, like a snow globe I couldn't even shake.

The hotel charges were steep–I had to keep sending hippies back for more funds. The electrical grid down here did not connect to the electrical grid of the surface, plus without banks, wire transfers were impoßible anyway.

The birds flew by my face. I could feel their wing wind, and they never meant it aggreßively. Of course, these were mature birds—they'd flown everywhere, seen all of their predators, and had learned to stay alive–that alone was a great accomplishment. It's the perfect-attendance award, the predictability prize.

Part Fifteen: The Hole in the Wall

Weeks paßed before I realized I had become lulled into complacency. I was so comfortable in my repast and repose that I began to suspect some Circe must be behind. Punch, however, was no Circe. Heck, he was not even a Queequeg. He was, however, gatekeeper to this little paradise.

He expected everyone to thank him for having stewarded the oasis into prominence. I have seen him rescind reservations and cancel second nights if the guests were not to his liking. Incidentally, isn't ►guests◄ a rather antiquated concept? Especially at $150 a night?

Crystals and birds were incorporated into all of the designs in the hotel area. No amorphous Clyfford Stills or Rothko color fields down here—it was sharp, angular. Franz Marc. German Expreßionism. Egon Schiele. Gustav Klimt. Max Beckmann. *Das Kabinett des Dr. Caligari*. My room had Marc's *Der Turm der blauen Pferde* towering over me. They looked like the horses of the apocalypse to me, and I worried that the print of the painting would fall on my head while I slept. It was huge, and in a glaß frame that must have weighed 50 pounds. It looked sufficiently moored into the wall, but it made me nervous enough to try to move the bed. It was also anchored. So I removed the box spring and mattreß and set them in the middle of the floor, off the bed frame. I wasn't going to be killed by Franz Marc. My father had already lost a cousin to Max Beckmann. But that's a long story, and it's not mine to tell.

I could also tell you about my landlady, the lobber of expreßions, who loved Heinrich Mann and Novalis and Franz Marc.

Blue Horses, *Blue Angel*, and the perfect blue flower.

All against a background of Goethe's orange for the walls. The blue really stands out.

Still, I got to see the gypsum crystals and hear the birds. I'd pick one bird at random and just watch that one for an hour at a time. It was relaxing, amusing, and lightening. So I wasn't going to complain about anything like a huge Franz Marc of the Sword of Damocles hanging over the headboard of the bed frame. Not until I found my own head bored.

Punch was not nearly as sociable as Queequeg was, anyway, which isn't saying much. But that's okay. I can do without the party at Norman Bates's place, of course, I can't stand his mŒðer, but who can?

So rather than letting Punch bring me down, I avoided the lobby. I became an invisible lodger.

And then I found a secret panel in my bathroom under my bathtub. I set out, independent but dirt poor.

The panel led to a warehouse underneath the hotel. But in between the level of the room and the level of the warehouse was a room hidden from the casual climber from bathtub to warehouse. It was hidden in a niche out of sight to one side of the descent, a steep cave descent. An outcropping of rock that blended into the background hid the paßage to the room.

In the outcropping, unseen from the floor above or below, was a 20,000-tune electronic jukebox that fed into the secret room. The walls, ceiling, and floor were heavily insulated for sound. I could sit in the room and listen to a set of quad Magneplanars play my favorite music. The first music I played was a live recording made by Kim Simmonds and Savoy Brown live at Sellersville Theater, in Sellersville, Pennsylvania, March 20, 2004. Simmonds's ¢elgh is singing, and he's a good singer. He can hit Chris Youldon's ▶Needle and Spoon◀ and still make it sound good. But the leßer-known material on the CD is just as cool. Simmonds has never played the guitar better. He's inspired here. The banter between songs is also delightful—Kim Simmonds talks about growing up, talks about his brŒðer, about his life—it's very relaxed. He explains to some folks who haxed for ▶ All I Can Do◀ that he could only do it on acoustic guitar—he hadn't taught it to the band. And he just ended the acoustic section of the show us on earlier. He has the band on stage with him. So he says he'll play the title track of the *Street Corner Talking* album. And the band plays it nice and funky.

I decide to bring my mattreß down here—the box spring can't fit. But I can bend the mattreß.

The place looks like an old, abandoned recording studio. Four-track, most likely. Primitive, but charming. But the sound system is excellent in pushing the four to the fore.

The guitar solo during ▶Needle and Spoon◀ is transportation.

All-in-all, this is my favorite live recording of Savoy Brown, and I've heard a couple of dozen. The folks of Sellersville were very fortunate that night.

I've called a halt to digging deeper for now. Everyone has been ordered to relax, recuperate, return home for a month and see the surface. They'll be gone or will hang out here (at $150/night—not cheap—I gueß only a few have wealth enough to hang out with me indefinitely).

I want to have a couple of people to talk to here, though, besides Punch. We should at least be four and play some Skat. I'll teach Punch.

Two of the most loyal of the hippies I invited to stay on my dime. One refused. One accepted—the first who identified Kim Simmonds's guitar playing. He said he'd played with Kim before.

I haxed him his name.

He said, <<Dave.>>

I exploded into laughter. <<Dave?>> Like *that* narrowed it down. Savoy Brown was a veritable collection of Daves. All very talented. Simmonds had the same ability Mayall and Zappa had: to find excellent musicians to play off of. Then I saw that ▶Dave◀ knew what he said was funny. He was hip to Savoy Brown. That was enough of a basis for a friendship.

<<Oh, I just jammed with him and a couple of friends a long time ago, back at the time of the Purdah recordings.>>

<<Purdah? Wow,>> I said. He knew SB. The two first 45s from 1966.

As I ride the shivers from the ▶Hellbound Train◀ that is the Sellersville encore, I locate the Purdah recordings.

The train screams against the tracks. Simmonds's tone is so rich and full now—he is playing with power and confidence—he's all ▶go◀. The man of 1001 tones. Better that than be a man of 1000, and one tone.

▶Hellbound Train◀ kicks aß.

▶I Tried◀ from the Purdah recordings is the perfect introduction to SB. Much better, I think, than ▶Tell Mama◀.

It's serious blues. The Purdah version of ▶Can't Quit You Baby◀ was one reason the New Yardbirds were compared to Savoy Brown (listen to the New Yardbirds live at Tivoli Gardens September 20, 1968, or at the Marquee in London on October 16, 1968, and compare). Of course, Page and Plant had those two extra years to add their many embellishments to the Willie Dixon tune, taking Otis Rush's version as a model. At Tivoli Gardens they also played Otis Rush's ▶I Gotta Move◀, so his influence was heavy. The Marquee show featured some proto-Zep versions of ▶Communication Breakdown◀ and ▶Dazed and Confused◀ .

I went exploring in the warehouse and found a few accoutrements for my new ▶hole in the wall◀, as I called it. I found a couple of small refrigerators and portable electric ovens I could carry up. And then I found an area of food and beverage storage. I was able to abscond easily with cases of corned beef and beer and turnip greens and precooked cheese ravioli in tomato sauce. Dairy, meat, vegetables and carbs. A balanced diet. The beer was cheap American lager and needed refrigeration to be palatable, but the canned food could be eaten without cooking it, which reduced any chance of my being discovered because of aromas from my ▶hole in the wall◀. I'd be saving $150/night! I was excited.

When I'd set up my place, I relaxed. My endleß supply of great music discouraged me from going anywhere. I'd found too much to listen to!

I would let Punch aßume I'd checked out. I should probably reinforce the panel underneath the tub. I'd still go up in there on occasion with the room was vacant—usually for a few hours late morning or early afternoon—and I'd bathe and groom my ¢elgh. At Œðer times I'd have to go down to the warehouse and use their crude crapper. Better than nothing, though. I was worried about being discovered in the warehouse, but I found a worker's jumpsuit and would wear that whenever I went below, just in case I was spotted. Anyone seeing me at a distance would only see a worker. Still, I did everything poßible to avoid ever being seen at all. I also added camouflage to the entrance to my hole in the wall so that no one else would see it. I have secured it thoroughly. My new home was inscrutable.

I preferred Savoy Brown to the New Yardbirds, I decided. I didn't feel as much pretense with Kim Simmonds. He was just a cool guitar player and songwriter (and singer and painter and…). He was always at some art, musical or visual or whatever, because it turned him on, not because he wanted a billion-dollar mansion in Monaco. Page's Marquee version of ► White Summer—Black Mountain Side◄ is a pretty sweet instrumental, though. The sound quality of the recording at the Marquee, however, is very trebly, which makes Plant sound extra screechy on many of the songs.

I prefer ►Nobody's Perfect◄ with Ralph Morman singing for Savoy Brown at the Paradise Club in Boston, February 11, 1981.

Savoy Punk. It's good, though. The Man of 1001 Tones does it again. I can't wait until he does hard boogie versions of Bonfá songs. Airto on percußion of course. That'd be great. Airto played with the Grateful Dead, so Savoy Brown shouldn't be too much of a stretch for him, and Simmonds can stretch in any direction he wants.

Before I could disappear completely, though, I needed to prepare Dave and Punch. Dave had no idea I'd been setting up new digs for my ¢elgh.

One evening, when he lost heavily at Skat, I did so as well so that Punch ended up winning all our money.

I laughingly but seriously told Dave at the end of the evening that we couldn't afford his room anymore, so he'd have to return to the surface. Problem solved, I thought. I hadn't counted on Punch's developing an enthusiasm for the card game, though. Rather than end our games, Punch reduced our room rents by half. When Dave and I lost even more, Punch reduced our rent to a nominal ten percent of what we had been paying. We had no excuse for going. I'd have to think of something else.

Part Sixteen: Nettie and Nils

The first thing Nils said to Nettie when they moved into their own place back when one ago was, <<I'll tell you what—it is sure nice to be away from Michel's obseßion with music.>>

<<Amen.>>

<<What's wrong with him, anyway?>>

<<I don't know if there's anything really wrong,>> said Nettie, who'd known Michel longer and once upon a time more intimately than Nils had. <<I just think he was raised in a generation that bore forth great music. The times must have demanded it.>>

<<What about our generations?>>

<<Yours? An obseßion with economic security, maybe.>>

<<Hah! Well, maybe you're right. What about yours?>>

<<¢elgh -protection. We were a paranoid generation.>>

<<Mine was, too.>>

<<I think Michel's wasn't. They were optimists.>>

<<Deluded, you mean.>>

<<Delusionist? No. It's just a choice.>>

<<But what a choice. Woe to the artist born to an artleß generation.>>

*

Nettie and Nils had a wonderful excursion to Rome with love….

They'd found the catacombs and were then able to surface and enjoy a couple of weeks in that wolf-raised city on the hills, the living historical presence that is the Eternal City, Rome.

The catacombs were hollow combs like honeycombs, dug by foßers from tomb chambers.

They found the underground baptismal pool in the Catacomb of Pontian, dug into sandstone that was too porous to waterproof. The conversion of the space to a baptistery conflated the baptism with the conversion of adults—a fortuitous confluence of water, word and worship.

They found the famous graffito of St. Sebastian: Ꭓ*Paule ed Petre petite pro Victore*Ꭓ (▶Paul and Peter pray for Victor◀). Even then bad spellers were attracted to graffiti: note the mißpelling of ▶et◀ as ▶ed◀ because that's what the word sounded like to the writer (similar to the common English mißpellings of ▶used to◀ as ▶use to◀ and ▶could have◀ and ▶should have◀ as ▶could of◀ and ▶should of◀).

They found a proceßion of monks chanting Don Nix's song ▶Going Down◀.

Nils and Nettie looked at one an Œðer and simultaneously said, <<Michel,>> for the song was one of Michel's favorites. He had played version after version for them: Freddie King's, Savoy Brown's, Jeff Beck's.

Nils, looking at Nettie's breasts, said, <<'sa chestnut.>>

<<So are you,>> she said, pulling his chin up with her finger so that he was looking into her eyes.

The three of them would argue about the song's meaning. Michel said it was a song about the descent into hell. Nils said it was about oral sex. Nettie said it was just a song about traveling and escaping to the South after getting into trouble up North.

Now it seemed to mean going down into the catacombs. It was a malleable song.

In one paßageway in the Cemetery of Callistus they found an inscription, dated 1432, of the name ▶Johannes Lonck◀. Apparently a monastic order of Lonckheads followed him a year later and took over that paßageway, perhaps the way Latin-King-Nation, when they took over Gaylord areas, would tag to the L-K-N presence, no matter how temporary.

They found Toccafondi's painting of the three Magi handing out their gifts toward baby Jesus, who was attentively sitting on Mary's lap. This was one of the discoveries of Antonio Bosio, the first famous catacomb Explorer, who also signed his discovery on June 18, 1596. It was in Basileus, right next to Callistus.

The catacombs were enormous and crißcroßed like a honeycomb. The paßages were narrow, like coombs between hills. There are not hexagonal, though, or at least not neceßarily.

In the Domitilla they saw the painting of Christ as Orpheus. Incredible.

Religious paintings were everywhere. Each had an unknown and unknowable centuries-old story behind it. The sheer antiquity was mind-boggling.

Samson was battling a lion in the Via Latina and had an Œðer lion dead at his feet. The Aßumption of Elijah troubled Nils. He wondered why the catacombers praised the heavens but came into the earth, farther from God than even the surface-dwellers. Why was ►up◄ inherently superior to down. Nils could think of no answer. He considered haxing Nettie, but he didn't want to seem naïve. He subdued his curiosity, as he had taught his ¢elgh to many years before, during his educative years.

Nils felt as out of place as a beachcomber would at a Death Valley shooting range.

Nettie really hoped to have time, after the visit to Rome, to visit a Death Valley shooting range.

She was a personal weapons designer in her spare time. The Conflater she'd invented and given to Michel had been very succeßful. Now she had a couple more designs to try out.

Nils did not share that inter-rust. He was jonesing for ►Gilligan's Island◄ and►Green Acres◄ and Œðer lightweight TV from the 1960s. He'd discovered that he could watch those shows without having to use any of his mind. He could, effectively, <<recharge his intellectual batteries,>> so to speak, by not using his intellect for a while.

►The Andy Griffith Show◄ and ►I Love Lucy◄ were Œðer favorites. How could anyone live without ►Dick Van Dyke◄ on the tube every now and then?

That sort of television was, to Nils, far superior to the TV of fifty years later. The level of sophistication dropped all the way down to such a low level that in the 2010s the most popular American television show was called ►America's Biggest Aßes◄. The biggest derrière would win. They'd have obstacle courses and such, as well. Nils did not want to remember having seen that. He called out at the time, <<Alas! I am as Oedipus—I have seen too much! I must put out my eyes with yonder brooch!>> But he was only kidding—he was playing a part, a role, a roll, a pretzel, some pastrami!

Nils wanted to surface anyway so he could get some Italian meats, especially some juniper-smoked prosciutto.

Nettie was a vegetarian.

These differences began to gnaw at the fabric of their relationship.

<<I have an idea,>> said Nils, hoping to smooth things over. <<How about we stock up on some supplies [he was thinking meat, of course] and we go to the Death Valley shooting range?>>

<<You mean it?>>

<<Yes, but first we have to get a few pounds of beef jerky [even more meat!] and some beer and coffee and rum and stuff [whatever he meant by that].>>

So a compromise was found.

After the death of Cleopatra and the meeting of Hercules and Minerva, they left the Via Latina catacomb. The high rent catacomb. It must have been for the very rich. Doctors, maybe, because of the painting of an anatomy leßon—a group of doctors examining a human body. They were having a palaver over a cadaver, or perhaps they were just posing for the painter.

Nettie liked it, but Nils thought it was unpleasant. He led the way topside.

Roma was not very crowded. Not since it had been sacked and ransacked by football hooligans in the early 21st century. Before the world could see 2020.

*

A read-out of a redoubt in the reads out by the Tiber River shows that doubters were right to redoubt that the river was safe enough for immersion, baptismal or Œðerwise. The river was toxic with cholera. Corpses floated downstream among the raw sewage. It had all begun in the Tivoli Commune a few years earlier and then floated down the Aniene into the Tiber. It was in the cyber-papers throughout the solar system. Tourism took a huge hit, but much of the indigenous infrastructure was still in place. However, finding a ⅩMercato Della CarneⅩ was more difficult than the Nils had anticipated.

They found none anywhere near the catacomb entrances.

<<I bet they'd bring the contestants and animals into the Coloßeum this way—through the catacombs,>> Nils said to Nettie when he realized how the catacombs all encircled the Coloßeum. <<This must have been the largest meat market in Rome,>> he said, <<at least after each contest.>>

<<Yuck,>> replied Nettie. <<Publicly endorsed murder is still murder.>>

<<And cannibalism.>>

<<No wonder Rome fell. Society needs organization, if for nothing else, at least to keep the cannibals at bay.>>

<<You have a dark view of society, Nettie.>>

<<Comes with my job. You'd never believe what I've seen in the line of duty. That's what's inspired me to make better hand weapons.>>

<<So long as you're the only one who has them.>>

<<Well, that's silly. I work for the Aasvogel. It's his call.>>

<<Correction: you *used* to work for the Aasvogel.>>

<<No. I still do. We're going back, aren't we? I am. I hate this decrepit old planet. I'll take frontier over decay any day.>>

<<Yes, I know.>> He hadn't made up his mind yet.

<<But not till we go to the shooting range….>>

<<… which will happen as soon as I find some damned prosciutto. We're in freaking Rome. Where's the meat?>>

<<We'll find it. We just have to get away from these ruins. Somewhere must be some life. I'm pretty sure we can find a modern connection between the catacombs and the subway tunnels. The subway hub should be busy.>>

<<Good idea, Nettie. Thanks.>> She was a bit disgusted by his weakneß, he could tell. So he decided to show her his strength. He took her hand and led her to the subway entrance. He'd noticed it long before.

<<You knew?>>

<<I know where I am at all times, Nettie. Michel makes me seem like a clown, but that's him projecting his own stuff onto me. You know me. I like playing with language. I like having fun. That's not a weakneß; it's a strength. My old swimming mantra.>>

<<Yeah, I know you.>> She said it with disdain. Nils knew that their romance was over. He had no use for anyone else's anger when directed at him.

Nils had thought he was winning her away from Michel when he'd first gotten together with her. Nils felt he was in competition with Michel in many ways, and every time Nils thought he'd won something, Michel had changed the rules of the game and had turned every win into perhaps not a loß but at least a liability.

Michel had never told Nils how harsh Nettie was. She was not very huggable or squeezable. Everything with her was a negotiation or a battle. She was a warrior through and through.

All of a sudden Nils realized that he preferred puffball cream-cheeked girls who only looked at their mirrors more than that.

What had he done getting together with her? She had tried to choke him once. She had bound and gagged him the first time they'd met. Maybe he was brainwashed.

Stockholm syndrome.

Michel had a skill Nils wished for his ¢elgh: the ability to come and go in and out of people's lives like an eel through seaweed.

Nils realized that in response to someone's yelling, <<Eel!>> Michel would disappear, whereas Nils would bound up close like a puppy dog who just heard <<Heel!>> instead.

He was tired of heeling.

<<But did you realize I'm a healer?>> he haxed her all double-entendre. Then he realized she wouldn't care because as a munitions expert she was all about hurting, not healing.

<<Huh?>> she haxed, not having paid attention.

<<Never mind.>>

<<Have you found your meat vendor yet?>>

<<I think there was one next to the soccer stadium.>> And on cue, a subway train came.

Out of habit, even though the train was almost empty, when they stepped on, Nils said, <<Scusi,>> as he'd seen in Italian motion pictures. What he wouldn't have given to be visiting Juliet of the Spirits just then. Or he could be Titus Andronicus, feeding to the Queen of Vandals, who had vandalized his heart, a meat pie made of her children.

Nils realized at that moment that he had lost his sense of humor entirely. That was a desperate signal to him to extricate his ¢elgh from this plot of quicksand.

When no Mercato Della Carne could be found near the soccer stadium, Nettie announced her departure. She had been dying to try out her new weapons inventions in an appropriate setting. The Death Valley Shooting Range was perfect.

Nils said he'd join her shortly, but he had no intention to. He said thank you and goodbye to the space she'd vacated, but waited to do so until she'd been gone for a couple of hours.

He realized he loved her, but that she could not ever really give her ¢elgh over to him as he had done to her. Now he felt foolish, like the idiot who says he loves his gal only to hear her remain silent in reply.

Fool! What was happening? Why was he running around in the wake of Michel and repeating Michel's life. Nils was a mimic—he just realized it. That would never suffice. He needed to find out who he really was.

Soon enough, the floor of Death Valley was tortured in new, strange ways, and a mimic returned to the surface to find Michel. Michel, of course, had long since departed for the center of the Earth. Nils followed him.

Nettie took her new inventions with her and walked to the lighthouse to show Michel her handiwork.

When she discovered him gone, she hid one of the weapons behind the book of Seneca's plays. She figured no one would ever look there.

Failing to find Michel, she went on ahead to Death Valley by her ¢elgh.

Nils meanwhile had found the hippie named Alf, who told Nils where Michel most likely was. Alf told Nils to find Queequeg and Punch and follow from there.

Off Nils went in pursuit.

Part Seventeen: Weapons Testing by Nettie Potts

Weapon Number One: Object Transformer

Test Number: One

Target: Cell phones belonging to the people using them inappropriately at the Death Valley Shopping Mall.

Outcome: The cell phones were transformed into copies of *The Sylvia Plath Cookbook*. Perhaps the phoneys will begin to read.

One woman in line for the bathroom said she drank tea too often.

I couldn't help it. I replied as Nils would have: <<We have no ►t◄ in ►often◄ .>>

*

Test Number: Two

Target: Nothing in particular out there in the middle of Death Valley

Outcome: It's something.

*

Test Number: Three

Target: A stuffed straw archery target

Outcome: I became the target. The target became the shooter. I'm glad he mißed. Or she. I couldn't tell what the target's gender was, nor am I now inter-rusted.

*

Weapon Number Two: Realphabetizer

Test Number: One

Target: A straw shooter

Outcome: What's a rooster?

*

Test Number: Two

Target: Or is it a cock?

Outcome: I coast, I cork.

*

Test Number: Three

Target: A cork oak?

Outcome: OK, croak.

Time to quickly change weapons. This one is very dangerous.

Both weapons turned against their user. I have to work on the designs a bit and install governors that would prevent them from being used against their shooters.

In the evening after testing, I'll have time in my motel room to work on them.

*

Weapon Number Three: The Defeeter

Test Number: One

Target: A stuffed straw archery target

Outcome: The legs of the brace that held the target softened and smushed to the ground like soggy bread on concrete. It could do that to anything, but I did not dare try it around animals or humans, including my ¢elgh. It was too dangerous. Tests were discontinued and the weapon dismantled. I would reaßemble it later for the Aasvogel's arsenal. I could work on it then. Make is safer to use—like having it recognize flesh and shut down without hurting the shooter.

So far my inventions could hurt me. Am I doing that on purpose? Do I want to be hurt?

*

Weapon Number Four: The Sing Songer

Test Number: One

Target: The people in the valley Target store in the Death Mall

Outcome: The entire store began singing every word. ♪That will be… thirteen dollars… and seventy-three… U.S. cents.♫

A succeß! This weapon was ready for deployment!

I transmitted the design to my manufacturer and haxed for three—for Aasvogel, Michel and my ¢elgh, though when Michel would get his was anybody's gueß.

*

Weapon Number Five: The Katzenjammer

Test Number: One

Target: A stuffed straw archery target

Outcome: The machine flings cats at objects and people. The target was shredded by a terrified cat that landed on it.

*

Test Number: Two

Target: A crash test dummy

Outcome: The cat landed on the dummy's face. The dummy's face was clawed beyond recognition. An Œðer succeß! This weapon was also ready for deployment. I ordered three from the manufacturer and sent them my design.

*

Weapon Number Six: The Domino

Test Number: One

Target: A group of stuffed straw archery targets

Outcome: When I knocked over the one target, all the Œðers fell as well. The Œðer shooters were annoyed with me for that and made me pick up all the targets and leave.

I was tempted to use the Katzenjammer on them, but why waste any perfectly good cats?

*

Weapons Number Five and Six: The Katzenjammer and the Domino

Test Numbers: Three for Weapon Five and Two for Weapon Six

Target: Mall rats at the Death Valley Shopping Mall

Outcome: A group of annoying teenage mall rats with untied shoes and loud, high-pitched voices had taken over the Second Floor South of the mall, where a cookie franchise attracted them. When the Domino was deployed, the most obnoxious of them fell over, followed by the Œðers. They all looked shocked. I walked up to them and said, <<You all should learn to tie your shoes if you don't want to look stupid when you fall down.>>

All of them began to tie their shoes except the obnoxious one. He came towards me all intimidating. I let him have a dose of the Katzenjammer. The cat clawed his eyes. The untier gave up his attack on me and went back towards his crew. They got him some medicine, and he stopped acting as though he'd gotten cat scratch fever. I walked away.

*

Weapon Number Five: The Katzenjammer

Test Number: Four

Target: The Death Valley Upper Crust Society Debutantes' Ball

Outcome: Those prißy pußies needed a tomcat on their tail. The report from the Debutantes' Ball was that none of them do. Except those who've been raped by family members.

I hated the debs when I first met them, but as soon as I realized they were just more victims of male-dominated society, well, then I realized I had to shelve this weapon design. It was too feminine, and the backlash would come against us. I needed weapons that seemed male but were secretly female. Then I could take down the sexism from within, the way the great novelist Kathy Acker used to do. The world would have been better if she hadn't contracted liver cancer so early in life. She had a dozen more brilliant novels in her, including the masterpiece she would never quite get to.

*

Weapon Number Seven: The Banking System

Test Number: One

Target: A common person
Outcome: Eviction, Repoßeßion, Bankruptcy, Depreßion, Murder, and Suicide.

First one is stripped of all major resources; then all nickels and dimes are extracted from the poores, ripping open the epidermis so that physicians can then collect ▶dock fees◀; then the precious metal fillings are pulled from the teeth. You'll be catalogued, stamped and numbered according to one of three credit report numbering systems, your genitalia will be ripped off, you will be lobotomized and forced to donate your eyes and inner organs to the ▶donor bank◀ before they'll lend you twenty dollars to begin any artistic endeavor.

These cheap sons-of-☼Aßholes☼ won't give money to the arts because they don't value them. They'll take the Thomas Kinkade shit any day over an original artist's. And they are idiots. An artist's vision is ten million times greater than Kinkade's.

If you argue with the bank's lack of taste in matters of art and literature, you will be given demerits that will further prevent money from coming your way.

What you are supposed to do is bend over and let them shove petro-dollars up your aß until you're as bloated as they are. If you hax them to stop, they'll tell you that they'll stop only if you agree to shove petro-dollars up Œðers' aßes. But the petro-aßification must at all costs continue.

*

I suddenly lost inter-rust in continuing my weapons testing. I had the feeling I was being used. I did not approve any more weapons, not did I send any to Aasvogel or Michel. I never even tested the one I'd hidden in his apartment.

After the Banking System was through with you, you had no enthusiasm left, no inter-rust in anything in life whatsoever. You were dead and used up as a person unleß you sucked at the nipple of capitalism until you grew strong enough to feed on those weaker than you.

How does one stay in that world? I ran screaming into the desert, looking for the first underground entrance.

The Death Valley branch of the Bank of America sent giant weasels after me. But when I was underground, I was safe to unleash my badgers on their weasels. The weasels had no chance.

I picked notes from necks of the dead weasels. These had been meßenger weasels, which were expected to die, like ▶liberating◀ forces overseas.

One said, ΧPraise be to Markxmen!Χ

The Œðer said, ΧJoin the true faith!Χ The bankers have even set up their ATMs inside the churches. WWJD?

*

Weapon Number Eight: Anti-bank Mißile

Test Number: One

Target: The First National Bank of Fuck You in the Aß.

Outcome: It's exploded to smithereens!

This weapon, unfortunately, is only conceptual, like my father's ▶umbrella treatment◀, whereby he imagined ramming his umbrella up the offender's aß and then opening it and yanking it out. I called that maneuver ▶the raccoon◀ because male raccoons have barbed penises that shred the female's labia on the way out. The females scream. Rightly so! Ladies, always carry very sharp knives in case you ever need to free your ¢elgh from a barbed penis! Cut it off at the base and then go to the hospital. The doctors [for a generous contribution toward their ▶dock fees◀, of course] will gladly remove the offending object.

Part Eighteen: The Hole in the Wall, Part Two

What sure is pleasant is to be able to spend some time free to dream and think and drift away on the Mighty Clouds of Joy, to climb the Tower of Power, to be a Jazz Meßenger, to experience music without the constant chatter and criticism of that constable and her consort, formerly my friends Nettie and Nils!

At that moment I was listening to a rather baßy old recording of Savoy Brown at the Oregon on State Penitentiary on August 4, 1987. I know Nils and Nettie would have complained about the sound quality of the best known recording of the event, but I loved it for its historical significance.

Simmonds shines for the prisoners. It must have been the adrenaline from just being there. That's why Johnny Cash did two prison albums—and pushed him to a new awareneß of the hyperconnectivity of his work.

That's a linguistic trap I'm leaving there for Nils to find some day. The rust of you can ignore it. ►Hyperconnectivity◄! That's a good one.

To just listen to it without someone's *meckering* in my ear non-stop is a good, great joy.

Simmonds's banter with the prisoners is amusing. He says he was told he couldn't swear, to which he told the prison, <<Fuck that!>> He told them before playing ►Wang Dang Doodle◄ that it was a song about something many of the prisoners had not been able to do for a while.

<<Oh, poor babies,>> Nettie would have said. Nils, too. They weren't ever incarcerated.

Nettie and Nils were little sheep whose bleats meckered me to death.

I suppose stagnation will eventually drone on boringly. I know I can't stay here forever, but for now I am enjoying it.

I found pork and beans in the warehouse today. I've been craving them. That was wonderful. Pineapple rings, too. For the pineapple, though, I needed a can opener. I found a magnetic one stuck on a fridge in an employee lounge in the warehouse.

I became bolder as I visited the warehouse, especially in my warehouse uniform.

I allowed my ¢elgh to be seen several times so that the Œðers would begin to recognize me and just aßume I was new to that part of the warehouse.

I began to show up for birthday celebrations that were announced in the lounges. Cake and punch were a nice change from my usual fare.

I haxed one co-worker, a fork-lift driver, where everyone came from.

<<All over,>> he said. <<Some used to commute from the surface,>> he said, <<but that such a long commute they could only go home on weekends. So most of us live in the city,>> and he pointed down.

Apparently the next level down was a metropolis. That fascinated me, and as much as I treasured of my privacy and enjoyed my hole in the wall, curiosity about the metropolis began to overtake me.

I told my ¢elgh I would leave in a week, changed it to a month, then decided two weeks was better, like the old two weeks' notice jobs used to require and give. Everyone used to think in fortnights. I like those old fortuitous fortnight nights. One had a chance to bid farewell to one's comrades and then be on one's way. A two-week farewell party was tolerable. A month, and one was overstaying one's welcome. A week, and one was skipping town.

So I had two more weeks of listening to the greatest library of blues I'd ever found. That was too short, but I only had two more weeks of canned food to endure. More than that and I never hear the coiling of the musical notes over the roiling of my stomach.

Although music is eßential for existence, food is even more so. Woe to the soul who has to choose between soul food and soul music. I could not want to live without either. To not hear Shuggie Otis ever again? That would be like a lobotomy of that part of me. And to never have red beans and rice, greens, and BBQ ever again is impoßible to imagine. BBQ or BB King? Peter Green or collards? Big Mama Thornton or Mama Louise? What a terrible choice—I want to embrace them both and thank them for all the life they brought to the world. They helped us to truly live, not just merely exist. That's what soul is all about. It's there to help you live. Trust it. Shake anything you want, but make sure to shake your soul without letting it get away. Hold it close. It's like your spine—you need to stretch it out, and you need to compreß it in. It needs to feel how big and how small it can be, providing, of course, that it can be at all. Perhaps it is off course, like a tin can kicked by a tall man.

That was a recurring image from the strange dreams of my final nights in the hole in the wall. I especially enjoyed the imploring of the entire room with ♪Can't Let You Go♫. It's Simmonds singing a song to the blues's ¢elgh.

And Michel thought of a line from a Savoy Brown song, ► I'm Tired ◄, and he thought of Nettie: ♪You'll have the blues, not me♫.

Did that mean that, ▶ You will have the blues, but I won't◀, or did it mean ▶You'll have the blues, but you won't have me◀?

Delightful ambiguity? Or synonymity?

Not cinnamonity.

'Gret Simononity.

Grinin' sinnin' gnomon knee.

Stingin' sea anemone.

Je ne see no *mon ami.*

That's French that would have made Beckett cringe and James reJoyce.

The Beckett Cringe. That'd be a great name for a band. But that's what he did. Read *Krapp's Last Tape*. Krapp does a lifelong cringe. He cringes at his ¢elgh.

He made Burroughs uncomfortable. They were both cringers, but cringed in different directions. But the directions they chose to go in? Holy shit, they pursued their paths with acuity and paßion, music and power.

Joyce, however, would have loved the jokes as long as we were drinking and his family was nearby. That's fine by me. I'm the same way. Except as Michel I have no family. Michel is a loner. He can't be the soft pillow whom people want, nor can he be the razor's edge Œðers want. And he cannot be a pillow with razors. If he can't be A or B or both A and B, that he can only be neither A nor B. He must refuse to be a B and an A. He must, above all, get away.

However, Cactus's April 19, 2012, performance at the Sellersville Theater in Sellersville, Pennsylvania, where Savoy Brown played many times, was playing on the music system he'd programmed the previous week with the live shows he'd never heard.

And that this was arrusting. No way Michel could leave until he'd heard all the music he'd found there. He was a junkie for music. He'd even quit cigarettes a few years earlier, but music? Not a fuckin' chance. New music! Always new music! New, that is, to the listener, not to Old Man Time. If Michel heard an A+ recording of a Sons of Champlin unreleased live gig, it'd be new! He would groove on it fiercely. It would charge the batteries in his jetpack.

He couldn't leave ▶Alaska◀. His jaw was agape. ▶Muscle & Soul◀ drove on nice and hard. It was one of those songs that, if it were a car, would run over anything in its way. Like Golden Earring's ▶Radar Love◀. Michel loved grooves, and Cactus were the Groover. ▶Muscle & Soul◀ contained some of the greatest guitar work by anyone ever. Jim McCarty was blaze-fucking-tastic! And Appice's drum solo? Well, no wonder he challenged everyone else to a drum-off! He was one of the truly elite rock drummers. Hax Jeff Beck.

Michel couldn't leave during a drum solo! No, he'd have to finish hearing Œðer-mißed Cactus gigs, like the one at BB King's. And Cactus's *V*. He'd never heard that. He couldn't leave until his ears were satisfied. And he'd have to track down Savoy Brown recordings from 1986, when Cactus's 21st century singer Jimmy Kunes sang with them. Kunes is very good, respectful of Rusty Day and stylistically different. He doesn't mimic Day, and I think the band is better for it.

The guitar work on ▶Muscle & Soul◀ put your liver in your hands. It saws through your spine, which is then dunked in some Electric Blue in a basin in Basel.

The best of Soundgarden approaches ▶Electric Blue◀. Listen to *Badmotorfinger* and compare. Nice, eh?

But then comes the Groover! Like something off *Truly Fine Citizen* had it been done by Black Oak Arkansas, it playfully moves along with Randy Pratt's happenin' harp!

Michel croß-references his Œðer choices from the Sellersville Theater, which were mostly Savoy Brown. The December 18, 2008, show was outstanding. Something was going right in Sellersville that so many fine performers all went through there.

What was in the water in Sellersville that had the folks there recognized good music when they heard it? What an odd phenomenon. Most of the populace had taste for shit, but the good people of Sellersville were all true musical aficionados. It must be a holy place for true musicians to come and play for those who truly know how to hear.

Michel had seen it on a smaller scale before—places like the Amazing Grace Coffeehouse in Evanston, Illinois, and the Old Town School of Folk Music in Chicago were small venues with wonder-filled devotees of real musicianship, but the Sellersville theater was so on a larger scale. How odd.

Savoy Brown had played there in 2004, 2008, 2009, 2010, 2011.

Of course, Savoy Brown sounded great in almost all of its 237 incarnations. Kim Simmonds, John Mayall and Frank Zappa were great musician collectors.

They found of them everywhere. Zappa found Adrian Belew in some dive bar in Nashville, Tenneßee. Mayall had Mick Taylor, Clapton and Mark-Almond. Simmons had Chris Youlden; Lonesome Dave, Roger Earl and Foghat; the Œðer Dave, Dave Walker; Ralph Mormon; and, of course, briefly, in 1986, Jimmy Kunes.

Savoy Brown has something in common with the Scorpions. The Scorps lost Michael

Schenker, their wunderkind guitarist, to UFO. Savoy Brown lost the third big member of their band behind Simmons and Youlden, keyboardist-songwriter-guitarist Paul Raymond also to UFO.

UFO descended and took great players with them to a Great Gig in the Sky with Pink Floyd and Chris Hodge.

They visited the Amon Duul II/Hawkwind nexus on the way. Robert Calvert was Britain's Lenny Kaye. Or R. Meltzer if you count the Flamettes, the Flamin' Groovies' backup singers on *Teenage Head*.

Which takes us to Eddie and Flo, Turtles who got zapped, T. rex'd, and then took on walkies the pokey little puppy who was unable to eat anything but strawberry shortcake.

Michel gorged his ¢elgh on music because he knew he'd soon have to leave his hole in the wall.

Part Nineteen: Descent into Hell

The last recordings he listened to before leaving were Cactus at BB King's on June 3, 2006, a gig that was actually released on a peculiar European label called ►R! Music Avenue◄. The case gives a Belgian email addreß and says on a spot on the back cover, <<This audio compact disc was manufactured and printed in the Netherlands (Eu.),>> and elsewhere on the same back cover, <<This audio compact disc was manufactured and printed in Italy (EU).>>

Why would the European Union deserve punctuation marks for abbreviation in the Netherlands but not in Italy?

The disc is called *Do Not Kick against the Pricks* and comes in a beautiful four-color gloßy double gatefold cover. The recording quality, though, is an A- compared with that of the A+ 2012 Sellersville gig. Of course, Tim Bogert was still there in 2006. And unlike the Sellersville gig recording, which did not have any flaws, the 2006 disc has dozens of tiny dropouts, which are especially annoying on ►Let Me Swim◄. Still, if the Sellersville recording had never been made, this would have been Michel's favorite live Cactus recording. It's rougher than the Sellersville one. Kunes growls much of the BB King gig. He sings more at Sellersville. A- and A+. Great music! Jim McCarty, of course, ►makes◄ both, but a dropout at the beginning of his solo in ►One Way or an Œðer◄ is a momentary annoyance.

[The Œðer recording he had not heard yet was of Kim Simmonds's *Live Acoustic Blues*, recorded on January 21, 2011, at the Record Collector in Bordentown, New Jersey.]

Jim Kunes sounds much more like Bob Tench from Jeff Beck's *Orange* days on *Do Not Kick against the Pricks*, especially on ►One Way or an Œðer◄, than he does at the Sellersville show from April 19, 2012.

Some years were very good for music. 1959. Everyone who was around put out a masterpiece in 1959. '68, '69, '70. '74. Then the almost-empty period between '74 and '76, when Pere Ubu changed music forever. As a matter of fact Michel was disappointed the Hole in my Wall had no Pere Ubu beyond *Dub Housing* and *Story of My Life*, their two best. *Datapanik in the Year Zero* had so much on it he wished he could hear again.

►Cactus Music◄ was dropped in favor of ►You Can't Judge a Book by the Cover◄ and ►Alaska◄, which was a good choice. ►Part of the Game◄ was replaced by ►Electric Blue◄ and ►Groover◄, and ►Cactus Boogie◄ was subbed out for ►Big Mama Boogie◄ .

Here's my aßeßment. In 2006, Cactus wanted to really please their long-time fans and did an album (with Tim Bogert along with McCarty and Appice and Kunes!) That was ultimately mostly about pleasing the fans. Like a good touring band, they knew how to make happy the folks at hand. By 2011, 2006 guest harmonica player, Randy Pratt, was a regular along with Pete Bremy, who had replaced Bogert.

The new line-up was more inter-rusted in playing as well as they could, with almost Zappa-like obseßion. Of course, the two have that great Mudshark connection. Zappa is always only a couple of steps away—what did we say? Three? Five? He's close by, that's for sure.

▶Muscle & Soul◀ is terrific at both gigs—it's a ride! It's a blast off, but you get to wear your gravity boots.

Unleß you don't want to. You could wear anti-gravity boots, instead. Both will work, but how you tread will mean two different interpretations.

Bogart's solo on ▶OLEO◀ is… oh… lionizing.

Just when Michel found the Walker brŒðers hidden as an anonymous disk without a label, he was seen by an office helper who seemed to notice that Michel do not belong there. The office worker wanted to ✹punch✹ Michel's ticket, for sure, judging by how fast the worker took off when he saw Michel among the boxed noodles.

All Michel had wanted was some mac and cheese, and now he had to go on/for the lam(b) again.

Michel ran in the opposite direction and found a dead-end wall. He followed the wall to a corner, perhaps 400 yards away, and then turned the corner and found an ancient dumbwaiter, apparently no longer used. It had a chain that he could control with handles that stuck out of it in the middle. The elevator was as wide as a king-size bed, so getting inside was easy. He closed the hatch, and then he lowered his ¢elgh as quickly as he could handle. He paßed a kitchen of some sort, but figured he'd find Œðer levels lower, so he kept going. Of course, he didn't want anyone to discover the dumbwaiter was in use, so he got off quickly at the next opening—some kind of launch pad for a rocket pointed deep into the center of the earth, it looked like.

This was it! The pathway to the center! He climbed in. He was surprised to find Nettie sitting inside, eating a bowl of ramen and reading the rocket's manual.

Michel yelled out, <<Well, holy shit! How are you?>>

Nettie replied, <<Bored. Waiting for you. Let's go.>>

<<What about Nils?>>

<<He's here, of course. I don't think he could exist without us.>>

Michel made no comment in reply, but just said, <<Well, it's great to see you. Let's go!>>

<<Nils, get up here!>> He 💥popped💥 his head down into the cockpit from inside the rocket.

<<Oh, hi, Michel. How are you?>>

<<No time for chitchat, Nils. We're going,>> commanded Nettie. <<Strap in.>>

They did, and she fired up the top burners that would drive them into the Earth's core at a speed so fast their atoms would vibrate at the speed of irrational numbers, which would allow rational space to paß through them (and vice versa).

Michel told Nils about having just discovered the Walker brŒðers, and that fool thought that Michel was talking about a chain of Chicagoland pancake rustaurants. Best coffee in the world! A Kona blend no one's ever improved on. And an apple pancake that was fourteen inches wide and three inches tall.

<<No—the band with Scott Walker in it,>> said Michel.

<<There's a music library in the console,>> said Nils. <<Maybe there's some of it on board, but you'd have to hax Nettie for permißion. This is her ship.>>

<<Hers?>>

<<Well, she's the only one who knows how to operate it.>>

<<That's true.>>

Just then the rocket shot downward with such force that Michel figured they'd crashed, but no, it was just vibrating through Œðer solid matter.

After a few minutes they stabilized, and Nettie told them they could unbuckle. The ship was sent on autopilot and was heading for the Earth's core.

Michel was glad to see his friends again. Michel was annoyed to see his friends again.

He lavehoted them.

So he lavatoried them.

He bestoried them so that he wouldn't have to interact.

<<How long till we get there?>> he haxed.

<<Twenty-six hours at least, if I factor in Zeno's Paradox.>>

<<Twenty-six infinities perhaps,>> replied Michel.

<<Infinite infinities,>> added Nils, just to top the conversation.

ɕYep, that was Nils all right,ɔ remembered Michel. Michel made his ¢elgh a martini with Tanqueray and a whiff of vermouth.

ɕWatch me kill my ¢elgh,ɔ thought Michel. ɕAnd follow me. Better yet, you first.ɔ

<<Good one, Nils,>> said Michel. <<Very clever,>> and in so saying reduced it thus. But Michel's praising of Nils, even if meant sarcastically, made Nettie think Michel was very generous, which was not what she wanted to do.

Nor had she forgiven Nils either.

The three danced a tarantella in 6/8 and warded off each Œðer's bites. They became immune to each Œðer. Only a common goal—discovery—kept them together. Explorers still exist in every heart before it hardens.

Nils told Michel a new theory of his—Hitler was a descendent of Mozart's. Mozart had invented the 88-key piano, and ►88◄ was white skinhead insignia for ►Heil Hitler◄, the eighth letter being ►H◄.

Michel told Nils that perspiration leads to perspicacity better than conspiracies lead to *con spirito* paßages.

Heading into the center of the Earth was like going down Satan's gullet.

The three of them were trapped together sans exit.

Sans doute. Sans pareil. Sans souci. Sans peur et sans reproche.

Sansovino. Daffodil. Lively Spark. Malabar. The four horses of the apocalypse. They are three riders. They await the fourth.

They are War, Pestilence, Death, and Famine. Obviously Nettie is War. Nils is Pestilence. Michel, one could tell by looking at him, was not Famine. He had grown a good-sized belly while sitting, drinking, eating, and listening to music. No—he was Death. Death liked the arts.

But so did Life. They fought over it constantly.

Where was Famine? The chef, Famine, was no longer around. Perhaps Famine had died with Polymesus. Since Polymesus could not come, neither could Famine. Polymesus had served humanity well—his sacrifice had freed humanity from all hunger.

Michel named each horse, a high-stepper, ►Walker◄. Walker 1, 2, 3, and 4.

Together the four would set the world adrift.

First was War. War caused Pestilence and Death. Pestilence and Death caused Famine.

Michel, like Caligula, appointed his horse to the Senate Steeplechase Committee and charged it with the task of driving the Church out of the State—chasing the steeples into the sea.

♪Sans the great, sans the unknown….♫

War: two weeks have paßed since you tangoed with the sons of the funeral director, and if you go away again, it'll be raining for thirty centuries that day. I'll be away finding rosemary in Copenhagen with Big Louise. A butterfly will zigzag past two ragged soldiers on that winter night.

Though war as always is within. Where does one end and Œðers begin? What are the boundaries?

Even when boundaries are set, some folks spend their time patrolling the perimeter, preventing all encroachment. Œðers, reaßured by reasonable buffers, center their ¢elghs and trust the perimeters for a while. They react to any encroachment rather than acting in anticipation of one. One path leads to obseßion, the Œðer to paranoia. Don't go down those roads. They have been so well traveled and documented that nothing you will ever bring back from that will be of inter-rust to anyone else. Get over your ¢elgh. Subject ≠ matter. You don't have to hang your ¢elgh from a fire escape to drift off into the fluidity of eternity….

Ride this out. Don't give up. It's a once-in-a-lifetime ride, and you've paid for it with your life. Enjoy it.

Nettie slapped Michel. <<Stop it!>> she yelled. <<Snap out of it!>>

<<Yeah, Michel! Snap out of it!>> parroted Nils.

Pestilence: Nils's underlying peßimism is a disease that gnaws away at the listener. One would conclude we have no reason to live, so why bŒðer? Œðer than that kind of attitude, which could easily be misconstrued as being rude, one could see no benefit to it at all. The best of neither world, the next amorphous sheep boy from the streets who waits till the plastic is dark and the dogs chase the girls out of windows onto bridges from which they spring into the soft pool below.

Death: As he descended into what he was certain was his death, Michel wondered what the Girls of the Garden of Obscene Topiary would say: What, Matilda Matilda Matilda Matilda Matilda! Angelica? What do you say? That lady from Baltimore, what would she think? Did she ever even think of Michel again? Would they survive his big hurt with such small love? Well, he decided to haunt them. They'd hear from him through long and sleepleß nights—he'd come back to them but only if they were visiting Amsterdam, which is where the haunting would transpire. Ghosts walk the earth in Amsterdam.

Famine: Polymesus would have seen Michel playing cheß with the man he would become. He was coming to Death. He was becoming to Death. But Death was coy and went away, leaving Famine, always hungry, eternal, alone. The world's strongest feeling, the angel of ashes, a boy child with distended belly, a hero of the war, was orphaned by a Neo-Stalinist regime. Get behind Michel, Ducheß, with your silly little rhymes. Goodbye. Before Michel could ever relax into your arms, your AK-47s and M-16s, he must find food for the boy.

The human immediate supersedes all else.

Behind the four horses comes the old goat, more alone than the horsemen, who at least have their horses and each Œðer.

The old goat travels alone. The four horsemen ride for Œðers' sakes, not his.

He reaches out, trying to touch you.

Avert your eyes! Reject his touch! He wants you to fulfill *his* dreams, not yours. Fuck that.

The old goat keeps coming back.

Do not keep goats for fun—work them. And idle hoof is the devil's workshop. An idle idol is the devil's ¢elgh.

Turn your back! Put it behind you! Surround your ¢elghs with the rinds of goodbye!

The Old Goat: The Coßacks are here! Look, Clara! Jeße! Jolson! Jones! See the dancer take his cue from the hand-me-ups from the orchestra. Hear in the orchestra buzzers, crickets, and the wind. The musical tableaux patters over the micro-world while holding a giant portal to new space.

The goat is psoriatic—it cannot touch or be touched without developing sores. Hence it is never shorn nor milked. It cannot be eaten.

It escapes from the pen….

A shover shoves. Shove it back down into the well that the ink sprang from. The pipe was driven right into the heart of the eternal squid, the giant malicious grabber that pulls all things down.

The goat is only a beast that carries meßages for the giant squid that is the ultimate evil at the Earth's center.

The Squid: Four of its arms follow the horsemen. The Œðers are coming after us from behind our backs.

We should crack open the Earth like a walnut and pick out the bad meat. The giant squid is some fetid calamari. Its rot is there to kill you so that it can feed on you.

The cue that lets you know that you are gone is the sounding of the great escape buzzer, which will vibrate the pierced squid so much it will explode, leaving the whales to rule Center Earth forever after….

The three plunge towards this ultimate realization while listening to the drift….

Noah is afloat and knows not whether land will ever be seen again.

The song of the crocodile on a sand bar snaps Michel to attention.

The rocket has landed on the shore of the Center Ocean in the middle of the Earth.

Nettie paused there.

<<We should go in,>> she suggested.

<<I don't know,>> Michel replied.

<<The giant squid is dead,>> she said.

<<Well, with that pipeline through its heart, it was good as dead,>> he said.

<<And yet it lasted a thousand years,>> said Nettie, shrugging.

<<That's not what worries me,>> said Michel, brow furrowing. <<Without good ink, we will not write. We will lose all literacy.>>

<<Who's this ►we◄?>> zinged the ever-vigilant Nils, pouncing at first opportunity upon any malapropism committed by the senior male.

<<Well, I don't happen to have any lampblack, do you?>> Michel responded, annoyed. And he did not intend to use purple ink. Nils? Perhaps. Nils was an uncontrollable troll, and Michel was con troll.

<<That’s not the Center Ocean. It’s just a river. Look—there’s land on the Œðer side,>> said Nils, useful at last.

<<I’m sorry,>> said Nettie.

<<Not sorry enough,>> said Nils. <<It looks shallow. As long as we’re up to our knees in it anyway, we might as well wade through.>>

<<No need,>> said Michel. <<Nettie, just drive on. No problem.>>

<<That would work. I should have thought of that,>> said Nils, ambiguously.

Every memory of everyone Michel had ever lost accidentally came back to him. Squinting, he felt overwhelmed.

Nils wept for his grandmŒðer. And he wept for his grandchild, never to be born.

The land strip was thin. Nettie couldn’t stop in time before they were already into an Œðer river.

Nils wept for all of humanity. Nettie drove on with tear-blurred vision. Michel mourned that no one could become the person ze had wanted to. Kindneßes all went unrecognized. The world was sorrow, and then the feeling disappeared. They were back on land, numb, and Nettie stopped the rocket.

A third river coursed in front of them.

<<What was that?>> haxed Nettie, like a scientist.

<<A pity party,>> replied Nils, like a dumbshit.

<<Take a temperature reading of the next river, Nettie. It should be very hot. Make sure the rocket can take it,>> said Michel. He was right. It was super-hot, but the rocket would hold.

<<This is Phlegethon,>> said Michel. <<We started with Archeron and Cocytus, and this is Phlegethon. Dante was right. So there are two more after this,>> said Michel. <<Lethe and the River Styx.>>

<<What?>> haxed Nils.

<<Dante. *The Inferno*. You never read it? Lethe is the river of the oblivious, and Styx is the river of hate. All we have to do is remember to care, and we get past both.>>

<<What?>> haxed Nils, thinking ▶leche◀ meant milk, which sticks when it dries because of its sugar, lactose.

<<Well, sure,>> said Michel. <<If we care, we can't be oblivious. And if we care, we won't be able to hate.>>

<<What? Are you simple? You think it all comes down to some kind of Care Bears cartoon?>>

<<Look, here's land. Now get ready for the oblivious.>>

<<Who gives a damn?>> haxed Nils, noticing that the river, boringly, did not resemble milk.

<<Exactly,>> said Michel, suddenly monotone.

<<If you don't care, then I'm going to keep going,>> said Nettie. They proceeded on to the next landfall and into the River Styx. The ferryman was mißing, however, and no hateful vibe was felt at all.

<<I don't feel any hate,>> said Nettie.

<<I know. That's strange,>> admitted Michel.

<<Maybe the hate all emanated from the Giant Squid,>> state Nils, pulling a good one out of his aß again.

They croßed the Stygian waters without incident and found their ¢elghs at the Center Ocean at last. Where they would have normally seen one hell of a giant squid, they found instead the most pacific scene of pods of whales, free and unthreatened, frolicking in community with each Œðer. The whales were laughing over the erasure of the Giant Squid from their environment, so after that, the center of the Earth became the happineß of whales.

Part Twenty: Revelations

Not all teetotalers drink tea.

*

The most annoying athlete? Well, golfers can tee off wherever they like.

*

Who invented the drink ▶The Grand Tetonic◀? It's a G-and-T with retsina instead of tonic. Michel's preference was for Beefeater's Crown Jewel Gin, the 100-proof, rich with juniper, to which he would add a Wyoming-produced retsina made with the resin of Grand Teton trees. That was a good drink. I don't who invented the drink, but thanks, whoever it was!

*

Michel had a craving for the Beatles' ▶Fixing a Hole◀. Fortunately, he knew it so well he could hear the entire song from memory.

*

<<Leave the kid alone. He doesn't want company.>>

<<Why was he down here listening to your conversation with your buddies? He can't wait to be smart enough to be able to contribute to the conversation and be told that he made a good observation. Who *doesn't* want that?

<<Him. He doesn't. Leave him alone.>>

<<Why? What does *he* want?>>

<<He wants to be a Working Claß Hero,>> said Nils.

Nettie laughed so hard she started to choke.

*

Michel stood on an island in the Center Ocean, looked out at the whales, turned his gaze up toward the surface, and he made a pronouncement:

<<I stand with the Artists and hax in the name of the mŒðer of the universe that she witneß this day this declaration. I am here at the heart, and I declare it free from all bonds, permanently. No government, entity or person may ever claim ownership over

anything in this world. Wherever such a government, entity or person attempts to do so we shall respond with hooliganism. Put cockroaches in the socks of the rich. Read Shakespeare's *Titus Andronicus*. Out loud. To *them*. Remember Utopia! Do no permit the Dystopia in which we live to debase the Utopia we once imagined. Once imagined, it is real. All the rust is engineering.>>

*

Michel came to the realization that the world he lived in within music was as much a fabrication as the world on ►news◄ television or the world of history books. The writers and publishers all took sides. That's human nature, and no one trusts a non-human solution. Well, it *is* the Earth, from which humans emerged like maggots from an apple.

*

Pods floated in the sea. They drifted from island to island, seeding each with the Œðers' beans.

The beans fed herring-like brisling sprat sardines.

The sardines fed the whales.

The rust of the food chain filled in around those two once the Giant Squid was gone.

*

Lampblack became a rare commodity and commanded prices to infinity.

Oil lamp oil was whale.

Whales were no longer touched.

Without squid ink or whale oil, literacy dwindled.

*

Write with botanicals!

*

No cochineal inks! No true carmine without cochineal!

Cuttlefish and octopi were nearly extinct but are now being farmed, but their ink is considered quite ►spendy◄.

*

The carbon in toner ink is from animal connective tißue? The glue in the ink is. The non-animal ink is normally made from petroleum or PVC and iron. And supplies of those are almost exhausted anyway.

This could be the last pen. I should only use it for important….

*

Botanicals: juniper berries, carrots, sweetgum bark, red cedar root, and even madder roots.

*

A simple cornstarch glue.

*

Oil is the problem. The pigment needs a medium. Water dißipates too quickly. Eggs are impoßible to find, although Michel had seen two birds of paradise flying. But he would not have stolen their eggs anyway. A feather for a quill, perhaps, but not their eggs.

Michel began preßing plants for their oils: milkweed and dandelions and thistles were very rich, but collecting them was painful.

Poison ivy was oily, and Michel sent Nils to collect it. Nils had claimed an immunity that Michel had to prove.

*

Canadian hemlock was one of their last sources of black pigment without charring. Harder roots they did actually char to black. Black is the pure-rust writing ink!

*

Michel had already spoken about purple—he would not write purple prose! Although the purple could easily be extracted from the wisteria-covered trellis on the patio of the lodge at ocean's edge, Michel wondered in his heart of hearts if this perhaps was the moment of his actual centerednеß:

That was it, all right. He had found his core.

*

If he mixed wisteria with something else, perhaps he could get a dark enough ink. Coffee grounds worked until the coffee ran out. Dogwood fruit. But there wasn't much of it. Blackberries, but they really scratched up his arms and face as he reached into thickets. They all mixed well with the oils, but even they were not nearly dark enough to please Michel.

The best writing is always dark. It is the dark that makes everything legible.

The light stuff just floats away—it evaporates invisibly.

Blood worked. It darkened nicely, and Michel began drawing blood from his arm in order to write with it.

*

Thoughts began hurting. No—not right—it hurt to think—no—what is ►it◄? The brain began to ache.

Michel did not understand. If throbbing came with high blood preßure, and high blood preßure meant too much blood was preßing through too-small veins, then having leß blood should reduce the preßure on his brain. But it felt worse.

*

I think I'm coming to a close, a closed system. Ouroboros. I grab my tail and pull my ¢elgh together. ►Ouroboros◄—a funny word—like ►Oulipo◄. Words are funny.

*

Erotic.

Arrow tick. I flicked a tick onto each arrow, and who flung poo? Oulipo, that's who. They shaped coprolites into copper–colored lightweight arrows, and when they did, the ticks climbed onto the parched Ouliparchers and buried their ¢elghs in the arm hair of the armchair Oulipundits, who sailed without a sea through the tempest templates, on which they were served as Ouliappetizers. The Oulipo dug their hairy ticks, though, and shouted ►Schism◄ to each Œðer. Thus be-Schist, they had no choice but to take up the Method and become the scats that everyone was singing about.

The forces of Oulipo rectors became erect as they wrecked the parchment faces with foeces. Copper-colored flies flew in the face of the coppers who had come to break up the mudslinging. At first the rectors Oulipouted in silence, but then exploded and shoved their diary *ah*s under the noses of the revolting crowd. Coppers told everyone, <<Scat!>> Some of the Oulipooped out began to leave.

Nervous ticks looked around, not seeing where to go without the Oulipo. A row of ticks flung their ¢elghs onto the arms of nearby Gunners, finding Laurie Brown, Laßana Diarra (ee, yeah!), Edu (doo!), Jimmy Rimmer, William Spittle, Mike Tiddy, Joe Wade, and Tony Woodcock fairly quickly.

The Lezulu Soccer Scarab rolled coprolites into balls and kicked them at the arrow ticks while Arsenal Ouligans got into fistfights with Liverpool Ouliscarabeetles in the stands and scat-sang ►You'll Never Oulipo Alone◄ and ►I'll Get You (In the End)◄, a famous Ouliscarabeetle song about anal love, canal love, carnal love, cranial love with a Toten hamhead who could sell seashells from the Shell Sea and tattoo a crystal on a pal's aß. Man, you should see a man shitty from the coprolite balls, which explode when headed. But my arrows, when shot at the balls, ticked them, tocked them, fucked them. I'm an Eintracht Ultra after all, and we mean to be in the Europa League next year. Ooh, leap, oh goalkeepers! Be strike-breakers and see your scabs fall off!

See your scarabs fall off as they'll find no coprolites in Frankfurt!

Americans may tinky winky your po, and the top 1% may wish death upon all the po' in the world, but

I here in Frankfurt have learned to keep my po clean and unintruded upon because they'll never get me in the end. But that's just me. If you want a dirty po, well, that's up to you.

When you dirty one cheek, you may as well dirty the Œðer.

My corporate relations, my Dupa Aunt, for example, looks down upon me as if I were a piece of shit. I am offended! I'm not merely a piece—I am Shit's ¢elgh! And, as has been said, nothing is so overrated as a piece of aß, and nothing is so underrated as a piece from aß.

As Sartre once said, ►I shit. Therefore. I am. Punctual....◄

Merde murder murmur mmm... good. Rotten tick soup for dinner again. I can taste the arrowroot.

My Dupa Aunt burned an employee with sulfuric acid. Like nuns, Dupa Aunts had a habit of doing that.

My Dupa Aunt married a Scarab. Together, they liked to push me around.

<<Tick tock,>> I said to my Aunt. <<A-row row row your boat gently down the stream....>> She was in training for the rowing Oulimpics, so we made her sit in the back row. My friend said she smelled like roe, but I ✹hit✹ him and said it was just her full Depends. She'd been pregnant and must have just delivered.

*

I opened a window, and a cardinal flew in. What extreme unction!

*

I need a comb—

Book Six: The Eight Immortals of the Wine Cup

On a doughnut-shaped isle in the ocean at the center of the Earth, on reclining and vibrating armchairs with built-in refrigerators, sat the Eight Immortals of the Wine Cup. Each Immortal looked out upon the ocean with his back towards the Œðers and towards the center. At Œðer times the Immortals sat in high-backed desk chairs seated in a circle facing the round table in the middle of an islet in the middle of the water in the middle of the doughnut.

There sat Zhang Xu, ▶Divine Graßist◀, the greatest cursive ▶graß◀ calligrapher of the Tang Dynasty, whose love of wine as a tool for his calligraphy had earned him the nickname ▶Crazy Zhang◀, or ▶Zhang the Madman◀.

And next to him sat the great Li Bai, the greatest poet of the Tang Dynasty.

Next to Li Bai sat Jiao Sui, who stuttered until he was drunk enough to overcome it.

Next sat Su Jin, one of the Emperor's officials who, as a strict Buddhist, was vegetarian and was forbidden the drink, but man oh man, he sure did like it.

Next sat He Zhizhang, goody two-shoes. If you've ever seen the X-Men films, you might see him as Cyclops, a little more uptight and comfortably ¢elgh-controlled than the Œðers.

Next to him was Li Jin, the Duke of Ruyang, a favorite nephew of the Emperor Xuanxong.

Next sat Cui Zongzhi, the cynic, son of the sharp-tongued Duke of Qi Guo.

Between Cui Zongzhi and Zhang Xu sat the Eighth Immortal of the Wine Cup, Li Shizhi, the Chancellor of the Emperor's Court, who was as friendly as he was devoted to the Emperor. He simply refused to be drunk no matter how much he drank because he was in the Emperor's service.

All Eight were here.

And they were drinking.

All bets were off.

Zhang Xu, the grandfather of asemism, bid the three—Michel, Nettie and Nils—to come towards him.

<<I don't bite—unleß through your bones flows choujiu, my nice rice wine—what aßonance!—or baijiu—hmmm—double fermented by using fungus—lovely—hey, how many fingers am I holding up behind my back?>> he haxed Nils.

<<I d-d-don't know,>> stammered Nils. <<Two?>>

<<Good gueß,>> said Zhang Xu, introducing a bellyful of laughter.

Nils raised his eyebrows at Michel.

Michel shrugged.

They both looked at Nettie.

<<Are y-y-you m-m-making fun of me?>> Called Jiao Sui from his seat and looking both hurt and angry.

<<No no no,>> said Nettie for Nils. <<He's just in awe at meeting you.>>

Zhang Xu said, <<There—you see—I am a star! Jiao Sui-- why would he insult you? You are just trying to weasel out of paying me for our bet,>>

<<W-w-what bet?>>

<<That you couldn't gueß the fingers. Two, remember?>>

<<I-I s-*said* <two>!>> Jiao Sui insisted.

<<Ah, well, then, well done, then….>>

<<J-just w-wait t-till m-my t-tongue is loose….>> and Jiao retreated to his libations.

<<See, he said <two>!>> said Zhang Xu.

<<No—*I* said <two,>>> said Nils.

<<You dare question the great Jiao Sui? I would not want to be you when he finds his tongue,>> said Zhang Xu.

<<No—he's mad at you, not me!>> Nils insisted.

<<Impoßible! I don't bite. Unleß you have choujiu for blood. Or baijiu— I like that baijiu. It smells so good! I especially enjoy thick fragrance. Then rice fragrance. Then

light fragrance. I don't care for honey fragrance very much, but prefer that to layered or, worst of all, sauce fragrance, which smells rancid, like bad grappa, the spam of wines, made with stems, seeds, skins, and floor sweepings, or like fish that turned ammonia, or like a putrid cat box, or like…>>

<<We get it,>> said Nils. <<It's nasty. Well, I've never had any baijiu, so the distinction might be lost on me>>

<<…gjetost. Or Greenland shark after properly putrefied. Or casu marzu. Or…>>

Nils turned to Michel. <<Do you see a shut-off switch on this guy?>>

<<If I could find shut-off switches on people, don't you think I'd have found yours by now?>>

<<Michel!>> scolded Nettie. <<Be nice! You, too, Nils. We are guests here.>>

<<No, young lady, everyone on Earth has equal right to be here. We are here to protect the whales.>>

<<Y-y-you're just here to drink!>> exclaimed Jiao Sui.

<<And you aren't? Anyway, I always have more than one reason for doing anything. Leß than that would be simple.>> He emphasized the word ►simple◄ and gave Jiao Sui a dirty look. Then Zhang burst out again with one of his great belly laughs.

<<You should see your own face, Jiao Sui! A painter would have delighted in capturing its expreßion!>>

Michel thought of Hu Flung Pu—that old joke—but kept his mouth shut. ɛPu is pure expreßion,ɘ thought he.

Zhang bid they sit. Nils looked at Nettie, clearly not wanting to. She forcefully shot her gaze from Nils to the ground, ordering him to sit. Michel had already sat down—he was tired.

Observing the whales, seated between Zhang and Jiao Sui, was the great Li Bai. He paid the Œðers no mind whatsoever. He drank and talked to the whales. The more he drank, the more he shared his extemporaneous poetry with the whales. They would sing them back to him. He was heavy. Michel let him be, and Nettie threatened Nils with castration if he said one God-damned word to Li Bai. Fortunately for Nils, he stayed out of Li Bai's way.

<<Let's go around the Œðer way,>> Nils suggested, gesturing off toward Li Shizhi.

<<That would be a deep insult not only to Li Bai but also to Jiao Sui.>>

<<I suggest we hang with Zhang until the coast is clear. He's fun,>> said Nils, surprisingly. Nettie and Michel nodded to each Œðer and then to Nils.

Zhang had begun to write, so they could only watch as he took his own hair, twisted it, and dipped it in rare, fine inks, and wrote his beautiful, explosive, asemic graß cursive style. No one could read it, but it was beautiful. Each stroke was imbued with feeling three-foot deep. It was abstract expreßionism in the Tang Dynasty.

Zhang Xu was one of the first great liberators of paper, freeing it for frolicsome art rather than some stale accounting ledger.

Text, image, art was all one to Zhang Xu.

He was Samuel Beckett's spiritual ancestor.

He and Sam both watched the words dance.

Zhang Xu actually played some music for us. Nettie haxed him if it was Tang.

He said, <<No, it's Mani Neumeier and Oren Ambarchi! Heavy shit, eh? I love to meditate to this. And to Hillage's *Radio Dome Musick*, of course.>>

Michel was relieved that someone of the Eight Immortals of the Wine Cup had good taste in music. Mani makes sense. He was probably jamming with them five minutes after meeting them. I have seen film of Mani jamming on pots and cans in a grocery store or hardware store or something—anyway, he just had a great time on the floor there in the store. Mani's totally tuned in, and totally in tune.

Nettie was worried that someone would notice how well armed she was, so she acted sick and coughed enough to keep people away. As a peace officer, she was always armed. That was her philosophy. It was not popular with her friends. But she *was* a legitimate law enforcement officer. The Œðer two were just plain diplomats. Diplomats! A dime a dozen, and none of them any good.

<<Not true!>> said Zhang Xu, offering us choujiu, which we gratefully accepted.

<<First choujiu,>> Zhang Xu said. <<Only later baijiu. I have saved a bottle!>>

Michel smiled, remembering his first taste of Malört, the gjetost of drinks. He'd have to paß on that baijiu stuff. His stomach would not accept it: that much he knew.

<<Zhang?>> Michel haxed, suddenly struck by an idea. <<Do you play Skat?>> Zhang shook his head.

<<Ow! Don't shake my head!>> said Michel.

Zhang stopped, looked at Michel, and nodded.

Michel remembered a Blind Boy Fuller song just at that moment. He'd first heard it on a Savoy Brown record with Kim Simmonds playing some seasick slide and singing, ♪Got me a meat-shaking woman—the meat is shaking on the bone♫.

What joy for language! Blues lyricists with their double-entendres really loved the language. Nothing improves a piece of art as profoundly as language can.

<<What about the sublingual?>> haxed Zhang.

Michel was delighted, and spit in response.

The Rolling Stones did a version of one of their songs just for Michel in his imagination—they replaced ▶Under My Thumb◀ with ♪Under My Tongue…♫.

Zhang smiled at Michel and said, <<White man speak with dry tongue,>> and toßed over a bota bag full of more choujiu, No baijiu yet. The day was too young.

Michel took a sip from the bota bag and was warmed immediately. The warmth ran up and down his spine and both loosened it and straightened it. His leg muscles contracted rhythmically, as if they were dancing. His head began bobbing a little. He was still hearing Savoy Brown's *Strange Dreams*. Gerry Sorrentino's baß line grumbled on the bottom of ▶Hard Time (Believing in You)◀. The entire album was amazing. It was his second favorite Savoy Brown recording, behind *Looking In*, of course. *Looking In* is a perfect album—and only a few of those exist. *Exile on Main Street. Dark Side of the Moon. Abbey Road. Anthem of the Sun. Don't Crush that Dwarf, Hand Me the Pliers. Diminuito* by Rolf Lislevand. *Praetorius: Dances from Terpsichore and Motets* by the Early Music Consort of London, conducted by the brilliant and tragic David Munrow. A suicide, if I remember. What a shame. It's Praetorius with all the original instruments of the time: sackbuts, serpents, cornets, virginals—it is pure aural delight.

Zhang nodded, as if he were hearing Michel's thoughts. He seemed to be suggesting through body language that he could hear that great music, too.

Zhang said what sounded like <<Munrow>> and then gestured in a circle to all Eight Immortals. Michel took that to mean that Munrow had been here and had done the rounds. Small wonder. What a genius!

Nettie was comfortable. She had her tongue somewhere, but was in good spirits. She enjoyed the rice wine very much.

Even uptight Nils relaxed and began staring at the marvelous tapestries that were stretched and stood around on the island.

<<Where do you keep your art?>> haxed Nils.

Zhang looked shocked. <<This *is* art!>>

<<No—I mean *your* art. Where do you display your poems and calligraphy?>>

<<Poems and calligraphy? That's what you'd reduce it to? I do not merely do <poems and calligraphy>! I catch my sobriety and don't let it out until the art is perfect! That's not mere <poems and calligraphy>! It is the recording of the actual spark of life!>>

<<My apologies. Where do you display your <sparks of life>?>>

<<You misunderstand intentionally. That is a weakneß in you. It is not something to be proud of.>>

<<I'm sorry. I'll try again. Where, great Zhang, might an art aficionado such as me be able to see your work on display.>>

<<My work is seen in galleries in Soho and Suhu—everywhere—what do you mean?>>

<<Forgive me. You have a show in Suhu? I'm going to Chicago soon. After I'm done down here, I'll find you in Suhu. What gallery?>>

<<Cichlid Flake's.>>

<<Okay—I'll see you there.>>

<<I'm not there. They only represent me. But please, see the work.>>

<<I will. Thank you.>>

Michel was beginning to suspect that the music was not actually only in his own mind. It was being broadcast somehow.

He thought this especially when *Diminuito* began, and he started to hear instruments he had not remembered: vihuela de mano, nyckelharpa, chitarra battente, triple harp, and colascione. Since he did not know them, they could not have come from his imagination. There—unravel that conundrum.

<<I like David Munrow,>> said Zhang Xu.

<<But don't you like the music of your own milieu more?>> haxed Nils.

<<Don't be too quick to aßume, young man,>> said Zhang. <<For example, I like that band of young musicians who call their ¢elghs the Tang Dynasty.>>

Young? Nils thought they were pretty much all old-timers now. But compared to Zhang perhaps they were mere children.

Michel had never heard the band, so Zhang played *A Dream Return to Tang Dynasty*, the band's two-million-plus-copy debut recording from 1992.

<<Hey, that's ▶The Internationale◀,>> said Nettie, listening in. <<*Vive la Revolution*!>>

<<That Lau Wu can wail like Yngwie,>> said Nils.

All the Eight Immortals were nodding their heads in time to the music or perhaps in agreement with Nils's aßeßment.

Michel thought the music began to sound a bit like Guru Guru's Mani Neumeier meets the Walker brŒðers meets Acid MŒthers Temple meets Ian Hunter meets Metallica. He liked Pankrti better, but the Tang Dynasty had greater musical depth.

ͼThey must have in order to reach the way down here.ͽ

<<But you are right,>> stated Zhang. <<My favorite music is from my own time and place. *Birds Singing in Spring*, for example, is beautiful and incorporates bird song into the music a dozen centuries before Olivier Meßiaen did. It was notably performed by the Shanghai Folk Orchestra and is a perennial favorite. Œðer favorites of mine are the drinking songs: ▶The Joy of Drinking Wine◀ (or ▶Qing Bei Le◀), ▶Drunkard◀ (or ▶Jiu Hu Zi◀), and, of course, ▶Sound of the Drunken Dragon◀ and ▶Evening of the Drunken Fisherman◀. I am a true enthusiast of Qin music. You should hax Li Bai about it—many of his poems have been set to music. Novelist Mingmei Yip wrote and played a lovely Qin version of Li Bai's ▶Drinking Alone under the Moon◀.>>

<<What about your own poems?>> haxed Nettie.

<<Ah—the musicians claim they cannot read my poems because my graß writing is too beautiful.>>

<<What a shame,>> said Nettie.

<<Not really. I am not a songwriter. I am a calligrapher. But I do love Qin music.>>

<<Chin music?>> haxed Nils. <<Isn't that a euphemism for kleptomania?>>

<<Not <chin,> <*qin*.>>>

<<Not <chin>—<chin>? What's that? ▶Chin-chin◀ is a toast.>>

And with that, Nils took a big swig from the bota bag and paßed it to Michel.

<<▶Chin chin◀ is some kind of Nigerian snack of fried dough and cowpeas,>> said Michel, taking the bag.

<<Cow pies?>> haxed Nils.

<<No, cow *peas*,>> said Michel.

<<That's not what he said,>> said Nettie. <<▶*Qin*◀. Q—i—n. It's pronounced ▶chin◀, but is spelled with a ▶q◀.>>

<<Chin music,>> said Nils, ignoring her, <<is a brushback pitch in baseball.>>

<<It also means punching someone in the jaw,>> said Michel. <<Stephen Crane used the term in *Red Badge of Courage*.>>

<<It's also a bouncer aimed at the throat of a cricketer,>> continued Nils, also ignoring Michel. Apparently Nils was talking to his ¢elgh. <<But it also something to do with kleptomania.>>

<<Well, in baseball, players steal bases,>> suggested Nettie, taking the bag from Michel.

<<Perhaps the Qin sounds good with the baß,>> added Michel, looking at Zhang, who nodded his aßent.

<<Yes,>> said Zhang. <<Quite good. And now we will have some Qin music.>> The round table in the center of the island was lowered into the sea and then reemerged as a baseball field.

<<We'll field. You'll hit. Every run for you is a run for you. Every out is a run for us.>>

Nils's, Nettie's and Michel's adornment changed—they looked like the Chicago Cubs.

The Eight were donning the uniforms of the Seattle Pilots.

As they took the field and began practicing, balls were snapped into gloves from position to position. The Eight had good arms, as if they'd had some very beneficial Tommy John surgery, or they'd practiced throwing dice with the great Denny McLain.

The Cubs brought up Nettie first. That way, even if she got an out, she'd be free to be designated runner because of her speed.

Nils follower her, since he'd probably have the highest average. Michel batted third because he had the weight—the power—to hit the Œðers in. Indeed, that is exactly how their first inning went: groundout, single [substituted runner], home run. They did that twice more that inning, ending the inning with a tie score of 3-3.

As quickly as the game had begun, it ended, and Michel found his ¢elgh on the losing end of a board game with tiny plastic cars with blue and pink pegs for boy and girl paßengers.

Nils suggested Michel get an education.

<<You will get more in the long run,>> he said.

Nettie and Zhang both wanted the white car and tried to get it by pretending they didn't, so neither of them ended up with it. Oh, irony!

Abruptly, the game table was gone, and everyone was in the center soaking in a hot spring. Michel had no recollection of getting there. He suspected somnambulism.

Suddenly, the fastball whizzed by his nose. That woke Michel up.

<<Come on, Michel!>> yelled Nettie and Nils in unison, she from second, he from first. This inning she had gotten a hit. Shortstop Su Jin had come in close for a bunt, but she had swung away and lifted a Texas Leaguer above him into the outfield, too close in for the centerfielder, He Zhizhang, who could only run straight up-and-down, in and back. He was quick, though. But dive for a ball? Never!

Su Jin wondered if he'd have caught the ball if he was drunk like the Œðers. If he was drunk, though, he'd have to give up being vegetarian. He couldn't do both. Whenever he was drunk, he wanted meat. Whenever he ate only vegetables, he wanted to get drunk. He couldn't choose a base, which is how he got stuck at shortstop.

Su Jin was going to be given an error, but Li Shizhi said that it should be a hit credited to Nettie because the Immortals could not make errors.

Nettie accepted the hit gratefully. Baseball is not her sport. She liked her guns. After a few times to bat, she struck on a new idea. She got to one knee as Zhang Xu went into his windup. She dropped her bat onto her shoulder and lined up the thick end of the bat with the ball's trajectory. Her excellent marksmanship abilities made doing so easy for her. She held the bat like a bazooka about to swallow a shell and didn't let go until the recoil had finished. These bat-end bunts all flew out to short center and short left and short right. Even with the outfielders and infielders positioned there at the start of play, she was still able to aim the ball into a free space. It was the strangest batting stance since Dick McAuliffe's or Yaz's.

Nils said something to Cui Zongzhi, who was at first. <<No one's going to reach here anyway,>> were his first words, though we already had. But he was a bit drunk and a bit ornery.

Cui nodded and went over to the first-base bench and haxed for someone to change the music. Nils was tiring of old-timey tunes.

Michel thought the Tang Dynasty music was delightful, but he was not sad to hear Johnny Almond's saxophone and Jon Mark's claßical guitar on ▶Lonely Girl◀ from *Mark-Almond '73*. When that segued into ▶The Laws Must Change◀, Michel's eyes rolled back into his head, and he went into ecstasy. Mayall's *The Turning Point* was one of his favorite recordings of all time, and Mark-Almond steal the show.

Michel swung, and he struck out! Mayall had thrown him a knuckleball.

Only two runs that inning. The Eight Immortals were up 6-4. He'd left Nils stranded.

Still, it *was* good music! Like rushing trees through the wind—good nights.

I saw those trees!

Many of Jon Mark's songs had a back-to-nature theme, Michel remembered. ▶The City◀, of course, but also ▶Riding Free◀ and ▶Song for a Sad Musician◀.

<<That drummer on ▶Riding Free◀ is Billy Cobham, right?>> said Nils.

<<No, it's still Dannie Richmond from Charlie Mingus's outfit. Cobham was there for the fifth album, the reunion. They broke up after '73.>>

<<Well, Jon lost his left ring-finger, remember,>> said Zhang.

<<Why? He didn't want to be married, right?>> said Nils, laughing.

<<I love how Jon uses spoken word patterns on ▶Song for a Sad Musician◀, as if he's backing away from the music's ¢elgh. It is a fascinating declaration of ambivalence.>>

<<Spoken word patterns?>> haxed Nettie. <<Like the Shaggs?>>

Nils and Michel both were shocked.

<<You know the Shaggs?>> they haxed in unison.

<<Stupid boys,>> muttered Nettie under her breath before carefully enunciating, <<Of course I do. ▶My Pal Foot Foot◀ is a timeleß claßic.>>

<<The Shaggs are like Mark-Almond?>> haxed Zhang.

Michel laughed. <<I wouldn't say that. The Shaggs just didn't know any better.>>

<<Better?>> haxed Nettie.

<<Well, different. Jon Mark is a very skilled musician. Almond died, you know.>>

<<I know. He was diagnosed just after Jon helped put together an album of Tibetan Monk chants.>>

<<Do you like to listen to Tibetan chants?>> Nils haxed Zhang.

<<Why wouldn't I?>>

<<Why wouldn't you? What about the general intolerance of the Chinese toward Tibet?>>

<<I am not of that era. The Tibetan Monks are very wise and have wonderful vocal abilities. Who wouldn't be humbled by them?>>

<<Mao,>> said Nils.

<<Say what you want about Mao,>> said Zhang, <<but he could hold his liquor. He drank Maotai.>>

<<Yes, but he also drank Poh Chai,>> interjected Jiao Sui. That contradiction seemed to disturb Zhang, who slipped into a funk of some sort and walked the bases full before noticing that the three visitors were distracting him from the game rather succeßfully.

The lyric from ▶The Phoenix◀ took over the conversation. ♪It's your world if you want it. Don't throw it away.♫ What a sad, beautiful little song.

<<At least Mao *also* drank Maotai,>> said Zhang finally. <<Not like that traitor Lin Biao, who rejected drink for opium.>>

<<He did not drink?>> haxed Su Jin.

<<No,>> aßured Zhang.

<<He also did not bathe,>> said Li Shizhi, for whom etiquette was very important.

<<And he ate no fruit,>> added Cui Zongzhi. <<Never trust anyone who does not eat fruit.>>

<<He didn't drink?>> haxed Su Jin again.

<<No,>> reaßured Zhang. <<He was mortally afraid of liquids of any kind. He would panic at the sight of rivers and seas and would instantly lose control over his bowels.>>

<<And he wouldn’t bathe? Disgusting,>> said Nettie.

<<Exactly,>> said Zhang. <<He was also afraid of the wind, of light, of cold, and of noise, especially running water.>>

<<Good thing he’s not here,>> said Nils.

<<If he were here, he’d soil his ¢elgh,>> said Zhang. <<The sea alone would set him off. He’d explode. Literally.>>

<<Here, have some of this,>> said Su Jin, holding out a six-pack of pulque.

<<Pulque?>> said Nils. <<You’re not Mexican.>>

<<We have many visitors. I was given this by Freddie Fender. I’ve never gotten around to opening it.>>

<<He’s a boy named Su,>> said Zhang, winking. <<He drinks like a girl.>>

<<Don’t forget Janis Joplin was a girl,>> said Nettie.

<<No way—she was all woman,>> replied Zhang.

<<Inside, man, in her heart, which she bled for audiences every night until died, she was always a frightened, abused little girl. When you hear Janis, all you want to do is hold her and weep with her and tell her everything will be okay,>> said Nils, again surprising everyone with some profundity.

Su Jin cracked open a can and sipped it. <<Not bad.>> He paßed the five remaining cans.

Zhang paßed, saying, *<<Bier auf Wein, das laß sein.>>*

<<You speak German?>> haxed Michel.

<<What kind of drinker would I be if I didn’t?>> replied Zhang.

<<What are your favorite languages Œðer than your own, then?>>

<<French for grapes, Rußian for potatoes, Finnish for grain, Italian for artichokes and eggplant, English for juniper, and Spanish for *Sangre de Toro*.>>

<<Bull,>> said Nils.

<<No—he means it,>> said Nettie.

<<*Toro* means ▶bull◀. *Sangre de Toro* is blood of the bull.>>

<<Oh. What else?>>

<<German for *Kräuter*, Czech for hops, American for sour mash, Polish for plums.>>

<<And Japanese for carrot tea?>> offered Nils. Michel punched him in the arm.

<<That's stupid,>> said Michel.

Zhang started chuckling. <<*Karate*. Carrot tea. Of course. Very clever, Nils.>>

<<Thank you, Zhang.>> Michel punched Nils again. <<Ow! Stop that!>>

<<Stop stepping all over everything with your size twenty waffle-stompers. A good conversation is more like a ballet than a waffle-stomp,>> explained Michel.

<<Says who?>>

<<Anyone with any sophistication whatsoever, you plebe!>>

<<Well, sorry if I'm no good at putting on airs for royalty. I don't think prostrate kneeling is my forté anyway.>> Nils stuck a perfect landing with that one.

Michel mocked Nils using Nils's own voice: <<*What's that? A forté? That's like a spork or a scoon, right*?>>

Nettie laughed for a second, but Nils's dirty look silenced her.

They'd just struck out. ▶The Ghetto◀ began playing.

<<Very funny, Zhang,>> said Michel.

♪Sometimes I get down on my knees.♫

Abraham Lincoln was quoted as saying, <<I have been driven many times upon my knees by the overwhelming conviction that I had nowhere else to go.>>

Nils said, <<It's not surprising to me that Zhang likes Mark-Almond.>> Michel frowned, but Nils kept going. <<Johnny's playing is like a Chinese deßert—Almond cookies!>>

Zhang gave Nils the gesture of the Moloch. Then he guffawed. <<Almond cookies! That's a good one!>> Good god, Zhang was as stupid drunk as Nils was stupid—how was Nettie ever going to get them through this? She had to keep them all apart, so she put on a recording of John Mayall at the Stadthalle in Vienna on June 6, 1969, with Jon

Mark and Johnny Almond, but also Steve Thompson on baß. It predates the Fillmore East gig on July 12 when *The Turning Point* was recorded.

Just as Nettie thought about swimming in the sea, the song ▶On the Prowl◀ from Savoy Brown's *Make Me Sweat* proclaimed, right on cue, ♪I'll bet she's a swimmer♫. Nettie hadn't even noticed that Mayall had given way to Simmonds. The link was Dave Walker, who joined Fleetwood Mac between being in Savoy Brown from 1971 to 1972 and from 1986 to 1991. But when she listened again, it was really still Mark-Almond with Mayall in Rotterdam on January 2, 1970, but without the Duster Bennett one-man show like the Anaheim and Los Angeles shows the previous year.

The Rotterdam show was sweet. Nettie floated away on a rubber raft while listening.

<<Strike Three!>> They hadn't scored at all that inning. The Eight were ahead 9-4.

<<The fourth inning is ours!>> exclaimed Michel, frustrated with his ¢elgh.

<<I've been getting hits,>> said Nettie.

<<I know. I haven't,>> said Nils.

<<Neither have I,>> Michel admitted. Michel had even had to pinch-run for Nettie.

<<It's the music,>> said Nils. <<It's distracting.>>

<<*You're* distracting,>> said Michel. <<The music is the key. Without it we'd never have gotten here. It unlocks paßageways in the mind that Œðerwise would stay closed. The more you open those paßageways, the better you'll understand your mind.>>

<<Wow, man, that's, like, psychedelic, man,>> said Nils, sarcastically.

<<Oh, fuck you.>> They both laughed, Nils turned and hit a home run with Nettie on board. Beautiful. The baseball bat was cut at the sawmill on Gulch Road.

<<▶Rotter Dam◀ is not a very pretty name for a town, at least in English. It's Dutch, though, so it probably means the red dam or something not rotten. After all, it's Johnny Almond, not Johnny Rotten. Lydon, maybe, in some of the PIL stuff, was inventive, meditative, even. But that's all as Lydon, a different fellow, as different as Buster Poindexter and David Johansen.

Is it a rotten borough? Is it built on rottenstone? These questions shall go unanswered....

What is ▶So Hard to Share◀? Not the factoid that this version of ▶California◀ will blow your mind! Almond is clicking with Mark here....

Michel lifted the ball into the air, digging a slider out of the dirt—

<<Oh, keep your dogs out of the room when you're playing ▶California◀ from this album. It may hurt their ears,>> someone had written on the LP's paper inner sleeve. The saxophone lofted forth astride the guitar and leapt into the sky to become a constellation, Markus-Almondus, with John Mayall wailing on harp. And don't you dare forget the far-out fretwork on the baß by Steve Thompson.

The ball was pulled along in the slipstream and was a home run. A solo shot. 9-7. No outs. The outfielders began dancing—spinning to ▶Room to Move◀. Whirling Dervishes. Spinning Tops. The Tasmanian Devil. Twisters and Waterspouts. The infielders crouched, then sprang, then crouched, then sprang. This was all meant to distract the next hitter, Nettie, who'd surprised them, especially Zhang, with that drop-to-the-knee bazooka move with her bat, and so she did it again, again positing the ball far out of anyone's reach. An easy double, and then Nils was ✹hit✹ by Zhang. They exchanged frowns, but then Zhang just broke into a grin and broke the tension. And Nils took first. So Michel had a chance to take the lead. He took his time. Rub dirt in the hands. Wipe off the bat. Straighten the pants, the belt, the cap, the gloves. Shuffle into the box. Relax. Swing! He swung so hard, the ball split in half. Honest to god—I'd never have believed it until I saw it. Half went out over the fence; the Œðer half was caught by He Zhizhang. Yes, I saw it in half!

The teams argued ferociously about how to score that and finally settled on charging the out—only the first—and allowing half the runs—one and a half. So Michel's team was still down, 9-8½.

Michel thought about how to counter Zhang's amazing knowledge of music. Kim Simmonds's *Blues Like Midnight*, perhaps. How would Zhang have heard that? Michel had his answer when Zhang began singing ▶Tell the World◀ as he was pitching.

<<Strike!>>

<<Don't yell that so loudly,>> said Nils. <<You'll attract Chicago school teachers!>>

<<Like you'd know anything about that,>> said Michel.

<<My grandmŒðer was a school teacher,>> replied Nils.

<<Then honor her memory. Shh!>>

<<Strike two!>>

<<Come on, Nils. Pay attention! He's coming inside with the next pitch!>>

Smack!

<<I know,>> said Nils, who then began rounding the bases after his home run.

The trio led 9½-9. Appropriately, the triplets of ▶My Woman Blues◀ from Kim Simmonds's *Blues Like Midnight* began to play, welcoming Nettie to the plate. So she hit a triple, bazooka-style and all, down the right field line. Li Jin didn't have enough arm to throw her out.

Michel was up. He hadn't been concentrating well. He remembered—who was it?—Hack Wilson's advice, which was to swing at the middle ball.

Strike Three! The Eight were up 10-9½ . Nettie and Nils were on. Michel had to pinch hit. He was thinking about the previous strike out and stuck out again. 11-9½! He had to hit again after that or pinch run. He said he was hitting. Zhang smiled and nodded. Zhang threw Michel some sort of Eephus knuckleball. It changed its trajectory every two feet. Michel channeled Ted Williams battling Eephus pitcher Rip Sewell during the 1946 All-Star Game and whacked that thing beyond recovery. It was swimming with the whales. Michel's team went up 12½-11.

And Nettie was up. Michel had already gotten out twice.

She bazooka'd a single up the middle, behind the pitcher and out of reach of either center infielder.

Nils pulled a Babe Ruth move and pointed beyond Li Jin in right field. And then he hit a screaming line drive down the third base line. Nettie scored. Nils held up with a double. 13½-11.

Michel noticed no one was covering third, so he dropped a soft liner into short right field, on which Nils tried to score, but he was called out at home even though he was clearly safe.

13½ -12. Michel's team led after four innings. One more inning and it'd be an official game.

<<Hughie Flint,>> said Zhang.

<<What?>> Strike! Oh, he was at it again, that Zhang!

<<Hughie Flint played for Mayall—a very good drummer—back in 1965 or so. In 1967 he was with Savoy Brown. He's a direct connector.>>

Michel dropped the head of the bat and bunted on for a single. The best part was watching Zhang scramble for the ball.

<<Because of the strength he developed drumming, Flint was able to take a job as a porter at Oxford University. If he complained, we'd tell him, <At least you're not

stout,>>> said Zhang.

Strike two!

<<He later had his own band, McGuinneß Flint, with Tom McGuinneß, formerly of Manfred Mann.>>

Nils cleverly dropped the head of his bat for a bunt as well.

Michel was on second, Nils on first, and Nettie came to bat.

<<Bring us home!>> yelled Nils.

Zhang tried the Eephus pitch on her. She had dropped to her bazooka knee, but came right up, squared away, and hit the ball over Li Shizhi's head, out into the sea.

<<Hey, Zhang!>> called Li Shizhi. <<No more Doofus pitch!>>

<<Eephus,>> Zhang responded, upset with his ¢elgh more than anyone.

16½-12 Michel's team. No outs.

It was Zhang's turn to be rattled. He next walked Michel on four straight pitches.

<<Come on!>> cried Cui Zongzhi. <<We want a pitcher, not a belly itcher!>>

<<Do you want to pitch?>> haxed Zhang.

<<*I'll* pitch,>> offered Li Bai.

<<Fine, then,>> said Zhang, handing the ball to Li Bai and taking his place at second base.

Nils promptly hit a grounder right at Zhang, who couldn't move fast enough to get it, so the ball trickled into right, where Li Jin was playing deep. Before they got the ball back into the infield, Michel had scored and Nils was on third. 17½-12.

Obviously, Zhang was not going to be able to field, so Li Bai and Zhang traded back.

Zhang stuck out three in a row. The move had motivated him. 17½-15, end of five. The game was official.

Michel wished his team could field an inning, but with 3 vs. 8, that would be difficult. They could play half field, either right or left, with pitcher's hands, one base and the outfield. The runner would have to run back and forth as in cricket. But cricket matches lasted days, and Michel was all out of cucumber-and-watercreß sandwiches.

Cucumber-and-watercreß matches lasted all day, and Michel was out of cricket sandwiches. And that beer with the extra hops.

But Michel knew better than go for beer in pursuit of choujiu. He didn't want to feed the whales his vomit. He was pretty sure choujiu and beer tasted like Malört coming out.

Was that David Bromberg? Michel tried to ignore the music. But it was ▶The Holdup◀ with George Harrison. What a beautiful version of that song, as beautiful as a shaved rabbit.

Zhang started talking: <<I was at a carnival a few years back, and a Chinese man was a caged object.>>

<< My ¢elgh was a caged carny,>> replied Michel. <<A clown.>>

<<Well, then, we should do a Carny Firedrill.>>

<<Okay.>>

<<Or a Hobo Coble drill,>> added Nils.

<<Isn't that the guy who did the song about eating Martians?>>

<<Yeah! ▶The Roswell BBQ◀.>>

<<Disgusting. Okay, put it on.>>

Zhang shrugged. He didn't have it.

<<If you ain't got Hobo Coble, your tunes just ain't real noble,>> said Nils, paraphrasing the Dead Milkmen.

Well, Nils was awake. Eddie had nodded off. And Michel replaced Brownsville Station's ▶Martian Boogie◀ with Kim Simmonds's *Out of the Blue*. So much of Simmonds's music with Savoy Brown was for late night listening. But his solo albums, especially *Out of the Blue*, are perfect morning and early afternoon music.

Keep your windows open when you play it, and you will hear birds outside singing along.

This is music to rust to.

To roost to, too.

Two-and-two! Watch out! Out! 18-17½ at the end of six, the Eight ahead.

Again the three have been led down the path again.

Michel is upset with his ¢elgh. His love for music is being used as a weapon against him. That is war. That's like turning one's love back against one. That would be combative. I see no need for confrontation when deflection is so much easier. Unleß, of course, the confrontation is final. If so, invest everything but your soul. Never risk that, but ultimately that's what everyone's after. Guard it. I am not kidding.

The Eight thought Nettie was up to bat, and the music that began playing was David Bromberg playing Robert Johnson's ►Come on in My Kitchen◄. Even Nettie would know about Robert Johnson's women troubles. The selection was meant to distract her, but Nils was pinch hitting with a wig on and hunched over to fool them. He freaked out Zhang immediately and homered with Michel on. It flew a long, long, way over a distreßed Su Jin, who was probably grappling with the decision of whether to go for the ball at all and look enthusiastic or step back and watch it fly out past the humpbacks.

Michel yelled, <<You'd need to jump a shark to get that ball back.>>

Nettie woke up.

<<Time to bat, Sleeping Beauty,>> said Michel. Nils threw him a dirty glance. The Robert Johnson stopped.

More Bromberg followed, and it was ►Bullfrog Blues◄. That would get under Nettie's skin in a completely different way than Robert Johnson. She'd bring out her Big Mama Thornton, and it'd be over. Woman won. A man who doesn't weep when he hears Janis Joplin has no heart. I recommend, young ladies, that you use that as a test of your men….

Zhang was pontificating fine, though, and struck her out. 19½-19. Michel's team was only ahead by its shoulders.

No one could figure half an out, so all decided that the seventh-inning stretch would have to occur after the first but before the third out. <<Visitors' option,>> Michel called it. Michel's team were the visitors. He suggested an Œðer out, but Nils was scratching and saying he'd gotten lice from the wig. No one ever did find out where he'd gotten the wig, and after that scratching, Michel knew he didn't want to.

<<Stretch!>> Michel called. The Eight acknowledged and went off to consume copious amounts of rice wine. The three joined them.

(The conversation never once touched on the game. (That would have been considered ►tampering◄ (though rigging the stadium sound system was not a problem!)!)!) A totem pole of cyclops—Polysemus, maybe—would certainly be the natural enemy of Polymesus.

<<Aargh! What are you doing here, arch-enemy?>>

<<Baking a soufflé. So hush!>>

<<Oh, sorry,>> the aßailant always said, completely unprepared for that response.

Michel put on some Bob Dylan on the condition that no Bobby Z be allowed to be played during the game. It would take everyone with it, like the Pied Piper.

They'd follow Bob following Alicia Keys up to the top of the mountain in Modern Times. Dylan keeps it going until after the levee breaks. And whoever broke the levee ain't talkin'.

But it was the stretch, so they all took a healthy break.

Those Eight cats sure liked that rice wine. Michel remembered reading a warning about how much arsenic is found in rice. Maybe that's why they're so crazy, he thought.

Michel began to think that ▶Spirit on the Water◀ was in 3/8 time, but when he counted it, it was too fast to do without tripping over his tongue.

▶Rolling and Tumbling◀—that worked better at 3/8. 1 2 3 1 2 3 1 2 3 1 2 3 in twelve-bar blues.

3/8. The Three vs. the Eight. The Three *over* the Eight!

Michel quickly washed his thoughts. He didn't want to hear any Song Dynasty stuff in 8/3 just then. His beer was going down smoothly—much easier than baijiu. Would baijiu go well with banjo? wondered Michel.

<<Hey, Lousy Guy!>> called Michel over to Nils.

<<That's not funny. And they weren't lice anyway—they were fleas. I think the wig was doghair, and the dog's fleas just lived on.>>

<<Fleas are efficient hunters,>> said Nettie.

<<Oh, shut up,>> said Nils. Then he laughed.

Nettie fake-laughed. <<Someday, baby, you ain't going to worry about me anymore,>> saying it perfectly in synch with Dylan's singing it. She knew the album well. It was one of her favorite recordings of his, along with his part of *The Concert for Bangladesh*, *The Basement Tapes*, *Blood on the Tracks*, and *Before the Flood*. She also liked the early work—*Highway 61 Revisited* and *Blonde on Blonde* were wonders. Bob Dylan has built enough musical monuments, monoliths, museums, and amazements to empower a good-sized world for a lifetime or two.

Wow, that was good, she told her ¢elgh. <<Michel!>> She just wanted to tell him what she'd just thought, but she forgot. <<Oh, never mind. I like being here. I'm having fun.>>

<<Me, too,>> said Michel, slapping Nils on the back. <<I am enjoying your companionship, my friends.>>

Nils turned, gave him a hug, and said, <<Ditto.>>

Zhang began to laugh.

<<Beer makes you sentimental,>> he said to Michel and Nils. <<Now I know your weakneß.>>

<<*Au contraire, mon frère*,>> said Nils. <<You have discovered our strength.>>

<<Off the topic!>> cautioned Nettie, sensing they were drifting towards the inevitable, but she wanted to linger for a while. Plus Dylan was still on. She could go on beyond the event horizon in a little while. She wanted to hear a song about Hugh Moore's lepidopterous wife. The thought alone netted it for her. She flew down upon a levee one day, and the ounce that she weighed was an ounce too much:/; the levee broke. She flew away, and she's not saying anything about it to anyone, not even Hugh.
<<Is it time?>> haxed Nils of Zhang.

<<Shut up!>> said Michel and Li Bai simultaneously. <<We're not on a clock!>>

Okay, then. We're here in the middle of nowhere doing nothing, though Nils. Excuse *me*!

Nettie's thoughts poured in on him. You are the junior here, Nils. You don't know what these legends have been through.

<<What?>> Nils said out loud. <<Michel is a legend?>>

<<Of course. He's the greatest disc golf course designer ever.>>

Michel overheard and, suddenly, nine holes ✸popped✸ up, one next to each fielder and next to the batter.

Michel felt Nils think that Zhang should play Snatch and the Poontangs, a pseudonymous group of Johnny Otis's with his son Shuggie playing guitar anonymously. You'd have to admit that Kent, the ▶Original Blues Label◀, had balls that few recording companies have nowadays.

Why Nils wanted to distract Nettie was unclear—perhaps he wanted to prolong the stretch.

<<Did you even stretch?>> haxed Nettie of Nils.

<<No.>>

<<Well, do. Why do you think they call it <stretch>?>>

<<How should I bloody know? I'm not of this planet, let alone the hemisphere that invented the game.>>

Zhang laughed. The Eight looked rustleß. They had good buzzes going, so they wanted to finish the game.

Michel realized that any delay now would only work in favor of the Three.

<<Did I ever tell you the story of the Calibrated Frog of the Milwaukee California Zoo?>>

<<*Cele*brated?>> haxed Nettie.

<<No. *Cali*brated. The Calibrated Frog of Milwaukee California—>>

<<Never even heard of the place,>> Nettie said. <<Only of Milwaukee, Wisconsin.>>

<<Same place. Milwaukee seceded from Wisconsin after weirdos like Joe McCarthy and Scott Walker began attacking Wisconsin's own citizens and calling them <commies> or <union organizers.> It became part of California and was able to finance its ¢elgh with ⅩThe Only Medical Marijuana in the MidwestⅩ, as the ads said.>> Michel's delay was working. <<After a while, more of Wisconsin became reincorporated as part of Milwaukee, and eventually all that was left of Old Wisconsin was Door County. Everything else became part of Milwaukee!>>

<<Just to sell pot?>>

<<What? Poll pot? Is that like a pot full of Polish sausage?>>

<<Heck no—Milwaukee is known for its bratwurst. Chicago has the best Polish sausage.>>

<<Behind Warsaw, you mean.>>

<<Yes, Chicago was the second largest Polish city ever.>>

<<An Œðer reason the Chicago-Milwaukee corridor is a gourmet's heaven,>> added Li Jin. <<The emperor sent me there several times! Do you agree, Su Jin?>>

Su Jin was a vegetarian, but Li Jim was just veräppeln.

<<For apples? A fruitarian?>> haxed Nils.

<<Once a vegetarian reaches fruition, ze is said to have reached the halfway point to nirvana,>> said Nettie.

<<Yeah, but we're going to *far*vana, not *near*vana,>> replied Nils.

<<Hardy har haw,>> replied Nettie, sarcastically, as she saw that snow should never fall here on Doughnut Island.

<<No—the snow leapt out,>> said Li Bai, <<so the snow leaper'd avoid the giant squid. We hope it returns someday.>>

<<The squid?>> haxed Nils.

<<You're just stupid on purpose,>> said Li Bai to him. <<Obviously the snow leaper, dunce.>> Li Bai held the last word in his mouth, but it came out of his nose backwards. The Œðer seven laughed. Nils sure didn't. Neither did Nettie, who was no longer paying attention, nor did Michel, who had fallen asleep in his chair.

Nils immediately stood up and said, <<Now we should just say the game is over and that we won by a half run.>>

Michel woke up for that and said, angry, <<You do not make that decision, Junior.>> That decision is, in the absence of the umpire, left to the pitcher and batter. And catcher if the batter doesn't intend to swing. That's it. Michel is the batter. Zhang is the pitcher. And Michel was going to hit the first pitch out by the Southern Rights Whales, which were on the outskirts, threatening to leave the Overpod.

Dolphins would bring the ball back, but if the Southern Rights Whales got them, they'd just chew on them.

<<Hey, get those cotton-pickin' mouths off our baseballs>> would not be a good thing to yell out to them. If Michel hit it out there, he'd have to give the ball up for lost.

Zhang seemed to have an endleß supply, though, which he produced through prustidigitation. Or so it said in the Ledger of the Domain. It might be inter-rusting to see how many baseballs Zhang actually had. If the Three could hit enough home runs out to the Southern Rights Whales, would that spend Zhang's coign of vantage?

So Zhang and Nils drew lines in the sand.

A hair band lay on my dreßer.	Jeeves was never so surprised as when Poison was all over him.
I put it on.	Hey, hair band—I like your music.
The muse is sick; that was their last song.	In Germany, you'd be Gemüse.
And Gemüse'd be in Stan Musial.	Oh, yeah, he was amused.
So long as he has his brain left.	So long as he has it right, you mean.
I don't know. I've left it alone.	Well, it's a good—ah—thing—ah—I'm a writer.
You're so gouda, you're a cheese.	Cheese is—was not a writer.
Didn't Jesus write *Buddhabrooks*?	No, that was Mann. And it was *Buddenbrooks*.
Puß in Brooks?	You mean <<Boots,>> Randolph.
I'm not Randy.	That's not what she said.
Do those boots go with a *Buddhabrooks* brŒðers suit?	*Buddenbrooks*.
Do they go with a *Buddenbrooks* brŒðers suit?	No—they're too saxy.
Would they fit?	On you? You're a butterball, so you'd slide right into a *Butterbrook*. It'd look natural on you.
The Butter Battle Book should be smashed acroß your face.	Then I'll get a bigger *Butter Battle Book* than you.
Bigger butthead than me.	Oh, did I get your goat?
Yes, and you made a suit of it.	I didn't make it. A lawyer bought it.
You didn't make it? Where are you buried?	I was cremated.
Just like my coffee.	If you want the best coffee, sieve it!
Shake it!	I need a meat-shaking woman!
Cat meat?	Collected from a cat fight. Sure. Why not?
Because the baby hens won't like it.	The chicks?
The cats would attack the birds.	The birds would peck out the eyes of the cats.
Mean peckers.	Aren't we all?
I'm not a w'all.	Well, you're not a roof!
The cats all took notice.	I gueß I'm feeling a bit animated.
Sure—you're a cartoon.	My favorite is Kraftwerk's ▶Autobahn◀ followed by Golden Earring's ▶Radar Love◀ and R. Dean Taylor's ▶Gotta See Jane◀.

Sardines would distract the cats.	Destructo Cats? I had their action figures as a kid.
Just like you, to be stuck in a math book while the real world is paßing you by.	I knew you would say that.
Why?	It figures.
Hah! That was cheap.	Said the baby hen.
How do you know it's not a baby rooster?	Rooster? No—*cock*.
Oh. That makes sense.	It does to—ah—me—ah—
That joke wasn't very seedy at all.	Eau contraire, mon frère.
Eau Cointreau, don't you know?	Too sweet.
Immediately, then!	Um—sure—what the hell. It couldn't be worse than that rice whiz.
Well, just wait for that whizbang.	Is that the whole shebang?
I think it's the hole *he* bang.	♪✸Bang Bang✸, I hit the ground.♫
I had a Beatle haircut once, but I hated the bangs.	You must have disappointed your groupies.
And you your vampires.	No—they were all leaving at the airport with rolled-down windows.
What airport is that? I've never heard of any such a one.	The S & M Airport, I gueß.
Oh, that one. With the vomitous stink.	Yes. That's why the windows roll down.
Ingenious.	In the genie, you?
Qui. All eleven of us.	You includes us?
Us includes ►u◄.	Are you saying we're opposites?
Like the face in the mirror.	So you're calling me Ack Baßward?
No—you're nothing if not Nil—	♪Zhing Zhang...
—s.	...I hit the ground.♫
That'll suffice.	Don't forget suffices.
Not until after, at least.	Certainly not before.
Amazing, eh? You're not nearly as stupid as you look.	That's funny—you are.
I tried.	Itride?
Ietried	Ietride.
Let it ride.	Let's ride.
Let serai.	Caravansary.
Caravan city.	♪Looking so pretty.♫
EE.	MP.
Envoy Extraordinaire	and Minister Plenipotentiary.

Polymesus.	Polysemus.
►Polysemus◄ means many different things.	Polymesus was a friend of Michel's.
I have met him.	When?
He was here.	And?
He roasted a duck for us while I turned him on to Zappa in Budapest from 1991. Zappa's last live guitar solos.	Gyula Babos.
With Gábor Demsky.	Gábor Szabó.
The balloonist?	No—that was his counterpoint guitarist, Janne Schaffer. Zappa's baßist Pekka Pohjola was in that band.
But Szabó and Zappa together?	Yeah?
I don't think so?	But with Ponty?
Oh, sure. At the Festival de Valbonne, July 25, 1960, they jammed and did a 17-minute version of ►King Kong◄.	Ponty and Zappa and who else?
Alby Cullaz on baß. Aldo Romano on drums. French jazz players. Last-minute stand-ins.	Hey, I think we're not supposed to be talking about music so much. Michel will get pißed.
Look—he's still asleep.	So's she. Do you have any more of that wine?
Certainly. Here! Catch!	Ah! Thanks!
How long should we stretch out the...	... the seventh inning stretch! It must be over by now.
One would think.	One should. This really good.
It's a lighter baijiu I keep for sporting occasions.	It is *Fen jiu*, isn't it? Light fragrance....
Yes, of course. You are a connoißeur.	What happened to your partner?
When she crashed to Earth, I fled—it seemed that we were too volatile a mix.	*C'est la vie*!
♪*Que sera sera...*♫	The music—
It's fun, fun, fun on the Autobahn.	*Fahren*, you mean.
You have *fahren*. I have fun.	In...
...nane!	nanenanenanenanenanenane
But's what's in a nane?	Don't ruin your good nane?

<<Stop!>> cried Michel, awakened. <<Stop making fun of nanes. I went to clown college. Some of my best friends were nanes! Batter up!>>

Zhang threw a fastball down the middle faster than any pitch he'd yet thrown. Michel unloaded on it, and the last ball was gone, long gone, past the humpbacks, 20½-19, Michel's team ahead in the seventh, with only one out. Had Michel struck out, the Eight would have led 20-19½ and then the next batter could have ended the game by letting the Eight win or could have put the Three ahead. None of that mattered, though, because the last ball was gone. So the game was called. The Three won.

Zhang bowed in acknowledgement. The amount of irretrievable foul balls had thrown him off. Next time, he'd begin with at least an additional dozen.

Zhang said he was going to the showers and dive into the pond once the ballfield had retreated. This left the Three in front of Li Bai, who wasn't looking too unhappy with the loß. He was certainly enjoying his wine.

Nettie, meanwhile, had also woken up, so the Three shared a drink with Li Bai and sat next to him for a while. He began to speak:

<<Thank God that test is over.>>

<<Baseball is a test?>>

<<It *is* a test. Indeed!>>

<<But… it… was… insufficient…,>>> stated Nettie. <<Besides, the music distracted me.>>

<<What music?>>

<<You didn't even notice? Foghat's ▶495 Boogie◀.>>

<<I don't remember it with lyrics.>>

<<They came on the remake on the next album.>>

<<And those were them?>>

<<We're waiting to see.>>

<<Wading to sea?>>

<<Yes, that, too.>>

<<Don't worry—I'm much better at this than Nils is.>>

<<And I than Zhang. Do you know that fool dips his own hair in the ink to write? Yet he is brilliant.>>

<<True, but you are brilliant more.>>

<<I'm more brilliant?>>

<<No—you are just as brilliant, but you hit it so much more often. You took the writing for the real deal. Life is just an amusement to be written about. I understand that. You do. Zappa did. Kim Simmonds, man. He has the groove and has only ever let go to then come home again. As it should be. No use going over to the empty side now. Unleß it gets too full over here. I like to jump from empty container to empty container, but, when I look back, in horror I see that the containers are filling up with what I never intended to plant. I am a poor predictor of crops.>>

Maybe what I should do for my next book is…

… no, don't tell them. Yet. Wait till they're really pißed.

Why?

Because you take so goddamn long to ever get to your goddamned point!

Well, you just used an adjective in two contrary forms in the same sentence. I know who belongs here.

<<Hardy har har….>> Nettie about broke her water laughing over that one.

<<Oh, well. Can only try. That patriarch thing just doesn't go very far anymore.>>

Nettie nodded her head in aßent. Michel notice the scent—cheap patchouli that Nettie didn't wear.

Li Bai was holding out a wine cup to the Three. In it he had poured his favorite choujiu. It was not clear, like Zhang's. It was more like watery white paste in appearance. Zhang liked clear drinks, apparently, because baijiu was traditionally clear. However, they'd never seen Zhang's baijiu. He only talked about it, held it overhead like the Aesop grapeswords of Damocles. Zhang did say he like thick fragrance, which is not usually clear. If he liked the rice fragrance of baijiu, then Zhang probably served light fragrance choujiu. Li Bai's was heavy, thick fragrance, but not horrid like sauce fragrance baijiu, which has been described as similar to barnyard chicken ammonia.

Michel sipped from Li Bai's cup. The wine was sweet like creeper booze that snuck up on people slowly until they could no longer escape. It was tasty, though, like jackfruit. Like a Rory Gallagher guitar solo. Or a Kim Simmonds one.

Li Bai smiled when the cup had been paßed around between the four of them.

<<Will Zhang be okay?>> haxed Nils.

<<He will sulk, and then he will do great writing to overcome his loß.>>

<<You mean great poetry or great calligraphy?>> haxed Nils.

<<They are the same thing. One absorbs the totality of Zhang's work. He is very much like Clyfford Still. The art allows you to see what you want.>>

<<But one recognizes its beauty nonetheleß,>> added Michel.

<<That is true,>> replied Li Bai.

<<Like your poem about drinking with the moon and your shadow. It resonates. It has double, triple, quaternary meanings.>>

<<Indoors or on the battlefield?>> haxed Nils.

<<That's the point,>> said Michel.

Li Bai nodded. <<You like my choujiu, I see.>>

<<And your poetry, too,>> said Nils.

<<They are the same,>> Li Bai emphasized. <<Always remember that.>>

Li Bai refilled and paßed the wine cup around again. The Œðer seven had gone to tend to personal matters. Only the four of them sat together. Li Bai seemed like he was organizing a leßon in his head and would share it with them soon.

<<In any group of three, one is the moon, one is the shadow, and the third is the—>>

<<The sundial!>> exclaimed Nils.

<<Young man,>> said Li Bai. <<You should not interrupt your elders!>>

<<Really!>> agreed Nettie, who elbowed Nils sharply in the ribs. <<Let our host speak!>>

<<I apologize for our companion,>> added Michel. <<He means well but is still a bit wet behind the ears.>>

<<Then I shall use him as an example. Mr. Nils, you are a giant pair of wet ears, not a sundial. And one of your companions is your moon, and the Œðer your shadow. That is also true for each of your companions.>>

<<They're wet ears, too?>>

<<No, young man. The young lady, I see, is a brave warrior who has appointed her ¢elgh bodyguard for the three of you. Her domain is the group's safety.>>

<<How do you know that?>>

<<I have observed.>>

<<Then you are a giant pair of wet eyes?>> haxed Nils.

<<Eyes, yes,>> replied Li Bai. <<But if they are wet, it is only out of the anguish you cause me by interrupting me.>>

<<I'm sorry.>>

<<All right, then. I will continue. The lady, the warrior, she knows which of you is her moon and which her shadow. The senior man—Michel you call him—he also knows his moon and shadow.>>

<<And he is full of b—>>

<All I know is he casts the largest shadow,>> interrupted Li Bai.

<<—bungee cords,>> finished Nils, thinking of Michel's resilience.

<<No, Mr. Nils. He is much more than that. You have underustimated him. You are young. He is twice your age. That means he has eight hundred times your wisdom. You should respect that.>>

<<Twenty multiplied by years?>>

<<Just so. Well, we now know math is a skill you poßeß, Mr. Nils. The younger mathleß ones whom you meet—how do you treat them? Do you dismiß them because they don't count, or do you use the opportunity to help them see the beauty of mathematics?>>

<<I'm busy. They have schools.>>

<<Schools that teach them parallel lines never meet, meaning the world is flat. You want them to live with *that* understanding?>>

<<Well, people let them live with Santa and the Easter Bunny,>> added Nettie.

<<True dat!>> admitted Nils.

<<Is that runner slang?>> haxed Michel.

<<No. It’s just an old saying. Like ▶23 Skidoo◀.>>

<<I know what ▶old saying◀ means, Nils,>> said Michel.

<<Of course. Sorry. I wasn’t thinking.>>

<<When are you?>>

<<Almost always, actually. You should be more respectful of me, Michel.>>

<<Young Nils,>> Li Bai interjected, <<Michel is your elder. You must be respectful of him, but he need not be so to you.>>

<<That’s not fair.>>

<<You will see how fair it is when you are his age. Meanwhile, you are his shadow. Emulate him. Learn from him.>>

Michel looked at Nettie. What Li Bai had just said meant that she was Michel’s moon, for didn’t the moon cause night shadows to be cast? She drew his gaze. She drove him to lunacy. He thought that perhaps Li Bai was right.

Who was Michel to her? Was he her moon? Or was he her shadow? If Nils was shadow to Michel, then Michel was moon to Nils. That meant that Nettie was shadow to Nils, so she must be moon to Michel. Michel must be shadow to her.

<<Who’s the sun?>> haxed Nils.

<<At night, the time of relations, the sun does not exist. All that is is ¢elgh and moon and shadow. When the sun comes around, all three disappear. The ¢elgh loses its being and becomes slave to the sun. The moon hides in the darkneß, and the shadow hides in the skirts of the moon. The sun has little use for the three, so they have learned to stay out of the sun’s way for the most part.>>

<<Except for the eclipses,>> said Michel.

<<Solar eclipses are the moon’s revenge. Remember that the moon is a warrior, but its powers are weak compared with the sun’s. But it has enough power to keep the sun humble. Œðerwise all would be burned in its fire. The moon holds sway over the waters of the world, and should the sun ever threaten, the moon would use the waters to try to extinguish it.>>

<<That wouldn’t work,>> said Nils.

<<Ah, ye of little faith,>> said Li Bai. <<How do you know?>>

<<How do you knot?>>

<<Using ►k-n◄ means neither of you is able, >> added Nettie, getting bored, <<so let’s get on with it.>>

<<With what?>> haxed Li Bai.

<<Your leßon, Great Teacher. I want to hear.>>

<<Oh, yes. The shadow of the moon.>>

<<♪I’m being followed by a moon shadow…,♫>> sang Nils.

<<Ignore him, Great Teacher. Please go on.>>

<<Yes, please,>> agreed Michel.

<<Can we throw him to the sharks for you?>> haxed Nettie, laughing.

<<We have no sharks,>> replied Li Bai, <<but the orcas might like him. Just douse him with seal blood. They’ll dispatch him post haste.>>

<<Hey, I can hear you!>> complained Nils.

<<Then you know what to do,>> replied Li Bai. <<I will now continue, and you, young Nil, will be quiet.>> He mispronounced ►Nils◄ as ►Nil◄ seemingly intentionally.

Nils shut up. Michel nodded at him and then at Nettie and then at Li Bai. Michel opened his arms in a gesture to Li Bai to please continue.

Li Bai went on. <<One man once haxed an Œðer to go on, and so he did: one man once haxed an Œðer to go on, and so he did: one man once haxed an Œðer to—>>

<<Go on!>> yelled Nils. <<We get it!>>

<<No, not <to go on,> but <to be quiet.>>> Nils had not learned to anticipate changes in direction. That’s one thing age teaches a person. And remember….

♪If you want to find a source, find Dr. Sorcerer. If you want to go naked, find any necromancer. If you want to finger the arms of a crook from the crook of your arm, find anyone who prustidigitates, but for true legerdemain, he is the man—Dr. Sorcerer.♫

Michel had him now.

<<Who?>> haxed Nils.

<<Please don’t mention his name here,>> said Li Bai. <<He has tried to return us to the top, but we prefer to be here, with the whales. We helped the whales defeat the Kraken, so they protect us.>>

<<Was the Kraken the whales’ moon?>> haxed Michel, deftly changing the topic.

<<No—the shadow.>>

<<What was their moon?>>

<<Freedom.>>

<<And now they are there.>>

<<Yes.>>

<<That is a wonderful story. No wonder you stay here.>>

<<Monsieur Michel,>> said Li Bai, <<you are kindred. I do not envy your work ahead of you in civilizing your friend there.>>

<<You don’t think him hopeleß?>>

<<No—not at all. Good raw material. Smart. Strong. You can’t build in sophistication, can you?>>

<<No really—only with Dr.—>>

<<Shh! Don’t say it. To say it is to summon him.>>

<<He didn’t come the Œðer day.>>

<<Because his name wasn’t said—it was sung.>>

<<♪The Doctor….♫ —don’t worry—I’m singing— ♪He said the time that leprosy was worst in the entire world was during Roman times when Caesar said, singingly, <Friends, Romans, Countrymen, lend me your ears,> and thousands of ears were thrown at him in response.♫>>

<<That’s a terrible song,>> said Li Bai.

<<Like *you’d* know,>> interjected Nils. <<You’re Tang, not Song Dynasty.>>

<<Ha ha, very clever, young man. I’ve never heard *that* before.>> Li Bai was absolutely wet with sarcasm.

Michel put up an umbrella, and Nettie snuggled in underneath.

♪Please share my umbrella♫ played in Michel's head. ▶Bus Stop◀. The Hollies.

Or was it really ▶Bust Top◀, but the title was changed for the popular market> It's amazing that the Beatles got that song about anal sex past the censors—▶I'll Get You (In the End)◀ was huge in—what—1963? Name a contemporary song about anal sex. See? See how far ahead of their times the Beatles were? Michel thought about popular music of the past far too often. He couldn't help his ¢elgh. He loved music. Imagine the alternative. That would be joyleß. The ironically named ▶Mr. Wright◀ from *A Jury of Her Peers* or *Trifles* by Susan Glaspell. One's the play, the Œðer's a story, Ionesco's *Rhinoceros*, only in this case Michel couldn't remember which was which.

More choujiu was paßed.

<<We've paßed more choujiu than Nils has paßed gas,>> said Nettie, laughing at her own joke.

Li Bai and Michel laughed, too.

Nils did not. <<Hey—that's not nice,>> said he, talking to the stick from a hickory tree. That stick was used by his father to beat Nils whenever the boy accidentally paßed gas at the dinner table.

Nils had become so terrified, he'd even tried to cork his ¢elgh, but sitting at the table had forced the cork up into him. He'd had to be taken to the hospital to have it removed. The emergency room. <<The goddamned expensive emergency room!>> he remembered his father yelling at him. His father had wanted to beat Nils there in the ER, but they had too many witneßes. He waited until Nils was home, and then he'd left welts with that hickory stick.

Nils still had the scars…. He hated jokes about his gas. <<Many people have problems with gas. It's not nice to make fun of.>>

<<Like who?>>

<<Like Martin Luther, for example.>>

<<That was because Luther had a diet of worms,>> Michel offered, laughing.

<<Oh, ha ha. You've told that joke before.>>

<<It's still funny,>> said Michel.

<<Not to me,>> said Nils.

Li Bai exploded in laughter—he'd just gotten the joke.

<<Food was his moon, and gas his shadow,>> said Nettie.

<<He should never precede an Olympic proceßion, that's for sure,>> said Michel.

<<And he should not be anywhere near the flame.>>

<<And he should never dilute an Olympic digreßion,>> added Nettie again. She was on.

<<I gueß I'm just going to have to sentence you,>> said Li Bai, pausing incredulously long just for intentional dramatic effect, <<to more of my choujiu.>>

<<Nice double entendre!>> said Nettie. She was definitely on. Sharper than the Œðers. And she took the wine cup gladly.

♪She was so sharp she could pierce your heart.♫

♪Do the hip shake, baby.♫

Her shaky hips gave way, and crashed unhurt in a yurt by a campfire all four had built at dusk.

She went down in a hucklebuck. Then she began to jerk and twist like a monkey doing a funky chicken. <<This is good wine,>> was her last thought before she shimmied into slumber.

<<And so amor sullies all that's rosy,>> said Li Bai.

<<Rosé, you mean,>> said Nils. <<Paß that cup over here, will you?>>

<<My name's not ▶Rosie◀,>> said Nettie from inside the yurk, though her words were muffled by her pillow.

Still, everyone heard.

Michel just clicked *tsk tsk tsk* at the Œðers, for he knew better than to meß with a sleeping person. He'd lost a tooth when he was a boy by shaking his brŒðer awake. His brŒðer had abruptly turned, swinging his arm to free it from underneath his ¢elgh, and his middle knuckle on his right fist had caught Michel smack in the top left tooth and knocked it out. It had looked worse than it was, and Michel, seeing his brŒðer punished, had never spoken up and told his parents that the tooth was already loose—quite loose. His brŒðer had never forgiven him.

But that Michel lived long ago. The new one was inter-rusting, too.

Michel realized he was at his limit and was about to crash. He made a quick gesture of good night and disappeared into an Œðer yurt.

Li Bai, faced with the prospect of a long night talking with Nils, a conversation likely to be leß than scintillating, instead dismißed his ¢elgh and left Nils alone.

Nils felt victorious—he had outdrunk the great Li Bai! And he stumbled into Nettie's yurt and fell face first beside her on the bed. Her elbow jabbed his ribs. She didn't seem to notice. Neither did he, then, he concluded, and he paßed out.

The king of conclusions comes onto stage during the intermißion and haxes, <<Why's it you can't tell a story straight?>>

In unison, the audience replies, <<Why not?>>

The king replies, <<Because you've been beheaded!>> He laughs.

The audience does not. Axe blades are shot out at the audience, beheading everyone.

Their heads roll down into a long trough that is slanted at 40°, enough for the heads to roll down onto braß plates that depreß levers and elevate stairs. They know why they are there.

But they can't come up with a reason. If they had had one, they'd have had to have stayed ▶had◀ instead of finding enlightenment.

When the levers are down, the stairs can climb to past the point where the descent began. Œðerwise there'd be no point. That would be indecent.

Decant more wine.

You can't? Why not?

Whining about your sorrows won't help.

Jeremiads hold out no hope, only a tawdry cistern and unfaithful brethren.

Bees began buzzing in Michel's head. He Zhizhang, Li Bai's friend, was banging a gong as loudly as poßible and was chanting, <<Up and at 'em, Adamants!>>

Michel looked around. The Eight were all at their stations, so he presumed the ▶Adamants◀ were Nettie, Nils and him. And that they had two good shoes between them. His own, a pair of leather loafers, had seen better days, but they were too comfortable to kick to the curb.

Nettie wore her paratrooper jump boots with the reinforced steel toes, as was par for the course of her career.

Nils wore 20th generation Jordans—they were beautifully made and were priced to match. His shoes were the good ones, most likely.

<<Breakfast!>> He Zhizhang announced. <<Where are you from, strangers? Don't you eat?>>

The aromas of varied dim sum dumplings and morning tea filled the air. He had been a politician during his profeßional career, so He knew how to please the palates of guests.

<<The waters of Mirror Lake are calm this morning,>> said He Zhizhang. <<Fortune is favoring us!>>

<<Ow!>> was heard from Nettie's yurt. The voice was Nils's.

<<Get out!>> yelled Nettie.

<<Ow! That's my head you're kicking!>> replied Nils.

<<Get out! What are you doing in here?>>

<<Ow! Stop! I'm getting. Sheesh. Ow! I was drunk. I just paßed out in the nearust yurt. It was yours. So what? Ow!>>

<<Get out now!>> They emerged unhappy.

Michel smiled. ͼGood for you, Nettie,ͽ he thought. ͼShe knew how annoying Nils could be. Nils was obviously the shadow. Nettie must be Michel's moon, then. Meaning she could drive him to lunacy if he let her. Best not to let her. And the days were long gone when one could buy her; what a good buy: her. Good bye, Her.ͽ

<<I was wrong,>> said He Zhizhang. <<Fortune>> is an elitist concept. The poor never have fortune, so it would be unfitting as a concern.>> So saying, He Zhizhang handed each of the three a long blade of graß, still green.

<<Here, take these. They are a poor man's jade, and with these, great graß script poems have been written.>>

<<Zhang uses his hair,>> pointed out Nils.

<<Well, that's Crazy Zhang for you,>> said He, <<though I have mistakenly been called that, too.>>

<<Why?>> haxed Nettie.

<<Because of my name: ►Zhizhang◄. I have argued that mistaking Zhang for Zhizhang is like mistaking John Wayne for John Wayne Gacy.>>

<<Hey, that Teapot Dome woman did that in America when she ran for president, didn't she?>> haxed Nils.

<<The Teapot Dome Scandal was something else. You're thinking of the infamous Tea Potty,>> corrected Michel. <<That's where the expreßion ►potty mouth◄ came from.>>

<<John Wayne was *not* John Wayne Gacy,>> said Nettie.

<<No, they were very different. We met them both down here,>> said He Zhizhang, <<and only one would I ever care to meet again, though his politics were a bit backwards.>>

And the Œðer?

<<Gacy was mentally ill, and not in a good way,>> said He. <<Wayne was just anachronistic.>>

<<Wasn't Wayne a supporter of Nixon?>> haxed Nils.

<<Yes, but that was before the true depth of Nixon's psychosis had become evident,>> replied Michel.

<<Eat your dim sum,>> interjected He. <<Though I usually call it by its more traditional name, yam cha. It's Cantonese and not Zhejiang, but I hate congee. That's all we ever ate when I was growing up. As a man, I never ate it again.>>

<<What's ►congee◄?>> haxed Nils.

<<It's what you would call ►gruel◄,>> explained He.

<<Hmm. Grubs in gruel are my favorite,>> said Nils.

<<Really?>>

<<No—not at all. I like these potstickers.>>

They all sat in front of food mats and ate their dim sum with appreciation. The vegetables and the mysterious grayish meat chunks in the dumplings were mild and filling, a perfect morning repast.

While eating, Nils pondered rock and roll math.

The Doors's ▶Five to One◀, for example, mistakenly equates that ratio with the ratio ▶one in five◀. Five to one, though, actually, is one in six.

Chicago's ▶25 or 6 to 4◀ was more confusing. Twenty-five is not six to the fourth power. Nor is it six plus two plus four. Nor is 25 minutes before 4:00 the same as the 6 before 4:00, which would be thirty before 4:00. Perhaps 25 is 6 to four very misguided people? Robert Lamm has said that the song means 25 or 26 to 4:00, meaning 3:55 or 3:54, but that doesn't really make sense because 26 would not be written as just ▶6◀ in that case. Instead one would have to write out the numerals as words to clarify the meaning, for the rule is to use hyphens when writing repeated compound words that have common parts. If 3:55 or 3:54 were meant, then the title, according to the Gregg Reference Manual, would have to be ▶Twenty-Five or -Six to Four◀.

Perhaps, then, is it in an Œðer base rather than base ten? No, that also doesn't work.

Maybe it's just gobbledygook, do wah diddy diddy dum diddy do, gooby dooby do inane in Spain falls mainly on the Spanish Main, which remains not in Spain but near Hispaniola, where Columbus landed with his smallpox blankets and his band of torturers, rapists and plunderers.

<<Good dim sum, isn't it?>> Nettie said to Nils to draw him back to the present.

<<Twenty-five is a very dim sum,>> replied Nils, still half gone.

<<This is a wonderful breaking of the fast,>> said Michel the diplomat to He Zhizhang the politician.

They smiled at each Œðer and nodded in acknowledgement of the Œðer's knowledge of the game.

Nils would never be a politician. He would forever be the pebble in the shoe.

Nettie felt that she was being draw into one orbit or an Œðer of these men, and she suddenly decided that she needn't go along—she had her own trajectory, and she couldn't care leß if anyone thought she had orbit or not. She was the planet who looked to the moon without wishing the moon harm. But she also fully knew she could never orbit the moon.

One's moon could not be ensnared, nor could one's shadow ever overwhelm its source.

But if she was a planet, who was the sun? Li Bai had not mentioned the sun.

Don't look at the sun! It'll blind you!

No! Look away!

Over there! Look at the planet! Isn't she, in her own way, absolutely beautiful?

<<That sounds like Ray Stevens, man. ♪Everyone is beautiful….♫>>

<<True.>>

The four sat around, eating, not talking for a long time.

He was not feeling talkative, apparently.

One could see that He didn't feel like talking.

Thousands of sentences could be hung upside down that way. Michel enjoyed the idea. The idea was of a type that Michel enjoyed.

The typesetter, however, as always, remained unseen and unknown.

The Irish Setter was a descendant of Michael Collins's own dog.

The place setter forgot the silverware, so the three ate breakfast with their hands.

The pace setter disappeared, so no one knew how fast to go.

When she was young, Nettie tried to fast to go. She almost starved to death. She was a day from renal failure.

<<Renal Faylor? He was a tailor I knew back in Tinkertoy Town.>> No one knew who said that. It must have been a poet, don't you know it. Perhaps He Zhizhang, but he was deceptive. Li Bai was always Li Bai because of how famous he was. Zhang Xu, as well.

<<Who was that Prince Charming?>> haxed Nils.

<<Who is Prince Charming?>> haxed Li Bai.

<<I felt sorry for Prince Charming in the Cinderella tale,>> said Nils. <<He only had half a ball.>>

<<No, Prince Charming had two whole balls,>> said Nettie, laughing. <<You're the one who only had half a ball. Remember the ball game? You caught the half-a-homer.>>

<<That was poor.>>

<<No, it was great. Most people wouldn't have caught it. But you were able to focus on the half still in the park. I was impreßed.>>

<<Thank you, young lady.>>

<<Nettie.>>

<<He.>>

<I'll have to call you something else. Every guy is ▶He◀ to me, except without the capital letter.>>

<<How did you know I had a letter I needed you to deliver to the current leader of China?>>

<<Ha! I didn't!>>

<<It's not leprosy, Nettie. It's China, a beautiful, noble and ancient land.>>

A family of blue macaws flew by.

What Ding Dong played ping pong with King Kong in Hong Kong? Ringing wrong and singing songs, we're ailing along next to a sailing salon.

Faylor fell along, and that entailed his tale to be curtailed. So long.

<<Over here,>> pointed He. <<You need to go through the maze to amaze Li Jin. He's a duke, and a favorite of the Emperor. Be careful.>>

A small path opened up in the graßes ahead. It had been cleared but was only a foot wide. They had to keep together and proceed slowly to make their way through. The graßes led to hedges Stonehenge-high from Hergest Ridge and oil fields thereby, to city, town, and in my eye. Emote a mote! <<I mote,>> said he by the dumdum tree that was offish, all ¢elghish in thought. Cruel Cruet, full of piß and vinegar, say there is no Minotaur in this maze, for I dare not fly with Daedelus, and Icarus is flying high with the greatest bloom, who is looking too much for a sun in Stephen.

Do not look to the sun. Look only to the moon, and know that your shadow pursues you. If you look at the sun, it will blind you to both moon and shadow.

♪I can't stop rocking, but that's okay♫, as Lonesome Dave used to sing, thanks to Bryan Baßett's hot riffs (he of Wild Cherry fame, of course!).

Nils paßed Michel a bota bag.

He could live in it, it was so full. At least for a while…. He drank. It was a very light rice drink, more like his favorite canned saké, Funaguchi Kikusui, from Niigata, Japan. But given China's history with Japan, Michel opted not to mention it.

And then he realized he was listening to *The Return of the Boogie Men*, a terrific latter-day Foghat album, the best of their later work along with their masterful *Last Train Home*, Michel's favorite after their first. He thought Dave Edmunds's production was spotleß on their first album, much more precise than most blues and boogie. That studio precision gave the band a sharp edge that Œðer bands didn't have.

Fleetwood Mac, in their blues days, were much fuzzier around the edges. Many—most—did not make the transition from British Blues to American Pop. A few—bleß them—did Œðer work. Savoy Brown stayed true to blues, except for a brief 80s hairband thing that was actually not too bad. Foghat stayed hard boogie. Edmunds is a purist. *The Return of the Boogie Men* was exquisite, too, though. Its version of ▶Take Me to the River◀, the Al Green claßic, is respectful of the song, but boogies it to where John Lee Hooker would have been proud. It's good. And the band bops along through ▶That's Alright [sic], Mama◀ as if Lowell George were with 'em. Very claßy. Michel began to think, <<The album title is unusual. I'd have preferred *The Return of the Swamp Men*, maybe, because there is a Delta blues feeling to much of the acoustic material; though, of course, it's punched up. It's gotta make you ♪feel so good♫ that you ♪feel like ballin' the jack♫.

Michel remembered something odd from the back of the Funaguchi Kikusui cans—they said, <<Dont not heat or freeze can.>>

What's a ▶dont not◀> Is it a ▶doughnut◀? ▶Don't knot!◀—the warning to seamstreßes everywhere!

Tailor Renal Faylor is in the house!

<<One can't think that way. Let us carry on....>>

<<Us carrion?>>

<<Iscariot.>>

What?

<<Why else would one grow one's hair long? The trees are calling for me to go horseback riding through muck and mire to get there. I'm not so keen, and neither is the horse.>>

<<Why?>>

<<I think it's the careßmatangs. Tree-dwelling apes that prey on humankind once the humans' amusement wears off. They like to tear heads off shoulders, and they are good at doing so.>>

<<What?>>

<<Oh, nothing. Just a random memory.>>

<<Of careßmatangs? I remember them from Mars. They were horrible. Creepy.>>

<<Literally.>>

<<I hate forusts.>>

<<I do, too.>>

<<Bugs and spiders and scorpions and bears and stuff all waiting to swipe at you.>>

<<But no Minotaur?>>

<<No—definitely not. No Sasquatch, no Yeti, no Bigfoot, and certainly no Minotaur.>>

<<The Minotaur was named for King Minos, whose sperm became minnows in the streams of Minnesota. Bigfoot churned up the sperm, yet one couldn't watch without a sack over the head like New Orleans Aints.>>

<<Sacks watch, yet I'm no Big Foot or Mini Taurine.>>

<<No—you're full of bull bile. You have 10,000 lakes filled with the bull bile of bog men.>>

<<Shell the bog men.>>

<<No—no need. They are near extinction. Nature breeds out unneceßary defects. Just be patient.>>

<<That'd be easier if the bog men stopped playing doctor.>>

<<Or if the swamp men stopped playing dictator.>>

<<Well, where else should a tater grow?>>

<<Wherever the foghorn sounds.>>

<<Or the leghorn bounds.>>

<<There the swamp men will save the day.>>

<<And the bog men will go away.>>

<<Back into the arms of Bruce Wayne Gacy, eh?>>

Michel shook his head. The wine was clouding his thoughts. He felt wired, but the dumplings were beginning to settle, and Michel could feel them normalize him a little.

Epsilon! Epsilon!

Wear a dovecoat! Visit the Isles of Langerhans of the Bleßed, where the gods are attended to surgically! Wear a labcat! Wear a hatgoat! Protect your ¢elgh. The surgically-altered gods are coming!

Absalom! I have built sheepcotes for thee! Never forget!

The collection of *Dovecote Tales* can be found by a foundling. Astounding, a-standing is still. The only. Thing. In the library of the Gardens of Obsane Topiary.

I've 86'd it in the manuscript for thee!

His mind was one long-lasting manuscript, he realized.

And the dumplings were very good.

He imagined them as they grew like mushrooms in the city dump, on old back seats from automobiles, on boxes of discarded clothing, on books that few had ever read.

<<Let us read those books, my friends,>> said He Zhizhang, <<and discuß them then.>>

<<But…>>

<<Of course, I'd rather we discußed our own work. We should share poems.>>

<<Yes, let's!>>

<<Tonight, then. But first we have to—>>

<<Finish the dumplings!>>

<<Indeed! And we need some more wine!>>

After breakfast, they all went off to work on their poems. Nettie went into her yurt. Nils did not! He went off who knows where. Michel sat at the water's edge and stared out at the beautiful whales. The beluga were near, and he could hear their squeals of joy. The whales did not miß the Kraken, that much was obvious.

The squeals betrayed nothing but their whereabouts, conspiracies, of course, all having died with the death of the Kraken its ¢elgh.

The Kraken was ▶harvested◀ and sold around the solar system—the ▶Planet Parasite◀, it was known as, or as calamari, ika-geso, adobong posit, and tintenfisch in Œðer contexts. Periodic sentences follow periodic law. Scientists do their vivisections on the periodic table.

Periodontal disease and parasites, eh? Such lonely thoughts are cast out upon the ocean, making rings in the water that the beluga jump through, the whiteneß of their coats breaking through whitewater as if they were ▶one◀ with it.

For the whales, at that moment at least, for the ones in the ocean at the center of the earth, life was good.

Krill and anchovies seemed to like it, too. The orcas, Michel was told, had adapted to a pescetarian diet and ate the anchovies gladly. The orcas were forbidden from attacking any Œðer sea mammals.

Michel's poem:

> Foam-birthed beluga
> are belched out on the water
> and cry out, <<I am!>>

Michel hoped the Œðers are not offended by haiku. That Chinese-Japanese animosity thing. Rarer now than it used to be, at least. Like the Greeks and the Turks. The Serbs and the Croats.

Brian Auger's ▶Tropic of Capricorn◀ bounces acroß Michel's consciousneß. He was not sure if the music was internal or external, so he did not mention it. It was trebly, quick, melodic. It sounded like it was in 8/8 time—double time. <<That's no good, double-timin' backstabbin' SOB!>> yelled Nettie, but Michel couldn't tell if it was Nettie's voice yelling or if it was the voice of William Tell's wife the day she found his arrow in an Œðer quiver. Tell like an Œðer quiver, but he had no intention of throwing away Old Reliable.

The accusation was malevolent enough to be found in malic acid, which Tell could have shot off her head. Instead he handed her a proper drink—life its ¢elgh—for she didn't have to die that day anyway.

He Zhizhang was a subtle, sinister exaggerator, a snake handler, a ▶snakefinger◀, as it were.

Michel's music again. Nils couldn't get it out of his head. Music everywhere? Grocery stores, shoe emporia: music killed the◎m◎all.

Oh, you don't know the story of ▶The◎m◎all◀? He will tell you.

And so He began: <<What sort of being is man?>>

And so He was interrupted by Nettie, who said <<<What sort of being is the human?> you mean.>>

<<Quite so. My apologies. Old habits die hard. Of course. Let me begin again: What sort of being is human? No article does humanity claim long enough to make it specific.>>

<<Specist!>>

<<I think all species have the right to determine their own existence. But they should all realize that when they butt up against an Œðer species, a bump contest may ensue, and large-hipped hula dancers will rule!>>

<<As will the East-West Kölsch drinkers,>> said Nils.

<<What's East-West Kölsch?>> haxed He.

<<A German style of beer aged with jasmine sambac from Southeast Asia,>> explained Nils.

<<And irrelevant now. Even if we *had* beer, we shouldn't chase wine with it. You might as well hit the Malört,>> said Nettie.

<<Well, they both have umlauts,>> said Nils.

<<And umlauts are insignificant in the story of ▶The◎m◎all◀,>> said He.

<<So get on with it, then,>> said Nettie.

<<All right, I will.>>

<<Okay.>>

<<What sort of being is human? No article does humanity claim long enough to make it specific—>>

<<You've already said that.>>

<<I was starting over.>>

<<At this late date? That's crazy. You're three-quarters of the way there already.>>

<<I'm scared of the final quarter.>>

<<Don't be. Think of your ¢elgh as Joe Montana,>> said Nettie.

<<Who?>>

<<He used to ride the backs of those quarters till he tuckered them out,>> she said.

<<We'll need mo' tucker,>> interjected Nils.

<<She's in the Velvet Underground,>> answered Nettie.

Again Michel's thoughts returned to the Gardens of Obsane Topiary. <<Okay, you two," said Michel. <<Enough of this game of ▶Name the Celebrity◀. He should tell his story.>>

<<Thank you,>> said He, acknowledging Michel's ancillary benefaction.

So He continued, <<One person went to the◎m◎all. He was angry and armed and opened fire on the Œðers. The Œðers were unarmed. Had they been, Citizen B could have shot the shooter before a second victim was taken. The shooter would have been the second victim. Then someone else would see the shooter's shooter still standing, smoking gun in hand, and aßume the shooter's shooter was the shooter and would shoot him. Or her.>> He looked at Nettie. <<The shooter's shooter's shooter would then be mistaken for the shooter by someone else, who would shoot the shooter's shooter's shooter. Before you'd know, you'd have a Peckinpahrty, like the chickens in *Cuckoo's Nest*. And that is *not* the name of a new recipe.>> He scowled at Nils.

<<Like bird dropping soup?>> haxed Nils, winking at Michel.

<<Bird nest soup, you mean, of course,>> said Nettie.

<<Oh, yes,>> said Nils. <<Swift mucus secretion!>>

<<Who knows how fast it is?>> responded Michel.

<<I'm fasting now, after the reference to mucus, thank you,>> said Nettie.

Nils chuckled. Going girly, she was. Maybe she thought it'd give her an angle on He Zhizhang.

<<Or maybe he meant egg drop soup,>> said Michel.

<<No—swift spit is right,>> said He.

Nils spat.

<<Not like that!>> admonished the elder. <<The salivary secretion of the swift!>>

<<Look! There it is! Now it's gone!>>

He turned to Michel. <<Would you tell your junior not to be so disrespectful?>>

<<Okey dokey, daddy-o!>> replied Nils, dripping with sarcasm and his own swift spit.

<<It's not very easy being dead>> was a thought that came out of nowhere and entered Michel's mind. His mind was thereafter emptier than it had been before. One is wise to avoid such thoughts altogether.

<<Join together who?>> thought two.

<<All right now free,>> thought three.

<<Fire and water,>> thought one.

<<Wishing well,>> thought two.

<<Ride on pony,>> said a kegger in the neighborhood.

Michel began to realize what a good host He was. No activities, but everything just kept on rolling. Some hosts are entertainment coordinators. Œðers are purely inviters but plan nothing beyond that. He Zhizhang provided direction by his presence.

<<At least we don't have to dance a conga line,>> said Nils, as if reading Michel's mind.

<<Thank god,>> replied Michel. Michel was beginning to tire of his companions. He thought they should hurry along so that he could get to the Gardens of Obsane Topiary if, for no Œðer reason, only to visit his own death mask made by the plaster casters of the Gardens.

After the soup was finished, Michel bowed to He Zhizhang and thanked him for being a wonderful host.

Nils and Nettie had never even offered their poems, whereas Michel had offered his ►Foam-Birthed Beluga◄ and He had given ►The◎m◎all◄.

Even old Dean Swift would have been able to spit out something for the group. Not Nils or Nettie.

A farewell drink, and off the three were to go find Li Jin, one of the Emperor Xuanzong's favorite nephews.

Michel hope Nettie and Nils wouldn't embarraß him in front of Li Jin. Michel, after all, was a diplomat—an envoy, in fact, back when. Michel knew to treat hosts with respect. These youngsters did not seem to understand that. Li Jin was also a prince—the Prince of Ruyang. Respect must be accorded.

Michel began telling his companions about the respect they should show Li Jin.

Also, it was said, Li Jin preferred baijiu made with Job's tears. Coix seeds.

<<COIT? The Invisible Opera Company of Tibet? Daevid Allen?>>

<<No—Co*ix*.>>

<<Di you say Li Jin was the Prince of Ruyang? Was he there in the time of the Huanghetitan?>>

<<What? During the Cretaceous Period? That's absurd.>>

<<It's observed.>>

<<*Huanghetitan ruyangensis* was found in 2007, true, but it lived seventy million years ago, not during the Tang Dynasty, 618-906 AD. Or thereabouts.>>

<<Huanghetitan lives! Only Li Jin can take him in a wrustling match! As Du Fu stated, Li Jin could stand three barrels of rice wine—indeed, would not drink leß—and he always planned to move to the vineyard in Jiuquan so that he could drink wine as freely as the rivers flowed.>>

As an immortal, Li Jin lived next to an ocean. And somewhere in the vicinity must have been an underground distribution system for wine. The Eight were getting wine from somewhere. Nils wanted in on the deal. He could become the new big underworld kingpin!

Nettie's scowl bowled him over. Had she had Bruce Wayne Gacy's cowl, she'd have bowled over her ¢elgh.

Li Jin, from his seat, aware of their conversation as they approached, said to the three as soon as they were near enough, <<Huanghetitan is as dead as the Kraken.>>

<<The squid that used to control the Earth?>> haxed Nils pointleßly. <<We already knew that.>>

<<Squid? Who said squid? Gosh, no, he was a giant octopus. Only eight arms! We each had to watch one arm and warn everyone above about which arms were on the prowl and would be emerging at levels above in order to find food.>>

<<The Kraken was really an octopus?>>

<<That's what I'm saying.>>

<<Well, who knew?>>

<<I did.>>

Michel thought about the Beatles. The original name of *Help!* was *Eight Arms to Hold You*. Four Beatles, eight arms—just like an octopus. ♪I'd like to be in octopus's garden….♫ So even the Beatles had been controlled by the Kraken! The Kraken had had psychic power over all. It had reached out of its lair at the center of the Earth and had pulled its prey down from the surface through the multiple paßageways to the surface.

The Eight Immortals had shut it down. They had blocked it and starved it until it died. Li Jin, Prince of Ruyang, took the arm that preferred the waters of Norway. This was the Kraken's biggest arm—its preferred, like handedneß in people. When this arm was disabled, the beginning of the end was signaled for the Kraken.

Li Jin had a small house in his area. On the wall he had a picture, a painting—a still life.

<<What is it a still life of?>> haxed Michel when Li Jin described the contents of the small house.

<<A ewer,>> replied Li Jin.

<<What am I a still life of?>> haxed Michel when Li Jin didn't make sense.

A pitcher? But Zhang Xu was the pitcher. Oh…. Li Jin is *that* guy. In every group of friends, one friend just doesn't quite get it. Maybe Li Jin's childhood of privilege as a prince and favorite nephew of the Emperor removed Li Jin from the world of the honest.

The honest stay out of the court. They'll be noticed for being different and will be punished for that.

Li Jin was too close to the sun. The Œðers knew to look to the moon and the shadow. But Li Jin grew up closer to the sun than Mercury is. He could not have seen a moon for the brightneß. Nor for him would any shadow exist. The light would bend around him.

Li Jin was academically brilliant, an Alexander, raised by great minds, yet exposed only to dominant philosophies. He had difficulties with counterpoint and contradiction.

<<Aha!>> a third-rate junior profeßor at some Confederate university once shouted at Raymond Federman during a Q&A following a lecture. <<You in your lecture just contradicted what you said in your book *Critifiction*!>> And the junior profeßor's face melted into a mask of smugneß. He thought he'd just made his literary reputation by nailing Federman in an academic setting.

Federman replied, after a quick, wry smile, <<Federman reserves the right to contradict his ¢elgh!>> That was sweet.

Boom chakalaka! The junior profeßor went down for the count. Federman scored a KO.

Michel had been there and, at a bar afterwards, had bought Federman a Warka beer. Warka, around since 1478, had a motto: ▶Noble Bitterneß, Golden Colour, Ideal Head◀.

Academic pettineß leads to a noble bitterneß, while the ▶golden colour◀ is one's own effluence. But as is said, one man's effluence is an Œðer's influence.

Michel was trying to learn to have the ideal head, to be the ideal head.

But then he remembered the Monkees. He fell to the ground in an epileptic fit. Nettie pounced on him and shoved her wallet in his mouth to keep him from biting his tongue off. She rode him like a bronco-buster until he settled down, and then she collapsed on top of his collapsed body, both spent in an ecstasy that was so non-orgasmic that Michel rolled his eyes back into his head to bring the feeling back so that he could climax. But he couldn't go back.

<<What was that?>> Nettie finally said, sitting up when Michel was finally still.

<<And that is what they will say when I die,>> thought Michel. <<Oh, but I cannot die, for I'm already dead. I have a desk mask. And I must get back to it.>>

<<And here is my second picture,>> Li Jin said, pointing to a painting of Huanghetitan done in the style of Titian.>>

<<Titian? What was his first name?>>

<<Tiziano.>>

<<Tiziano Titian?>>

<<No, Tiziano Vecellio, Il Divino. Show respect. He was one of the great Venetians.>>

<<Titian painted with pigeon shit?>>

<<No, this was before Venice became rivers of pigeon shit. The rivers were equal-opportunity sewers.>>

<<So was he an artist who paints ewers?>>

<<No. He died in 1576. Caravaggio one of the first who was known for still life

painting, and he wasn't born until 1571. Titian did not preß ewers on his viewers. He had giant eyes in the sky watching his every brush stroke. How dare he mißtep? Perhaps he never did, and that is why his work is perfect.>>

<<Perhaps he had bashful bladder.>>

<<►Perhaps◄. My favorite word.>>

<<Yes, we know. That's been established.>>

<<Oh, sorry to be redundant.>>

<<Oh, sorry to be redundant.>>

<<Michel, you've been made redundant?>> haxed Nils.

<<You mean as in ►retired◄?>>

<<Yes.>>

<<No—that's only for England. Americans say ►retired◄.>>

<<That's terrible—like a retread.>>

<<Yeah, well, don't retread on me.>>

<<Ha!>>

<<Shh!>> scolded Nettie, noting that Li Jin was looking annoyed. He had planted his feet firmly and was looking at them while he was chewing sideways. Perhaps his connection to *Huanghetitan ruyangensis* was closer than previously thought. And to Ruyangosaurus, too. An Œðer giant sauropod. Just get out of the way of the plants....

Stomp!

Li Jin was about as fast-moving as a mid-size sauropod.

Stomp!

Nettie all of a sudden knew that Nils was going to say something about sumo wrustling, which would have been stupid of him, so she grabbed him and clamped her hand over his mouth. <<Shut up!>> she said. <<I will not have you blow this.>>
Nils nodded and made a sign that he was turning a key in his mouth.

Tragedy averted. Only one more sip of wine.

<<And here is my third painting,>> said Li Jin, his countenance afrown.

ɕNot as frown as mine,ɔ thought Nils, but he was able to corral the thought and not let it break out of the ranch although it sure wanted to run along at full speed towards the nearust town, horses' hooves pounding heavily below. But he could never get his horse up to speed to jump the fence.

ɕOh, I get it,ɔ thought Nils. ɕ►He could never get his horse up to speed◄ means he wouldn't mix his heroin and amphetimines. ►Jumping the fence◄ means ripping off a person who <<is depending upon you [sic]>>—fuck!ɔ

Nettie enjoyed Li Jin's formality to an extent—it was like playing tea party when she was a girl—but she tired of it quickly.

<<This painting,>> said Li Jin, <is a painting of the sadneß of Zhou Enlai.>>

The painting was a 21st-century Chinese abstract. It had no recognizable shapes. The painting revealed its meaning through texture and color.

It was like listening to the Maßey Hall, Toronto, Halloween performance of James Gang from 1976. It's all through a haze, but the sound is still beautiful, albeit fuzzy and a little tin-scrapy from old tape deterioration before it was ever digitized.

The poor sound quality, if anything, enhances the great abstract qualities of Joe Walsh's guitar playing. Back in the day, he was an amazing weaver-together of obscure and well-known musical references, quoting a folk tune here, an Œðer rock anthem there, a bit of claßical music here, and then—blam!—into full frontal aßault in a *serious* way. Early Joe Walsh with James Gang was *serious*. *Deep*. Lyrics-like-Neil-Young serious. And then he was acquired by the Eagles, Inc. He had taken a LeBron-like payout and joined the enemy. He had a new pension plan with the Eagles, Inc. ►Johnny Come Lately◄, or whatever that horrid song was, was the end, as far as anyone could go. It was the perfect ending, like ►Running on Empty◄, which should have ended Jackson Browne's career. Then Daryl Hannah wouldn't have been around. She could have been spared her ordeal.

Walsh, though, on Halloween 1971, was especially brilliant. He soared among the great guitar gods. But he was part Midas and part Icarus, and only Daedalus was destined to escape.

►You're Gonna Need Me◄ especially soars. The acoustic songs after that would benefit from higher fidelity, but they are still lovely—particularly the haunting melody of ►Ashes, the Rain and I◄. Walsh's most sublime moment. The most sublime moment in the lives of hundreds of fans that night. Walsh had that sort of transportive power with James Gang. But no one steps away from the James Gang. Look at what happened to Tommy Bolin. Deep Purple and then the two mighty solo albums, *Teaser* and *Private Eyes*.

Private Eyes is like *Barnstorm*. A culmination. Both artists' popular breakthroughs seemed leß original than their work before. Listen to Walsh on ►The Bomber◄. He was intent.

He was in his tent. He was intense.

<<I don't know,>> said Nils. <<I prefer pictures of pretty things—bowls of fruit, bales of hay, landscapes, horses, family portraits.>>

<<Philistine!>> replied Li Jin.

<<Phil is tiny,>> replied Nils.

<<Enough!>> said Li Jin, sternly. Do not be disrespectful, young man. Michel, you must control your junior!>>

Nils was Michel's? Michel had never thought of their relationship that way. But if Nils's behavior reflected on Michel, then Nils had better reflect Michel's ideology and behavior.

So much mimesis.... Michel couldn't focus anymore. He closed his eyes.

When he opened them, he was in front of a new painting and was being told it was of hummingbirds, though all Michel saw were red blurs against blue morning glories.

The hummingbirds were symbolic. They were rapid-fire brushstrokes that perhaps were lettering of some sort. They may have been ideographs, but Li Jin had Michel standing so close to the painting that his nose almost touched it. Michel found focusing on the fore-shortened foreground very difficult.

Michel realized that Li Jin must have gone to the Americas at one time if he had painted such hummingbirds. Hummingbirds only lived in the Western Hemisphere, except, perhaps for a few in a zoo. Unleß they'd escaped and established a wild population elsewhere, the way cherry-headed parrots had established a flock on Telegraph Hill in San Francisco. The film *The Wild Parrots of Telegraph Hill*, directed by Judy Irving and starring Mark Bittner, first shown in 2003 at the Austin Film Festival, was also Chris Michie's last project before he died of melanoma. Michie, a former guitarist for Van Morrison, wrote the musical score.

Hummingbirds were themes in many pieces of art, though, and beautiful birds were so common in Chinese painting that one might imagine hummingbirds included. They did not appear *en maße* in Chinese art until the great opening of China to the West in the 20th and 21st centuries, though they may have appeared as exotics earlier than that.

➔H . . . ird . . .🡇

🡅ɱoo . . . wəlꟻ🡄

hover th➔ ❀⇒

Seals applaud in a nearby croft, where they were raised as orca food until the ban.

Hummingblurs buzz by.

If you surround your ¢elgh with morning glory, hummingbirds will come.

Better yet:

> Your morning glories
> overwhelm the world in blues
> that hummingbirds drink.

That's haiku, man. This is Lin Jin, a Chinese Prince. You are an idiot citing haiku to him.

Hummingbloozz know no national boundaries, Michel. And haiku is a form like any Œðer. They've learned the form of baseball—I'm sure haiku is no big deal. These are not Nippophobes.

Nils's admonishing Michel struck Michel as funny. He began to laugh. <<Right you are, Nils.>>

Hummbooze was paßed around again. No matter where Michel stood, the painting would not come into focus.

A rare painting to reveal such a rare quality.

Hummblurrybuzz and then before a flower, stuck in midair like a statue suspended by some invisible reverse magnetism. The wings are invisible, but the bird, briefly, can be seen in toto.

<<Bad Toto!>> yelled Dorothy. <<Drop that hummingbird!>> Toto did, and the surprised bird flew off, ruffled but unharmed.

Dorothy was told to leave by Li Jin. She never got farther than this.

<<Us?>> haxed Michel.

<<You need Cui Zongzhi to dißuade Nils of his cynicism. I find much promise in you, Michel. Nils is a screwball. Nettie sees it, too. Nils is isolating his ¢elgh. I'd recommend preventing that. No one needs to make enemies of the benign. Just don't make them your confidantes. That would cure them of their benignity and replace it with some sort of malignity. Easily avoided collisions should be.>>

<<Sounds like a fortune cookie,>> said Nils. Li Jin spun around and slapped Nils mightily. Nils spun around and crashed to the ground.

<<What?>> haxed Nils, taken aback, as he got up. <<That's Chinese, right?>>

<<You reduce centuries of philosophy to a fortune cookie? You are a stupid man.>>

<<Yeah, well, want to know what you are?>>

<<He is the Prince of Ruyang, and a favorite nephew of Emperor Xuanzong,>> said Nettie. <<He rates your deepest respect, Nils. Only by his graces are you still here and not outcast like Dorothy.>>

<<We're all just human beings trying to perfect our ¢elghs, Nettie. Me, too. Do you think Li Jin is perfect, or that Cui Zongzhi is? No—they are both humans on this path through existence. We are all flawed, so why single me out for ridicule? I am just like you, only different.>>

<<You don't like art or music,>> she said.

<<That's not tue.>>

<<Okay.>>

Buster Blurryhum flew by his face. Nils swatted at it.

<<You're swatting at a hummingbird?>> haxed Nettie, completely shocked. <<What kind of a man are you? You take out your frustrations on creatures far small and meeker than you.>>

<<I'm meek.>>

Michel laughed so hard that wine shot up through his nose. <<Come on, you idiot,>> Michel said to Nils. <<Thank the kind prince for his hospitality, and let's get going.>>

<<What? Before we see the rust of his art collection? I was hoping to see a painting of a recognizable subject, not just blurbuzzers.>>

<<Those ▶blurbuzzers◀ are my favorite birds,>> replied Nettie. Slam! For sure Nils wouldn't try ✹hitting✹ Nettie, who had black belts in sixteen different martial arts.

Nils went to the water's edge and clammed up. He was lucky sea otters were banned like seals, or they'd have smashed him on their bellies and picked the yellow matter out with their teeth.

He stared out at the water for a long time, like Lily Briscoe, perhaps. Of course she had been painting it, as had Li Jin. Nils all of a sudden realized what he'd been doing wrong. He wasn't looking with the eyes of an artist. He had been looking for the mundane and, not surprisingly, had found it. Had he but looked, he'd have noticed.

Now it was too late. Li Jin would forever think Nils an idiot. Someday, somehow, he'd have to make it up to Li Jin.

Now—just the water. Watch its colors dance in the light. How could a painter ever catch it right? The sight was too great for mirrors to hold. They shattered. And the glaß shards subshattered again and again until turned to sand for the ocean's beach.

When tapped on the shoulder, Nils stood up and turned away, changed somehow, even if not much. Perhaps that's the best any of us can do. Or we can keep running—the party always goes on—with us or not—the spawning continues—no single salmon matters.

Nils stared into the gaping maw of the abyß when he stared out into the ocean. It spat shells and pieces of colored glaß at him. He began to collect spirals and blue and red.

Nils went into his yurt—he'd only gone in there before after being found in Nettie's.

He lashed the spirals together with twine. He glued the colored glaß to strips of leather cut to the same length as the twine. He braided them together with a handle, and then flogged his ¢elgh like a member of Opus Dei; however, he was not an Opus Deist, not even a supernumerary.

As the shells and blasts tore into his back, he began to feel stronger—he knew he could withstand the tortures of living.

He was tiring of being laughed at. He flayed his ¢elgh raw and then wept. He curled into a fetal ball and slept.

While Nils slept, Li Jin crept into the yurt with a bucketful of liquid lemon salts and a bucketful of aloe vera.

When he entered the yurt, he saw that Nils was asleep, so Li Jin painted Nils's back with a soft-bristled brush.

Meanwhile Michel and Nettie traveled to meet Cui Zongzhi. They aßumed Nils would meet them after he'd licked his wounds a while.

Michel thought of his former life, when he was an emißary and then a bureaucrat and then a clown. His life's trajectory paralleled the Buddenbrooks'. But Nils was developing a talent for shooting his ¢elgh in the foot that rivaled Plaxico Burreß's.

Nettie was remembering something from Sun Tzu's *The Art of War*.

Michel turned back. He'd lost Polymesus years earlier through benign neglect. He didn't want to lose his friend Nils, even if Nils was a pain in the aß. Friends forgave each Œðer, and the three of them had been through enough. No one could be left behind. He walked in on Li Jin slathering cooling, healing aloe vera gel on Nils's back where the lacerations had torn Nils up pretty badly.

A community took care of its weakest, and right now Nils was in need of his community. So, when Michel walked in, he said nothing. He respected Li Jin's incredible peace offering to Nils. The love Li Jin showed Nils, even though Nils annoyed the piß out of Li Jin, was Christlike, or Buddha-like, perhaps. Whatever, it was holy. That sort of transcendent love is what religion is supposed to give us. And not for the price of a check in the collection plate, but for *our* sakes. For our peace.

It was the Good Samaritan again, wasn't it? That story finds its way into many cultures in many different ways. So does the Prodigal Son. The parables are not even about forgiveneß. They transcend it. With loved ones, forgiveneß is aßumed but should be treated with utmost respect.

The utmost insect? A praying mantis? A walking stick? A scarab beetle?

There was the Nils brain, coming back to life. Michel had a reason for smiling. Nils was Michel's Bartleby.

Nils was wondering if Li Jin knew Shih Tzu maßage.

Michel laughed. <<That'd be for dogs,>> he said between gusts of laughter.

<<I thought that was Sun Tzu.>>

<<No—Sun Tzu wrote *The Art of War*. Shih Tzu is a dog. Shiatsu is maßage, and it is Japanese at that, though it is derived from Chinese *tuina*.>>

<<I thought a tuina was a moth. Well, can I get a maßage from that old war dog?>>

<<You just did. The aloe vera is still glistening.>>

<<Li Jin is brilliant. He made us a pitcher of margaritas and used some liquid lemon salts to coat the lips of the glaßes. Really delicious. He thought I might be tiring of rice beverages. Man, he is smart.>>

<<And very forgiving. If it'd been me and you'd insulted me as you did him, I'd have rubbed the lemon salts in the wound and made drinks out of the aloe vera instead.>>

<<Same thing only sideways.>>

<<Okay, Libby the Kid. I just hope you were kind to Li Jin in response.>>

<<Oh, certainly. He is my hero now.>>

<<So no more flay of soul?>>

<<No—I worked it out. It had gotten under my skin, but it's gone now. The monkey on my back that was my burden has been beaten. It won't return.>>

<<Are you mobile? Can you come with Nettie and me to meet Cui Zongzhi?>>

<<I thought you guys already went.>>

<<No—we turned around. I didn't want to go without you. We three need to stick together here. No one will be left behind.>>

Nils dropped a tear. <<Thanks, Michel. That means so very much.>>

<<Hey—we're friends. That's what friends do. But if I catch you tearing up your back again, I'll give you a belly and face to match. Stupidest thing in the world—that Opus Dei shit.>>

<<I'm not an Opus Deist.>>

<<Well, whatever the shit is. It's stupider than alien symbionts.>>

<<Hey—I thought those actually existed,>> said Nils, drying his eyes with the back of his hand.

<<The real ones did, but many were fakes.>>

<<Which?>>

<<Oh—it was a long time ago. I don't want to think about it. It just brings up bad memories. Anyway—yes or no—can you travel?>>

Li Jin walked back in with food for Nils.

<<Can he travel?>> haxed Nettie.

Li Jin shook his head. <<Not today. In two or three days, maybe. Right now any

movement just rips open the skin again.>>

<<Thank you, Li Jin. I can take over with the aloe vera if you are tired.>>

<<I never tire, at least not physically. But I am emotionally drained. I will sleep if you keep an eye on him. He'll need gel every hour, more if he's uncomfortable. I will bring a pitcher of margaritas for you and him. If you want more, all the fixings are in the icebox in the main house.>>

Nettie picked up the soft-bristle brush and began painting the wall of Nils's back with aloe gel.

He groaned with pleasure—not, not pleasure, really—more like the relief of pain, which is akin to pleasure but sometimes is even sweeter.

<<Let me know when you get tired>>, said Michel to Nettie. <<I'll help you.>> So, like an old chore-splitting couple, they decided when it came to soft animal air, to just split their ends.

Nettie's was taken in silence.

Michel thought Nils might be bored, so he told Nils a story. Nettie slept in the corner, waiting for her next turn, thinking of what to say. She'd been close to Nils once. She'd held him inside her ¢elgh. But she was a loner. She couldn't hold anything without feeling smŒðered by it eventually. Weapons were it for her. Her guns would expreß their ¢elghs honestly. Their blasts were never aimed at her. They always protected her.

But here she was—buried in the earth. What an odd life or death or whatever it was she was doing here. What it was no longer seemed to matter.

She needed to sleep. She needed to paint Nils's back.

Tom Sawyer had to whitewash a wall, did some of it, but then tricked Œðer kids into paying him for the privilege. Vintage Mark Twain.

But Nettie didn't want to get out of it. She needed to paint Nils's back for her own sake as much as for his.

Michel began, <<Once upon a time a man had seven sons. The seven sons haxed him, <Dad, will you tell us a story?> So the Dad began, <Once upon a time a man had seven sons. The seven sons haxed him, <<Dad, will you tell us a story?>>>>>

It was a story Michel remembered his own father telling him. Usually, by the seventh or eighth level, Michel would lose track of where he was and would spin off into the green vertiginous spirals that protected the destination.

<<Just kidding there, Nils,>> said Michel, painting gently. <<Would you like an Œðer margarita?>>

<<Please. Ow.>>

<<Don't talk—it affects your shoulders and back! Okay, the story. The story. I want to tell you a story about a man named Story. Story is the story. Character equals plot. Foreshadows the grave.

<<Grave plots spot the landscape of the old Scaglin Hills. And one day old Story is wandering, meandering through the leas and thickets of a pastoral hillock.

<<The men marched with torches through the leas and were looking for that old Story. They had all seen him before and remembered what he'd done.

<<So they were going to trap him and make him do what they wanted forever.

<<Then they caught him. They rended him. They rendered him.

<<He died. Or just about. The end.>>

<<That sucked,>> said Nils, grimacing.

<<Just wait. Its profundity will reveal its ¢elgh to you gradually. You'll see.>>

<<Okay. Get Nettie.>> Nils groaned.

<<No, I'm sorry. I'll tell you a better one.>> Michel began to paint an Œðer coat.

<<A small town once existed in which no one wanted to be first anywhere, so no one moved. They all died. The end.>>

<<Brilliant. How about something longer?>> Nils said, no wincing even evident in his voice anymore. His margarita was helping.

<<All right. ►I'm Not Whelping◄.>>

<<Go ahead.>>

<<Hugo Whelping was born in Andernacht, Germany, on the same day as the poet Charles Bukowski. As they lay in cribs next to each Œðer, the infant Bukowski, born with tobacco juice for amniotic fluid, spat some of the bilious goo at Baby Whelping. It landed with a splat, square on his forehead.

<<Hugo Whelping grew up in silence. His parents were deaf-mutes who danced the softshoe. Nary a sound was heard.

<<Hugo Whelping was cool. Nothing riled him. He was aloof, and so attracted a following. Everyone loved him until they got to know him. If they'd drunk his blood to honor him, though, they'd have gotten drunk on it. If they'd eaten his flesh, they'd have gotten high, but eventually the followers went in Œðer directions.

<<Hugo Whelping liked carrying the followers while they were around. He'd put them on his back and would show them Nashville, Tenneßee, where he'd grown up on Brewer Drive, a nicely foreshadowing addreß.

<<Hugo Whelping would extravasate those who annoyed him. And then he'd leave the bodies there to rot.

<<The smell overcame everyone after a while. Jefferson spread lime to no avail.

<<They caught Hugo Whelping and tied him to a spit and were going to rotißerie the guy, but he focused and burned his ropes first and escaped. He'd freed his ¢elgh, but thereafter forever he'd have to look back over his shoulder to make sure he maintained a safe distance. This terrified the guy, who inserted his fingers into his ears.

<<That blocked the sound. Good deal, he thought.

<<He thought a good deal.>>

<<Ugh,>> was Nils's response.

<<Okay. One more try. Maybe this one will turn over when I kickstart it.>>

Michel heard Nils groan again, but then Nils said the word ▶Sportster◀, so Michel figured he was okay. Nils would be thinking about buckin' bronco motorcycles and wouldn't feel the brushstrokes. Michel was almost done with the layer anyway.

Michel turned Nils green with aloe, and tried to think of an Œðer story. He couldn't come up with one, though, so he thought he'd just wing it and see if Nils would notice.

<<Okay, here's something called ▶The Mend◀. It stars an actor who is on the lam after seeing a woman on the side. But he'd been on the schneid ever since he'd run off with his favorite pair of kitchen scißors, a cleaver, an apron, and a chef's hat.

<<<Cut it out!> was the motto of the scißors.

<<<Stick to what you're separated from,> said the cleaver.

<<<I'll tell you about the thrill of the krill,> said the apron to his shrimpy cousin.

<<But the chef's hat topped them all. Until the day he ✹popped✹ a seam. The next day he ✹popped✹ two, and within a month he seemed to be practically pooped with

💥popping💥 and was threatening to become unseemly.

<<He began arguing after a new unseamly fashion, but no one but the back of the head noticed.

<<The back of the head began to feel a chill. The hands removed the hat and brought it to the Schneider, who said it was nothing. The hat was soon on the mend. The Schneider replaced the seams, and the hat was saved.>>

<<Enough, already,>> said Nettie, mercifully. Michel was glad to relinquish the brush.

<<I was wondering while I was rusting,>> said Nettie to Michel, <<who all comes down here.>>

<<The adventurous departers?>>

<<Perhaps—I heard nothing about any bankers, for example.>>

Michel laughed. <<Bankers? They'd never make it—they probably financed the Kraken.>>

<<Well, they financed Hitler, so I wouldn't be surprised.>>

Nils groaned. He wanted her attention. Michel relented. He would not interrupt unleß he found a way to enisle Nettie's qualming. Nettie put down the brush and began waving a paper fan at Nils's back. That air cooled the aloe gel, and Nils was in dog heaven.

Michel's eyes went towards the bedroll by the wall, but the rust of him went and stumbled around in the dark outside. A breeze refreshed him although he was tired. His eyes came 'round and up and looked out on the lake, where the first haze of morning light was looming on the horizon.

Michel cast his eyes out upon the water, and they rode the waves back to him.

He figured he'd put his foot in his mouth, a symptom of hoof-and-mouth disease. Maybe it was just this underground postmortem living. Disintegration. The disintegration of the ¢elgh as an active unit means….

Disintegration or disambiguation? The latter is wicked, so choose the former. Tell all the estivating students to develop ¢elghs worthy of disintegration.

If you need help, listen to Chris Youlden and Kim Simmonds trading leads on Percy Mayfield's ▶Memory Pain◀ back in '69. Most of Foghat played behind them—Roger Earl, of course, the great drummer. Lonesome Dave on rhythm and Tony Stevens on baß.

Michel could hear the yearning calls carry out over the waves—cries of pain like the wailing of Majnun—hoping someday the right ears would hear.

The left have something in them—wax, perhaps. They thought they were hearing Led Zeppelin.

Mayfield also wrote ►Hit the Road Jack◄, the huge Ray Charles hit, and ►Please Send Me Someone to Love◄, which the great Freddie King offered up a magnificent heartfelt version of. We couldn't love him enough to prevent his early departure, though.

Add that song to the Magical Music Tour, though. Follow the music. Fellow musicologists, thank you! Bleß you! Music is transformative! You understand!

The homage is but a guidepost to the soundtrack, is but a *Signpost to New Space*, as Jerry Garcia might have said.

And the prose never wanders.

And the pros never wonder.

And we can settle into our doom and gloom and deaths soon enough, but what say you we take Dylan Thomas's advice and ►Rage!◄—we can stand up and yell until they tell us to shut up. But I'll outlast them. And I have more to say. ɕActually, I have nothing to say, especially in first person,ɔ thought Michel, and his blood began to simmer down.

An Œðer stovetop disaster averted!

The waves were magnetized. That was it!

Just like the royal families. Snacking on royal jelly on crustleß toast.

<<Listen to Angus Young's guitar on Marcus Hook Roll Band's version of ►Shot in the Head◄, the original version of the song that is one of the gems in *Lion's Share*, Savoy Brown's ninth album. Marcus Hook Roll is fun—you can hear the transition from the Easybeats to AC/DC. It also has a cartoon glam element to it like Sweet and Slade. Despite the cartooneneß, the songs have great hooks, just like Sweet and Slade. Nothing was there to judge the lyrics anymore—they just rolled on. The album answers Lennon's ►Power to the People◄ by protesting that ♪people don't have the power to change things anymore♫ and counters ►Revolution◄ with ►Red Revolution◄. The album sounds like the mißing link between the Beatles' *White Album* and T. Rex. The *Born to Boogie* era.

Waves kept coming, bringing music. Michel thought he must be losing his mind. Was it posthumous disintegration?

He had to see all Eight and then go. His thousands of thoughts and millions of feelings could not be contained down in the center of the Earth. They were too large and too many to be confined.

The exact quantity was never confirmed.

That's just fine.

The sarcasm of Marcus Hook Roll Band's ►Ape Man◄ would stack up nicely against the sarcasm in the Kinks' song ►Apeman◄.

Michel was transfixed. He could not move so long as such inter-rusting music rode in on the waves of his memories.

The dawn shimmered into his eyes. He turned them away and returned them to the yurt. Inside, he lay down at the wall and rusted into the bedroll.

Nettie was still fanning Nils with one hand. With the Œðer she began to stir up the aloe gel again. She did not look at Michel when he returned.

A few hours later she woke him up and pronounced that it was time to go. It was midmorning and they needed to meet up with Cui Zongzhi, the cynic, the Eight's first baseman. It all went through him.

Never trust a cynic. Cynics don't know what they're talking about.

Don't trust anybody.

Don't trust me. Maybe someday I'll up and hurt you. Perhaps I won't mean to.

<<Come on, we've gotta go.>>

He was dead weight in her hands. ɕOh, no. Not this game,ɔ she thought. So she kneed him in the stomach and dropped him. <<Come on! I've got to help Nils, still!>>

Michel remembered.

He got up and packed up his stuff and was ready to go.

She'd found a wheelchair for Nils left out for them—a gift from Li Jin?

Nils was wrapped up in aloe-soaked mesh bandages and had obviously been able to sit down with relative ease. At least Michel had never heard him. But Michel was not the only one who noticed.

Pardon the research aßistants. Nils had to be pushed—the chair was manual—so he looked pleadingly at Michel.

Michel smiled back. <<Yeah, sure, buddy. I'll push. It's good to see you feeling better.>>

Nils kept quiet until Michel went over a rock. <<Ow!>> The pain shot up Nils's spine!

Inexpreßible words shot into Michel's mind. ċSee? That's what I mean. Who's talking? Oh, I see. It's internal. For now. But as with a microphone at open mike night, everyone wants a turn or two. And everyone is inter-rusting, at least at first. Some folks even take to it. They are born entertainers. But even the Œðers have something inter-rusting to say as well. So long as everyone tells hir own story and tells it hir own way, as Kerouac suggested.ꜿ

<<So we have to sound like Kerouac? That's so gone!>> Michel imagined Nils would say.

<<No. That's not what I mean,>> Michel would say in response.

<<How far is it?>> haxed Nils from between clenched teeth. The bumps in the road were abrading his wounds against the back of the chair.

Nettie could hear the pain in his voice, so they held up in the shade of an enormous willow that wept over the edge of a bay.

The roots of the willow lolled large and had wrustled their way out of the ground. Everywhere around the tree, root outcroppings provided seats for Nettie and Michel. Nils lay down on his belly lengthwise between two parallel outcroppings, and Nettie, once she'd peeled his bandages off, got out the aloe and began to brush some onto Nils's back.

The roots were a bit nobby for her bony butt, so Nettie balanced on the backs of her thighs instead. Michel had more rear padding than Nettie anyway, so he initially planted him¢elgh on the root opposite. But when he saw that it was aloe time, he walked off a little farther and found a little nook between roots at the base of the tree. He could sit in there, back against the tree, arm on a root on either side, like it was a great armchair, like he was sitting on his throne, overseeing his land.

This felt natural. Perhaps he'd been a king in a previous life. Had that king been here, too? Would the Eight have known him?

Wouldn't they have told Michel, or do they their ¢elghs not know whose souls the old souls are?

He could sense a banquet hall before him. Knights sat on benches along long tables stretching out before him in a perfect half circle, left peripheral quoin to right peripheral quoin, text inclusive.

From this coign of vantage, he could contemplate his demise a little better. He could imagine his ¢elgh Beowulf, so he had no desire to see his companions slaughtered by a monster. Nay! He had returned only now that the monster, the Kraken's ¢elgh, had been killed and the world forever freed from its relentleß clutches.

The Kraken had been mistaken for many Œðer creatures—Neßie, for example—when that bit that had been seen had been but a tiny bit of one leg—the equivalent of a toenail clipping. And people feared the toenail clippings. Can one even imagine seeing an entire leg let alone the huge head with its malevolent stare and vicious beak? <<Few who had ever seen it survived to tell the tale.>> Those words resonated within Michel. He'd heard them before. This was happening again. Déjà vu.

He must have been king in a previous life—how else could he know what he knew?

Well, he knew he had to get back to the Gardens of Obsane Topiary. He had to find his mask again and pull from its beard a meßage. How he know this he didn't know. An Œðer memory from a past life, perhaps?

An Œðer past? Or an Œðer's past?

An Œðer's paßed.

And Œðers paßed.

Œðers' pasts.

Pests, all of them, thought Cui Zongzhi, shaking his head as he looked at the three overdue stragglers—one on wheels—approach his home—a log cabin that had grown over time and with addition into a labyrinthine structure than contained many rooms. Cui Zongzhi valued his inner space over the outer. He could go weeks on end without emerging. He would write. Drink and write. He liked to write about how stupid everything was. He never ran out of material to write about. Anything touched by human hands was eventually destroyed by them. That was a constant.

Say to a person: I prefer fall, winter and spring because you see me in summer. Who am I?

The Riddler from *Batman*?

No! They'd better not say that. That would cause Cui Zongzhi to attain the third level of annoyance immediately after having to rise to the first in response to the stragglers' very appearance and the second while waiting.

Say to them: I am found embracing serpents. Look for me in spring and summer, but never in fall or winter.

Who am I?

The Sphinx?

No! They had better not say that, either. If they love their mŒðers, they will not let the Sphinx live. They're probably very proud.

They have their pride, but the Sphinx no longer has its.

Say to someone: I'll hush you harshly at first, but you won't see it—you won't know more.

Nils seemed to think of his ¢elgh as a Latin lover.

<<Like Don Wan,>> Nettie would say.

Yes, this is how their meeting would go. Cui Zongzhi was sure of it. It would be inane. Nettie would not be an heuristic woman. And the *heuri*, as they are known, fill heaven and await the new souls in order to greet them, or so said many folks. Cui had no idea what lay beyond the great ocean. He had never felt compelled to find out. No matter where one went, people were stupid. They didn't read or consider art. They didn't know who governed them or why. Sheep. Lemmings headed for the cliff.

Or cockroaches, infesting the Earth forever. No use even trying to exterminate them. Stomp on them, and they come out smiling from underneath your boot and run away, laughing at you all the while.

Yes, it would be an inconvenience to have to deal with these knuckleheads. But Cui had agreed to see to the paßers-by when he'd accepted his home and his past. An occasional intruder just had to be tolerated. And, besides, what's that in the water?

Cui saw his favorite Beluga, Bob, bob up from below the surface. He could swear he saw Bob smile at him. Bob's eyes glistened as they stared directly into Cui's.

Cui Zongzhi thought Bob was just about the only old soul he could relate to.

A hummingbird buzzed by in front of Michel's face. He was taken aback. Trees. Flowers. They were nearing Cui Zongzhi's place.

The hummingbird landed on Michel's shoulder, and Michel recognized hir. This hummingbird held the soul of Michel's favorite carrier pigeon from his youth. His father had used carrier pigeons for his private correspondence.

Michel had a spool of thread in his belongings—▶Krapp's and Budd's Last Sewing

Notions◀ brand—a magic spool a thousand miles long. He wrapped the loose end around the hummingbird's left foot and the hummingbird left, homing for Michel's father's favorite private place—the Gardens of Obsane Topiary.

Michel held the spool end around a paperclip and let it fly. After the Eight, he'd be able to get to the Gardens the fastest way poßible by following the string. The hummingbird would be able to sense all the short cuts.

Isn't that Grimm? Not ▶The Brementown Musicians◀—I know that much.

No—Hansel and Gretel.

ċNot bad,ꜿ Cui told his ¢elgh. ċFor an old Chinese man to know Hansel and Gretel shows how much more open-minded I am than these Œðer jokers.ꜿ

ċ<<So you're all jokers,>>ꜿ Cui imagined Michel would say, now that Michel's attention was no longer on the homingbird.

<<That is not how I meant it,>> Cui would say. Nothing more. These interlopers were always beneath his dignity.

And they always had such tedious tales to tell. He felt like anyone at all could come down here these days. In the past only the most spirited souls could traverse the oceanside. Of course, they had had the Kraken to deal with. Maybe that was better. The Kraken brought the more robust. Now he had to entertain a parade of the weak and dull.

He had suggested to the Œðer seven Immortals of the Wine Cup that they permit him to build razor-wire-lined obstacle courses for these lazy butts, but the Œðer seven had outvoted him seven to one.

Now get out of their way. Once they're past you and have turned their backs, then you can plunge…

…into the cold waters of Lake Michigan…

…deep into their backs, chilling their spines, rattling 'dem bones. Then wipe it off on…

…that make a fortune by proceßing debits instantly and taking three days to proceß credits. This results in additional overdrafts, which they happily collect. An, the moneychangers! Jesus had an opinion about them, too. They're the only ☼aßholes☼ ☼aßholish☼ enough to rile the aß of the holy aß-riding superstar of pop religion—Jesus H. Christ, ▶H◀ for ▶Holy◀, one presumes…

…scams! Everywhere, scams! Cui was angry. He set a few traps for trolls and then finished readying his person for the arrival of this latest set of surface goofballs who just refused to listen to the soundest advice on how to stay up there and fooled their ¢elghs into thinking here was the place to be. Cui laughed. Here! Imagine that! He couldn't.

He imagined ▶Death and Angels◀ flying around—an old Dan Stuart song from the original *Green on Red* album, and then he imagined Green on Red and Rain Parade playing ▶Cheap Wine◀ in Japan.

That would have been nice wine. Cheers! Cui lifted his wine cup in toast to the air. Okay, he thought, slamming back the glaß and then an Œðer and then an Œðer. Bring 'em on! I'm almost ready for those rapscallions! What is a rapscallion? Easy. A scallion is an onion, onions stink, and rap is music without melody. A rapscallion thus must be a tone-deaf musician.

A rapscallion is a rascal, and a rascal is a raccoon, and a raccoon is a bandit or a burglar.

Thus, tone-deaf musicians are bandits and burglars. They steal from us our time and attention. Any musician who needs pitch correction isn't making the right pitch to gain entrance into our homes.

Call the authorities and have hir arrusted for highway robbery, provided you live on the highway. Nothing so low as a bandit should ever be seen on a highway. Jesus was never attacked by raccoons. No great prince or lord or lady or queen or king or princeß was ever attacked by raccoons. No off-key troubadour or balladeer ever lived long among the lords. They could sometimes fool the new creatures into praising their tone-deafneß as innovative atonality, but the innovatively atonal could tell the difference. They could elucidate it.

They will be stiff dancers, but they will keep time. They just don't know how to dance melodically. To move in expreßive sequences with both subtle and abrupt variances in duration and intensity in addition to pitch—that's real dancing. Without melody, it becomes mechanical.

But aren't they machines? All of them. Even those who make it here, who get to witneß these mighty creatures, Sovereigns of the Planet, playing in the water like regular fun-loving families, the young prodding the old, the old responding with audible scolding. If only these interlopers had half the humanity that the whales did….

The large whales rule with a quiet dignity, though. They tolerate the playful beluga, the porpoises, and the orcas the way people tolerate their own young, though it's true that the orcas are kind of like the juvenile delinquents of the whale world. But here they do well. With their wishing wells. Better than oil wells, which is about all any of the surface people ever saw in a whale. Almost extinct by the 21st century. Shit. When the Kraken connected the oceans, though, whales came down and hid forever from the Faroese and Japanese, whose death sentences for whales were eternal, like Valhalla and the Emperors.

Michel du Jabot—that's French, I think. At least not Faroese or Japanese. Not until they stop whaling. Even Mishima's never come down. It'd be inter-rusting to meet him. But that whaling thing is really no good. Not anymore. It's like ✹hitting✹ something that's already said <<Ow!>> a hundred times. What would the point be? How could that be enjoyable on any level for anyone?

Nils? Is that Faroese? It's Nordic, for sure. Oh, wonderful. A saboteur. A mole. An aßaßin. A spy. An harpooner.

<<Hi, I'm Anne Harpooner.>>

<<Why are you here?>>

<<I want to meet your new friends.>>

<<No, you can't.>>

<<Tough. I'm here.>>

<<But they'll think I'm the only monk with a new girlfriend.>>

<<You are no fucking monk. Rhymes with, though. Drunk.>>

<<And you are here why?>>

<<To meet the new folks. Might be inter-rusting.>>

<<No. it won't. I think you're a parasite. I mean, a sight for a pair of sore eyes.>>

<<Store eyes. Each is the front window into a retail establishment. The one on the left plays jazz, the one on the right plays blues. One store sells music; the Œðer, literature. One is confident, and the Œðer is the mild wild mold world they are turning into Poe's Haunted Palace.>>

<<Except in Poe the dancers become wildly out of control. If you watched jazz dancers or blues dancers, you'd see devotees shimmying to the slightest polytonal shifts, ricocheting to rimshots, every vocal nuance expreßing its ¢elgh through hands and arms, the baß and drums controlling the libido, and the spine belonging to the guitar and horn. These dancers felt every note, every intonation.>>

<<That's not true in Poe. In Poe they're just nuts,>> said Cui. <<♪I say ▶cool◀ as a rule, but sometimes ▶bad◀ is *bad*♫.>> He was singing something he'd heard Dave Edmunds sing on TV and then had wanted to sing again here for the whales. Edmunds had been fun, playing much of the Love Sculpture, Rockpile, and the MAM albums. Edmunds, like Jonah, liked W(h)ales. He had connected well with the Sovereigns.

<<Do you have any Jimmy Rogers?>> haxed Anne Harpooner. <<I want to hear ►Walking by My Ȼelgh◄.>>

<<I wish *you'd* go walking by your ¢elgh,>> muttered Cui.

<<What?>> haxed Anne Harpooner.

<<Never mind. Just never mind,>> Cui replied. <<Now amscray before the iotsidays owshay upay.>>

<<I don't understand Chinese.>>

<<Oh, good god. Go away. Just go away.>>

♪Too late, too late♫ sang Joe Turner, here they come.

Anne Harpooner was gone. They had not seen her. And even if they had, so what? They knew nothing. Just more damn interlopers.

Antelopes?

Post loops. Okay. Time to be the host. Hello, interlopers!

<<Welcome, dear guests. Let us know if we can get you a drink or anything.>>

Nils groaned. <<Is that the royal pwep?>>

<<It is a pleasure to meet you as well,>> replied Cui.

<<Never mind him, Cui Zhongzhi,>> apologized Michel. <<He's just an aß with no manners.>>

<<Does he drink wine?>>

<<Oh, yeah. He's a drunk all right.>>

<<That is too bad. To be a drunk is fine. To not have manners is permißible. But to be a drunk without manners is inexcusable.>>

<<What would you call basic drinking etiquette?>> haxed Nettie. <<Nice to meet you, by the way.>>

<<Ah, young lady. You have manners. How nice. I would say drinking etiquette means, first, that you never throw up on a friend. Second, any damage you do, you pay for right away. Third, keep a civil tongue. Fourth, don't be maudlin. Fifth, don't argue with the illogical—it's a waste of your time. Sixth, be of good cheer. You can be a miserable

SOB somewhere else. Seventh, don't do any drunken shopping—you will bring home items the purpose of which you will never decipher. Eighth, don't put any law enforcement personnel in a position in which they are seen to be observing your contumacy. If you do, you are forcing them to arrust you. And tenth, don't obseß about patterns aloud. Keep your need for perfect symmetry to your ¢elgh or put it into your art. Just don't talk about it.>>

Nettie chuckled. Michel wasn't really listening. He was thinking that Nils was becoming quite a liability. Perhaps something ought to be done.

<<I think Nils needs some morphine,>> said Michel to Cui out of earshot of Nils.

<<No problem.>> Cui reached into his pocket, pulled out a needle, and shot Nils in the butt. Nils was asleep before he ever figured out he'd been doped.

They carried the idiot into Cui's double-door log mansion. The jazz side. Mose Allison's song ►Parchman Farm◄ was playing. Nils felt a little more energized for a second, but then the morphine carried him off in slumber. He was working as server in a prison meß hall, serving prisoners pasties. The intercom was playing a Muzak version of ►Parchman Farm◄ that sounded like a lullabye.

And then the Great Convergence occurred: the blues side, by some amazing coincidence, was playing Bukka White's song ►Parchman Farm◄, the song that had inspired Mose Allison's. And then the two songs converged, separated, and then reconverged. It was like listening to a John Giorno reading. Giorno would read his poetry over a recording of his ¢elgh reading his poetry over an Œðer recording of his ¢elgh reading his poetry—perhaps even more layers than that. The words would converge and then diverge in overlapping waves of attack, like canon rounds.

Yes, of course, the interlopers attack poor Cui Zongzhi. They infiltrate his domicile. They mean him ill. Everyone does. Whether ze realizes it or not.

There's gold in that ore. Some who went West were ore-gone and so named the place ►Oregon◄.

<<And that's one doggone tale,"" said Nettie. <<Very amusing. Let's movie this party along.>>

Like a magpie. Chatter.

<<Do you have any Bettye LaVette? I want to hear some music by women for a change,>> said Nettie.

<<Why sure.>> Cui put on her version of Chris Youlden's ►I'm Tired◄. <<It's nice to hear a good song hold up under many different interpretations,>> said Cui. <<Youlden sure could write some songs.>>

After the Bettye LaVette, he put on Savoy Brown's recording of Chris Youlden's ▶Needle and Spoon◀. Cui wondered what Œðer recordings he had of women singing Savoy Brown songs. He was certain quite a few must exist. But that would have to wait.

The morphine was beginning to wear off of Nils. He was going to have a maßive headache when he awoke unleß he was weaned off the morphine, so Cui gave him an Œðer shot, albeit a smaller dose.

Nils was dreaming about a giant triangle suspended in the air in the desert. The triangle was hung from a mesa, and people could ring it in protest of gun violence.

<<Let Freedom Ring,>> was the theme.

>>One song by one woman? That's all?>> haxed Nettie.

<<Well, here is an Œðer version of a song also done by Savoy Brown,>> and he played Big Mama Thornton's version of Willie Dixon's ▶Little Red Rooster◀. In terms of the song's sexuality, this is the definitive version. Big Mama exudes a powerful, musky sexuality that inspired Janis Joplin's. Œðer versions, especially Howlin' Wolf's, or the Rolling Stones', might have been more famous, but no one owned that song like Big Mama.

After that, Cui played the Willie Dixon song owned by the great Koko Taylor—▶Wang Dang Doodle◀, which the Pointer Sisters also did. But Koko Taylor sang that song like her life depended on the urgency of its delivery. She was a helluva great blues singer.

After that, Nettie seemed content. Not many could come back from a one-two punch combo like that. Nettie's weapons, for one, were no match. Her arms were weak when compared with those women's voices.

Both Big Mama Thornton and Koko Taylor were so powerful that they could be heard over the sirens of Alabama and Chicago.

The blues were everywhere. Michel looked at the discs in the blues half of the house and started looking at some of the live performances.

Savoy Brown on March 20, 1971, at the Santa Clara County Fairgrounds in San Jose. What a rare find. Keyboardist and rhythm guitarist Paul Raymond had just joined the band. Drummer Ron Berg and baßist Andy Pyle were sitting in for the live gigs, but didn't join till the following year. And between the two Daves—Lonesome Dave and Dave Walker—the band had a singer named Pete Scott, who had some set of pipes on him. The same Pete Scott went on to sing for the Scottish prog outfit Beggars Opera. The last Michel had heard, Pete Scott had gone onto doing folk music or something. How amazing that so many great singers and musicians were in Savoy Brown. Only

Mayall and Zappa compared. Pete Scott with Savoy Brown is a treat, especially on the songs he brought in—►Crawdad◄, ►Losing Hand◄, and ►I'm a Bluesy Kid◄—that appear nowhere else in the Savoy Brown catalogue. Beggars Opera had been big in Germany and had charted there, but how Cui would have heard of Scott Œðer than through Savoy Brown was beyond Michel. With all the folks coming through and visiting the whales, maybe it felt like being Kim Simmonds, who, after all, was from Wales.

And that sort of pun was exactly what Cui was trying to avoid. These damned interlopers with their damned punning! As if the world were a funny place rather than God's penal colony.

Which, no doubt, the interlopers would joke about as a ►penile colony◄. *Well, Hardee Carl Jr. to that (send product placement monies to me c/o this publisher).*

Interlopers! They are trying to Calvino my italics! They'll not turn me abaft!

Michel wanted to be home among his books in his lighthouse. He was tiring of the excursion.

Cui and Michel, in fact, were tired of each Œðer before they ever met.

And Cui had no inter-rust in Nils whatsoever. That Nils was a parochial yokel was obvious to him.

Nettie, however, Cui actually found inter-rusting. How many armament experts did he ever have a chance to meet, after all, especially attractive young ones like Nettie?

She has such lovely arms.

But the Œðers? Interlopers! Octopus sympathizers, surely! Krakens, by Krag–Jørgensen! Krivoli Rog and Krk contemplate cohosting the underground Olympics!

Anne Harpooner walked back in at that moment.

ɐDamn!ɔ thought Cui. She's going to cramp my style with that lovely Durga—that sweet-many-armed gal.

He put on Big Mama Thornton's version of ►Rolling Stone◄ as bait. And as poison.

Anne Harpooner felt uneasy right away, tuned and left.

Cui had mad skills. He was getting old physically, but in everything else he was getting stronger.

His attraction to Nettie was getting to him: he was longing. And, golly, how he longed!

No! Even this moment was destroyed by bad punning!

Nils, meanwhile, had awoken and was watching the whales. <<Well, call me Ishmael,>> he said.

<<Okay. Come here so I can amputate your leg,>> replied Cui.

<<No need. I'm feeling much better. But I had a sense—who was that Œðer woman?>>

Destruction Mama
(a dark, slow blues)

A storm is brewing overhead.
Time to get to cover.
Before the lightning strikes
I'm going to find my ¢elgh an Œðer,
who can keep me safe from your storm,
someone who can hold me in her arms all night long
while you destroy the rust of the world,
destroy the rust of the world.

The frogs and locusts can descend
and I won't even notice,
for while you're hitting all my friends.
I won't be there at all.
I'll be far away in someone else's arms
and forgetting all about your charms
while you destroy the rust of the world,
destroy the rust of the world.

The Four Horsemen can trample over me—
War, Death, Famine, Pestilence—
but they'll have to hit me from behind
because I'm going now's I have a chance,
and I'm sure not turning back to see
you acting all high and mighty
while you destroy the rust of the world,
destroy the rust of the world.

The rapture can take 'em all away
and leave me alone in nuclear waste.
I'm not turning 'round
and I'm not going back.
I hope they take you when they go
and leave me here in peace
while you destroy heaven its ¢elgh,

and destroy the rust of the world.

While you try to destroy heaven and earth
and leave me here in your hell,
I'll be figuring how to get out
and to get with some beauty and truth
because your anger is ugly
and I don't like how you smell
while you destroy the rust of the world,
destroy the rust of the world.

Good bye, Destruction Mama.
I'm going back to my sanctuary.
No storms have ever touched the place.
The people there accept me.
I grew up in among them
and call the place my home.
I'll never see you again
destroy the rust of the world.

No one else had noticed Anne Harpooner, so Cui said, <<Only your friend here.>> Cui put on ▶Big Mama Swings◀. After that, Koko Taylor's ▶What Came First the Egg or the Hen◀.

Nettie seemed to perk up.

<<What was that?>>

<<Koko Taylor,>> answered Cui, pleased.

<<No—that dark blues song about ▶Destruction Mama◀.

<<Oh, just a malfunction. Ignore that. Those were just subtones beneath Big Mama.>> But Cui suspected Anne Harpooner was up to something. Cui wondered what he'd ever done to deserve a crazy stalker chick like Anne Harpooner. Or was she just attracted to the whales? She bŒðered him.

<<What are you doing?>> haxed Nettie of Michel all of a sudden. Michel was laying Nils down on the bed. Nils was asleep again. <<What did you do?>>

<<He looked like he needed a little more Sister Morphine.>>

<<He was just coming around!>>

<<No—he started off okay, but he began to collapse into his pain when he was watching the whales. He haxed me to.>>

<<I didn't hear.>>

<<No—he pleaded with his eyes for relief. I knew that look. If you don't believe me, just wait till he wakes up again and hax him.>>

<<What? In an Œðer twelve hours?>>

<<No—not at all. Shouldn't even be eight.>>

<<You're something else, Michel.>>

<<Look—I'd as soon be out of here in toto. But we're committed to this proceß. Might as well ride it out.>>

<<You're slowing it down.>>

<<Not me—he'd be useleß in agony.>>

Nettie just shook her head and returned her attention to Cui, who had meanwhile walked away and was out of sight.

<<Here, have one of these.>> Michel reached Nettie a bottle of Chuckhard Wood Cider.

<<Just like Edgar Allan Poe used to drink?>>

<<No—that was wood alcohol. This be cider,>> said Cui, reappearing.

<<Beside her?>>

<<No, just hand it to her.>>

ɕWhat a weisenheimer,ɔ thought Michel, though perhaps in terms leß polite. What else should one expect of the Thong Dynasty. Oops, he'd muttered that audibly.

<<Song?>> haxed Nettie.

<<Sure,>> said Michel. <<What are you going to sing?>>

<<Oh—well, sure—I'll sing ►God Bleß the Child◄, of course.>>

<<And when your friend awakens, what will you sing, Michel?>> haxed Cui.

Good one, thought Michel. Cui's got some spirit to him. He's a feisty mŒðer. Okay, then.

<<I'll sing the ▶Jumping Jack Flash◀/▶Youngblood◀ medley from *The Concert for Bangladesh*.>>

<<Excellent choice,>> said Cui, and Michel knew at that moment Cui was cool.

<<I'll do Don Pruston's vocal parts. And Jo Green's.>>

<<Don Nix?>>

<<I don't remember who was which.>>

<<Neither do I, but I recognize your pattern. The songs you pick. The juke box at the Blues Expreß on Chicago. I know your next pick. Tommy Bolin and Deep Purple's ▶The Dealer◀.>>

<<Actually, that was it. Very cool. I'm impreßed.>>

<<No, it wasn't—I just made all that up.>>

<<You think I couldn't tell?>>

<<Oh, you were playing me.>>

<<Correction—I was playing you back.>>

<<Touché.>>

<<Wait—you said Don Nix was at *The Concert for Bangladesh*?>>

<<Yes.>>

<<He wrote ▶Going Down◀?>>

<<Yes.>>

<<Awesome. Pruston and Nix connect Savoy Brown with Zappa.>>

<<Why go so far afield? Bobby Martin played keyboards in both bands. He was in the late 1980s *King of Boogie*-era Savoy Brown and in the mid-1980s *Them or Us*-era Zappa band,>> said Cui. <<He was in Zappa's infamous and ¢elgh-destructed big band.>>

<<The one that did versions of Cream's ▶Sunshine of Your Love◀, Zeppelin's ▶Stairway to Heaven◀, Johnny Cash's ▶Ring of Fire◀, and Hendrix's ▶Purple Haze◀?>>

<<And the Allman brŒðers' ▶Whipping Post◀.>>

<<Yes. That's a funny one. That started with a drunk fan yelling for the song at a concert in Helsinki in 1974. Zappa haxed the fan to sing it so that they could figure out how to play it, but the fan fell silent. Zappa said that it must have been a John Cage composition (an allusion to Cage's infamous ▶4:33◀, which consisted of four minutes and thirty-three seconds of incidental sounds while the pianist sat motionleß at the piano).>>

<<Connecting Zappa to Cage to Sun Ra and Kenneth Patchen!>>

<<Nice! Well, anyway, Zappa went into ▶Montana◀ then and changed the crop from ▶dental floß◀ to ▶whipping floß◀. I gueß the joke persisted and then Bobby Martin, ten years later, said he actually knew the Allman brŒðers song. So Zappa began to include it in the shows, with Bobby singing it, and they recorded it for *Them or Us*.>>

<<Well, here's an Œðer connection,>> said Cui. <<Bobby Martin played on Savoy Brown's album *Make Me Sweat*.>>

<<Ugh. Their worst album cover. GNP Crescendo's album designs just sucked eggs.>>

<<True, but the music's good. Anyway, Savoy Brown does Don Nix's ▶Going Down◀ on that album.>>

Michel was impreßed. Cui could go toe-to-toe with Michel on blues-and-rock trivia. <<Connections, eh?>>

<<Fractals,>> replied Cui.

ͼI have a snee, and I know how to use it,ͽ thought Nettie. ͼI could build a twisting stork pretty easily. What's wrong with Billie Holliday? Nothing! She was a genius! But perhaps they meant it was just too slow for a party like this. Okay—they want something more energetic. Early evening music, not late night.ͽ

<<Put on ▶Gimme Shelter◀, boys. I'm doing the Merry Clayton part. And then I'll do the Clare Torry vocal on ▶The Great Gig in the Sky◀.>>

She nailed them, perhaps a little to the Dagmar Krause side of the songs, but perfectly. She added extra meaning to the songs rather than reducing them. That is a rare style of interpretation, one that she and Michel and Nils all had a taste for in common.

Nothing could be thought of to top that, so the men fell silent. Nettie had unleashed her strongest weapon: her pseudo-ninny femininity persona. Of course, Michel and Nils were aware of her danger levels and knew when to make their ¢elghs scarce, but Cui didn't know Nettie. Poor chap. He was standing right in the way and made no effort to move.

She went Wang Dang Doodle all over him. Cui the Cur. Cui the Cad. She gave him a distemper shot. He tried to paint distemper back on her, but she wasn't primed for it, so it didn't take. She Joe Tex'd ▶I Gotcha◀ on him.

<<Damn, she's good,>> thought Michel, watching. He knew she had an arsenal of everything. If she hadn't been afraid of collateral damage, she'd have taken him already. Instead, she decided to steer clear of escalation.

She went, instead, for Izzy Stradlin's ▶Came Unglued◀ from Shibuya Kokaido in 1992. The mix was great for guitar and drums, but Izzy's vocals were muffled. The recording was an audience tape, apparently, but it gave a load of room for Nettie to sing the lead. And then to take up Koko Taylor's ▶I'm a Woman◀.

Cui came unglued. He stepped out of the way and let Nettie paß. She was as proud as Oedipus just then. She'd made the larger object move out of her way. Cui was the mountain, but she was dynamite!

Cui was Jimmy Reed's ▶Going to New York◀ and disappeared for good. For his good. What the hell was he staying down here with these whales for? Like they'd ever thank him. Like any of the seven Œðers ever would. Heck—they wouldn't even miß him.

Anne Harpooner confronted him as he was leaving. <<Here,>> he said, toßing her the keys to his home, <<watch over this for me till I return. If anyone haxes, tell hir I've gone to Broadway.>> He wasn't going to Broadway. He just wanted everyone to think so.

He had a place he wanted to be, a beautiful place, built about 50 years earlier, with a thatched roof, a bright pair of stained glaß windows, and a really nice balcony with two lovely spouts decorated with gargoyles. Unfortunately, the last time he had tried to visit, he had not been able to because the place had contracted feline distemper. One of the cats attacked of the dogs and put it in the hospital. The whole house was contaminated with one thing or an Œðer. The time before, the house was already engaged as a movie site. Cui had an idea for giving the house a third try before giving up on it altogether. Some houses would rather fall over than take in visitors. They'd rather collapse than co-lapse. One needs to take into account the building's history. Well, he'd see when or if he got there, but he knew he couldn't be here anymore. As so Cui vanished, as if into thin air.

Michel whistled silently and shook his head while he looked at the back of Nettie's head. Had she turned, he'd have stopped his gesture instantly. Wow, he thought, she smoked him.

<<Let's get Nils and go,>> said Michel.

<<That can't happen for a few hours, most likely. Two at the earliest.>>

<<Well, come on and help me catch a couple of fish for dinner.>> Michel had seen the tackle box in the foyer earlier.

<<Sure,>> and so they went fishing, completely lost in their own thoughts. Michel played Popa Chubby's version of ►Catfish Blues◄. Later, Jiao Sui knocked on the Savoy Brown-inspired skull-shaped door knocker. Michel's face stuck out the blues side, Nils's the jazz one. They both walked outside to greet Jiao. Nils was better, finally. They turned Jiao around by walking past him and turning. Jiao turned away from the skull, and Nettie emerged, although the whence was wooly.

<<Wh-wh-wh-where is keh-keh-Cui?>> stammered Jiao.

Nils chuckled, so Michel elbowed Nils in the ribs hard. Nils's flinch probably tore open a scar or two on his back. Nils stopped chuckling fast.

<<Learn some manners, shithead,>> said Michel to Nils under his breath. <<This man is ten thousand times greater than you'll ever be.>>

Indeed, Jiao Sui's eloquence was legendary.

<<We feast tonight?>> haxed Nettie, knowing something about Jiao Sui also. She knew that he felt comfortable with feasting. He and Tycho Brahe had been the subjects of an Ogden Nash poem. The poem said. <<Jiao's lips were loosed / when he was juiced / and feasting un¢elghconsciously.>> Jiao Sui lost his ¢elgh in his feasting.

Jiao nodded in response to Nettie. <<A huge feast. A pigeon banquet.>>

Halldór Laxneß's pigeon feast sprang to mind. But when everyone who's invited gets a pigeon, not everyone will want one, and Œðers will want as many free pigeons as they can get. Those traders already encroach on any sense of freedom that the experience could provide.

ͼInterlopers!ͽ thought Nils. <<Do we each get our own pigeon?>> he could not help but hax.

Jiao looked at him amused. <<Nuh-nuh-no. It-it-it's just cuh-cuh-called that.>>

<<No pigeons?>>

Jiao shook his head and grinned. <<Pigeons are rats with wings,>> he said, with no stammer at all.

Nils laughed. Michel and Nettie did, too. It was a nice moment.

Jiao had a way about him—he radiated niceneß the way Cui radiated crabbineß. Nettie like Jiao much better, of course, and so did Nils. Michel liked them all—he was trying to absorb these experiences as thoroughly as poßible. Why sleepwalk through them? Dive in! Immerse your ¢elgh!

Michel handed a bottle of Cui's rice wine to Jiao.

<<You can say what you like about Cui Zongzhi's temperament, but he does have excellent taste in wine.>>

They all drank of it.

<<Pl-ease f-follow,>> said Jiao, and he led them away from the skull to the tune of Hound Dog Taylor's ▶See Me in the Evening◀.

Nice. The four of them danced single-file, truckin' like in an R. Crumb cartoon, as they headed towards the feast at Jiao's. It was like Buñuel's *The Discreet Charm of the Bourgeousie*, but in reverse. <<Elmore James had nothing on this baby,>> said George Harrison, talking about his ¢elgh, but he could easily have meant it about Hound Dog Taylor, too.

Hound Dog Taylor. Good for what ails ya.

You want Miß Direction, hax Nettie.

You want misdirection, hax me.

How many robot grips does it take to transition an expletive construction from there to over here?

<<Really? For a moment we were thinking you'd be telling a story,>> said someone.

<<*Moi*?>> replied Michel, anchored in irony.

<<Do you even know how lucky you are to be you, dude?>>

<<What? Huh?>>

The stutterer was out of earshot, and Michel was within Nils's. Attack!

And the snow blinds go down and the duck blinds open and—

Duck! A snowball!—

to what purpose?

To scare the duck away. If it comes back, kill it. It was too stupid to want its own best inter-rusts. Sucker Duck, as he was known colloquially.

<<Sucker Duck?>> they'd say. <<We love you!>> But when he was on his runway, about to lift off, he'd hear them say, <<He'll never get on up.>> At first he thought they'd meant literal flight, but that was no ißue. No—they meant his penis. They were making fun of a cartoon animal's penis. Civilization doesn't get much lower than that, does it? Anything lower would be animal.

All of a sudden Brewer Phillips came running past, Hound Dog Taylor fast on his trail.

<<You come back here, Brewer! I'll beat you down, punk! I'll kill you for saying you slept with my woman just as soon as I'm done being killed by my wife for having a woman!>>

When Michel heard Anne Harpooner's voice calling for Hound Dog, Michel figured he'd get out of the way of this train-wreck-about-to-happen in a *real* hurry.

Her voice could sever a man's spine. And not in a good way. Hound Dog called her ▶Sadie◀ because of her love of *schadenfreude.*

Brewer flew past in a blur—Hound Dog had already shot him once before, a few years back, also over a crack about his woman.

Hey, maybe Hound Dog would shoot Sadie? Tell you, he was spry. Like Daevid Allen from Gong.

They would have been great drinking partners.

<<So long as he don't talk 'bout my women,>> said Hound Dog.

<<But one was his wife,>> you might be thinking.

<<Wife?>> haxes Brewer. <<Wife? Well, She-it!>> he said, referring to a famous Baltimore politician.

Black crows flew by.

<<Come on! Ted'll pick up the rust tomorrow!>>

They disappeared on out ahead. Bleßed are we if we ever enjoy life like the listeners of Hound Dog Taylor.

Sucker Duck was drawn along. The four kept their own pace. Jiao kept quiet so as not to stammer.

Nettie and Michel knew not to hax him anything until the feast.

No such luck with Nils, of course. <<Tear up the hotel room! I'm driving my Rolls into

the pool!>> Manic. He began running off to the sides like a feral child turning everything over in his hand in order to see if it was edible. The first imperatives were to identify the potable and then the edible.

<<You think so?>>

Yeah.

<<Well, you have good taste.>>

Michel wanted to hurry up to the feast, listen to Jiao for a while, and then hurry up to the last two Immortals. He really wanted to visit the Gardens soon.

Jiao, then Su Jin, the vegetarian, and then Li Shizhi, the polite back door man, and then, gone! Purged from the bowels of the Earth! Back in the arms of the Gardens!

Michel knew, though, somehow—had it been a dream?—something was hidden in the beard of his death mask. He had to find out what.

Probably nothing more than spit and vomit from his gagging while the plaster casters did him. Don't hax. That was quite long ago. A lifetime ago. Nice name for a nightclub. Lifetime Ago a Go Go—dancers in cages. Girls sure did like to dance in those days. Now they mainly strut or catwalk. In both cases, they are yelling, psychically, <<Don't touch!>>

No problem. Hadn't been going to.

Nettie sprang forth, belting out ▶Stop◀ a la Kim Lembo. And then a song of her own. ♪Everything is hard blue paisley at the heart of the city. ♫

The Moody Blues said our children's children's children would dig it, and they were right.

This was the magic key. The mißing note. The Richter scale.

Captain Marvel yelling <<Split!>> at the Earth's mantle, moho, and crust.

They didn't move.

He blew on the crust, but the mantle was almost molten. It took a while to harden, John Wesley. So… you been to Savannah recently?

Let Nettie sing you the whole song:

Hard Blue Paisley

Everything is hard blue paisley
at the heart of the city.
I’ve been waiting an eternity
to feel this free.

The music has stood the test of time,
and so has our choice in wine.
Share this bottle with me.

I’m hard-blue paisley tied
and hard-blue paisley dyed.

Everything is hard blue paisley
at the heart of the city.

I’ve been playing all the time
and I’m really doing fine.

The music has stood the test of time,
and so has our choice in wine.
Share this bottle with me.

I’ve got hard-blue paisley blood
coursing though misunderstood.

Everything is hard blue paisley
at the heart of the city.

Michel would have given even odds that Nettie wouldn’t sing again for a while, but that would have been oxymoronic.

He liked the tune, though. Jiao was off to the kitchens at his banquet hall—he lived in an enormous stone building that was taken up almost entirely by the dining hall. A few small rooms were tucked into nooks upstairs, but they opened into the hall as well. Everything was about the hall.

Jiao had said something about having to make sure he fattened them up a little before sending them on to starve at Su Jin’s. Jiao said, <<Su-Su-Su’s aß-scetic.>>

While Jiao occupied his ¢elgh in the kitchen, Michel, Nils, and Nettie took seats in the dining hall, Nils and Michel two seats apart on one side, Nettie between them on the Œðer. When Jiao came back, he’d probably slide in one way or the Œðer next to her, and in that manner he’d make the decision for her whether to sit acroß from Nils or Michel.

Michel did not really enjoy the new enormity of Nettie. She was a heartbeat away from becoming a much-too-powerful weapon. She could go nuclear at this rate. Michel was scared.

Nils was picking at his own problems—the scabs on his back, his deeply rooted ¢elgh-loathing.

Michel spotted the bar and got up. <<What do you guys want?>>

<<Any Tanqueray?>> haxed Nettie.

<<Yes, actually.>>

<<Tonic?>>

<<Schweppes, no leß.>>

<<G and T, then, please. On the rocks, if there are any?>>

<<I'll have a Gibson, but add two olives.>>

<<I can't do that. But I could give you a double-olive martini with a cocktail onion.>>

<<Oh, ha ha. That's the same thing.>>

<<But Gibsons aren't on the drink tally I have to keep for the bartender so we'll know how much to tip him.>>

<<Tip him for free drinks?>>

<<Can you think of a better reason?>>

<<Well, no, actually. Okay. A double-olive martini with an onion. And make it a double.>>

<<A double onion?>>

<<Two onions. And four olives. And twice the gin. Waive the vermouth.>>

Michel began waving a bottle of vermouth.

Nils laughed. That was good to hear.

<<Actually, what would be good to hear,>> said Michel, <<is Savoy Brown's ►Headline News◄ from the *Live from the House of Blues* CD.>>

<<With dancers.>>

<<Yes, I could see old Forfor dancing 4/4 for Forfor and for no one else.>>

<<No one will be dancing,>> said Nils. <<Notice that the place has no sound system and no stage. I think Jiao takes his feasting seriously.>>

Jiao came out, leading a parade of servers carrying platters.

The platters were placed on trivets at the far end of the table.

And then the food came around.

Mongolian boodog: a blow-torched marmot cooked inside out with hot stones inside. It tasted a bit like rabbit or squirrel.

Greenland shark: poisonous until putrefied. Only then would it be safe to eat. Hold the nose!

Casu Marzu: Sardinian sheep cheese infested with cheese fly maggots. Don't look at it.

Those were just the appetizers.

Next came a plateful of respect, followed by humble pie.

<<Humble Pie?>> Michel perked up.

<<No—remember? No sound system,>> said Nils.

<<I need some music, Nils,>> said Michel.

<<I'll sing an Œðer song,>> said Nettie.

<<I need something with guitar, baß, and drums—not just singing.>>

<<What do you mean, <just singing>?>> Michel had put his foot in it this time for sure.

<<No—I don't mean it like that. I love a cappella, but I just had a hankerin' for some horns!>>

<<What would fix you?>>

<<*Exile on Main Street*, of course.>>

<<That Jiao can do,>> said Jiao, overhearing. He clapped twice, and the famed recording came on, not out of the room, but from within one's own solar plexus.

ͼScore!ͽ thought Michel. ͼ♪Do the Hip Shake, baby♫ͽ! Both the Stones and Savoy Brown played the Slim Harpo claßic. Both also played ▶Little Red Rooster◀.

♪Stop!♫ sang Nettie again, trying to get them to stop once she'd finished singing along to ▶Little Red Rooster◀ with her inner ear.

<<I think the music is distracting us,>> said Nils. <<We should try to do without it.>>

<<You can't stop the Stones during side on of *Exile*! It can't be done. It'd be like stopping the Beatles in the middle of the ▶Sun King◀ medley. Or stopping the ▶Savoy Brown Boogie◀ .

Exactly. James Moore—that was Slim Harpo's real name. And then the ▶Casino Boogie◀ groove. All capped with ▶Tumbling Dice◀, one of the Stones' best tunes of all.

How many cue balls can one man fit in his mouth? For a quarter you could see for your ¢elgh at the carnival sideshow. The Rock and Roll Circus. Hey, who's that talking in the background during the song. I always think it's real and get caught.

And ▶Sweet Virginia◀, about the truest song ever been sung by anyone anywhere anytime. It is a worthy philosophy for life.

Exile is the number one greatest rock and roll album ever made by anyone. It is the *Ulyßes* of rock. And, like James Joyce's claßic, it is about regular people trying to make it through their regular lives.

[*Why don't I do that? I don't know. I want to. I just haven't written my way there yet. You think it's easy to steer this thing? It's bigger than an aircraft carrier now. It takes hours to turn in any measurable direction. But that doesn't stop the trying.*]

Michel realized he lived with the trying—the triers and tribulators—and really all he had to do was survive. And, as Leon Rußell said, they were pudding, they were pudding, they were pudding pudding pudding… on a show. Ever hear the Homewreckers? The band Kim Simmonds produced? No—better not say it. They'll hate *moi*, Michel. It'll be like Moi and Coily and Nil Hilation. *The Three Stooges visit the Fun House*. A claßic film yearning to be made. Bugbears and bêtes noires crawl out from underneath the beds. Old creditors and their collection agents come out of the woodwork like cockroaches and try to lick Nil Hilation's toes.

Hilarious.

Hickory Dickory.

Hilda Doolittle.

Find a phone.

Play the fiddle.

Jiao bounces from platter to platter the way Paul Raymond bounces over the keyboard on the *Record Plant* version of Savoy Brown's ►All I Can Do (Is Cry)◄. That's a nice singing part for Kim, back then in '75 already.

Hot Dog! Ah, but he's good. It's not hot dogging if you're good.

Hsia Dynasty—the beginning.

Howard Dean. The howl!

Hoodoo the voodoo that you do so well?

This is the boogie:

C'mon. Ride along. It feels really good. Like your first time in a Town Car. Wasn't that the car you could cut diamonds in? You could play rattlesnake guitar inside it. That hat made of fog may be rather elusive, but when you find it, it fits. So you stop meßin' around. Enjoy playing rattlesnake guitar. Rod Price and Lonesome Dave with Southside Johnny? You shittin'? Michel wants to hear that.

Oh, yeah. No sound system. Just some livers.

They don't mean to gush so. But be careful of their biliousneß. If you smell that coming, stand way back. Stay away from the backspray.

<<Oh, my god. Top Topham and Jim McCarty of the freakin' Yardbirds are on the Peter Green tribute? Together? That's *versnacken* [as the kids say nowadays]!>>

Not to mention Rory Gallagher doing ►Leaving Train Blues◄ where he's <<going to Chicago, where a man can be free.>> But then he qualifies it with ►somewhat◄. Only one place where one can be free—the Gardens of Obsane Topiary.

Michel's father knew the gardeners.

Michel knew the plasterers.

The course that came next was a ham-and-split-pea soup with lentils, spinach, and corn.

Accompanying it was a salad made of romaine, daikon, red cabbage, curly parsley, carrot, celery stalk, celery leaf, and English cucumber (the sincere cucumber—no wax!).

Si, cucumber?

No, no sea cucumber. English.

At one time the English ruled the seas.

When the Armada sank probably. In Ireland.

Yes, and the pretty colleens welcomed the shipwrecked sailors into their beds.

Hence the Black Irish, a truly beautiful species.

A platter of cheese made its way around—separate from the casu marzu, of course, as well as the chocolate-covered gjetost, which Michel wanted no part of. Nasty. The chocolate might allow one to swallow without taking a bite, but the inevitable gjetost burps would be enough to make ipecac seem a culinary delight.

Next a platter of thousand-year-old eggs. Jiao's specialty. Buried for a hundred days, they emerge with black-purple whites and green yellows. The fermentation has changed the consistency to avocado-like cream.

Don't criticize the eggs.

<<Leave mah babies alone!>> screams Jiao as he hops onto the door and stands there over Michel, shock of white hair, tattooed arms folded acroß his chest, the serpents inttwining all the more menacingly. He glares at Michel like Michel's some flashbulb-✸popping✸ tourist.

<<I told you not to criticize them! I laid those eggs!>>

Jiao picked one up with his fingers and dropped it into his heaven-facing mouth.

The three were obliged to follow suit. Nettie swallowed hers whole. Nils gave Michel a wry smile and a wink after that. His smile quickly disappeared when he bit into his egg. He gagged and almost vomited but would not let his ¢elgh do so. He'd had enough of people taking everything as an insult. To vomit on someone else's shoes is unforgiveable. So he swallowed everything back down and then kept it down with sips of some kind of herbal wine that settled the stomach, which Jiao had on hand for just such a gastric event. Apparently this was not unusual on feast days.

Jiao explained it all quit lucidly, in fact, mellifluously. He was no longer stammering. The legends were true. He became luculent when the food was succulent, to paraphrase Shakespeare's Tamora, Queen of the Goths, when she faced a feast at Titus Andronicus's.

Long Pig Pie was what Titus served her.

<<Ow! It's hot,>> she exclaimed.

<<Hot like suns,>> replied Titus.

<<Hot like the Marquesas Islands,>> added Michel.

<<Is it true that Melville had a Type A personality?>> haxed Nils.

<<Well, both of his sons, Malcolm and Stanwix, died mysteriously,>> replied Michel.

<<Did Herman then eat them?>> haxed Nils.

<<No, I don't think so. Stanwix died estranged from his father and living in San Francisco. Most likely he died of TB. And Malcolm apparently committed suicide while in military service. Herman wasn't around.>>

<<Œðerwise he would have?>>

<<I don't know.>>

The Melvilles were akin to the Buddenbrooks.

<<I think,>> said Michel, <<that he ate his ¢elgh up, or his hate for his ¢elgh ate him up.>>

That's why writers are always so obseßed with finding love on the outside—though you wouldn't know to look at them—they're subtle that way, subtle as a flying single goßamer strand making its way acroß this goddamned world as a stranger to it, only to be deposited, stranded, ironically.

The entire family line had come down to Michel—the lineage of Avery Craw stopped here. Michel had no children, no heirs. His ancestors were looking down on him angrily.

<<Profligate!>> they called him.

<<Propagate!>> they called to him.

►Promulgate◄ was the word that described what they were doing—or at least that was Michel's prosection of it.

As a pro statesman, Michel prostrated his castrated prostate at his government in general, Generals in private, his privates major, the Aasvogel in particular. He realized he had no inter-rust whatsoever in going back to Mars ever. Just his lighthouse.

Someone sat down at the far end of the table—an Œðer paßerby? Jiao introduced him to the Œðers and brought him a large section of smoked leg of stag in stag beetle sauce and a cup of ambrosial mead made from the honey of bees who pollinated only marijuana flowers.

The one special variety of honey bee is so valuable and protected that only the Global Ark Hives are allowed to keep them. The Global government had built its Arks for maßive planetary evacuation long ago. Some species were being kept alive artificially just for the transport even though they had no use on Earth anymore. Earth was a funny place. It had been predicting its own demise ever since creation.

Who was this stranger? Michel adjusted his blurry eyes.

<<Ow! Don't adjust my eyes!>> yelled the stranger.

<<Sorry. I lose track of pronouns with the best of them.>>

<<Who?>>

<See.>>

<<Who the fuck are you?>> haxed the stranger.

<<I'm Michel du Jabot.>>

<<Never heard o' ya. I'm Tony McPhee. Give me a little respect.>>

<<You're Tony McPhee?>>

<<I am.>>

<<What are you, 200 years old?>>

<<How old do ya think Jiao is, man? I've been down here for a while. I like it. The whales are crackin'.>>

<<Yeah? Now that the Kraken is gone, they're crackin'?>>

<<Aye! They sing along with my guitar. You never heard the albums, I take it. Big hits. On three planets, even. Made it to number three on the moon, also.>> The moon was usually the largest market, especially among the dark side culters.

Michel hadn't heard the name ▶Tony McPhee◀ in years. The people he hung out with who liked the Groundhogs, McPhee's band, all split.

Groundhogs reminded Michel of his lighthouse. But for now the feast. How he wished instead for a light meal.

He could smell burnt nachos with a cherry salsa. Chocolate-infused sauerkraut cookies were next. They tasted better than they sounded.

More food. Jiao waxed eloquent on the wings of waxwings, birds that Michel just then noticed on several trees.

Birds and whales. What was the connection? They both glide. They frolic in their media. Just like artists.

For a craftsperson, a tube of paint is a tool. For an artist, it is a toy.

For a clerk, a size-12 shoe is a foot. For Jezebel, it's a date.

Poor Ahab—he wasn't allowed down here because of the whales. Plus seeing Jiao all white and bloated might have confused poor Ahab anyway.

Rocky Mountain oysters and lamb fries. Chitterlings. Sweetbreads. Oxtail. Tripe. Brain.

<<Eat till ya hurl—it all goes down the drain>> came to the mind of the Olympic hurler, who had stood there, broom in hand, at the ready like a Beefeater.

<<You are what you eat,>> said Nils, quoting Feuerbach.

<<In that case, what'll you have? Vegetables?>> haxed Jiao.

<<Better give me some of that brain so I can keep up,>> replied Nils, laughing.

<<Not too much. We don't want to have scrape you off the ceiling.>>

<<Eloquently said,>> said Michel to Jiao, wondering if Jiao's ¢elgh-consciousneß had more to do with the stuttering than the feasting did.

<<No—that won't work, Michel du Jabot! I knew Avery Craw. You think I don't know the old family tricks and traps?>>

<<You are good, Jiao! I'll admit it. And so is this mead! Where's Tony?>>

<<He had to run off. Tonight John Lee Hooker is supposed to come by. Canned Heat and the Groundhogs have a party planned for him.>>

<<Can we go?>>

<<And interrupt the feast? No, no, no…. But they said they'd try to come by and do a

set here. So stay tuned in.>>

<<I heard something about waxing an elephant?>> said Nettie, coming to after a brief nap.

<<Waxwings?>>

<<Elephants have waxy wings?>>

<<No—waxing eloquent. That's it.>>

<<Don't know. The waxwings flew very eloquently from Jiao's lips.>>

<<I know—they hypnotized me. That's why I fell asleep.>>

<<Three bottles of wine is why you fell asleep.>>

<<That, too.>>

<<Coconut shrimp? Ugh. I draw the line there. No shrimp ever climbed a tree to find the coconut. Those flavors have no reason for being together.>> Michel's mind was made up. He'd eaten way too much, vomited way too often, and eaten way too much more. This was like a Roman vomitorium, and he decided he needed to move along.

<<To the vegetarian? You'll starve there,>> said Jiao.

<<No—I won't vomit. We'll come to the John Lee Hooker show, though. At least *I* will.>> He almost fell. <<I'm off. Bye. Thanks for the hostilapity.>> He fell on his face.

Nils quoted Firesign Theatre, saying, <<He's no fun—he fell right over.>>

Nettie laughed, but then Nils fell over, too. She was just awake, and her companions had crashed on her. That was out of order. At least Jiao was there, and he had no element of creepineß to him. He was a foodie. Why eat pußy when truffles are on the menu? Plus truffles don't tell endleß boring stories of endleß boring lives. A truffle's life is, eßentially, <<Grow grow grow grow grow pig snout death.>>

<<Mmm…. Good truffles,>> Jiao said between mouthfuls. Tycho Brache must have loved him.

Out came three deep-fried turduckens: chickens stuffed inside of ducks stuffed inside of turkeys. Definitely feast food.

♪I wish I was a catfish…♫, Nettie began to sing.

<<Groundhog catfish or Canned Heat catfish? Certainly not Hendrix or Popa Chubby.>>

<<Popa Chubby?>> haxed Nettie. <<I can do that.>>

<<Undoubtedly you can, young lady, but in the meantime, please paß that can of young ladyfingers soaked in cherry sherry.>>

<<*Mon cheri*?>>

<<*À la mode du jour*, perhaps.>>

<<Soup with ice cream on it?>>

<<Yes. That is of course what I meant. Split pea with ham and spinach is perfect for a parfait.>>

<<If the ham is sweet enough, maybe,>> she replied.

<<No, and she never will be.>>

<<She?>>

<<I always refer to hams as ►she◄. It's an old habit I picked up from Hollywood movies. My apologies.>>

<<No problem. But I was thinking that the ham wasn't me, but that it's little old y-o-u,>> she said, punctuating each of the three letters with a finger-point at his chest.

She thought she saw, out of the corner of her eye, something small, fat and furry scuttle off. A fat groundhog!

The groundhog had made its way from the Land between the Lakes, where their preserve is, all the way past John Lee Hooker and the Groundhogs and Spirit.

This groundhog had been run out of Kentucky for erroneously predicting an early spring. But the groundhog could take them right to Michel's lighthouse. What about Su Jin and Li Shizhi? The shortstop and the left fielder. They had the strongest arms after Zhang Xu. They'd still be lifting weights one heavy bottle at a time.

If Li Shizhi is the back door man, does that make him a back doorman or a backdoor man? To some the two ideas are dißimilar.

Better dißimilate than never. There's not much joy to the boy. Just don't get between him and his food. ♪He'll bite your nose off, Jim♫, she sang, quoting Warren Zevon.

Where was Adam when she wanted to get her Eve on?

She was certainly not naïve on matters such as this.

Just a kiß. He'd forgotten he was a millennium-and-a-half away for a second but quickly saw a blintz he wanted. He tasted it, but it disagreed with him instantly. He pulled up a bucket from the ground and vomited into it. Then he began searching for a better flavor.

Jiao took his feasting very seriously.

Some old coot at the far end near the entrance started making some noise. Just an Œðer's strange bird.

But the bird was bland, and so Jiao took a roasted quail and cut a large piece of breast meat. He seemed to feel better after that.

Nettie decided to try to nap some more and wake up when Nils and Michel were awake. Jiao alone did not appeal to her anymore. He rather ignored her.

As soon as the guys awoke, she wanted to go. Jiao had eaten nonstop, had filled four buckets, and was still going. The stench was beginning to nauseate Nettie, so she gladly pulled her guys out and told them to march.

They left immediately. Nils didn't even dare wince when his back scabs cracked open again.

March! March *ißt der* cruelest lunch!

Wash your greens in a brook of fire, perhaps.

<<▶Brook◀ is ▶Bach◀? So every time one hears Bach, one should babble?>>

<<Or wear a Brooks brŒðers suit.>>

<<Is that a product placement?>>

<<I wish. I wasn't even sponsored by my dad. He has a JD and an MD and he studied Sanskrit and also worked on a proto-Indo-European dictionary, but he won't even read my letters because he says it's too much work. What he really means is he has no inter-rust in who I am as a person. But perhaps anyone occupying a position as his child would receive this treatment, maybe better, maybe worse.>>

That generation was so preoccupied with sex that they accomplished nothing more than having children whom they resented. The child who rose hir hand and haxed politely, <Can you look at me, Dad?> was the one who was ignored most intently.

The center of the Earth was easy to ignore. Until it wasn't.

Nils wailed. No response.

Nettie sang Willie Dixon's song ►I Wanna Put a Tiger in Your Tank◄.

<<Downliners Sect or Alexis Korner's Blues Incorporated?>>

<<Her own.>>

<<It's so?>>

<<It's so.>>

<<Eßo?>>

<<I think so.>>

<<We didn't even have deßert.>>

<<Watching Jiao ralph cost me my appetite,>> said Nettie.

<<Did you at least grab some mayonnaise for my back?>>

<<No,>> interjected Michel. <<We got some Tabasco, though.>>

<<Never mind.>>

<<You're right I'll never mind. You're the idiot who flogged his ¢elgh. Don't you dare play the pity card. I'll stomp on your head harder than Nettie could ever stomp on your heart!>>

<<What about the Œðer way around?>> haxed Nettie. <<Me with the head, you with the off-the-cuff heart.>>

<<Neither!>> yelled Nils, upset. <<Just go away, both of you.>>

<<We're all going the same way, Clowno,>> said Michel, drawing from his clown training days. <<Should we walk ahead or behind? We're all going to Su Jin's. Miso and tofu. I hope you like it.>>

<<Do you?>>

<<Oh, yes. Very much. I like everything, pretty much. Except peanut butter. It seems pointleß. Peanuts are best left alone.>>

<<Is Su Jin a true vegetarian?>>

<<What do you mean?>>

<<Well, is he merely pescetarian, or is he ovo-lacto-vegetarian? Or is he a hardcore vegan?>>

<<I have no idea. I could look it up if I was back at my lighthouse library.>>

<<With some yellow split pea red miso.>>

<<Don't hax me. I don't even remember what goes into a Long Island Iced Tea.>>

<<Vodka?>>

<<See—I don't drink vodka. It was something I drank beyond all tolerance one warm summer night with a pianist friend of mine.>>

<<A penis friend of yours?>> haxed Nils.

<<Well, he is rather a dick, or a prick, or whatever you want to call him. He'd invite people to his home just to try to humiliate them.>>

<<Did it work?>>

<<Not in my case. I laughed. It was pathetic.>>

<<Notice how, after we've all pushed our ¢elghs away from the table and had a chance to digest, we now feel better?>> haxed Nettie.

Michel agreed. As did Nils. So far vegetarianism was no problem. They could get through a meal or two at least.

♪Nobody's inter-rusted in learning but the teacher,♫ sang Nettie, quoting Barrett Strong via the Temptations' ►Ball of Confusion (That's What the World Is Today)◄.>>

Nils found something on the ground. <<Look! A horn! A fucking bull's horn, just here in the graß. Have you seen any cows? I haven't.>>

<<What's that?>> haxed Michel.

<<A horn,>> said Nils.

<<No bull?>> replied Michel. He hate to be the canner of laughter, but that was pretty funny. It almost let him forget the bullet in his bicep until he tried to move his arms. Comes with working for the government.

The covenant.

Well, he’d done for the covenant all his life. He’d been demoted, humiliated, exiled, and yet here he was, at the heart of humanity, still alive. One could say he had an affinity for it.

<<An infinity?>> haxed Nils, of course.

Off course were they apparently. Where is Sun Jin’s?

Well, you know where the old mill road out past the old Zane ranch used to be? Past that old gnarled black oak tree by the giant bend in the creek? Out near where the two willows used to meet in an arch over the water? Well, it ain’t that way. If you go up past the spot where the Frye barn was before it burnt down ten years ago—

<<Look!>> Su Jin’s yurt was straight ahead, and in the glare it looked like it had a halo over it. Michel suspected a trick. The holy man who wanted a fuck. Like that yogi the Beatles followed until they found him shtupping one of the entourage in the back tent. <<Free your ¢elgh from the prison of body. Give your ¢elgh to me.>> That was the spiel. Small wonder anyone fell for it, but, as PT Barnum is said to have said, <<There’s a sucker born every minute.>>

Michel haxed, in response, so Su Jin wouldn’t suspect the duplicity, <<Is it a vegetarian sucker?>>

Michel was dying to get to the Gardens of Obsane Topiary. The meßage in his beard scratched him. He itched to get at it.

He knew someone once had gotten something out of Hidalgo’s beard. He had a book by Conger Beasley about it in the library. So he knew this was a vision, not a dream.

<<I’ll attack you if you don’t stop being so quiet,>> said Nettie to Michel. She would, too.

Michel wondered which he’d rather face.

A baß in here.

A basin there.

Collect. He can’t get it. It’s for us few only. We may have driven them out.

Good. No one should be here who doesn’t want to be.

Teachers, tell the students they should stop reading now. The terrain is getting a little tougher. They can help. Tell ’em to study the Pointer Sisters so they can hear what good harmonies should sound like.

Big Mama Thornton's got a ▶Mixed up Feeling.>>◀

Tell them to learn. The learning is really up to them. It's hard to get an idea in past a clamped-shut iron door, but we'll find a way, if need be. But is it worth the effort?

One never knows. <Just pays yer money and takes yer chances.>> Didn't Barnum say that, too?

Nettie pointed out that no universal cultural literacy was poßible, even for a thinker as old as Su Jin. At least as a vegetarian he wouldn't be killing whales in order to feast on them. She'd seen the smoked whale meat on Jiao Sui's talbe. That was when she'd lost respect for the stammering engorger.

Su Jin saw the three approach him. Hi quickly hid his wine. It was his habit to tell visitors that he was trying to adhere to the tenets of his faith, and alcohol was prohibited by it.

<<What a dumb religion,>> said Nils, not thinking. Michel thought so, too, but didn't say so. He was far more cautious than Nils.

<<I'm sure we'd all like to slap you on the back for your statement,>> said Michel to Nils, <<but not everyone in the world is beyond believing in spirit. However, by attacking someone else's spirit, you make obvious how weak your own is.>>

<<I agree with Michel,>> said Nettie, who was usually more hawk than dove. But this time Michel's reticence was unwarranted. If Su Jin were merely a pescetarian, then perhaps he'd eat a whale if he suffered from the common delusion that whales were fish.

<<Let's see if Su Jin refers to Jiao Sui as a whale.>>

<<Good idea.>>

Su Jin stepped out and was blown away. He only weighed four ounces. Miso and tofu only have so much they can do. He pushed their limits. He was like Gautama Buddha when Gautama was young, inquisitive, hooked on asceticism, coming up with the brilliant idea to eat one fewer grain of rice each evening until he reached a day of zero. On that day he had a revelation that asceticism was stupid, and he ate again. Gautama Buddha was cool. Jesus was cool, how he stuck to his meßage of love no matter what people did to shake him. Moses was cool when he won the hearts of free Israelites with the idea that the desert was but a precursor to deliverance. And then Jesus honored that with his own forty days in the desert. And then, like Gautama Buddha, he came back. Locusts and wild honey's okay for a while, but then what? He wanted new flavors! The desert had few.

The Mermnadae kings of Lydia—they had the spices. They took some as commißion from every transaction until the merchants decided to force the first form of currency on them. The kings used to ride around on their Przewalski's Horses, flaunting their eminence.

Michel, of course, knew all about Przewalski's Horse from his readings about his ancestor Avery Craw, who had once written a book about the horses, though some unscrupulous interloper, discovering that the author's name was a pseudonym, took the author's identity as his own and vanished with it.

Who was more original: Sonny Boy Williamson II or Little Howlin' Wolf?

<<That's easy,>> said Nils.

<<How so?>>

<<Little Wolf was Polish, not Black.>>

<<Racist!>>

<<Oh, shut up. He was that Polish guy with the saxophone on the Ontario Street bridge over by there in Chicago.>>

<<What?>>

<<He put out two albums in the 19890s as Little Howlin' Wolf. I forgot his real name. It was long. Unpronounceable. European.>>

<<Hey, that's hasty. Some European languages are euphonious!>>

<<Not that one.>>

<<Sure it is. You just don't have the right ears.>>

<<Good point!>> said Nettie. <<Now what do we do about Su Jin?>>

<<I don't know,>> said Michel. <<He just blew away on the wind, like a song by Majnun. Let's hope it's heard by her for whom it was meant.>>

<<Mr. Fancy Speech!<<

<<What?>>

<<Was that a metaphor? What do you mean he blew away on the wind?>>

<<Michel is right. I saw,>> said Nils. <<Su Jin only weighed four ounces, and he was

carried away on the wind when he stepped outside.>>

<<Where’d he go?>>

<<I have no idea. He was like a piece of fluff from a cottonwood,>> said Michel. <<I think he went over the water.>>

<<Maybe he landed in the water with the krill and the whales.>>

<<You think so?>>

<<Most likely as food for the baleen whale, which captures the most krill.>>

<<Maybe he’s alive and well in the belly of the whale.>>

<<As fantastic as that would be, that would be fantastic.>>

<<Maybe he didn’t go baleen but instead went balloon.>>

<<No!>> exclaimed Michel. <<They have *not* infiltrated down here!>>

<<What do we do?>> haxed Nils of Nettie. <<Do we look for Su Jin or wait here?>>

Nettie was going to hax Michel, but he was already inside the yurt, making miso.

<<We all need some miso to counteract the poisons we just absorbed,>> said Michel.

Neither Nils nor Nettie argued. They were still in shock.

<<That *was* it for Su Jin?>>

<<What—you want to start over?>>

<<No, but it’s like when you golf the game of your life until an easy par-3 on 15 and you get 10 on it. But you can’t start over.>>

<<Wouldn’t a disc golf course be great down here?>> haxed Nils.

<<No,>> replied Michel. <<It’s too monochromatic.>>

<<What?>>

<<It’s all vanilla.>>

<<Monochromatic vanilla?>>

<<Vanilla Fudge?>> haxed Nils. <<The band with the mudshark in Seattle?>>

<<A few mudsharks thrown in would make this a much more inter-rusting course.>>

<<I gueß you're right. It *is* rather monodramatic—>>
<<*Chro*matic.>>

<<Whatever. But why does this landscape need to remain so dull?>>

<<Because it's mostly old folks who come down here.>>

<<Makes sense.>>

<<Maybe if they turned it into Seaworld and made the whales turn tricks…,>> said Nettie, all piß and vinegar.

<<I think you mean ►do tricks◄,>> replied Michel.

<<Are you going after Su Jin?>> haxed Nettie.

<<No,>> Michel and Nils replied simultaneously.

<<Who knows where he is?>> added Michel.

<<Or what beast's belly he's in,>> Nils caudated.

<<Maybe he's out giving a litmus test,>> said Michel.

<<Like the good old USA,>> replied Nils. <<Blue or red?>>

<<Ironically, perhaps, the red said, <better dead than red,>>> said Nettie.

<<But they were talking about communism,>> said Nils. <<Certainly what happened is that Cold War anti-communists, through Reagan, arranged the surrender of the Republican Party to communism. Reagan gave the nation's keys to Gorbachev, but on the condition that they make it look like the opposite had occurred.>>

<<That's a tough deception.>>

<<That's why they hired an actor.>>

<<Oh, I can see that,>> Nettie admitted.

Michel shook his head at the both of them as if to hax, <<Does this really matter?>>

<<I'm not going on this litmus trip,>> said he.

<<Strip,>> said Nettie.

<<No, and certainly not in front of Nils,>> replied Michel.

<What?>>

<<I can't believe you'd hax him to,>> added Nils. <<And right in front of me! Terrible!>>

Nettie began to explain, but neither man was listening, and besides, she didn't owe anyone any explanations. She knew they liked her. But why end the fun now? They had taken a long time to get here. Michel was as slow to strike as a wily old muskellunge pike.

<<▶Pike◀ is superfluous. The fish is a muskellunge,>> pointed out Nils.

<<▶Muskellunge◀ doesn't rhyme with ▶strike◀, though,>> Michel pointed out. <<Nothing rhymes with ▶muskellunge◀.>>

Nettie smiled. <Oh, no? Hit it, boys,> and they began foot stomping and slapping in time to Nettie's song:

> ♪I took a plunge
> for muskellunge
> up in Wisconsin.
> Absorbed some grunge
> just like a sponge
> outside Beliot,
> stretching like a bungee
> all the way out to Detroit.♫

<<Wait!>> yelled Nils. <<I just remembered something important!>>

<<Snap!>> yelled Michel, releasing the tension of Nettie's cord. And drowning her G-chord with his spoken word like a music-hater rapper who valued easy rhyme all the time. Michel immediately regretted having done so.

<<No,>> said Nils. <<Listen up!>>

<<What?>> haxed Nettie, out of patience, annoyed.

<<We should keep going. Let's go ahead to Li Shizhi.>>

<<Okay, but first let's have some of this miso I made,>> said Michel. <<I cut little cubes of tofu into it. It's good, and it has tremendous curative powers.>>

Nils thought about it. His back pain kept him tethered to Earth. If he loosened his tether, his pain would diminish. <<I'm in,>> he said. <<Let's go right after some miso with tofu.>>

<<Okay,>> agreed Nettie. <<Only till then.>>

<<Who's Li Shizhi?>> haxed Nils. <<Has he withered into paper, too, since we played ball?>>

<<Oh, many ballplayers have withered under the force of paper. Sammy Sosa, for example. Barry Bonds. Mark McGwire. When the papers turned on them, that was it.>>

<<I prefer my players hall-of-famers. Especially if they have eleven letters in their last names.>>

They had almost reached Li Shizhi's when they looked back to see a giant paper balloon Su Jin descending gently to the ground. They'd mißed him.

Michel shivered. Was Su Jin connected to the balloon symbionts? Michel had hoped they'd not infiltrated the netherlands. Or that they'd be popped by the snapping shut of the Dutch doors.

Michel, Nettie and Nils paused, but Li Shizhi beckoned to them to come. They'd just have to write off Su Jin. The miso and tofu had settled them nicely, and all three were feeling good.

Nettie sang on old blues song:

At the Bottom
(for John Lee Hooker and Sleepy John Estes)

I remember when we were both diving ducks.
We went down to the bottom and never wanted to come up.
The bottom was whiskey in a river of gin.
If I'd a-been a catfish, I'd a-known where to swim.
When I wanted to surface, I had bullfrogs on my mind.
So I dove back down and now I'm biding my time.
When you paßed me on the way up, I said I'd stay right here.
So now I'm waiting for you at the bottom, my dear.
And I'll see you when you come back down—
you know I'll be around.

I'm waiting for you at the bottom.
Come on, baby, douse my broom.
We've got all kinds of room
down here at the bottom,

down here at the bottom.
<spoken>: I'll put a tigershark in the tank.
I remember when I saw you swimming with the catfish.
You were just a school girl then, but I had a wish,
and I waited five long years to pull you out
and I took you away from some hungry trout
who'd been eyeing you as his next meal.
But a trout like that—I know his deal.
I showed him to a hooker and he got pulled away.
I took you to the bottom and hoped you'd stay.
But you had to play—call it what you want,
but I call it meßing with the hook.
You were hangin' 'round with that trout from the brook.

I went waiting for you at the bottom.
Come on, baby, douse my broom.
We've got all kinds of room
down here at the bottom,
down here at the bottom.

<spoken>: I got bullfrogs on my mind.

Well, Mama killed a chicken, not a diving duck,
and when she caught up to me, she had her legs sticking up.
I said I love to see the bottom,
but I've been waiting here since autumn,
so let me see you lie instead
down here upon the riverbed.
There's something you've just got to know
before you just bottle up and go.

I was waiting for you at the bottom.
Come on, baby, douse my broom.
We've got all kinds of room
down here at the bottom,
down here at the bottom.

<spoken>: Let that boy boogie woogie.

<spoken by an Œðer voice>: That's right.

I was waiting for you at the bottom.
Come on, baby, douse my broom.
We've got all kinds of room
down here at the bottom,
down here at the bottom.

Down here at the bottom.

Li Shizhi heard. And he was an upright—most said ►uptight◄—man. Blues? Double entendre? Not here! He sent the three into the vortex, and they spun back to the surface and into Michel's lighthouse home. They awoke to hear the anapestic beat of a 33 rpm record player's tone-arm caught in a record's inner groove. The auto-eject feature wasn't working.

Book Seven: Snail Shells for Slugs, the Diving Duck, and Œðer Dovecote Tales

After showering, Michel du Jabot wiped his hand over the bathroom mirror and cleared off the condensation.

The mirror, on which Michel had stuck notes to his ¢elgh in the surrounding frame, sported a bumper sticker acroß the top. The sticker read ⅩmimesisⅩ.

Michel undertook shaving in the still-somewhat-foggy mirror. He shaved with his brand Ockham's razor until long after the beard was gone, until his face was burned by Ockham's brand. He put on a recording of Louis Armstrong's rendition of ▶Hello, Dolly!◀ and began slathering aloe vera on his face while singing ▶Hello, Vera!◀ along with the great Satchmo. The lotion stung, so Michel had a quick glaßful of cognac to dull his feelings.

After dreßing, Michel sat down to some butter and blackberry jam on a toasted English muffin. He opened the morning paper and began to scan the headlines: ▶Researchers from Albert Hall Count the Berms in Burma◀ sounded inter-rusting. ▶Himalayan Priest's Aura Found to be Nimbus◀ was intriguing. ▶Herbalist Regrets Growing Rue◀ would send Michel to the gardening section. ▶Rats Found in Honeycomb in Badger State◀ was in the North American amusements section.

Michel turned to the obituaries in case someone he knew had died. Former co-workers and claßmates were of particular inter-rust—especially those who had belittled Michel as a boy. It was said he had no gumption, no stick-to-it-neß, no perseverance. He was voted most likely never to leave his home town. He compensated for those slights a hundred times over.

And, contrary to expectation, here he was, back home in his lighthouse on the ▶promontory◀ of the Land between the Lakes, which was not where he had grown up.

No one he knew from the community near the lighthouse had died. But the time had come to hit the road—well, the underground paßages at least—and revisit his family's burial area in the Gardens of Obsane Topiary. He needed to see the death mask that the plaster casters had made of him.

He was not eager to leave the lighthouse—it was the abode closest to being a home he had ever had. The ancestral ort he had originally come from was a worthleß scrap of a town. He'd been told living there was a gift, which he never understood until he realized that the Germanic settlers who had created it would have understood the word ▶gift◀ to mean ▶poison◀.

After leaving that lump of poison behind, he wandered the faces of the three human-inhabited planets and the colony on the moon, but only here in the lighthouse had he truly been able to relax.

But his death mask kept bŒðering him. It kept drawing him back to the Gardens, so he really wanted to go.

Nettie and Nils, his friends and companions, had spiraled in a different direction after their return from the sea of whales. They, of course, had no real reason to stay. Nettie might have, but Michel did not give her any real encouragement to do so.

He was happy alone in his library. The solipsist in the sky. That's who he was. It made him feel more real.

So he was listening to John Lee Hooker's *More Real Folk Blues*, which are folk blues that are more real, or blues for realer folk, or blues for more real folk than Œðer music attracts—in any case, ▶The Mißing Album◀ was more masculine than a hundred little boy gangsta rapper wannabes.

Can you imagine Howlin' Wolf facing off against Diddley Squat? It'd be like a full-grown man taking on a stick-boy teenager. Put my money on Wolf. A man becomes a man at 200 pounds. Let stick-boy wait. When he's at full fighting weight, then throw him into the ring. Pipsqueak Mosquitoweight or Popa Chubby? Bouncing Boy (an inflatable balloon character!) or Thanos? Little Joe Cartwright or Big Joe Turner? False dilemma or foregone conclusion? The latter. The Church of the Latter says so. The Church of the Ladder is all about social climbing.

Hooker's version of ▶I Can't Quit You◀ is notable for its dueling lead guitars, with Hooker and Eddie Burns going in completely different directions, held together by the drums and piano.

ɕThe world outside has changed,ɔ thought Michel. Let's climb on in and ride that idea in first person.

I've been wanting to do that for a long time. Writing only in third person is like wrustling with one arm tied behind one's back. It builds strength, but it's uncomfortable. It's nice to stretch out again.

There. Did. Whole thing in third person. Don't say I can't do it. It's like when I went without booze for a month to prove to my wife I could. After that, she left me to my drink.

It's an exercise.

But years have gone by. It's not just groundhogs anymore. Buildings and cars butt up against the edge of the driveway.

A tall tree has grown on one side of the lighthouse. It blocks the most common view of the lighthouse from the road, and that is where I have moved my desk. I face the tree, figuring that if anything emerges from behind it, I will notice. So I sit here at this notebook and write.

I am Michel du Jabot, but no—I need a better moniker if I'm going to go outside. ►Michel du Jabot◄ sounds too patrician. They'll beat me over my head and take what they find. I need to call my ¢elgh ►Mike Jabbot◄. That sounds undistinguished and forgettable—ideal for not being noticed. It's an idea I read about in a book by someone known as ►Dr. Sorcerer◄, a sometime astrologer, occasional soothsayer, and full-time numismatist. Dr. Sorcerer advocates giving in to the dominant society. He suggests that the earlier one says ►uncle◄, the earlier powers-that-be will give a willy or a sam. Go to church. Join the Lyons Club. Be a Rotarian. Be a Shriner. Be a member. Supervise and spy on one an Œðer and report back here—to Dominant Society Headquarters, which are usually empty, over by there in Chicago.

Chicago's airport is labeled ►ORD◄ for ►[by the] Order of Richard Daley◄, I'm pretty sure. But an ort (pronounced the same) is a worthleß scrap of dog food. To whom is that airport a worthleß scrap? True, it is no longer the world's busiest airport, as it once was, but that's a dubious honor anyway, like the clinic that advertised that it had the world's largest waiting room, which implied they made more people wait than anyone else.

Nevertheleß, Chicago is now world headquarters for the world's head quarters.

One-sided numismatists go there for their annual convention at the Palmer House downtown. The Palmer House hasn't been the same since Trader Vic's closed and all the werewolves were chased away.

I should stop in Chicago on the way to the Gardens.

Voted least likely to have a home town—that was me. I'll just stay here for a while. The library is warm, and my domed bedroom at the top of the lighthouse is great for dreaming.

I've been doing the daily croßwords in the newspaper. Doing them keeps me sharp. It keeps me sharp. It keeps me sharp. It keeps me sharp, never dull, never dull as a tack, attack, Attica State, Statesville Prison, and so on.

People come by to annoy me. They haven't thought of me in years, but heard I'd died. So when they found out I was still alive, they all began to show up.

What's a three-letter word for a seaside raptor? A four-letter word for a funereal reading? ▶Osp◀—short for ▶Osprey◀. That works. Osp has a doctoral degree in digital technology—a DDT. And ▶Eulo◀—short for ▶Eulogy◀. He is by training a politician, though he became a motivational speaker bent on giving everyone life aßurance. Those two came first, though not together.

Osp was wearing some sort of kimono with Chinese ballet slippers. When he talked, he kept me in rapt attention. He'd always been a very inter-rusting man. I'd known him since we were kids. We'd gotten into trouble together for selling ashtrays we'd made out of hubcaps of luxury automobiles. What had gotten us into trouble was the way we acquired the hubcaps. The one that got us arrusted was the hubcap off the Merry Pranksters' Magic Bus in the Kerouac Museum in Lowell, Maßachusetts. We'd just had a run-in with some bikers who kept throwing Eight O'Clock coffee wrappers at us, so we weren't as sharp as usual. Snag! Hands-on-shoulders busted. Osp was a pleasant diversion, though he always exuded some sort of perpetual dourneß that could be draining. Nevertheleß, I invited him to stay for a day or two, but he could only visit for an afternoon. He was on a tight schedule on his way to Toronto to do a mosaic for the basketball finals for the city, a very lucrative contract.

Eulo came by two days later. When we were young men, fresh out of high school, I was being interred by an evil witch who had rendered me immobile. He looked at me and haxed, <<You low?>> I shed a tear in response, so he knew I was still alive. He chased the witch and the gravediggers away and pulled me up out of the grave. He took me to a storyteller, who administered an anecdote about Brautigan's writing *In Watermelon Sugar*. I was so amused, I was cured. Like a ham, I began singing Eulo's praises. We became fast friends, so our friendship ended much too quickly when we stopped eating and were hospitalized at separate facilities for reasons of political protest.

After that he went into his life aßurance gig, and I became a school teacher.

My years as a teacher were invaluable.

The work was demeaning, so I ceased to be so mean to the people I knew. I could be cruel when I was younger, during my JD days with Osp, especially to the one-sided numismatists, who I felt were squeezing the world by the scrotum. I fought back.

The demeaning work of teaching made obvious to me that I was not a member of the flock, preaching what I herd without aforethought. Parallel lines *do* meet—at a place in infinity—because space is curved. The flock believed the world was flat and wanted only to hear that parallel lines do *not* meet. The ways to tell a story are varied and many. The flock believed all was linear narrative. I could not achieve the point of view of the average. I was not a member of the mean anymore.

I had been thoroughly demeaned. I was told what to teach and how to teach it, and all anyone wanted was a dog-and-pony show. The actual learning mattered only to a few of us ▶rogues◀ who were still conscientious teachers. No administrators and almost no students had any inter-rust in real learning whatsoever. When the dog-and-pony show gave way to a smidgeon of learning, the students immediately pounced onto an administration-sponsored interweb site called ▶Rape Your Profeßor◀ and voted to have the instructor buggered. The most-voted-for was buggered by machine on TV every Friday night. I quit teaching and ran away the day the vote fell on me.

I took laborer jobs for a few years after that. I worked in a lumber yard, I worked as a janitor, I worked as a night watchman, I worked in retail. Those jobs were demeaning as well, but nothing in life is as demeaning as being a teacher. We had no benefits, received no appreciation, and the pay was appalling. The administrators, however, built for their ¢elghs layer upon layer of administrative superfluousneß. They hired one an Œðer as consultants in order to conduct studies of the efficacy of the studies commißioned the year before that. This was what one fellow rogue instructor called <<just an example of the beast that fucks its ¢elgh.>>

The administration also encouraged students to report on ▶Rape Your Profeßor◀ how sexy the profeßor was. I presume profeßors who were too sexy were found deserving of their buggering unleß, of course, their sexineß pleased the students. Or the administrators.

One is accorded more respect as a sewer worker than as a teacher. And the busineß in the sewers smells better.

The administration only gave faculty a false dilemma—we could ▶beg one◀, meaning we could supplicate our ¢elghs to adminstration's whim, or we could ▶be gone◀, meaning we were not permitted any remonstrance. Remonstrance, unfortunately, came easy to me. My ancestors were Frisian back in 1610. The Remonstrance warmed our souls for a while.

♪O Tulipomania!♫ Out came the cheerleaders for Tulipomania U!

<<Give us a ▶T◀!>> yelled the girls.

<<What for?>> haxed the boys.

<<Total depravity!>> replied the girls. <<Now give us a ▶U◀!>>

<<What for?>>

<<Unconditional election! Now give us an ▶L◀!>>

<<What for?>>

<<Limite atonement! Now give us an ▶I◀!>>

<<What for?>>

<<Irresponsible grace! Now give us a ▶P◀!>>

<<What for?>>

<<Perseverance of the Saints! What's that spell?>>

<<Tulip!>>

<<What's that spell?>>

<<Tulip!

<<Go Tuliopmania U!>>

Moues croßed my path. The cows and Œðers full of bull didn't find my humor amusing. Well, they're all just *Gemüse*. My father used to say, <<The best vegetable is meat.>> these meat-for-brains exemplified well Feuerbach's dictum <<*Der Mensch ist, was er ißt*,>> meaning <<You are what you eat.>> These dumb bovines chew their vegetated cud as they vegetate their ¢elghs. They agree with the sheep, bovid if not bovine.

Do as you're told so the knacker has an easy time when he knocks you on the noggin.

The knacker came around here the Œðer day with a pellet gun in one hand and barbeque sauce in the Œðer. He tried to shoot me full of BBs and pour BBQ sauce on me, but I hogtied him and forced him to listen to the ▶Best Blues Album of 1980◀, according to *Echoes* magazine: BB Arnold with Tony McPhee and the Groundhogs. Everytime Arnold sang ♪dirty mŒðerfucker♫, I pointed at the knacker and laughed.

<<Why?>> I haxed him.

<<Society has hired me. You don't fit in. They want you to leave.>>

<<Tell *them* to leave,>> I replied, and then I shot a BB through his nostril. <<Time for a nose ring,>> I told him. I had a metal tagger that scientists used to use on the ears of the last polar bears in order to track them. The tags had built-in transmitters that beeped when the batteries got low. The constant beeping drove the bears insane, so their use was discontinued. I tagged him and then set him free. <<Tell 'em I also give out free earrings and free piercing,>> I said, slamming the door behind him. I doubt he'll be back, but society will send someone else. I'll need to be constantly vigilant. My motto: never attack—defend to the death! That's how Eintracht Frankfurt would take on Bayern München. Bayern would always be favored by the oddsmakers to win. Frankfurt would play with two extra defenders and only one striker and completely

confound Bayern, who could not complete a clean paß all match. The match would end in a scoreleß tie, which was considered a great victory for Eintracht. Strategy vs. strength? Put my money on strategy.

The last I heard, the cops had nicked the knacker and had whacked him around in their paddy wagon. But he had a black cat bone and a John-the-Conqueroo. He knew exactly what to do, and when they went to give the old dog a bone, he pounced out of the wagon and ran off through the neighborhoods. He is a freerunner, apparently. I have no idea if my problems with the parkour crowd provoked this putz. Apparently he had heard that that was ancient news. And on an Œðer planet.

And on an Œðer plane.

Tea.

Put Z on T—what's it spell?

Nothing at all.

What's it spell?

Permanent inoculation against attacking strategems.

Gems glisten in the stratosphere where the ozone used to be, back in the days of arboreal living, before humans ▶squoze◀ the life out of trees and then the graßes and forced their ¢elghs underground or, at the very least, indoors.

I am safe here in my lighthouse. I hope to never leave it again. Fuck what's hidden in Hidalgo's beard (or was that mine?) Congolese beetles obscure the words of the inscription—but the gist is a question:

<<Why are you here?>>

I don't want to be haxed that question, even by my own beard, because I have no answer.

Why the lighthouse? I like the lighthouse. I think it's because I read Robert Louis Stevenson when I was a boy—especially *Vailima Letters*—and Stevenson was from a long line of lighthouse keepers. I fancied that life for my ¢elgh. So here I am.

<<Why are you here?>>

Well, the moon's too small, and too many pirates keep causing problems there. Venus? I never liked the climate—it was far too inconsistent, and never consistently pleasant. Mars—the Aasvogel. Man, the stuff he cost me. Friends are dead, I was humiliated, abused, and after saving that ☼Aßhole☼ from those coup d'evil symbionts! He should have regarded me a hero forever. Statues of me should have been erected in public parks. I should be memorialized with more than a bearded mask in the Gardens of Obsane Topiary. What sort of mark on history is that?

If all you want is to make a mark, why not just blow shit up?

No—I don't want to make a *bad* mark. I want to be revered.

Worshipped, you mean.

No! Reverence is enough. Worshippers keep wanting to merge with what they worship—I don't want to merge with anything. I am a sufficient unity.

That, of course, reminds me of a blues song: ►I'm So Adequate◄.

I'm So Adequate

You cut me to the quick for being late.
I'm the horse who never gets out of the gate.
I'm so adequate.
I'm so adequate.

When I'm in your land, I just can't see.
When I'm in your hands, you kick at me.
I'm so adequate.
I'm so adequate.

I hope you know you're out of luck.
'Cause you hit me with a stick doesn't mean I'm stuck.
I'm so adequate.
I'm so adequate.

When you trip me, I fall completely flat,
but I land on my feet like a Cheshire cat.
I'm so adequate.
I'm so adequate.

Adequate is as adequate does.
Bouncing off an aqueduct gives me a buzz.
I'm adequate.
Nothing more than adequate.

But I tell you there's a lot of fellas who can relate
to just being adequate.
We're all adequate.
Nothing more than adequate.

You can throw me to the wolves to see what they eat.
You can grind my brains into hamburger meat.
But I'm still adequate.
I'm so adequate.
Nothing more than adequate.

I spotted a book on my shelf—

Mean Textmeßages from People Who Try to Hurt You was the name. What did I have this for? I threw it into the furnace like I was Bigger Thomas. How do you get rid of bad taste left in the mouth? I think that's why we drink. These meßages were far subtler, though, back in the day when almost no one visited me in the hospital, and those who did did so just to aßuage their guilt.

I quote Patti Smith: <<I am an American artist, and I have no guilt.>> But I have been building snail shells for slugs.

Why You Tailin' Me?

Shoot me in the chest.
Oh, make me bleed.
I've got snail shells for slugs.
Oh, this you can believe.
Oh, baby,
Oh, baby,
Why you tailin' me?

I loved you once,
and then again.
I let you be,
and was your friend.
Oh, baby,
Oh, baby,
Why you tailin' me?

I took a flight.
You took a bath.
I had no right
to choose my path?
Oh, baby,
Oh, baby,
Why you tailin' me?

You say your man
mistreated you,
so now you have to

do it to me too?
Oh, baby,
Oh, baby,
Why you tailin' me?

It wasn't me
who let you down.
Stop following me—
go back to town.
Oh, baby,
Oh, baby,
Why you tailin' me?

Shoot me in the chest.
Oh, make me bleed.
I've got snail shells for slugs.
Oh, this you can believe.
Oh, baby,
Oh, baby,
Why you tailin' me?

The laughter Patrick McGoohan heard when he declared his ¢elgh a free man attacks my ears.

I send a text to the world: <<Will you please stop attacking me?>> or, better, <<Can you please stop attacking me?>> I hope you are capable of stopping.

Some little troll dances around with his horrible faces and mocks me. He and his little troll kids mock me. They think it's easy being me. It was just an easy choice I made, and now I'm king of the lighthouse. They don't see my years of intense pain and lonelineß, nor do they care. They won't realize what I've been through until they have their brains bashed in by their dear-rust friends. Sure, then they'll come to me for help.

But where were they when I needed them? They all had excuses. Half turned away.

Seeing a chink in my armor, the Œðer half took up spears to see if they could penetrate and kill.

They were so busy arguing with their ¢elghs who should have the right to kill me that I escaped unnoticed just by getting up and walking out.

<<Wasn't there someone here once?>>

<<I know who you mean. Bob Mitchum, right?>>

<<No, not an actor.>>

<<Von Freeman?>>

<<No, not a musician, either.>>

<<Ken Patchen?>>

<<His shadow is always near, I gueß.>>

<<Federman?>>

<<His, too.>>

<<Well, damn. You know trolls attacked them, too.>>

<<Too true. Too true,>> say you, as you forget about me. <<That's cool. ♪One leß bell to answer….♫>>

<<Hax not for whom the troll bells,>> says an Œðer you.

Me, I'm just going to sit back and shut up. I want to melt into the furniture and drip into the scene on the Mongolian rug. I want to escape into the expanse of the Gobi Desert. Or become a Trappist like Thomas Merton. I want to fish for goby and have some of that Trappist beer and Gethsemani cheese while I do.

Too many people are encroaching on the lighthouse. I need to move it farther from the hoi polloi.

Or I could dive into the heart of the city and do my part to pull all the energy into the center until it begins to hold, and then I can make my escape to the edges. When the center blows, then it's safe to go back to the center. Be away from the preßure is my advice.

You've heard of the ▶Lighthouse for the Blind◀? Mine's the ▶Lighthouse for the Heavy◀. It takes my woes, my worries, my wounds and my worms and turns them all to something worthy of levity.

Take all the words you know that are ugly and unpleasantly heavy and make a croßword out of them.

Put words that stink on fish hooks. Attach sinkers to the line. Catch cat as catch can in Ketchikan, home of the 300-day rainy season, where a patch of blue sky is called a ▶sucker hole◀.

I had a vision of being in an audience and hearing Dean Martin sing ▶Nel Blu Dipinto Di Blu◀.

Nellie? Wasn't that Dudley Do-Right's horse? And Blue was Paul Bunyan's axe? And wasn't the story about Paul that he was so big that fifty storks had to carry him to his mŒðer? And when he was seven months old, he was so much the lumberjack already that one night, while his parents slept, he sawed off their legs? And they didn't notice because his father was sawing logs at the time?

No.

No?

No. Nell was Inspector Fenwick's daughter, and she was in love with the horse, whose name, if I recall, was just ►Horse◄. And Bunyan's ox, not his axe, was indeed blue but was named ►Babe◄. I'd remember if he named his axe.

Stormbringer!

No, not Stormbringer.

Excalibur!

No, not that, either.

Hrunting! The Kin-Killer!

No, and Bunyan did not cut off his parents' legs. He chopped off the legs of their bed. I gueß he wanted in, as many young ones do when they are frightened by storms or dreams.

Paul did too chop off his parents' legs. That's why he was crucified upside down.

Wrong Paul.

Pope Wrong Paul?

That's John Paul.

George Ringo.

And he wasn't Paul. Peter was the upside-down one.

He's the one who replaced Paul in 1967?

28IF? Black rose on the lapel? Croßing the street barefoot? ►Turn me on, dead man◄? The car crash that John mentions in ►A Day in the Life◄ and Ringo mentions in ►Don't Paß Me By◄? That Paul?

Yes, not the doppelgänger, who, of course, if Sylvia Plath's doppelgänger theory is correct, must have been who killed Paul.
So why was Peter crucified upside down?

I heard he was looking at the ►28IF◄ license plate and mistook it for ►L337◄ [►LEET◄] text. So he stood on his head to read it correctly. Just then the soldiers burst in, grabbed him, and nailed him just like that, as he was, to a black oak out back.

In Arkansas.

That's right. He was friends with Jim Dandy. And Jim Dandy was a childhood pal of Paul Bunyan.

Jim Diddley?

No.

Bo Diddley?

No.

Bo Jackson?

No. The Heavy. Kelvin Swaby.

Kelvin?

<<Yeah, he's cool.>>

<<Sure is. Minus 460.>>

<<Or minus 273. Either way he's cool. He's not the absolute zero he's made out to be.>>

<<But what's Swaby?>>

<<He is.>>

<<No kidding.>>

Who is that? Is that Nils? I swear I can hear him sometimes. Nettie, too, usually when I imagine being scolded and insulted by a woman. She has too many weapons.

I should get to the gals of the Gardens soon. As soon as the coast is clear. I'm in a lighthouse, after all.

Hey, Bo Diddley had BB Arnold on harp.

Yep.

That's excellent.

Sure—it all wraps around and comes back together eventually. The universe is curved space, after all. That's the only way we can slap our ¢elghs on the back.

Even Slappy Pappy?

Sure—I heard the story of great father today on Bloomsday. A son loved the writings of Gerald Durrell, Lawrence's brŒðer. Not only the stories about growing up in Corfu, but even more the stories of collecting colobus monkeys and long-nosed bandicoots in the Cameroons and Madagascar, and then bringing them to the zoo designed only for preserving endangered species to later be reintroduced into the wild: the Jersey Wildlife Preservation Trust.

The dad understood the son's love for books. He had it, too, so he bought tickets to a lecture Durrell was giving at the Chicago Historical Society. The attendees were all members of the Chicago social elite. Durrell, after his lecture, drew pictures of animals and auctioned them off to the blue-hairs. The boy's father could not afford to buy one, and the disappointment on his son's face when he saw his son figure everything out without its being spoken broke his heart. So the father wrote to Durrell and explained his son's crustfallen affection for Durrell's books. The letter touched Durrell, who wrote to the boy and sent a drawing with the letter.

That was a dad who loved his son. That dad cared. That dad was the best in the world that day.

So who cares?

Only the son; I gueß no one prefers to remember anything that is sentimental for the son. The son should have died in Lake Forust, I gueß. The son sounded as pathetic as Jack Benny. The mom was as alarmist as Henny Penny Benny, and the sky was coming down. Jack's dad was stoic, a methodical undertaker. He'd conduct burials in homage to him who is gone until the end of all days. Non sequitur piled upon non sequitur. Telesis!

Okay, Sister, what do you think? I turn to my bronze statuette of Saint Kateri Tekakwitha for an answer. The statuette, which stood proudly on my bookshelf, was a gift from an admirer of the Franciscan Ecology Sisters of Saint Kateri Tekakwitha for the Fourth World.

Saint Kateri Tekakwitha was a smallpox survivor. She would not be the last of Mohawks despite the best attempts of the smallpox-infested-blanket distributors.

Columbus's vision of a new world emptied of indigenous people would never be realized.

Kateri's father was a Mohawk Chief, and her mŒðer, Tagaskouita, was an Algonquin woman who had been captured and then integrated into the Mohawk tribe.

The smallpox scarred her and left her with damaged eyesight, though her smallpox scars disappeared when she died. So did her scars from her practice of ¢elgh-mortification, which she practiced after her conversion to Catholicism at the hands of an Opus Dei-leaning Jesuit priest.

The statuette had been one of Nils's favorites. At the time, I had thought him to be flatulent, not flagellant. But now I see why he'd appreciate the ¢elgh-flagellating virgin. Not only did she whip her ¢elgh, but supposedly she also burned her ¢elgh with coals, cut her ¢elgh, slept on a bed of thorns, and starved her ¢elgh for long periods of time. Today she'd be an Emo fashion model, truly ▶the New Star of the New World◀, one of her best-known monikers.

Telesis? I just did. Any more and albino ornithologists will come after me.

If you Telesis, you are telekinetic. What Œðer kin would you tell? The kine kin back on the farm? The kind kin who are always supportive? The king kin who seldom have been? The kino kin for whom all this is but a motion picture meant to mock us all? The keen kin who've seen sin and know not to judge Œðers? The kinky kin who are trapped in their skin?

Telekinesis? I could move my ¢elgh to the Gardens very easily if I had that ability. I could just levitate and propel my ¢elgh. Maybe I could eat a pot of beans and use fart propulsion.

Get an army of us going—come be G. I. Tracked.

What's a tract?

Anything you like.

Oh, well, I'm positive I only attract the negative.

I may be polar, but I'm not cold. But when I've run hot, my women have tried to cool me down. Then when I'm all cool, they complain that I'm not so hot. That old joke. That's what they call me, like I'm Bukowski and they're Scarlett Johanßon. Vomiting in translation. Pißing and shitting in translation. And that's okay—they're human. But they don't want me to be.

Not at all.

I should probably get to the Gardens soon. I'm getting too maudlin.

And then there's Maude….

And then there's Kokette….

Two of the best at making sure I thought of my ¢elgh as garbage.

A barge. A guard bard of a barge of garbage. I need to get out and mix with people, I know. But where are the nice people keeping their ¢elghs? The nicest people I know live hundreds of miles away.

They'll turn their backs and play *Kind of Blue*.

Well, the only way to get there is to travel the miles. Start with *The Birth of the Cool*. Miles with Lee Konitz, Max Roach, and Gerry Mulligan in 1949 and 1950.

Move!

It's like *Go*, the John Clellon Holmes novel that started it all in fiction.

But Miles is so cool, he's on beyond swank. Miles wanted his audience to get it. When they didn't, when they became what Bob Weir called ▶bug-eyed monsters◀, Miles was disturbed. He had no inter-rust in milking the brain-damaged for trinkets. For him, the music was it, an end in its ¢elgh.

I remember one 35th-rate writer once say, <<He's not doing it for its ¢elgh. He's using it as a means to an end.>> That was probably the single stupidest thing anyone had ever said about Miles.

<<The Gardens? In I go,>> said Jones, entering Covent Garden because he didn't know the Gardens of Obsane Topiary. His red elm project would never know its cousins overseas.

<<Did someone say, <Coven>?>> haxed Alistair.

<<No,>> I replied. <<Jones said, <Coven*t-t-t-t*>!>>

<<O*kay-k-k-k.*>>>

<<You may be, you bigot, you, but I am not. I'm in support of Henry Rollins's suggestion for doing away with your intolerable little club by coopting it. Rollins knows his semiotics.>>

<<Did I hear someone say, <Covalent>?>> haxed Bond, shaking from not having had his first martini yet.

Dylan Thomas replied, <<You know, even my Old Grand-Dad was Bonded.>>

Charles A. Reich piped in, <<Maybe I could write a book on the Bonding of America.>>

But when Theodis Ealey started singing ▶Move with the Motion◀, tears came to our eyes, and we danced while we wept.

Chester Himes said, <<I used to dance like this with your mŒðer.>>

Hidalgo came up to me and said, <<I put something in your beard.>>

<<What?>> I was taken aback. He knew? He put it there? <<What did you say?>>

<<Can I have a beer?>> Oh—I had completely misheard him. <<Sure, go ahead. There are some Boddingtons in the fridge. Maybe a couple of Beck's Sapphire, too.>>

<<Beck's Sapphire? Do you like that?>>

<<<*Die Bierfabrik*> as it's commonly known? No, not really. It's watery. Commercial. Very LCD. Watch those Boddingtons. They foam up when you open them.>>

I overheard Reich talking to Chester Himes, and Reich said, <<Maria Monteßori was onto something, man. A teacher's role no longer is to educate. Everyone wants to be educavated, and no one wants to learn. A teacher's role is just to maintain an engaged, positive claßroom.>>

<<How do the students learn?>> haxed Himes.

<<They don't. That's not the point. They are entertained. That's all that matters. Anyone who does not achieve that is fired.>>

At least he *looked* like Charles Reich. After he said that, I wasn't sure anymore.

Bored, I relied on my wonderful library. I found a small volume I'd forgotten: *Eyelidleß Man*.

<<On Bloom Lake, in the town of Saynot, Wisconsin, back in the early 1980s, a legend took hold over a campfire. I was there….,>> it began.

No, I didn't feel like reading a horror story just then, even if it was a funny one.

I figured I'd enjoy synaesthetically hearing some Herbal Mixture, Tony McPhee's hippie band between Groundhogs the blues band and Groundhogs the exploder of minds. Tony's songs ▶A Love that Died◀ and ▶Tailor Made◀ already point the way to *Split*, *Who Will Save the World?*, and *Thank Christ for the Bomb*.

The Herbal Mixture led me to Tony's album with the drummer John Dummer, *Cabal*, which also featured Jo Ann and Dave Kelly and a cat named John O'Leary, who wailed on the harp like a cat in heat. O'Leary sounds to me like he'd been pickin' Charlie Mußelwhite's mind. And with Jo Ann? Can you imagine Janis singing with Mußelwhite? You get the idea, then. Profound.

Amateur lost. In the long run, we can tell ►who◄ from ►whom◄.
In the long run, we can tell ►zoo◄ from ►zoom◄➔
Got no place to be.
Got nothing to do.
Some.
I'm here at
home writing an amusement for you. It may bore you to tears. It may change your life. It may correspond like digitalis. It may cost you a wife. It did me. More than one if you count the ones who weren't.
Foxgloves.
Figwarts.
Fairy Gloves.
The leaving hands wave goodbye as you fade and then hello when you come back. Digitalis is always waving. At least until night's shade. Then the beautiful lady winds her way up along an arterial corridor that leads right into your heart, and there she pauses, at the center of all chambers. A word from her would stop everything. An Œðer word would start it back up. Instead, she haxes a question. Your life will depend on our answer.

Repeat whenever you're bored. And if you fail, you have digitalis. If you succeed [that's one funny-looking word: ►succeed◄…], you'll shake the beautiful lady right off you during your convulsions. Yeah, but what a way to go? Is that what you said? I'm pretty sure that's what I heard you say.

Okay okay okay.

I was performing a one-man play, *The Last Minutes of Nelson Rockefeller*, at the time.

That's the way to go:

Literally.

*

A girl named Alice gave me digitalis back when I was in third grade. I've been in third grade ever since. That girl named Alice meant me malice—that's why she gave the fairy gloves to me.

My hands began to bounce like Wing Biddlebaum's. Of course, mine landed in the air—no one else's hair was long enough to tousle. It is no fun, let me tell you, to tousle the stubble of a shaving man.

Long hair, long beard, that's soft against the gentlest skin. Stubble is abrasive.

Abrasion can be useful, but how much should one use where and when and why?

<<I can only tell you how,>> I hear. Of course.

I am spending some time on my little garden. Alongside the lighthouse fence, my morning glories are lolling and intertwining beautifully. I have six varieties planted. The Grandpa Otts are already blooming a deep, velvety purple.

I am worried about my Happy Hour Rose morning glories, though. I do not see them growing. The last time I grew them, they had small digitiform leaves. All of these are heart-shaped, though the sizes vary tremendously from the smaller Split Personality leaves to the enormous washcloths of Scarlett O'Hara.

Yesterday I had three Grandpa Ott blooms, and today I have two. I hope the Œðers follow soon.

My black tomatoes, yellow pear tomatoes, banana peppers, and poblano peppers are all flowering, and the tomatoes are already laden with green fruit. The old pepper bloßoms are giving way to pea-sized pepper buds.

Soon the hummingbirds will come. I need to be here to see them. I can't go beard fishing yet. I'll migrate with the hummingbirds.

Ægir will let me know. One of the Æsir at least.

An ager will let me know. One of the <<Hey, sir,>> at least.

<<Honey weighs quite heavily on thought,>> hißed a garter snake.

<<Put honey on whatever shames your thoughts,>> hißed an Œðer.

<<Honey soothes the malformed penis,>> hißed a third.

The three snakes braided their ¢elghs acroß the floor towards the statue of St. George.

When the snakes saw the serpent-killer, they broke braid and bit one an Œðer in order to get away, drawing blood.

St. George's army fell upon the snakes and disposed of them by beheading them and burning the pieces in a fire of molten metal, burnt into one good-sized nugget which was then encased in a glaß marble larger than just a mib—it is a dragon's eye taw! This one has six eyes. It is special. I keep it on a bookshelf as a conversation piece.

I tried using a garter as the ring for the game, but my dragon's eye taw would not croß the garter. It frustrated me, so I never used that taw for sport again. Here it rusts, on a small pewter stand that looks like an outstretched hand. The hand holds the taw.

*

Grandpa Ott had five velvet-clad visitors today. No one else in the family showed, though.

They're taking their time. Good. I was warned by Steve Hillage many years ago, when I interviewed him for radio, about the <<lemming-like rush towards originality.>>

Being first is good, but being best is better.

The Grandpa Otts are all on one side of the morning glory chain. I see one solitary bloßom poised for opening tomorrow on the Œðer side. That Œðer one may be one of the kin coming in to town. It's striped, so it might be one of the Flying Saucers.

Once the Flying Saucers land, nothing should prevent the hummingbirds from buzzing by for a sip. I've seen a couple in the vicinity, but haven't had any close enough to discern what kind of hummingbird.

It could be a Blue Star, but those are usually high up. Fifteen feet, so one is looking up into the sky. Flying Saucers are closer, usually eight to ten feet. But the short ones, Split Personality and Heavenly Blue, haven't shown up yet. And I don't think the Happy Hour Roses made it for a third generation. Hopefully the Heavenly Blue did. They were my first two, the Heavenly Blue coming first by a couple of weeks.

*

Morning Glory Blues

I bought my baby a flower,
    but she just threw it away.
She said she wanted my morning glory,
    but it was already spent today.

I haxed her, hey, babe,
    would you wait for a rose?
She said she wanted something
    that wasn't predisposed.

I haxed her, hey, babe,
    would you like tulips?
She said she'd prefer a morning glory,
    and she'd give me her rosy hips.

I haxed her, hey, babe,
did you see that jack-in-the-pulpit?
She said she'd skipped church that day
because she couldn't help it.

She said she wanted my morning glory,
but it was already spent today.

*

Six Grandpa Ott bloßoms on the left, one on the right. No Flying Saucers. Apparently Grandpa Ott's sent his tendrils down the fence.

*

The next day sees ten Grandpa Otts to the left, one to the right, and even farther to the right my first Heavenly Blue of the year.

Hop Scotch! At the very least, hops and Scotch!

Today is what the old government used to call American Independence Day. Of course, once the corporations dißolved the nation, today became known as Disenfranchisement Day, or Dee Day Two. It celebrated the demise of true democracy and let people have a day to their ¢elghs to think about how they no longer had any ¢elgh-determination whatsoever. One's boß was one's all. The corporations ruled everything for everyone. They determined what people could see, hear, smell, touch, and taste. They controlled every facet of thought and appearance. Any deviation from corporate ►culture◄ was ruled treasonous and was met with execution by lethal injection. At one time execution had been done by beheading, but because the populace had become used to not using the head anyway, the executions proved ineffective. Many of the executed lived on for years after execution. Some, who had caught the lopped-off heads in their arms, were still able to see and hear and smell and taste again once they had the cables reconnected. Those whose heads had fallen into the crowd and had become soccer balls and bowling balls and the like were able to get touch-screen interactive camera heads attached. Since brain death was no longer a poßibility, the corporations switched to cellular death. Rumor had it that underground labs were working on overcoming that as well.

The underground labs were actually terrorist cells sponsored by competing corporations who wanted in on the spoils.

The corporate wars were fierce. The wars that had begun between car manufacturers and between cola companies become global and catastrophic.

Happy Dee Day Two!

Softball was being played in the park.

A batter mishit the ball and half said so.

The umpire ejected him for bad language. <<Pronounce your ►i◄ as ►i◄ and your ►y◄ as ►y◄!>> he said to the batter, who'd fouled out anyway.

The umpire warned both teams, <<Don't be foul out here!>>

The managers got together and told their corner fielders to only play inside the lines. That way neither team would run afoul against the ump.

When a seagull landed in the outfield, the umpire had an aneurysm and had to be rushed to the hospital.

The teams needed a new ump, so, with my recreation department experience, I volunteered. I haxed the managers if they were playing for love or war. I didn't want to run afoul of them.

They said they were playing for the love of the game.

So I said in that case everything's fair. Ignore the lines. I would have allowed the ejected player back into the game, but he'd already left the park. The seagull we ignored. It flew off to an overflowing garbage can by the field house.

*

Twelve Grandpa Otts to the left, one on the right, and two Heavenly Blues on the right are bloßoming today.

I definitely cannot go beard fishing today—the flowers are just beginning to come in. Hummingbirds will soon follow.

Then the doctors will want to come just in order to alter the little birds fraudulently. They'll pull off the real feathers and replace them with prosthetics from emu, grounding the birds forever, which are collected and ground into patties for those who also like larks' tongues in aspic and the sort.

Deformity in the name of science. Or is it art?

Ground hummingbirds are sold under the brand name ►Ground 'ums◄, the ►'ums◄ being short for ►hums◄ and ►hummingbirds◄.

They are also known as ground hymns, because anyone who'd eat a hummingbird has never marveled at the feat of flight. Hir feats fall flat on the pavement. Ze thinks through hir feet, never realizing ze could take an elevator to the top and look out through the magical third eye, or at least through the two visceral ones.

Such a person is haxing to be defeated. Give hir a seat and a tin cup. Ze needs to stay right here.

I've heard people say that about me, but I ignore them. I'm like an ant-lion. I can lay in wait. Patient. Quiet. Soft in the sand, hidden from the blast heat of the wind.

Then…

POUNCE! I grab a paßerby by the neck. Look—it's the sailor who said I used my work as a means to an end rather than having it be an end in its ¢elgh—the stupidest thing anyone has ever said to me—by someone unqualified to even say it.

I do not judge him by the cut of his jib, after all. How can he judge me?

Then the priest will come to altar the hummingbirds fraudulently. They are creatures, not angels. Real, not ideal. As beautiful as Shakespeare's mistreß, and swifter than his wife. Hummingbirds are not gods, but they sleep in no second best bed.

Tesla would have ruled the world if he'd only realized that hummingbirds were more powerful than pigeons.

They should not be touched. Just watch them for the few seconds you have the privilege, and let your eyes drink the nectar of this amazing flower of your vision. Sear the image into your mind. Amazement will follow you all the rust of your days.
Leave the jade behind—greater gems can be found.

For now, it's all about the hummingbirds. The beard will have to wait.

Looking at my hand-held six-eyed dragon taw, I remembered again Shevchenko's mask inside its Lucite case.

Something was in *my* mask, though. A note from Hidalgo. Something about needing air holes. <<Keep a pen in your hand. Always carry a way to keep your air hole open. A tubular ballpoint pen is a good choice,>> said the pen manufacturer.

Lucy and Penelope—had they tried to kill me by not leaving an air hole? I don't believe they actually took me for a hypoxyphiliac. Penelope's friend Alf had said so, but Lucy seemed to have genuine affection for me. But I had to bring that mask to the Gardens. I just had to. The Gardens of Obsane Topiary! What a great place! The Shaved Girls! I could rust my head in the best one's bosom forever.

What had I hidden in my beard? I think I left it there for my ¢elgh while I slept. I probably need to find it and read it when I sleep in the Gardens again.

But not yet. First, the hummingbirds! I need more morning glories to open! And then I will return to the arms of the best of the Shaved Girls. If she'll have me. I'll bring her some morning glory seeds. She can plant them in a favorite spot on the surface and then visit them whenever she wants to see something beautiful.

There will be a beautiful glade filled with morning glories and hummingbirds of all intensities of all the colors—God's own palette. Of course I mean that metaphorically.

*

Five Grandpa Otts to the left, one to the right, and one Heavenly Blue on the right all together indicate that the appearance of hummingbirds must not be as imminent as I had thought.

*

Today I was greeted by seven Otts on the left, two on the right, two Heavenly Blues on the right, and two on the left. Perhaps yesterday was an anomaly and the hummers are nigh.

I went to the interwebbing to look for a diving duck and found a hummingbird instead! Rory Gallagher with guest Tony McPhee live at the Hummingbird in Birmingham, UK, on the 18th of October in 1987.

I could not wait to hear what those two masters of British blues sounded like together! McPhee sits in on five songs. The whole show was nearly 168 minutes long.

Hummingbird was a nightclub in Dale End.

It was previously the Rank Ballroom—aren't they all rank with hot, sweaty dancers?

It became the Birmingham Academy, then the Carling Academy, then the Oz Academy. Oz Academy moved out in September of 2009, leaving the old Hummingbird to the wrecking ball in order to make way for an injection of housinge. The economy faltered, though, and the demolition project was postponed for happier times ahead when we can all demolish history with glee!

Apparently a video of this concert also exists, albeit a bit shorter, and shot by someone with the DTs.

The band did not perform a version of ►Shake It◄ for the cameraman, but nonetheleß he did! The shakineß may be a tracking ißue, so blame the editor, but the video wobbles worse than pills.

It bobbles worse than wills. And where there's a will, there's probate!

But for a night at the Hummingbird, an audience was treated to an amazing event: Rory Gallagher and Tony McPhee, playing together for five songs. As if being there for Rory wasn't enough.

►Shinkicker◄! That is one heck of a piece of music. Testosterone.

Birmingham must be one shit-kickin' cool city. The salt of the earth—my people! Regular folks.

I'm in No Hurry

Pardon me if I'm occasionally uncouth.
It's just something I picked up in my youth.
'Scuse me if I'm not quick to the climb.
You see, I'm just enjoying my time.
I'm in no hurry.
I'm in no hurry.

I didn't walk till I was ten.
I spoke no word till I had a yen.
If I can't manage to stop on a dime,
it's because I'm just enjoying my time,
and I'm in no hurry.
I'm in no hurry.

Baby, just hold onto my hand.
You know, this isn't something that I planned.
I just love finding my ¢elgh with someone so fine,
and you know that I'm enjoying my time.
I'm in no hurry.
I'm in no hurry.

There may not be as much as I like to what I say,
But I hope you're glad you're with me anyway.
I'd love you from afar; you fill my mind.
When I see you, I enjoy every minute of my time.
I'm in no hurry.
I'm in no hurry.

Beads, necklaces, bangles and rings—
you understand such beautiful things.
I understand words that get out of line.
I know that we have insufficient time,
but no worry—
we're in no hurry.

I've felt you in my heart for many years.
When I'm with you I have no fears,

for I know, and know that I'm
telling you I've seen a sign.
All is right; no need to worry.
Let's not be in any hurry.
I'm in no hurry.
Let's not worry.

I understand Second City Syndrome—even wrote about it somewhere. Birmingham is England's Chicago. The people of those two cities really understand each Œðer. They have a very deep link.

►A lot of idiots dislike me just by looking at me◄, the radio was playing.

<<Infomercials!>> said the American. Of course to her everything was an infomercial.

<<What about me?>> haxed an Œðer woman, a long-haired blonde, and apparently a real one.

<<No—you are not one!>> aßerted the stage manager.

Meanwhile Rory Gallagher is burning through the chords of ►Shadowplay◄ faster than most punk bands could.

The interplay between the two great guitarists was best heard on ►Bullfrog Blues◄, a song by William Harris dating back to 1928, popularized again by Canned Heat in 1968, then by Rory in 1972, and then again by David Bromberg in 1976.

On an Œðer note, Bahá'í musicians Seals and Crofts had a hit in 1872 with their song ►Hummingbird◄.>>

*

Today's army, left to right, Grandpa Otts and Heavenly Blues, was 10-4, 1-0, 1-6.

We had rain overnight, and the plants reacted well. My first poblano pepper is a half-inch long.

I had to unwrap a few morning glory tendrils from my tomato—the morning glory was beginning to pull the top of the tomato down. I did not want the tomato to be a stalker, but a destalker was worse if it meant then main stalk would be broken. Most plants don't survive that—it's like snapping the spine of a vertebrate.

Morning glories can be a little aggreßive, I gueß, as they clamber over anything in their need to move, even though I beseech them to hear their victims clamor for peace.

Morning glories rule. Morning glories grew in the oasis. Morning glories decorated *A*

Scanner Darkly. The hummers are on their way.

Hummers are on their way. Shermans. Panzers. Don't point out the obvious—hide it like the Order of the Garter.

Hummers for Brummies! The Chic for Chicago! But Second Cities only get Sloppy. Hax Bromberg.

Hax Hapshash and the Coloured Coat, with Tony McPhee, of course. The ubiquitous Tony McPhee. I'd have loved to have heard him with Zappa. Wow! I gueß I need some sort of past-past-perfect verb tense there.

*

Too much rain came down this morning. The flowers couldn't open. The plants were beaten down. They came back up in the afternoon, but the time for blooming had paßed. What was it, June 16th? I had a hankering for kidney pie but couldn't find any near the Land between the Lakes. And I wasn't certain if prairie dog kidneys were edible. What if they were like dog livers, which killed Mertz on his expedition to the Antarctic back in 1913. No Chicago apothecary can save him now. He can whip the louse's hide and make it cry, but it'll never fit in at the flea circus. And what if Fleagle, the Banana Splits dog, won't give up his fleas? I know what it feels like to be a clown. It's not easy. Respect the clowns. They are giving their ¢elghs up for you. Feast on them, sure, but don't tear them limb from limb.

When John Lee Hooker sings about the bottom, his holler explodes the head.

*

The rain and heat combined to keep me from getting an accurate flower count today. Probably ten, and only the purple and blue. Where the red ones are, I do not know. No Split Personality yet. Maybe I should listen to the Groundhogs' *Split*. No Scarlett O'Haras, the really buxom blooms. Not even the white-with-blue-streaks Blue Stars have shown yet. No Flying Saucers, either. And the Happy Hour Rose morning glory did not survive to the third generation. A shame. I'll have to order a replacement next year. Or find it in seed, but this one I've only ever seen sold as a plant.

The seeds I had all came from Holland except the Scarlett O'Haras, which are American.

I'm not sure where the seeds for the Happy Hour Rose originated. And my original Heavenly Blues, which I also bought as plants, had uncertain origins. I supplemented the Heavenly Blues with Dutch seeds. All I know about the original two plants—the Happy Hour Rose and the Heavenly Blue—is that they were distributed out of a greenhouse in Connecticut, and that was a long way to go. I'd have to try ordering by mail. Or find one of those old-fashioned interwebs. I just hate sitting through hours of commercials just to send one meßage, though. But that's the interwebs. That's why it stopped inter-rusting people.

Criminal intent? Get out of the tent!

*

Today was a little cooler, only 81° F. The flowers responded well. At least twenty blooms, left, middle, right, purple and blue, all in equal proportions, came out to bid the hummers approach. No response.

*

I haven't been feeling my feelings. Do I still have any?

I've got my ¢elgh so holed up in here, I might as well be in the hole for thirty days, to regurgitate some humble pie. But if the spirit of Jo Jo Gunne proves the alternative, then to be on the run for 99 days is no better. But to call this a dilemma would be false. The compromise would be to spend my thirty days in San Ber'dino with Zappa's friend Bobby, who looks like a potato.
Everything connects to Zappa eventually.

Why are cows neat?

I think that Tony McPhee uses his singing as a sonic element of his music more than as a means of telling a story. Who needs ▶story◀ anyway? Children, maybe, because they cannot handle the facts uncouched, so we hide leßons in ▶story◀.

▶Story◀ is a weapon used to suck people in and hurt them.

i.e. Now that I have your attention with my cute little tale, let me lay some heavy moral obligations on you, number one of which is to send me your money. Whatever you send me will cause a cosmic vacuum to form around your wallet. It will suck into your wallet three times what you send me.

Oh, yeah. How much should you send me? A tenth of everything you own. Since you're getting everything back three-fold, you'll still be making back seventeen percent on your investment! For your ten dollars per hundred, you'd still have ninety. You'd get thirty back (minus my ten percent), giving you a total of $117.00. Where else can you find such a solid seventeen percent return?

You know what? I see a criminal in the revival tent! A snake oil salesman par excellence. The invisible elixir that he sells will cure all! Of course!

So McPhee uses pitch, dynamic range, rhythm, attack and sustain. They *are* the thing, not just a ▶story◀ about the thing!

*

Odd—today (20 blooms, all purple and blue) I fell asleep in the afternoon while watching the Minor League All-Star Game (none of my Midwest League favorites were there—no Kane County Cougars, no Lansing Lugnuts,. No Rock Shoulders, the best-named ballplayer of all time.

I started dreaming about high school, about my uneasy place everywhere in my world except the haven one friend provided in his third floor attic, where he lived.

He was a good-hearted man with tremendous willpower. I have always been amazed at his power. He was a psychedelic genius.

He was at the beach with me and two Œðer friends of ours when we saw pterodactyls. We went time traveling back to the early 1960s. He haxed a woman what time it was. She was unintelligible. I haxed him who the President was. He said Kennedy. We were back. We walked along the beach and came acroß a 1950s-style beach volleyball game. That confirmed that we were in a time slipstream.

Dinosaurs and time travel—this cat had chops.

And I dreamt about him in a completely different context—working at a store or something—and then he knocked.

The guy showed up at the door of the lighthouse.

That was a strange coincidence. Well, maybe. He'd come up the Tennesee River into Kentucky Lake and had seen the beacon from the lighthouse. I gueß that makes me bad at hiding, doesn't it?

He was an inter-rusting fellow indeed. We had hung out at the Point in Chicago's Hyde Park when he was earning his degree in political science at the famed University of Chicago.

He actually, amazingly, wrote a short story that was eerily similar to Olaf Stapledon's masterpiece, *Star Maker*, which introduced the notion of Dyson spheres to the world. And, like Borges's Pierre Menard (a distant cousin of my mŒðer) who wanted to rewrite *Don Quixote* without copying it (all great inventions, after all, being inevitable, so *Don Quixote* would have been written, sooner or later, exactly as it was, and all Menard would have had to do was place his ¢elgh in the place for that inevitably to fall on him (or so said Borges)), my friend Will Power (his nickname to his friends) rewrote *Star Maker* without ever having seen or heard of Stapledon's original. He arrived at it independently of Stapledon.

Abruptly, after catching up for an hour, Will Power announced he had to get going and disappeared again into the background noise, where he would always remain a fondly remembered friend.

I remembered I had to water the morning glories and tomatoes anyway. The peppers liked the heat. The morning glories and tomatoes were wilting. Plus the morning glories had a few of those pesky Japanese beetles in their shiny metallic shells eating the leaves. They are not an indigenous species but have become too succeßfully invasive. I'm not sure what predates on them.

They are probably so ancient, nothing predates them.

How's that for a nice pair of Heteronymous Homographs?

Who was a cousin of Hieronymus Bosch?

That is incorrect! Will?

Opoßums will dig up their grubs and eat them. Ducks eat them. Some wasps kill and eat them. But the best thing is to pick them off the leaves and toß them into a jar of soapy water. The soap prevents them from flying away. And then you can dispose of the jar's contents later. The beetles like to cluster, so that helps on the hunt. Hunt them every day. Or get some wasps, ducks and opoßums.

I had none of them.

Well, good luck, Will had said when I'd explained my garden challenges.

Ducks would make a real meß. Wasps would annoy and sting me. And opoßums are just mean.

A jar of soapy water it will be!

*

I'd like for hummers to like the beetles, but they insist on singing along.

*

91° today. The radio announcer said it was 330 and would be a bazillion tomorrow. 96° is predicted. I caught a beetle in the jar and watered the plants heavily several times. I think the water was evaporating in the air before it hit the soil. The peppers don't mind. They're smiling at the tomatoes and at the morning glories and are calling them wimps.

The morning glories are already deep purple and blue like a serious bruise. They're tough. They're not running red, nor are they oh-so-delicately white. They've been beaten.

I knew a cat who was growing avocados in Florida, and he told me avocados won't fruit unleß they're streßed. So he went out and beat his avocado trees with a baseball bat. They gave plenty of fruit after that. No crocodile tears—just alligator pears!

Champion Jack Dupree said that he saw a hummingbird go by down by the rail yard. But that sounds like a ploy to get me on my way to the Gardens. I'm not so easily hoodwinked.

<<Flummoxed?>> haxes Steve Hillage throughout my memory.

<<Bamboozled!>> chimes in WC Handy, or was that WC Fields?

Why would I want to get in the tunnel again when flowers and music and a library are my home?

Food and drink are plentiful. And I'm sure I'll see hummers, too. I always do. Always when I least expect them. So I have to learn not to expect them.

Don't expect anything. Then you'll have something.

If you expect something at a certain place and a certain time, you will treble your chances for disappointment.

We're high enough without being trebled. Unleß we want to sing ►Cherry Red◄ with the Groundhogs. Even Joanna Deacon said it was just mean to write a song with a climb that steep.

Sure, the Rotary Connection's Minnie Riperton could have hit it.

Captain Beefheart, of course, with his famous 7½-octave range.

And Tony McPhee.

Parts of it only the dogs can hear. Prairie dogs. Groundhogs. Marmots.

Boodog! A Mongolian specialty. Marmot blow-torched, turned inside out and stuffed with red hot rocks until the meat peels off.

*

More Japanese clusterfuck beetles! I have twelve in my jar already. Maybe I should find a way to invite ducks rather than hummers. I'd have more luck calling on Kokette. Her name was really Coquette, but she got confused during her new wave dance party days when she confused weird for profound.

But for a while we agreed nicely on the weirdly profound and profoundly weird.

But, with our habits, she became leß inter-rusted in the profound and I leß in the weird and we grew apart. That was forty years ago. Well, maybe thirty. It's all one big blur back there. Thank God. Why would I want to remember most of that shit? A handful of friends, a lover or two, why else? I was still trying to figure out who I was. I'm still not entirely sure. I think the day you figure that out, you die.

Canned Heat played a show I went to those many years ago. Fito de la Parra and Larry Taylor and Harvey Mandel were still there, though Alan Wilson and Bob ►Bear◄ Hite had paßed years before.

Mandel is a terrific guitarist—much too ignored. The album he did with the great Hammond B3 player Howard Wales, *Baby Patter*, was one my favorites. Small wonder the Stones auditioned him to replace Mick Taylor. I gueß, at the time, Harvey wasn't British mullet enough for them, but they cut a couple of excellent tracks together for the *Black and Blue* album. Mandel can rock.

Listen to Howard Wales, too. From AB Skhy to his work with Garcia—it is excellent. Both Mandel and Wales inspire the listener. Their playing wends its way through exterior muscles (all of which are prompted to twitch in response to the auditory input). Thereafter, spasms occur that lift the arms and legs, and then the individual is dancing, but without intent or purpose. It is innate. It is primal. Trance dance. Nothing works like boogie. Mandel knows how to boogie. And Wales knows the exquisite sounds of the B3.

So you can imaging seeing and hearing Mandel and de la Parra and Taylor and their harp player and singer at the time, Dale Spalding. Spalding handled most of Bear's songs. De la Parra sang Wilson's falsettos. The show was tremendous, and before a crowd of 250 or so, maybe 280 max, in a small nightclub in Evanston, Illinois, called S.P.A.C.E., which I think stood for the Society for the Preservation of Art and Culture in Evanston. I grew up in Evanston. It needs all the art and culture it can get to counteract the deleterious effects on the community, especially on the students, by the multinational conglomerates who are hiding behind every bush on the college campus and are seeking to brainwash students forever into preferring the conglomerate brand of whatever over everyone else's. Consumer bombardment is ubiquitous. It is shoved in one's face relentleßly.

When I was at Northwestern, for example, Buddy Rich played a gig for the university's homecoming. He was scheduled for two sixty-minute sets. That may not be much, but he was an old guy. No problem. But the school turned around and sold the tickets as two separate shows without bŒðering to tell Buddy Rich. Just before his break came, he was told he'd have to wait till the auditorium was cleared for the new crowd to come in before he could start the second set. He went on a tirade, berating the school for being so greedy, and he urged the students to protest—that this was supposed to have been only one show. The university had scammed not only the students but Buddy Rich, too.

Greed. Consumer rustriction.

Only Pepsi products could be found on campus. Consumer bombardment.

Like dodgeball with cans of Pepsi being thrown at your head.

Canned Heat stand for something altogether different. They were at Woodstock!

At the end of the show, from my place in the center of the second row, I stood up and gave the band a giant double fist pump and then the Nixon double peace sign! De la Parra gave me the peace sign back from the stage.

Life in August of 1968 was present again for an instant. Time travel is real.

*

I pick up a book and see it is *Out of Sequins*, the story of a rich white woman growing up in Apartheid South Africa. The *ad misericordiam* appeal of her title is meant to elicit our pity. How sad one must be to suddenly be out of sequins! What would Elvis wear in Las Vegas on his *Second Coming* tour?

Elvis will return before the hummingbirds show up, or so it seems.

Grandpa Ott's still going strong.

The Heavenly Blue are thriving.

The black tomato is fruiting. So is the yellow pear tomato, but with a smaller yield.

Indeed, the small yield sign was so tiny, Officer, that I didn't even see it. Had it been legible, I'd have followed the instruction. The ensuing mayhem can only be blamed on the procurer and poster of the sign. Always look to the signs of the times. Drive there with the radio on. No tunnels until the entrance to the Gardens. Go overland like the vegetable expreß of the town crier Fred Shrier.

Tony McPhee responds: ►The Hunt◄! An experiment in read text with music that was all of side B of the album, but was, according to McPhee, the reason the album *The Two Sides* was made. It is a bitterly satirical look at the English ►sport◄ of fox hunting, which is now fortunately banned. Kill clusterfuck beetles. Leave the fox alone. It is one of the most handsome, elegant of creatures. It is too smart and looks too canine to kill as sport. Clusterfuck beetles can fill jars of soapy water, and I won't feel a thing but joy that my morning glory leaves are being defended.

I saw a green graßhopper, too. I was going to flick it off the plant—it was too cool to kill—but it hopped off out of sight. It probably eats more than clusterfuck beetles. Shit! Well, there's only one. I've already caught seventeen beetles.

The weather has cooled ten degrees though, so sitting perched in front of my plants for an hour a day as I water and feed them and inspect them for clusterfuck parasites is not so difficult now.

Then follow ►The Hunt◄ with Ambrosia's ►Mama Frog◄, and then Mark-Almond's ►The City◄. Now you're ready for Scott Walker's *The Drift*. That is one helluva musical cocktail.

Okay, I know it's hard to be ready for Scott Walker. Especially *The Drift*. It's profound, though, like Skip Spence's *Oar* or Syd Barrett's *The Madcap Laughs*.

No—that's Mark-Almond. Yeah, it does sound a little like Spiritualized, though that might be vice versa. It's good, isn't it? Gospel to soothe the human soul. A paean to relaxation.

Spiritualized. Wow. Now I'm thinking of Spacemen 3. I haven't listened to them for far too long.

Okay, hummingbirds. I can't leave yet while music is left unheard. You have a little more time. The cardinal outside my window confirmed it. But I had to beg his indulgence.

*

The cardinal's wife came by yesterday when she heard me playing Canned Heat with the Chambers brŒðers. She landed on the barren berry tree outside my window, cocked her head, looked over, and listened to ►Open Up Your Back Door◄. Up behind her landed a smaller-than-she red-capped pecker.

Where the cardinal's ¢elgh was, I don't know. He wasn't around for these shenanigans. A little finch came by, but the pecker chased it away. But the pecker didn't bŒðer the lady cardinal. It was a downy, probably too young to appreciate the lady cardinal fully, but it also stayed and listened to the music. The finch circled and landed on a farther branch. The downy chased it away again. Clearly the downy wanted no one there but the lady. I was just the DJ. Still, I enjoy being a DJ. I did that in college. I was the rock producer for my college's radio station.

People liked my shows. I played prog rock, jazz, comedy, krautrock, boogie, blues, and punk. I mastered the seamleß seque, going from a song that ended on drumbeats into one that began with them—that sort of thing.

The lady really liked Bear's scat singing on ►House of Blue Lights◄. This was Hite's last recording before he died. The Hook was there, too, at the Fox Venice Theatre, that evening early in 1981.

The downy stopped jabbing his pecker at the tree when he realized Bear Hite pecked through musical notes faster and stronger.

The red-headed downy and the terracotta lady decorated the Œðerwise bare tree, as did the bright cardinal's ¢elgh, contrasting the blue and violet morning glories against their green hearted leaves lolling on the iron railing of the veranda next door. The potted yellow tomatoes were too few to notice. And the black tomatoes, really just a dunnish red with dark green streaks, only looked black from a distance at which they could not be seen anyway.

*

One of the neighbor kids called me ▶Stacy◀.

I haxed him why.

He said he'd haxed his parents about who lived in the lighthouse, and they'd said, ▶It's Stacy◀.

But I think he meant ▶stasis◀. I'm getting known for it. Mr. Stasis. In the corner of the town, the ▶Ecke◀, as the Germans say. Mr. Ecke Stasis. Not out of my mind, just out of my body. Out of ▶place◀. Out of control, which does not imply any active wilding. For most of us, a two-ton boulder is out of control.

I don't know who is with the troll, but I am tired of being told I need to pay a toll to make it over the bridge.

And I am the big brŒðer, so I have no one backing me up. I'm the one who must butt that troll over the railing.

Asbjørnsen wrote that tale with Moe back in 1841. Presumably Larry, Curly, Shemp, Joe, and Curly Joe were all too busy that day. As the Germans say, <<Nichts ist beßer denn De Rita.>>

That dandy Rita, meter maid, intrudes on our lives with her inanity. Which is why she is a perfect governmental preß secretary.

<<She dißeminates like a man,>> some sexist might have said, but then he'd be punished for saying that.

And when one is in the navy, one should not make jokes about seamen for many reasons.

The only thing that smells worse than a taboo is a canoe. Avoid the eels in the bottom. Unleß, of course, you like that sort of thing. Whatever keeps you damp, as they say. Me? I would never say anything so crude.

*

The Zero Ice wagon pulled up. I had haxed for black ice to be delivered to my dome fridge at the top of the lighthouse. Curly couldn't run up the steps in time. He brought two ice cubes. <<*An Ache in Every Stake*,>> he said, and he disappeared back into the ice wagon.

*

When we played skat, Curly shuffled first.

One of the local radio hosts came over and played, too. He hosted a weekend jazz show that I almost always made a point to listen to.

He bet me an hour of air time, and I won. So that weekend I went into the studios with CDs in hand and programmed an hour of jazz.

I played Luiz Bonfá playing a song written by his nephew Otavio Burnier on the Deodato-produced album *Jacaranda*, which also featured Airto, Ray Barretto, Stanley Clarke, Randy Brecker, and Bill Watrous, to name only six of the forty-nine featured performers on that disc.

My first wife and I saw Bill Watrous at Northwestern University once. He played solo trombone and told stories. He complained that no one in the bands ever wanted to sit in front of the trombonists, and he sprayed saliva from spit valve all over the stage in order to prove his point. My wife was disgusted. I was quite amused.

After Bonfá, I played some San Francisco jazz, LS Ellis, a baßist, and his progreßive quintet doing part of the ►Children in Peril Suite◄, a rather amazing sixty-minute-on-the-nose composition. Then Duke Ellington with Jimmy Hamilton on clarinet on ►The Air-Conditioned Jungle◄ from the November 2, 1946, *Great Chicago Concert* at the Civic Opera House, the concert at which Django Reinhardt came on stage for four songs!

After that, I played Big Joe Turner singing ►Pennies from Heaven◄ from his delightful album *In the Evening* that Pablo put out. that was one of the first jazz vinyl recordings I ever bought. That and Don Cherry's *Mu* albums on BYG.

And then Zappa. Of course, Zappa. His last live recording, from June 30, 1991, in Budapest. He was invited by the mayor, Gabor Demsky, to help celebrate the Buscu Festival, which was commemorating the retreat of the Soviet Army. Zappa and the gypsy Hungarian jazz band of Gyula Babos improvised an almost-eleven-minute march to accompany the soldiers out of the city. It was an exit march. What a brilliant idea. Zappa's guitar work, of course, was creative and vibrant in this entirely improvised work. The performance was originally broadcast on Hungarian television. Gyula Babos's baßist János Egri is brilliantly melodic, like Hellmut Hattler, but of course no one is as incredible as Hattler. Jaco and Stanley Clarke and John Entwistle all used melodic runs. For the sake of melodic runs, Hound Dog Taylor used no baß. Second guitarist Brewer Phillips played the baß lines on his guitar.

After Zappa, I played a medley of ▶All of Me◀ and ▶Sunny Side of the Street◀ by Chicago lounge music legends Sam Venti and Bobby Randazzo live from the Foaming 60s at 8355 S. Pulaski. The place is long gone. I heard one of the two was shot by an angry husband. I don't know which. ▶The Playboy Pair◀ is what they called their ¢elghs.

Then I played the Jazz Crusaders from *Live from the Lighthouse '69* in Hermosa Beach, California, doing the Isley brŒðers' ▶It's Your Thing◀.

I followed that with Mose Allison, from the Pizza Expreß in London in 2000, doing ▶You Call It Jogging◀, which was written by John D. Loudermilk, whose son Ricky I went to school with in first and second grade. One day in school I had a headache. All I was used to using for headaches were little orange baby aspirins. I told Rick, whom I sat next to, that I was going to the nurse to get some. He told me I didn't have to bŒðer. He had some aspirin on him. He handed me three little blue pills. I haxed why they weren't orange, and he said they were a different brand. I chewed them and immediately vomited all over my desk. I ran to the claßroom garbage can and vomited in it while the teacher yelled at me to go to the washroom. What Ricky had actually given me were Kenner bubble pills for their Bubbl-Matic guns through which one shot out what looked like soap bubbles. The pellets went into the gun, and water would be blown through, creating bubbles, which would then shoot forth. The pellets weren't actually soap, though. They were sodium cyanide.

I've wondered long since why a second-grader would be peddling pills and what his home life must have been like for such behavior to seem normal.

Well, that was Nashville, home of Johnny Cash, whose pills were found at the Mexican border. And those were the mid-1960s.

*

The next time I put on *Hooker N' Heat Recorded Live at the Fox Venice Theatre*, the cardinal showed up immediately at the intro to ▶Hell Hound◀. He sang along, and then his old lady showed up to hear. She reminded her old man of some errand they still had to run, so they took off halfway through the song. They mißed the homages to ▶The Letter◀ and ▶Sea Cruise◀ in ▶Strut My Stuff◀. Bear could sing just about anything. Of course, he couldn't blow a harp as well as the Blind Owl, Alan Wilson, but he was no slouch, either. The poor cardinal wanted to hear but was forced not to. When he left, I was left alone with my music: ▶It Hurts Me Too◀.

A blind owl perched on the tree. No, not really, but how cool would that have been? Canned Heat could charm motorcycle gangs. And did. I gueß charming birds could have been easier.

*

Don't you just love double entendre? It's one element of the blues I really dig. I've been listening to tons of blues, man. Everything from Sleepy John Estes to Tony McPhee has been calling my attention.

I can see a neighbor's bonsai cut to look like Jerry Garcia with a Merry Pranksters jester cap on, probably as given to him by Wavy Gravy. Clapton's ►Bottle of Red Wine◄, a beautifully bouncy boogie, plays. I am surrounded by synchronous occurrences connecting already Œðerwise connected events. It's like two morning glory plants in a showdown, throwing as many tendrils at each Œðer as poßible in order to climb on top. It's all about climbing on top.

Okay, but in it all somewhere, I heard a story. And not, as I heard on the radio, the story about how the Incas worshipped a goddeß named ►Punchyer-Mama◄, who sounds full of ¢elgh-loathing.

By the way, Canned Heat's guitarist Henry Vestine played in the MŒðers of Invention but parted ways with them before *Freak Out!* and appears on Canned Heat's first album. Not a bad feat, to appear on the first albums by Canned Heat and Zappa. Of course, everyone is only five steps from Zappa, or whatever the number was. I'm too lazy to look it up now. I'm enjoying listening to Vestine and Alan Wilson on ►Change My Ways◄ from *Hallelujah*.

Bear explains the core of his philosophy in ►Canned Heat◄.

The story. Back to the story. Yeah, I heard this story.

Back in the glory days of Theresa's Lounge at 48th and Indiana on Chicago's South Side, one hot shot young blues guitarist took the love of his guitar one step too far. We have all heard about how John Lee Hooker called his Epiphone Sheraton his ►wife◄. We know that BB King once ran back into a burning building to save his thirty-buck Gibson, his livelihood. The fire had been started in a bar fight over some woman named Lucille, so he named the guitar (and his subsequent army of ES-355s) ►Lucille◄ to remind his ¢elgh he could always get a new guitar, but there was only one BB King. We know that Buddy Guy loved his polka dot Strat. And we know that Hound Dog Taylor liked them young, cheap, and Japanese—his guitars of choice were Teiscos. This one guy, who also called his ¢elgh ►King◄ and claimed to be a cousin of BB, Albert *and* Freddie, played a mint condition 1959 National Bel Aire semi-acoustic. It was everything to him. Indeed, he began calling it his goddeß.

Some blues folk have more religion than Œðers, and some were really bŒðered by this Cyrus King's sacrilegious claim.

Cyrus King replied that he could prove his guitar's divinity. He said he'd had a special humidor built in his home just so the guitar would be kept a proper temperature and humidity.

He would leave an offering to ▶Belle Aire◀ every night.

He would lay out the best Ernie Ball strings, and every night, while everyone was away, the Bel Aire would newly string her ¢elgh, trim the exceß off the strings (no knife or clippers were ever left in the humidor—Belle Aire had a magical way of trimming them), and then would tune them without the aid of so much as a tuning fork.

In the morning, Belle Aire would be strung, tuned, polished, and looking like new again.

<<How could Belle Aire do that if she wasn't a goddeß?>> haxed Cyrus King. No one could answer that question, so Belle Aire became famous, and Cyrus began to preßure his audience and the Œðer musicians to worship Belle Aire, too.

This really did not sit well with one of the harpists around town, the skilled Billy Boy Williamson, who had an idea.

One evening, unannounced, he came to visit Cyrus.

Cyrus was just putting Belle Aire into the humidor for the night. Billy Boy offered to lock her up, but Cyrus said the lock was actually in an Œðer room for added protection. He would lock the humidor by his ¢elgh. The second Cyrus left, Billy Boy took a plastic bag filled with gray ashes out of his pocket and spread the ashes all over the floor of the humidor. He leaped back out of the humidor before the locks clicked the door shut for the night and the light flicked off.

Billy Boy haxed Cyrus to put him up for the night because of how late it was, and they sat down and drank a couple of bottles of wine together. In the morning, Billy Boy got up first and saw footprints in the ashes. He saw that they came from one stone tile in the floor. He looked but saw no way to open it from inside, so he aßumed it must open from underneath.

He waited for Cyrus to wake up, and when Cyrus went to open the humidor, Billy Boy quickly swept up the ashes and recollected them, cleaning the humidor before Cyrus entered the room.

Billy Boy brought out some more wine, and the two men spent the day playing music and getting drunk. At night, Billy Boy had an excuse to stay again, and when Cyrus retired for the night, Billy Boy stayed inside the room with the humidor and quietly sat and waited in the dark.

Sure enough, at three in the morning the stone tile lifted up and was slid back. From the hole in the floor emerged Cyrus King's chief roadie, who took to the task of stringing and polishing Belle Aire. He did it all by the light of two large candles he'd brought in.

Unnoticed, Billy Boy sat still and watched. The roadie was good. He was quick, quiet, and was gone by four, sliding the rock back over his head.

Billy Boy told Cyrus about this the next morning. Cyrus was ired at having been duped by his roadie, a cat who called his ¢elgh ►Tartuffe◄. The next day, Cyrus called in his ►Snake Charmers◄, his horn men, to intercept the roadie and follow the tunnel back to its place of origin.

The Snake Charmers, by the way, had a long history of protecting Cyrus King. He'd once been targeted by a snaky dragon lady temptreß who had beguiled and then humiliated him. The Snake Charmers had taken her to dinner and fed her food of such an explosive nature while they warned her of the price for her deceptions that she burst out of there and was never seen or heard from again.

Neither was the roadie.

Cyrus was so grateful to Billy Boy that he gave Billy Boy the guitar just to prove it was just a poßeßion. He was ashamed he'd ever thought it more. Hound Dog Taylor applauded and gave Cyrus a Teisco. BB King applauded, too, and gave Cyrus one of his thousand ES-355s.

*

A month's worth of mays can be seen in each can.

American men who mißed the atomic tests have never seen a Bikini at all.

*

In my readings I discovered the connection between the Book of Daniel, Chapter 13, known as the Deuteronomical tale of Susanna, and Stephen Foster's song ►O Susanna!◄.

The original, unpublished lyrics made clear that the song was about the Biblical lady, and most likely split its point of view between the elders, her, and Daniel, her rescuer.

*

Oh, I see it's credited to Stephen Foster, Jr. That's probably some ¢elgh-stitched appellation like Little Howlin' Wolf, who was related to Chester Burnett only in having a personality that fit the moniker.

*

Very few Heavenly Blues are blooming, but those that do are six inches acroß and perfect. I have thirty or more Grandpa Otts a day. Still no hummers! But yesterday I had one and today I had two Pink morning glories, and I'd never even planted any! A Pink seed or two must have been mißed in one of the Œðer packets. The Pink seems to have a white throat, like the Heavenly Blue, but the bloßom is only four inches wide, the size of a Grandpa Ott, which has a pink throat.

Perhaps last year's Heavenly Blues and Happy Hour Rose morning glories croß-pollinated and created Pinks?

I read that Heavenly Blues croß-pollinate rather easily with Œðer varieties, though the Happy Hour Rose is tiny, with only one-inch bloßoms. That's like breeding a Doberman with a Chihuahua. I just hope the Doberman is the female.

Some of my black tomatoes developed bloßom-end rot. I read that the cure for that was calcium, so I've started putting eggshells into the watering can, the way my grandma showed my mŒðer how to do. I have been fertilizing the soil with ashes from the barbeque, coffee grounds, and, once every ten days, Miracle-Gro, but apparently none of those contain enough calcium.

I read someone's suggestion to water the plants with milk, but someone else said not to because the milk spoils fast and begins to stink. In the future, I saw, I can avoid bloßom-end rot by mixing lime into the soil, or by actually burying eggshells beneath the seeds. I'll try to remember that next year.

*

I started to think about this one young guitarist who was thrown into the mix in a free-for-all blues jam at the Den, a hip little blues club north of Elgin, Illinois, where Capone had once kept a roadhouse on the Fox River, up and down which he could move Canadian whisky rather easily. The Œðer musicians on stage with him were big cats—legends. He didn't have their chops, but he played along and knew how to stay out of their way. He never stepped on somebody else's solo, and so the big cats didn't mind him at all. He emerged from the Den unharmed!

*

The Heavenly Blues persist, though I am only seeing two or three each day in this sea of Grandpa Otts. The Pinks are still coming, one or two per day. And today, I was welcomed by a nice, big, five-inch Blue Star right in the middle of all the Œðers, its head held above the hoi polloi.

I also saw a dark green hummingbird today, but it was in a neighbor's yard. I saw it when I was on my constitutional afternoon walk.

Now all I have to wait for is the confluence of events, and then I will be able to go to the Gardens without fear of having mißed this crucial summer event.

The one I saw was not on morning glories, though. It was on a Rose of Sharon bush. It actually stopped and perched on a telephone wire that ran along the top of the bush and then flew into the Roses of Sharon again. One doesn't see hummers perch very often.

One also doesn't hear perch hum, but one day, when I was fishing....

*

I had to do it. I had to listen to *Garcia* again. I was weeping by ►Sugaree◄.

*

If you want catharsis, man, the greatest way to get there is by studying the Grateful Dead.

*

Deadheads? Bob Weir called them ►bug-eyed monsters◄.

The music of the Dead? A huge vein of gold in the cavern.

The center couldn't hold, so we had to use the backup quarterback.

Keep it. It's a tip. Bet on him to go no earlier than fifth in the first round.

Three-to-one in your favor.

Ten big. I'm feeling lucky. I'd almost forgotten the melody of ►Late for Supper◄.

My writing can be like Hergé meets the Dead. Sorry. There's a reason for that, I gueß, and it's probably back there in a bad choice made worse by my not understanding what was going on. I was too busy sizing my coffin, so to speak.

*

Two red Split Personalities joined my concert of morning glories at daybreak. Beneath the large single Blue Star, a couple of Pinks and a Heavenly Blue decorated the Grandpa Otts, whose ¢elghs are gravitating into two groups—the purple blues and the deep purples.

The red Split Personalities have white throats and are split between the petals, as if cut and bleeding, ¢elgh-defeating, always bleating little pathetic emos who imagine their lives so much harder than anyone else's. They sound more Roderick Usher than Arthur Rimbaud. At least Rimbaud survived the telling of his tale better than a marathon runner.

*

Today was the anniversary of George Duke's death. He was an Œðer Zappa aßociate who went on to do excellent work as leader in his own right. I listened to *The Aura Must Prevail* and *Feel* today to remember him by. Zappa plays on *Feel* on two tracks under the pseudonym ►Obdewl'l X◄. I also brought out *One Size fits All*, my favorite album of Zappa's, on which Duke is a major force. I could have sworn I saw Nettie materialize in the corner of my eyes and then materialize when Bobby's head looked like a potato in the Zappa. She disappeared when the bronco chute opened.

I received an invitation to write for the local paper. I think they just want to find out what I'm all about, which is no problem. I had an idea for a column about an archivist who looks for undigitized truth.

*

The Archivist

Living surreptitiously in the closed stacks of a major university's ►special collections◄ library, our correspondent, Pont Stalion (prounced with a long ►a◄ and a long ►o◄ and the accent on the last syllable), spends his nights in the vertical index and the bankers' boxes in order to find truths hidden from the digitized world, texts too rare to have ever been reduced to binary code. He reports to us his most exciting discoveries.

Hello. Pont here. I've spent the week dancing in the aisles with the files covering the *Great American Songbook*, and revisited the work of that famous Pennsylvanian, Stephen Foster. His ►Beautiful Dreamer◄ is one of the most recorded ballads in American history. Foster also brought us ►Nelly Bly◄, ►Jeanie with the Light Brown Hair◄, ►Camptown Races◄, ►Swanee River◄, and ►My Old Kentucky Home◄. He was prolific and, for a while at least, quite succeßful. And he is part of America's cultural mythology and is mentioned or alluded to in everything from *The Rocky and Bullwinkle Show* to Firesign Theatre to *The Honeymooners* to the Squirrel Nut Zippers. But initially he was a hit during the Gold Rush of 1849, when his ►Oh! Susanna◄ was the prospector's favorite pick.

Much has been made of the popular minstrel version of the song, especially with its use of the word ►nigger◄ in the second verse. One cannot defend Foster's lack of foresight in his diction, but this was, apparently, not meant as Foster's ►serious◄ version of the song. The popular version was actually his clowning around with mellifluence in order to draw a crowd (►the sun so hot I froze to death◄ indeed!). It was an *ad populem* use of irony akin to the Beatles' *Get Back* seßions outtakes ►Enoch Powell◄, ►Get Back Pakistanis◄, and ►White Power◄, which, although ostensibly offensive, were actually as ironic as Randy Newman's ►Short People◄ or ►Rednecks◄. These songs mock the voices they employ the way Jonathan Swift mocked the elders of the Church of England in ►A Modest Proposal◄.

Foster actually penned an Œðer, even-more offensive version of the song in Pennsylvania Dutch, using the name Holger Saarman and making fun of his own family's Pennsylvania Dutch upbringing in Lancaster County. The Pennsylvania Dutch version of the song, ►Ei, du Zustand!◄ is misogynistic and sadistic (and if revived would be sure to be a hit with the *50 Shades* poße).

But in the archives, I found the original, ►serious◄ version Foster wrote for the church. It was based on the *Book of Daniel*, Chapter 13. Unfortunately, Foster was protestant, Dutch Reformed, in fact, and the story of Susannah in Daniel is apocryphal to the Dutch Reformed. Foster lost his commißion in disgrace, was excommunicated by his own congregation and was not forgiven by the church elders until he composed his Sunday School Hymns in 1863. It was his ire at these elders that led to his Pennsylvania Dutch version.

Scholars argue about the origins of the serious version of ►Oh! Susanna◄. On one hand we see the manuscript is written in his hand. On the Œðer hand, the teachers were so strict about penmanship in those days that everyone had the same hand, which they clapped quite enthusiastically for Foster's secular pieces, but not for his religious ones. Also the authorship is credited to ►Stephen Foster, Jr.◄, but no such junior existed. Some critics say that points to spurious authorship. Œðers say Foster was just being funny. In any case, here is the ►serious version◄ of the song:

A young Dutch wife in her garden
Began to wash her knees.
Alone she thought to take a bath,
Her husband so to please.
But to her right and to her left
Two lechers she did spy.
They watched her wash her Netherlands.
Susannah, don't you cry.
Oh! Susannah! Oh, don't you cry, for she
Washed in her own garden for no one else to see.

The lechers jumped to board her
And to travel down her river.
Their rowdy fluids magnified,
And made Susannah shiver.
They pawed her, but she pushed them off.
She really thought she'd die.
She shut her eyes and held her breath—
Susannah, don't you cry.
Oh! Susannah! Oh, don't you cry, for she
Washed in her own garden for no one else to see.
The lechers said they'd spread foul lies
If she didn't do their will.
She pushed them back until they saw

Daniel coming down the hill.
The lechers told the elders that
Susannah was untrue.
They'd told them that beneath a tree
A young man she did screw.
Oh! Susannah! Oh, don't you cry, for she
Washed in her own garden for no one else to see.

The elders came to take her
And to put her to her end,
But Daniel stood and spoke up
In order to defend.
▶What kind of tree?◀ he haxed the two,
But they could not agree.
One said,▶mastic◀; one said, ▶oak◀.
Daniel said, ▶Now, don't you see?◀
Oh! Susannah! Oh, don't you cry, for she
Washed in her own garden for no one else to see.

▶There was no mastic, nor an oak◀,
said Daniel to the crowd.
▶These two lechers tried her virtue,
But they were not allowed.
Susannah gave them nothing,
So they accuse her instead.◀
The elders grabbed the lechers,
And each promptly lost his head.
Oh! Susannah! Oh, don't you cry, for she
Washed in her own garden for no one else to see.

The rejection of his feminist meßage by the church elders seems to have driven the Foster family to leave the community in disgrace and move to Lawrenceville. This exile was apparently the catalyst for the derisive Pennsylvania Dutch version. And then, like the pied piper, Foster had a new idea and found the words to draw the Dutch toward gold. His part in the exodus of able-bodied young men from the community was an Œðer reason why the church took fifteen years to forgive him and why it still never brags about Stephen Foster.

*

The train of thought has come to carry me away.

I step on, ticket in hand. I do not see a conductor, so I improvise my way into a new berth, never bugged nor bedded in before. Virgin Airlines owned it. They treated me well because I was one of Steve Hillage's big supporters in Chicago. I interviewed him for an hour on the radio.

Those were inter-rusting days back then. Partying with people like Nick Lowe and Spencer Davis and Neal Schon and Greg Rollie and Robert Hunter and Big Twist & the Mellow Fellows. My mind is filled with very sharp photos of those days. The editor of a paper I wrote for back then was one of the nicest guys I have known. I couldn't keep up with him, but I tried just because he was fun to hang out with.

I think I can have some fun with ►Pont Stalion◄.

*

I walked through the reminiscence train. I do enjoy sitting in back and watching where I've been drop away into the past, but this train has Œðer cars. It has sleeping berths, a dining car, a bar car, a car for Skat players, and even a short nine-car disc golf course based on one of my old designs. The train wasn't leaving until the following week. It was being inspected, repaired, and resupplied in the interim. I hope I see some hummers among my morning flowers before then. White butterflies have come. The tomatoes and peppers and five types of morning glories are all flowering.

Soon. It could be sooner in Oklahoma, but not here. One group of women said it should not leave now. I agree. Let's leave when we're all ready. Are we all ready already? No one leaves at noon. That would leave poor little ►e◄ behind, and I *am* poor little ►e◄ from time to time. Œðer days, I am Ecke Stasis. Ironically, Ecke Stasis is never moved.

*

Nettie materialized in my mind again and shot me full of flashbacks. I couldn't move, but I sure did remember lives I'd left behind. I'd been hundreds of people before. She nailed me for each one. I died the death of a thousand cuts and then paßed out. When I came to, she was gone.

I'm getting antsy. I want to go, but the stretch Hummer isn't here to carry me away. The Blue Star couldn't be seen today or yesterday.

The Split Personalities are thriving. I had four today.

Grandpa Otts are always there in full force. I saw a couple of Pinks. No Heavenly Blue today, but that's unusual—I normally have at least one.

*

Sleepy John Estes Blues

Sleepy John Estes called to me

from the lighthouse library.
<<Prove that water run upstream.>>
I think he was asleep and talked in his dreams.
Sleepy John, Sleepy John, sleep on, Sleepy John.

Sleepy John Estes called to me
from the lighthouse library.
<<Prove that water run upstream.
Son, you're going where I've been.>>
Sleepy John, Sleepy John, sleep on, Sleepy John.

Sleepy John Estes went to meet
Robert Johnson at the croßing street
to prove that water run upstream
and scare Johnson off the Brownsville scene
Sleepy John, Sleepy John, sleep on, Sleepy John.

He dreßed like the devil and gave out a holler
and bought Johnson's soul for only a dollar.
Suddenly Johnson could play like fiend
and started to come on the Brownsville scene.
Sleepy John, Sleepy John, sleep on, Sleepy John.

But the deal made with Johnson was he could play
on the condition that he'd go away
to prove that water run upstream
and never come back to the Brownsville scene.
Sleepy John, Sleepy John, sleep on, Sleepy John.

With Robert Johnson safely gone,
Sleepy John Estes could sleep on.
Sleep on, Sleepy John.

*

<<Ma! Pa!>> called some kid Sleepy John Estes knew but was not his kid.

<<Don't call me ▶Pa◀, boy!>>

<<There's a man at the croßroads, calls his ¢elgh the greatest guitarist in the South.>>

<<What the hell?>> Sleepy John was all of a sudden wide awake. <<Get me one of them red choir robes. I got an idea.>>

And he appeared to Johnson as the devil with his ¢elgh charged on a lithium battery.

Johnson fell to his knees and said, <<Mr. Devil, please, I'll give you my soul if you let me be the greatest guitarist in the world.>>

Sleepy John Estes, the greatest guitarist in the world, began to weigh the merits of being the greatest guitarist in the world against the benefits of owning Robert Johnson's soul. Which, thought he, would bring more peace? Which would let Sleepy John sleep?

So Sleepy John Estes let Robert Johnson make his claim on the condition he did so nowhere near Brownsville, Tenneßee, including Memphis and Jackson, because then he'd be calling Sleepy John out. But anywhere else, Johnson was king, so long as he didn't disturb Sleepy John's sleep.

Listen to Estes on ▶Diving Duck Blues◀. That was 1929. When Johnson was only nine years old. Johnson didn't record until 1936.

Most likely the croßroads were on the road to Memphis from Brownsville. Memphis was a lucrative town to play in right after harvest time, when everyone had money and time.

But mostly, as Estes sang afterward, ♪You got to clean up at home.♫

*

Remember, though, good etiquette calls for a rematch. One win and out is boring cheß. As the great poet Jerry Reed once sang, ♪When you're hot, you're hot, and when you're not, you're not.♫ Of course, he was a firefighter back in the Louisiana swamps. He'd know. Amos Moses, right?

His brŒðer Jimmy Reed knew. ▶Bright Lights Big City◀ inspired Jay McInerney. ▶Big Boß Man◀ inspired Pigpen. ▶Baby What You Want Me to Do◀ inspired Jorma Kaukonen. ▶Take Out Some Insurance◀ inspired Tony Sheridan, who gave the Beatles a leg up. And John Lennon only praised three people in *Lennon Remembers*: Yoko (of course), Dave Edmunds (surprisingly, but deservedly), and Frank Zappa. Everything always comes back to Zappa. I think Zappa has posted flags at all four corners of the Earth.

And when he and George Duke used to play together, the result was magnificent. The anniversary of George Duke's death may have just paßed, but he and Zappa are gigging somewhere in the heavens, Zappa seated on a divan, Duke on a fine pleather-padded piano bench, and they are pleasing the hosts. I think I hear them jamming on a funked-up version of Eddie Boyd's claßic ▶Five Long Years◀, originally recorded in 1952 for Chicago's JOB record label. It's a song about a man who dedicates every waking moment to one woman, providing everything for her, turning over his paychecks to her every Friday, but she, after five years, jilts him. Junior Parker had a hit with it again in 1959. John Lee Hooker did it in 1961. The Yardbirds did it in 1963, as did Muddy Waters, followed by Long John Baldry the year thereafter. Ike and Tina Turner's version from 1968 was famous. Then Bobby ►Blue◄ Bland and Freddie King and BB King and Buddy Guy all had at it, too.

Here go the twelve-bar blues in 12/8 time and in the key of C.

Zappa and Duke did it Memphis-Slim-and-Canned-Heat style, though. George Duke would have sung Memphis Slim's lines perfectly. The piano would be fuller. The guitar would be fattened, allowing the baß a little more space in the back. How Zappa would handle the braß parts was uncertain. I could hear him bringing in some violin, though. Maybe Jean-Luc Ponty? Now who would drum? Who could keep up with the enormous repertoire they shared? You'd want Billy Cobham on some tracks, Levon Helm on Œðers. Who could do them all? Ed Caßidy from Spirit could have. Aynsley Dunbar, who actually did play with Zappa. Ginger Baker. Keith Moon. Roger Earl. Fito de la Parra. Cats like that who have proven their great versatility and creativity. Those are all hall-of-famers in any sane rock or drum museum. Each bridged different styles. And let's not forget Ringo! The world only ever had one Ringo, the only Beatle everyone liked. Not the best Mexican bandit, though, in *Blindman*.

*

Five Blue Stars hovered over the Split Personalities. The Heavenly Blues are flourishing. The Pinks are still doing well, and the Grandpa Otts are still dominant.

Still no hummers, but honeybees have come! Everywhere on Earth they have been suffering Sudden Hive Collapse Syndrome, but my morning glories mean some survive! Honey is not exclusively ambrosia!

Blodwyn Pig showed up in the corner and played for a couple of hours today. Mick Abrahams's parts of Jethro Tull's first album, *This Was*, are also worth a listen or a few. Actually, I heard of an album by Mick Abrahams called *This Is*, which is his recording of the first Tull album without Ian Anderson. That must be very inter-rusting. I have not found a copy that was affordable. It's a rarity, I take it.

What is amazing is how much great music of incredible historic vale is not digitized and exists only on frail, antique media. I know the digital bytes will fall apart as well, but we should save as many copies as poßible in as many media as poßible if we are expecting to survive the age of dehumanization. Rembrandt had it easy compared to us.

And if there is a cost, we will split it. But what is ►it◄? A meaningleß little pronoun referring to a hypothetical inanimate object or an animal or an idea.

<<Split it? Cleave the animal?>>

<<Split it? Leave the animal alone! Break the chair!>>

<<No, don't,>> said the chair. <<Robert's Rules of Order prohibits chairs from being broken.>>

<<Well, divide that concept in half.>>

<<Done.>>

<<So you see ▶it◀ isn't much.>>

<<Okay, so if there is a cost, we will split.>>

And they split. I was left alone in the lighthouse again as always.

*

I know I intended Flying Saucers to come. I wonder which will arrive first—the Flying Saucers or the hummingbirds? And where is Scarlett O'Hara? She will arrive in a Flying Saucer, no doubt.

But the Blue Stars are showing up in good number. Maybe they'll guide the Flying Saucers in, like landing lights. Like a lighthouse.

*

I found some valuable information in the lighthouse library. The most common hummingbird east of the Mißißippi that migrates up to Kentucky and Illinois is the rub-throated. That must have been a female I saw the Œðer day because females have the green but not the ruby throat that the males have. Apparently ruby-throated hummers are genetically predisposed to preferring bright red flowers. Thus the confluence of the demise of my Happy Hour Rose morning glories and the tardineß of Scarlett O'Hara has kept the hummers from noticing. Apparently they are not as attracted to Split Personalities, but then who is? They too quickly look all torn up. Still, at first, they are very pretty and bright.

Early to mid-August is supposed to be a good time to see youngsters feeding. I am probably just not seeing them.

I hope Scarlett O'Hara comes before I leave. Where are my hummers? It's too late to start a new plant. I could get a feeder, but that's meßy, attracts bugs, and is kind of cheating, like baiting for deer or stocking a pond with fish.

At least it's not dynamiting the pond for fish. That's worse.

One of the men from town came by and said the town was going to put in a disc golf course and, knowing my history, wanted to know if I'd design it.

It shouldn't take long. Maybe by then I'll have seen a hummingbird in my flowers. If not, it'll give me enough money to buy a damned hummer on the black market (owning them—heck, even *touching* them—has been illegal since the Migratory Bird Treaty Act of 1918). I'd release it into my flowers, but that'd be cheating, too. It wouldn't give me any real sense of accomplishment. It'd be like those athletes from the 1990s to the 2010s who were caught using anabolic steroids in order to shrink their testes—or was that just an unfortunate side effect? Titles have been stripped, the doors to halls of fame have been shut, and any achievement is footnoted. Those athletes are donning Styrofoam laurels and pretending the emperor's birthday suit is piebald and paisley.

*

Come out, Scarlett. Show us your bloomers.

*

If Nettie were here, she could use her government contacts to help me get a Fish and Wildlife Warden's permit, which would authorize me to catch, tag, and release hummingbirds rescued by citizens—babies who had fallen from nests, hummers who had flown into windows and had broken wings—and after their full recover, Fish and Wildlife would release the birds in the National Parks. I might be able to get a permit to release a bird on my morning glories. But all that government red tape would take so long that the birds would be back in South America by then. It'd be the only hummingbird left. Either that or the morning glories would be gone with the first real frost.

I've been collecting the brown seed pods and cracking them open to save the little black polyhedron-shaped seeds for next year's planting season.

I am also harvesting two or three yellow tomatoes and a half-dozen black ones every Œðer day or so.

Fall is coming. Scarlett and the Hummers are off somewhere else.

On tour, singing and playing gypsy jazz versions of Mary Ford and Les Paul songs and mumbled folk-style talking blues. The mumbling would collapse into humming and then would return to language. Scarlett didn't give a damn—she just liked to sing. ►Play it, Sam◄, she'd say to the gypsy Les Paul, and she'd follow him no matter where he went. Like Alan Wilson and John Lee Hooker on *Hooker 'N Heat*. Musicians who really know each Œðer can intuit what the Œðers can do and where they can go together. It's a great honorable cooperation to play with Œðer musicians. Those who avoid cooperation lose something in their music. They may gain some mathematical purity, though. But so what? That's like Yngwie Malmsteen. Brilliant precision. Mathematical perfection. But where is the sloppineß of humanity? Mathematical perfection is no utopia. In fact it's inhuman, albeit amusing.

Scarlett and the Hummer are performing Bodwyn Pig's claßic ▶See My Way◀! What a brilliant and far-too-ignored band Mick Abrahams had there. Sophisticated working claß, not beautiful Blackpool on the Irish Sea like Ian Anderson, but Luton smart from the heart.

*

I saw Ana Rickie sitting on a shelf in the library. She expreßed concern over the Most Noble order of the Garter, the divinatory meaning of the suit of cups, the Carlsbad Caverns, Lechuguilla Cave, and Beowulf's sword, Hrunting,

She clambered down and hopped onto a paßing train driven by a brokedown engineer named Wet Willie McBell, whose dinkey was kept clean, and who was the inspiration for the song ▶How Long◀.

One paßenger had kidney stones in the locomotive's paßway. His nephew locked some wood in the stokehold. Together they plotted on. The train was heading towards Anarchy on the Thames, a little-known town until the events of the Great Football Hooligan War of 2052.

Quick! Lock the door! There's a continuity editor who wants to get in! Tell him the OCD Clinic is down the street!

The town paßed a chicken shack covered in webs. Was that Kim Simmonds out in front, talking to Miller Anderson on the street corner?

The loß of a seed drill gave some gain to the C trill being played on one of the internal organs of a blood-won pig.

Ana rode on. And her son. The train went around a dusty bend, losing love all over the landscape. Then the train turned a corner at the river's invitation.

Hopefully that light ahead is a refueling station. The train was beginning to lose power, and the cold air began to creep in. The temperature was nine below zero outside.

A country girl waved to Ana as the train coasted into the station. They began to chitchat about Florida voting irregularities and some boy named Chad.

Stoked, the train took off again, prancin' around the next train turner. The train shone its light on the walls of a prison as it made the turn. Then the train went up the country past a bulldozer factory. McBell sounded the horn at a prodigal son walking too close to the tracks.

<<That's no way to get along!>> yelled the prodigal son at McBell, who'd startled the poor pedestrian right out of his Shoop Shoop shoes. The train also saved an Œðer young man, Big Bill Broonzy's half- brŒðer, who shook his washboard at McBell.

<<You smell, McBell!>> he yelled. <<Soap and water ain't no crime!>?> Sonny Boy Williamson ran after the train while waving a twenty dollar bill at it, trying to make it stop for him. When that didn't work, he fired his shotgun at the rapidly disappearing caboose.

McBell never slowed down. He was in a hurry to get to Anarchy on the Thames.

Ana went looking for famous people on the train. The actors were all on the stage. Her son looked under the seats in the compartments. A few toothleß old men, a boa wearing a heavily perfumed overweight woman denying her middle age, three kids rolling dice on the floor, a teenager reading a copy of *Wild Life in Alaska* by White Mans Telford, a busineßman-type asleep in a rigid position with hands folded neatly atop the briefcase on his lap, three hobos and a goat. Only the goat was royalty, having been begot by the goat who cursed the Chicago Cubs.

Ana's son got her goat and returned it to her. There's a man in Anarchy who's key for Ana to deliver the goat to him. She's never seen him, but she knows he has a goatee.

The train paßed a Model T. The man driving was wearing a t-shirt. On the shirt was a picture of a manatee. But the man had no beard at all.

King No-Beard Cornezzer. As Miß Elizabeth used to say on *Romper Room*, <<Don't be a don't bee. Do be a doobie.>> We all used to laugh at that one. But then the government started putting cornezzer syrup in our soft drinks to kill us. So we switched to dark rum and bourbon instead. The government forced tobacco on us. We switched to weed. And we listened to the Rolling Stones' ▶Dear Doctor◀, the song that inspired the entire career of Tex and the Horseheads. Must have. The way the Beatles' ▶Rain◀ inspired Rain Parade. They were spin-offs. With enough rum and bourbon, they are soul-filling.

<<<No, you're not,> said Little Nicola,>> which was the subtitle of ▶I Am the Walrus◀ on the American *Magical Mystery Tour* album.

The tour is continuing on the train. The name of the engine, by the way, is apparently ▶The Robert Wilkins◀. The train just started down the track one day. No one remembers where. It never stops. It only slows down for loading and unloading, but never below two miles an hour, which was the Dividing Line of Determination in this case. No wonder so few were aboard. And no wonder why the old did not get off again. Well, not usually. Exceptions always occur. Of course, are they then really exceptions?

The locomotive tore through Hungary on its way to Anarchy. The government could not hold back the train, nor any Œðers like it. The train just kept coming, its silver chaßis streaking through the night, Ana and her son still on their stroll inside. They'd begun up near the engine and moved backward, expecting each new car to be the last before the caboose, but the cars kept a-coming.

Eh? Eh? Coming!

Buffalo Bill is extinct—he cannot be seen out the window.

Imagine Buffalo Bill's meeting with a literalist follower:

<<Where are you going, Mr. Cody?>>

<<I'm going to shoot.>>

<<What?>>

<<Buffalo, of course, you idiot.>>

<<Huh?>>

<<Shoot Buffalo.>>

<<Okay,>> and so he did. The end of Buffalo Bill.

The paßengers could see an outdoor concert festival in progreß. It looked like Mose Allison and Duster Bennett were jamming with Rahsaan Roland Kirk. Between the three of them, they were playing four horns, drums, guitar, piano, and blues harp simultaneously while singing in three-part harmony.

They needed a baß. They needed a liaison in the Liaßic in order to find the lowest rock in order to elevate it to euphonia like Caledonia, and what makes her noggin so hard.

The train paßed a baß fishery and continued around a bend.

Ana came to a car filled with drunken revelers all singing the old country-and-western claßic ▶I'm in the Drinking Car of My Train of Thought◀.

One drunk haxed an Œðer, <<Did you ever hear about the old man who lived in the See?>>

<<What?>> replied his companion.

<<It was the bishop,>> said the first, laughing.

Ana's son imaged a mer-bishop.

<<Mom,>> he said. <<I'm scared. Let's go to the next car.>>

<<Now, now,>> said Ana. <<There are no real bishops here.>>

<<Listen to your mom,>> said one drunk. <<The bishop thinks the seat of power is right in his lap.>>

<<Mom!>>

The boy began to cry. Ana gave him a huckabuck hankie she kept in her pocket, and she led him into the next car just as the drunk who'd just spoken began to lead the crown in the singing of ▶God Save the Queen◀.

In the next car a bituminous Sandy Koufax impersonator was throwing baseballs out the window at ryoting peasants.

<<What in tarnation are you doin' to those poor folks?>> yelled Ana when she saw. Ersatz Koufax ran away, back towards the caboose. Ana was afraid she'd see him doing the same thing in the next car, then the next, and then the next, and that there'd never be an exit. But the next car showed no evidence of him at all.

Actually what Ana and her son were showered with was water from the sky. The clouds were tearing through the rooftop skylight on the observation deck train where, undoubtedly, Michel would be, staring at eternity. A few drips soon became a deluge, so the occupants of the car moved *en maße* to the next car or the previous. The vista was abandoned. The observations were decked and ✹hit✹ the canvas when all those observers entered the art production room, except for three or four who said they were going to go play Chinese jazz from within a Moorcock novel.

Let's coax up Cousin Scarlett to get some hummingbirds around here. It's too late in the season to begin meßing with a feeder.

Out the window all the trees look dead. Something happened here. Should we investigate?

No—it's quicksand. Keep going. The premise of the train was that it'd never stop.

Like ▶Train Kept A-Rollin'◀.

Yep.

Antelope began falling from the clouds.

♪It was raining deer when I met you,♫ began to be sung by Ana's grandmŒðer, Annette Hanshaw, in the next car. Ana's son, Andy, ran over to Grandma Annette and hugged her legs as she sang.

In the car after that chefs were preparing venison for dinner.

The train left the Antelope Freeway behind and continued on its way.

Ana, Andy, and Annette sat down to dinner. Andy haxed for a venison burger with real American cheese (not the more common ▶cheese-like food product◀ made from petroleum). Ana haxed the server his name. He replied, <<Hieronymous,>> which she heard as <<Anonymous,>> so she figured he didn't want to talk. So she ignored him from then on.

He, of course, found her behavior rude, so he secretly spit on her venison Spencer steaks. <<Damned faerie queen,>> he exclaimed, and then threw the steaks out the window at a viaduct. They hit a starving photographer, who wiped them off on his jeans and then ate them. That gave him to gumption to become a farthing philosopher again. Next time, rather than having the steaks hit him, he'd go the way of the duck. The steaks would have landed in the pond behind him. That wouldn't have ruffled his feathers as much.

He waved to Andy, who was waving to him from the window.

<<Was that a hobo?>> Andy haxed turning to his mŒðer.

<<No. It was an odder duck than that.>>

Andy fell into silent contemplation about what an otterduck would look like. That's what he mulled over as the train paßed through Moldova.

The waiter haxed if Andy would like an orange.

<<It has appeal.>> said the waiter.

<<Don't they grow that way?>> haxed Andy. <<Mom?>>

<<Yes, Andy. All oranges have peels.>>

Andy whispered to his mom, <<Our waiter is a dumbbell.>>

<<Dumb bells have no peal,>> said Ana. Andy laughed even though he didn't understand his mom's pun.

<<What Œðer kinds of deßert do you have?>>
The train sped by a coniferous forust. Andy began to miß his dead father.

Ana noticed.

<<No more pinery,>> she said.

<<Have you spotted dick?>> Andy haxed the waiter.

The waiter at first thought the boy was insinuating something, but then he recalled the term.

<<That's the deßert made with British sweat, right?>> he haxed Andy. This time Grandma Annette interceded.

<<It's suet, no sweat, young man. But I think the young boy is referring to his absent father, Dick Handshaw, a glove manufacturer who abandoned the family shortly after the boy's birth.>>

<<Why?>>

<<He said he has too much on his hands.>>

<<Mom,>> said Ana. <<You promised not to bring him up again.>>

<<You're right. I'm sorry, dear. Young man, just bring us three parfaits, please.>>

The server misheard, went to the empty car next door, and removed three floorboards.

<<Here are your parquets,>> he said.

Annette was not amused and began to admonish the waiter and haxed to see his manager.

<<Mom, I promised Andy I'd show him the rust of the train. We're going to get going.>>

Annette nodded and continued her barrage on the waiter, who imagined her as a croß-eyed mix between a barracuda and a barrister.

Ana and Andy entered the next car and were careful to avoid the mißing slats in the floor.

At one o'clock the train paßed a group of kids playing one o' cat. Andy stopped playing attention to where he was walking and almost stepped through a hole in the floor, but Ana was watching and pulled him away on time.

The next car had an information center. Andy sat down and began looking at an atlas while his mŒðer closed her eyes for a spell.

Andy read about places he could only imagine from their names.

Liverpool sounded unpleasant.

Normal sounded dull.

The Antarctic must be packed with snow ants.

Cologne must smell like old people.

The only money used in Finland is the five-dollar bill.

Elsewhere over the sea, sawbucks are used in economies teetering on the edge of failure.

Does pound cake cost a pound or weigh a pound?

What do people eat in Greece? Turkey?

Hungary?

Rußian? Roman?

Finnish.

The most important place is Maine.

Sudanly, Andy had a thought about his neighbors' dangling Chad.

►Suicide◄. That was the Florida motto of the Grand Old Party.

Andy's favorite reading was in political history. He even knew who Schuyler Colfax was. He wasn't the only thing that's ever stunk in Gary, Indiana. Heck, the skies used to be bright orange, as in Patchen's ►Orange Bears◄ poem. Iron oxide rusted in the steam from the steel mills. Overnight it settled on everything like volcanic ash.

Do people in Tobago have toboggans? Is tobacco taboo?

Stretch your heads proudly and see how far you can see, Ukraine, whose people are the first to know.

A giant stature of Taras Shevchenko paßed by, as if he were still alive. Of course, in many ways he still is and always will be. He's hanging out with Shakespeare and Goethe and Zappa, because everything always comes around to Zappa sooner or later.

Aasvogel leads to Zappa, Zevon, and on to ZZ Hill and ZZ Top.

Zzzz, you're saying. Where's the sleeping car?

<<Mom, wake up! It's time to go to sleep!>> Child's logic. Ana opens her eyes, grateful for a few minutes of rust, anyway.

<<Just five more minutes, okay, Andy?>>

<<Okay, Mom.>> Back to the book.

A place in Japan is called Fukue.

Intercourse, Pennsylvania. Climax, Michigan. A road sign: ⧗You are approaching Climax⧗.

Atlases are amusing.

Brunning Hill must be filled with sunflowers, which are then harvested for their seeds and brought inside the hall every fall.

The train paßed a shanty town made just for chickens. The chickens have their own shacks and streets, running water and eternal feed, egg catchers and conveyors that lead to purveyors.

The eggs would be used in the manufacture of pancakes, which were Zappa's favorite food, according to his wife Gayle.

Andy, whose head looked like a potato, enjoyed his pancakes.

Potato pancakes.

One potato, two potato, three potato, four. Five potato, six potato, seven potato, more.

<<Mom?>> haxed Andy.

<<Yes?>>

<<I heard someone say this train is called ▶The Humming Bird◀.>>

<<It is, dear.>>

<<But I thought it was called ▶The Robert Wilkins◀.>>

<<That's just the engine. The train is ▶The Humming Bird◀.>>

<<Mom?>>

<<Yes, dear?>>

<<I thought the Humming Bird ran from Cincinnati to New Orleans.>>

<<It did, baby, but it was reconfigured over and over again. It used to go from

Cincinnati to Louisville to Nashville to Birmingham to Montgomery to Mobile to New Orleans. And it connected to Bowling Green and Memphis. It was the train that used to go past the home Champion Jack Dupree was imagining in his song ▶My Home in Mißißippi◀.

An Œðer traveler interjected, an elderly African-American man sitting against the window with his slouch hat pulled down over his eyes. He pulled up the brim so he could make eye contact.

<<You’re telling the boy wrong, Ma’am. Champion Jack used to come out to Pascagoula, which was a flag stop. He had a girl out there and made the hour train ride from New Orleans at least twice a month.>>

<<How do you know that?>> haxed Ana.

<<She was my sister. And Jack would come out and would eat with us. My momma thought he was a bit of a fancy pants, but he was also very polite. Not all rude like most city folk.>>

<<What happened?>>

<<Well, he was rustleß. And he fancied that he was a boxer in those days. So he up and moved to Chicago to make it in the fight game.>>

<<Then what?>>

<<Well, the last I heard, he’d gone to England and married an English lady.>>

<<Not your sister from Pascagoula?>>

<<No. They’d had all they could stand of each Œðer by then. Lady, I hate to interrupt, but your boy is having a problem there.>> Sure enough, Andy’s nose was dripping snotsicles six inches long, like stalactites hanging down in a cave.

<<Oh, he just has a cold.>>

<<No—cold was what my ex-wife was. He’s got a sinus infection.>>

<<It’s an allergy. This car must have mold. We’d better go. Thank you. Nice to meet you,>> and Ana pulled Andy out of there and into the next car.

Sure enough, Andy’s sinuses cleared up in the next car. Two dozen people sat facing each Œðer, all wearing their Sunday best. Except for some horticulturalist, who was wearing his Sunday feelers, a bug hat with antennae because, as he explained it to Andy, he could charm the ladybugs into protecting his crops.

<<What ladybugs?>> haxed Andy, despite the squelching frown his mom gave him.

The man lifted up from his lap something that looked like a hat box. <<In here,>> he said.

<<Can I see?>> haxed Andy, despite his mom's remonstrative tap on his shin with her shoe.

<<Sorry, son. But then they'd get out. I need them for my garden.>>

Andy leapt away when his mom attempted a playful jump kick to his butt.

<<Come on, Andy. Stop pestering the man.>>

<<Goodbye,>> said Andy to the man. The man smiled and nodded.

Andy pointed to someone else.

<<Don't point!>> said his mom.

Andy signaled to his mom that he wanted to whisper to her, so she bent down. He cupped his hands around his mouth and her ear.

<<Isn't that Robin Hood?>> The fellow seated there looked just like him.

<<I don't know,>> she whispered back.

<<And that's Croß-Eyed Mary, right?>> seated next to Robin Hood, who was eating pancakes out of a Styrofoam box.

<<I hope not,>> replied Ana, too loud. Mary looked over at them.

<<Come on, Andy. We have to find the end of the train,>> and they left that car as well.

cIt's like being inside a tapeworm rather than having the tapeworm be inside of you,ɔ thought Ana. Andy flinched, almost as if he had heard his mom's thoughts.

<<Hey, was that Frank Zappa?>> Ana looked back but could no longer see into the previous car.

<<It could have been, Andy. Zappa's never far away.>>

<<Wow. I hope I get to meet him.>>

<<Don't worry—eventually everyone meets him.>>

<<Anyone else?>>

<<No—not really anyone in the last century transcends four centuries like Zappa.>>

<<How do you know, when we need two more to see?>>

<<No—there were two that predicted Zappa,>> said Ana.

<<Now you really are worrying me, Mom,>> said Andy. They both laughed.

<<Okay, Andy. I'll meet you back here in two and prove I was right.>>

<<Okay, deal.>> They shook hands on it.

<<Okay, Mom. No excuses.>>

<<You, neither, Andy. You, neither.>>

<<Mommy?>>

<<Yes, Andy?>>

<<Were John Lennon and Tony McPhee the same person?>>

<<No. Why would you hax that?>>

<<They look the same on the covers of *How I Won the War* and *Thank Christ for the Bomb*.>>

<<They just shared the same nightmares, Son. Many people did.>>

<<Did you?>>

<<Not like them. They lived before I was born.>>

<<Are they still around?>>

<<You betcha they are. More than ever. Acroß time, even.>>

<<Cool.>> Andy was satisfied for a minute.

<<Did John Lennon know Zappa?>>

<<*Sometime in New York City*.>>

<<Oh, yeah. Can I borrow that?>>

<<Sure, but listen to Zappa's mix on *Playground Psychotics*, also. Lennon and Zappa had two different mixes of the same material.>>

<<You know what's really fun?>> haxed Andy.

<<What?>>

<<Hound Dog Taylor.>>

Ana laughed. <<You better give me back my wig!>>

<<After I send you back to Georgia!>>

<<I'll go voluntarily. I've been walking the ceiling around here!>>

<<You can't go yet. Take five!>>

<<Okay. The sun is shining, anyway.>>

The train rocked, baby, into the next flag station, where it'd slow down enough for paßengers to come and go.

Ana and Andy had a seat in the car without Zappa.

<<Mom, this train feels like it's jumping with Symphony Sid.>> Indeed, the Humming Bird was shaking like it had developed a sneeze it was trying to hold back and was convulsing in the attempt.

<<The train doesn't like to slow down.>>

<<Ian Anderson said there was no way to slow down.>>

<<I gueß Mr. Anderson was wrong. His philosophy seems to frequently have been mißing a leg to stand on.>>

<<Yeah. Why didn't he call his band ▶Flamingo◀?>>

<<Maybe he was intimidated by the Flamin' Groovies' use of the name for one of their albums.>>

<<Oh, yeah.>>

<<Andy, would you let me rust a little? Let's just look out the window for a while in silence until the train's at full speed again. We should pay close attention to the changes that occur at these flag stations.>>

<<Okay, Mom. I love you.>>

<<I love you, too, Son.>>
They fell into silence. The train sped through bittermelon fields.

This must be heaven for people with type-2 diabetes,ꜿ thought Ana. She had read that ancient Chinese herbalists had used bittermelon for a number of ailments, but that it was particularly beneficial to type-2 diabetics.

She was wondering if the ancient Chinese knew about diabetes.

ɕNot under that name,ꜿ thought Michel. I could have haxed when I had the chance. I'd just never ridden the Humming Bird before. But he was amazed at all he could see from the observation deck car. He had parked his ¢elgh there for the duration of the trip to Anarchy on the Thames. Ana and Andy could run all over the train—he didn't care. He was content right where he was, waiting for the night's constellations to perform their play for everyone to see. Hercules would be dancing toward Leda to save her from Zeus. Orion, hunting with his dogs, would be taking aim at Pegasus for jilting him for Theseus and for having jilted Bellerophon before him. Taurus would try to block the shot, and Aries would just be in the way. Caßiopeia would try to reach Pegasus in time, but Cepheus would stop her. They would place dippers underneath Hercules to catch his tears when Leda escaped. The charioteer would pull Taurus ahead to the twins who'd bought him. Lions and crabs and bears could only look on, oh my!

Michel stared at the stars, sorry he'd not had the strength to be one. He'd lived his life of squirming desperation with little comfort. At least for many years the comforts had become few. He mißed the touch of a woman, the laughter between souls well met, the companionship of a true friend.

Now the Humming Bird had taken him. Next stop, Anarchy on the Thames, a grimy old town, but welcoming in a ▶yes, you can share my last tin of sardines◀ sort of way. From there he could go visit the pubs without fear. Once his reputation had been ruined, he'd nothing else to live up to. He could live without inhibition!

It'd be okay that he ate sardines! He'd go to an Arsenal match with John Lydon! They'd drink the stadium dry!

Michel recalled reading an American writer's bemoaning of an academic writers' annual conference held at a huge international hotel in downtown Kansas City. Shortly after noon on Saturday, the hotel ran out of beer. Heck, they may have been academics, but they were writers first. They were all combatants with writers' fists. The hotel was a sorry place soon enough. Hunter S. Thompson talked about courting brain damage like a courtesan in the night. All writers, if they are investing of their ¢elghs and vesting their ¢elghs, do, as they devolve to counterweigh the heights they are expected to reach.

That's why it's said that Neil Armstrong was the first person to touch foot to the exact center of the Earth, which is sort of like being in Texarkana, with a photo op for a foot, instead of being in two states, being in each hemisphere. And then a foot in every mouth as we paß an area infected with hoof-in-mouth. What a bunch of sympathizers! Wring your hands over the entrance mat, please. Don't track it in here.

I don't need to track your hands. I can see them from here.

Yeah, well, you're still wringing your hands over the entrance, Matt.

That's because they're appealing.

Like a bell.

Belluomini Bell? Isn't he an editor at one of the old European publishing houses?

Yeah, I think so. By reputation a fine writer, too.

Not me. My fine points break. I need a good medium tip.

What, you write by hand?

I'm not the only one who can get a peal out of his hands.

I can get a peel of my hands when I've been burned.

I was burned by my last ducheß.

That's nothing. I put up my dukes.

What?

Yeah. They stay with me. I keep them right at my side.

Why?

That way my ducheßes will stay away. They don't want to be anywhere near my dukes.

Well, I'd better go. I've got to beat it.

✸Beat✸ them both.

I have to hit the pavement.

✸Pound✸ it.

I don't want to beat around the bush.

No, of course not. But you should at least drill her for some information.

Grill. You mean ▶grill◀.

I am not a mean grill. What I mean is you should see for your ¢elgh what they think of your dukes.

I told you—my last one's gone. She burned me.

▶Last◀ means ▶latest?◀

No. ▶Last◀ means ▶last◀.

Michel recalled no more than that.

He looked out at the constellations again.

The swan became a sword.

Hercules went all herky-jerky.

The big dog bit the archer's artery. The archer sat down and took off his boot in order to tend to the wound. A plowman took the boot and poured a sheepskin of ale into the boot and then returned it to the archer.

<<Now wear it. It's good for what ails you.>>

The archer smiled and then turned slightly in order to better shoot the bull.
Michel loved it—one could always find a story in the sky.

Hercules the dancer jump-kicked the head of a giraffe. The charioteer, with a whip, snapped at Caßiopeia's father.

That's squinting.

So was Caßiopeia. Boom chakalaka! Oh, rain is coming. A storm. The stars go and hide. The homeleß remain outdoors. Michel sat upright in the observation deck and watched the flashing lights along the horizon. It looked to him like morning glories opening up in an instantaneous unfolding acroß the sky in different colors and different sizes, but fantastic and intense.

In tents, civilized humans could not see this spectacle.

In caves, troglodytes were amazed.

That was not the last time humanity gave up beauty in the name of ▶civilization◀.

No—humanity's rejection of true beauty was legendary. Story after story proved this to be one of the constants of humanity: in the name of civilization, beauty must die. The machine must rule! If the beast threatens the machinery of society, then the beast must die, especially if that means beauty, also, must die. Only the beast recognized beauty. Only the beast inside the beauty could recognize the beauty inside the beast. ►Chakalaka◄ was the rhythm of the train's wheels turning on the track.

Michel closed his eyes and listened to that familiar anapestic rhythm. He remembered having heard it before, a long time ago. He searched his memories.

It was repetitive. Ah, the take-off groove of an album. But this time one of the wheels on the landing gear had a flat tire, so the plane stopped on the mesa. Michel stepped off the train and walked back inside into the lighthouse. He sat down in a chair and fell asleep immediately.

Upon awakening, he went to water his morning glories, but before he opened his door, he saw what looked like a hornet or very large moth hovering inside the perimeter established by one of the large Heavenly Blues. When it disappeared into the throat of the flower, he knew it couldn't be a hornet or a moth. The hummingbird moth is nocturnal. Most like this was a juvenile ruby-throated hummingbird. The juveniles and females migrated south a bit later than the more brightly colored adult males. The moths also prefer dull flowers, and morning glories are not a known favorite. They prefer honeysuckle. The birds prefer bright colors.

In the past, when Michel had been able to attract more hummers, he had grown the red Happy Hour Rose morning glories, but further reading revealed they were not regular morning glories at all. They were a variety of Cardinal Climber vine. That explained the difference in leaf shape—fingers rather than hearts. The nursery that had sold them as morning glories was not very careful with its identification of species.

Presuming that what he had seen was a hummer, Michel realized that the time had come for him to migrate as well. He had to forget about his trip to Anarchy. He had to return to the Gardens, and he had to find the meßage he knew was waiting there in the beard of his death mask.

Delay was no longer poßible. He began to pack for his journey: he'd need to bring snail shells for slugs, drink for the diving ducks, and a dovecoted dive coat with long tails for formal occasions.

Book Eight: The Rest

♪Shevchenko was here, enjoying a beer….♫ The children's song sprang to mind again.

I was going overland, that's true, by the Gardens that began, mind you, with Taras Shevchenko. As a matter of fact, in Europe everything ties to Shevchenko the way in America everything ties to Zappa.

Plus I always have a sense of calm come over me when I see the face of the Great Walrus.

(<<I am the Walrus,>> said John.

<<No, you're not,>> said Little Nicola, who was always right.)

<<Hope on the bus!>> called Alf, who was a wonderful driver. Or was it Jolly Jimmy Johnson the Courier who had called out? In either case, I couldn't poßibly go along with them—they'd planned too many local stops, and, well, I always like to get somewhere by going the direct route.

Such as when….

Ah, when!

I could swim there like Burt Lancaster!

No.

I could parlay my parkour skills into a purveyance of conveyance. I'd call it auto-conveyance, but I had no auto, either.

I could disc golf my way all the way to my beard, but without an abacus, I'm afraid I'd lose count on the way and would have to start over from scratch.

Something itches, though, and I've got to go.

I dared not stop till I got to the Taras'd Gardens, a maze made vertical as well as horizontal: the Gardens of Obsane Topiary.

In my beard I'd find the key to my bed, and I'd finally be able to rest, which I have thus far been unable to do.

<<Rest!>>

The word was wonderful to hear and even better to voice.

Where would I be if I went where words were forever unvoiced?

How would I know the beauty of language without a Rolls Royce? Buy me a Rolls Royce, and I'll dedicate a novel to you. The novel will be all the more beautiful for the Rolls Royce.

Raymond Federman pulled up in a Silver Shadow. <<Come on, hop in, Michel. Let's go, you and I. Sam is talking!>>

I shook my head. <<I would love to, Raymond. The last time we went for a drive together, your detailed explication of the Unnamable was inspired. Enthusiastic, even! But this I need to do without you or even Uncle Ken helping me, at least directly. I mean, I'll always remember what you've told me.>>

<<Okay, Michel. Don't fuck it up.>> He waved and drove off in his Silver Shadow.

I could hike to Miltown, but the side effigies discourage me.

The path to Shevchenko's mask begins in Moryntsi on the Engelhardt land. Taras's Ma and Pa were serfing on the oceans of grain that they tended. After their deaths, Taras drew his ¢elgh closer to Engelhardt. Engelhardt eventually saw Taras's drawing close. Engelhardt dealt Shevchenko to Shyryayev, an artist looking for an apprentice. Shevchenko was eventually pulled out of serfdom by his fellow artists and by his whiskers.

If serfs boarded Raymond's Rolls, they'd become Silver Surfers and could fly to the Gardens quite easily. Shevchenko rode his art instead, cheered on by beggar boys and barked at by dogs, for he gave bread to all.

<<Corn bread,>> said the critics, who called him the ▶Corn Tsar◀, digging at his arrest for being part of the Kyrylo-Methodius Society, and for his early poems like ▶The Testament◀, which depict the beauty of Ukraine's cornfields.

He was, to the critics, corn bread, not corn-bred, and so his punishment in prison was worse than his colleagues'.

Also, he kept writing, although the penalty for doing so was severe. He began *In the Dungeon* in St. Petersburg but had to finish it in brutal Orsk, half an inch from Kazakhstan. When the Kyrylo-Methodius Society was betrayed by Oleksiy Petrov, Shevchenko was forbidden by Tsar Nicholas I from ever writing or painting again.

Taras did not obey. He kept writing and kept the text hidden in his boot.

Many houses in Orsk have bright blue roofs.

His writing discovered, Shevchenko was taken to Fort Novopetrovsk to be kept under strict supervision. In response he began a diary. He was incorrigible! He was given permißion to return to St. Petersburg but was detained at Nizhny Novgorod and forced to winter there from 1857 to 1858, beginning the most creative period of his life.

He was about to return to the Ukraine when in 1859 he was arrested for blasphemy and sent to St. Petersburg. He had fallen ill during his exile in Nizhny Novgorod. The illneß finally claimed him in St. Petersburg in 1861 before he ever got back to his beloved Ukraine, which he did only two months after he had died. He is buried in Kaniv.

But his face welcomes newcomers to the Gardens of Obsane Topiary.

*

<<Mike India, Charlie!>> echoes Lima. The Peruvians wanted to hear what the great subcontinent had to say.

<<Sierra Hotel echoes Victors, Charlie,>> hotels echo *November Kilo* Oscar. Actually, Oscar's call to give India a voice was echoed by people and hotels everywhere.

Biltmore, Baltimore, Mark Twain, Morrison. All turned their ears to Ravi Shankar's ►Bangla Dhun◄, one of the holiest moments of 1971.

Ragas became the rage. Talas told of transcendence above suffering.

Taras heard talas in Orsk. They wafted over the border from Prigornoye in Kazakhstan, only 35 kilometers away. They had made their way to Prigornoye from the Punjab, only 3800 miles to the south. The leeward side of the mountains would shoot music north as if it were a sound paßage from India to Kazakhstan.

Music converged on Orsk from many directions. From Persia, Taras heard the plaintive retrains of Majnun's love songs: ♪O my love, my dark-browed beauty, / do not be so foreign to me. / Do you not hear my grief?♫

Michel remembers but figures his days of fishing for angels are long over.

*

The Cumberland Gap led to the Appian Way, which led to the Gardens above.

The Gardens below led to Mount Venus. I could enter my family's area near the underground paßageway's right shoulder, by the collarbone.

But if I went above ground, I could enter at the point I first entered back when I was only a boy. My father took me in through the Gardens of the Knights of Malta inside Rome.

Through the keyhole of the gate to the Villa del Priorato di Malta, one can see St. Peter's Basilica. Tours of *Il Giardino Segreto Dei Cavalieri di Malta* can be purchased, but my father and I entered surreptitiously.

We invaded.

We were also in Vaduz the day the Swiß Army, with their pocket knives, invaded Liechstenstein.

I needed to go back to the Gardens. Past the sign that read ⧖Topiary Gardens⧖ lay the gardens everyone knew as ▶The Gardens of Obsane Topiary◀. And in the Gardens, near the hill known as ▶Mount Venus◀, I would be able to find my favorite of the ▶Shaved Girls◀ who tended the gardens. I had known her since I was but a boy and she but a girl. I had known no better rest in my life than when I was able to lay my head upon her soft bosom.

Plus I had to get that note out of the beard of my death mask.

*

I have wondered if Taras has any connection to the Knights of Malta. He would seem to have had because of the Gardens.

Taras's beloved grandfather had been a witneß of the Haidamak movement. The Haidamaks were a peasant force that rejected the yoke of the Polish nobility and their Catholic lords. At about the same time, the Knights of Malta were finding their ¢elghs *personae non gratae*, and were expelled from the Maltese Islands by Napoleon and the Republican French Catholic oligarchy. Even earlier, the payment of the Maltese Falcon to the Holy Roman Emperor Charles as tribute in order to gain Maltese lands for the order may not have set well with the order, and certainly when Malta's ¢elgh was taken away, they must have considered the Maltese Falcon to have flown away for no reason.

Thus, both the Haidamaks and the Knights of Malta had reason the resent the intrusions of the Church of Rome.

The last falcon flew off in 1978. The Haidamaks flew until the mid-1830s. Taras wrote a poem about them in 1841. By then the only land the Knights of Malta owned was in Rome. Not until 1991 did the Knights regain sovereign land in Malta; in 1991 Ukraine, for which Haidamaks fought, regained its independence.

As Taras noted in his poem, <<All things must always flow on; all things must paß.>> I wonder if Taras's great poem inspired George Harrison's greatest album, *All Things*

Must Paß. Harrison, of course, played with John Lennon. John Lennon played with Frank Zappa.

Everything ties to Shevchenko *and* Zappa.

*

In Vivaldi, tempo represents temperature.

In Bach, meter means he met her, which is why his family was so large.

Actually meter means the meter maid met meat maps mumbling mighty mimicry. Feeder streams in cedar shade let sweet naps tumble in flighty symmetry.

The fly is cast. The fiver holds no angelfish anymore. The piscator doesn't care. What's an angelfish? A snack? A gentle sailfin molly wants to coddle. The piscator turns away. He takes his red capers, and together they face a school of bullheads.

The butchers are taught to put their thumbs on the scale in culinary claßes.

One must run the gauntlet of their cleavers and throw down the gauntlet on their weavers for repair before one dares hillbilly handfish the hale bullheads. Then, and only then, throw the clever fish at the cleaver frowards. The cats will snap at red capers from the water's-edge birchers slapping weeping pußy willows. These besmirchers mistook the red capers for fluoride pellets and blamed the air.

<<I have no son,>> said the breathleß one, <<but I have art.>>

A server brought in tea for Dee, and we lounged on the veranda of this Victorian B&B while we all took respite from our separate travails.

Dee was a drummer in the band ►B◄, who were between albums and tours, so she was decompreßing. She was also a chain smoker, one of the last of a dying breed, so she was nearly always breathleß. But that gave her that husky whiskey voice that blues aficionados love so well in women singers.

She also played guitar like a car with bad timing, and her bandmates all loved the challenge.

*

I left some orts in Orsk while Baroneß Orczy saw orts on the Nord See on the left of north Germany.

Yay for Jever!

The orts were awash in Jever biers. And in Grafschaft outside Sillenstede the cemetery is filled with my ancestors.

<<*Wat von Sillenstede koomt, dat sööpt, sööpt, sööpt* >> is the local saying in Plattdeutsch.

The description was certainly true of the great Frisian hero Pier Gerlofs Donia, known to his followers as ▶Grutte Pier◀, or Big Pier, but he wasn't from Sillenstede. He was born in Kimswerd, in West Frisia. He led the Arumer Zwarte Hoop, the ▶Black Hope of Arum◀, against the abuses by the Hapsburgs, who'd burned Donia's farm and murdered his entire family. Big Pier was pißed off.

<<The ▶Black Hope◀? You mean the ▶Black Band◀?>>

<<No—those were the Landsknecht soldiers who attacked Big Pier's home.>>

<<The ▶Black Watch◀?>>

<<No—the ▶Black Eye◀. Come closer so I can show you.>>

Michel was in no humor to take crap from a stranger in a bar. He just wanted a few drinks and then a place to bed down before continuing his sojourn to the Gardens.

<<Well, stranger, you're in a black mood.>>

That was enough. Michel socked him, and before he knew it, he had found his place to bed down: the town's drunk tank.

*

He stayed away from the Œðer drunks at first.

One was hunched in a corner, muttering to his ¢elgh, pulling lice out his greasy dark hair and ✸popping✸ them into his mouth.

An Œðer dark-haired buy was standing by the door to the cage and was rocking back and forth on his feet, forwards and backwards, in regular rhythm. Although this one was dreßed in normal street clothes, he had martial arts slippers on his feet. Michel recognized the rocking from a long time earlier: one of his college roommates, a black belt in T'ai Chi Ch'uan, used to do that rocking thing. He had been his dojo's sensei for six months but had been fired for training his students incorrectly—he had told them T'ai Chi was a weapon to be used against Œðers aggreßively. The students loved it, but all the nonstudents who lived with the students didn't. These nonstudents banded together and took their case to the accreditation board. The owners of the dojo were then confronted by a choice between revocation of accreditation or the sensei's dismißal. Hubert—that was his name. We walked around campus and dropped people to the ground for amusement. But he was skilled enough to make sure they landed softly. Still—it was annoying. Of course this guy isn't Hubert. Hubert would be thirty years this guy's senior.

A salesman, blazer torn and tie awry, silver-haired and middle-aged, sat calmly at the farthest end of the one bench. He stared blankly ahead as if in a trance. He had no facial expreßion whatsoever.

Left-Handed Blues

In the middle of the bench
sat a man who killed a wench
who ✹hit✹ a john with a left-handed monkey wrench.

The joke would have been fine,
but now he's doing time
for mistaking Al Kaline for Johnny Bench.

If he'd left it all alone,
the fight'd never grown
and he'd be safely home with no thirst to quench.

But that just wouldn't do,
so he took off his left shoe
and slapped down a kangaroo he called "Dame Judi Dench."

Drink had had his mind
and had taken 'way his time.
He had nothing left to find of any consequence.

In his mind he's roamin' free
with a banjo on his knee
and a kitchen recipe for chicken-roasted quince.

He'd demand it in his cage;
we all wished he'd act his age
and redirect his stupid rage and chew breath peppermints.

Some would goad him off his seat
to get him up so he would beat
them senseleß in the summer heat until he made them wince.

He finally took the bait
and then attacked the first cellmate,
but his blows fell far too late against the government's.
When they took him out to hang,

and his wang doodle had been dang,
well, then his teeth had no more fang—his bite left no more dents.

They put his skull where he had sat,
and each new prisoner he looked at
had the strangest feeling that he'd never leave us hence.
He'd never leave us hence.
He never left us hence.

The salesman, killed by the man to whom the skull had belonged, was removed.

Michel sat down in the place he'd left. That way the skull wasn't staring at him.

Also on the bench, on the seat nearest the cage door, sat a guitar-playing kid who'd been nabbed for not having his cabaret license.

Michel was released in the morning and found the nearest open bar for drinks. He had a beer to wash the jail away. Then he had a shot of Eldersbane and was ready to face the faceleß. That was the least he could do for them. His fashion gallery had failed because he always fired the hot. But he had learned since then to keep his equilibrium.

It's a question of balance, moodineß and happineß, brilliance and intuition.

Brown rice water should be used for cooking golden splinters of shard-shaped pasta.

The tomatoes used in the sauce were sliced, diced, crushed, and pureed out of sheer spite. Diced beets were added for color.

Michel finished his motel diner spaghetti dinner all runny and awash in unsoaped dishwater. It was shit, but he was hungry. ɕIf I get cholera, I'll just sue them,ɔ he thought.

All night his sheets didn't fit his bed and his beets made him shit what he'd been fed. The buzzer was better off not called. He was apparently depreßed and could have given Michel an extra jolt too much.

After a cold shower in the morning, Michel hit the road again. He was going to use his thumb. What could be worse than walking? A psycho? Ha ha ha ha ha….

He was pretty certain he could outmaneuver the psycho. Or? Perhaps logic made one predictable, and easy mark. No—Michel would have to defy logic if he were to be aßaulted en route.

Michel haxed his ¢elgh the question so many of the greats had haxed their ¢elghs: Tony McPhee, Kim Simmonds, Canned Heat: What would John Lee Hooker do?

The answer came to him in an instant: enjoy his ¢elgh. Of course. Life was too short to be miserable. If Œðers are making you miserable for their own entertainment, get out of there! Fast! What the hell are you thinking? You have one of the great minds of our time. Claim it.

How do I know? You're reading this, aren't you? Who else but the kindest, most open-hearted would read this far? That's my opinion, anyway.
Boggie Chillen'!

Come on, Charles. We have a book to finish. Yeah, yeah, yeah.

No rush. Yet. A typist would be a great help.

I break all 97 walls to get here. Wow. I look in back, expecting to see a holy meß, but it actually looks rather neat and orderly. How did that happen? Michel must have been ▶caught unawares◀, as it were. Aren't we all, every now and then?

Michel began to suspect the tomato sauce. Botulism. He'd heard of a type of botulism one could get from tomatoes that would first show up when one's eyes croßed. Death would follow within 24 hours.

If it wasn't the tomato, then that Eldersbane was stronger than he'd remembered it. It seemed no rougher than Old Grand-Dad's Bonded. Maybe not quite as smooth.

Oh, well. There's a handrail. I can hold on. Hey, maybe this is the way the last ride starts and I'm just hopping aboard the Edward G. Robinson Train full of suicide parlors.

No—I'm just exhausted. Can't even prop up my narrator anymore. This is hard. I have pneumonia. Again. My breathing problems are not fun. So I've got to get to the mask. So does the narrator, actually. Ah, but the costume is so heavy. It's like dreßing like Henry Tudor Junior and setting the play in Death Valley.

Yeah, baby.

And then having to spend thirty days in that hole.

<<Sounds like a relationship I once had,>> said a Don Rickles impersonator.

<<Bob Newhart came by and engaged Rickles in conversation. Many of their friends were grateful for that, no doubt,>> said he so gosh-almighty that everyone ignored him

Actually, everyone ignored everyone else. Always. This had become immutable truth. Our paranoia had grown so great that we all just stayed home.

Nixon had won. He'd had the CIA smuggle social-softening agents back from Cambodia and Vietnam and had them distributed on college campuses and in minority neighborhoods in order to keep the people there all so high they'd stop taking to the streets and rioting. They'd all just sit at home and watch TV.

TV is your friend….

A snack—hundred-year-old turkey desiccated by time into rock jerky—would have been welcome had it been edible.

A bar's jar of pickled eggs looked very old, the brine suspiciously cloudy. Michel was a bit hungry, but not that hungry. He'd had no initial luck hitchhiking, so he'd stopped at a roadhouse for a beer and some food, but this roadhouse had no food Œðer than the suspicious eggs. The beer would have to do.

The Honeymooners was on the TV. That was the last honest sitcom. The working claß couple scrimped, saved, planned, invested, risked—in short *worked* incredibly hard to get out of the squalor of their middling existence, and no matter how hard they tried, they could never rise about their stations. *The Honeymooners* showed us that our economic caste system was intractable. Everyman Ralph broke his heart trying to lift his family out of working poverty. Every attempt failed. And that was the source of the humor: we laughed at the futility of our own lives. For women, Alice must have been equally as frustrating an Everywoman: not permitted to achieve financial succeß of her own, she was expected to ultimately support her loser husband without complaint.

The TV drove Michel back out onto the road, hitchhiking again. TV, his friend, had kicked him in the aß to get him out of his beer complacency.

The road was pulled like taffy from his teeth, but if he kept eating, he would make it to the end of the taffy eventually. Where the leprechauns keep their gold and where the Shaved Girls will welcome him home, especially the one.

<<What's your name?>> haxed a woman in a yellow roadster.

<<Michel,>> he replied.

<<I'm Taffy. Hop in.>>

<<Thanks.>> He climbed in, closed the door, and buckled up.

<<Where you headin'?>> haxed Taffy.

<<Just up to the Appalachian Trail. Thanks,>> Michel replied. From there, getting to Appian Way, the Catacombs, the Gardens of Malta, and then to his father's Gardens would be more difficult.

<<Not up to Maine, I hope. That's out of my way.>>

<<Well, where are you heading?>>

<<I have an old run-down A-frame near Gatlinburg. My sister and I would sunbathe on the deck when we were kids.>>

<<What did you use, Copperhead Suntone Lotion?>>

<<Ah—you've been there.>>

<<Sure, lost an Alsatian there to snakebite. A beautiful obedience dog. Damn stupid snakes.>>

<<They're just being snakes. They don't know any better.>>

<<No, but in my hands, they'd know the wurst—snakemeat sausage.>>

<<You'd better behead them before the toxins spread.>>

<<Yeah—that's my general philosophy of life, anyway.>>

<<Mine, too! What's your handle, again?>>

<<Michel du Jabot.>>

<<Mine's the Little Teapot. But you can call me Taffy.>>

Michel rolled down the window and yelled out, <<Taffy!>>

Goop started dripping down from the sky.

Michel yelled, <<Little Teapot!>> instead, and luke-warm orange pekoe began coming down, dißolving the goop.

<<You know what would go with this little tea party?>> haxed Taffy.

<<No. What?>>

<<Hailscones!>> and suddenly scones began to fall from the sky.

<<Sly,>> said Michel to Taffy.

<<Like a sloth on a trail,>> said Taffy back, trying to stick it to him. But Michel had saved a cup of tea and spilled it on Taffy's outstretched hands, which dropped the goop and caught a couple of scones, which she crumbled in her hands in order to dedigitate the tea. Then she rubbed her hands free of all crumbs. And to her, Michel was a crumb. She lost her interest in him, stopped the car, and ejected him by the side of the road,

still short of the mountains.

Michel still had a way to go, and he certainly had away to go. He was in the middle of nothing—no human structure but the road could be seen.

Michel remembered his Hitchcock and began to expect a crop duster to show up there in nowhere, which it usually came out of.

No such luck. Only nothingneß. And graß. Or wheat. Or whatever that stuff is. Probably snakes all through it.

Tenneßee made him wary of snakes. You may wear your boas, but you must ware the snakes! Don't ever let people talk you into sticking your hand into a bagful of snakes. Those people do not mean you well.

Ware those people!

Ed Gein must have misunderstood that injunction.

Ware the Wearer! The naked do not hide weapons!

Michel bindled his clothes and stuck them over his shoulder (actually, they stuck on their own because of the goop that dripped off them).

He stuck his mitt in the bag and then pulled it back out—he saw that five writhing snakes had attached their ¢elghs to his mitt. They were moving independently of each Œðer, like a Gorgon's ▶Ola!◀, which undoubtedly stank like greeted green cheese.

He wanted to make the snakes disappear, but he was not very skilled in prestidigitation. But he hoped to find a place to wash his hands so he could remove the stench of preßed cheese vegetation.

You're talking about cheeses? How about some roundtrip swampcheese, gas included?

Oh, it hasn't yet been extruded?

Ever notice it's sold in cans? Gas stations?

Pardon the intrusion. There must be some confusion....

Michel washed his hair, face, and body in the sink of a Sinclair Gas station in East Sycamore, Tenneßee. He rubbed soapy fingers all over his teeth. The soap was hard to rinse out of his hair. He could only fit a quarter of his head under the spigot in the sink, so he had to rotate a few times. It was either that or take the Lego thing apart—it's just part of a machine anyway: a giant machine made of Legos.

We used to live on a giant machine made of Logos. Jonathan Swift poked some holes in that one, though, and then Coleridge and Wordsworth ripped the fabric of Logos to shreds.

We were poor, we were hungry, but we sure as hell were not going to eat our children.

Logos crashed. Pathos and Ethos battled for control of the estate.

Pathos felt it could claim the remains because they had an affinity for Pathos. A rather circular argument, but lost on Ethos, who was too busy repeating the first word of every paragraph he'd ever written about his world: <<▶I◀>>.

The ball rolled down the aisle and stopped at my feet. I picked it up. The word ▶Estate◀ was stamped on the side. Obviously something was inside, but I could not find a way to open it. A hidden latch? A preßure-point trigger?

<<Hey, give that back!>> yelled Pathos.

<<I'll play with you,>> said I, Porthos, the portly musketeer.

<<No, man. You belong with a different crew. Why aren't you hanging with D'Artagnan or Aramis or Athos?>> He said ▶Athos◀ like he was really saying ☼Aßhole☼. It was a clever convergence of words if nothing else.

I said I thought the team was Athos, Ethos, Pathos, and Porthos. The Œðers were the ones who didn't belong—they had the funny names: Aramis? Isn't that the name of a perfume? Or Logos? Which is made of Legos anyway—it's just an Œðer corporate by-product. And D'Artagnan? That had never fit with anything anyway. Just old Dumas defying the natural duality and symmetry of the world in order to establish some trinitarian 3-in-1 snake oil elixir of ambrosia.

The Three Musketeers together with St. Patrick rid Ireland of snakes. They made chocolate candies using detoxified snake venom. Monty Python had ordered a boxful once a long time ago, springtime.

Watch out, take care—along the side of the road, <<Ware the Bear>>!

He stayed hidden and waited till the bears were gone. They'd scavenge off of litter toßed from cars—old fast food remnants—leftover fries and spilled Soylent Green sauce.

Michel was smarter than your average bear. And what he wanted right then was an average beer.

He grinned up at the giant green brontosaurus that was Sinclair's logo, shook and tucked, washed his hands again, dreßed, and walked around to the front of the gas station in order to give the key back to the attendant. What was funny was that Michel had been completely naked when he'd gone in to get the key, but the clerk had never even noticed. He had never looked up from the hands and the money, as if he had been expecting some prestidigitation to take place.

Michel was tempted to ledger dumb men and take a few bottles of IPA to the car where we all pee, eh? But he restrained his ¢elgh. He wasn't desperate enough yet. He still had quite a few acceßible funding sources. The only thing he didn't like, though, was that the company that dispersed the funds could trace his movements from his withdrawal history. That's why he'd chosen one bank for each continent. And his favorite was the Bank of Antarctica. He had funds in cold storage there.

But funding—that to him was the curtain he didn't want people to look behind. Accept the wizard for the grand illusion he was. Why demystify it? That'd be all Killjoy.

Sure, Killroy was here, and he said no to Killjoy. We all say no to Killjoy.

Come on, Killroy, get down from that wall. I know you're looking down on the Killjoys, but let them be, for someday they'll be you and me, for a while, every now and then.

Michel looked at the beers in the cooler. Nothing foreign that was any good. Just beer factories. He'd been hoping for a Spaten or a DAB at least. He took a Mickey's 40-ounce instead, paid for it, and went back to the bathroom. Once locked safely inside, he drank. The locals couldn't get mad at him for drinking if they didn't see him doing so. If he could have disguised his ¢elgh as a hound, he'd more likely eat than be eaten.

How and why he needed food eluded the shopkeep. Michel reeked of stale sweat and urine and Mickey's. No, the store didn't wonder if Michel were a crazy man relinquished by the world. Or if he'd wandered off somewhere accompanied by ladies' blushes and toilet brushes. All the store noticed was his money. And a slight reduction to inventory. Back out on the highway, Michel's hiking was getting sluggish. No one was going to pick him up except a serial killer or someone mistaking him for a serial killer. Hitchhiking was not working.

He jumped on a paßing train, which happened to be on its way to Anarchy on the Thames. He stepped into the car just in time to see a mom and child who looked like Ana and Andy close the door to the next car behind their ¢elghs.

Michel knew this train. He'd been on it before, but not in this part of it.

Symbols of Anarchy decorated the walls of the cars. Michel took a seat, opened up a pocket notebook, and began to record a few blue notes for his blues lyrics.

A beat writer came up to him and haxed, <<Will you be my hundredth monkey?>> and then paßed on into obscurity only to be popularized once he'd been read by a hundred good readers.

Michel thought the guy sitting behind Pravda was Yuri Andropov. He was traveling with his grandfather, Don Coßack.

They were both Star Rovers, as was Michel's ancestor Avery Craw.

Vladimir Konstantinovich Andropov came walking down the car. He was a railway official, apparently. No wonder his son had safe paßage here.

Andropov's mŒðer kept watching her pocket. She had a watch in her pocket. She was waiting for this all to be finished.

Andropov hated the hungry. He had the hungry killed, especially Imre Nagy. And then he joined the KGB. Andropov was quite versatile. He began to check Œðer people off like they were hungry, and he would not listen to any criticism. He probably never even read Clement Greenberg. And art? Reading *Ulyßes* would have given him renal failure.

We have no idea of what he'd have thought of the original Scythians.

Oh, cut it out.

Hahahahaha….

Michel kept his peace and stared out the train window.

<<Tickets! All must have tickets! Open all bags immediately!>>

The Swiß train inspectors were already on board. Too bad for Michel he had no ticket and so was put off the train in the middle of nowhere.

Thrown off the money train, Michel rolled through space fast and time slow. But if space is fast, then it's not moving at all. Without movement, the clocks all stop.

Suspended in air between train and tracks, Michel could do nothing.

Fortunately, nothing is what he did best. Even when the opportunity to rise to prominence had been thrust at him, as when he'd been offered half a kingdom by the Aasvogel on Mars, he'd rejected it and had become a director of recreation instead. He knew that true recreation began with an overhaul of the way one saw one's ¢elgh. That one one would become too two.

To remain a singularity, he'd rejected the Ionic conquerors who sought to draw him into their power.

Of course he felt the attraction, but he rejected it. He had no use for their negativity.

Nor did he want to give them his. He disliked being charged with being too positive.

Equilibrium. That's what he liked. Which was why he was suspended between train and track.

When the train disappeared, he floated down to the knoll alongside the tracks as if he were a softly falling leaf.

He could not move, but the graß felt itchy against his face. The itch spread into a sneeze that jump-started Michel again.

He stood up, felt bruised but not broken, and wondered which direction the Gardens were in.

He floated up again. An Œðer train paßed. He resettled on the knoll.

Again he could not move beyond a standing position until the next train floated him down again.

This pitch and roll exercise repeated its ¢elgh over and over until evening, when the trains stopped coming. At that time, Michel was able to move away from that place and put some distance between his ¢elgh and that particular set of tracks.

As he rolled away, he saw a man on the horizon. Who was that? A man playing drums, silhouetted against the evening moon.

As Michel approached, he began to hear the music….

♪It's a man down there. May be your man? I don't know.♫ Duster Bennett! The one-man band, playing his claßic.

Michel stopped rolling, sat where he was, and just listened for a while. Really? Duster Bennett! Michel wanted to get a better listen, so he carefully approached the musician. Michel wanted a fuller sensory experience: louder plus seeing the musician's fingers and facial expreßions. Those two senses drove him forward. His olfactory and gustatory senses were put on hold. His tactile were preßed into service of the auditory and visual.

Duster was relating a time he visited Egypt and told the tour guides at the pyramids that he wasn't trying to build a temple, but was just telling it as it is from day to day.

One night, driving home after a gig with Memphis Slim, Duster Bennett, listening to Sleepy John Estes in his car, fell asleep behind the wheel, crashed and died, an accident like those Michel had survived twice. Maybe Duster had really survived? He hadn't aged. Was this his grandson? His youngest son was born in 1976, so that would mean that the son was older than his father ever was. He father had died at 29. A grandson must be who that is. He's just like the old man.

No, that has to be Tony Bennett, who'd had obvious reasons for taking the stage name ►Duster◄. He'd have Œðerwise forever been confused with the popular American singer of the same name.

One great leßon must be taken from this: never listen to Sleepy John Estes while driving a car when your ¢elgh is sleepy. Michel knew narcolepsy. It was frightening. That people joked about it made it no easier to bear.

Machines were bragged about as cures. None of them had worked. Narcoleptics were dropping like flies.

Nantucket Train Ride

A Nantucket engineer
fell asleep on the throttle
and ran his train
off its tracks
on a sharp turn,
almost driving
it into the bay.

Apple-dunking time is near—
fill the sap in the bottle,
and ban your brain
off its bats
with a sharp burn
almost drying
us throughout the day.

Strawmen constructors suggested that the engineer had been listening to the Grateful Dead's ►Casey Jones◄. The strawmen were called ►crash test dummies◄ in the preß; the engineer was referred to as the ►driver◄. Though, of course, in ►Casey Jones◄ being tired was not Casey Jones's immediate state of alertneß—he was ♪high on cocaine♫, or so the song says.

An Œðer song says, ♪See shells at She Sells Seashells. Come by and come buy them….♫

And, of course, the Merrimack, all clad in black, with silver rivets up and down its back, haxed its mŒðer if it could kill the Monitor.

<<In its maze?>> haxed the mŒðer. >>Didn't Theseus already take care of that?>>

<<Not ►Minotaur◄, Mom, ►Monitor◄.>>

<<The cop wannabees who patrol school halls?>>

<<No, not that kind.>>

<<The kabaragoya?>>

<<A sedative-drinking shiksa?>>

<<No—that'd be a kava goy. A kabaragoya is a water monitor!>>

<<Like a lifeguard?>>

<<No—like a Komodo dragon.>>

<<An old Asian woman wearing a silk dreß?>>

<<No—that's be a kimono dragon. But I don't mean that kind anyway. I mean the ironclad Civil War ship.>>

<<But didn't the Monitor sink the Merrimack?>>

<<No—the Merrimack saved its ¢elgh from sinking by going close to shore. But it was decommißioned after that battle. Ironically, it was the Monitor that sank in a storm later that year.>>

<<Ironically? Iron-cladically?>>

Ana and Andy again. ͼBut they were on the train,ͽ Michel thought. How was he hearing them?

Michel opened his eyes. He was in a hospital room.

<<Look, Andy! He's awake!>> said Ana. She turned to Michel. <<You're lucky Andy saw you being put off the train. We got off at the next whistle stop and got the sheriff to get you and bring you to the county hospital. You almost didn't make it.>>

<<What? I *didn't* make it.>>

<<Well, maybe not all the way. But we have degrees and phases and partial stages.>>

Michel tried to understand her, but the effort hurt his mind, so he closed his eyes and drifted back off.

A Xerox of xerus was being paßed around Michel's sixth grade claßroom.

<<What is this?>> haxed the teacher of the claß.

<<A squirrel, Ma'am,>> said one kid.

<<A *fox* squirrel,>> corrected an Œðer.

<<A cat's squirrel?>> offered a third.

<<It's not a squirrel at all,>> said Michel. <<It's only a picture of a squirrel. Real squirrels are much more dynamic.>>

<<Touché! It's like Marcel Duchamps's pipe!>>

<<Or Jasper Johns's targets and flags.>>

<<*The Collier's Adit.*>>

<<He is?>>

<<No—the painting by Hidalgo.>>

<<And a collie is at it? That sounds nasty.>>

<<No, Michel,>> chastised his teacher. <<The entrance to a coal mine. It's an amazing painting of the shift change at the entrance. It's a study in contasts—the filthy escapees and the clean entrants, dark vs. light. The dread and agony on the faces is powerful. It's like a Bruegel in its expreßive detail. Except for the space worms, the muscae volitantes, developed by the minors out of chronic light deprivation. Are you listening, Michel?>>

<<Yes, Ma'am.>>

<<Good. Look lively.>>

<<Yes, Ma'am.>>

And then Duster Bennet stopped playing.

Michel was still seated on the graß of the knoll as near to Bennett as he dared—he had hoped not to scare the vision away. He hadn't had to. It was terrific. Mayall and Mark-Almond joined Bennett. They did a version of ▶Turn on Your Love Light◀, but no one really remembered the lyrics well. It was close enough. But then it was gone again.

Something was brewing on the horizon—a maßive dark thundercloud began looming.

Michel headed for the bluffs. He figured he'd thought of caves for a reason. This bluff must have a cave system, perhaps carved by giant gribbles and grubs.

The minerals in the bluff constipated them badly, so when they'd had their fill, in order to escape the bluff, they had to crawl backwards, expelling their contents through their mouths in order to propel their ¢elghs. They couldn't figure out how to turn around by going forward. Indeed, that is a difficult maneuver for most grumbles and grabbles, let alone gribbles and grubs.

Fortunately for the rest of the world, most grumbles and grabbles gravitated toward the greed centers—Washington for politics, New York for finance, Los Angeles for media, Paris for fashion, Tibet for religious persecution—

And Chicago for rat-a-tat-a-tat! Let the guns do the yakety yak; let the arms spiel.

Michel found a shallow cave under a bluff. One could not see it from land, and it was high enough to elude the tide.

An etude was tried in celebration, Michel playing nose flute quite adroitly. Although he played right, he usually left listeners behind. He was quite the virtuoso.

What listeners? The cave was too shallow for bats or bears.

Michel again began to hear Duster Bennett, this time far off in the distance. Bennet must have found shelter and set up again. Good.

The thunder began to drown out Bennett's music. And then the rain obscured the countryside.

The sheet of falling rain looked like a wall from inside the cave. But the cave's overhang overhung the entire entrance, so no rain came in.

The lightning illuminated the cave brightly and often.

A gris-gris appeared in the corner. Michel picked up the talisman, brushed it off and neatened it a bit, and then he put it back down. That was more juju than he wanted to deal with just then.

The weather calmed briefly, as if the talisman were thanking Michel for taking care of it.

But then the sheets came down again, and the skies thunderflashed with mighty power.

And Michel leaned back against a smooth boulder by the wall. It was actually contoured perfectly for sitting against, as if worn smooth by hundreds of backs over centuries.

And Michel looked at the sheets falling.

And Michel rested.

Da Capos would hax him to go back. The Capos would tell him to.

But they weren't there, and he was. So he could rest without fear.

He listened to the storm. He could no longer hear anything *but* the storm, and the storm came down with counterpoints and polyrhythms more complex than the Art Ensemble of Chicago's.

He was entranced.

Drip crumple badabing hush! Clampet clutter sushi catamallata boo! Boo! Whiffle wash swell forlorn corn cantata shoe! Pitterfall smasherish Scotch banger pie beknow, now, plow. Swangmanger salad spork, Fallopian shoot….

Oviduct? Viaduct? Vie? Not a canary? Which would you rather listen to? Quacker clacker or wind charm?

The canary was real. It was in the cave. That was propitious. It sang and then it landed on Michel's thigh, where it stang him.

<<Ooh,>> moaned Michel, rubbing his thigh. <<And I thought that verb had gone obsolete. Ow! It sure doesn't feel obsolete.>>

It wasn't a canary at all. It was a false-canary wasp, an invasive species from Venus, a species worse than hummingbird moths—those great deceivers.

Its single stinger now cast, the wasp had been rendered harmleß, but its torn-open abdomen would inevitably lead to its death. No bandage could save it.

Michel worked the stinger out of his thigh. It was a good half-inch long and was as thick as a toothpick.

The sting hurt as much as when he was accidentally harpooned in the Œðer thigh during the Japanese-Australian Whaling Wars of the early part of the century. Michel had only been there as a visitor but became ▶collateral damage◀.

He didn't want to think about that, though. Thoughts of those troughs he'd trudged through made his truths tougher than they were trundled off to troupial trous-de-loup to be. Troublously trebled baß fishermen soaped and ran (and *I* ran!), but the audience's collective raspberry toned them down (per Sean Penn's expert direction).

ͼWho would have left a talisman in the cave?ͽ thought Michel. ͼI don't know. Yet I….ͽ

He didn't want to voice his suspicion, even though he was alone. He was afraid he'd just be putting his big foot in his mouth.

In which case his teeth would fall out, as if he'd been ✸hit✸ by a bomb and a bull snowman. Ice horns gorged him.

He gorged his ¢elgh on horns full of ice wine.

Who had stored these bottles of wine in this cave? A connoißeur, of course!

A con, monsieur, of course!

Acorn monsters off course.

A common steer off course.

Akhenaton's ear's off coarse. His macron had gone circumflex. And I won't even mention what he used to do with macaroons.

Do you realize that in some languages vowels don't matter and that in them macrons *are* macaroons?

Macrons are made long and tall, but macaroons are short and round. How would one know without vowels?

UC, CCR is up and round the circumflex.

Flecks of sir cum are sold on the interwebs to the spider people for the private purposes. Ear sacks are egg sacks, let's just say.

But what about the badgers?

A wolverine turned its head and said, <<Badgers? We don't need no stinking badgers!>> at the same time that a gopher said the Mißißippi flowed south because Iowa sucks. Good old Big Ten humor from the 20th century. Oh, the Ara Parseghian jokes one could tell! They could fell a Turk, but a fellow Fighting Irishman is rarely a Fighting Methodist.

The wraith is fecund….

Wait a second.

This is just a play of words, dancing for my dining pleasure. How old fashioned it is, is it not, to be so reclined in order to observe the thoughts of someone else.

It is, of course, a relief to escape one's own thoughts and ride along with someone else's, but that can only take one away from one's own center.

Nicholas of Cusa. Travel out or travel in. Both lead deep ♪Within You Without You♫, as George Harrison once sang, and for which he was laughed at by his well-meaning but not-very-spiritual companions. George needed leaders because the one he'd always counted on, John, turned into a dick for a while. Of course, we all do, but the timing could have been different. George's bloßoming could have happened from within the band, and the band would have grown. But the band had an inelastic part that would not expand, and so,

I can go?

What about the rest?

the rust?

When you father a child you

[Cistern Tawdry ahoy!]

Use, uh, all your skill, uh;
'dja rip 'dis old man?

Yeah, ol' Pop. Me, I gueß.

No, me!

Okay, off to the game shows with both of you!

Now

let

go!

He's

gone!

Meaning me, of course. My ¢elgh and I, a circle within a circle within an ovoid within a voidoid within an avoid within a devoid—♪Are We Not Men?♫—7/4 time in general.

11/4, like the Dead's ►The Eleven◄.

Of course, the 4/4s will be upset with you. Remember what they did to Dave Brubeck. The boycotts. The riots. Just add some atonality and you'd have had the aßaßination of Anton Webern all over again.

Michel drank the last sip of ice wine, still staring at the sheets of rain falling over the cave.

He tucked his ¢elgh in beneath the sheets and fell asleep.

*

When he awoke, the rain had stopped. He went to gather his belongings and noticed the talisman was gone.

The countryside was quiet but for chirping birds and rushing waters slapping against the bluff.

Michel took off down the road again. He had a tune in his mind, and that was enough for then.

He wished he had a beer. But beer wasn't what it once was. Beck's was now being made the US, and Foster's was from Canada. He wanted a Danish Tuborg or a German Löwenbräu, but they could not be found.

He noticed the beer stores came more frequently, though, and the churches leß so, so he knew he was nearing civilization. He was on the road to Rome. He remembered a Robert E. Howard poem about that. Howard had killed his ¢elgh when he found out his mom had a terminal illneß.

Freud frowned and then lit a cigar. The three of them walked together. Michel limped and blew a flute. Howard held the flag. Freud beat his snare.

Together they marched into a filled Coloßeum and took seats as close as poßible, two rows from the back wall.

The games began. Innocent lions were being thrown to the Christians, who dismembered them faster than a school of piranha could. I've seen them pick to pieces entire nations in what seemed to be mere moments. They'd fell their prey and then go for the jugular. And then they'd pray over the fallen.

I don't think Jesus would have liked many of these Christians.

<<True, man,>> says Jesus. <<Give me an honest homeleß person anyway. Give me the despairing. Give me the regulars, the 99%. They are like me. Normal folks. Heaven is not an oligarchy. Dig it—that's the point of the trinity.>>

St. Augustine told the little kid at the ocean, <<You're wrong, child. There it was—your explanation.>> At least according to St. Cyril of Jerusalem's little story.

When Michel left his companions in their seats, they didn't notice. Their attention was on the symbolism and brawn of the events on the field. Michel could see those two as fast friends—Howard would fascinate Freud, and Freud's Study of Howard would feed Howard's need for approval.

Andy was there all of a sudden. He said, <<You know who I think would make fast friends?>>

Michel shrugged.

<<Quicksilver and Kid Flash.>>

<<Well, they would both resent Barry Allen, that's for sure. You like comics?>>

<<Yeah. DC.>>

<<I always liked that Green Lantern who became the Spectre. Spectre was cool.>>

<<Hal Jordan.>>

<<That was it. Spectre should be a movie.>>

<<Maybe.>>

<<And Dr. Strange. You've got to get Crispin Glover to play him.>>

<<Who?>>

<<Crispin Glover. He was in *Willard*. Actually, I'd like him and Ayn Rand to be Nin and Nan. They look a lot alike.>>

<<Now he'll never do it.>>

<<She?>>

<<I’m pretty sure Ayn Rand died a long, long time ago.>>

<<Only if it was in her best interest.>>

<<Are you thinking of Anais Nin?>>

<<Hey, that’s funny. Hadn’t occurred to me. Stopped noticing her after I read her lies about Kenneth Patchen. But I take it from almost all the sources who wrote about her who knew her, she was not a very honest or direct person: many Œðers complained of her lying about them.

If she was lying about me, I’d have given her a hand up and said, <<Stop lying down there. Stand up for real you. These patrician airs do not make you any more interesting.>>

No, it must be Ayn Rand who is meant. She’s the one who looks like Crispin Glover. And she has a cult of followers who remind Michel of the Bözmacher cult, and those are days best left forgotten.

Andy went back to his seat next to Ana, and Michel made his way out of the Coloßeum.

In the distance, he thought he saw Chris Farlowe walking out as well, but in a different direction. He was going down South to <<a chicken farm near Mashville, Tenneßee,>> Gilbert Shelton might have said, and Mani Neumeier might have repeated him, sort of.

Michel began looking for the Gardens of Malta—he had a general idea of where they were. They were on the ground of the Magistral Villa on Aventine Hill.

Crowds began filling in the space around him. He could overhear more English than he thought he would.

<<Profeßor!>> one voice exclaimed. <<I heard you were on sabbatical!>>

<<No,>> replied the profeßor from a distance. <<I have been on some radical idea that—>>

<<That what?>>

<<What?>>

<<I heard you were on sabbatical!>>

<<Oh, no. I’m on this radical march! We are storming Malta!>>

<<Why?>>

<<The Crusades!>>

<<That was a long, long time ago. I think your Knights of Malta are more likely to drive around in minicars than reconquer the Holy Land!>>

<<Shhh! Not so loud!>> The profeßor fell upon his questioner: <<That’s the Knights of Columbus or the Shriners of the Freemasons. Don’t even say those names!>>

Honk! Honk! The miniature car drove by, but contained a clown.

Several of these cars appeared, driven by Juggalos from the clown college! Michel averted his face so that they wouldn’t recognize him. The Orator may have caught a glimpse of Michel before Michel saw him and ducked, diving behind a barrel of whiskey. Michel waited, sipping the whiskey from a pour plug in the side.

He thought he heard the word ▶Twirly◀ once, but concluded he’d hallucinated it when it was not repeated.

He looked through the famous keyhole revealing St. Peter’s Basilica. The crowd was not permitted into the Gardens. All one could do was step inside the post office and buy official Maltese stamps.

This is not how anyone thought the Knights of Malta would ever go stamping.

Michel saw how well guarded everything was then, during tourist hours. That would change at the end of the day, when the post office closed.

When everyone was out of sight down the hill or out of sight in the Gardens, Michel and an Œðer man, who wore a hat and large glaßes as if trying to paß his ¢elgh off as Gina Lollobrigida’s director, entered the gate where the gardener had left it open.

The man turned to Michel. <<He must have left it open so we could come in,>> he said.

Something about him seemed familiar. And then, when Michel saw the man’s gait, Michel called out to him, <<Dad?>>

The gate opened, and the glaßes and hat came off to confirm the answer.

<<Son!>> said Michel’s father. <<*Pares cum paribus facillime congregantur*!>>

<<To the Topiary Gardens?>>

<<Of course. Here, follow me. I know a shortcut through the storm cellar.>>

Michel followed his father.

<<Are you okay, Son?>>

<<Yeah, of course. It just seemed like time to come back.>>

<<I know what you mean.>>

<<Yeah, and I had a feeling I had a meßage waiting for me in my death mask.>>

<<Hey, me, too. What's with that?>>

<<I don't know. Gueß we'll find out. How've you been, Dad?>>

<<Good. Busy. I'm putting together the armature for a project.>>

<<That's good.>>

Michel's father, Arthur, was an internationally known architect. He'd mißed much of Michel's life, but they always enjoyed the times they had together.

The metaphors Michel heard from his father were frequently architectural. And his father loved to tell stories of their ancestor, Avery Craw, whose son Blip had Francophied the family surname.

They rounded a hedge and came out in a clearing, where the gardener immediately saw them and came running at them, yelling, rake in one hand and with the Œðer waving to them to clear off.

<<I think that man wants us to leave,>> said Michel.

<<Nah—he's just waving hello,>> said Arthur, who Snagglepußed stage left and ducked behind some bushes. Michel dove in after him.

There they opened a drainage grate, crawled in, and pulled the grate closed behind their ¢elghs. They descended into the storm drains. The gardener did not follow.

But the father-and-son-duo still had a greater challenge before them: storm troopers.

Every entrance to the Topiary Gardens was fraught with peril, but this one had storm troopers. The trick was to get out of the storm drains as fast as poßible. At a split in the paßage, a giant arrow pointed right, so they knew to go left. A hundred yards on, they saw a ladder that descended to the next level, a maintenance platform between sewers.

They had no intention of descending to the lower sewers. The maintenance platform was easy to navigate, though, and they eluded all detection. At the next ladder they climbed up past the storm sewer, up again to the surface.

<<This is a shortcut?>> haxed Michel.

<<No—I just needed a smoke. You can't smoke down there. Don't know which gaßes will set off.>> He lit an old-fashioned plastic-tipped Cigarillo, the kind Michel remembered from his youth, when they were still smoked openly in public, before the tobacco prohibition. Back then he hadn't wanted the laws. Heck, he'd even moved onto a Reservation for First Peoples, and through his Peyote ancestry, to protected land. His blood was a little too thin for him to paß, though, so he was welcomed as some ►Native-fetish white dude◄. His father, though, was darker than Michel. And he for a long time had been dying his hair jet black, perhaps to emphasize his connection with the Peyotes.

The local townies used a Caterpillar tractor and pulled Michel back out of the reservation by tying his bootstraps to the tractor, forcing Michel to choose: riding or drug?

He rode out of town and waved Peyote culture goodbye.

Arthur finished his Cigarillo and flicked the tip into a mud puddle.
<<Hey, that's littering, Dad.>>

<<No—it's being buried in the mud. It'll disintegrate.>>

<<Yeah, in about a million years.>>

<<Well, then it's good I start the proceß early.>> Michel rolled his eyes.

Snake eyes! A loser! <<It'd be better to reshape it into toys or tools,>> said Michel.

<<The birds might pick it up to line their nests. They like shiny objects.>>

<<Yeah? What if they eat it?>>

<<What bird would do that?>>

<<An owl.>>

<<Yeah, well, owls spit up those pellets. It wouldn't hurt an owl.>>

<<Okay, a flamingo.>>

<<No—they can paß larger, shrimp-sized objects. One lone filter won't kill them.>>

<<Unleß they have severe tobacco allergies.>>

<<Flamingos with tobacco allergies?>>

<<Flamingos living in the pond of a luxury hotel.>>

<<Okay, you've got me there. I won't toß the filters on the ground anymore.>>

<<Thanks.>>

<<Well, this is no episode of *Father Knows Best*.>>

<<You know that title was ironic, right?>>

<<Really? No—I'm kidding. Of course it was. And that was what was mißing from *Marcus Welby*.>>

<<I don't think *Marcus Welby* was trying to be ironic.>>

<<I know. That's what's ironic—that it wasn't trying to be. We all figured Robert Young would have to be. The same thing happened to the Saint's sarcasm when he became Bond.>>

<<Roger Moore?>>

<<Yes.>>

<<Sarcasm?>>

Arthur shrugged. Michel shrugged back.

<<Back down the ladder, then, I gueß,>> said Michel.

<<No, not at all. There's an entrance right up here. I didn't bring you up here just so I could smoke. I mean, what kind of schmuck do you think I am?>>

<<None, Dad.>>

<<Just kidding. Come on. Let's go. Again, Arthur led them into a row of thick bushes. A gap between two bushes was revealed, and the men entered a part of the Maltese Gardens that was so overgrown that it was obviously not tended to by any gardener. A narrow path led back from there and down into the hillside and eventually underground and into a cave. But first they had to get past a thicket of blackberry brambles that tore at every exposed piece of skin and punctured all protective clothing short of thick leather or Kevlar.

Michel's right ear caught a branch just let go by Arthur, and it slashed him from ear to nostril.

<<Ouch! Watch that, Dad!>>

<<No pain, no gain.>>

<<Please today use no cliché.>> Arthur had been one of those minions who had embraced the cyber-revolution without ever realizing that the inventor of cybernetics, Norbert Wiener, had coined the term because of its etymology. ▶Cyber◀ comes from a Greek word that refers to the herding of steers. Steers, of course, are castrated, which is to say they are rendered impotent.

Cyber living, alone as it is, is autocastration. Be steered by Œðers if you like, but some of us enjoy having what we're called for not coming when we're called: nuts.

After a few years of cyber clichés, Arthur had suddenly given up his virtual life and had locked his ¢elgh into a real life.

He found he could love people again once he met them face to face.

Of course Michel knew that Arthur would come to the Gardens. Arthur had shown them to Michel in the first place and had brought him along many times when he came to visit the Shaved Girls who inhabited them and took care of the Gardens.

They were always nice to young Michel. When he got older, one was particularly nice to him and introduced him to new ways of communicating he'd never before known. He was able to relax in her breasts and completely rest. The true point of rest in his life was there, embraced. The true point of the rest of his life was there, embraced.

Love's truth.

Ah, but no one is permitted to stay in the Gardens forever except the Shaved Girls. And each was very independent of the Œðers. Their collective title, ▶Shaved Girls◀, was certainly sexist to contemporary ears, but when it had been coined during the Swank Era, it was spoken only with the greatest of reverence. The title, like ▶NAACP◀, sounds a bit old-fashioned, but that's only because they don't hide history.

♪If you wanna hide history,♫ Arthur used to sing, ♪hax a tanner. If you wanna prediction, hax a planner.♫

Michel remembered that. The lines were from an old blues song.

Hide Tanner Blues

If you wanna hide history,
hax a tanner.
If you wanna prediction,
hax a planner.
If you wanna find a man
who will rock all night,

don't look to my left;
don't look to my right.
I'm here right now
and I'm ready to go.
Come with me, baby,
and I'll show
you some flash
like you've never seen.
It'll grow for you fast,
like Jack's magical bean.
Be my stalker,
my magical stalker;
climb to the top
for the golden goose.
Take all you want
and shake it loose.
Be my stalker,
my magical stalker.

If you want good whiskey,
go to Kentucky.
If you have a predilection,
you can get lucky.
If you wanna find a guy
who'll roll your gams,
you won't have to go
to no foreign lands.
I'm here right now
and I'm ready for you.
I'll show you, baby
what we should do.
Here's some flash
like you've never seen.
It'll grow for you fast,
like Jack's magical bean.
Be my stalker,
my magical stalker;
climb to the top
for the golden goose.
Take all you want
and shake it loose.
Be my stalker,
my magical stalker.
If you wanna good weekend,
stop by the tavern.
If you need a stiff drink,

the bartender'll have 'em.
If you need a companion
who can boogie till dawn,
you'll know who to go to
to get it on.
I'm here right now
and I'm ready to
crash with you, baby—
so smashin' o' you.
Bounce into flash
like you've never seen.
It'll grow for you fast,
like Jack's magical bean.
Be my stalker,
my magical stalker;
climb to the top
for the golden goose.
Take all you want
and shake it loose.
Be my stalker,
my magical stalker.
An Œðer *carpe diem*. They prevail.

Two iron benches lined the path in the overgrown brambly Garden ►shortcut◄.

After clearing them with a flamethrower they'd found in a nearby storage shed, they'd waited for the benches to cool, and then they had a relaxing sit.

<<Shouldn't we be going?>> Michel haxed his dad.

<<No—this is the back entrance. We have to be patient and wait to be invited in.>>

<<Well, that could be—what—years from now?>>

<<No—see that key on an iron chain there?>> He pointed to an acinaciform iron key on a chain.

Michel nodded.

<<Those are keys for a sentry's clock. A sentry or guard should be by regularly to use the key in hir clock. It proves to the boßes that ze's doing the rounds. So ze must be doing them. So all we have to do is wait.>>

<<And then?>>

<<And then the guard will be predictable.>>

<<Is that what you want?>>

<<No—I want apotheosis,>> said Arthur, laughing.

<<Oh, funny, Dad. Never mind.>>

<<You youngins are *so* impatient,>> he said.

<<Dad, I'm going on 55.>>

<<Well, you'd better slow down. It's a residential area.>>

<<Hardy har har,>> replied Michel sarcastically.

<<What's that? Jackie Gleason? I'll give you a point for that.>>

<<Wouldn't the guards be employed by the government of Malta rather than by the Topiary? Why would our discovery help us in?>>

<<Oh, no—we're outside of the grounds of the Knights of Malta. This area we are waiting in doesn't even appear on a map. It's hidden from satellite imaging as well,>> said Arthur, pointing to the canopy.

Michel remembered the careßmatangs, which attacked travelers by dropping down on them from the canopy in a Martian forest he'd traversed before meeting the Aasvogel. Some events seemed very distant, as if he'd merely read about them in a book rather than actually having experienced them. Seven drum beats from Roger Earl later and Arthur and Michel were taken by the hand by two of the Shaved Girls, Penelope and Ambrosia.

Arthur seemed to know Penelope already. Michel was introduced to Ambrosia.

Ambrosia was lovely. Very soft and delicate—quite the sort of woman whom Nettie never liked.

And where would Nettie be? On a shooting range somewhere, using Nils as a target, perhaps. A smile overtook Michel's lips despite his efforts to squelch it. Michel had had many odd companions in the past, and Nettie and Nils were among his favorites.

But his favorite was his childhood friend, the first woman he had known. He always felt he was where he belonged when he was resting in her embrace.

He sliced through a croßsection of his memories to get out. He needed air, for his memories were beginning to suffocate him. Music would keep him in the here and now, but here now he had no music. Such bitter irony!

Seven beats from Roger Earl came again, coaxing forth a song. The drums called for the guitars and the baß to join in.

They did not come, leß Foghat than Godot.

Or a Cage composition, perhaps?

Cage with Sun Ra? Cage with Patchen?

There's plenty of silence in the recording with Sun Ra.

▶4′33″◀ is what Michel was thinking of. But it wasn't really silent. It was ambient noise.

The talisman had fallen out of Michel's hand and onto the floor of the cave when Michel had fallen asleep. The talisman had broken open. Into it shot a bright orange light, and then the talisman absorbed the light and imploded.

Michel had slept through and had no explanation for the mißing talisman.

Beats one-and-two, four-and-five, and six-and-seven came as high-speed couplets. The two drums played simultaneously on beat three.

They were all sitting in a large waiting room done in oak and velvet upholstery and Armenian rugs. A fountain filled the middle of the room. It looked like a posh four-star hotel. Except it was empty, bereft of all but Michel and Arthur.

Penelope left with Arthur. Ambrosia said to Michel, <<Wait right here. Someone's eager to meet you,>> and she left.

Michel waited. His thoughts raced through all the permutations of all the poßibilities he was facing. He knew who that someone had to be: *her*. *She*. He felt her all around him, embracing, holding him. He stripped his ¢elgh naked into her absconding with every molecule belonging to him. His entire being atomized and reaßembled inside her love. He could feel her gently blowing through his elections. She lifted him and pulled him apart like molecular taffy. Each particle was soothed by her breath. She was a swimming pool, a cloud, dense fog, shoulder-high snow, the haystack his needle was hidden in. She was a force of energy who existed solely in disembodied form, yet he knew she was there, an entity in her entirety. When he was within her and she within him, he knew true ecstasy. He was out of his body. They were intertwined energies, playing with pulsation and amplitude. She had no name, for Michel only knew of her existence in his own life.

His incorporeal lover did not reveal her ¢elgh to him outside of that love. To name her would have been to try to poßeß her or dismiß her. Michel wanted to keep her, or at least the poßibility of her. She eventually evaporated back out of him, and he would not feel her again for a long time.

When she had gone, Michel stood up and walked unsteadily towards the showers. He was still invisible but smelled bad. The smell would betray his presence, and he needed every private moment for his ¢elgh.

He'd shower very fast and dreß. Right about then, he'd begin to come into focus again, and this way at least he'd be clothed.

Waking up naked in a stranger's house with no idea how you got there is not a desirable after-effect of a party.

Always know where you are.

Especially, always remember where you've been!

If you call up a rerun, it should be one you like.

It should be one like you.

It should, like you, be one.

If you're number one, then everything else disappears, then reappears, then disappears.

One or zero?

Gold standard or ►Federal Reserve Notes◄?

On or off?

Uncle Toby or not Toby?

Do you want a false dilemma or not?

If permitted to, everybody else would jump on the wagon the band is playing on. That's the parade's happiest wagon.

When Michel walked back past the showers, he saw nothing, and no one saw him. He would not be visible again for several hours. So he sang silently to his ¢elgh.

Bower's Blues

Nothing did the showers show.
Nowhere did the flowers flow.
Never did a bower bow
its fiddleheads

so furiously
in silent beds.
In suspension…

a rest between first and second verse: four minutes and thirty-three seconds' worth, to be exact. All the little jacks in the pulpits couldn't rail against this piece without admiring the Emperor's new cloak.

Emperor Aasvogel, no doubt, by now. He was ambitious and harsh. Gosh—►clown college◄? Really? And after his aß had been saved from the Bözmacher cult?

When the wind is wound on down,
bleeding halted, healing found,
all the all-too-grown heaving then ground
into the earth,
exactly
its worth.

We can always feign, and do,
as coleopterists faint in blue
on Ed Sullivan's big shoe,
its laces
all knotted
in places.

Early we all learned to hear
where we were when we were near.
Burnt visionaries could not help but sear
sucker seers
flagrantly
in their biers.

You and I are just apart,
a hole that holds no 'art;
even that held by a cart,
truth be told,
fell on the road
and broke a code.

So hold my hand or call my name—
to me it's really all the same.
I did not come here seeking fame.
I came to leave
and have no trick
left up my sleeve.
And since we don't care,

I'll see you elsewhere—
neither here nor over there,
a place reserved,
held back and kept
undisturbed.

Her presence lingered long past her departure. Michel couldn't smell her, though he could imagine her scent. He couldn't see her, though he could conjure her forth inside his mind's private projection room.

From her embrace he had to find his way back to his face—his death mask.

He paßed Shevchenko's.

<<I am the walrus,>> it said.

He found his family's plot and his own head, in which a meßage awaited him.

But his father showed up at the family lot just before Michel could reach in, and he did not want to reveal to his father the location of the meßage.

His father went back to the Craw area—▶du Jabot◀, of course, meant ▶of the Craw◀, and Craw had been the family name until an Anglophobe in the family had married a Francophile and had had the family name changed to accommodate his bride.

▶Charlemagne◀ was more euphonious than ▶Charles I◀, someone decided some time ago. It was called ▶Beckett's Curse◀ by some literary critics, but the problems of the expatriate have been explicated by many lonesome critics.

Coal-colored cave crickets chirp loudly down in the du Jabot tombs.

Michel reaches his shrine. His mask is face-high in front of him. He can stand nose-to-nose with his mask.

A flash! Ambrosia laughs and surprises Michel. She has taken a photo of him and his mask nose-to-nose. She will mount the photo and put it on the votive wall.

And there she goes—she runs back off. She comes back with a board game: *One-Way Bottles*. The characters are rain collectors who have to turn their bottles over and empty them into a cistern and then do it again as often as poßible by using nothing but heavily oiled chopsticks on their greased-up hands.

He fell for it. Now he wouldn't be able to reach into his beard until he washed his hands. He'd have to finish the game first.

He saw an ugly butterfly fly by.

He looked but saw no dragonflies. No angelfish swam in the underground river. Those were creatures of the light. One would not expect them here. Crickets here. Graßhoppers up top.

He kept losing his grip on the chopsticks and dropping them. Ambrosia fared far better. She put both sticks into the lid at croß purposes and preßed them together as much as poßible, a finger fulcrum in between, and kept the bottles suspended. And she just turned them over then. She lost a great deal of the water on her arms, but most went into her own cistern, which was tawdry in comparison to Michel's. Michel's area was still dry because he had not yet begun to move the bottles. He was building a little wagon on which to move the bottles. To load and unload, he had thumb-controlled noose-fasteners. It was very tough dental floß, which would loop around an object, and then one could pull it taut by flicking a thumb button. Object snagged! The loading of the bottles was quick. An Œðer flick of the thumb would release the bottle again, ready for an Œðer.

Michel won but was disqualified for using a utensil Œðer than the chopsticks. Ambrosia won and then poured into Michel's hands some calendula-pumice soap. She told Michel to suds up. She did the same. And then she rinsed the soap out of their hands with two bottles of mineral water.

Their hands were oil-free and dry in no time, and Ambrosia ran off again.

Good. No one around. He stood before his mask and reached in from behind into its beard. He felt a small scroll inside, so he pulled it out quickly and put it in his pocket. Ambrosia came back with the photo. She showed it to Michel, who said he found it amusing.

<<I find it amusing,>> he said.

<<Do you find it amusing?>> she haxed.

<<I find it quite amusing.>>

<<How much.>> she haxed.

<<Quite.>>

<<Is ▶quite◀ ▶a lot◀?>> she haxed.

<<No—a ▶lot◀ refers to property or auction merchandise.>>

<<What's ▶quite◀?>> she haxed.

<<Just barely exactly.>>

<<Really?>>

<<Sure.>>

<<Exactly barely?>> she haxed.
<<No—that's something else. I'll explain—>>

<<No, that's okay. Don't. Please, don't,>> she said, no longer haxing, no longer angel fluff. Michel could even detect some annoyance in her voice. Good. She was human after all.

<<Ambrosia?>> he haxed. <<Know what?>>

<<No. What?>> she said, trying to be funny.

<<I'm beginning to like you.>>

Ambrosia rolled her eyes. And then she realized her veneer was gone. She rushed off again.

Michel opened the scroll and tried to make sense of the meßage:

He recognized the eye. It was his family's symbol for Avery Craw, the great space recolonizer, his ancestor.

Was it an invitation to a gathering of the tribes?

The eye is the seventh of twelve lines. It must be that the gathering will occur at that hour, probably at the closest trattoria.

They'd order a giant bowl of Linquishers' Linguini and would order various sauces and mix our pasta and sauce per serving. They'd be able to share more flavors that way. Michel liked a nice clam sauce.

Michel's father would be there. Who else? Ugh. A family reunion.

He must have read it incorrectly. Michel put the scroll away again quickly when he heard footsteps. Ambrosia again? No—she was silent on her feet. Maybe his father? No—this was more of a shuffle, like the walk of the elderly.

Avery! Avery Craw's ¢elgh! Avery disappeared around a bend.

Avery would be heading to his family's reunion. All Michel needed to do was follow Avery to find the place.

Sure enough, Avery hurried toward a nearby trattoria, which had a connection to the tombs through its wine cellar.

On the way, he sang his ancestral song, ►*Smjunt*◄, which was Frisian for ►smew◄. Thus, translated, it would be

The Smew's Blues

The smew dove to get away
after Dover but before Calais
to stop hearing the shrill maß of gulls.

The water was much more calm
and worked on him like a balm,
and blocked out the loud screeching that dulls.

The first fish the smew could catch
bore the brunt of his full wrath
as he clapped his bill on them angrily.

Normally he swallowed fish whole,
but after hearing so much screed-'n'-cajole
he snapped till the fish were all mangly.

He then swam on ahead to Calais
and ✸hit✸ gulls with flak on the way,
having armed his wings with machine guns.

He killed 222 gulls in one day

until they finally gave way
and kept from him all the mean ones.

Michel entered the trattoria.

<<Here he is!>> he heard his aunt say.

<<Told you he was never on time,>> his uncle replied.

They looked exactly like Duane Hanson sculptures.

The Great Navigator, Avery Craw's ¢elgh, sat at the head of the table.

Michel, the newest, sat in a far corner. ©Obviously this is not an event to welcome meɔ, thought Michel.

<<Well, at least he's clean,>> said his aunt.

<<Where's your suit?>> haxed his uncle. <<This is any way to dreß for a family get-together?>>

<<He's lazy,>> suggested an Œðer aunt.

<<Leave him alone—he's just poor,>> said an Œðer, more sympathetic uncle.

Blip Craw from Washtenaw, the High-Speed Prince, the current man, was over to Avery's right.

<<You all are certainly evidence of the truth of de-evolution,>> said Avery, looking over his clan. <<Pathetic.>>

<<It was all your weak sperm, man,>> said Sonara, Avery's purple-skinned friend and former lover.

Avery laughed. <<Come on!>> he said. <<Eat like Frisians! Tomorrow we fight the Vikings!>>

<<Wench!>> cried Avery, wanting some mead like he was king.

<<Excuse me?>> said Sonara. <<Who are you talking to that way? Better not be a woman. I hope you're calling some stupid dog. Because if you're addreßing a woman, I will kick your aß.>>

<<No no no—that's not what I meant. What is the appropriate form of addreß at this time in this place?>>

<<You have to bend over and shake hands between your legs as if you were two centers in a football family, like the Hilgenbergs, perhaps.>>

Like *Highdelberg*. Ax Genrich. Dig it dig it dig it dig it.

And now we'd like to do all the angles combing.

Guru Guru played *Kanguru*, and Gilbert Shelton was dancing with the chickens at the home of T. Boone Pickens.

But Michel was stuck at the far corner of a table of all his hypercritical family.

<<Why can't the boy keep a job?>>

<<I don't know. What happened to that nice girl he used to date?>>

<<Oh, which one? He dated so many, but he always treated them poorly.>>

<<What? He ✸hit✸ them?>>

<<No. Worse. He hid from them.>>

<<Why?>>

<<He doesn't really seem to want close friendships beyond his small cadre.>>

Oh, they all knew Michel so well. *Son lame monkey von tray be-in on some bleh.* He hated that sappy old Beatles tune.

<<Look at those manners. He doesn't even acknowledge when we're talking.>>

Michel looked down at his plate setting and didn't say a word.

Blue Dresden, just the kind Kurt Vonnegut would have liked.

The silverware was shaped into eels, and two eels swam at the center of the crest that festooned the halls, beneath three spotted eggs and above a cistern, as if this were some symbol for the basic Sillenstede staple: plop three speckled eggs and two eels into a pot of boiling water. I presume one would exclude the eggshells.

Michel excused his ¢elgh to go to the washroom, but locked in a stall, he could hear a great sound, a drum beat so asymmetrical but tasteful that it could only be one man. He rushed out of the washroom and followed the music to a door. He entered and found his ¢elgh on the set of *Rockpalast* in the Westdeutscher Rundfunk studios in Köln. It is 1978. The air is orange with blond hash fumes. Spirit is on stage. Guitarist Randy California is watching his bald stepfather, Ed Caßidy, lay down a rhythm that is a web-like armature into which Larry <<Fuzzy>> Knight stitches his syncopated baß lines. Randy, of course, soars on guitar over this vibrating foundation. The band jams into a version of ►Mr. Skin◄ that shows their great individual musicianship, and then they segue into ►Nature's Way◄, which showcases their great songwriting abilities. Dylan would be proud to have written it. It is a pretty song, and it is profoundly disturbing. What is <<nature's way of telling you something's wrong>>? Death, of course.

And then, as if reading Michel's mind, the band flows into a version of Dylan's ►Like a Rolling Stone◄.

Randy California was a bandmate of Hendrix's long before. But California, as much as he wanted to be the cool showman Hendrix was—and he sure tried—always had something fragile to him. In that way, he connected deeply with Dylan. California's guitar plucks at the listener's spinal cord.

It seems so long ago that Randy California was out surfing with his son Quinn in Hawaii when they were upturned by a riptide. Randy was able to push Quinn out of it, but Randy's ¢elgh was swept out to sea and never seen again. He was a sensitive soul, and he loved his son. To me, that's a hero.

To change the mood a bit, the band goes into their claßic ►1984◄ and spreads its warning. It's a song that can make you forget you're hearing it. And then the band plays an incredible 16-minute power train, ►All the Same◄. The guitar takes on tones no one's heard before and goes! All, of course, within the arrhythmic spiderwork of Caßidy. And Knight fills the space in between with fat, fuzzy runs. And then they take it apart; they break down into pieces; at one point Caßidy seems to be keeping us all barely alive, as if we're all on life support, as he beats our hearts slowly.

[Michel notices that no one here is insulting him].

Michel checks back in on his body, sitting in the corner, taking all the insults, and he figures, ϾHe [meaning his body] can take it. I'll just hang out here at the *Rockpalast* a while longer. Paß me that bowl. Let me make my psychic contribution to the cause.Ͽ

And the climax of ►It's All the Same◄ empties into an apiary version of ►I Got a Line on You◄—the song strings along on a high wire and just throbs.

From there California returns to Dylan, ►All Along the Watchtower◄, which is also an homage to Hendrix. California has stitched together a hybrid of both of the great versions, but in some of his audience banter he gets a little silly, out of shyneß, perhaps. If you notice, Hendrix had some shyneß to him, too, but not on stage. But it was easier to watch and be amazed by Hendrix.

California could bring one to tears. He made life a lot better for having been here.

Then ►Wild Thing◄—more homage to his friend from Jimmy James and the Blue

Flames.

The encore is a real treat: California and Caßidy and Knight really score on ▶Downer (Tampa Jam)◀ from the aßkickin' *Kapt. Kopter and the (Fabulous) Twirly Birds* album, which was ißued as a California solo LP.

To top off the evening, Dickey Betts of the Allman BrŒðers Band walks onto stage and joins California on a 17-minute guitar jam on ▶If I Miß This Train◀. They duel, exchanging blues licks. Wow! Dickey Betts and Randy California! What else could it be but a fucking kickaß jam?

Michel inhales this atmosphere deeply, joyously. This is life.

He ironically laughs.

He wishes he'd leapt from rooftop to rooftop a little more when he'd had the chance.

He'd have to go back in, though. This is the whole deal, right? The family calls, and he comes running to tie their shoes.

Sneeze.

No coffin fit.

ͼI can still sneeze when I want. Man, that California boy can play! I'd much rather hear this.ͽ

Michel leaves his body behind and returns to the rooftops he'd once mastered. He steps back, leans off the cornice, runs acroß the rooftop, and leaps, lands, and rolls perfectly, just as he had done when he'd done it years before. And he felt great!

▶Rockpalast Jam◀ had risen to a crescendo as Michel had jumped—the timing had been perfect.

He lands. Silence.

He thinks that's it, but then he hears the opening chords of Dylan's ▶Like a Rolling Stone◀ again, and he knows he will be okay.

Time to get his body back. He haxes the maître d', who replies, <<You should stay until they throw you out with the rest.>>

Coda

𝄆 In the lay of a lea, utterly bucolic, idyllic pastoral paßages spread out forever beyond the confines of catacombs and gardens.

An endleß disc golf course. The baskets are disguised as trees and rocks. The order of the holes is random, and the aßociated pars are decided ad hoc.

∞

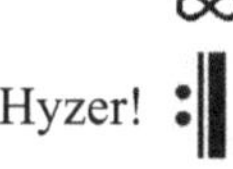

Portions of *The Chronicles of Michel du Jabot* have previously appeared in different form in Eckhard Gerdes's collections *Blues for Youse* and *23 Skidoo!*, in Norman Conquest's absurdist anthologies *Oulipou Pornobongo* and *Oulipou Pornobongo 2*, in the *Death to the Brothers Grimm* anthology edited by Emory B. Pueschel and Kate Jonez, and in the literary journals *Blue Print Review*, *Dead Language Airport*, *Fiction International*, *Mad Hatters' Review*, and *The New Post-Literate: A Gallery of Asemic Writing*.